Three Complete Novels

CATHERINE COOKSON

The Love Child

The Maltese Angel

The Year of the Virgins

WINGS BOOKS
New York

This omnibus was originally published in separate volumes under the titles:

The Love Child, copyright © 1990 by Catherine Cookson
The Maltese Angel, copyright © 1992 by Catherine Cookson
The Year of the Virgins, copyright © 1993 by Catherine Cookson

This edition contains the complete and unabridged texts of the original editions. They have been completely reset for this volume.

This 1996 edition is published by Wings Books,
a division of Random House Value Publishing, Inc.,
201 East 50th Street, New York, New York 10022,

http://www.randomhouse.com/
Wings Books and colophon are trademarks of Random House Value Publishing, Inc.

Random House
New York • Toronto • London • Sydney • Auckland

Printed and bound in the United States of America

Library of Congress Cataloging-in-Publication Data

Cookson, Catherine.
   [Selections. 1996]
   Three complete novels / Catherine Cookson.
      p.   cm.
   Contents: The love child—The Maltese angel—The year of the virgins.
   ISBN 0-517-14836-6
   I. Title.
PR6053.0525A6 1996
823′.914—dc20
                                              95-39499
                                                CIP

8   7   6   5   4   3

Contents

Contents

The
Love Child

To Jack, with my warmest thanks
for keeping me on the straight and
narrow—legal-wise. May you
continue to sing in the mornings
to Kathleen

If you are the bastard of a king, an earl, a lord,
Although the shame will still be there,
You'll get a cut from the world's fare;
Your mother too will have her share.

But if you spring from the loins of the poor,
Your mother will be classed a whore,
A Strumpet, a Gillyvor or a sot,
And her bread will be dearly got.

As for you, the stain is red,
And qualifies you for any man's bed.
But should you rear and stand aside
And demand to be a virgin bride,
Prepare for ridicule and disdain.
Base-born, a child of Cain,
A bastard,
And that you will remain.

The fairest flower o' the season
Are our carnations and streak'd gillyvors,
Which some call nature's bastards.

From *The Winter's Tale* by
William Shakespeare

THE LOVE CHILD

Part One

The Family

ONE

"*I* tell you, Dada, that's what I mean."

Her face bright with merriment, the young girl read again from the magazine: "Ladies and farmers' wives will benefit equally from the scented sachets on their pillows. The fragrance is derived from rose petals, sweet briar blossom—" At this point the dark, bright eyes lifted from the page and swept over her family before she went on, gurgling now, "Cow pats, well ground, as in Farmer Cox's boxings, sold by the pound and dampened, for poultices on the chin, and boils where boils have never bin . . ."

Her voice trailed off and joined the peals of laughter as, dropping the magazine on to the low oak table, she turned and clung to her sister, the while her two older brothers, their bodies bent forward, made guttural sounds and their younger brother, Jimmy, lay on his back on the mat before the open fire, his legs in the air treddling as if he were on a mill; the youngest of them all, a nine-year-old boy, leaned against his mother's side, and she drooped her head until it touched his, and they shook together.

The father hadn't openly joined them in their laughter; but rising from his seat at the side of the fireplace, he slapped his daughter playfully on her bent head, saying, "One of these days, Miss Clever Clops, that tongue of yours will get you into mischief. Now come on, all of you! It's half-past eight and bed is calling."

Slowly the laughter subsided, as one after the other of the family rose to their feet and wished their mother good-night. First, there was Oswald and Olan, the eighteen-year-old twins, like her, both dark but different in stature, Oswald being almost half a head taller than his brother, and broad with it, and he, bending and kissing his mother on the cheek, said, "Now, I've told you, Ma, you're not to get up to see us out. We're big enough and daft enough to cook a bit of gruel and heat a pan of milk." But to this Maria Dagshaw answered, "You see to your business, my boy, and I'll see to mine. So, go along with you both." When, however, her son Olan bent towards her, she gripped his arm, saying, "D'you think you'll be able to stick that driving and the winter coming on?"

"Don't you worry, Ma; anything's better than the mine; I would drive the devil to hell twice a day rather than go down there again. And the smell of the bread, anyway, keeps me awake. A wonderful new idea, isn't it, Ma? To send bread out and about to the houses?"

"Well, they do it with the tea, why not the bread?" said Nathaniel.

The two young men turned and looked at their father, and Oswald said, "You're right, Dada. And Mr. Green said there'll be other commodities on the carts before long. If they can carry stuff into the market on a Saturday, why not carry it round the doors, Monday, Tuesday, Wednesday, Thursday and Friday."

"Well, there's something in that." Nathaniel smiled on his sons and there was pride on his countenance. "Good-night," he said. And they both answered, "Good-night, Dada."

Nathaniel now turned to his daughters, saying, "You two scallywags, get along with you into your bed before trouble hits you."

"Oh, you wouldn't whip us, Dada, would you? Oh, you wouldn't! Oh, you wouldn't!"

"Stop your antics, Cherry, else you'll see whether I will or not. And you, Anna, stop your jabbering in bed. And don't shout up to the boys else I'll be in there with a horse whip; you're not too old to be skelped. D'you hear me?"

"Yes, sir. Yes, sir. Three bags full." At this the two girls joined hands and were about to run down the long room when they turned again and doubled back to their mother, whom they kissed on both cheeks, while she smacked playfully at their bottoms.

When the door had closed behind them Nathaniel turned an unsmiling face towards his wife, saying, "Those two are so full of the joy of life it frightens me at times."

As Maria said, "Oh, don't say that," her fifteen-year-old son, Jimmy, looked at his father and asked him a question: "Why does it frighten you, Dada? Because they laugh, and sing, and Anna can make up funny rhymes and stories? What is there in that to frighten you?"

Nathaniel walked towards the fair-haired boy, who was a replica of himself when young. "I'm always afraid they'll be hurt eventually," he said. "And you know why, don't you? I've explained it to you."

"Yes, Dada, I know why. But as you said, the boys have weathered it, the girls are weathering it in their own way and I in mine, because I have learned to fight like Ossie has taught me. Nobody insults Ossie, either in the village or in the market. And they won't me either, because as I grow I'll become stronger. Anyway, I can use my fists and feet to match any two . . ."

"Jimmy! Jimmy, quiet. You've heard me say the pen is mightier than the sword and from that you can gather the tongue is mightier than the fist or the foot."

"No, Dada, I don't, not when you're dealing with Arthur Lennon or Dirk Melton."

"You should keep away from them."

The boy now turned to his mother, saying, "How can I, Ma, when I have to pass through the village to get to the farm?"

"Well, I take it back in the case of Arthur Lennon." His father smiled down at him now. "Being the son of a blacksmith, he's tough. But still, as I've always said, if you can use your tongue, it's better in the long run, because you know you can confound people with words. Only"—he smiled now—"you've got to know what your tongue's saying and not let it run away with you." And his voice now rising, he looked down the room and cried, "Like my dear daughters do!"

"Oh, Nat."

"Well, they are listening behind the door."

"They're not; they'll be in bed."

"I know them." He now turned to his son, saying, "And I know you, young fellow. Off you go; and take Ben with you, if you can drag him from his mother's arms." He bent down and ruffled the brown-haired boy who, when he turned his head and looked up at him, caused a strange pang to go through his chest as he asked himself again how he had come to breed this boy, who had the look of an angel in a church window and the manner and gentleness of a female and the questing mind of someone twice his age. He was the seventh child and a seventh child was always different. But Ben was so different that every time he looked into his eyes he thought the gods must be jealous of such as he, and he feared their decree that the good die young.

The boy kissed his mother on the cheek and drew himself from her hold, then put his arms about his father's hips and laid his head against his stomach; and for a moment there came on the kitchen a silence that lasted while Nathaniel led his son up the room to the ladder that was set at an angle against the end wall. And as he helped his son onto it, he said softly, "Don't let the boys get you talking; they've got to get up in the morning. You understand?"

"Yes, Dada. Good-night, Dada."

The boy turned from the bottom rung and laid his lips for a moment against his father's cheek, and Nathaniel watched him climb, then disappear through the trap door and so into the long roof-space that held four beds, but which allowed standing-room only down the middle of it.

When he turned from the ladder it was to find Maria standing at the far side of the long trestle table, which was already set for a meal with wooden bowls, wooden plates and a wooden spoon to the side of each plate. In the middle of the table stood a china bowl of brown sugar, and at one end of it was set a bread-board with a knife across it, while at the other was a wooden tray holding eight china mugs.

Maria was looking towards them as she said, "We'll have to go careful on the milk until Minny is back in working order again. What d'you think she'll have this time?"

"Well, if William's done his duty it could be twins. Let's hope triplets, but that's too much to ask. If she comes up with one nanny we'll be thankful. Come and sit down."

He went round the table and put his arm across her shoulders and led her back down the room towards the fire. And there he pressed her into the seat he had recently vacated, and with the liveliness of a man half his forty-four years he twisted his body into a sitting position at her feet, and laying his head on her knee he remained silent for quite some time before he asked quietly, "How long d'you think it can last from now on? The twins are near men, the girls near women."

"Oh Nat. You mean, our way of life?"

"Yes, just that, Maria, just that; our way of life and this present happiness that has grown and matured in spite of everything."

"It'll last as long as we're together, and nothing can part us except death. And then if you were to go I wouldn't be long after, and I know it's the same with you."

He put up his hand and placed it on hers where it was resting on top of his head, and in a low voice, he said, "It's been a strange life, hasn't it?"

"And it'll go on being strange," she replied; "it's the way we've made it."

"Yes. Yes, you're right. And consequently they'll all have to fight their way through it, each one of them. Yet they know where they stand, even down to Jimmy. He's a wise boy, that one. And then there's Ben. He doesn't somehow need to be told, he knows it already. He's imbibed it, whether from the others or the atmosphere in the house, but he knows he's one of a family that lives apart . . . You know what tomorrow is?"

"Yes, I know what tomorrow is, dear. It's the seventh of September, eighteen hundred and eighty and the anniversary of the day we first met. As if I could ever forget it!"

There was a pause now before he said, "I can see you as if it were yesterday standing at the schoolhouse door. You were holding a lantern up high and it showed me your face as you said, 'Can I come in? I want to learn to write . . .'"

There was another silence, and in it Maria saw herself walking into that schoolhouse room. It was a bare and comfortless room, but in the middle of it was a table on which were books and papers. She had looked at them as if they were bread and water and she were starving with a thirst for both.

He had told her to take a seat; and when he asked her, "Haven't you attended this school?" she had shaken her head and said with bitterness deep in her voice, "No; nor have I been allowed to go to the Sunday School so that I could write me name."

When he had asked her why, he had watched her jaws tighten as her teeth came together, before she said, "Because I would be breakin' into a fourteen or fifteen-hour day's work for me father. I am from Dagshaw's farm down the valley."

"Have you no brothers?" he had asked.

"Huh! None. I am the only one, an' I save a man's wages, perhaps two, for they will only work twelve hours. Some prefer the mines to workin' for him."

"Couldn't you talk to him or stand up to him?"

"You can't talk to him; he's an ignorant man. But I have stood up to him with a shovel afore now; it can't go on, though. Me mother put it to me to come to you. She said, if I could write me name and read perhaps then I would get a good position in a house, not just in a scullery. She herself was from better people than my father but they died of the cholera and she never learned to read or write."

He had said to her, "You should have come to school."

At that she had abruptly risen to her feet and said, "If I could have come to school I wouldn't be here now, would I? And if he knew I was here now he'd come and lather me all the way back. Then God knows what I might do to him, because I hate him. I would likely end up in the House of Correction, for there's murder in me heart at times. Me mother feels the same an' all."

"But it's dangerous for you to come this way in the dark at night, and not only that, your name . . . If it was found out you were visiting me so late . . . You understand?"

"Aye; yes, I understand. I'd be careful though. But you're afraid, aren't you? You're afraid, an' all; an' you're a respectable man."

He had smiled at her and said, "Not all that respectable," which caused her to peer at him through the lantern light and say, "Oh aye; you must be the school teacher with the drunken wife who caused an uproar in the village?"

It was some seconds before he answered, "Yes. I am the school teacher with the drunken wife."

"Oh, I'm sorry. I'm sorry. It was just the carter's prattle. I thought that man lived faraway in Gateshead Fell or thereabouts, because I had heard of you as a kindly young man."

He had smiled wanly at her as he replied, "News doesn't travel half as quickly in Africa as it does in this quarter of the land."

"I won't trouble you any more," she had said, "cos you've got enough on your plate," to which he had replied quickly and with a smile, "Let's risk it. Twice a week, Tuesdays and Thursdays at about this time. But should there be anyone here I shall open the curtains and you'll see the lamp-wick up high."

After going out of the door she turned to him and said, "I'll never forget this night . . ."

Nathaniel turned his head now to gaze up into her warm, dark eyes and, as if reading her mind, he said, "Did you ever forget that night? Because that's what you said to me: I'll never forget this night."

"How could I, ever?"

"But it's a long time since we have spoken of it. We hardly spoke of it at all at first, you remember, because what followed was so painful."

He dropped his head again onto her lap and looked towards the fire. The wood had mushed itself into a deep, dull, scarlet glow and in it he envisaged all that followed the night she first came to his door.

Within a month she could write her own name and copy and read aloud complete sentences. And during that month Nathaniel's wife had visited him again from her mother's house in South Shields, with the intention of staying by his side, as she had put it. But he had warned her that if she stayed then he would pack up and go, as he had done two years previously, except that this time he would leave no address. And she would have no support from him. That was the ultimatum, and she left, cursing him.

But that visit had brought him before the Board of School Managers in the Town Hall at Fellburn. They informed him that his wife had again disturbed the peace in the market place; that it was disgraceful and should another such incident happen he would be relieved of his post, because such unedifying goings-on were not to be tolerated when connected with a man in his position: a schoolmaster should be looked up to, not only by the children, but by the elders in the community, as a paragon of virtue and knowledge, a man in some ways on a level of respectability with a Minister of God. Did he understand?

He understood. And with this he had written a letter to his wife, which he knew would be read to her by the same penny letter-writer who composed her demanding scribes to himself. He told her of the situation, emphasising the fact that if she once again showed her face in the town or the nearby village, he would lose his position and consequently she would lose her support, because as he had already warned her, he would leave and she would never find him again.

But that day, when he walked out of the Town Hall, he knew he would already have lost his position if it hadn't been for Miss Netherton. Apparently the question of his conduct and dismissal had been put to a vote and it was only Miss Netherton's vote that had saved him.

Miss Netherton was a power, not only in Fellburn but also in the surrounding countryside. It was generally known that her people had owned quite a large area of the town. And even now, although she lived in Brindle House, which was no size in comparison to Ribshaw Manor, which had once been her home, she still owned a number of properties in the village as well as in Fellburn. Moreover, she was connected with big names in Newcastle, and further afield still.

He had been tutoring Maria for three months when one night their hands accidently met, and they did not spring immediately apart, but only slowly did the fingers withdraw from each other, while their eyes clung in knowledgeable confrontation of what had been happening to each of them. Even so, no word was said.

Then December came, and something happened in that month that changed their lives. Tuesdays and Thursdays were the nights for instruction. But it was on a Friday night of this particular week that she visited him. He had been to a meeting with the Church Elders. He had wanted to put on a Christmas play in which all the children would take part. The Elders were willing to countenance this, but insisted that only hymns should be sung. It was almost ten o'clock when, frustrated and irritable, he entered the house and lit the lamp; but then there was a knock on the door, and when he opened it there she was standing shivering.

He had pulled her swiftly into the room, saying, "You're like ice. What is the matter?"

"I . . . I had to see you. My . . . my mother wants your ad . . . advice," she had stammered.

He had pushed her down into a chair, pulled the curtains, taken the bellows and blown up the fire. Then he had rushed into the other room and brought back the cover from the bed, and when he had put it round her, his arms remained there and, looking into her face, he said, "How . . . how long have you been waiting?"

"An . . . an hour. It doesn't matter."

"But why have you come?"

She had pressed him gently from her for a moment to put her hand inside her coat, and she brought out a stiff, yellowish-looking bag about nine inches long and four wide and, her voice trembling now with excitement, she said, "We were cuttin' down wood, mother an' me. There was a tree leaning over; the wind had got it. It wasn't all that big, perhaps ten years' growth, big enough to make logs, you know, so we pulled on it and brought it down, and . . . and as I was chopping off the branches, me mother went to hack off the root. You see, it had left quite a hole where the roots had been dragged out, and as she bent over it she saw this bag sticking up at the bottom of the hole. And she pulled on it. She had to pull on it because the end seemed to be stuck; it's very sticky clay soil. Anyway, she called me and said, 'Look!' And I said, 'What is it? Open it.' And for a moment she seemed frightened. You see it was tied at the top with a cord, but it's broken, as you see, because when she touched it it fell away; and the bag was stiff, brittle. Feel it."

He felt it. Then her face brightened as she said, "Guess what we found in it?" He shook his head and said teasingly, "A fortune?" only for his surprise to be shown by his open mouth when she replied quickly, "It could be. I don't know. But look!" and she had withdrawn from the bag a cross; not an ordinary cross in gold or silver or brass, but one studded with stones.

After gazing at it he had pulled the lamp further towards them and bowed his head over it. And then he had said, "My God!"

"That's exactly what me mother said: my God! She says it may be worth something."

"Worth something? Oh, yes; yes."

Her hand now tightly clasping the bag, which seemed to crackle under her touch, she had then said, "If he knew . . . Father, that's the last we would see of it. So mother said to bring it to you and ask what we should do."

He had sat back in his chair and after a moment said, "Well, this could be classed as treasure trove, you know, belonging to the Crown. A priest or monk must have buried this years and years ago, likely during the Reformation."

"The what?"

"The Reformation. The breaking up of the monasteries. We must talk about that sometime. But this, I don't know. Once you let it out of your hands I think that's the last you'll see of it; I mean, of the money it might bring to the authorities. This has been known before. Or the ritual will pass through so many hands that your prize-money would be worth nothing when you got it, and it might take years." Then after a pause he added, "But then, there must be someone in the city who buys stuff like this. Look; will you leave it with me? I'll try and get advice. I think the best person to ask is Miss Netherton."

"Oh, aye, yes, Miss Netherton, from Brindle House? They say she's a nice lady."

"Well, she has helped me. But at first I won't say who you are, just that you have something you would like to sell on the quiet, and could she advise you. Will that do?"

"Oh, aye. Aye, I know you'll do your best. Oh!" She had put out her hands and touched his cheeks; then the next minute her arms were about him and his free arm was holding her, while his other was extended straight out, gripping the precious find. And thus they stood for some time before, slowly, he laid the cross on the table and, pushing the rug from her, he then held her body close to his, and so tightly that they could scarcely breathe. When eventually he pressed her from him they looked into each other's eyes before their lips came together, and long and tenderly they remained so.

When it was over she leant against him as he muttered, "Oh, my dear, dear, dear one." And what she said was, "I've loved you from the minute I clapped eyes on you. I knew it was only you for me. Even if your wife had not been what she is, it would have made no odds. I would have loved you in silence all me life. But now I'm yours an' you are mine for all time."

And so it was . . .

He brought his gaze from the fire and again looking up into her face he said, "There are fiends in this world, but thank God there are friends too. And if ever there was a friend, Miss Netherton has been one to us all these years."

"How old is she now?"

"Oh, I should think in her early sixties, but she's still so brisk, and she has some spirit in that small frame of hers. She must have just been in her early forties when I first saw her as one of the School Managers. But I'll never forget the night I went to her with the cross . . ."

Again he turned and looked towards the fire. The embers were almost dead now, showing but pale grey and dull rose, yet in them he could see himself standing in the drawing room of Brindle House. Ethel Mead had shown him in, and Miss Netherton, on entering the room, had greeted him warmly: "It's a bitter cold night. What brings you out in it? But first, before you tell me why you're here, would you like a drink? I can offer you port, whisky, brandy, or, on the other hand, a cup of tea or coffee."

He had said, "I would be pleased to have a cup of coffee, Miss Netherton. Thank you."

He had watched her pull on a corded, tasselled rope to the side of the fireplace, and when Ethel Mead entered, she had said to her, "A tray of coffee, Ethel, please"; then had said to him, "Come and sit by the fire. But first let me have your coat."

He had taken off his overcoat and she had laid it on the arm of an upholstered easy chair, then, sitting opposite him, she had said, "I hope you're not in trouble again."

"No; not this time, I can say, thanks be to God." They had both laughed and her quick rejoinder had been, "You must instruct Parson Mason on how to say that, because he irritates me every time I hear him drawling it out. Besides me, his Maker, too, must be tired of it."

Again they had laughed together; and then she had waited for him to speak, but his first words caused her some surprise. "Would you mind if I didn't tell you my business until after the coffee has been brought in?" he had said.

However, after a short pause she gave a little chuckle and said, "Not at all. Not at all."

Until the coffee arrived they had talked about the school and the Christmas concert and she had remarked, "All that fuss about hymns. We get enough of hymns on a Sunday, the adults twice and the children three times. We have a surfeit of hymns. But it was six to one this time, so I thought I'd better let them win, eh?"

Looking at her he had thought what a marvellous woman she was and had wondered why she hadn't married. Some man would surely have found life at least jolly married to a woman like her.

The coffee came and a cupful was drunk before he said, "This is very private business I want to speak about because I think, in a way, it could be illegal."

"My! My! My! Let's hear it then. It will be a change to deal with something really illegal and not all the little piffling things that come my way."

"A friend of mine is in dire poverty; in fact, both she and her mother are in dire poverty and lead a life of hard work and restraint. They were pulling at a fallen tree prior to sawing it up when, underneath the roots, the mother found something that I'm sure you will think is very precious." He now put his hand into his inner pocket and drew out the stiff leather bag, and, handing it to her, said, "See what's inside."

A minute later she was staring down at the cross on her palm and, strangely, she too called on God: in her case, it was: "Dear God in heaven! How beautiful. How very, very beautiful." Then lifting her eyes to his, she said, "Where did you say she found it?"

"In the woodland attached to a farm. They own the farm, at least the husband does. Unfortunately, the mother and daughter are treated like serfs."

"Oh. Oh. I could put my finger on that farm. Is it Dagshaw's? Low Meadow Farm?"

After he had moved his head slightly in acknowledgement, she said, "Oh, yes. Yes, he's an awful man, that one. I wonder how he came by such a distinguished name, because there are other Dagshaws, you know."

"Yes. Yes, I know."

"And so the mother found this? Well, it is a precious find." But then, her head jerking, she asked, "What do you want me to do?"

"I thought you might be able to advise them what should be done. If it is treasure trove it will go to the Crown, won't it?"

"Yes, I should think so; and then that's likely the last anybody will see of it."

"I . . . I thought as much."

"That is until it appears in some museum years hence, or more likely goes to a private collection. But if they were to get money for it, what would they do with it?"

"Escape, I think. I know the daughter will, and I should think the mother, too. The mother is originally from Cornwall. By what I can gather, her father was a Spaniard and there are relatives still living there."

"But what will the daughter do?"

It was a long moment before he answered, "She will come to me. We have discovered that we love each other."

The small body in the chair seemed to stretch and bristle slightly. "But you are a married man, and your wife is . . . well, you know what your wife is. Will she allow this to go unheeded?"

"All she cares about, ma'am, is that she gets enough money for her drink. But even my stipend from the school hardly supplies that. Yet it keeps her at bay."

"You mean you intend to work all your days to keep your wife at bay?"

"Yes; if need be. I had two years of literal hell living with her; I could stand no more. I had done everything in my power to help her. When we married, I did not know that she was addicted to drink. She and her mother were very clever in that way. I lodged with them for a time, you see."

"Oh. Oh, that is often the way: lodgers should be warned against all landladies and their daughters. I've heard of this before. Anyway, do you know what will happen to you if you go ahead and take this girl into your house, because she is a young girl, isn't she?"

"Yes. But the thing is I won't have a house in which to place her; so, if she wishes to stay with me, we will likely have to take to the road until I find other kind of work."

"Oh." She got to her feet, really bristling now. "Don't let me hear you talk such nonsense! You with your brain and capacity for teaching. And let me tell you, you shouldn't be teaching in that little school such as you're doing, you should be in the university taking a higher course. I have listened to you. Oh yes, when you haven't noticed, and I have seen your method of teaching. You're worth something more than a village school; and supposedly being the power behind that school, I shouldn't be saying this, but your pupils . . . what are they? What intelligence? Will any of them get anywhere? They will be able to write their names and recite the alphabet, perhaps read a little and chant Jack and Jill. But then, you don't just Jack and Jill them, do you? You drop in bits of Shakespeare and Pope. I must tell you something funny in the midst of all this seriousness. When I said to the chairman of the Board that you were a clever young man and you spoke of Pope, he got straight on his feet and cried, 'That's it! We'll have no popery here.' And I couldn't stop my tongue from yelling at him, 'Don't show your ignorance, Mr. Swindle. Pope is a great writer; Alexander Pope not Pope Alexander.' God help us! Some of those men on the Board should be put to the bottom of your class. But now, back to this gem."

As her fingers stroked the stem of the cross she whispered, "Rubies, sapphires, diamonds. Oh my! There's a great fortune here. But who is there who might pay its worth? Take this to a jeweller, one of the less distinguished in Newcastle, and what will he offer you for them? A hundred pounds, two hundred at the most, and then sell it for thousands, perhaps even tens of thousands. I don't think you could put a price on a thing like this. Anyway, if they give it up, it will definitely go to the Crown. Oh, and I couldn't bear that. I wish I was a very rich woman."

When his eyebrows were raised she said, "You're surprised that I'm not. In comparison with some, yes, but in comparison with others, no. One time when my family owned the manor and houses all around and had their fingers in all kinds of pies, yes; but that was when I was very young. I had a father who delighted in travelling in grand style and gambled in every city in which he stopped, and left the affairs of his estates and works to others. Is it surprising that he should come home, together with my lady mother, and find that he had been rooked right, left, and centre? And that those he had left in power and had authority to sell to advantage, had sold to his disadvantage and feathered their own nests? But still, even when the manor had to go and all the works, this house, this ten-room small establishment, remained, together with Fox's farm and a number of houses in the village and a few of more value in the main thoroughfares of Fellburn and Newcastle. I live by my rents; so, of course, I am rich compared with many people. But"—her voice sank—"I am not rich enough to buy this. How I wish I were. Look; could you leave this in my care until tomorrow? I can promise you I won't sell it on the quiet." She laughed, an almost girlish laugh, then said, "There's a plan forming in my mind, but I need to work it out and make sure it is the right one for those two women; and for you, because if you intend to take this girl to yourself you will need money, whether it is yours or theirs. Will you do that?"

"Yes, Miss Netherton."

They had shaken hands like old friends.

Maria didn't come to the schoolhouse that night, and so he was to see Miss Netherton again before he could tell her his news. And what Miss Netherton suggested the following day was, she would, in a way, buy the cross from them over a period of time. If she were to take a large sum out of the bank her agent who saw to the estate would wonder why; but it would be quite in order, owing to her generous nature, to pass over Heap Hollow Cottage and an acre and half of land, the transaction to be duly signed as a deed of gift. Also, she would be able to afford the sum of two pounds a week out of her private income, which could be divided equally between mother and daughter. And an immediate payment of twenty pounds in cash to the mother would enable her to travel to her people in Cornwall. This arrangement was to last until the whole had totalled five hundred pounds, which would cover practically five years ahead. Of course, it would be a personal arrangement and they would have to trust her; although she would put the transaction in writing herself, as it would be unwise, because of possible enquiries as to why her generosity was stretching over this period, to do it legally.

Did he think Mrs. Dagshaw and her daughter would agree?

Would they agree?

When, that night, he told Maria of the arrangement she burst into tears and her sobbing became almost hysterical. What he did not tell her was what Miss Netherton had said concerning their association: Did he realise, she had said, what the reaction of people in the village and round about would be towards them should they decide to take up their abode in the cottage? Would it not save a lot of trouble if he remained at his post as a teacher and the girl lived in the cottage and cultivated the land? They could still see each other. But the way he was suggesting would bring a great deal of trouble on their heads. And to this he had replied that, be that as it may, he was determined that they should come together, and for the rest of his life he would look upon her as his true wife.

It was Maria herself who said, "What will they do to us should we go there and live together?" And he had answered, "Well, we'll find out, won't we?"

And they were to find out . . .

He got to his feet now and, taking her hands, he pulled her up towards him, saying, "Come to bed. You've got a lot of cooking to do tomorrow for the big tea and I've got that patch to turn over to get the frost at it. And then I've the two Fowler boys from Fellburn in the morning. They're both as thick as deep fog, but nice all the same. But they'll have to work some, and so will I if they want to get into that fancy school. Yet, why worry? Their father will buy them in if their brains won't. But it's that pit lad, Bobby Crane, I'm interested in. I hope he can cut across without being noticed after coming up from his shift tomorrow."

"It's risky for the boy, don't you think?"

"Yes, but he wants to carry on, and that's the main thing. He's got a lot in his napper, that boy, and he wants to get out of the pit; but God help him! He'll be out soon enough if they know he's learning to read and write. Still, who's to give him away except his own lot; and there are those among them that will do just that, because they're as bad as Praggett and the owners. They think that once a man can read and write he'll never go down a shaft again; and that's true in a way, for who but a maniac would go down there if he didn't have to eat and feed his family? Here!" He handed her a spill. "See if you can get a spark from the ashes and light the candle, and I'll lock up and put the lamp out."

Together they walked down the deep shadows of the room to the far end where the ladder went up to the trap door and where, to the side of it, was the door of the girls" room, and opposite the one that led into their bedroom.

Within ten minutes of entering the room they were lying in bed, side by side, their hands joined as usual; and now he said to her, "Go to sleep. I can tell when you're thinking. There's been enough thinking for one night. Good-night, my love." He turned slightly on his side and kissed her, and again he said, "Go to sleep." And she answered, "Yes, I'm almost there."

But she was far from sleep, for she knew that he had been thinking of the past, as she had been, and, her eyes wide now, she stared into the blackness and she was back to the day when she first saw this house. And she looked upon it now as a house and no longer a cottage, because it was twice the size it had been on that day.

She could see the grass where it grew up to the window sills of the long, low, one-storeyed building, and when they had pushed the door open the smell of staleness and damp had assailed them. But she could hear Nat's voice, as he looked up to the roof, saying, "That's firm enough. There's not a slate missing. And look at the size of the room; it must be fifteen feet long. And this other one." He had hurried from her and through a door, then had shouted, "This is the same length, almost." He had then climbed the ladder, and she had heard him stumbling along overhead, and he had called to her, "It's quite clear and there's piles of space."

Down the ladder again, he had taken her hand and run her through the rooms to one of two doors at the far end. The first one led into a scullery-cum-kitchen, about seven feet square. Then they were out through the other door into the yard. And there, as if stuck onto the end of the house, were two byres, and beyond them a stable; and across a grass-strewn, stone-cobble yard was a coalhouse and a privy. But what was much more noticeable was the large barn. It was an old erection, and although the roof was gaping in many places the timbers were sound.

She could hear him saying, "It's wonderful, wonderful." And she had thought so too, but she was speechless with the promise of joy to come. But what she did say to him when they returned to the house was, "Wouldn't it be wonderful if this could be one big room. Could you break the wall down?"

"Why not, my love?" he had said. "Why not? We'll take the wall down and we'll make a fine kitchen of that scullery. And as for that fireplace—" he had pointed. "Out will come that small grate and we'll have an open fire, a big open fire."

"But where will I cook?" she had said.

"You'll have a fancy oven, my love," he had answered. "There's a show-room in a foundry in Gateshead Fell; I've seen it many times. We'll choose a stove with an oven and a hob and a flue leading upwards, connecting with this main chimney. Oh, we'll do wonders here, my love." And they had kissed and he had waltzed her round the uneven floor.

When at last they were outside again he said, "Miss Netherton tells me this used to be a splendid vegetable garden; and it'll be so again. And we'll have a cow."

"I'd rather have goats," was her immediate reaction.

"Then we'll have goats, dear."

How wonderful that day had been; but how they'd had to pay for it; how terrifyingly they'd had to pay for it.

Three days later, her mother had left the farm, leaving a letter for her husband, a letter penned by Nathaniel; and the irony of it was that Mr. Dag-shaw had rushed to the schoolmaster's house in a rage and asked him to read it. And it was with pleasure that Nathaniel had read his own writing:

"I am leaving you and going back to my people. I have known noth-ing but cruelty from you all my married life. I've had our child; she too is leaving you. It is no use you coming after me and trying to force me back for my people will protect me. If you remember, they never liked you. It was by chance that we met, a sorry day for me, when I visited my late cousin in Gateshead Fell. But now it is over and you will have to pay for slaves in the future. I do not sign myself as your wife because I have been nothing but a servant to you. I sign myself Mary Clark, as I once was."

Nathaniel had said that the man had looked thunderstruck for a moment, and then had said, "D'you want payin' for readin' that?" And Nathaniel had answered, "I do not charge for reading letters, and that one has given me the greatest pleasure to convey." Her father, she understood, had screwed up his face and peered at Nathaniel as if he were puzzled by the answer. And it was a full two weeks before the puzzle was solved for him, and then only when he went into the market, where some toady commiserated with him about his daughter disgracing herself and going to live with the schoolmaster in Heap Hollow Cottage. And didn't he know the village was up in arms and the schoolmaster had been dismissed and the vicar had practically put a curse on them both?

Perhaps it was fortunate that the day her father confronted her, in such a rage as to bring his spittle running down his chin and his hands clawing the air as he screamed at her, was the day the second-hand dealer from Fellburn had brought his flat cart full of oddments of furniture, including a bedstead, a chest of drawers, a wooden table, two chairs, and a large clippie mat, besides kitchen utensils, and when he saw the red-faced farmer raise his hand to the nice young lass who had sat up on the front of the cart with him and had chatted all the way from the town, he had thrust himself between them, saying, "Look! mister. If you don't want to find yourself on your back, keep your hands down, and your voice an' all." And her father had yelled at him, "She's my daughter and she's turned into a whore," to which the man retorted, "Well, if that's the case you won't want anything to do with her, will you? So be off! For I'll be stayin' till her man gets back from Fellburn where, she tells me, he's on business."

At this her father had yelled, "He's not her man, he's a schoolmaster who's been thrown out of his job. He's a waster, a married man."

"Well, if that's the case, to my mind he's a nice waster, from what I saw of him yesterday. So will I have to tell you just once more to get goin'!"

At this her father had thrust his head out towards her as he growled, "I'll see you crawling in the gutter. D'you hear? And I'll have the village about your ears. They won't put up with the likes of you; they'll stone you out. And you're no longer akin to me, nor is the one that bore you. Not a penny of mine will ever come your way. And you'll rot, d'you hear? You'll rot inside. You filthy hussy, you!"

And at this she had cried back at him, "Well, as a filthy hussy I've worked for you since I could toddle, never less than fourteen hours a day and not a penny piece for it. An' the clothes on my back, an' my mother's, were droppin' off afore we could get a new rag. An' then they weren't new, were they, if you could manage to pick up something from the market stall. Even the food was begrudged us; we only got what you couldn't sell. Well, now you've got your money in the locked box in the attic, I hope it's a comfort to you, because you'll never have any other."

She felt sure he was going to have a fit. And when she saw him turn his cold, glaring eyes on the man, she knew what was in his mind: she had told a stranger about the locked box in the attic. He would go back now to the house and move it, perhaps bury it, like the cross had been buried. At the thought of the cross she laughed inside. If he'd had even an inkling of what they had found, he would have gone mad, really mad.

She had watched him walk away like someone drunk; but after he disappeared round the foot of the hill that bordered the hollow to the right of the cottage, her knees began to tremble so much that she felt she would fall to the ground. It was only the dealer's kindly tone that steadied her when he said, "Well, if I had to choose atween him and the devil for me father, I know which side I'd jump to. Now don't take on, lass. Get yourself inside and if there's any way of making a hot drink, be it mead with the poker in it, or tea, or a small glass of beer or what have you, I'll be thankful for it, for like yourself I'm froze to the bone. And in the meanwhile, I'll get this stuff unloaded; then we can put it where you want it."

She had blown up the small fire in the grate, then had put a pan of water on and made some tea.

An hour later, after the dealer had gone, she pushed the bolt in the door and sat crouched shivering near the fire, waiting for Nathaniel's return. And when he came she had flung herself into his arms and cried while she related her father's visit and his last words to her. And what Nathaniel said in reply was, "Well, it's what we expected and we've got to weather it . . ."

The onslaught began a week later when the barn was set on fire. She could see herself even now springing up in bed to see the room glimmering in a rose glow and to hear the crackling sound of wood burning. They had rushed out and made straight for the well but had stopped when, with both hands on the bucket, Nathaniel had said, "It would take a river to put that out. A bucket is no use." But she had cried at him, "The sparks! They're catching here and there in the grass: if they spread, they'll get to the cottage."

The rate at which they were able to bring up water from the well would have been of little use had it not been that the grass was still wet from rain earlier in the day.

In the flickering light they saw shapes seeming to emerge from the shadows and a voice came through the night so high and loud that, for the moment, it shut out the crackling of the burning barn as it cried, "It'll be your house next, the whore house." And so, maddened, Nathaniel had been about to rush in the direction from which he thought the voice had come when voices from different areas began to hoot and yell.

The following day Miss Netherton, after looking sadly on the burnt-out frame, said, "Well, I expected something like this. But it's got to be put a stop to in some way else your lives could be threatened." And Maria remembered thinking, They're already threatened.

The following week they had brought home the first goat. She was a sweet creature, already in milk, and they thankfully drank their fill from her; at least for the next three days, before she was found with her front legs broken.

She remembered holding the poor suffering animal in her arms and crying over it as if it were a child, her first child. Nathaniel had gone to Miss Netherton's to ask if Rob Stoddart, her coachman, or the lad, Peter Tollis, could come and shoot the animal and put it out of its misery, because he himself had never handled a gun. But from now on, he said, he would learn.

The matter of the goat had incensed Miss Netherton and she had her coachman drive her into the village and to the Vicarage. And there she had told the Vicar that if he didn't stop incensing his parishioners against her tenants, as she had called them, he would in future be doing without her patronage. But, apparently, he had said that whatever she did, he would carry out God's will. So, following this, she had walked boldly into the bar of The Swan, an action in itself which caused comment, because no woman ever went into the main bar of a public inn. But there she had addressed not only Reg Morgan, the innkeeper, but also Robert Lennon, the blacksmith and his eldest son, Jack, as well as Willie Melton and his son, Dirk, who were painters and decorators, and she reminded them that of the thirty-two cottages and houses scattered around, she owned seventeen.

Next she had gone to the King's Head and there again, in the main bar, she had addressed Morris Bergen and his wife, May, and John Fenton, the grocer, and two pitmen from the nearby pit, Sam Taylor and Davy Fuller, who were known as louts and would do anything for an extra pint of ale. And addressing the latter two, she had pointedly reminded them that the owner of the mine was a friend of hers.

For the next four weeks they were left in peace. However, Miss Netherton had warned them to keep clear of the village, even if this meant going a mile or so out of their way across the fields and over the quarry-top to reach Fellburn to do their shopping, which they did in the middle of the week, so evading market day.

Then the climax came. It happened when they were walking just inside the copse that adjoined the Hill, or the Heap, as it was called, and from which the cottage had derived its name, that Maria let out such a fear-filled yell as she cried at Nathaniel, *"Don't move!"* and its effect on Nathaniel was immediate: so abruptly did he halt his step that he almost fell on his face; then she pointed to a distance not two feet away from where he was standing and hissed, "A trap! A man-trap!"

"No!" He had stood stock-still, gasping. "Not that. They wouldn't."

"They would. Oh, they would."

"That settles it!" said Nathaniel. "I'll have the law on them. Traps are forbidden now, even for animals. And whoever set that could be having their eyes on us this minute, waiting for the screams. Will you stay there near it?" he asked her, but immediately changed his mind. "No; I will," he said; "you run to Miss Netherton's and tell her. Tell her to come and see for herself. Then I'll take this matter to the Justices. I'll have a constable here and someone who can release that trap without losing a limb."

She had picked up her skirts and run and had burst unceremoniously into Miss Netherton's kitchen and, finding no one there, had dashed into the hall, there to be confronted by the sight of the lady herself accompanied by two gentlemen. They had been laughing together but stopped, and Miss Netherton, leaving them, came towards her quickly, saying, "What is it? What is it, Maria?" And she had spluttered, "They've set a man-trap. Nat nearly stepped into it, he's . . . he's guardin' it. Will . . . will you come and see?"

"A man-trap!" One of the gentlemen had stepped forward. "Where is this?"

She didn't answer because Miss Netherton was already saying, "There is a feud going on between two friends of mine and the village. You remember the schoolmaster we talked about? I rented him a cottage, but those in the village have burnt down the barn, they have crippled his goat, and now they are aiming to cripple him or this young girl here."

"Well, we can put a stop to that, can't we?" The man had nodded towards her, and Miss Netherton had explained, "Mr. Raeburn is a Justice of the Peace and he will settle this once and for all."

The outcome of this and of what had come to Miss Netherton's knowledge through her coachman and the carpenter in the village, Roland Watts, relating to the person who had set the trap, was a visit from the law to the innkeeper of The Swan, the consequences being that Reg Morgan had to appear before the Justices on the 17th of March to answer the charge of unlawfully setting a man-trap to the danger of human life and limb.

Moreover, every tenant of Miss Netherton's in the village received what was then a law letter. It was written on thick paper and came from a firm in Newcastle. It indicated to the occupants that were Miss Netherton's tenants in Heap Hollow Cottage troubled in the slightest form in the future, the recipients of the letter would be given immediate notice; and it went on to indicate that it was up to them to see that the outrageous incidents against Miss Netherton's tenants ceased immediately.

So they were left alone; and they spoke to no-one except Miss Netherton and her small household or Roland Watts in the village, and the dressmaker, Miss Penelope Smythe, should the latter happen to meet them, which was rarely.

When the twins were born they did not go to the Parson to ask if he would christen the babies. But he had a field-day in the pulpit on the Sunday, for his sermon reached the greatest length yet, an hour and twenty minutes. And Miss Netherton had laughed when later she related to them: "He hadn't any voice left at the end of it; just enough to upbraid certain members of the congregation for falling asleep."

A kindly parson in Fellburn had christened the children, but the record went as follows:—

> September, 24th, 1862. Oswald and
> Olan, base-born sons of Maria Dagshaw,
> begotten by Nathaniel Martell.
> Baptised October, 20th, 1862.

This entry into the church register hurt her in some strange way, for she had imagined herself to be past hurt. But she was grateful to Parson Mason and his wife, Bertha, who had been kind to them both and who had laughingly said, "Your children being christened here makes them subjects for parish relief. But let's hope they never need it." And Nathaniel had answered, "They never will."

But from the birth of her sons began the spitting. It started with the women. She'd be walking through the town. It could be on a Wednesday or a Thursday, any day but Saturday, when the town was turned over to the market, but two out of every three times she entered that town she would hear the hiss and spring aside only too late, for her skirt would be running with filthy mucus and she'd see the back of a woman or women walking away from her.

At this period they never passed through the village.

Annabel had followed the boys. She had been born beautiful, more so even than she herself had been. But she was of a strange nature, strange in such a way that it seemed to stretch to opposite poles within her, one to a depth of quietness and serious thinking, the other to laughter, gaiety, mimicking and quick temper. What was sad, however, at least to herself, was that her daughter, so intelligent, clever in so many ways, was still a sort of maid to Miss Netherton. When she said, "sort of maid', she included being a companion to the older woman, for did not Miss Netherton take her shopping when she went into Newcastle, and when visiting the museums; and twice had taken her to a theatre show? She knew she should be grateful that her daughter was paying back some of the debt they owed to that very kind lady; yet, she couldn't help but have her own plans for her daughter.

And then Cherry came, and she was as fair as her father, with merry blue eyes and a tripping tongue. They were foils for each other, her two daughters. Each caused gaiety and laughter in the house where there would have been none without them, for the twins were sober young men, and Jimmy, at fifteen, was a questing boy, wanting to know the ins and outs of everything, impish in a way. And then there had been one born into life, already dead.

Her last-born was Ben. Why had they called him Benjamin? The name didn't suit him, but it happened to be the name of Miss Netherton's father. Miss Netherton had allowed that to be used, then why hadn't she let one of the girls be called Mary? for that was her name. But she would have none of it. She said she didn't believe in passing on names, it made the recipient feel fettered in some way. Nor did she believe in the role of godparents. The role of godparents, she said, was to be guardian to the spiritual life of the child. But how many godparents dare enforce their authority? She could see no spirituality in choosing a godparent for a child, only the hope by the parents that it would be a beneficiary at some future date.

She was very forthright in her thinking, was Miss Netherton. But she had constantly been a guardian angel to them all, and still was.

The payment of money for the cross had ended a year after Jimmy was born. But they had managed, because by that time they were on their feet, so to speak. The barn had been rebuilt, the wall taken down between the two rooms, a bedroom built for the girls at one side of the house and their own at the other. The vegetable garden yielded all that they needed in that way for most of the year. The apple, pear, plum, and cherry trees that had been planted in the second year now gave abundant crops. The four goats supplied them with milk and cheese, the twenty hens with eggs and a fowl for the table every now and again; and the ducks that splashed in the artificial pond that the lads had dug at the bottom of the land, gave large, greenish eggs in abundance and young ducklings by the dozen each year . . .

She turned on her side and felt the waft of Nathaniel's quiet breathing, and she told herself once again how she loved this man; more than loved him, adored him. Yet, it would be a sin to think about that if she had been a church-going Christian. No-one should be adored but God. But what were church-going Christians? Women who spat at you; men who drove their carts through the middle of narrow lanes and pushed yours into the ditch. When that had happened for the countless time Nathaniel had made a stand: "We'll go through the village in future," he said, "straight through the middle." And this he did, and the sight of Dagshaw's Gillyvors, as she knew they were called, brought folks running to the cottage doors and the men coming out of the inns.

But as the years went on it would seem that the villagers took no notice of them, especially when the whole family sat upon the flat cart, while Nathaniel sat erect on the high driving seat. She always saw to it that every one of them was dressed in their best when they went through the village. And Nathaniel always drove straight down the middle of the street. One day they met the coach from the Manor. When, some way off, the coachman waved them aside, Nathaniel returned the salute in the same manner and drove his cart steadily forward until, at the last minute, the coachman pulled his horses sharply aside and drove them onto the broad grass verge.

When a head was thrust out of the coach window and a voice yelled at him, "What in hell's flames do you mean, man?" Nathaniel had cried back, "The public highway is for all men, and it runs through this village."

Again this incident was brought to Miss Netherton's notice, and what she said to Nathaniel was, "You're tilting your spear at the castle gates now, I hear. Well, you'd better keep your visor down. Still, I wouldn't worry; their arms don't stretch all that far around here. The one that bawled at you would likely be what I term the carp among the salmon. But his father is all right, quite a pleasant man really, and the younger son too. But I wouldn't say the same for his wife. There's a vixen if ever there was one. Why do nice men allow themselves to become ensnared?"

What would they have done without Miss Netherton? But oh, she wished she would do something for Anna: get her a position of some kind worthy of her brain and intelligence. She had hinted at it more than once, yet here the girl was, seventeen years old, near eighteen, and neither one thing nor the other: not quite a servant and not quite a companion. But she must get to sleep; it would soon be four o'clock in the morning.

Part Two

Anna

ONE

$\mathcal{M}$aria had cooked all day; the table was laden with her efforts: there was a currant loaf and a rice loaf, and caraway seed cakes, yule do's made from pastry and decorated with pieces of ripe cherry; there was a large earthenware platter containing two chickens, already dismembered, a bowl of pig's-head brawn; and there were moulds of soft goat cheese and a platter of unsalted butter standing at both ends of the table, besides two crusty loaves. It was a fare that would have done credit to a banqueting hall, and Maria surveyed it with pride.

She was now thirty-six years old and the little mirror in the bedroom told her that she looked her years but that she was still a beautiful woman. She hadn't lost her figure through childbearing and her carriage was erect. But there was a deep age in her eyes. How could it be otherwise, for over the past nineteen years the life of ecstatic love had been mingled with fear and humiliation not only for herself but for her brood, for they each one carried the stigma of their birth and would do so until they died. But would she have had things otherwise? Yes, oh yes. If she had been the acknowledged wife of Nathaniel her eyes would not have admitted the pain, for then she would have been the wife of a schoolmaster. And her children would have been free to wander at will from the time they could toddle, whereas they had all been kept to the boundary of the wood, the hill and the garden, and they had no friends, except for Miss Netherton.

She turned from the table as two voices hailed her from the kitchen, one saying, "We are home, Ma," the other, "What can I smell?" She went quickly down the room now, saying, "What I can smell are muddy boots and sweaty stockings. Have you left them outside?"

She was met at the kitchen door by her two sons, both in their stockinged feet, and Oswald, laughing, said, "Oh, Ma, let's get near the fire and put our slippers on. It was actually freezing coming over the fields. I'll bet there'll be an early frost the night."

As both young men pulled crackets from the wall to sit down opposite the open hearth, she went to a box at the side of the fireplace and, taking out two pairs of moccasin-like slippers, she threw them onto the mat between them, saying, "You're a bit early, aren't you?"

"Yes, Ma, we've been good boys and Mr. Green let us off. And we've got some news for you, too, both of us."

"Oh! Good news?"

"Yes. What other news would we bring?" Olan smiled up at her.

"Well, will it keep till the others get in?"

The twins looked at each other, smiled, then Oswald said, "Yes, Ma, it'll keep. Where's Dada?"

"He's in the barn with the pit lad."

"Oh, the pit lad." Oswald stood up, then added, "That poor beggar. We heard in the town there's trouble at the Beulah mine. They've been routing out some of the men from the cottages, putting them on the road because they've been agitating."

"I thought they couldn't do that now," said Maria.

"Oh, they can do that, Ma. The men have only got to mention union, I understand, and they're for it."

"God help them if they've got to live out on the moor this winter. D'you remember three years ago? There were six families out there. Four of the children died, besides an old man and woman. The young ones, I understand, eventually made it to Australia. Still"—her tone lightened—"come and look at the table."

"I could smell it down the road, Ma."

Oswald punched his slender brother, saying, "You can smell food from Land's End to John O'Groat's. But look at that." He gazed on the table; then turned to his mother, saying, "My! you have been busy, Ma. And where've you hidden all this stuff for the past days? It wasn't in the pantry yesterday. If it had been it wouldn't have been here today, would it?"

They all laughed now, then turned as the far door opened and Nathaniel came up the room with his youngest son by his side; and while the young boy stood, open-mouthed, gazing at the table, Nathaniel turned his gaze from it and onto Maria, saying quietly, "You have put some spreads on that table in the past years but I think that's the best yet."

Maria pursed her lips at the compliment, while her eyes shone with the pleasure of it. Then she asked, "How was your pupil?"

"Doing nicely. Fine. Oh, if I could have that lad every day he would go some place, far beyond me, in what I could teach him. He just gollops up knowledge. I've never known anyone like him."

"I golloped up your knowledge, Dada."

Nathaniel put back his head and laughed; then looking at Olan, he said, "All you golloped up, my son, was food. And what have you got to show for it? You're as lanky as a bean pole."

"Aye, but I'm strong with it. You can't deny that."

"No, you're right. I can't." And Nathaniel slapped his son on the back;

then turned to Maria again, saying, "We're going to wait until they all come, aren't we, no matter what time?"

"Of course, of course," she said, nodding emphatically. "But let's hope Mrs. Praggett doesn't keep Cherry late tonight."

"She should stand out for her time. She's paid for eight till six," said Oswald; then on a laugh, "Even if Mr. Praggett decided to throw his bairns into the river or down the mine shaft. Eeh! she was funny, wasn't she, that last time she described the row he was having with his wife when she tipped the dinner over him? It's a good thing she sees the funny side of it else she wouldn't stay there five minutes."

They were laughing again when the door of the kitchen opened and Anna came into the room. And it was her walk that brought the rest of the family to concentrate their gaze on her without giving her any greeting, because her step was slow and the pose of her head suggested hauteur, but on reaching the end of the table her manner underwent a change as she gazed along its length, but then was resumed as she addressed her father, saying, "Mr. Martell, I have news for you, and for you, Maria Dagshaw."

"Such news, daughter, that portends a rise in your station in life, an elevated rise, into the aristocracy, say?"

"It could be so, Mr. Martell. It could be so."

"Let up, you two." Oswald flapped his hand towards them. "Anyway, you're not the only one that's got good news. We have too, Olan and me here, but we're keeping ours for the tea."

"Oh. Oh," she exclaimed, and laughed; then her manner returning to normal, she looked towards Oswald, saying, "You really have good news?"

"Yes. Aye, we have."

"Oh, I'm glad. Well, I'll keep mine an' all for tea. And Dada, when the postman brought Miss Netherton's mail he said he had a letter for you. Here it is." She put her hand into the pocket of her short coat and handed him an envelope.

After looking at it, Nathaniel glanced at Maria. Then, turning from them, he went to the small desk that stood in the corner of the room and, picking up a paper knife from it, he slit open the envelope and read the letter.

When Maria, who was watching him, saw one hand go down to the desk as if for support, she went hastily to him, saying quietly, "What is it?" He did not answer her, but turned his head and looked into her eyes. Then gently pressing her aside, he walked across the room and through the door that led into their bedroom, and she followed.

"Nat. Nat." She was sitting on the edge of the bed beside him now. "What is it? What does it say? Who is it from?"

Slowly he handed her the letter and she read it, and it was a long moment before, in a pained murmur, she said, "No, no. She wouldn't do that. Five years. Oh, Nat."

He was holding her close as he murmured now, "But it wouldn't have altered their situation; they would still have been classed as . . . as gillyvors."

She didn't pursue his statement for her mind was crying, No, but it could have altered my situation, and in other ways, too, it could have been a relief.

She lifted her head from his shoulder, saying, "Shall we tell them?"

After a moment's thought he said, "No. Not till after they have given us their news. They're full of it, whatever it is, and it seems good. But after the meal I will tell them."

The meal was over, they were all replete and they had said so in their different ways and congratulated their mother on the wonderful feast.

"Now who goes first? I think ladies should have the choice, don't you, Oswald?"

As Oswald nodded down the table towards his father, Anna said, "Mine can wait. Let Oswald and Olan tell their news."

"As you will. As you will."

"Well, go ahead, Oswald."

All eyes were on the bright-faced, bulky form of the eldest of the family. And he, looking directly at his father, said, "Mr. Green has asked me if I would like to manage his other shop in Gateshead Fell."

"Oh! Wonderful!"

"Managing a shop!"

"All by yourself?"

"Will you get more money? Double pay?"

"Be quiet. Be quiet." Nathaniel waved them down. "And listen. Go on, Oswald."

Oswald took a deep breath before he said, "Of course, it isn't as big as the Fellburn one and it's in rather a poor quarter near the river, but it's got prospects. I am to do part of the baking to begin with, nothing fancy, you know, like our present shop, just plain bread, rye, brown, and white, and teacakes, griddle cakes and yeasty cakes. Of course, the drawback is, I have farther to go, yet I start at the same time in the morning. But on three times a week he is letting Olan, here, pick me up when he's on his round."

"How much money are you getting? Twice as much?"

"No. No, Mr. Moneybags." Oswald laughed at Jimmy. "But I'm going up to seven shillings a week and what stale bread I'd like to take away with me at night."

"Stale bread!" Cherry's voice was indignant. "There won't be much stale bread left around that quarter if it's a poor one. Anyway, tell him we don't want his stale bread."

"You'll tell him no such thing." Maria silenced Cherry with a cautionary hand, then went on, "If I can't make use of stale bread for puddings then there's plenty will be glad of it, especially if we have company on the moor again, as you said earlier, Oswald."

Oswald now nudging his brother said, "Tell them your piece."

"Well—" Olan ran his fingers through his hair, then smoothed each side of his cheeks as if he were straightening side whiskers, before sticking his thumbs in his braces and declaiming, "I've been put on commission."

"Commission? What d'you mean?" This question came from various quarters of the table; then Olan explained. "I am to take the cart filled with trays of fancies and, as Mr. Green says, break new ground. I approach private houses and inns and such like and ask them if they would be interested in placing an order with the firm of George Green, High Quality Confectioner,

Established 1850. And for every order over a pound I get one penny commission."

"*A penny?* What's a penny to brag about?" Jimmy was butting in again. "It's something to brag about when twelve of them make a shilling, bighead," replied Olan.

"Yes, Olan's right." His father was nodding down towards Jimmy now. "A shilling is something to brag about."

"It might be, Dada, but how long is it going to take him to earn it?" said Jimmy, practically.

"Well, that remains to be seen," replied his father. Then looking at the slightly dampened Olan he added, "Doesn't it?"

"If the weather keeps fine I could make it in a week. Anyway, Mr. Green is supplying me with an oilskin cape and cap and also covers for the trays. So he's thought about the weather."

Jimmy was laughing now as he put in, "But what about the poor horse?" And when Anna's hand came out and slapped him across the ear he laughed louder, and at this they all joined in.

"Well now, that's us settled." Oswald was looking towards his sister. "Out with it."

All eyes were on Anna now, and she, looking up the table to her mother and father, her voice low and her mien deprived of all aping hauteur, she said, "Dada. Ma. I'm to be a pupil teacher."

The news brought no response for a moment; then it seemed to animate each one of them, for they all rose at once and crowded round her chair and the questions flew at her from all sides, until Maria shouted, "Stop it! all of you, and listen."

When the hub-bub had died down it was Nathaniel who, holding out his hand, caught his daughter's and drew her up from the chair, saying, "Let's all go down to the fire. Good news should always be spread around the fire."

A moment later they were all sitting or crouched round the mat, their eyes on their beautiful sister, and in what sounded like a tearful voice, she began, "Miss Netherton took me in this afternoon. Apparently it's been under discussion for some time. I am to take up my position at Miss Benfield's Academy For Young Ladies next week."

"The Academy For Young Ladies. Oh! Anna." Cherry's arms were about her and the sisters were hugging.

"She never let on to you?"

Anna looked at Maria, saying, "No, Ma; not a word. The only thing is, she has been pushing all kinds of books towards me over the past weeks, not only English and history, but . . . well, things that went over my head." She turned now and looked at her father, saying, "Not that they would have gone over your head, Dada, philosophy and such. But, as she said, I won't need anything I've read of late in the Academy, nor for some time and with the little ones, but . . . but it may help me later on to put over my English and history to the muddle-minded minxes that grace Miss Benfield's decaying mansion."

"Is it a mansion?"

"No, no." She shook her head at Maria. "It's a terraced house on two floors and has a basement with an iron grid over it." She glanced towards her father now, saying, "It looked as if the wash-house was below, for steam was pouring up through the grid and there was a smell of soap-suds. But up above, oh, all was different." She wrinkled her nose now. "Miss Benfield was dressed in black satin. She's big—" She made a sweeping motion with both hands over her chest, then she glanced at Cherry and said, "I wanted to giggle when I first saw her. Remember that poem, The Bosom Of The World: Where all nature is unfurled . . . ?"

"Now, now, be serious." Her father was nodding at her. "Tell me what she said."

"Well, it wasn't what she said, it's what she expected me to say. She just asked questions, and mostly about you."

"Me?" He dug his thumb into his chest.

"Yes. Were your parents alive; what had they been. I said your Father had been an engineer but both of them had died of cholera."

"What was the house like, the classrooms?"

"Oh, Dada, grim. The one room I saw upstairs was partitioned off and there were eight desks in one part. What I suppose is the drawing room is the main classroom. The dining room, too, had been partitioned off; part of it is called the music room."

"How many teachers are there?"

"I think there are just two; Miss Benfield and another one."

"It doesn't sound like a very high-class establishment to me."

Anna now looked at Olan, saying, "Nor did it to me and I'm sure it didn't to Miss Netherton. But, as she said, I have to begin somewhere. And once I get a year or so's experience I'll be able to pick and choose. I'm . . . I'm sure, Dada, it's the best she could do for me at the moment."

Her expression was serious and so was Nathaniel's, for they both knew why it was the best Miss Netherton could do for her at the moment: a bastard and one of a family of bastards would not be classed as a fit person to instruct young ladies.

"Well now, what more news have we? Anyone else got a surprise?" Anna looked around the family.

Nathaniel still didn't say, "I have news, surprising news." It was Jimmy who next gave his news: "Well, nothing happens on a farm that you could call news, except today Daisy kicked a bucket of milk over. And Farmer Billings raged about the byre, cursing. He used some words I'd never heard before and Mrs. Billings chastised him, you know, how she does in that churchy voice. "Enough! Enough! Mr. Billings," she shouted. "Be grateful you have milk to spill; you won't find any in hell." And you know what he shouted back at her?" He chuckled so much now that he almost choked. " 'Go and boil your head, woman! Go and boil your head!' "

Nathaniel allowed the laughter to die down before, looking down on Jimmy, he said, "He didn't say any such thing, not Farmer Billings."

"He did, Dada. Honest to God."

This aroused more laughter, because Jimmy had spoken almost as Farmer Billings would have.

But Maria quickly intervened. Looking at Cherry, she said, "Have there been any high jinks in your establishment?"

And Cherry, her face still wide with laughter, said, "You wouldn't believe it; but it's been 'My dear Florence' and 'My dear Mr. Praggett'. They've been cooing like two doves the last few days. And I wanted to say to her, 'Look, woman; don't let yourself be hoodwinked. He's no dove. You should know that by now.' He's a dreadful man really. He gets so mad at times that he actually jumps. He does, he does. Like the day I told you about when I'd just hung a line full of washing out and he came rushing out the back way and straight into it and got tangled up in his wet linings and brought the whole line down—remember?"

They remembered; and just as on that first occasion, so the room was filled with laughter.

The laughter trailed away as one after another they turned their attention to the young boy who was saying quietly now, "I'm going to be a doctor when I grow up."

The statement, made with such emphasis, brought no response from anyone for a moment. Then his father asked gently, "Why this sudden decision to be a doctor, Ben?" and the boy's answer was firm as he said "Because I want to mend things, like . . . like sores on legs, Dada."

"Sores on legs . . . ? Who has sores on legs?"

"The children that came into the wood this morning."

"And they had sores on their legs? What were they doing in the wood?"

"Gathering blackberries, Dada. They were very small, not as big as me. They had no shoes on and their feet were dirty and they had sores on their legs."

Nathaniel rose from his chair and picked up his son from the floor and held him up in his arms. And looking into his face, he said, "And you will be a doctor some day, son, and heal sores on legs. God willing."

"What if he's not, Dada?"

"What if who's not?"

"God. God willing. You said the other day you were willing to help the pit lad or anyone to read or write, but what if God isn't willing?"

A shiver ran through Nathaniel's body and he repeated to himself, Yes, what if God isn't willing? This last child of his, this small, strange and continually happy child filled him with foreboding, even fear at times.

He did not resist Anna's taking the boy from his arms and standing him on the floor again. He hadn't been aware that she had risen to her feet, but he could count on her always being there at moments such as these: when life became so frightening he seemed to become paralysed by it.

Maria was standing close to him now, saying, "Tell them our news. It's time."

"Oh, yes, yes, our news. We have some special news for you. But first of all I must say something to your mother that I have longed to do for the last nineteen years." And now he took Maria by the shoulders and pressed her down into her chair. Then dropping on to one knee, he looked into her face and said, "Maria Dagshaw; I love you. Will you marry me?"

"Oh! Nat. Nat." Maria pulled her hands away from his and covered her face with them; and now they were surrounded by their children, all saying in different ways, "Oh! Ma, Ma. Oh! Dada, Dada."

"Dry your eyes, my love." Nathaniel picked up the corner of her white apron and gently drew it over her wet cheeks. Then, sitting at her feet now, he addressed his family, saying, "I have never kept anything back from you. You have all been brought up to face the situation that we brought upon you by our love for each other. Yet, in spite of the so-called shame, I doubt if there is a happier family in the whole of the country. So now I will tell you the news I received, that Anna brought to me tonight, the news that should have been delivered five years ago. It has happened like this. My wife, as you know, was addicted to drink. In order to keep her from plaguing me, I had to find her five shillings a week for her lifetime. I used to send her a ten-shilling note once a fortnight, care of the letter-writer, the penny letter-writer, you know. Well, his letter tells me it was only by accident that he found out my wife had died five years ago. After her old mother had missed two visits to collect the money, he thought he'd better take it to the address he had been given. It was a kind of lodging house, and the landlady greeted him as if he was a relative of the poor, lonely old woman. It must have been through questioning her that he learnt my wife was already dead. The man, the letter-writer, didn't want to be implicated in anything unlawful, so he thought he had better do some explaining."

He paused before saying, "So five years ago I could have said the words I said a moment ago to your mother: Maria Dagshaw, will you marry me? But still"—he moved his head slowly—"we would have been no happier than we are now, and, unfortunately, our marriage cannot erase the stain we have put upon you all."

"Oh! Dada. Dada." The girls were kneeling by his side, their arms about his neck, while Maria held her hands out towards her sons, and they crowded round her; and it was Olan who said, "Whatever happens in life, Ma and Dada, I'll always thank God that I was born of you, and Oswald, being part of me, says the same, don't you, Oswald?"

"Oh, yes, yes, Ma . . . Dada."

"And Jimmy is proud of you, too, aren't you, boy?"

And Jimmy, his voice thick, muttered, "I don't know, being connected with you two is nothing to shout across the water. Anyway I can disown you once I can buy my farm."

The result of this was a rough and tumble on the mat with the twins, and Anna shouting, "Stop it! you hooligans. Look! you'll have him in the fire."

When order was restored again, Oswald asked quietly, "Where will you be married, Ma?"

Maria glanced at Nathaniel and said, "We haven't got that far yet. Certainly it won't be by the Reverend Fawcett in the village. Parson Mason will do it, and gladly, I'm sure. He christened all of you."

"Yes; your mother's right." Nathaniel now rose and, pulling Maria to her feet, said, "What your mother and I are going to do now is put on our coats and take a walk as far as the wood, because there's a moon out tonight and after proposing marriage one should always walk in the moonlight with the beloved." He hugged Maria to him for a moment; then addressing his family again, he added, "And you lot will clear the table, wash up the crocks, tidy the room, then away to bed, and by the time we come back we want to find this room absolutely clear."

"Slavery, that's what it is, nothing but slavery."

As Jimmy was getting his ears cuffed again, this time by Cherry, Nathaniel and Maria went out into the moonlight.

The family set about their separate duties: Oswald lifted up the large black kettle that was half crouched in the embers of the fire and took it into the scullery and poured the water into the tin bowl that Anna had already half filled with cold water.

Not until this was completed did she say to him, "Well, what do you think about their news?"

"It's not going to make much difference to us, is it?"

She looked up sharply at Oswald, and the flickering candle-light seemed for a moment to turn him into a man, and she asked softly, "Have . . . have you minded?"

"I wouldn't have been human if I hadn't."

"And Olan?"

"The same; yet not quite. Well, you heard what he said. What about you?"

"Oh." She paused for a moment and looked at her hand sluicing a piece of blue mottle soap round and round in the water; then she said quietly, "Just now and again when I heard the word."

"The word. Aye, it twists your guts up, doesn't it? If it were only the one word used, bastards, you'd get used to it, but somebody comes up with a new one, gillyvors, base-borns: base-born child of Maria Dagshaw and Nathaniel Martell, it says on our registration papers."

She brought her hand out of the water, shook it, then dried it on a rough piece of towelling hanging from a nail on the cupboard door to the side of her and, turning to him again and using the pet name that her father didn't like, she said, "I'm sorry, Ossie, but they couldn't have done anything else the way they felt. And they're wonderful people. You *do* understand?"

"Oh, yes." He put out his hand and patted her cheek, saying, "Don't you worry your head about what I say, Anna. Of course they are wonderful people. It's all the other buggers that are not."

"Eeh! Ossie"—she pushed him as she chuckled—"don't let them hear you swear. By the way, do you know the real meaning of gillyvors?"

"Yes, we are the real meaning, what else is there?"

"Well, if you break it up, a gilly is a woman of easy virtue, vor is her offspring, so there you get gillyvors or gillyflower."

"Is that so? Well, Ma's no woman of easy virtue. Anyway, we've got this far, so I suppose we'll weather the rest, God willing. Oh—" Oswald laughed quietly—"God willing. What do you think about Ben and his question? It shook Dada, I could see."

Her voice serious now, she said, "Ben's questioning would shake anyone; at times he seems too good to be true . . . Sh! Look out! Here they come."

With the others now crowding into the kitchen with dirty plates and crocks, all serious issues were swamped in joke and chatter and chastising— the happy façade had been resumed.

TWO

"*I* can't believe you'll not be popping in the door tomorrow morning. I'm going to miss you, my dear."

"And I'll miss you, too, Miss Netherton. Oh, yes. Yet"—Anna smiled—"I'm not going to the ends of the earth, not even into Newcastle, just into Fellburn, and to . . . *Miss Benfield's Academy For Young Ladies.*" They laughed together now, and Miss Netherton, putting her hands on Anna's shoulders, pressed her away, then surveyed her up and down, saying, "You look very smart. Your mother is a very handy woman with her needle. In fact, she is a very handy woman altogether. Do you know, I've always envied her. Yes, even in her plight and her struggles. What would I not have given to have a family, to have a daughter just like you. But there it is, man proposes and God disposes. But come; we must get away if you are to arrive at your post on time." Her hand went out again now to Anna's head and she said, "How nice it is to see you in a hat. Why must the young and the old be expected to wear bonnets? I could never stand them."

She turned now to Ethel Mead, who was standing apart, and called to her, "Doesn't she look beautiful, Ethel?"

Ethel adjusted her winged, starched cap, then the shoulder straps of her bibbed white apron before she said, "Well, I've always been learned that 'andsome is as 'andsome does. So, I suppose you can say the same for beauty."

"Oh, don't hurt yourself in your praise, Ethel." Miss Netherton laughed, then added, "Is that all you've got to say to Anna?"

The elderly woman now turned and looked at the slim young girl, and, her face softening, she said, "I hope it's a good start in life for you, an' I wish you well."

"Thank you, Ethel, thank you so much." Yet even as she spoke she knew that whereas Miss Netherton was sorry to lose her, Ethel would be glad to see the back of her, for she was devoted to her mistress and was naturally jealous of anyone she imagined was taking her place in Miss Netherton's affections.

But in the yard, Robert Stoddart showed sincere heartiness and goodwill as he assisted her into the brake, saying, "Up! with you then, miss, and let's get you to that school an' knock sense into those bairns. What d'you say, ma'am?"

"I say the same as you, Rob: let's get her there; but we'll never arrive on time if you stand chattering and arranging rugs. We can see to ourselves. Get up, man!"

Anna exchanged a smile with the neatly dressed, small lady now sitting opposite her, and yet again she thought, how wonderful this little woman is. How she could talk, even chatter to her servants, whom others would class as menials and beneath their notice, and yet still hold their deep respect.

There were those, however, beyond the household, who regarded her with fear, for wasn't she a property owner?

As they reached the village she told herself to sit straight and hold her head high, for they could do nothing to her when she was with Miss Netherton. Only once before had she ventured to pass through the village on her own, and she had ended up in the wood crying her eyes out, while beating her fists against the tree trunk, imagining she was pummelling the face of the blacksmith's younger son, who had made a gesture to her that she would never forget, and which she knew she dare not speak of to her ma or dada. As peace loving as her father was, she knew he would have gone into the village and taken a whip with him, for his fists would have been no match for Arthur Lennon.

Miss Netherton now leant towards her and in a raised voice to cover the noise of the wheels on the rutted road and the trotting of the horse, she said, "There's one thing I'm not sure of, and that is how Miss Benfield will view that lovely dress."

"Why?" Anna now drew the sides of her cape apart and looked down on the grey woollen dress while adding, "It's plain."

"Yes, my dear, it's plain for many occasions; but the waist is not straight. You see, it comes to a point, as does the neckline. I never thought about asking her if she had any rules on uniform. Still"—she flung her arms up— "what does it matter? The children will like it, and they'll like you. You'll be a figure of interest. Oh, yes, compared with the other two I saw." She chuckled now. "I didn't ask her if she had a decent cook, but anyway, I'm sure you'll get enough to sustain you at dinner time. It is in your agreement that you get one meal. I understand that the children leave at four, but that the teachers have to tidy up the schoolrooms and check the work that has been done during the day. You will soon get into the routine. But there's going to be a snag with the winter coming on. It will be dark and although the two miles or so will be nothing to walk in the summer, it will be quite different later on. And the nights are cutting in quickly now. Have you thought . . . ?"

"There's a carrier cart leaves the market at ten past five. I shall get that."

"Oh, well, that won't be so bad; but you'll still have the fields to cross."

"Father or the boys will meet me; at least, someone will."

"Ah!" And Miss Netherton sat back against the padded rail of the brake. "We are about to enter the underworld. Sit up straight. But then, you are sitting up straight; you always sit up straight. But don't look at me, look from side to side. Keep talking, chatter about anything; look amiable, as if you were used to this early journey every day because, you know, they'll be at their doors and gates before we reach the end of the village. John Fenton will stop cutting his bacon and he'll call to his wife and his mother to come and see, and she'll say, 'Where're they off to at this time in the mornin'?'"

Miss Netherton went on chatting and looking around, as she had bidden Anna to do, and she, taking up her mood, said in a light tone, "Mr. Cole is unloading a carcass from his hand-cart. There's a young man with him; I suppose it's his son."

"That'll be Stan. Yes, that'll be Stan, the apple of his mother's eye . . . or the orange in the pig's mouth."

Anna only just managed to stop throwing her head back and letting out a peal of laughter. Then she muttered, "Mrs. Fawcett, the parson's wife, has just emerged from The Vicarage Lane."

"Oh, I must bow to her. How far is she down?"

"She'll be in your view within the next"—she paused—"ten seconds, I should say."

The parson's wife had stopped on the grass verge that surrounded the village pump, and Miss Netherton, looking as it were across Anna's shoulder, inclined her head to the woman and smiled, whilst saying under her breath, "Just turn your head slightly. Don't smile, just glance at her, then look at me again and go on talking."

It was like a scene in one of the little plays that she wrote for Christmas, so that they could all join in.

Miss Netherton was saying, "By the look on her face I think she's going to have a seizure, and they will have to send for Doctor Snell. You know, I think my driving through the village is the only entertainment they ever have."

At the end of the straggling street the road began to narrow to become no wider than a lane, and it was here that they met up with an approaching gig and Miss Netherton, standing up and looking over Rob Stoddart's shoulder, said, "Pull into the side a moment, Rob, and pull up."

The open carriage had been approaching at a pace, but now the horses dropped into a trot and were brought to a stop by the side of the brake. Two men were sitting in the front, and the one holding the reins touched his cap and, bending forward, said, "Good day, Miss Netherton. You're out early."

"Apparently I'm not the only one, Simon . . . or you, Raymond." She turned her head slightly to address the other man and he said, "I could give you two hours or more, Miss Netherton; I've had a gallop already."

"Oh, my goodness! You have almost done a day's work." There was sarcasm in the tone. Then looking at the man she had addressed as Simon, she said, "Oh, Simon, may I introduce my companion, Miss Dagshaw. Miss Dagshaw, Mr. Brodrick."

The man's eyes had widened just the slightest, and there may have been a slight hesitation before his hand went to his cap again, as he said, "Pleased to make your acquaintance, Miss Dagshaw."

Anna gave no reply, but inclined her head in acknowledgement. Then her gaze was lifted to the other man. He was looking at her through narrowed lids, but he did not acknowledge the introduction.

And Miss Netherton, quick to notice this, put in hastily, "Well, we must be away or we'll be late for an appointment. Good-bye, Simon. Good-bye,

Raymond." The two men again touched their caps in salute, and Rob Stoddart said, "Gee up! there." And they went bowling down the lane.

It was some minutes before Miss Netherton spoke; and when she did it was to ask the question: "Do you know who those gentlemen were?"

"Yes."

"Oh, you've met them before?"

"No. But I've seen them in the distance when the hunt was on, or in the early morning, when one or other of them rode past the bottom of the land when making for the moor. I . . . I didn't know who they were until Dada pointed them out to me."

"Well, if you ever write that story you are always talking about, you could do worse than set it in my previous home; you could even use our family, for you would find good material there. It wouldn't be so exciting as this present family, though, because there was no malice in it."

"There is malice among them?"

"Oh, yes. Yes. There are very few saints in the world, Anna; we're all a mixture of good and bad. Well, those two brothers have got their share, with more good than bad in Simon, but more bad than good in Raymond; at least, that's how I see them. And from my experience, it's the good one that always gets hold of the rotten end of the stick. Simon is the younger by a year, so Raymond is in charge of the estate, the farms, and some of their business deals, such as the Beulah mine. They don't own it, but have a good share of it, and by all accounts he is a hard enough task-master. The brothers are like chalk and cheese, as brothers often are. Poor old Simon has tied himself well and truly to that house, with his mother, wife and child."

At this point she took a long-handled umbrella and poked Rob in the back with it, saying, "Do you purposely look out for holes in the road, man? I won't have a tooth left in my head shortly."

Rob answered with a grunt and went on talking to his horse as he guided her over the rough pot-holed track.

Anna said, "The mother is an invalid, I understand?"

"Yes. She broke her back while holidaying in Switzerland some years ago and has been on a spinal carriage ever since. Well, that's when she's not in bed; but she can be wheeled about on this carriage, you see. And Simon has that job most of the time; she never lets him out of her sight. But I must admit he's very fond of her."

"The father? Isn't he there?"

"No. Arnold Brodrick travels. My own papa and he could have been brothers in their desire for travel, although in Arnold Brodrick's case it's to get away from responsibility, a sick wife and a vixen of a daughter-in-law. Now, you could get your teeth into that family for a story, as I said. Oh, yes, yes. By the way, have you written anything lately besides those little rhymes of yours?"

"I . . . I started, but the only thing I could write about with any strength of feeling was our family because, I've got to face it, I've had no experience of the world. Nor have any of us, have we?"

"Well, I won't say that. I think you've all had experience of reactions of some members of the world, and forcibly. And you know, Anna"—she now leant forward and gripped Anna's knee—"it isn't ended. In your own particular case, and perhaps that of Cherry, it's just beginning. Men can fight the stigma in their own way. Although they feel it deeply, the male in them won't let them admit it. I've known some even to brag about it; at least, if their lineage just might have been connected with those in high places. Your mother and father, you know, and of course you do know, have defied convention, they have spat in its eye; but they picked the wrong place to do it, near the narrow confines of a village. If they had chosen to live in the city or some large town it could have passed unnoticed, or nearly so. But if one desires to be burnt alive, then I would say go and live in a village and do something that half of them would like to do but haven't the courage. Oh, it's amazing how frustrated desire can appear under the heading of righteousness. But it's been so all down the ages. I think I've said it to you before, I'm sure I have"—she tossed her head and laughed now—"I've said so much to you. You're the only one, you know, I can talk to without keeping my tongue in my cheek. But what I am going to say now is, you must read the Greeks, more philosophy, Plato, Aristotle. Your father, naturally, hasn't touched on these except for his own entertainment. He's immersed in the later Roman period, isn't he? But you would garner wisdom from Aristotle. Well, just give it another name, common sense. Of course, you will find that philosophers, being human beings, will contradict themselves here and there, and each other. But you can blow away the chaff from the wheat and use it to your own advantage.

"A-ha!" she now exclaimed. "Here we go into the street of learning. You know, my dear"—again she was bending forward—"I wish I could have started you off in some better place, but I know you understand the reasons. And as I've also said, do a year or so here, by which time you will have had experience, then maybe I'll be able to talk sense and charity into one or two scholastic friends. At least, I hope so. Females, you know, are much more difficult to deal with than men. I prefer men any day in the week. In fact, I don't like women. Did you know that? I just don't like women. Of course, in your case you will have to look out for both men and women, for from the looks of you, you will have trouble with the former in one way and with the latter in more ways than one."

Wasn't it odd, Anna thought, that this kindly, lovable benefactress should have that one flaw: she would never let her forget that she had an obstacle to surmount, that there would always be this obstacle, but it was not surmountable. However, she put out her hand and gripped the older woman's, saying, "Whatever happens to me from now on, there won't be a moment of my life in which I will stop thanking you for what you have done for me, and not only for me, but for my family. Now, don't get up. I'll have to be on my own from today but I shall slip across tonight and tell you all my news and how I have implanted wisdom and knowledge into five- and six-year-olds, or perhaps the nines or tens . . . never the fourteens. I think I'll be a long time before I reach the fourteen-year-olds in Miss Benfield's Academy."

"Go on with you! And my wishes go with you. You know that." She pushed her towards the back of the brake, where Rob had pulled down the step, and as he helped her to the ground he said, "Best of luck, miss. Best of luck." Then leaning towards her, he whispered, "Knock it into 'em. And I bet you'll have to do just that with some."

"Shut up! you, and get back about your business."

Anna gave one last look at her friend before walking towards the green-painted door and pulling on the iron-handled bell.

The brake had disappeared half-way down the street before the door was opened and a small dishevelled maid of no more than twelve years old pulled the door open, let her enter, closed it, then, adjusting a none-too-clean print cap, said, "When you come, I 'ad to show you to the dinin' room. It's down 'ere." She crossed the narrow hall and opened a door from which stone steps led down to the basement.

Anna followed her, but at the bottom step she paused for a moment and gazed in amazement at what she saw was the kitchen. But all she could take in was the rough stone floor, a black stove, a wooden table, and to the side of it a stone sink, and, at the far end was the grating through which she had seen the steam emerge. It was that grating that afforded the only light in the room.

Then the little maid was knocking on a door, and when she received the command to enter, she pushed it open and stood aside, and Anna walked into what was used as the dining-room, but which she recognised instantly was just a part of the kitchen that had been partitioned off. On the far wall was the sash window that should have given light to the whole room.

Miss Benfield was sitting at a table on which there was the remains of a cooked breakfast: there was a greasy plate in front of her which showed the traces of egg yolk. Another person was also in the room; she was standing behind a chair.

Miss Benfield looked steadily at Anna for a full minute before she drew in a sharp breath; then, as if diverted by the slight throaty noise the other woman had made, she turned to her, saying, "This is Miss Kate Benfield, a relative, and my first assistant."

Anna looked at the woman across the table and inclined her head and smiled, but she received no answering smile, merely a slight movement of the head.

Anna thought she had never seen anyone with such a miserable countenance, and on this admittedly slight acquaintance, she appeared to be the antithesis of her relative. The only resemblance was in their height, both women being tall, but this one was thin, so thin she looked emaciated.

"You are not suitably dressed."

"What! Why?"

"When you speak to me, you will address me as Miss Benfield."

"Why do you consider me not suitably dressed, Miss Benfield?" She turned her glance quickly from the big woman to the slight one because she thought she had heard her gasp. Then again she was looking at her employer, for she was saying, "You wish to be a pupil teacher, then you should have some idea of how such a one should appear before a class of children. The uniform is as Miss Kate's here: a white blouse and a black skirt, that to reach the top of your boots or shoes." She leant her head sideways, observing Anna's grey skirt, which was showing an inch of stocking between the hem of her dress and the black laces of her shoes.

"I'm afraid, Miss Benfield, that I do not possess a black skirt and white blouse, at least, that is, at present, but I have a dark blue dress and I will come attired in it tomorrow and until such time as I can acquire a suitable uniform."

Miss Benfield was on her feet, her huge chest heaving as if being assisted by a pump. "You are getting off to a bad start, young woman. Now, let me inform you there is a way to address me and there is a way not to address me. And if you wish to continue here, and rise in this establishment, you will learn that, and quickly. Your tone is anything but deferential, which manner you would be wise to adopt in future. Have I made myself plain?"

"Very plain, Miss Benfield."

The breasts rose and threatened the buttons on the black satin blouse; then the indignant lady turned to her first assistant and said, "You will take Miss Dagshaw and introduce her to the duties required of her today."

The first assistant turned sharply away and made for the door and, after staring at the woman's back for a moment, Anna turned as abruptly and followed her through the kitchen, past the little maid, who was scooping ashes from the hearth, up the dark stone stairway and into the hall; thence down a passage to a room that had been partitioned off.

There were no desks in this room, but there were two long, narrow tables, each with its backless bench, and so placed one in front of the other that the children sitting at them would be facing the blackboard attached to a wall. There was a cupboard opposite the door, and this Miss Kate Benfield opened. It contained four shelves; and she started at the top. Taking down two boxes, she pointed to the pieces of cardboard inside, saying briefly, "The alphabet. You know how to teach that, don't you? You hold them up like this." She picked up a piece of cardboard. "You ask them what that is; then you make them all repeat it ten times. Then, according to how far they're advanced, you do, cat, dog, rat, mat, sat, and fat. You've done this, I suppose?"

Anna made no response, so the woman put the boxes back, saying, "That occupies the first hour." Then pointing to the second shelf, on which there were a number of tattered-backed books, she said, "Nursery rhymes. They'll know some of these already, having learned them at home." She was now pointing to the third shelf. "These trays are for clay," she said. "You'll find the clay in there," and she pointed to two tin boxes. "But you won't need these until the afternoon. They are getting tired by then. But these"—she was lifting some picture books from the bottom shelf—"these are for the last hour in the morning. You can hand these out if they are getting restless, and ask them to tell stories about the pictures of the animals or birds. Think you can do that?"

"I should think so." Anna's tone was cold and it wasn't lost on the woman, for she said, "Well, you knew what you were in for, and you're starting at the bottom."

There was something in the voice that didn't match the countenance and caused Anna to say, "Thank you for your help. You're right. I'm starting at the bottom. By the way, may I enquire what relation you are to Miss Benfield?"

"Cousin."

"Oh."

"Yes, cousin." The head was nodding now and it seemed to Anna that she might have said something further about the relationship but, the hall clock striking nine, she said, "That's fast. It's ten minutes to. The horde will be arriving at any second now," and on this she smartly left the room.

Anna turned and surveyed the small room and the cupboard, and her thoughts were not that very soon she would be attempting to teach small children for the first time but that she would be spending the whole day in this airless, dusty little square. And when her mind touched on her home she closed her eyes for a moment as she muttered, Oh, dear God! I don't think I can stand this.

"*Quiet now! Quiet now!* Go to your rooms." The voice brought her eyes springing wide and a hand to her throat. She was here and she must stay and put up with it. There was Miss Netherton to think about, besides her ma and dada.

"*Miss Dagshaw.*"

She started slightly as she heard her name bellowed from the hall, and she hurried along the passage, there to see Miss Benfield surrounded by eight small figures, while other children were making their way up the stairs. It would seem, though, that there was some impediment on the stairs, for a number of them stopped, so blocking the way for the rest, and they all turned and looked down on her.

Leaving the small children, Miss Benfield smartly stepped into the passage and almost hissed at Anna, "Haven't you the sense to take off your coat and hat? Are you thinking about teaching the children like that?"

Bristling now, Anna said, "Well, will you kindly tell me, please, where I can hang my coat and hat?"

Miss Benfield swallowed; then, turning to the children, she said, "Margaret, show Miss Dagshaw where the teachers' room is."

The small girl sidled past Anna, hardly taking her eyes from her; then ran back along the corridor, turned a corner and pushed open a door.

"Thank you."

Anna now saw that the teachers' room consisted of two cubicles, the first holding three wooden chairs, a two-foot-by-one table, and a row of wooden pegs attached to the wall. It also had half a window and this was uncurtained. But when she pushed open the door in the partition she saw that the other half of the window was covered by a yellow-paper roller blind and that below it was a wooden frame with a hole in it, and directly below the opening was a tin bucket.

She closed the door quickly, drew in a long breath, took off her hat and hung it on one of the hooks, with her cloak under it. Her cloth handbag, in which was her purse, she kept in her hand; then, opening the door, she made for her classroom, which was but a few steps away.

The children were already seated, eight bright faces, well-washed and well-fed-looking faces, and as she returned their stares she wondered at the parents who would allow their children to be taught in a place like this.

"Good morning, children."

"Good morning, miss." The voices came at her one after the other. There followed a silence in which she wondered what she should say; then she was saying it. "I am your new teacher and so I hope you will help me to get over my first day. Will you?" There was silence for a moment; then, "Yes, teacher. Yes, teacher. Yes, teacher." She looked at the four little children sitting upright on the first form and said, "Now, tell me your names." And pointing to the end one, she said, "Yes?" and one after the other they said their names, some in a whisper, some loudly: "Mary. Sarah. Kathleen," and she herself, smiling at the fourth one, said, "And I know you are Margaret."

"Yes, teacher."

After she had been given the names of those on the back form, she said, "Now, shall we start with the alphabet? You usually start with the alphabet, don't you?"

"No, miss; you call the register." It was Margaret again.

She looked helplessly towards the open cupboard. She had no register. She hadn't been told about the register.

"Oh. Well, we'll see about that later . . ."

There was no actual break until twelve o'clock, except that which the children contrived for themselves by asking: "May I leave the room, miss?" And one bright spark caused a giggle. When coming back into the room from her excursion, she remarked, "It stinks."

At twenty minutes past eleven, if she was to judge by the hall clock striking the half hour and it being ten minutes fast, there were one or two yawns, so she decided to brighten things up in the rhyme section by getting the children to demonstrate the words as much as possible by the use of their hands. Looking through the book, she picked *Jack and Jill* and said, "Now children, let's be Jack and Jill, shall we? What did they do first?"

"They went up the hill, miss."

"All right, we'll all go up the hill."

Eight pairs of arms followed her actions and clawed their way up the hill.

There were only six rhymes in the ragged cloth books, and when they had finished demonstrating the last: *Hickory, Dickory, Dock, The Mouse Ran Up The Clock,* and she said, "Well, that is all," one child called out, "Tell us another, miss," and this was echoed by the others, "Yes; let us do another, miss. Please."

She put her head back as if thinking; and she was thinking of all the nursery rhymes her father had taught them and the funny little rhymes she herself had made up, dozens of them. But she had better stick to the well-known ones . . . Which one would be good for demonstrating?

'There was a little man'? Yes, yes; she would do that one. She said aloud: "I know a nursery rhyme. You can all act to it. It is called, 'There was a little man.'"

And so she began:

"There was a little man,
And he had a little gun—"

She stopped here and said, "Well, make a gun. You know, a gun." She used both arms stretched out now as if she were holding a gun to her shoulder. Then she went on,

"And his bullets were made
of lead, lead, lead, . . ."

"And his bullets were made of lead, lead, lead," they repeated, then there was a chorus of, "Bang! Bang!" Followed by high laughter, and, "Do it again, teacher! Do it again!" So she did it again, going through the whole rhyme this time, and the responses grew louder and the laughter became higher. Then suddenly the door burst open and the first assistant appeared, her face expressing amazement.

"What on earth!"

"We are just demonstrating a nursery rhyme."

"I heard." It was a low whisper. Then, "Come outside for a moment."

In the dark corridor the woman said, "She just needs to hear that and you'll be out of the door. Bullets through the head; I've never heard such a thing."

"It's a nursery rhyme: There was a little man, he shot a little duck . . ."

"Well, I've never heard of it. I'm just in the next room. I couldn't believe my ears at first. Look"—her voice sank—"if you want to remain here, stick to the rules."

"I don't know whether I want to remain here."

"Well, that's up to you. But I'll say this much, I think you'll work out all right, for you're the best teacher we've had for a long time. Now, take my advice and go in there and tell them they mustn't repeat that nursery rhyme, that's if they want to see you again. I'll leave it to you to work out how you'll do that. So far, from what I've heard, you seem to be able to cope with most things."

Again Anna wanted to thank this miserable-looking woman. She also wanted to step round the corner, go into that smelly cubicle and put on her hat and cloak and go home.

And admit defeat?

She drew in a long breath and returned to the classroom.

At five o'clock Miss Benfield called Anna into the downstairs classroom and reminded her of her dissatisfaction with her apparel. She also said that, from what she had overheard, her discipline needed a great deal of improvement, and, if she did not like the meal that was provided then she had better bring her own.

To all this, and probably to Miss Benfield's surprise, Anna made no reply. She was feeling tired and weary. Moreover, she was cold. The whole house was cold. And she was hungry . . .

When she reached the market square, the carrier cart had already left, and she had never known herself to be so near to tears. She would have to walk; the twilight would soon be on her, and if she didn't hurry it would be dark before she reached the cut, which was the shortest way home. That path, at one point, passed close to the edge of the quarry, and although the quarry wasn't all that deep, she wouldn't like to fall into it in the dark. But then her father might still be waiting for her. Yet, if he saw that she wasn't on the carrier's cart, would he stay there? No; more likely he'd go back and get their own cart out.

She had been standing on her feet for most of the day, and so by the time she had left the town and had taken to the country road her step had slowed.

And when she reached the cut, she wasn't surprised to find no-one waiting for her.

The cut, as it was called, ran between open green fields, through a small copse, then uphill onto the edge of the quarry, which was no more than thirty feet at its deepest point and extended over hardly an eighth of an acre. It was said that the demand for its stone had already dwindled before it was half dug out. Going away from it, the path once again ran between open fields, until it merged into the moor. At one point it crossed the bridle-path to the village. At the edge of the moor another hardly discernible path led to their own patch of woodland which, in turn, gave way to the hill and there, in its shelter, was home.

As she rounded the bottom of the hill, she saw in the distance the lights on the cart picking out Neddy's rump, and she went into a stumbling run now, shouting, "Dada! I'm here!"

It was Jimmy who heard her first, and his voice echoed back to her: "She's here, Dada!"

In the yard they were all about her, questioning, but her father's voice rose above the rest, demanding harshly, "Where've you been? Why weren't you on the cart, girl?"

"Oh, Dada, let me get in and sit down. I'm worn out. One way and another, I'm worn out."

In the kitchen Maria said, "You've had us worried, dear. You see, you're not used to the town and . . ."

"Ma, let me take my shoes off."

Eager hands were now at her feet and they took her shoes off and lifted her cold soles towards the blaze of the fire while rubbing them.

"May I have something hot, Ma?"

"Yes, my love, yes. It's all ready; some mutton broth."

"What happened?" It was Oswald bending towards her now.

She turned to look over her shoulder, saying, "Wait till Dada comes in" —she smiled wanly now—"and I'll tell you, right from the beginning at nine o'clock this morning. No; ten minutes to, onwards."

She had finished the soup and eaten two large slices of bread and pork fat before Nathaniel came into the room. He seemed to have taken his time unharnessing the horse and stabling it, and Maria looked at him anxiously while making a motion with her head; then he was standing in front of her, saying, "Well! let me have it. What kept you? It was all arranged that you would come home on the cart."

Anna let out a very audible sigh, then said, "Do you want to hear the whole story before you eat, or after?" At this there was laughter; but when he said, "For my part, before," there were slight groans. So she told them exactly what had happened, from the meeting with the head of the establishment in the so-called dining room, the condition of the kitchen, what she was expected to teach, the watery stew with the grease floating on the top, which she couldn't stomach at dinner time, the first assistant for whom she felt sorry, and lastly, what had prevented her from catching the cart, which was the lecture from Miss Benfield.

"She can't go back there again, can she?" Maria appealed to Nathaniel; and he thought for a moment, then looked at his daughter and said, "Well, it's up to you. Why not leave it until after we have eaten properly and then you can tell me what you intend to do, and I will go across to Miss Netherton and give her a report, because I can see you're all in."

"Dada." She looked up at him and, her voice soft, she said, "It's your fault, you know; you've made it too easy for me all these years."

THREE

*A*nna continued to teach at Miss Kate Benfield's Academy during the remainder of September, then through October and November, and she had experience with all the children, from the five-year-olds right up to those of fourteen, who were classed as young ladies.

It should happen that Miss Benfield, the first assistant, who usually supervised the nine-to-eleven and the twelve-to-fourteen children's classes, was subject to severe bouts of head colds, during which she sniffed, blew and coughed a great deal until, hardly able to stand, Miss Benfield the elder would allow her to go to her room . . . wherever that was. Anna never found out.

When this happened Anna would take one or other of these classes on alternate mornings and afternoons and, of all Miss Benfield's classes, she liked taking those of the older girls, for she knew they enjoyed her teaching, although twice she had been pulled over the coals by Miss Benfield for taking liberties with Shakespeare. Miss Benfield had insisted that she herself would choose passages that the girls must learn by rote and from which they must not deviate.

In the course of her teaching she also had to deal with religious instruction. There was no Bible in any of the classrooms, but prior to the religious lesson Miss Benfield would hand her a copy, having marked a particular psalm or proverb that Anna must read to her class, then ask them questions about; after which they were to write a short essay on the subject.

It transpired that today she had marked the Thirty-sixth Psalm: "Wickedness confronts God's Love". It consisted of twelve short verses; but, of course, that wasn't enough for Miss Benfield, who had also marked the first part of the Proverbs: the Proverbs of Solomon, Son of David, King of Israel. And Anna was instructed to tell her pupils they were to write a short essay on the word "wisdom".

So here she was facing nine young ladies, so-called, five of the age of fourteen, four of the age of thirteen, and their faces were full of interest. She was aware that they liked her, and with the exception of one girl, she liked them. And yet it should happen that this particular girl was the brightest of them all. In fact, Miss Lilian Burrows, Anna considered, was too advanced for her age and she was sure that the knowledge she had acquired hadn't all come from Miss Benfield's Academy. .

So she began.

"Well now, you are all aware what day this is"—she made a little moue with her mouth—"and you know what lesson we have on a Friday."

"Oh, yes, yes."

"Oh, yes, teacher, yes."

The scoffing retorts came from them all. They still had to address her as "teacher" even though she had earlier pointed out they could call her Miss Dagshaw. This had caused another storm in Miss Benfield's bosom. The only one to be addressed as "Miss" was herself. Would she please remember that!

Anna had, on that occasion, said she would try, and the bosom had swelled still further. There were many nights she caused her brothers and sisters to roll on the floor when, with a pillow pushed down a bibbed apron, her dark thick shining hair dragged up to the top of her head and her feet turned outwards, she performed a remarkable imitation of the mistress.

"Not Proverbs again, teacher!"

She looked down at the pained expression of a pretty girl sitting in the front desk.

"I'm afraid so, Rosalie; but we are having the Psalms first."

The groans were so audible that she turned and looked quickly towards the door, then said, "Shh! Shh!" And when quiet was restored she said, "Now listen carefully. This is the Thirty-sixth Psalm and it is headed, 'To the chief Musician, A Psalm of David, The Servant Of The Lord'. Just write. " 'A Psalm of David.' "

She waited; then after a moment she said, "It deals with wickedness that confronts God's love." She glanced around her, then began to read.

The transgression of the wicked saith within my heart, *that there is* no fear of God before his eyes.

For he flattereth himself in his own eyes, until his iniquity be found to be hateful.

The words of his mouth *are* iniquity and deceit: he has left off to be wise, *and* to do good.

Verse after verse she read until she reached the twelfth one. When she had finished she said, "As you know, you will have to write a short essay dealing with the wickedness that confronts God's love. Shall I read it again?"

"No, miss, no. Anyway, we read that psalm some weeks ago."

One bright voice piped up now, saying, "Miss Pinkerton read it on her last day here. She used to almost stutter."

"She didn't!"

"She did."

"She didn't! She had a lisp."

The two combatants turned to a third girl who said, "She didn't reign long." Then this girl, looking at Anna, said, "You know, teacher, you've stuck it the longest. But anyway, I hope you go on till I leave; I'm going into Newcastle at Easter."

"Oh my! Oh my! She's going into Newcastle at Easter."

At this point Anna rapped her ruler on her desk, saying, "Now! now! No more chatter. Let's get on. You don't wish me to read the psalm again and so we'll turn to the essay."

It was then that the bright spark, Miss Lilian Burrows, put up her hand, and in a high, superior, affected tone, said, "Read us something from the Songs of Solomon, teacher, please."

Anna's eyes widened. Here was someone who knew about the Songs of Solomon. She looked at Lilian and said quietly, "How many of the Songs have you read, Lilian?"

"Oh"—the girl shrugged her shoulders—"I've been through them all. I know bits and pieces here and there. Do you know them, teacher?"

"Yes. Yes, I know them."

"Where did you learn them? In Church? Sunday School?"

"No. I have never been to Sunday School. My father taught me; he's a teacher. I have been reading them since I was quite young. They are difficult to understand at first; but they are beautiful."

Lilian stared at Anna; then slowly she stood up, her quiet demeanour vanished and the bright bragging spark took over. In a voice belying that it was from a fourteen-year-old girl, she began,

"The voice of my beloved!
behold, he cometh leaping
upon the mountains, skipping
upon the hills.
My beloved is like a roe or a
young hart."

Anna stood amazed; her lips were following each word; in fact, keeping in time with the girl. Then she heard her own voice joining in with the words:

"behold, he standeth
behind our wall, he
looketh forth at the
windows, showing
himself through the
lattice."

She herself paused, but she couldn't stop the flow of the young girl who, head back, was oblivious to where she was as, her voice getting louder, she went on:

"My beloved spake, and said unto me,
Rise up, my love, my fair one . . ."

"That's enough! That's enough!"

The rest of the girls were staring at their companion, watching her as she let out a long breath and then slowly sat down.

Now they transferred all their attention to Anna, waiting for her words of chastisement; but she couldn't chastise the girl, even though she knew she should, because what she had put into those lines had nothing to do with religion. Looking at her now, she asked her, "Does your family pray together?"

The girl gave a loud "Huh!" by way of answer; but then said slowly, "No; we don't pray together."

There was uneasiness in the room. The girls were not fidgeting but looking straight at her, and now she said, "We shall all deal with the Song of Solomon later; now, we shall write our essays . . ."

Nothing seemed to go right for the rest of the day and when, later, during the uncomfortable ride home on the back of the cart, she saw in the distance a speck of light from her father's lantern, she felt she wanted to jump off the cart and run to him and feel the comfort of his arms and the solace of his quiet voice.

But when the cart stopped, Nathaniel had actually to help her down, so stiff was she with the cold. And the carter called to Nathaniel, "There's snow on the way; had a flake or two way back. Glad to get home the night. See you Monday, lass."

"Yes. Thank you. See you Monday."

"You're freezing. Here, put my scarf round you."

"No, no; I'm all right. Just let's hurry."

"You'll not be able to keep this up if the weather breaks. You're shivering like a leaf. Anyway, what kind of a day have you had?"

"Awful. I'll tell you about it later."

"By the way, we've got visitors."

"Visitors?" When she paused in her step he pulled her forward, saying, "Come on. Come on."

"Who are they?"

"Two pit families. They had been on the moor; I hadn't seen them. Apparently they had been coming into the wood at night to get shelter from the wind. They had erected a kind of tent against the wood pile. That gave them a bit of support. But they must have scampered off at first light. It was Ben who brought them in; at least, he brought five bairns to the door."

"Five?"

"Yes, five; the oldest one about seven: rags on their feet, practically the same on their backs. Your ma brought them in and gave them broth, but she said she couldn't let them stay in the house, and rightly, for their heads were walking, they were alive. Anyway, the father of two of them came down and apologised. He was a decently spoken man. I asked him how long he had been out and he said a week or more, but that they would have to make for the poor house shortly; he couldn't see his wife and bairns freeze to death out there. So I had a word with your ma and she was with me, as I knew she would be, and we told them to bring their bits and pieces down. They hadn't much; they had sold what furniture they had for grub. They did have some bedding and cooking utensils. Anyway, there's plenty of dry hay in the barn, and I lit the boiler in the tack room. We keep nothing much in there; only Neddy's harness and odds and ends. The men rigged up a kind of cooking stove, so they can eat in there and be warm. And as your ma suggested, they can have a wash down—she would, wouldn't she?" He laughed. "She's worried about Ben being near the bairns and picking up the army from their heads. I told her Ben must have been in touch with them for days; so she'll scour him tonight to make sure."

"Life's very unfair, Dada, isn't it?"

"In some cases it is, dear, but I must admit that many get more than their share of unfairness."

"You did."

"Me? Oh, no, I didn't. I've been very lucky, my dear. Your ma's had a deal of unfairness, and you and every one of you, and there's more to come, you know that; but not me. There's many a man who'd envy the six children such as I have." He put his arm around her shoulder and pressed her to him.

"Dada."

"Yes, my love?"

"Do you think there's anything bad about The Songs of Solomon?"

"Bad, about The Songs of Solomon? They have some of the most beautiful lines in the Bible."

"Yes, I thought so too."

"What makes you ask such a question?"

"Oh, something that happened today. I'll tell you about it later; all I want at this moment is my feet in front of the fire, a bowl of hot soup in my hands and Ma's fingers gently rubbing the back of my neck and her voice crying at the rest of them, 'Leave her alone! Let her eat.' You know, Dada, I look forward to that scene every day from one o'clock onwards. And I wouldn't exchange it for Solomon's Temple."

Their laughter joined and their arms linked, they went into a slithering run, with the lantern swinging from Nathaniel's extended arm, and they didn't stop till they rounded the foot of the hill and saw the welcoming lamplight from the house.

FOUR

𝒪n the Monday morning Anna did not arrive at Miss Benfield's front door until five minutes to nine. The carrier's horse, an old and wise one, had been wary of the road and its thick coating of frost, and so the journey had been somewhat slower. But as soon as the door was opened by the little maid, she knew that this wasn't going to be an ordinary beginning to another week of repetitious lessons, and hand-clapping to keep her own and the children's fingers flexible, because the young girl, poking her head forward, said, "She wants to see you," her thumb jerking rapidly and indicating, "in the big room."

Anna went to draw the pins from her hat, but stopped; if Miss Benfield was calling her to boot in the main room, something was afoot.

"Good morning, Miss Benfield. It's a very cold . . ."

"*Be quiet!* Don't give me any of your pleasantries. I wonder that you dare show your face in my house."

Anna stared at the woman for a few seconds before saying, "Would you mind telling me, please, what you mean by that remark?"

"Corruption. *Corruption.*" The last word was almost yelled.

For a moment Anna thought the woman had gone mad, that she had lost her senses. But this thought didn't altogether surprise her. So her voice was level as she answered, "I don't understand you."

"You understand what the word 'corruption' means. You have corrupted my girls."

Now she did understand her, and immediately gave Miss Benfield her answer: "You must be out of your mind," and even dared to add, "woman."

The chest heaved twice before the woman could say, "Lilian . . . Lilian Burrows and The Songs of Solomon. Now do you understand?"

She knew both Lilian Burrows and The Songs of Solomon; but she didn't really understand, until Miss Benfield said, "Lilian had a cousin and some friends with her on Friday evening and"—the bosom heaved again, and Miss Benfield swallowed deeply—"when they returned home they told their mother that Lilian had recited pieces to them from the Bible, funny pieces that they hadn't heard before, and that they had giggled." The bosom rose, and on the deep deflation, she said, "Just imagine it. Just imagine it."

"Yes, I can imagine it. She's a very bright girl and it would seem, Miss Benfield, that you are acquainted with the Songs of Solomon."

"I . . . I may be. I am an adult, I understand the meaning, the real meaning of the words of Solomon; but a young girl would put a wrong construction on them. And mind, not only a young girl would do so. And you have imbued this child . . ."

"I have done nothing of the sort."

"You deny it?"

"Emphatically I deny it. Lilian is well acquainted with that part of the Bible, and must have been for some time, because she can rhyme it off."

"Yes, under your tuition, as she said."

"What!"

"Don't pretend innocence, young woman. That child would never have thought of reading such things; in fact, she would have not been aware they were in the Bible, but your corrupt mind introduced her . . ."

"Shut up!"

Miss Benfield actually took a staggering step backwards, and her mouth opened and shut as she sought an answer; but she hadn't time to bring a word out of her froth-smeared lips before Anna cried, "I have never read anything to my pupils except that which you dictated. Lilian Burrows is well-acquainted with the Songs of Solomon, and not with those alone, from what I judge."

"How is it, then, that she could tell her parents that you have been reading them for years."

"Because I told the class so. When the girl stood and recited line after line of a particular verse, the second to be exact, in which, you will remember, Miss Benfield, occur the words, 'The voice of my beloved! behold he cometh . . .' "

She stopped here and Miss Benfield made no sound, but just stared at this daring, beautiful creature whom she had disliked on sight, this bastard child of wicked parents whom, she told herself, she had taken in out of pity and whom she felt had inherited some strange power, an evil power, for in her eyes there was knowledge that shouldn't be there. And, too, her bearing was such as could only be promoted by pride supplied by the devil.

A thin stream of saliva ran down from a corner of Miss Benfield's mouth. She opened her tight lips while at the same time pointing towards the door, saying, "Get out! Leave my house! You've sullied the name of my school and I will see that you find no engagement in this town for your corrupting talents and I'll make sure that Miss Netherton's influence will not aid you in any way in the future."

Anna stared silently at the woman for some seconds before she said, "This is not a school, Miss Benfield, because you have no knowledge to impart. You are an ignorant woman. The little teaching that is done here is supplied by your cousin, that poor downtrodden woman. If the school board were to examine you, you wouldn't have a livelihood, you wouldn't even be allowed to teach in a village school, because the standard there would be so far above you it would be as a university compared to this house. So, I would like you to remember, Miss Benfield, that when you are blackening my name and my ability to teach, I shall not restrain myself from giving my opinion of your establishment.''

As she turned away she thought that the woman was about to have a seizure, and when she opened the door it was to see the children coming in, but before that it was to cause the younger Miss Benfield to take a springing step away from her.

For the first time she could see what could have been a smile on the thin, worn face of the first assistant and she did not lower her voice when she said to her, ''Stand on your feet, Miss Benfield. Face up to her, because without you there would be no Academy For Young Ladies.'' She had curled her lip on the last four words.

When she watched the thin, weary woman bring her teeth tight onto her lower lip, she put her hand quickly out towards her, saying, ''Do it. Make your own terms.'' She took a step backwards, then said, ''Goodbye.''

The children were surprised to see their nice teacher making for the front door and the first assistant scampering after her.

Anna was on the pavement when the woman spoke, her voice coming in gasps as if she had been running: ''Thank you,'' she said. ''I'm glad you came.'' And again she said, ''Thank you.'' And this time her head was bobbing.

Anna said nothing in reply; she could only raise her hand in a gesture of farewell; then she walked past more children escorted by very young so-called nurses and here and there a parent, who looked at the new young teacher in surprise, for she was not going into the Academy but was walking away from it, and it being only nine o'clock in the morning.

The farther she walked into the town the further her anger rose. That dreadful woman. How dare she say her teaching would corrupt? Even if it had been she who introduced the Songs of Solomon, even so, how dare she!

There would be no carrier-cart going her way until twelve o'clock. She paused outside the station. She could get a train to Usworth, but then she would have as far to walk again to get home; what was more, she had never been on a train, and she didn't know how to go about it. Part of her mind told her now that she must do something about that, too, in the future.

The market-place was almost empty. She crossed it to walk down Victoria Road and past the park at the foot of Brampton Hill. Here, the shops on one side of Victoria Road petered out, but did so grandly, with the imposing structure that held the post office on the ground floor and the Registrar of Births and Deaths on the second floor.

She was actually walking blindly when the voice said, ''Oh, I'm sorry. I beg your pardon.''

The man, who had turned from fastening his horse's reins to the horse post at the edge of the rough pavement, put out his hand and gripped her arm as she almost overbalanced.

''I do beg your pardon. I didn't see you . . . Miss . . . Miss . . . you are Miss Dagshaw, aren't you?''

She blinked at the man. He was the one who had acknowledged the introduction that first day, when Miss Netherton had driven her to the school, and here on her last she was meeting him again.

"Are you all right?" He was looking into her face, and she closed her eyes for a moment before she said, "Yes, thank you, sir; I am all right. It was not your fault. I . . . I wasn't looking where I was going because"—she now forced herself to smile—"I was in a temper, which could even be translated into the saying, blind with rage. So you see, it is my fault. But I am all right, thank you." She made to move away, but his concern having obviously changed to merriment, she stopped, and he went on to say, "I won't dare ask what has put you into a rage. But I understood from Miss Netherton that you were in a teaching post?"

"I was, sir, up till about"—she considered—"until twenty minutes or half an hour ago."

His shoulders began to shake again, and she herself laughed. The sound came out in small jerks. Then, remembering who she was, and who he was, she adopted a more sober air and her voice sounded slightly prim as she said, "Good day to you."

As she went to move past him he stopped her with his hand, which did not touch her but was held a foot or so from her as he said, "Since what you say suggests that you are no longer a teacher, at least for today, may I enquire if you are on your way home?"

"Yes. Yes, I am."

"And you mean to walk?"

"Well, sir, having no other means of propulsion except my legs, I mean to walk."

She watched him bring his chin into his high stiff collar for a moment; and further, she noticed that the points of it did not cause a ridge of flesh to form beneath his jaws, as with most men who wore such collars. And then he said, "You know, you sounded just like Miss Netherton. Your turn of phrase and wit is a replica of hers."

Very likely she *was* talking like Miss Netherton because she had patterned herself on her mentor's speech for many years; but as for wit, she couldn't see that she had said anything at all that could merit that word.

"Look," he was saying now, "I've just got to slip into the post office; I want to send a telegram. So would you allow me to give you a lift home? If nothing else, it would take the weight off"—he paused—"your means of propulsion."

As she looked from him to the high, two-wheeled gig with but two seats, she asked herself if it was the right thing to do to accept his offer. What would Miss Netherton have done? Oh, she would have said, let's get away. But there was a great difference between herself and Miss Netherton in relation to this man. He was one of what was termed the gentry. In his eyes, even being a sort of school-marm, she would still be considered a menial, and she didn't like that thought. She never felt like a menial. Miss Netherton had never made her feel like a menial.

"Thank you. That's very kind of you."

"Well then, would you care to come in out of the cold and wait while I do my business?"

She had never been in this post office. When she had gone to buy stamps for her father it had been from the small office near Bog's End.

"Thank you."

He said no more, but went a little ahead of her, and pushed open the door to allow her to pass into the large bare room that was cut in half by a counter.

"Take a seat; I won't be a minute." He pointed to a form fixed to the wall, and she sat down and watched him go to the far end of the counter and speak to the assistant, who handed him a form on which he then wrote something before handing it back, together with some money.

There were three other customers in the post office: one was walking towards the door when, as Simon Brodrick turned from the counter, he stopped and in a loud voice cried, "Well! Hello, you. What are you doing here at this time of the morning?"

"Oh, hello, Harry. Oh, just sending off a wire."

"How's everyone? Haven't seen you for two or three weeks. Missed you last time when Penella came over. What about next week?"

They were near the door now. Anna had risen to her feet and Simon Brodrick put out his hand towards her, but didn't speak. He opened the door and waited for her to pass him. And when they were in the street he did not introduce her to the man but, touching her elbow, helped her up onto the steep step of the gig, then onto the leather seat, before turning to the man, who was muttering something that was inaudible to her.

Simon loosened the horse's bridle from the post and took his seat beside Anna; then looking down at the man, he said, "Give my regards to the family," then shook the reins as he cried to the horse, "Gee up! there," and off they went.

Anna didn't hear what the man replied, if he replied at all; she only knew he had all the while stared fixedly at her and that she, returning his gaze for a moment, experienced a feeling of embarrassment and unease.

They had passed through the outskirts of the town before Simon spoke, and then he said, "Will you be looking for another situation since, as it seems, you have lost or left your present one?"

"What? I mean, pardon?"

His voice a tone higher now, he said, "Will you be looking for another situation?"

"Not yet; well, not until after the holidays. In any case, I think I'll have difficulty in finding one."

"How's that?"

"Well, firstly I don't think Miss Benfield will give me a reference, judging by our last conversation."

"Oh, a battle of words, was it?"

"Yes. You could say that, Biblical words."

He turned towards her and there was a note of surprise in his voice as he repeated, "Biblical words? You were arguing about the Bible?"

"Part of it."

"Really?"

She could tell by his tone that he was interested, and amused. She also told herself that he appeared to be a nice man, easy to talk to. So she heard herself saying, "I was accused of corrupting the young ladies by allowing one of them to read a passage from the Bible."

"Accused of . . . you mean, certain passages of the Bible touch on corruption?"

"It would appear so."

"May I ask which?"

She looked ahead as she said, "The Songs of Solomon."

She saw his hand jerk on the rein and she knew that once again his shoulders were shaking, and there was laughter in his voice too as he said, "You were teaching your pupils the Songs of Solomon?"

"No." The word was emphatic. "One of them was out to teach me. She didn't know that I was acquainted with that part of the Bible and had been since Da . . . my father introduced me to it years ago. The girl was bored with the Psalms, so she stood up and had rendered part of the second Song to the entire class before I had the wit to stop her. Then it appears that she entertained some friends at home with her repertoire."

She drooped her head as she said, "There was a meeting of parents and a storming of Miss Benfield." Then after a moment her head came up as she ended, "And I was accused of corrupting young minds."

"The Songs of Solomon."

"You find it funny . . . amusing?"

"Yes. Yes, I do. And you do, too; I can tell by your tone, at least now. But you were in a fury, weren't you?"

"Yes. Yes, I was. Have you read the Songs of Solomon?"

"Yes, but many years ago in my schooldays, during the period of wrong constructions and false values."

There was a sober note to his voice now, and she said, "Is that how you look upon youth?"

"Yes. Well, at least mine. But you, now; I'm sure that your values will be utterly right and your constructions without error."

"I don't mind being laughed at. Dada . . . my father, oh, why do I say that when I always call him Dada?" She twisted her body in the seat as if in defiance. "So, I will repeat, Dada often laughs at me and my ideas. I'm quite used to it."

She was surprised when he made no reference at all to her last words and she thought, Oh, now he's recalling the gillyvor bit and Dada is the cause of it. And when, looking straight ahead, he remarked, "You would like to be put down at the quarry end, wouldn't you?" she felt she had surmised correctly.

"How do you know that?"

"I know that you don't often travel through the village; I'm a friend of Miss Netherton's."

"Oh. Yes, of course. And yes, I would like to be put down at the quarry end."

About five minutes later he pulled the gig to a halt. The conversation had become desultory: he had spoken about the weather and the roads. But quickly now, he alighted from his seat beside her and went round the vehicle to hold out his hands to assist her to the ground. And when they were standing facing each other, he said, "I must tell you something before you go, and I want you to believe that I'm not laughing at you. I'm not easily given to laughter, you know, but I haven't laughed as much as I've done this morning for a long, long time; and I would like you to know that I've enjoyed your company and our conversation to the extent that I can't look back to a time when I felt more interested in what a human being had to say. It is a great pity, at least I feel so, that I shall be deprived of such conversation in the future. Goodbye, Miss Dagshaw; and thank you."

His hand was held out to her, and after a moment's hesitation, she placed hers in it, and as their palms touched they looked steadily at each other.

She was moving away, walking with a straight back, down the narrow path towards the quarry. She knew that the gig was still there, and she wondered why she felt so strange, that she wanted to burst into tears, when just a short while ago she too had been laughing.

"Miss Netherton will be upset."

"No, she won't, my dear." Nathaniel put his hand on Maria's shoulder. "She'll understand."

"You know, Nat, I become afraid for Anna at times. Her tongue is too ready: she comes out with things she should keep in her head, the things that you've put into her head. You know that?"

"Yes, I know, and I'm glad I've done that one good thing: I've made her think and be honest in her opinions, as well as fearless. Our children are all honest, but she is outstanding." A smile came on his lips now and he shook his head as he said, "Oh, I do wish I had been in on that last conversation or battle of words she had with Miss Benfield. If she said only half of what she thinks she said to that woman, then I am proud of her."

"It'll get her into trouble some day. That's what I'm afraid of, Nat."

"Well, my dear, if she gets into trouble it will be for a righteous cause."

"I don't know so much. You know what she said to me about the man who came out of the post office with Mr. Brodrick?"

"No."

"She said, 'He looked at me in an odd way, Ma, sort of surprised yet familiar.' You see, Nat, underneath all her cleverness, she has still got to learn about life and men. I know exactly what was in that man's look because, there she was, about to drive away with Mr. Brodrick."

"It was Simon Brodrick she was with, dear. If it had been the other one, Raymond, then I would have been anxious. But Simon is a married man with a three-year-old son."

"Yes. And you can add to that, his wife is known as a vixen. And if you are to go by the tales that Miss Netherton's Rob gets from Robert Grafton, the coachman over there, then there is hell let loose in that house at times between him and his wife. And another thing, the two brothers don't seem to get on. The Raymond one acts God Almighty, if you can believe all you hear, and he's hated at his pit."

"Well, it isn't exactly his pit, it's his father's; at least the share that he holds; the other two owners keep out of the way. One, I'm told, lives on the South coast, at Brighton, where the life is as high as it is in London, and the other is abroad. But getting away from our dear Anna and her escort, to that poor lot in your barn. The men have gone into Gateshead Fell this morning to see if they can pick up work there. If one of them could get a job, he has a relative in the town who could house them, he says. Anyway, I shouldn't be

surprised if sometime soon I shall be having a visit from one of the pit offi-
cials."

"*Why?*"

"Oh, to tell me what'll happen to us for harbouring agitators, trouble-
makers, riot-rousers. One thing, they can't turn *us* out of *our* house."

"Well, that being the case, what could they do?"

"Oh, there's all kinds of things they could do."

"What's on your mind, Nat? What could they do? Tell me."

"They could enclose the land roundabout, taking in the quarry."

"That's a right of way, has been for countless years. They can't do that."

"Possession has always been known to be nine points of the law, dear.
They'll do it first, then leave us to fight it afterwards, by which time we'll
have a hard job to get out of here unless we go through the village; and that
means all of us and at different times. And I can't escort every one of them,
not from four o'clock in the morning onwards."

"He couldn't do that; he would be cutting off his nose to spite his face. I
mean, Praggett would. Cherry wouldn't be able to get there, and Anna
wouldn't be able to get to Miss Netherton's."

"Oh, yes, Anna would. She would go through the village. And yet I
couldn't see that going on long before there would be trouble. Anyway, dear,
let's talk about us. Tomorrow I'm going to see Parson Mason. You know, all
those weeks ago, when I went to him, I think he would have been willing to
marry us then if it had been left with him. But the dear Bishop got to know
about it. And through whom? None other than the Holy Reverend Roland
Albert Fawcett. Were we not two wicked persons? In the eyes of God we had
sinned, and grievously. We had given birth to six wonderful children, happy,
well-formed, intelligent children who could more than write their own
names, they could pen a complete letter, even knowing how to address the
person in question. Moreover, they possessed a sense of humour and here
and there a gift of wit. They were whole in mind and body. But they were
gillyvors, bastards, and in the sight of God, full of sin inherited from their
parents."

Nathaniel now walked down the length of the room and stood near the
window that looked on to the frost-coated vegetable garden, and he said,
"You know, I'm really of a mild nature, Maria, you know that, but on the day
when I came out of the meeting in that vestry I was so burnt up with righteous indignation and rage that, just as Anna said she had the desire to hit out
at that woman this morning, well, I wanted to lash out; and on that day I
could see myself flailing those so-called men of God, all except our dear
Reverend Mason. Anyway, his letter says the matter is settled and I go in
tomorrow to propose a date." He turned from the window now and came
back to her, and he was smiling as he added, "Do you think they'll arrange
the service for midnight?"

She looked up at him and, answering his half-smile, she said, "Could be,
if they want the devil there."

"Oh, my dear." He pulled her up towards him, saying now, "There is a
God. I know there is, although I feel at times he is blindly furious at what
goes on down here among his so-called Christian community. Anyway, let's
forget ourselves; at least, let me forget myself for a moment and talk about

what's going to happen to our beautiful daughter. I mean, how she is to get work anywhere near enough for her to travel home? Fellburn is out of the question. Gateshead Fell is not much better; the righteous are there too. There's only Newcastle. She could manage that on the cart in the clement weather, but in the winter, no way could she make that journey."

"Nat, leave Anna's future to take care of itself; I've got a feeling it will. I've always had a strange feeling about our eldest daughter. I've no such worries about Cherry. But about Anna, somehow I think her future's already written down in the book."

He stared into her face for a moment before he said, "You're a witch; so who dare cross a witch!"

"Yes; remember that, Nathaniel Martell. Odd that"—she turned her head to the side and she smiled—"I'll become Maria Martell. Sounds nice. Yes"—she nodded—"I could grow to like it."

He slapped her playfully on the cheek, then went out.

When Nathaniel crossed the yard towards the barn where the children were playing with a skipping rope, they stopped when they saw him and moved together almost into a huddle, and he went to them, saying, "Give me the end of that rope." After a moment's pause one of them picked up the end of the rope from the ground and, slowly approaching, handed it to him.

"There now, you take the other end and we'll see what the rest can do. Come on with you."

When the rope was swinging, he cried at them, "Come on! You can skip." Then he went into the children's rhyme his pupils of years past had sung:—

> All in together, girls;
> Never mind the weather, girls;
> Lift your toes and then your heels,
> Skip high or you'll coup your creels."

Apparently this was known to the children, for they took it up, and their giggles and laughter brought the two women from the far end of the barn to stare in open-mouthed amazement at their benefactor. This kind man, whom they'd heard for years described as the fellow in Heap Hollow who had bred a family of bastards had, to their surprise, turned out to be a gentleman. Their men said so, so he must be. Then one of them happened to turn her head and look towards the wood, with the result that she nudged her companion hard with her elbow, saying, "Oh, look out for squalls. Look who's coming. Oh, he'll put a lid on it."

The other woman now looked towards the approaching man and cried to the children, "Leave go! and come on in, all of you. Come on in!"

When, startled, they obeyed her, one of the women cried to Nathaniel, "See who's coming, mister!"

Nathaniel looked towards the man fast approaching him; then he turned to where the women were hustling the children through the open barn doors and said, "It'll be all right. Don't worry, it'll be all right."

He did not, however, go forward to meet the man but walked towards the house, and was standing by his front door when Howard Praggett came to a puffing standstill about a yard from him.

"You know who I am," he began straightaway, "and I know who you are, and you know why I'm here, don't you?"

"No, Mr. Praggett; I have no idea why you're here. It is your first visit. Would you care to come in?"

"You can drop your politeness, mister. I know all about you and your tongue. I'm going to put it to you plainly; you're breaking the law, you know, in housing that scum." He jerked his head towards the barn.

"I will answer the second part of your accusation first, Mr. Praggett. I object to the word 'scum'. I am housing two miners and their families because you have turned them out of their cottages and they have nowhere to go but the open moor, on which at least the children would soon have perished. Now, as for the law, what is the name of this law I am breaking?"

Howard Praggett thrust his head first one way and then the other from the band of his collarless reefer-coat before he said, "They are criminals, agitators, rioters."

"If that is so, why aren't they in the House of Correction? Why haven't they been called up before a magistrate?"

The man's face had become suffused with a purple tinge and again his head jerked from side to side before he said, "You think you're a clever bugger, don't you? But wait until Mr. Raymond . . . Mr. Raymond Brodrick gets back from London. He'll point out laws to you. And he'll have them into the House of Correction for inciting workmen to riot, as those two did last night in the dark, going from one house to another, trying to bring the men out . . . when they're quite happy and know they've got a square deal. Aye, you can sneer and laugh, but they're eatin' and they're housed and their bairns are shod."

"Oh, that surprises me. Three of those children back there are barefoot and—" Nathaniel's tone now lost its bantering and became bitter as he ground out, "You say they can eat and they're housed. Do you know I'd insult a pig by placing it in one of those mud-floored, stinking hovels that you call houses for the men. And the stench from that pit village can be smelt for miles. I considered Rosier's was bad enough, but your place can beat it. Now I'll bid you good day, Mr. Praggett. And you can tell your master, when he returns from the big city, exactly what I have said. You can also tell him that my barn will be open to any other of his men you decide to victimise."

The man stepped back from him as if in order to stretch his arm out and give room to his wagging finger. In a tone of voice that sounded almost like that of an hysterical woman, he cried, "And your daughter will be out of a job. I'll see to that. She'll be one less for you to live on."

As Nathaniel raised his arm, fists clenched, Maria's voice cried out from the open doorway, *"No! Nat. No! Don't!"*

Praggett backed away from him, shouting, "If you start that, you'll get the worst of it. I could knock you flat because you've never done a decent day's work in your life. Flabby bastard!"

Maria was now gripping Nathaniel's arm, whispering, "Let him go. Let him go. It would only mean trouble."

They remained close together until the scurrying figure disappeared around the foot of the hill.

"Don't let it upset you. Come on inside. You're cold, I've made a drink."

Inside the house, Nathaniel slowly lowered himself down into a chair and, resting his elbows on the table, he dropped his head onto his palms, muttering as he did so, "He'll make trouble."

"Well, we're used to that. As for sacking Cherry, his wife will have something to say on that point and she'll likely emphasise her words with the frying pan."

He raised his head and looked up at her. "That's what they must all be thinking, that I'm living on the children's wages."

"That's ridiculous. They'll know, as they seem to know everything about us, that you do coaching for the children of two of the best families in the town."

"They'll forget about that." He sighed now as he said, "It's been a funny week-end. The harmony of the house has been broken somehow: first, those two poor families coming in on us; then, this morning, Anna turning up out of the blue like that, and that woman accusing her; and now our latest visitor. What next, I wonder?"

"A cup of tea; it's always heartening. And I'll give Anna a shout; she's down by the wood-pile." Maria laughed. "She said she had to take it out on something, so she had better get a chopper and the saw in her hand."

Anna had certainly taken out her feelings with the chopper and the saw. They had previously felled a tree and during the last hour she had stripped it of most of its branches and had cut them into the required lengths on the sawing block and heightened the wood-pile with them.

The wood-pile was arranged against the railings that skirted the boundary of their land. Beyond was part open rough land, part farmland, and it was very rarely that she had seen anyone crossing it except on horseback, when it was usually the Hunt. She hated the Hunt and the hunters because their beloved dog, Rover, had been killed on the occasion of a Hunt. It had become excited and jumped the fence and raced after the riders, and was trampled on. Unlike the hounds, it had not been trained to avoid horses.

She had added the last logs she had sawn up to the wood-pile when her attention was caught by the sight of a riderless horse. She put her hand across her brow to shade her eyes against the weak winter sun that cast its own particular and peculiar white light and, to her surprise, she saw that it wasn't a cart-horse but a saddled one: the reins were trailing on the ground and it was trotting gently and making towards her. Then, coming into sight from around the hedge that bordered part of the field away to the right, was another strange sight: a man was running erratically after the horse. He was calling out something; suddenly he stopped, and Anna watched his arms go up in the air as if to ward off a swarm of bees or wasps. Then, quite distinctly, she heard him utter a weird sound. It came to her like a cry for help.

As she saw the figure fall forward, she herself let out a startled cry. Within seconds she had climbed onto the pile of logs, dislodging a number as she went, and from its flat top she jumped down into the field beyond.

As she ran towards the prostrate figure the horse came towards her and she could see that it was limping. It stopped as if it expected her to do something; and as if it had spoken she shouted at it, "In a minute. In a minute."

As she neared the man she stopped, for he was writhing on the ground: he was lying on his back and there was foam round his lips. She noticed that his teeth were clenched but that there were two missing from the upper set. She had never before witnessed anyone in a fit but she knew instinctively that this man was suffering such a seizure. And now she forced herself to go to his side, and as she knelt down by him she took hold of one of his arms, which he was still attempting to flail and, gripping the wrist, she said, "It's all right. It's all right." The spasm was subsiding now; his body was rocking from side to side but slowly, as if he was spent.

She groped in the pocket of her coat, an old one that she wore when out working in the garden. There was a piece of linen in it, not a real handkerchief, but it was clean, and tentatively she went to wipe the man's lips; but her hand stayed when his lids suddenly lifted and his eyes gazed upwards. They were blue eyes, as deep a blue as you could find in the sky on a summer's day. She saw now that he wasn't, as she had thought at first, elderly but a man perhaps in his middle forties.

Slowly, he turned his head towards her and his lips moved, but no sound came from them at first; but then, after a moment, she thought he said, "Sleep." And she felt sure she had heard aright, for he closed his eyes and turned his head to the side.

She rose from her knees and stood looking down on him as she muttered, "He . . . he can't stay here. It'll soon be dark."

She turned about when she thought she heard her mother's voice calling, and looked towards the wood. The horse was standing near the wood-pile now. She again knelt down by the man's side and, shaking him gently by the shoulder, she said, "Wake up! Wake up! Can . . . can you stand?"

The eyelids flickered as if they were about to open again; then she heard him sigh, and he turned his head as if on a pillow. It could have been he imagined himself to be in bed; so, she thought, there was nothing for it, she must fly back to the house and get her father.

Rising quickly, she picked up her skirts and began to run, and she was half-way across the field when she saw her father. He was standing within the railings to the side of the wood-pile, patting the horse's muscle and she called to him, "Dada! Dada! Come here."

His voice came back to her asking, "What is it?" He obviously hadn't seen her before, or the man, and as she neared him he called, "Where has this horse come from?"

She leant against the railings, gasping, as she said, "The man . . . the man who was riding it"—she now flapped her hand against the horse's neck—"he . . . he had a seizure. He's lying back there in the field."

"Seizure? What d'you mean, seizure? Did he fall off?"

"I don't know. The horse is lame; it was coming here, and then he appeared. He must have been chasing it, and then he had this . . . well, I suppose it was a fit."

Nathaniel screwed up his face. "A fit? How d'you know it was a fit?"

"It couldn't have been anything else. Come, please."

As he turned hastily from her to make for the wall that abutted the railings, she said, "Look, you can jump down here from the wood-pile. I did . . ."

As he stood looking down at the figure who had turned on his side and who was now apparently fast asleep, Nathaniel said, "Dear, dear! God love us! Yes, he must have had an epileptic fit. There was a boy at school; after he'd had a bad one he always slept straightaway. Look, we can't leave him lying here. Run back and tell your mother and bring that piece of canvas that covers the straw. We'll have to have something to carry him in. And another thing"—he stopped her as she was about to run from him—"tell the women, the pit wives, to come; we won't be able to manage him on our own."

Nathaniel now knelt down by the man and loosened the cravat at his neck, and in doing so exposed a fine wool shirt which, like the riding jacket, was of the best quality. He was of the gentry, but from where? He couldn't recall having seen the face before. He knew of the Wilsons by sight, from The Hall, but they were at least three miles away. And the Harrisons from Rowan House. And then there were the Brodricks. He had only once seen the old man, although the two sons, Raymond and Simon, he had passed a number of times. This man he was sure he hadn't seen before. He must have come quite some distance. But why, being subject to fits, did he take to riding out alone?

It was a full five minutes before Anna, Maria, and the two pit wives arrived, and he wanted to say to them, "Where have you been? You've taken so long," for he was feeling somewhat helpless and frustrated. But what he actually said was, "Put a sheet on the ground, and we'll lift him on to it."

"Who is it?" Maria was asking the question; and when he answered her, "I don't know," one of the pit women stepped forward and said, "I do. But however has he got this far? He hardly goes out. 'Tis Mr. Timothy, the mistress's brother. I used to work there years ago . . . at the Manor. He was all right once, but the fits started when he came back from foreign parts. After the mistress was hurt with the snow coming down on her. They thought she was dead. She might as well be, 'cos she's hardly moved since. But, 'twas from then they said he had his fits."

All the time the woman was talking, they were lifting him on to the sheet, and now, as if the pit wives had done this before, each took up a corner of the canvas sheet near the man's head and, as if taking charge, the same woman nodded from Nathaniel to Maria, saying, "Yous take yon end." Then turning her attention to Anna, she said, "And you, miss, better get a hold of that horse, he's wanderin' again. Well . . . one, two, three, and up! with him."

There was no way of getting their burden into the wood except to walk him along its edge until they came to the gate. In the meantime Anna had run towards the horse calling to him the while; and when he stopped and waited for her, she caught at the bridle, saying gently, "Come on with you. Come on."

After stabling the horse and calming him down, she hurried into the house. They had laid the man before the fire, and she asked, "Has he come round?"

"No sign of it yet," said Nathaniel, and looking at the two pit wives, he said, "Thank you for your help;" then spoke to Maria, saying, "We've got to get word to the Manor because it looks as if he's going to be like this for some time. And anyway, they'll likely be worried and out looking for him by now.''

The two women were already making for the door, and the one who had done all the talking turned and said, "Well, we'll do anything for you, mister, because you've been kind to us. But that's one thing we couldn't trust ourselves to do, nor let our men do it, I mean, go up to the Manor, 'cos we wouldn't be able to keep our mouths shut; an' the men would likely use more than their tongues.''

"That's all right. That's all right. We'll get word to them. Thanks again. Are you all right over there?''

"Oh, aye, sir, warm and comfortable, and that boiler next door is God's blessin'.''

Maria waited till they had gone before exclaiming, "Well, *we* can't go, can we, so what's to be done?''

"The best thing, probably," said Nathaniel, "is to get word to Miss Netherton. She will let Rob drive to the house and then they can take over. Would you go there, dear, and ask her?" He had turned to Anna, and she, looking down on the man, said, "Yes, I'll go." And then added, "I think he'd be more comfortable with a pillow under his head.''

"Well, leave that to me, will you?" And Maria pushed her aside. "You get about your business and I'll see to mine.''

Outside, Anna again picked up her skirts and ran; and ten minutes later, out of breath, she was knocking on Miss Netherton's front door. And when Ethel Mead opened it she exclaimed, "Oh, you! What's up? And look at the sight of you." She pointed to Anna's old coat but Anna ignored her remark and said, "Is she back yet? I mean, Miss Netherton.''

"No, but she should be any minute. It's near on dark now so she shouldn't be long; she hates being out in the dark. Sh! . . . Listen. There they are now." Anna ran across the gravel drive and as the trap came to a stop Miss Netherton, looking down on her, cried out, "What on earth!''

"I'll explain it later, Miss Netherton, but at the moment will you allow Rob to go to The Manor and tell them Mr. . . . Mr. Brodrick has been hurt and that we have him in the house.''

"Mr. Brodrick?" Miss Netherton put out her hand to Rob and said, "Hold on a minute, Rob, until I know what this is all about." Again she said, "Which one? Raymond or Simon?''

"Oh, not those. I understand . . . I think it's . . . well, the pit wives said it was Mr. Timothy.''

"Good God! Tim. What was he doing near your place?''

"I think he was riding, but the horse went lame. I saw it running across the field, and . . . and then he came in sight. He . . . he"—she looked from one to the other—"he had a sort of seizure.''

"Oh, God above! He had one of his fits. Look, Rob, I know it's been a longish drive but get yourself over there and tell them what's happened. Was he hurt?" She was speaking to Anna.

"Not that I know of, but he seemed to want to sleep, just to sleep.''

"Yes, he would. Well, go on, Rob; don't stand there. You'll hear all about it when you get back.''

The old man said something that could have been in the nature of a grumble, but he turned the horse about; and Miss Netherton returned her attention to Anna, saying in much the same way as Ethel had done, "Why are you dressed like that?"

"Because I've been sawing wood."

"Sawing wood? What do you mean, sawing wood?"

"Just what I say, sawing wood. I came back this morning. I'm finished."

"Oh, dear! Oh, dear! Let me get in and sit down."

Inside the hall she said to Ethel, "Get me out of this gear, will you? And I want a cup of strong tea. We'll have two cups of strong tea. And bring the decanter in, the brandy; I've had the most trying day and I need sustenance. Now, young woman, come along and tell me the reason why you got the sack, or you left, whichever it is."

As briefly as possible Anna described what had happened. When she had finished Miss Netherton gazed at her and said, "Well, you've done it this time. Of course it wasn't your fault, I know, but The Songs of Solomon! Let me tell you, and I could bet on it—" She leaned forward now and there was a grin on her face and a deep chuckle in her voice as she said, "I bet those songs are Miss Benfield's bedtime reading. But having said that, she's going to make hay out of this. And she was right, you know, there isn't much chance of my getting you set on, at least in Fellburn. Anyway, the weather's terrible and for the next few weeks you'll be saved from that journey. And you may come and talk to me again. That'll make you mind your p's and q's and stop you corrupting young girls." She laughed aloud now, and Anna with her.

When Ethel brought in the tea tray there was no decanter in evidence and Miss Netherton said, "You've taken your time over that. And where's the brandy?"

"I didn't bring it. Remember what you said: you told me not to bring it in before seven o'clock 'cos you just go to sleep after; you don't get any work done."

"Bring that brandy in, woman! and this minute, or you can pack your box tonight."

"I won't bother, I'll only have to unpack it in the morning."

When the door closed on the maid there was a look of glee on Miss Netherton's small face and she said, "It's so nice when your servants are obliging and courteous and, more than anything else, subservient."

Their laughter mingled again, but softly; then watching Anna pour out the tea, she said, "Take that coat off, you look dreadful."

"I can't take the coat off because I'm going immediately after I drink this cup of tea. I want to know what's happening to that man."

"Oh, he'll survive. But I wonder why on earth he got on a horse; he couldn't have been on one for years. He spends most of his time in his room or in the conservatory. He grows the most beautiful orchids, you know, and he writes. And he's a very nice fellow at heart, different from the rest. You know that Simon and Raymond's mother, she's the invalid, broke her back enjoying herself in Switzerland? Never liked her. Couldn't get to like her. But there you are, I'm such a hypocrite: I go there and I talk to her and at bottom I'm sorry for her; but more so for Simon, and being married to that upstart of a vixen who's no better than she should be. And I'm sorry for the boy, too, that's Simon's son, you know, he's only three, coming up four . . . What! You're going now? Oh, well, I suppose you must; but come over first thing in the morning and let me know what transpired. Better still, I'll go over there and find out all about it myself, because there'll likely be the devil to pay. Raymond's valet is supposed to see to Tim, too, because Raymond spends half his time in Newcastle or Scarborough or London. It's Simon who sees to that place, and that's ruined his career. Go on with you, then. Go on. You're dying to go. But come over in the afternoon and stay to dinner. Don't answer me back. Go on."

Anna went out smiling, and as she tucked up her skirts and ran the whole length home again, she felt a sense of well-being and happiness. Perhaps it was because she was free and tomorrow she'd be able to enjoy the company and gossip of that little woman.

At the moment, however, there was that poor man with his fits. She wondered if he was awake yet.

The man was awake, but only just. Even so, Maria took Anna to one side before she whispered, "He seems to be a little"—she tapped her head—"he asked where the angel was."

"The angel?"

"Yes, that's what he said: 'Where's the angel?' What did Miss Netherton say?"

"She's sending word to the Manor. She seemed to know all about him and said he was a very nice man, but unfortunately had these fits."

"Is he touched? I mean . . ."

"She didn't seem to think so. Anyway, there'll be somebody here soon from the Manor. Don't worry."

She went down the room to where her father was sitting in his chair by the side of the man, who certainly looked to be still asleep, and she exchanged a glance with Nathaniel before kneeling down and gently putting her hand on the man's brow, but then quickly withdrew it as the eyelids lifted. The eyes were open wide now and staring at her; and the face went into a smile, the upper lip moved and revealed the gap in the teeth as he said, "The angel."

She turned her head quickly and looked from her father to her mother, and Maria nodded at her, as much to say, There, what did I tell you?

The man now sighed and said in quite an ordinary tone, but slowly, "I thought I had died at last. You are not an angel."

"No, sir." She laughed softly down on him. "In no way am I an angel. Anyway, I think they are all fair-haired."

He continued to look at her; then he asked quietly, "Where am I?"

"You are in my home. This is my mother and my father." She pointed to the two figures now standing to the side of her.

He looked up at Nathaniel and Maria and after a moment he said, "I am sorry. I am sorry for troubling you. My illness is no respecter of time or . . . or place."

He made an effort to sit up, and Nathaniel, bending quickly, put his arm around his shoulder. "Are you fit enough to stand, sir?" he said.

"I . . . I will sit for a while longer if it will not . . . inconvenience you."

"Not at all. Not at all. You are welcome to stay as long as you like. We have sent word to the Manor."

The man had been looking at Nathaniel, but now he closed his eyes and his head dropped back as he said, "Oh, dear me."

"Would you like a cup of tea, sir?"

The head came forward, the eyes opened and his gaze rested on Maria for some time before he said, "Tea? Oh, yes, yes; I would indeed be grateful for a cup of tea."

"We could make you more comfortable in this chair." Nathaniel pointed to the wooden armchair, but the man said, "Would you mind if I sat here a little longer? I've . . . well, it is a long long time since I sat on a rug before a fire. It is very pleasant; indeed, yes."

"By all means, sir; but we'll make you more comfortable. Pull the settle nearer, Maria, and Anna, fetch another couple of pillows."

A few minutes later their guest was sitting propped up, supported by the weight of the settle, and with a cup of tea placed on a cracket to his side.

"Do you take sugar, sir?"

Looking at Anna, he said, "No, I don't, but thank you. Yet I have a sweet tooth, a very sweet tooth." Then he turned his head and stared at Maria, who was standing to the side of him and said, "And I love sweeties."

Maria paused as she thought: he said that just like a child, and yet he sounded sensible enough; and in her kindly way she now answered him, "And so do I, sir, but I rarely get a chance to indulge myself, because my family are there before me whenever I make toffee."

He smiled. "You make toffee?" he said.

"Yes, once a week; cinder and treacle."

"Cinder and treacle." What he would have said further was interrupted by a voice, crying, "Ma! Ma! It's me; I've got the push. He gave me the push, but the missis says I've got to turn up in the morning. They're going at it . . ."

Cherry's voice trailed away as she entered the room from the kitchen and she stood open-mouthed for a moment, looking at the man sitting on the mat. "One of these days, daughter, you'll come in quietly," Nathaniel half-grumbled at her. "This gentleman has had a slight accident." Then looking down on the man, he said, "This is my daughter, Mr. . . . ?"

"Oh. How do you do?" The inclination of his head was towards Cherry; but then he turned and looked at Nathaniel, saying, "My name is Barrington, Timothy Barrington."

And to this Nathaniel answered, "And ours is Martell." He glanced towards Maria as if he were saying, Well, it will be in a few days' time.

When there came a knock on the door Anna, being nearest to it, opened it and standing there she made out the figure of the man who, earlier in the day, she had laughed with and who, for no reason she could understand, had made her want to cry.

"I understand . . . ?"

"Oh, do come in."

He stepped into the lamplit room, then turned and stared at her, shaking his head, and she had the feeling he was about to remark on this being their second meeting in one day; but then, becoming aware of others standing round the fire at the far end of the room, he apologised: "I am sorry for the inconvenience," he said.

"There has been no inconvenience to us, sir." Nathaniel was coming towards him. "Will you come in, please?"

Simon Brodrick followed Nathaniel up the room towards the fire; then stood as if in amazement, looking down onto the mat to where Mr. Barrington was sitting, and said with some concern, "Oh! Tim."

And Mr. Barrington answered, "Oh, Simon; now don't you start. I just had to get out else I would have exploded."

"Well, you did explode, didn't you?"

"Yes. Yes, I suppose I did, but I was going on the fact that it hadn't happened for . . . oh, weeks and weeks. Well . . ." His voice trailed away.

Simon now dropped onto his hunkers and the two men looked at each other, and for the moment it was as if they were alone, such was the way they spoke, for Simon said, "If you wanted to ride so badly why couldn't you have told me? I would have come with you."

"Yes, I knew you would, but, my dear fellow, I'm sick of people; I'm sick of close proximity, even of you." He now lifted a hand and pushed at Simon, and as Simon got to his feet he looked at Maria, and began, "I'm sorry we've had to inconvenience . . ." only to be interrupted by Timothy Barrington saying, "I'm not, Simon. No, I'm not sorry this has happened, because these dear people have been so kind to me and they have let me sit on the rug by the fire. How long is it since you sat on a rug by a fire, Simon?"

Simon looked down on him and said, "As usual, you are well enough to talk and prompt an argument, but are you well enough to get on to your feet?"

"Yes. Yes. Give me your hand."

Between them Nathaniel and Simon drew him to his feet, then sat him in the wooden chair. Once seated, he looked about him, taking in first Maria, then Nathaniel, then the small boy who was standing by his side, then the two girls who were standing together, one very dark and one very fair, and both beautiful. Then he sighed and, turning his head towards Simon, he asked, "What did you bring?" And when Simon answered, "The coach," of a sudden he put his fingers to his mouth and felt the gap in his teeth, saying in some surprise now, "I must have lost the two of them when I fell." And now he started to laugh but stopped abruptly and, his eyes blinking, he looked at Nathaniel as he said, "You must think it's a very queer fellow who is partaking of your hospitality. Perhaps on our further acquaintance I can prove to you that I am just odd and not all that queer."

This brought a laugh from Nathaniel and he answered, "Odd or queer, sir, it would be my pleasure; in fact, the pleasure of all of us, were you to partake of our hospitality whenever you feel so inclined."

"Splendidly put. Don't you think so?" He turned his head and looked at Simon, and Simon answered, "You wouldn't expect it otherwise from a learned man. Mr. Martell is a teacher, a tutor."

"Is that so? Well, sir, I shall certainly take you up on your invitation. But now I really must go, for indeed I have outstayed my welcome."

When, with the support of Simon, he stood up and walked towards the door, Anna noticed he didn't look as tall or as big-built as when he was lying down. His height would be about five-foot seven and, although he was thick-set, his figure was in no way bulky.

At the door he turned and said a single, "Goodbye," which included them all. But Simon Brodrick said nothing until, with the help of the coach-man, he had placed his errant relative in the coach and had then hurried back to the door of the house, where Maria and Nathaniel were standing with the girls behind them, and here, looking first at Maria and then at Nathaniel, he said, "I'm indebted to you. But about the horse?"

"Oh, yes, the horse." Nathaniel turned to Anna: "You've put him in the stable?" he asked.

"Yes. He'll be all right there until morning."

"Thank you. I'll send for him first thing."

"He'll have to go to the blacksmith; he sprang a shoe."

"Likely that was the reason for . . . for the trouble. Thank you again. Good-night."

They all answered, "Good-night"; then they watched the driver turn the coach and make for the field gate that led on to a rough path on the edge of the open land and connected with the coach road.

When the door was closed, Nathaniel looked from one to the other and said, "What a day! My two daughters have been sacked from their posts, I have been assailed and told that I might end up in the House of Correction, and now one of the scions of the aristocracy has an epileptic fit and ends up on our mat"—he indicated the mat with a sweep of his hand—"and further, another scion drives his coach to our door and we are thanked most gra-ciously for our services. Do you realise, Miss Maria Dagshaw, that this day could be a turning point in our lives?"

And Maria, taking up his tone, said, "I do indeed, Mr. Martell. I do indeed. So much so that no-one must sit on that end of the mat; I'm going to cut it off and hang it on the wall."

"Oh, I'd leave it there until the boys get in," said Nathaniel; and Anna joined in the general laughter, even though she was thinking: Turning point in their lives? Her Dada could be naïve at times; nothing could alter what they already were, what he himself had made them; not even their forthcom-ing marriage would or could erase the stain. And whatever condescending patronage they might receive from The Manor wasn't going to help either. Oh no. Nevertheless, she was experiencing the same feeling as she had done when, withdrawing her hand from Mr. Simon Brodrick's, she had then turned from him and walked along the quarry path.

FIVE

The news seemed to set the village on fire: those two from the Hollow had nerve to go and get married after breeding that lot. And what d'you think? Miss Netherton was there, at the church, so it was said, and also at the do they had when the lot of them returned home. And that wasn't all. Oh, no. It was unbelievable but true, flowers and fruit had been sent from The Manor. To that lot of scum! And why? That's the question, why? Oh, there was something behind this, and you needn't go very far to see the reason for it. Tommy Taylor could tell you; he saw them with his own eyes. He was picking up the letters for the second delivery when he saw Mr. Simon Brodrick with that young piece. She came into the post office as bold as brass and waited for him, and then he handed her up into the gig. *He saw it.* And what was more, he saw Mr. Harry Watson chatting to Mr. Simon while she sat perched up there. Now, if you asked him, there was the reason for the flowers sent to the Hollow. But the nerve of that young hussy. Like mother, like daughter.

Some said they were surprised that it was Mr. Simon she had caught, and him married with a three-year-old son. Now had it been Mr. Raymond, they could have understood it. Yet, who could understand any decent man going within spitting distance of one of that litter. And that particular one was supposed to have been in a position of a teacher in Fellburn. Well, that surely was another cover-up, 'cos who would take her on? They would like to bet that young gillyvor had a house there, and what she taught wasn't the A.B.C.

This was the talk in the village before the end of the year 1880, but by the beginning of March, 1881, the villagers were dumbfounded by the news that that one was being taken on at The Manor to instruct the young son in his letters and such. And not only that, Mr. Timothy, the one that had fits, had been seen walking across the moor with her. What next! What next! But to think the hussy had the nerve to push herself into the house, and under her mistress's very nose. But there was one thing sure, she wouldn't reign long there, not under the young Mrs. Brodrick, she wouldn't. If she got wind of this, she would skin that one alive, for didn't she have a temper like a fiend? Well, there was going to be sparks flying. Just you wait.

But here and there in the village, there were those as well as a farmer or two round about, who dared to voice their doubts about this general opinion of the young gillyvor. Nobody had seen her out riding with Simon Brodrick since that day Tommy Taylor saw her. As for her walking with Mr. Timothy, well, there was some talk of her finding him in the field, when he had a turn on him, and he had been taken into their house.

That couldn't be true, they were told; it was well known Timothy hardly moved out of the grounds.

Yes, that was true. But why keep on about them down in The Hollow; the couple were married now; they'd had the ceremony performed as soon as it had become possible.

Yes, they knew that, but it didn't make any difference; the bairns were still bastards.

But, said the moderate ones, you couldn't get over the fact that they were all well spoken and in decent jobs and they kept themselves to themselves.

As Miss Netherton said, after listening to Ethel, who related the gossip she had drawn out of Rosie Boyle, who came in from the village daily and acted as a housemaid, it could be that there were now two camps of thought in the village, and it wasn't before time. But she'd be sorry if the day ever came when all the inhabitants turned into kindly sensible people, to include the parson and, of course, his wife, because then she would realise they had all died, including herself.

Part Three
The Child

ONE

"Must you go to this house, Anna?"

"It isn't that I must go, Ben; I want to go. I want to teach and it's an amazing opportunity that's been offered to me, practically on the doorstep, you could say. What is wrong, Ben?"

The boy took her hand as they walked across the frost-spangled ground towards the wood, and in an affectionate gesture he leant his head against her arm for a moment as he said, "I shall miss you."

She stopped and looked down at him. "But it will be the same as when I was at the Academy, even better. I don't have to be at the Manor until nine and I leave again at four, and the journey will be over in a flash, because they are being kind enough to take me back and forth in the gig. You'll see much more of me than you did last year."

His eyes were showing a sad expression, more so than usual. Suddenly, she stooped down to him and, taking his face between her hands, she said, "What is it that's troubling you, Ben?"

"I don't know. It's just that I don't want you to go. I feel sad at your going."

"Did you not feel sad last year when I went to the Academy?"

"No. No, I never felt sad then."

"Oh, Ben." She pulled him suddenly into her arms, and he pressed his head against her waist and they hugged each other; then she took his hand again and they walked in silence for some way, until she said, "The others were happy for me when they left. Oswald and Olan, didn't they make you laugh when they dipped their knee to me? And Cherry, look how she acted the goat and said how she was going to cock a snook at Mr. Praggett. And Ma and Dada and Jimmy are so glad for me. There's only you, and now you make me sad because you're so very dear to me, and you are not wishing me happiness in my new position."

"Oh, I am, I am, Anna. I wish you to be happy. All the time I wish you to be happy, all the time I wish you to be happy."

"All right, all right. Then don't get depressed; but what is it?"

"I don't know, Anna, just a sadness inside me."

"Oh, Ben." She looked down on him, troubled: Ben to say he was sad. He was the happy one, yet there was something in this small brother of hers to which she couldn't put a name. Was he fey? No, no; there was nothing pixyish about Ben. He was a boy, a highly intelligent boy. He had the power to learn so quickly. At times he surprised her, for he seemed to know the answer before half the question was put to him.

As she looked towards the wood, she could hear the sound of the axe coming from the far end. Her father was at the wood block and she must have a word with him before she went; she must say something to him that she couldn't say in front of her mother, in case it should worry her. So now, looking down on Ben, she said, "I want a word with Dada. Look; go over to the gate and as soon as you sight the gig, come back here and whistle. Will you do that?"

"Yes, Anna; yes." He ran from her and she now hurried through the wood. And Nathaniel, stopping his work at her approach, called, "You're ready, then?"

"Yes, I'm ready, Dada. And it looks as if you've kept out of my way."

"Perhaps you're right, dear, perhaps you're right. But now you're all ready and set to go?"

"Not quite, Dada; I want to say something."

"Well, say it, my dear, say it."

"I'm frightened."

"Frightened? What about?"

"I don't really know. I'm like Ben. I asked him why he didn't want me to go to The Manor, and that's what he said: he didn't know."

"If you feel like that, my dear, you shouldn't go. But who are you frightened of, or what are you afraid of? Not the teaching?"

"Oh, no, not the teaching, Dada. You know that. And it isn't so much that I'm frightened, it's that I have taken a strong dislike to someone."

"Whom have you taken a dislike to? You've only been there the once."

"Yes, I know, but that was long enough. It's the child's mother."

"Now that doesn't augur good for your stay."

"Oh, I don't think she'll trouble me much in the schoolroom. The nurse indicated that she never bothered about anything but her painting and horse-riding. And from what I gathered from the talkative old woman when I met her, the mistress took long spells in London and abroad. I also gathered that there was little love between the old nurse and the young mistress, although she's not all that young; she's over thirty."

"What exactly has made you dislike her?"

"Everything about her: the tone of her voice, how she looks at one. I didn't tell you, but she surveyed me up and down as a farmer might a beast in the cattle-pen in the market. I fully expected her to prod me." She gave a little laugh here and, leaning towards him, she said, "Can you imagine the result of that action, should it have happened?"

Nathaniel laughed outright now. "By! yes, I can, and that would be the end before the beginning of your tutoring. And you would likely have ended up in the House of Correction instead of me, and I've been threatened so many times of late. Now, my dear, whatever you do and whatever the provocation, you must endeavour to keep your temper."

"But, Dada, I don't feel that I've got a bad temper. Well, what I mean is, not a regular bad temper. I have to be aggravated beyond endurance before . . ."

"Oh my! Oh my!" He had his hands on her shoulders now. "Would that we could see ourselves as others see us. I am a mild man, they say—some pity me for my mildness—but there was a time last year when, if I hadn't been checked by your ma, I would surely have laid out Mr. Praggett. But I am a mild man"—he shook his head at himself—"who prefers to fight with his tongue. But none of us knows what we are capable of until the circumstances arise. It all depends upon circumstances and the feelings they arouse in one. There would be few murders if it weren't for the circumstances leading to them. We'll have to get on to that subject sometime, my dear; circumstances. Ah, there's Ben's whistle. Is that a signal that your golden carriage has arrived? Come on. Come on. And make up your mind, my dear, that the only time you will raise your voice is in laughter or in defence of someone, or extolling someone's good points."

"Oh, Dada, shut up! Stop your preaching." She turned to him and, throwing her arms around his neck, she kissed him, saying, "I love you. Do you know that? You mild man, I love you." Then, as if in embarrassment, she hurried ahead of him.

It was a young lad who was standing by the gig. He took off his cap as Anna and Nathaniel approached; then said, with a broad Irish accent, "I'm Barry McBride, miss. I'm for to take you to the house. If you'll get up, if you're ready, we'll be away, 'cos I'm a bit late. I had a bit trouble with him." He thumbed towards the horse. "He's fresh."

Anna glanced from Nathaniel to Maria, who had now joined them, and Ben who was by her side, and she said, "I'll be away, then," and there was just a suspicion of the Irish twang in her words which brought a twinkle to Nathaniel's eyes and he answered, "I would, then. I'd be away with you and not keep Mr. McBride waitin'."

"Oh, sir"—the boy turned to Nathaniel—"I'm never mistered. I'm just McBride, number two."

"Oh," said Nathaniel, "number two? Why number two?"

" 'Cos I'm the second stable lad. Me brother, he's number one. He's by the name of Frank, but we're both called McBride."

"Oh, I see, I see." Nathaniel nodded as if the explanation had enlightened him. Then putting his hand under Anna's elbow, he said, "Up! you go then and away."

McBride number two now put his cap on, went round to the other side of the gig and seemed to launch himself up in one movement into the narrow seat beside Anna. As he did so the whole vehicle swayed, and when McBride number two called, "Up! Milligan," the horse seemed to rear slightly before turning around and having to be checked to prevent his going into a gallop.

So quickly did they leave the front of the house and make for the gate that she had no time to wave a goodbye, for it was taking all her attention to hang on to the iron rail support of the seat to keep her balance. But once on the road and going at a steadier pace, she called to him, "Why do you call the horse 'Milligan'?"

"What is that you're after sayin', miss?"

Raising her voice, she cried, "Why do you call the horse 'Milligan'? It's a strange name for a horse."

"Oh, that, miss. Well, 'tis the yard's name for him. He's really called Caster, but he's got this fightin' spirit in him. You see, miss? An' the Milligans are like that. There's three of 'em in the pit, Rosier's pit, an' two in the Beulah, an' if they're not at each other they're at anybody that passes their way, 'specially us. We're kin, you see, by birth, cousins. An' this one here is the spitting image, in his manner, like, of Michael the eldest, who kicks out at his own shadow. He shouldn't be used for the gig at all. But they want to quieten him down, they say, an' there's as much hope for that as the man prayin' for heaven while he's shovellin' overtime in hell. But what's my opinion? for it counts for little in the stableyard."

Anna hung on tightly to her support, because her body was shaking now, and not only from the motion of the gig, as she thought, Well, whatever happens between times, I'll surely be entertained on my way there and back if I can differentiate between Michael the cousin and Milligan the horse . . .

As they bowled up the long drive, McBride number two said, "It's me orders to drop you in the back way, miss. I questioned that to number one, you bein' a learned lady, and as usual he said for me to keep me gob . . . mouth shut, an' use me eyes an' just open me ears for orders. So it isn't me doin', miss, that you be dropped at the back door."

"That's quite all right, Mr. McBride."

"I wouldn't be doing that, miss, as I said back yonder, I mean 'mister' me; they'll scoff me lugs off."

"Very well, I'll remember . . . McBride."

"That's it, miss; give everybody his due, nothin' over and nothin' under, an' the world won't rock."

She mustn't enter even the lower precincts of this establishment laughing, but oh, how she wished her Dada or Ma or any of them could have been on this journey with her. She looked at the red-haired boy as he helped her down on to the flagged yard, and again she had to compose her face as she imagined the effect on them all, were he sitting on the mat among them of an evening.

But, within a moment or two, there was no need for her to make an effort to compose her features, for after McBride number two had led her to the back door amidst a stoppage of work in what had been a busy yard, the door was opened by a young girl whose uniform told Anna that she could be termed a menial, and yet her features were expressing a look that didn't complement such a position, for, whether she was aware of it or not, the look on her face expressed disdain.

At first, the girl didn't speak, but walked ahead of Anna through a long, narrow boot room, then across a large scullery, before thrusting open a door and exclaiming to someone beyond, "She's here!"

Anna stepped into the kitchen, to be confronted by three pairs of eyes, and immediately she took in the situation. The hostility was almost visible, and she met it as she meant to meet all such. Addressing the big woman in the white-bibbed apron and large starched cap, she said, "Will you kindly inform Mrs. Hewitt that I am come and wish to be shown to the school-room . . . ?"

As the cook said later, when seated at the head of the lower staff in the servants' dining room, you could have knocked her down with a feather. The cheek of that one, and the voice. Why! Miss Conway didn't talk like that and she was a lady's maid.

The cook, now addressing one of the girls standing near, said, "Go and fetch her."

What followed this, as the cook again said later, almost caused her to flop on to the floor, for that one dared to walk up the kitchen and cast her eyes over the array of china on the long dresser, then turn about and sort of examine the bread oven and the stove. If Mrs. Hewitt hadn't come in at that moment, she would surely have let her have it.

When Mrs. Hewitt came into the kitchen, she approached Anna, then looked at her in silence for a moment before she said, "Will you come this way?"

Her tone was civil but her mien stiff.

Anna followed her out of the kitchen into a corridor, from which a number of doors led off. The end one was open and showed the outside yard, and the housekeeper, pointing, said, "You'll go through this door when taking the young master for his walks." Then again leading the way, she mounted a flight of stairs and, stopping on the landing, she again pointed, this time to a door on her left, saying, "Never use that. That leads to the gallery and the house."

She opened the other door and they now ascended a flight of stairs which led on to a wide landing, almost like a room with a sloping roof on one side. A number of doors led off, and the housekeeper, unceremoniously opening one, stepped into a room, saying, "She's arrived, Eva."

"Oh, come away in. Come away in."

"How's your back?"

"Oh, the same, Mary. I can't expect any change in it now. By the way, did you see Peggy on the stairs?"

"No. No sight of her."

"By! I'll put a cracker in that one's drawers afore I'm finished. She's been gone fully five minutes with the slops. Sit down, lass." The nurse flapped her hand towards Anna; and the housekeeper said, "She knows the rules'; and turning to Anna, she said, "I've explained them to you, but they'll be put in writing. Today, though, you'll be sent for at half-past ten; the mistress wishes to see you. Is there anything more you would like to know?"

"Not at present, thank you."

The housekeeper's bust could in no way be compared with that of Miss Benfield as regards its size, but nevertheless it followed the same action as that lady's and expressed its owner's thoughts more than words could do at the moment.

The housekeeper now turned a knowing look on the nurse, then abruptly left the room. And Eva Stanmore, looking at Anna, chuckled as she said, "It would be advisable, lass, if you altered your tone when speaking to them above you."

When Anna made no answer the old woman chuckled again and said, "You likely don't consider them in that way, eh?" And when Anna again made no reply, she said, "Well, it's up to you. Yet, I suppose if you went on your knees you couldn't change people's opinions. There's a lot of ignor . . . ramuses in this world. Anyway, the child's all ready. He's sitting in there waiting, as good as gold; not that he's always as good as gold, but he's got quite a bit up top for his age and he's interested in somebody new coming to look after him. He seemed to like what he saw in you the other day."

"I'm pleased."

"Aye, well, that's your room." She pointed across to what was evidently her sitting-room. "There's a cupboard in there for you to hang your clothes, and the master's put in the things that you'll need: slates and pencils and things like that. And, of course, the child's got his own bricks and toys."

Anna had risen to her feet and, as she made her way to the door indicated, the nurse said, "You're a funny lass."

At this Anna stopped and, looking down on to the wrinkled face, she said, "And you're a funny woman, but in a nice way," and they smiled at each other before the old woman said, "Go on! you." And she went.

The schoolroom was well lit by two long windows, and standing gazing out of one was her charge.

At her approach he turned quickly, and she held out her hand and said, "Good morning, Andrew."

"Hello. Good morning. Did you see the horses going out? Look." He grabbed her hand and drew her to the window, then pointed downwards, and she saw three horses being led from the yard.

"I have a pony."

"You have? That's splendid. You like riding?"

"Yes, when I don't fall off." His mouth went into a wide grin.

She took off her hat and coat and hung them in the cupboard, then looked round the room. It was quite comfortable. There was a wooden table on which there were books and slates, pencils and paper, already laid. An abacus was standing to the side of the table. There was another table against the far wall on which were coloured blocks with letters on them. And what struck her was everything looked new and unused. At the far end of the long room a fire was burning brightly in a small grate, which had an iron guard around it. And what she found unusual was a large leather armchair set to the side of the fireplace. Did that indicate she would have time to sit down and relax?

When she stood by the table examining the plain exercise books and those for copying scripts, the child said, "Papa bought them, but I have a lot more, and my colouring books."

"Show me."

He ran to a row of low cupboards that took up part of one wall and, kneeling down, he opened one of the doors and pulled out an assortment of books, including cloth ones, and as he strewed them round him, he looked up at her brightly, saying, "I like making pictures, not learning letters, just making pictures."

Anna picked up one of the books and looked at the splash of colour on a page, and she nodded down at him and said, "And yes, yes, you're very clever at making pictures. But I'm sure you'll be just as clever learning your letters. And we'll paint the letters, too, and the numbers."

"I can count up to ten."

"Oh, that's good. Come on, let me hear you."

As she caught his hand he tugged her to a stop, saying, "Will you take me for a walk this afternoon?"

"Yes, my dear, yes, if you would like that."

"I would like that, please."

She had the desire to stoop, sweep him into her arms and hug him. As she looked down into his face and he looked up into hers she knew she would love this child.

Betty Carter, the upper housemaid, came for her at twenty past ten. She didn't greet her in any way; she just stared at her.

A few minutes before this, nurse had called her from the schoolroom into her sitting room. There she said, "You will have to go in a minute or so. I'm not gona say anything. It wouldn't be any use, would it, to tell you to keep your tongue still, no matter what's said to you. You're of that type, and being brought up as you have been, you're at a disadvantage, fallin' atween two stools, as it were. Well, go on; get along with you."

Anna took no offence at the old woman's talk, for she had felt she was going to like her and that, in what she had said, she was wishing her well.

She was now on the middle landing and going through the forbidden door, and without moving her head she took in the broad corridor, with its four deep bay windows. From this, they passed into an upper hall. Here a balustrade bounded an open gallery, and from it a grand staircase led down to the ground floor.

Two corridors went off the gallery and the maid, walking quickly a step ahead of her, led her down the one to the right-hand side, which had a number of doors on one side of it, while the wall opposite was hung with pictures. They turned a corner and into yet another corridor, a shorter one this time, and at the end of which was a flight of three steps leading up to a door, and on this Betty Carter knocked twice.

There was quite a long pause before the order came to enter. And the next moment Anna found herself walking past the maid and into a large room, bare except for a long wooden table on which there was an array of jars containing brushes, a number of palettes, and a great quantity of paints. Opposite this table, some lying against the wall and some on the floor, were a number of canvasses. But standing by an easel, which was set at an angle to a long window, was the lady to whom she had been bidden to present herself.

There was also another person in the room, and she recognised him as the second man in the gig. He was standing some distance from the easel and, unlike his companion, he turned and looked at her with a hard penetrating stare. Then without speaking at all he strode past her and the maid and left the room.

Betty Carter now approached her mistress who, it would seem, was unaware of her presence, yet when the girl spoke while dipping her knee and said, "I brought her, ma'am," her mistress said, "Very well. You may go."

When the door had closed on the girl, Anna slowly walked up the room until she was about six feet from the woman; and there she stopped and waited. She watched her put her head to one side while staring at the canvas on the easel, then put out a hand and stroke some paint on to it. But it was only after she had turned completely round, placed her brush and palette on the table, then wiped her hands on a towel that was laid by the side of a bowl of water, did she turn and look fully at Anna, saying now, "You know you are on probation?"

Anna hadn't been aware that she was on probation, but she answered, "If you say so, madam."

"I do say so." It was a bawl. The woman was glaring at her now, her face suffused with temper. And Anna returned her stare, until the woman turned to the table again and squeezed some paint out on to the palette, then picked up the brush and returned to the easel. And once more she was applying the paint to the canvas. There was no sound in the room, and Anna was about to say, "May I take my leave, madam," when the woman said in a surprisingly quiet tone now, "How long have you known my husband?"

The question forced Anna to screw up her face in some perplexity, as she said, "What did you say, madam?"

"You heard what I said, girl." The eyes were still directed towards the canvas, but the voice had changed. It was deep and seemed to have a threat in it. And, in answer, her own tone changed: she forgot the nurse's advice and admonition as she said, "I don't understand you, madam. I have only known Mr. Brodrick for a matter of months. I first saw him and the gentleman who has just left when out riding with Miss Netherton."

"You are lying, girl."

"I am not lying, madam. I don't lie. I have no need to lie. I have seen your husband twice since that time: the first after I left my post in Fellburn and had missed the cart and had to walk home, when your husband was on his way to the post office and he kindly offered me a lift part of the way. The other time was when Mr. Timothy had a seizure and we brought him to our home and your husband came to collect him. Then, I had a letter asking if I would take the post and . . ."

The woman turned to her now and held up her hand, crying, "Enough! Enough!" Then she stood looking at her, staring into her face, which she felt to be flushed, and with an imperious movement of her hand she said, "You may go."

Anna did not immediately turn about, but returned the woman's stare for a moment, and when she did turn she was halted again by the voice saying, "Girl!" and she stopped in her walk, but she did not this time turn round and the voice went on: "You will be wise if you forget our conversation. You'll also be wise if you watch your tongue and speak only when you're spoken to, and then briefly. I hope you understand me?"

Still Anna did not turn round but walked ahead towards the door.

The woman's scream almost lifted her from her feet.

"Girl!"

Slowly Anna forced her body round and she wouldn't have been surprised if, like Mr. Timothy, the woman had gone into a seizure as the words were flung at her like darts: "Don't you dare! ever dare stand with your back to me when I'm speaking to you. Do you hear me? Answer me!"

"Yes, madam, I hear you."

"Well, hear you this: you will stand there until I give you leave to go."

Before the last word hit her she was almost pushed on to her face by the door being abruptly opened, and then a voice said, "Oh, I'm sorry. I'm sorry. Oh, good morning. You arrived, then."

She looked at the kindly face of Timothy Barrington, and at this moment she had the desire to burst into tears, for his warm greeting coming on top of that woman's tirade was almost too much for her.

When he held the door open for her, she did not wait for the order of dismissal from her mistress, but walked past him without a word. And she almost fell off the second step into the corridor.

Some minutes later, when she reached the top landing and was making for the schoolroom door, Peggy Maybright, coming out of it with an empty coal-scuttle in her hand, exclaimed, "Eeh! What's the matter with you, teacher? You look like a piece of lint."

She didn't answer the girl, but went into the schoolroom and closed the door none too gently.

The child was sitting at the table and he turned and said, "I can't count with Peggy, teacher; she's silly."

What she should have said in admonition was, "You mustn't call anyone silly." Instead, she sat down opposite him and when she rested her head on her hand he enquired, "Have you a headache, teacher?"

As she was about to say, "Yes, dear, I have a headache," the door leading into Nurse Stanmore's room opened and the old woman called to her, "I'd like a word with you if you have a minute. And you, Master Andrew, keep on with what you're doing, that's a good lad."

Reluctantly, it would seem, she rose from the chair and went slowly towards the nurse, who, still holding open the door, now closed it behind them, before turning to her and asking, "She go for you?"

Anna swallowed deeply, then said, "Yes. Yes, you could say she went for me."

"What about?"

"Nothing that I can give any reasonable answer to. She . . . she just went for me. Whatever I said . . ."

"Did you cheek her?"

"No, certainly not. I just spoke and answered her questions."

"Sit yourself down. You look shaken."

"No, and I must tell you, I don't intend to stay."

"Ah, now, come on. Come on. If it's any comfort to you we've all gone through the mill with her, some of us for no reason. She's got a temper like a fiend. The house has never been the same since the day she stepped into it. Sometimes I think she's not right in the head but"—she nodded now knowingly—"she's all right in one direction, that's where blokes are concerned.

Why, in the name of God, Master Simon took her on and didn't let the other one manage her, God alone knows; but he's dealt with her in his own fashion, and it's put years on him. If it wasn't for madam, his mother, he'd be gone long afore now. Anyway, it's about time for her trip to London. She goes up about this time of the year, sometimes stays a couple of months, going round exhibitions and things. But it's my opinion she goes around more than exhibitions. Oh aye, I know what I know. So be a good lass, and I'll bet you a shilling when Mr. Simon gets word of this, she'll leave you alone. And he's concerned that the boy should be learning his letters and such. To tell you the truth, I'm glad he's taking an interest in him. He didn't seem to bother much afore, except that he told me to get him out of those petticoats and into pants. But as I said, you don't usually breech them till they're five. But you know what he said to me? In that case, by the time he was five, he'd be playing with dolls. So the poor bairn is going to be breeched shortly. Making him old afore his time, I say. But there you are, that's today. Look, hold your hand a minute and sit yourself down in that chair."

She now almost pushed Anna into the leather chair before going to a cabinet at the far end of the room, from which she took out a bottle and a wine glass, which she then filled from the bottle and said, "Drink that."

"What is it?"

"Nothing but what could do you good. It isn't spirits, 'tis herbs. I have it made up specially, as me mother did afore her. It's a cure for most things except"—she laughed now—"bad legs, rheumatism, and heartache. Oh, and I've known it help that, an' all. Anyway, it'll pull you together."

The potion tasted very nice, like honey, but with a tang to it; and after draining the glass, she said, "It's very pleasant-tasting."

"Aye, I've always found it so meself. And you'll find it'll work on you the lower it drops into you."

Anna rose to her feet and, looking at the old nurse, she said, "You're very kind, and . . . and your kindness contrasts with the feeling against me I've already experienced since coming into this house."

"Oh, take no notice. We're not all alike. But some can't help being ignorant. And there's always a mixture in every household. Now, go into the boy and give him of your best."

Anna looked at this old woman, and again kind words were about to be her downfall, so she turned swiftly away and went into the schoolroom and began to give the boy . . . of her best . . .

It was about an hour afterwards when a tap came on the outer door of the schoolroom and after calling, "Come in," she rose to her feet at the sight of Mr. Timothy Barrington entering the room.

"Am I disturbing you?"

As she said, "No, not at all," the boy jumped from his chair, saying, "Oh, Uncle Tim, have you come to take lessons?"

"Well, I need them, Andrew, but I don't think Miss . . . Dagshaw will have time to bother with me, because you have such a lot to learn. What are you doing now?" He was looking down on to the table, then he exclaimed, "Oh, you have drawn a dog!"

"No, no"—the boy laughed now—"silly; it's a cat."

"But where are its whiskers?"

"I haven't put them on yet, Uncle."

"Oh, I see. Well, I think you had better, and put some legs on it, too. Then let me see what it looks like when you complete it. Go on. Do it carefully."

As the child scrambled back onto his seat again, Timothy walked to the window, saying, "You have a lovely view from up here, Miss Dagshaw. A most pleasant room to be taught in. I remember the schoolroom at my home: it was so dull, the windows very high. I understand they were placed so in order not to distract the pupils. And, of course, in a way, I can understand the reason. We were five young boys and three young girls, the result of my father's second marriage. His previous one had only produced my half-sister, who was past fifteen when I came on the scene . . ."

He laughed and said, "Don't look so perplexed, but is it any wonder, the way I keep jabbering on? Madam"—he pointed now towards the floor—"Mrs. Brodrick senior is my half-sister."

Anna nodded. "Yes. Oh yes, I understand," she said.

He leant towards the window and in a lower voice now, he said, "You've had a taste of Mistress Brodrick junior's temper. One wall of my sitting room also happens to be the wall of her studio. Her high notes at times penetrate through it. I knew you had been called to the throne room; I saw you from the far corridor. I . . . I just want to say, don't let it disturb you. Simon, my nephew, will, I am sure, make things plain to his wife that it was he who engaged you, so you will not be so disturbed in the future. I . . . I am so sorry you have been subjected to this on your first day here.

"My sister would never have allowed such a thing to take place. By the way"—he glanced at her—"perhaps you know she is an invalid, but as soon as she feels able, she would like to have a word with you."

"Thank you for your concern, but I don't think I shall be able to stay on."

He turned quickly towards her and said, "Oh. Oh, give it a chance. I mean, don't let this . . . well, it will upset his father"—he nodded towards the boy—"very much if he knows that his wife is the cause of his son's being deprived of your tuition. Do, please, re-consider. Anyway, she is leaving for London shortly. She spends a lot of her time there and"—now he smiled—"when that happens the house returns to normal." He leaned towards her and in a conspiratorial whisper said, "Without exception, we all breathe easily during the respite and gather strength for the next onslaught."

She was forced to return his smile; then, quickly changing the subject, he asked brightly, "How is your family? And that cheery sister? I have meant to come across and visit you but . . . but I've been rather taken up with my own doings. You see, I . . . I write . . . well, I'm interested in history, but now and then I write silly stuff, like poetry." He whispered the word, and she actually laughed as she said, "You do? How interesting! I, too, attempt to write silly stuff."

"That's wonderful! Wonderful! I must read some of your work."

"Oh, no! Never. It's merely rhyme, not real poetry . . ."

"Look! Uncle . . . there."

They turned towards the table to see the boy holding out a sheet of paper. Timothy took it, and looked at the drawing and exclaimed in admiration, "Oh! yes. Yes; *that* is a cat."

"It isn't, Uncle; I've changed it into a dog. Don't you know the difference?"

Timothy looked at Anna. "I am stupid," he said, "I am the most stupid fellow on this earth. I must go away now and look up books and learn to know the difference between a dog and a cat." Then, turning to the boy again he said, "You can laugh. You can laugh heartily like that, but everyone isn't able to draw like you can. I must be away now, I really must. Be a good boy. Goodbye. I'll pop in tomorrow, if I may?" He glanced towards Anna, then said, "Goodbye, Miss Dagshaw."

"Goodbye, Mr. Barrington . . ."

She was sitting at the table again guiding the child's hand to make the capital D, while saying to herself, What a nice man. And to be stricken like he is. It isn't fair. Oh yes, it was true, as the nurse had said, there were kind people in this house.

And those same words she repeated later on that evening, while sitting with the family round the fire, telling them of her experiences during the day. However, she omitted that part of the interview with the mistress when she was asked, "How long have you known my husband?"

There was a meaning in those words, she knew, which would have upset her parents.

"She sounds a bitch," was Oswald's opinion, and this was confirmed by Jimmy: "She's got that name all round," he said; "she doesn't care what she rides over. She went straight through the turnip field. She thinks she can do owt she likes on the land because the farm's rented from them. But Mr. Billings went to the house and had a stop put to it. Some say she must drink, but I don't think so, because she's like that first thing in the morning. I've seen her riding to the moor, braying the horse with her whip as she goes, and it giving its best . . ."

Also, it wasn't until they were in bed that she said to Cherry, "Mr. Timothy asked after you," and Cherry said, "Did he? Did he now? Isn't that nice of him." Then she added, "Why didn't you say so before?" and Anna replied, "Well, it would have sounded as if he was singling you out; he hadn't particularly asked after the boys or Ma or Dada. He called you cheery; I thought he was saying Cherry."

"Ooh!"

"Now, now; don't get ideas."

"Who's getting ideas? Don't be silly; he's an oldish man and the poor soul is . . . well, you know . . . But it was nice of him to ask after me."

They lay quiet for a moment; then Cherry asked, "Do you think you'll ever fall in love like Dada and Ma did?"

Again there was a pause before Anna answered, "There are very few men like Dada about, so I doubt it. What about you?"

"I doubt it too; but I wish there were, at times, I wish there were."

Anna didn't take her sister's words up and say, "Yes, so do I," she said, "Go on, turn round and go to sleep. It's late, and the morning will be here before we know where we are."

TWO

$\mathcal{A}$nna had hardly begun the lesson the next morning when the door was opened unceremoniously and Simon entered. And when the child ran to him, crying, "Oh, Papa! Papa! Have you come to take me for a ride?" He patted the boy's head, saying, "No, not this morning. But come." He held out a hand and drew the child towards the door leading into the old nurse's sitting room and, opening it, he called, "Are you there, Nanny?" And when, getting up from her chair, the old woman said, "Oh, yes, I'm here, Master Simon. And you're up afore your clothes are on, aren't you? What is it?"

"Keep the boy with you for a few moments will you, please?"

"Yes. Yes. Come here my dear, come here."

Simon pressed the boy towards her, then closed the door and, now turning to Anna, he said, "Good morning."

She was standing by the table and it was a moment or two before she answered, "Good morning," giving as much emphasis to the words as he had done.

He walked up the room and from across the table he began to explain why he had interrupted the lesson. "I didn't return until eight last evening, when I was informed that you were subjected to some annoyance yesterday."

"*Oh, please. Please.* It is over. Perhaps it was partly my fault. You see, I . . . I have never been in service and therefore I'm not acquainted with the procedure."

"Oh." The words came out on a long slow breath, and he dropped down on to the child's stool, at the same time pointing to her chair and saying, "Sit down. Sit down." Then, after a moment during which he gazed down on the blocks from which his son had been learning his letters, he said, "If you are to remain here, or, I should say, come daily and teach the boy, then I'm afraid that sooner or later you will be subjected, I am sorry to say, to my wife's temper. I am speaking to you now as I would to no other member of the staff in this house. They, of course, are used to her manner, they don't need to have it explained, and so I am relieved of the embarrassment . . ."

"Please, please, don't continue. I have no wish to cause you embarrassment. I understand the situation. Should your wife wish to see me in the future I will endeavour not to arouse her ire in any way. I . . . I am not without fault; I have the unfortunate knack of speaking my mind and I have not as yet learned to be subservient."

She watched his face now break into a smile and his head wag for a moment before he said, "Oh, Miss Dagshaw, you will, I think, in your life achieve many things, but subservience, never. You are your father's daughter, if not your mother's, and they certainly have always been anything but subservient to opinions or gossip. And from what I gather, there's another strike impending and your father is likely to arouse the wrath of the coal gods by sheltering some of the outcasts."

She stared at him. This family owned shares in the Beulah mine—his brother saw to the running of it, so she understood—and yet, here he was, speaking disparagingly of it. This was a strange house, a strange family, all at odds. And she was finding it hard to understand, for she had been brought up among eight people who thought as one about most things.

He was saying, "How are you getting on with the boy?"

"Oh, it's early days yet; in fact, merely hours, but I find him most receptive and bright, and he's a"—she paused—"warm, loving character."

Again his head was moving, but slowly now as he repeated, "A warm, loving character. Strange, that."

It seemed that the next instant he was standing on his feet, so promptly had he risen from the table.

"My mother would like to see you sometime later today," he said. "She is an invalid, you know, but I can assure you that your interview will be different from your experience of yesterday."

She made no reply, and he stood looking at her for a moment before he said, and quietly, "I'm . . . I'm glad you're here . . . I mean, to see to my son. Also that you find him of a warm and loving disposition."

Something puzzled her about these last words as she now watched him walk towards the far door, open it and say in quite a loud voice. "Well, back to work! young sir. Back to the grindstone!"

"Oh, Papa, Papa, did teacher show you my drawing?"

"No. No, she didn't. And Andrew"—he bent down to him—"you must call your teacher 'Miss' not just 'teacher', Miss Dagshaw."

"Miss Dog . . . shaw?"

"No; Dagshaw."

Anna had come down the room and, looking at the child, she said, "I think it is too much of a mouthful: 'Miss' will do."

"What is your Christian name?"

She paused before she said, "Anna, Annabel. I'm usually called Anna."

"Well"—he had turned to his son again—"you will say Miss Anna."

"Mis . . . sanna?"

"No. Pronounce it correctly. Not Mis . . . sanna, Miss Anna."

The child now said on a laugh, "Missanna."

"Oh dear me!" He looked at Anna, saying, "You'll have to work on that one, Missanna."

She smiled at him, then held out her hand to the boy, and as they went up the room she heard the door close and his voice, subdued now, talking to his old nurse.

It was two o'clock when Betty Carter again entered the schoolroom unceremoniously. Standing just within the door, she looked to where Anna was sitting at the table going through some books and she said, "Madam wants to see ya."

Anna closed two books and placed them on top of a small pile, before she got to her feet and walked towards the girl, saying, "Thank you. If you will lead the way."

On the landing, before following Betty Carter, she gently pushed open a door and looked at her charge taking his afternoon nap; then, closing the door gently again, she walked towards where the girl was standing impatiently at the top of the stairhead. Once down the stairs, this impatience showed itself further when her hurrying step became almost a trot, and when Anna did not follow likewise, the maid stopped abruptly in the gallery, muttering, "Anything the matter with your legs?"

Anna did not answer, she just looked into the narrow plain face, and with a gesture of her hand told her to go on, which in no way placated her guide, for the girl now glared at her, opened her mouth as if to let her have it, decided against doing so and went down the main staircase at a rush and so into a large hall which appeared dim even with the light from two tall windows, one at each side of a glass-framed partition, leading to what she imagined to be a vestibule and the front door proper.

The girl now nodded towards two male servants who were standing surveying them, then carried on through what, to Anna, appeared to be a maze of corridors before stopping at an embossed, grey-painted door. Having rung the bell to the side of it, the girl stood facing the door until it was opened by a woman to whom she said under her breath, "Madam wants to see her."

The elderly maid looked over her informant's shoulder at the slim young person standing erect; then, turning her attention to Betty Carter again, she said, "Very well. We'll call you when you're wanted."

The girl, after throwing a sidelong glance in Anna's direction, walked quickly away, and the older woman said, "Will you come in, please?"

The tone was pleasant, the smile was pleasant; it was as if she had entered a different house; and this was confirmed when the maid escorted her across a hall, this too painted in a pretty grey colour, then into a small sitting-room, where a woman, dressed in a nurse's uniform, had just entered from a far door. And she stopped and looked at Anna for a moment, then said with a smile, "Will you come this way, please? Madam will see you now."

As she entered the large room, Anna immediately took in the furnishings: first, that there was a lot of furniture; and then that the bed was placed near the tall window at the far end; but it was the couch in the middle of the room and facing another large window that drew and held her attention. Perhaps it was not so much a couch as a bed, for lying on it was a figure, with the head resting on a single pillow.

The nurse now led her to the foot of this bed and from there she looked at the pale face topped by a mass of white hair, and was immediately struck by the brightness of the eyes. They were large eyes, what she would call intelligent eyes: all the life that should have been in the body was in them. They did not move over her but were riveted on her face. And then the person spoke, and to Anna's further amazement the voice was as alive as the eyes when it said, "Bring Miss Dagshaw a chair, please, nurse."

A chair was brought, and Anna thanked the nurse and sat down, and once more she looked up the length of the inert body to where the head was moving slightly now, which movement brought the nurse to the bed, saying quietly, "Would you like to be raised, madam?"

"Yes. Yes, I would, just a little."

The nurse crossed the room to a door, opened it and spoke to someone. And now there came into the room a man in a white overall and he went straight to the head of the couch and began to wind a handle.

When the lady said, "Three turns, Mason," the bed slowly tilted, and now it seemed to Anna as if she and the invalid were at eye level.

"That's it. Thank you. And, nurse, will you please tell Miss Rivers that I shall need her in about five minutes."

"Yes, madam."

Anna was aware that they now had the room to themselves.

"How are you finding my grandson?"

"I find him an apt pupil, madam, and of a nice disposition."

"And of a nice disposition?"

"Oh, yes, madam, a very pleasing disposition."

"How do you intend to instruct him?"

Anna paused before she answered: "Well, madam," she said, "I think he should become acquainted with the whole of the alphabet, and that he should be able to count up . . . but gradually, to a hundred, during which time he will be doing little addition sums and also putting his letters into one syllable words."

"That seems very practical and will lead to when he is due to have a tutor . . . I understand you have been educated by your father?"

"Yes, madam."

"How did he instruct you?"

Again Anna paused before she said, "Mainly through reading, just reading."

"Just reading?"

"Yes, madam. He is a great reader."

"What did he advise you to read?"

"History, geography, and literature."

"Literature? What books did you read?"

"Well, madam, the ones I remember most are those of Mr. Daniel Defoe and Dean Swift. He first told us the stories, then would get the older ones in my family to read parts aloud—" her lips moved into a smile as she added, "pretending that he had forgotten a particular section."

"Have you many books?"

"Not as many as we would like, madam."

"We have a good library here; you have my permission to take the loan of whatever you need."

"Oh, thank you, madam."

"How many are there in your family?"

"I have two brothers older than myself, madam, a sister a year younger, and two brothers younger than her."

"You are also a friend of Miss Netherton's, I understand."

"Yes, madam, I am honoured to be that."

There was a long pause now while Anna had to bear the scrutiny of the bright eyes; and then the lady said, "I am sure you will instruct my grand-child well. One last thing: should at any time you feel that you wish to speak about anything that might be troubling you while you are in this house, then I would wish you to speak to the child's father or to Mr. Barrington and they will convey the matter to me. Thank you, Miss Dagshaw."

As if a bell had rung on the lady's last words, the door opened and a young, plainly dressed woman entered, and with one last look at the seem-ingly disembodied lady on the bed, Anna rose and said, "Thank you, madam," and dared to add, "for your kindness." She did not dip her knee but inclined her head gravely forward. Then she took two steps back from the foot of the bed, before turning away to walk to the open door, by which the nurse was awaiting her.

The nurse smiled at her and she returned the smile; then she was handed over to the maid who had let her in and had been addressed as Wilson.

Wilson smiled at her, and she smiled back, and when the door was opened for her, Anna turned to the woman and said, "Thank you." And Wilson said, "You're welcome." And this exchange brought the waiting up-per housemaid's mouth agape.

As Anna followed Betty Carter back to the nursery, she noted that the girl was no longer galloping; she also realised that having left madam's quar-ters, she had entered another world, and in the main, a hostile one.

Again around the fire that evening she described the events of the day, mak-ing much play of her visit to the older Mrs. Brodrick. And she finished by saying, "Well, now, that's me. What's happened to the rest of you?"

"Well," Maria said, "a number of things have happened; but first of all, I hear that Miss Netherton's not at all well. She's been in bed today, so I think tomorrow morning, before you take your jaunt in the gig, you should slip over and see how she is."

"Oh yes, I will. Number two could go that way, I should think."

Nathaniel looked at Anna and said, "Yes; why not?" And she smiled back at him, saying, "Why not indeed! I've just to tell my coachman to change his route and that'll be that."

When Oswald pushed her and she almost fell off the cracket, they all started to laugh and Nathaniel put in, "Well, he is her own coachman; and he's a comic, if ever I've heard one. But now, Oswald, tell Anna your piece of news."

Oswald now stuck his thumbs inside the straps of his braces and waggled his fingers, then put his head on one side as he said, "I've been offered a position."

"I thought I knew that. You told us about Mr. Green."

"Oh, that's old stuff. Manager, I could be now, with Olan under me."

"With Mr. Green?"

"No, no. With Mrs. Simpson."

Jimmy, now bending forward in silent laughter, slapped Olan on the knee as he spluttered, "Pies and peas, with or without vinegar."

They were rolling on the mat again until Nathaniel cried, "Give over! both of you. Behave. And listen. Go on, Oswald."

"Well, it's like this, Anna," Oswald said. "You see, we go to this shop now and again near the river front for a pie and pea dinner; they're always good quality and it's a clean place. There used to be a man serving, elderly. Well, he was the boss and he died. The mother and the daughter did the baking and such and they had to get a new fellow in. Well, he rooked them and so the daughter went up into the shop and got a lass to help her. But there's some ruffians on that front, you know, especially from the ships. Well, 'twas last Wednesday I had told Olan here that he should try servicing round that quarter, and why not try the pies and peas place? So we decided to meet at twelve when the break came, and he brought the tray in with a few odds and ends he had left. The place was a bit full and we had to wait our turn, and it should happen that two drunken fellas started to take liberties with the lass behind the counter, and when one of them leant over and grabbed the front of the lass's frock and in doing so spilt a bowl of peas, she screamed. And so I went to stop him . . ."

"Went to stop him." Olan laughed. "That's how he got the lump on his jaw and his black and blue cheek. It was supposed to be from a bread tray falling on him."

"Never!" cried Maria now. "You didn't tell me that."

"Well, there was no need, Ma. And shut your big mouth." He had turned to his brother, who was grinning at him. "Anyway, when the shop was clear the mother thanked me, and then she asked me what my job was. And so I told her, and I said this was my brother, and she invited us both into the back room."

Oswald now looked directly at Anna as he said, "The top and the bottom of it is, Anna, she's asked me if I'd manage the shop. And I can have Olan here as an assistant. Before her man died they had been thinking about taking the empty shop next door to turn it into a sit-down place, you know. And she said, later on we could have the rooms upstairs if we wanted them. But I shook my head at that."

There was a nudge into Oswald's side from Olan's elbow as he said, "Tell her what she offered us."

"Well, me twelve and six a week to begin with, and Olan, ten shillings; a rise every year and our cart fare paid for as long as we travel."

Anna shook her head slowly as she said, "That's wonderful, marvellous. Are you going to take it?"

"I don't know." Oswald thumbed towards his brother now, saying, "We thought we should put it to Ma and Dada. And, you see, I'm nineteen turned, and although Mr. Green's been very good, he's got two sons and a daughter and I can never see me getting much further than the little Bogs End shop, or Olan either."

Nathaniel smiled now at his sons as he said, "Would you mind if I took a trip and had a look at this money-making pies and peas business?"

"Oh, yes, Dada; I'd like you to see it. And she's a nice woman. They're both nice. Apparently they've had three men in since her husband died and with the last one the takings went down by half."

"How old is the woman?" It was Maria asking now, and her sons looked at each other; then Oswald said, "Much older than you, Ma."

"I'm glad to know there's somebody in the world older than me," said Maria, and this brought forth more laughter; then Olan said, "In her fifties. Not as old as Miss Netherton, but about fifty."

"And the daughter?"

"Oh, she's getting on an' all." Olan was nodding his head. "Twenty-something, I would say. Wouldn't you?" He looked at Oswald, and Oswald said, "I should think about twenty-four, and that's getting on for a girl; I mean, a woman."

Maria exchanged a twinkling glance with Nathaniel, then said, "Well, they seem stable women. But I think it's wise what your dada said; he should go and have a look at the place."

Looking closely at Cherry, now, Anna said, "You've been very quiet in all this. Hasn't Mr. Praggett done an Irish jig on the table for you, or amused you in any way? Hasn't he thrown Janet or Lucy downstairs?"

Cherry didn't answer but her father put in quietly, "Cherry witnessed something disturbing coming back tonight. You know the pit lad, Bobby Crane? Well, he was attacked by two other pitmen and they threatened what would happen to him if he didn't stop coming here. Apparently he wrote out a notice, well, in large printed letters, for one of the men who was pushing the union and our dear Mr. Praggett found out. And two of his henchmen set about the lad. The sorry thing is one of his assailants happened to be his cousin. And my brave daughter here"—he put his arm round Cherry's shoulder—"did some screaming, then took up a staff and actually hit one with it. I think they were so astounded at this that they went off, just aiming verbal abuse at her. Anyway, she helped young Bobby here and he's now over in the barn, sleeping I hope, after your mother's administrations."

"Oh, I am sorry. And oh, Cherry, you were brave to stand up to them . . . Poor Bobby. What will he do now?"

"Well, he's not going back to the pit," Cherry said. "He's made his mind up. He's asked if he can stay in the barn tonight; but he's going into Gateshead or Newcastle tomorrow and he says he'll take anything; he might even sign on one of the boats."

As if aiming to lighten the conversation, Ben said, "You didn't tell them about Jimmy's bull, Dada."

Nathaniel looked down on the boy. "No, I didn't," he said. "And for once my erudite son has kept his mouth shut. But that points to a very good quality in him, because what he would have to tell would be in praise of his courage, too."

Jimmy was now sitting with his hands between his knees, his head down and his gaze turned towards the blazing fire, and Anna, looking towards him, said, "He's fought a bull?"

"As much as. Well, it should happen from what Farmer Billings told me, and with pride, that he had taken Rickshaw to the market. Rickshaw, by the way, is the name of the bull. I always thought a rickshaw was a Chinese one-man carriage, but the bull was called Rickshaw. I wonder why."

Jimmy's head came up and round, and he muttered, "Because its rump swings," then turned to gaze into the fire again for, amid laughter, his father was continuing, "Well, the herdsman was there and he was supposed to have control of Rickshaw and to take him around the ring. Well, Rickshaw was in a pen and the herdsman opened the gate and went to lead his charge out. But Rickshaw thought differently. Apparently he must never have liked the herdsman, for he put his head down and it was the herdsman who went out."

They were all in different stages of laughter now, some smothered, some high, some emitting squeals at their mind pictures as Nathaniel went on, "Then Farmer Billings said there was a scattering of people all about, but Rickshaw didn't charge. He just walked forward, and my son here put his hand out, got hold of the nose piece and spoke to him, then led him quietly into the ring."

Jimmy's head was once again turned towards his father, and he was spluttering now as he said, "Only because I was dead in front of him, Dada, and I thought, if he was going to toss me I wouldn't go so far if I held on to his nose piece."

Nathaniel himself was laughing loudly as he said, "Modesty. Modesty. You used your wits and, as you've told me before, you liked old Rickshaw, and that you used to talk to him and give him titbits. He liked turnip, didn't he, and crusty bread?"

As the laughter died down Anna wiped her eyes and looked at her young brother. "We're all laughing, Jimmy," she said; "but that was a wonderful thing to do. You could have been hurt, too. Anyway, tell me, is Mr. Billings going to put your wage up?"

"That'll be the day for celebrations. He'll likely give me a bag of turnips, knowing that we grow our own."

"Wait and see. Wait and see," his father said, then added, "Now we'll get to our small nightly duties, whether it's washing our face and hands or helping to set the table, and then to bed. But I myself will go to sleep tonight on the very warming thought that I have three very brave children . . ."

Anna did not rise immediately with the others, but sat gazing into the fire for a moment, seeing there the child who needed love so much, sleeping in that garret room. For after all, that's what it was, no matter how nicely furnished. Then one after another she saw those members of the household she had so far met and she reflected, in comparison with her family, how loveless they all were.

She started as her father's hand came on her shoulders and he said, "Where were you? What were you thinking?"

She looked up at him and said, "I was thinking how lucky we all are." And he said simply, "Thank you, daughter."

THREE

$\mathscr{A}$nna had three more encounters with the mistress before she left for London. The first one left her shaking and lying in the hedge. It was on a Sunday. She had been to see Miss Netherton, who was recovering from a very bad bout of bronchitis and had been ordered by her doctor to take a holiday, preferably in Switzerland.

This she had emphatically rejected at first, but after she was told that one of her lungs was affected, she had reluctantly succumbed to the suggestion. She had told Anna she would be leaving within the month, but in her inimitable way she had added, "I'll be back before I get there because I can't stand foreign places. Foreigners don't know how to make tea."

It was a very cold day, the night frost having remained on the ground, and now it was two o'clock in the afternoon. She had come along the coach road from Miss Netherton's; then after clambering up the bank and crossing the stile, she had walked along the quarry path. There had been a lot of rain before the cold spell had set in and so there were many glassy patches along the way. The rain, too, she saw had brought a fresh fall from the quarry top; soon, she thought, they would be unable to walk along here, unless the hedge was taken down.

She had just passed the part where the path narrowed to within a few feet of the quarry edge when, to her amazement, she saw in the distance a horse and rider. Towards the far end the path was bordered on one side by Farmer Billings's fields, but it eventually petered out into the moor. Because of the obstacle presented by the stile and the bank, she had never known a rider to use this path.

From this distance she couldn't make out who the rider was, but she noted that the horse had been pulled up. But then, to her utter amazement she saw that the animal was being urged into a gallop and that it was heading straight for her.

The path, although not so narrow here, still had the quarry on one side and no outlet to her right except the bramble hedge. She had no time to think, only to scream, as she fell back on to the hedge as the horse flashed past her, its smell in her nostrils and the face of the woman driving it looking down on her.

She didn't try to rise, for her weight was bending the hedge and taking her downwards, but the scream was still high in her head and it was yelling at her: She meant that! She meant it! She could have killed me. She wanted to. She's mad. Oh, my God! She's mad.

She was now lying almost prone in the bushes; the branches were entangled in her clothes and she couldn't push herself forward. She wanted to cry out now with the pain from her hands as the bramble spikes pierced her woollen gloves.

Slowly and painfully she drew herself back and into the field, and there she lay for some minutes, until she felt able to pull herself to her feet and retrieve her hat that was perched on one of the bushes.

She had adjusted her clothes and put her hat on when she heard the horse's hooves again, walking now, and she stood as if petrified, telling herself that she couldn't run across this field because a horse could easily overtake her. She was standing stiffly looking over the broken hedge when the rider drew up and stared at her. And then in an ordinary tone the words came to her: "My horse was startled. It must have been a rabbit. Anyway, you shouldn't be walking along this path, it's dangerous. Are you hurt?"

She made no reply. She couldn't reply. She just stared back at this woman, this terrible woman, this frightening creature, who, shaking the reins, now said, "Well, if you will walk along byways, that's your affair."

She was still standing rigid when the sound of the horse's hooves faded away.

When she reached home and her mother exclaimed at the condition of her coat and her bleeding hands, she told her she had slipped on the ice and fallen into the hedge, and her mother seemed to believe her. But her father looked hard at her, and she returned his stare and they understood each other.

Later, when they were alone together, he said, "Was it from the village?" and she said, "No, Dada; it was a horse-rider and I had to jump out of the way."

She knew he was puzzled by her answer but she didn't enlighten him further.

Their second meeting was in the schoolroom.

Simon often visited the schoolroom now and it was shortly after her visit to his mother that he said, "I understand that you would like to borrow some books from the library, but I'm afraid"—he smiled—"there's nothing elementary enough for school use up here."

Then, as his mother had, he too asked, "Have you many books at home?" and she had answered, "Not as many as my father would like, but he *has* collected a number over the years." And to this he had said, "Well, if there are any he would care to borrow, you must take them."

This morning he had visited the schoolroom early. She had just set out the books and equipment that would be necessary for the lesson. As always, the child had run to him, crying, "Papa! Papa!" And he had stooped and picked him up, saying, "You're getting heavier every day." Then looking at Anna, he had asked a question: "Everything all right?"

"Yes. Yes, thank you."

"He is behaving himself?"

"He always behaves himself, sir."

He had looked towards the window and remarked, "It's a lovely day, cold, but the sun is bright." Then he had added, "I shall be away for the next two days, perhaps three; I'm going to London."

Before she could make any comment the child had said, "Will you take me to London one day, Papa?"

"Yes, yes, I hope I shall. That's if you remain a good boy and do what you're told, and learn your lessons."

"I shall. I shall, Papa."

He had put the child down and, stepping towards Anna, had looked her straight in the face as he said, "Should there be anything you need, or advice, my uncle will be in the house. And, of course, there is always my mother. You just need to ask if you may see her."

When she made no answer he had said softly, "You understand?" And then, inclining her head, she had said, "Yes, I understand. But I hope I won't have to trouble them."

"I hope so too. Well, goodbye." He had smiled at her, then patted his son's head. He had not, however, left by the door leading into the nurse's sitting room, but by that leading to the landing, and there he had turned and looked at her again, his face straight, and when once more he had said, "Goodbye," she too had responded, quickly, "Goodbye. Goodbye, sir."

Why should she have felt troubled? She had sat down at the table opposite the child and when he said, "Papa is big, isn't he?" she had said, "Yes. Yes, he is, dear."

"Will you take me to your house some day, Missanna?"

"I should like to, but I would have to get permission first from your papa."

"You could ask Uncle Timothy."

She had wagged her finger at him, saying now, "We'll get on with our letters, shall we, Andrew?" And he, laughing, had said, "Yes, Missanna."

It was about half past ten in the morning when the second encounter took place. Katie Riddell, who always brought up the child his hot milk and biscuits at this time, scurried into the room saying, "She's on her way."

"Who's on her way?"

"The mistress of course, who else?" And the girl poked her head forward. "At least she was making for here. She's not usually around this part in the morning, so look out." She plonked the tray down on the table, looking at the child as she did so and saying, "Hello, Master Andrew." He answered, "Hello Katie"; then she went out as quickly as she had come.

Anna felt a tightness in the bottom of her stomach: it was as if her muscles had suddenly contracted. She made herself go about her duties: she put a bib on the boy, tying the tapes into a bow at the back; then she poured out the milk from the jug into a cup, and he said, "Why don't you have milk, Missanna?"

"Because I prefer tea." Even whilst saying this, Anna half turned her head quickly towards the door leading into the nurse's sitting room, from where the sound of a voice was now coming, and it certainly wasn't that of the old nurse going for her assistant, Peggy Maybright.

When the door opened to reveal the figure dressed in a riding habit, had the circumstances been otherwise, Anna's thoughts would have been, She is beautiful! As it was, they were to tell herself she must keep calm, and she must keep her tongue quiet.

She noticed immediately that the child didn't jump from his seat as he would do when either his father or his uncle entered; he got down slowly to go and meet his mother, and greeted her in a most polite manner. "Good morning, Mama," he said.

"Good morning, Andrew. What are you doing?" She looked towards the table.

"I am going to have my milk, Mama."

She now walked up to the table, looked down on to the tray, then turned her cold gaze on Anna and said, "He should not be eating off a tray; a table should be set apart."

"I shall see to it, Mistress."

"Yes; yes, you will see to it." She now looked around the room as if she hadn't seen it before and when her gaze was halted as she saw an easel, the child cried excitedly now, "Papa bought that yesterday for Missanna to write on. It is called a black . . . board."

His mother now walked towards the easel that supported the blackboard, and the child in his excitement ran to it and said, "This is a weasel."

"Easel."

"Weasel. Yes, Mama, weasel."

"Say, easel."

"It . . . it is difficult, Mama, to say weasel."

The eyes were turned on Anna now. "Why haven't you done something about this?"

"It is an impediment of a sort, Mistress. I'm aiming to cure it, but it will take time."

It was as if the child sensed the hostility and aimed to soothe it by saying, "I know my two-times table, Mama, and I can count on the ab . . . a . . . cus. And Missanna says I am . . ."

"Who is this Missanna?"

"Why"—the child put out his hand—"teacher is Missanna. Papa said I had to call . . ."

Now the voice was so loud that the child shrank back as his mother yelled at him, "She is the *teacher* and you will call her *teacher*. You understand?" She was bending down to him, her hand tapping her skirt as she spoke. And it was a moment before the child answered, "Yes, Mama."

As Anna watched the woman slowly straighten her back and turn towards her, she had an overwhelming desire to respond physically to this woman— she could see her hand slapping that face—for there would be no reasoning with her.

And when she said, "In future you will report his progress to me every week when I'm at home. You understand?" She couldn't answer her; she couldn't force, "Yes, Mistress," through her lips.

"I am speaking to you, girl!"

Now she was answering, her words coming fast: "I am aware of that, Mistress; you leave no doubt in anyone's mind to whom you are speaking. Well, I am speaking, too, and let me tell you I have no need to put up with your treatment. I was engaged for this post by Andrew's father and I shall take my orders from him. Is that plain?"

She watched the colour drain from the peach-like skin; she watched the high collar of the riding-habit move in and out as if the woman was choking; and she was prepared for the onslaught. The words were fired like bullets from a gun and the report of them as loud, as she screamed, "You insolent slut, you! You low-born insolent slut! Get out of my sight before I take my whip to you!"

"Mama! Mama! Don't! Don't smack Missanna."

The sight of her son throwing his arms protectingly around Anna's hips and pressing his head into her waist was too much. Her hands reached out and, grabbing the collar of the child's blouse, she actually flung him across the room; and his screaming died away as his head hit the skirting board and he became still.

There followed a deep momentary silence, until the door from the sitting-room flew open and the nurse hurried in crying, "Mistress! Mistress! What have you done?"

Penella Brodrick was now leaning against the table, her hands gripping the edge, her body half over it, and she didn't answer the nurse, nor even turn her head when she heard the child begin to cry now, but seemingly having to make an effort to drag herself up straight, and with one hand held out before her as if groping her way, she went from the room.

"Missanna. Missanna."

"I am here, dear. Don't cry, don't cry. Let me feel your head." Anna felt the back of the child's head, where a bump was slowly rising, and as she picked him up from the floor the nurse said, "Cut?"

"No, only a lump."

"My God! She could have killed him. But you . . . you, lass, your tongue'll get you hung. I've never heard anything like it. One thing sure, she's never been spoken to like that in her life . . . Bring him in and lay him on the couch."

A few minutes later, when the child was tucked up on the couch, the nurse stood beside the fire and, looking down on Anna, who was now actually shivering, she said, "Lass, lass, you've got to learn to still that tongue of yours."

"How . . . . how could I? The things she said, the way she went for me."

"Aye, I heard it all; I've sharp ears. She takes some standing, I'll admit that, by God! she does. And I'll say this to you; you know nothing of it. There's never been a day's peace in this house since she set foot in it. Of course it was her upbringing; she was spoilt from the day she was born. She was one of the Harrisons. Rotten with money they were, on their mother's side anyway; French, she was, so they tell me, and the father Irish, as mad as a hatter, died on his horse blind drunk, they say. The mother had relations in Newcastle and was married to one of the shipowners. The mistress came to a dance here with them. I remember the first time I saw her. We were watching from the upper gallery. She had all the men around her like a queen bee, but from the beginning she had her eye on Mr. Simon and he on her an' all, it must be confessed. An' then in the weeks that followed, Mr. Raymond an' all came into the picture. The three of them were always riding together, and be at this or that do, too. Then, of a sudden, her mother yanks her back to France; she had a Count or some such in her eye for her. But what does she do? In no time she's in Newcastle with her maid and, I understand, enough luggage that would have filled the hall here. And then started the tug of war as to who was going to get her, Mr. Raymond or Mr. Simon. But who did she really want? There seemed to be a tussle. Anyway, she marries Mr. Simon, and mind, she could give him three years, although she doesn't look her age."

The old woman walked towards the couch and looked down on the child, whose eyes were now closed as if he had fallen asleep; and almost under her breath she said, "From the minute they came back from the honeymoon there was a change. Nobody knew what had happened. Nobody knows to this day what had happened." She now glanced sideways at Anna as she added, "A body can only guess, but it's wise to keep your guesses to yourself."

"I can't stay here, nurse. I love the child, but you see it's impossible . . ."

"And the child loves you, me dear. He's been a different boy since you came. What company am I for a bright little lad like that? What can I learn him, or Peggy Maybright, for that matter. She can't even play with him, doesn't know how. All she's good for is fetchin' and carryin'. Look, me dear." She now pulled a chair up and sat in front of Anna. "She'll be gone in a day or so. Conway is skittering around, already packing, they say. The clothes that woman has, you wouldn't believe. They say she changes from her shift up twice a day. The flat irons are going in the laundry from sunrise till the moon shows up. So, me dear lass"—she patted Anna's knees now—"stick it out. Mr. Simon's for you and Mr. Timothy an' all. Oh aye, Mr. Timothy. And from what you didn't tell me what went on when you met madam, I understand it was pretty plain sailing down there. So you see, just give it a day or two more, perhaps a week at the most, and you won't know you're in the same house."

"She doesn't seem sane, nurse . . . I mean, there's no reason for her attacks."

"Oh, that's what you think. As for being sane, she's sane all right and it's the devil's saneness. And you think there's no reason for her attacking you as she does? Why, that woman is as jealous as hell of anyone Mr. Simon has a good word for. She dismissed her other maid. She was a good-looking lass with a fine figure, and she came across her one day talking to Mr. Simon and the lass was daring to laugh at something he had said, and out she went on some pretext or other. Now Conway, her present one, is as plain as a pike-staff, with a sour puss on her. Come on, lass, cheer up. I'll brew us a strong cup of tea. An' look"—she thumbed towards the couch—"there's somebody sitting up and taking notice. Not much the worse; but that isn't his mother's fault, because she could have brained him."

The child now came towards Anna, saying, "Are you hurt, Missanna?"

"No. No, dear, I'm not hurt."

He climbed upon her knee, put his arms around her neck and, his face close to hers, he said, "You won't go away and leave me, Missanna, will you?"

She looked back into the innocent countenance and she paused a moment before she answered him: "No, dear," she said; "I won't go and leave you."

That evening, again sitting around the fire, she did not relate the events of the day to the family, merely saying that things had gone as usual. In any case, the interest was focused on the affairs of Bobby Crane, who had been offered a job of sorts in Gateshead Fell, the terms of which were under discussion.

There was a small boat-builder on the river bank who wanted an apprentice, someone willing to learn and around the age of Bobby, who was now seventeen, but the wage was very poor, only seven shillings a week, and, as Bobby said, he could never pay lodgings out of that and live. So would Nathaniel allow him to sleep in the barn until something better came along? But he fancied this job as he would be working under the open sky. Rain, hail, or shine, it wouldn't matter to him as long as he was on top of the ground instead of under it. And the hours were good, half-past seven till half-past five with a half-hour off for dinner. He had offered to pay two shillings a week for his sleeping quarters; the rest he would need to live on.

Nathaniel had shaken his head at this point and said, "God help him. However, I have already told him there would be no rent charged for any sleeping quarters here. And Oswald, too, if he takes this job of managing the pies and peas shop, which is in his mind to do, then out of his good wage he has promised to pay for a dinner for the lad and there'll always be a bite left over here for him at night." But her father had ended, "What I'm really pleased about is he's more than anxious to keep up his learning, so anxious that he is determined, after he finishes at half-past one on a Saturday, he'll go around the markets and see if he can pick up some cheap books. He's got the bug all right."

It was Cherry who put in at this stage, "He's even speaking differently; I couldn't understand the pitmatic at first. And he looked quite nice today. Ma had given him one of Olan's coats."

Here, Olan created the usual gale of laughter by saying, "Olan had only two coats and now Olan's got only one."

Leaning back against the head of the settle, Anna looked around at the fire-illuminated faces and for the countless time she told herself there couldn't be another family on earth like this one. Then that little streak of fear crept into her thinking as it had been wont to do of late: What if something happened to break it up? Yet what could happen? Nothing, except they could marry and go away . . .

Marry, did she say?

Who would want to marry them? At least, Cherry and herself. The boys might stand a better chance, but it wouldn't happen in the village or hereabouts. Oh, no, never hereabouts. But why worry about her family? they could certainly take care of themselves. What she had to worry about was that house, or the mistress of it, and the little boy who had grown to love her, and she him.

FOUR

𝒯he mistress was leaving for London; and the bustle made itself felt on the nursery floor when Betty Carter rushed into the schoolroom and, addressing Anna in her usual fashion, said, "Give him here! Peggy Maybright has to get him ready for downstairs; the mistress wants to see him."

"Leave him alone!" Anna almost snapped the girl's hand from the child's arm. "He doesn't need to be got ready except that his hands need to be washed, and I will see to that. If you have to accompany him downstairs, kindly wait outside."

Anna watched the girl draw herself up to her full height before saying, "One of these days . . ."

"Yes? One of these days, you were saying?"

The girl flounced out of the room, and Anna said to the child, "Come along, dear," and went over to the table on which stood a basin and a ewer of water, and as she poured out the water the child said, "Why don't *you* take me down, Missanna, to see Mama?"

She paused for a moment before she said, "Your mama hasn't asked for me. Anyway"—she was drying his hands now—"it is you your mama wants to see. Now, be very polite, won't you? And tell your mama you hope that she has a nice holiday."

She now took the boy to the door, where Betty Carter was standing with her arms folded and the light of battle in her eyes. And when Anna saw her thrust her hand out towards the child, she said quietly, "You have no need to take his hand; he is quite used to walking alone. Go along, Andrew."

She watched them as far as the top of the stairs, where the girl paused a moment before glancing back at her.

She returned to the classroom, closing the door behind her, and leant against it for a moment as she asked herself: How was it that she engendered such animosity? Surely it wasn't solely because of her birth? Could it be her manner towards people? But look how well she got on with nurse and Peggy, and how nice madam's servants were to her. And there was the housekeeper, Mrs. Hewitt. She was very civil towards her . . . well, most of the time. Sometimes she appeared to be on her guard. Why this should be she couldn't imagine. Was the animosity towards her because she spoke differently? Perhaps. Well, she had her father to thank for that and she did thank him. And thinking of him reminded her of the book he said he would like . . .

It was during the child's rest hour that she decided to take advantage of the permission granted to her to use the library, for her father had mentioned that there was a certain book that he would like to read and which he had been unable to get elsewhere. She had made a note of it: Pope's translation of Homer's *Iliad* and of his *Odyssey*. They would probably be in such a library as was in this house.

She knocked on the nurse's sitting-room door and when the voice said, "Come in. Come in, my dear," she went in and was greeted with, "You're just in time for a cup of tea."

"If you don't mind, nurse, I won't have any just yet. I'm going to take the opportunity of slipping down to the library. I told you I had permission."

"Aye, yes, you did."

"Well, where is it? Where do I go from the main hall . . ."

"Oh, you don't have to go near the main hall. When you get to the foot of the stairs here you'll see a door opposite. Now that doesn't lead into a bedroom or such, but into a passage; then a flight of stairs leads down to the West wing, and when you land in the corridor there you'll see an oak door right in front of your eyes. It stands out from the rest for it has a rounded top. Well, that's the library, and a splendid room it is an' all; but I don't know if it's much used these days."

"Thank you, nurse." She was about to turn away when she recalled that there was something she had meant to ask the nurse. And so tentatively she said, "The master. The child doesn't speak of his grandfather."

"Huh! That's easy to explain. He's very seldom here, 'cos he travels all over the world digging up bits of crocks here and there."

"He would be what you would call an archaeologist then."

"Oh, would he?" The old woman's eyebrows moved upwards. "Oh, you learned ones put names to things, don't you? Well, my explanation for what he is would be a digger up of the dead."

"Oh, nurse."

She went out laughing, and, following the old woman's instructions, she came to the black oak door with the arched top, and when she opened it and looked down the long room she could only gasp at the magnificence of it. It had a painted, domed ceiling, and at the far end were two long windows which apparently looked onto the garden, for she could glimpse the trees in the distance. Slowly she walked towards the highly polished mahogany-topped table that was flanked by a number of carved high-backed chairs.

She stood at one end of the table and put her hand down on the head of the animal whose curved body formed an arm of the chair, and she stroked it for a moment as if in appreciation of the workmanship. Then she turned her head first one way and then the other, and finally her gaze came to rest on the wide stone fireplace with a log fire smouldering in the hearth. The logs, she noticed, were at least four times as long as those they cut for their fire at home.

Above the fireplace two antler-headed animals seemed to be staring down at her. She looked away; she didn't like animals turned into trophies; it put her too much in mind of the cruelty of the stag hunt.

At each side of the fireplace enormous glass bookcases filled the walls, but it was the long wall opposite the fireplace that particularly held her interest. Apart from a door at the end and two small alcoves, the entire wall was made up of bookshelves holding what must be, she told herself, thousands of books.

She stood with her head back, looking upwards and wondering for a moment how anyone could reach a book from that top shelf, when she saw at the other end of the room near the door by which she had entered, a kind of double stepladder; it was on wheels and had a platform on the top.

She smiled to herself. That's how they would reach the top shelf. Oh, how her father would love this room. She could see him spending his entire day here.

She walked to one of the alcoves. The recess was about two and a half feet deep and four or five feet wide. There was a padded bench attached to one side and a flap table at the other. The table, she saw, was hinged, and once one sat down it could be lifted up practically across the knees. The little place suggested study and she could imagine the two brothers, when they were young, being made to sit here while their tutor sat at the centre table.

She ran her hand along a row of books. She must find her Dada's book and get back before the child woke and needed her. But how was she to go about finding Pope? Well, she supposed it being a fine library the books would be in alphabetical order or, at least, divided into sections.

Thinking of alphabetical order, she began to move along the shelves and soon noticed brass slots holding cards. The one she was looking at read "17th Century"; and the books here were certainly in alphabetical order. And so she moved along to the next section which, as she had expected, read "18th Century". This should be it. And yes: there was *The Essay On Man*. She took it from the shelf, and looked farther along, and was not disappointed: she took down Pope's translation of *The Iliad* and his translation of *The Odyssey* in one volume. Her dada had already told her the story in the form of mythology; it was almost, to her, a fairy tale. This translation was in poetic form, and immediately she had the feeling she would never tackle reading it. She liked a straightforward story, one written by Mr. Charles Dickens or Mrs. Gaskell.

She wasn't sure when she actually became aware of someone talking. She rose from the seat in the alcove and looked up and down the room. Perhaps it was someone walking in the garden, but they must be talking loudly for their voices to penetrate these thick walls.

She now walked down the room towards the window and as she did so she had to pass the other door in the room. She noticed it was an ordinary door and that it was slightly ajar, and she was actually startled as she recognised the mistress's voice coming from the room beyond. She had assumed she had already left the house.

She was about to turn and tiptoe up the room when the words that came to her halted her movement, because the voice from the other room was saying, "You'll come over to France, won't you, darling? Promise me?"

The master had been gone from the house these last two days and now the mistress was talking to someone and using endearments.

"I promise you, my love. I promise you."

"But what about next week?"

"I'll be up there like a shot if those damn savages behave themselves. But if they come out on strike, well, I'll have to be here, at least for a time."

"Why can't the other two come and take their share? I've told you you should suggest it."

"And I've told you, my dear one, I'm single-minded in everything I do, what I own, what I manage, and . . . and whom I love."

As her mind opened to the situation presented by the words she had overheard, she turned and at a tiptoeing run reached the alcove. There, having quickly grabbed up the two leather-bound volumes that were farthest from her, she made to snatch at the Addison and Steele book; but so hasty was her action that it slipped from her fingers. Had it fallen on its edge it would have made little noise, but it landed flat on the floor with a loud plop!

She was in a panic as she stooped to pick it up, for she heard the door being pulled fully open, and, trembling, she stood up to face once again the startled but infuriated stare of Penella Brodrick.

Raymond Brodrick was at her side, and it was he who spoke. His voice light and over-hearty, he said, "Ah! Miss Dagshaw; you are sampling the library?"

Before she could answer she watched the woman, as she thought of her, move swiftly towards her, demanding now, "What are you doing here?"

"I am choosing some books, Mistress."

"*How dare you!* Choosing some books, are you? Who gave you permission to come into this room, or anywhere near it?"

"Madam did." She did not add, "And your husband."

The woman turned and said to her brother-in-law, "Did you hear that? I ask you, did you hear that?"

"Yes. Yes, I heard." And he looked at Anna and asked quite politely, "Did my mother give you permission?"

"I would not have said so, sir, nor would I have dared to take the liberty of entering this room if I . . ."

"I've told you! I've told you!" Penella Brodrick cried at Raymond. "The insolence of her! She wouldn't dare talk like that if he . . ."

"Be quiet! Be quiet!"

"I won't be quiet." She swung around to Anna again, ordering her: "Put those books down."

Slowly Anna put the books on the table and immediately Penella Brodrick grabbed one up and, reading the titles aloud, she cried, "Pope's *Essay On Man!*" She cast a glance back at Raymond, then added, *"The Iliad* and *The Odyssey!"* Then the furious look still on her face she cried at Anna, "Don't have the effrontery, girl, to tell me that you can read or understand these books!"

"They are for my father. Madam gave me permission to take a loan of them. But yes, I could read and understand them and . . ."

"Penella! Penella!" Raymond had his hand on her upraised arm.

The books were now flung to the floor; and the words came out on spittle as the woman cried, "You insolent bastard! And you are a bastard, every inch of you and from a litter of bastards, birthed by a whore . . ."

Anna gripped the edge of the table as she watched Raymond Brodrick almost dragging the infuriated woman down the library and through the door. She felt she was going to faint: her legs gave way beneath her. She dropped onto the alcove seat and, folding her arms on the narrow table, she was about to lay her head on them when once again she heard the voice; and now she turned a fear-filled glance towards the panelling as Raymond Brodrick's voice came to her quite plainly, almost as if he were sitting at the other side of this narrow table, saying, "Why do you hate her so?"

"Because he's flaunting her at me."

"You don't mean . . . ?"

"Yes, I do mean. He's never away from the nursery now, and he hardly ever went there before, and you know the reason why."

"Penella, look at me. You say you love me."

"I do, I do, Raymond."

"Well, if you love me, why are you so concerned about whom he may be taking to bed? He doesn't have you, so he's bound to have someone. It stands to reason . . . You still care for him, don't you?"

"*No, I don't*. What I feel for him is hate. He's not a man. How could you expect me to feel anything else but hate for someone who's tortured me for years with his silence? He ignores me except on occasions such as when he told me to leave her . . . that bastard alone. Yes, do you know that? He's warned me what will happen if I go up there again."

"But you never did frequent the nursery very much, did you? The child was always brought down. You've got to stop this, you know, Penella; it'll burn you out. Your body isn't strong enough to carry the hate you have for him, and now apparently for her, and your love for me. One is bound to cancel out the other."

"It won't. *I am* strong enough. Why don't *you* hate him? You don't, do you?"

"No; I don't know. I did when he married you. And I hated you an' all, didn't I?"

"Oh, Raymond, Raymond, take me away."

"Now, now; don't go into that again. I can't, not yet, not as long as mother is alive. When father is away the control is in her hands. Although I am the eldest she is still the boss and, as you know, every penny that passes through her books is seen to by her . . . *dear secretary.*"

"I have enough money for both of us, darling."

"You have enough money for yourself, my dear one, and your extravagant tastes, but not for us both. Anyway, I like the life I lead. You know I do. I like to work and I like to play. Now, come on; the carriage is waiting and has been for some time now. If all goes as arranged I will see you next weekend in London, then within a fortnight in Paris. And I'll have another break in January, if you're still determined to stay away that long. Away you go now! But let me straighten your hat and kiss you once more."

In the silence that followed Anna raised her head, then lifted her hand

and pressed it tightly across her mouth as if to still the emotion that aimed to tumble from it: the amazement, the disgust, the knowledge of the situation that had been revealed to her and the fact that she was implicated in it made her feel sick. She couldn't stay in this place, she couldn't; she would have to go.

As she attempted to rise she felt dizzy, so dropped back onto the seat. It was as if she had suffered a physical attack; and she almost had. But had she done so, it couldn't have hurt her more than had the verbal one: *You bastard!* It had a dreadful sound. The word implied something bad, dirty, much more so than did gillyvor; and yet they both meant the same thing. And she had called her mother a whore . . . Ooh!

She actually sprang up, and then toppled back against the panel of the alcove as the hand touched her shoulder. She thought for a moment the woman had returned; then she was gaping up at Timothy and he was saying, "Oh, my dear, I'm sorry I startled you. I . . . at first, I thought you were lost in reading, but then . . . Oh! my dear, come." He held out his hand to her and his voice was light as he said, "Just a few inches farther and you would have been through that panel. It's artificial; there used to be a door there, you know."

She turned now and gazed at the panel and she mouthed, "A door?"

"Yes." He was nodding at her. "There were originally two doors leading into the other part of the library," he pointed up the room, "and there was only the one alcove and the boys used to fight over it when they were studying. So their father had that panel put in and the seat and the table, and that mercifully solved the problem."

She shook her head, then took his proffered hand as he said, "Come and sit in a more comfortable chair," and, as if she were a child, he led her around the long table to a leather chair standing near the fireplace.

"Sit down for a moment, my dear." He chafed her hand, adding, "You're cold." He took up the pair of bellows lying at the side of the fireplace and blew on the dull wood embers until the sparks began to fly up the chimney; he then drew a chair forward from the table and, after placing it by her side, he sat down and said quietly, "Tell me what happened to upset you so."

She was gazing down on her joined hands as she said, "I . . . I can't explain, except to tell you that I . . . I must leave here."

"But why? She's gone, and all tension has gone with her." He paused. "Did you see her before she left? I mean . . ."

Her head came up sharply and, looking at him, she said with some bitterness, "I not only saw her I heard her and almost felt her. She was going to strike me. If it hadn't been for Mr. . . ."

She stopped as abruptly as she had started. And when he said quietly, "Go on," she said, "No, no."

"Raymond was with her?"

When she remained silent he turned his head slowly and looked towards the alcove; then he looked down at his hands now as he said, "You overheard them talking in the next room? That's it, isn't it? And what you heard must have amazed you; and when she knew that you had overheard . . ."

"No, no," she put in. "No, I don't think she knew I had overheard anything. Yet I don't know. I dropped a book and . . . and that must have told her there was someone in here, and unfortunately at any time the sight of me seems to arouse her anger, but today she . . . she did not believe that I had been given permission to take the loan of books and she called me names."

When she stopped abruptly, he did not speak nor did he question her further, and so they sat side by side looking towards the fire until he said, "She is a very unhappy woman; and not very intelligent. She's to be pitied, in a way. It is because you are young and learned and—" he smiled now before he said, "beautiful". Then he added quickly, "Don't shake your head. I'm sure your mirror doesn't lie to you, and moreover, your straightforward and natural manner must infuriate her, for you do not act like the servant class. You are not subservient in any way because . . . well, you are an unusual girl, you know, and come from an unusual family . . ."

"Oh, yes, yes"—she nodded now—"I come from an unusual family, and I'm never allowed to forget it . . ."

"Please. Please. I meant that as a compliment, believe me, for I admire your father and your mother and honour them for the stand they took and the way they have brought up you and your brothers and sister. You're all better educated than many in the large mansions similar to this house." Then again a note of laughter in his voice, he said, "You must admit you're a very unusual crew."

She wanted to smile at him. He was such a nice man, so kind. He treated her like an equal, as did Mr. Simon . . . Oh, Mr. Simon. And for that woman to think that she and her husband . . . She would never be able to face him now. Yet he may not know of her suspicions. What had she said? That he ignored her, didn't speak to her. Then there must be a reason. Well, didn't she know the reason? Hadn't she heard the reason? But why did they live together? Hadn't Miss Netherton said something about him being very fond of his mother, and she of him? But that surely wouldn't keep him tied to a woman like her if . . .

"That boy up there loves you."

"What? Oh, yes, yes, the child. And I'm very fond of him, too."

"Well, then, how can you talk about leaving? If I know anything, Penella will not return before Christmas, and if she decides to go to France, where she still has relatives, it could be three months before she comes back. She has stayed away as long before now. Come." He took hold of her hand. "Promise me you will stay with us. Anyway, what will happen to me if you go? I will only have to trudge across that moor to see you, and you know what happened on the moor the last time I trudged. And my poor horse, too, had sore feet, or a sore foot . . ."

As she rose to her feet now she did smile at him, saying, "You should have been a diplomat; in fact, I think you are one. By the way, may I enquire how you have been feeling lately?"

"You mean the epileptic seizures? Oh . . . don't be embarrassed. I have ceased to worry about them. But, strangely, I have been free of them for weeks now. I'm on a new medicine. I had just begun taking it that day you came to my rescue and, you know, I have not had a seizure since. No; I lie. Well anyway, not a serious one, a petit mal, as it's called, once or twice, but that's all. They first started after a shock, you know. We were in Switzerland, my sister and I, and I saw the avalanche coming. It would have enveloped her, and I remember screaming a warning to her; and then it enveloped us both. But now my doctor thinks it may not be epilepsy. He has another name for it. You see, it all happens up here." He tapped his head. "One of the main cells decided it's not getting enough attention so hits out, and down I go fighting! And that's odd, because I'm not a fighting man. I'm a coward, an extreme coward."

"Oh, Mr. Timothy, I think . . ."

"What do you think?"

"I think you're the nicest man I've ever met."

She watched the colour of his face change: it was as if he were blushing, and he turned from her abruptly, saying, "Don't say that. Don't be too kind to me or I may take advantage of it."

"I'm sorry. I didn't mean to up . . ."

He turned towards her again, saying, "You didn't upset me, my dear, anything but. Anyway"—his tone changed—"now that the coast is clear from dragons, dwarfs, and gingle-gill-goollies, I would like to bring Andrew across to visit your family sometime."

"Oh, you'd be welcome. But tell me, I have never heard that word before, gingle-gill-goollies?"

"Oh, that. It's one of my home-made ones. I make up such for children's tales. Do you like fairy tales?"

"I was brought up on them."

"Did they not frighten you?"

"Yes, some of them did."

"Just some of them? Most of them did with me. We had a nanny who fancied herself as an actress and she read some of the very early ones and they are horrific. And she used to scare me to death. So I write fairy stories that have happy endings. You look surprised."

"No. No, I'm not, because my father has told me that Sir Walter Scott wrote fairy tales."

"Do you read Scott?"

"Not much. I . . . I'm not very fond of him. I find his writing . . . well, rather laborious. Do you like him?"

"Yes. Yes, I must confess I do like him. But then I have more time to indulge my fancy. I admit he takes some getting into."

They were walking towards the library door now and she said, "I would like to say thank you, Mr. Timothy. You have been of great help to me."

"Ah, well, then there's going to be no more talk of leaving?"

She sighed before she said, "Well, not for the present."

"That's good news. Now we can look forward to a happy Christmas, eh?"

On the drive home she wavered as to whether or not she should tell at least her mother what had transpired in the library; but then she knew her mother would surely confide in her father and the implications of that woman's suggestion would trouble them both, as it did herself. So she decided to say nothing for the time being, and she was even able to laugh at Barry's chatter as he endorsed the household's relief at the departure of the mistress.

"There's one I know'll thank God for her goin', an' that's Milligan, 'cos that poor beast's been run off his four feet. He used to duck his head every time he saw her comin' into the yard. I'm tellin' you, 'tis God's truth an' could be borne out by everybody in the stables. That horse used to back away from the door an' kick like hell. Beggin' your pardon, miss, but he did. The devil himself couldn't have used his hooves quicker than Milligan when she went to get on his back. Oh, 'tis like a ton weight off each of us; an' everyone else, too. The lasses are different in the kitchen. You can have a crack with 'em an' not be afraid of jumpin' out of your skin an' into the horse trough."

Laughingly she enquired, why into the horse trough? to have the answer, "Well, after the mistress's tongue has lashed out at you, you're stingin' all over. D'you know, she can swear like a trooper. She can beat our Frank. He's the first stable lad, as I've told you, miss, an' he learned from Ben Sutter. You know, he was in the Army once an' he was taught by the devil himself, who was the Sergeant Major, he said, an' there's not a word he doesn't know that you could get locked up for."

Oh, she liked Barry McBride. He was another one she would surely miss when she left the house, as leave she must some day, and that some day would be the day that woman stepped foot in it again.

FIVE

$\mathcal{I}$n the weeks leading up to Christmas, 1881, Timothy had three times brought the child to visit them: each time on a Sunday so the whole family would be present; and the boy had been enchanted with the long cosy room, but more so with its occupants and they with him. So it was proposed by Maria that Mr. Timothy and the child should be invited to their usual Boxing Day party.

Oswald, Olan, Jimmy and Cherry all worked till late Christmas Eve in order that they should have Christmas Day as a holiday; as Oswald and Olan, who had now taken up their new positions in the pies and peas shop, worked up till one o'clock on Boxing Day, as also did Cherry and Jimmy. But by three o'clock they were all present, washed and changed and ready to meet their guests: besides Timothy and the child, Miss Netherton was coming and also Bobby Crane.

The lad had spent Christmas Day with them and surprised them with his ability to play the penny whistle almost as well as Oswald could play on the little flute that Nathaniel had bought him for his tenth birthday, after having heard him blowing through a reed. In consequence, the get-together around the fire after Christmas dinner had been a jolly affair.

Now it was Boxing Day and party day and the room was packed. The tea had been merry and noisy, the centre of attraction being Andrew. Everybody seemed intent on making him happy and if his squeals of delight were anything to go by they had succeeded.

When at last the meal was over the family helped to clear the table, which was then pushed to the far end of the room in order to give space for some games, and the child became so excited that Miss Netherton said to Mr. Timothy, "What d'you bet me that nurse hasn't to get up in the middle of the night to somebody being violently sick?"

"No, no." Timothy shook his head. "If he's going to be sick I'll see that it happens before he goes to bed. But what odds? Did you ever see anyone enjoy himself as that child has done?"

As Anna and Cherry moved the two lamps into a safe place, one on each end of the mantelpiece, and put the pair of two-branched brass candelabra, holding wax, not tallow, candles, on the window sill, the child, pausing in his jumping up and down, looked about him with open mouth, then turned to Anna and said, "It's like the story you tell me about Cinderella's palace."

This brought a great hooting laugh from Nathaniel and a chuckle and the flapping of the hands from Maria. But Timothy, standing near the boy, looked around him, as the child had done, and said, "Yes. Yes, you're right, Andrew. It is like Cinderella's palace. But there's more than one princess here; there are two princesses and two fairy godmothers. And then there's the king of the castle—" He extended his hand towards Nathaniel, and, turning to the laughing boys, he added, "His sons, the princes."

"Can we have a party tomorrow again, Uncle?"

"What!" This was a hoarse whisper from Timothy now. "Do you want the king to throw us out? This is a special day; it only happens once a year."

Gauging the moment to be right to start, Nathaniel cried, "What game are we going to play first? " 'Here we go round the mulberry bush' ", eh? What about it, you two musicians?" And nodding towards Oswald, he said, "You know the tune," then turning to Bobby, he added, "Do you? It goes . . ."

"I know how it goes, Mr. Martell."

"Then let's join hands. Come on! Come on!"

And so to the faint, sweet music of the two pipes they joined hands and danced and sang as they went:

> "Here we go round the mulberry bush,
> the mulberry bush, the mulberry bush,
> Here we go round the mulberry bush
> On a cold and frosty morning.

What do we find on a mulberry bush,
a mulberry bush, a mulberry bush,
What do we find on a mulberry bush
On a cold and frosty morning?

Nothing at all on the mulberry bush
nothing at all, nothing at all,
Nothing at all on the mulberry bush
On a cold and frosty morning.

The leaves have gone to feed the worms,
to feed the worms, to feed the worms,
The leaves have gone to feed the worms
On a cold and frosty morning."

After they had danced and repeated the rhyme three times, Miss Netherton stopped and, panting, sat down in a chair and cried to Nathaniel, "I've never heard that variation before."

"No, I don't suppose you have. I made it up years ago for a little class I had when I was dealing with the making and spinning of cloth, and so on. And I discovered that the silk worms were fed on the mulberry leaves."

"How interesting."

"Another game! Another game! Let us play another game, a dancing game, Missanna. Missanna, like the one in the book."

"Oh, that was a polka."

"Oh! a polka. Not for me. Not for me." And Timothy sat down now beside Miss Netherton, and Nathaniel, turning to Oswald, cried, "Play us a polka." And holding out his hand he said, "Come on, Maria. Jimmy, you take Ben; Anna has already got her partner." He laughed to where the child was clinging to Anna's hands. And before he had time to appoint a partner for Bobby, he saw Cherry go over to him and hold out her hand, and he noticed that the boy hesitated a moment before getting to his feet, and they all laughed when he said, "I've got wooden legs." And while Oswald played a brisk tune, Miss Netherton and Mr. Timothy clapped in time with the music.

After one and another had dropped out exhausted and laughing, Nathaniel said, "Well now, it's time for a little rest and some sweetmeats." So, going to a side-table, he picked up a large box, lifted the lid and, looking around them all, he said, "This is a gift from our dear friend, Miss Netherton." And after they had all helped themselves to a sweet and nodded towards Miss Netherton, saying, "Thank you, ma'am," she said. "Thank you all for a most happy day."

It was Jimmy now who put in, "Tell us a story, Dada. One of your ghosty ones."

"Blind Man's Buff!"

They were all looking at Andrew now and laughing, and Nathaniel said, "Well, I waive my right: the guest of honour's wishes must come first. Blind Man's Buff, it is."

"Missanna. Missanna be blind man."

"No; you be blind man," said Anna, bending down to the child. And he, now gripping the skirt of her dress and attempting to shake her, said, "No! you be blind man and catch me."

"All right. All right. Dada, let me have a bandage."

"Have my green muffler, my Christmas Box."

She looked at Jimmy and, laughing now, she said, "Oh, thanks, Jimmy. That'll do fine."

It was as the boy scurried from the room to fetch the muffler that the sound of a horse neighing turned the attention of the party towards the door, and Mr. Timothy exclaimed, "That'll be the carriage. I said six o'clock, but it's only half-past five."

"Oh, no, no, Uncle Timothy; we can't go home yet. Please, please."

"All right, all right."

It was as Nathaniel went to open the door that there came a rap on it, and when it was opened Timothy was the first to exclaim, "Oh! Simon. What a nice surprise! Come in. Come in," only to turn swiftly to Nathaniel and say, "Dear me! Dear me! Here I am taking liberties. I'm so sorry."

Nathaniel was laughing now as he addressed the man at the door, saying, "Come in by all means, sir! And you're welcome."

"Oh, Papa, Papa, we are having a lovely party. We have danced and sung and there are nice things to eat and . . ."

"All right, all right, I'll hear all about it later." He patted his son's head. "But first let me say, how do you do? to Mr. and Mrs. Martell and thank them for entertaining you." At this he turned and, looking at Maria, he said, "It is very kind of you to put up with this rowdy boy and his equally rowdy uncle," which caused a little tentative laughter; and then he turned to Nathaniel, saying, "Thank you, sir, not only for today, but for the kindness you have shown in the past, and mostly for allowing your daughter to impart her knowledge to my son."

The words were very formal and for a moment they seemed to dampen the atmosphere, until Miss Netherton said in her usual imperious voice, "Well! don't stand there, Simon; come and sit down for a moment. They are about to play Blind Man's Buff."

He did not however obey her but, looking from the child to Timothy, he said, "Don't you think you have both already outstayed your welcome?"

But before either of them had time to speak Nathaniel cried, "Not at all! Not at all! We could go on all night. Just let him have one more game. Please."

"As you wish. As you wish." Simon was smiling now, and he went and stood near Miss Netherton's chair while Oswald, taking the scarf from Jimmy, doubled its length in four; then going to his sister, he said, "Turn round, and no peeping, mind," and after tying the scarf at the back he swung her about three times, crying, "Ready! Set! Go!"

With hands stretched out before her Anna groped towards the giggles and the whisperings and, taking up the pattern of her playing the game in the nursery with her pupil, she called, "Where is that big fellow who won't learn his lessons? Where is he? I'm sure he's over here."

Now she turned about and made her way towards the fire. She knew this because of the heat that was meeting her. And once her feet touched the mat she swung swiftly to her left and made a dive for the armchair, and from behind it there came giggling and scampering. And when Cherry took up the chant in which the boys joined,

"Name the one you want to catch;
name the one you want to hold,
if you dare be so bold,"

she answered,

"I name the one I want to hold:
It's Master Andrew, I make so bold."

When she heard the child's giggle she made a little run in his direction and knew that someone had suddenly lifted him up out of her reach.

Then the chant changed:

"Move round, move round,
The blind man can't see.
Be quick! Be quick!
Or he'll catch thee."

She could hear them all changing places, and again she was going down the room towards the fire, saying now, "You should give me a word." And when she heard Oswald say, "Ma'ah! Ma'ah!" like the nanny goat, she knew he was standing near the kitchen door. She did not move in that direction but towards the big armchair again, and she knew the child was there by the suppressed little squeak he made, and she guessed he would be standing up pressed against the back of it. And so, thrusting her hands quickly out, she made a dive for him. But she had misjudged the distance, and she realised her hands were gripping the lapels of a coat. She felt them lifted from the coat she held and heard a child's voice shouting with glee: "You've caught Papa. You've caught Papa. You've caught Papa. Not me, you've caught Papa."

In the next second Anna had pulled off the scarf, and there she was looking into the unsmiling face of Simon. Withdrawing her other hand sharply from his and amidst the laughing and chatter, she picked up the boy from the chair and forced herself to say lightly, "Why didn't you give me a better signal?"

"I did! I did! Missanna."

"Well, you didn't squeak loud enough."

"Can we have another game? and then you can catch me and . . ."

"No, no." It was his father speaking now. "I think you've had enough for one day, and everyone has had enough of you, too. Moreover, the horses are outside and they are getting very cold, as is Grafton. And you know, when Grafton gets cold, what he does."

"He shouts."

"Yes, he shouts. Oh yes, he shouts." He was smiling now, and he looked towards Timothy who, smiling back at him, said, "And, more than shouts."

Miss Netherton, now moving across to Simon, said, "I've ordered my trap for half-past six, but I'd be more comfortable in your carriage if you would care to drop me."

"It would be a pleasure indeed."

"Well then, I'll get into my things."

There was bustle and chatting, and then they were all crowded round the door and Timothy was saying, "I cannot remember when I've enjoyed myself more, and I have no words with which to express my thanks. I can simply treat your kindness with impertinence by saying, may I come again soon?"

Nathaniel's and Maria's assurance that he knew he would be welcome at any time was drowned by the laughter brought about by Miss Netherton saying, "Take my arm, you philanderer; you would make a wonderful professional beggar." Then, turning to the family, she spoke to them as a whole, saying, "You know what I think. I haven't this fellow's tongue, so I can simply say, thank you for a most happy time."

Robert Grafton had now come forward and was swinging the lantern to show Timothy and Miss Netherton to the carriage and the child was saying his goodbyes to all in turn, shaking each hand and saying, "Thank you. Thank you." Then as his father lifted him the child put one hand round his neck and of a sudden, reached forward and tugged Anna towards him by gripping the front of her dress and with his lips pouted out he kissed her, an audible kiss on the mouth. For a second her eyes were again looking into Simon's, and she gave a slight gasp and tried to loosen the child's hand from her collar.

But he held on to it and said, "I will see you in the morning, Missanna?" and she stammered, "Y . . . yes, in the morning."

"I love you, Missanna."

She was feeling that even her hair was on fire. There were laughing murmurs all around her; and Simon was saying, "You must forgive my son for expressing his feelings so publicly," and to Nathaniel and Maria he said, "You'll be glad when this invasion is over."

Amid loud protestations he nodded from one to the other, then said, "Good-night. Good-night all," and made his way towards the carriage.

They stood and watched the horses being turned on the frost-bitten ground and they remained standing round the opened door until the side lights of the carriage had disappeared through the gate and onto the narrow road.

With the closing of the door, there was a general expression of shivering and a making for the warmth of the fire, and although they talked and chattered about the events of the day, a quietness now seemed to have descended on them, and presently Oswald said, "It's one of the nicest Christmases I can remember, and we've had some nice ones, haven't we, Dada?"

"Yes, Oswald; we've had some nice ones, but as you say I think this is the nicest. I suppose it's because we've made a child happy and he needed to be made happy. He's had no life, no child's life, from what Anna tells us. He's to be pitied, in a way." Then turning his gaze onto Bobby, who had his head down, he said, "I don't retract on that, Bobby. There are many worse things than an empty belly in this world. You can't live on love, I know, but it helps a slice of dry bread to taste as if it had butter on it."

"Oh, I know, I know, Mr. Martell, I know what you mean. An' I've watched the bairn the day; it's just as if he had been let loose."

"Have you enjoyed yourself, Bobby?" The sudden enquiry brought his head sharply round to look at Cherry, and he stared at her for a moment before he said, with a grin, "You know, if I knew you better I would say that was a bloomin' silly question to ask me." And this wrought a change back to laughter, his own being the loudest: but then, with a slight break in his voice, he looked at Maria and said, "You'll never know really what you've done for me this Christmas. What you've all done for me. To me dying day I'll remember it. Whatever else happens in me life I'll remember this day." He turned to look at Cherry again and said, "You've got your answer." And she laughed, her mouth wide, saying, "I can see how they wanted to throw you out of the pit; you talk too much."

Their reactions to something funny was back, and again there was general laughter, for the whole family had noted and remarked on how the young fellow hardly ever opened his mouth; and Anna had asked her father: "Does he talk much when he's learning his reading?" to be told, "It's forced in a way, but it's getting better."

They weren't late in going to bed, and it was after the two girls had lain silently side by side for some time that Cherry said softly, "I like him."

"Who?"

"Bobby."

This caused Anna to turn on her side and face her sister, and say, "What d'you mean by that, you like him?"

"Just what I said."

"Which I take it to mean, you more than like him?"

"I'm not quite sure of that, Anna; but I've never sort of felt like this about any other boy. Not that either of us have had the chance to meet boys. But there's those from the village you see now and again walking through the fields on a Sunday, in their best suits, and to my mind Bobby seems to stand out. He did, even in his pit clothes; and he's got a mind and he thinks. But . . . but I'm older than him."

"Oh, yes, yes, a lot older, a year and a bit! What is he? Seventeen, and you're eighteen, just gone."

"Don't laugh. It isn't right that age should be like that; the man should always be the older."

"Don't be silly! It's how you feel, it's got nothing to do with age. Look at Miss Alice Simmons from Bowcrest, she who married last year. Remember? She's thirty-four, they said, and she married a man of twenty-five."

"Well, that lot can make laws for themselves; the higher you're up the less it matters . . ."

"You had better not let Dada hear you talk like that; he'll ask where all your learning's gone? And I'll say this: if you like Bobby, go on liking him; but get to know him better. And anyway, you know nothing could happen for years."

"I know that, but I can but hope."

"Well, go on hoping, dear; it's better than no hope at all."

She turned away and onto her side and after a moment Cherry said softly, "There's someone interested in you an' all; but there's no hope at all in that quarter, and I feel sorry, I do."

"What d'you mean? What d'you mean?" Anna had turned back again and was half-sitting up in bed.

"Oh, lie down, you know what I mean. You could see the way he looked at you when he was holding your hands in Blind Man's Buff. And I think I'm not the only one that noticed. Dada isn't blind to that kind of thing."

"Cherry! Cherry Dagshaw! Shut up! D'you hear? Don't ever dare bring that subject up again, to me or anyone else. *D'you hear?*"

"All right, all right. Lie down."

Anna lay down, and after a moment Cherry, with a big heave, turned on to her side, saying, "If I had my doubts before how you felt, you've dispelled them now."

Anna was for flouncing round again but she stopped herself by gripping the edge of the feather tick. She would have to leave that place; there must be no waiting.

Part Four
The Blow

ONE

*T*he winter of 1881–2 had been a severe one. There were days when the roads were impassable because of the heavy falls of snow; and conditions were made even worse when the thaw set in.

She hadn't kept the promise to herself to give up her post, telling herself that the child needed her. However, she was relieved, yet at the same time sorry, whenever the weather made her visits impossible.

The severest snowstorm occurred in February. It went on for four days. Huge drifts blocked the roads, trains were unable to run, and when eventually the thaw came the rivers overflowed their banks, flooding much of the land in and around the villages; only the moors seemed to escape. And perhaps this was as well, for in the second week of March, two pit families and a single man made their home on the moors, at least on the edge of it and as near as possible to Nathaniel's woodland fence, in order to get a little shelter from the trees.

They had been there for three days before Nathaniel and Anna, having gone down to the wood-pile to replenish the house stock, came across them; and they were aghast at hearing the sound of a child coughing its heart out under one of the tarpaulin shelters, three rough habitations that Nathaniel wouldn't have offered as shelter to his goats. The company consisted of three men, two women, and five children. One man had a fire going in a holed, square, tin box and had erected a tripod over it on which a kettle was swinging. And when Nathaniel spoke to them across the railings, saying, "Dear! Dear! This can't go on," the man said, "We ain't takin' any of your wood, mister."

"I'm not talking about wood," said Nathaniel, harshly now. "I'm talking about the conditions under which you are living and that child coughing in there." He pointed to the tarpaulin and makeshift walls of oddments of furniture. And he said, "You only had to come and ask. You know you could have used the barn; others before you have done so."

The man came towards the fence now and the other two men and one of the women followed, and it was the first man who spoke, saying in a quiet voice, "Aye, I know that, mister. You've been very good, and you needn't have been, with what they've done to you and your lot. But we didn't want any more trouble to come on you. So we'll be all right here for the next day or two, then we'll shift. We're goin' into the town. We'll get something; if not, the workhouse will have to keep us. But that'll be over me dead body. I'll swear on that. And we'll all see our day with that lot back there." He thumbed over the moor in the direction of the mine. "Livin' on the fat of the land, they are. We're turnin' out more bloody coal now than we ever have; three times as much as twenty years ago. I know me figures, mister. I know me figures. I'm a union man. That's me trouble, I'm a union man. The three of us here are and there's many more back there an' all. If they'd only have the bloody guts to stand up for what they think an' come out. That's why we're here, you see. We tried to get them out. Stand together, I said. And what happened? That bloody keeker, Praggett, put his oar in again."

"Why is it always Praggett who seems to have the last say in the evictions?"

"Oh, well, mister, he just works to orders an' all. There's only one there who has a good word for us and that's Taunton, the engineer; but he's got to watch his step. It's been worse since Morgansen, the second owner, come up from London and put his neb in: they should get themselves bloody well down below and see what goes on in order to let them live like lords. But I suppose Morgansen's come 'cos of his lass is goin' to marry Brodrick. An' he's lordin' it an' all since his old man died. But we'll see our day with the lot of 'em. They can do nowt about it. The union's growin' and it'll swell an' swell an' suffocate the buggers, and I hope I live to see it."

Looking at the man, Anna could see just how he had talked himself out of his job: he was a box-thumper. And yet he had a cause, oh yes. But what was this about Mr. Raymond going to marry the other mine-owner's daughter? That was something new. Oh dear, what about his brother's wife? She recalled the day she listened in to his protestations of love, so what would she do now? How would she react?

She was wintering, as nurse had called it, in the South of France; and she remembered nurse adding laughingly, "I hope she summers there an' all," to which she had mentally agreed, for the house was a different place without her personality. And except for the two weeks it had been in deep mourning for the loss of the master, Arnold Brodrick, the news of whose death had only reached them a week after he had been buried in some remote area abroad, the house had taken on a peaceful air. And she had felt herself to be accepted more and more by the staff, with one or two exceptions: the upper housemaid's manner, to say the least, was still offensive. Maybe it was because she had been bred in the village and was the blacksmith's niece.

Her father was saying in a puzzled tone, "Why won't you accept the hospitality of the barn? It is weatherproof and warm and your wives could cook in the tack room. And that child needs shelter other than that erection, if I'm to go by that racking cough."

It was one of the other men who answered this, saying, "We would like to, mister. He won't tell you"—he pointed to his talkative companion—"but Praggett tells us that if any more of us are given shelter from you they can ring off the land and then you would have no way out for your horse and cart, and the only other way on foot would be through the village. And we know that you've had trouble there as well."

Nathaniel's indignation seemed to put inches on him and his voice was loud now as he cried, "They cannot enclose us, the moor is common land. And we are bounded on two sides by Farmer Billings's land."

"Aye, well, you know, sir—" The man was nodding at him and in a quiet voice he said further, "Billings only rents the farm from the Brodricks. It's their land, you see."

"But Mr. Brodrick would never allow it."

"Aye, you would think so, but . . . but Morgansen's got a bigger slice, so I understand, of the cake, and Brodrick must be out to please him, I suppose, seein' as he is goin' to join his family. Strikes me it's a business deal as much as a marriage. Anyway, that's it, sir. We didn't want to get you into a fix like that, for they say Morgansen is tougher than Brodrick."

"There are public rights of way that even all the Brodricks and Morgansens have no control over. Now, take down those ramshackle attempts at cover and get yourselves into the barn. You can have the boiler going in a short time and hot water and hot drinks for that child. How are you off for bedding?" He was looking at the women now, and one of them said, "Well, sir, not too bad, but it's a bit damp."

"Then get it over and get it dried off. Look, carry your things along to the gate there. Until the weather gets better you'll have to make journeys back to the wood-pile to keep the boiler going. There's plenty of wood, so you needn't worry about that or anything else . . . Fencing us in indeed!" He turned about now and, taking an armful of logs, he said to Anna, "Come. Did you ever hear anything like that? What will they try to do next?"

"Well, they've said it before, Dada, and they'll likely carry out their intent, and leave us to fight it after."

"Just let them try. What a pity Miss Netherton's away! She would have gone over there and blown them up. She knows the law. For two pins I'd go myself . . ."

"Please, Dada, don't get involved any more than you need. I'll be going over tomorrow. I'll see Mr. Simon; perhaps he will be able to do something, although, as he says, he washes his hands of the mine and all its business. He doesn't like what's going on there any more than you do. As for Mr. Timothy, I think if he had worked there he would have been the first one to go on strike."

On entering the house Nathaniel cried, "Maria! Maria! Come and hear the latest." And when Maria emerged from the kitchen saying, "What is it now?" he told her, and she listened in silence as she stood drying her hands. Then she asked quietly, "What if they have the authority?"

"They haven't the authority to take in common land, moorland."

"But it must belong to somebody. They just haven't bothered to rail it in before now."

Nathaniel looked from Maria to Anna; then going to a chair, he dropped down onto it, and again remarked, "I do wish Miss Netherton was here. I know nothing about law. I've been stupid enough all my life to deal in folk-lore and fairy tales, never getting down to the basics. I'm an idiot, a pleasant idiot, that's what I am."

"Yes. Yes, of course you are, dear." They were standing one at each side of him now, and Maria, stroking his hair back from his forehead, added, "I've known that for a long time and I've wondered how I've put up with it." Then Anna laughed and Nathaniel looked at her and said, "She means that. Under that pleasantry she means that."

"Yes, of course I do. And now what we all want is a nice glass of elder-berry wine, heated."

When Maria returned to the kitchen Nathaniel looked at Anna and, all the steam going out of his tone, he said, "If we can't get the cart out, how will we manage to get the hay and animal feed in, and our groceries? And then there are the boys; if the moor is cut off they'll have a mile and a half to walk, and have to pass through the village to get on the old coach road."

"Well, don't worry about that, Dada, they'll do it. Or they can stay in the town, you know: there's those rooms above the shop that they're always talking about. I'm sure Mrs. Simpson would like them there permanently. As for Bobby, he'll tramp with them, and then there'll be less likelihood of their being set upon than if they were on their own; even though we know, and they now know, that Oswald is capable of taking on two men, as he's already proved. That leaves Cherry and me. Now, Mrs. Praggett will see that Cherry gets there all right or you'll soon know what'll happen to *Mr. Praggett.*" She laughed now. "As for me, well, Dada, I'm thinking seriously of leaving the tutoring."

"Why? Now why? I understood the child isn't to be put under a male tutor until he is six?"

"Oh, there are numerous reasons; the main one, of course, is that the mistress will be home shortly and I couldn't risk another up-and-downer with her without hitting her."

He returned her smile and said, "I understand"; then taking her hand, he added, "I understand more than you know. I think you're a very, very wise girl, and I love you dearly."

"And I you, Dada, because you are an idiot, a folklore fairytale idiot." And bending, she put her arms round him and kissed him. And Maria, at this moment entering the room and carrying a tray holding three mugs of steam-ing wine, said, "And I'll be expected to manage him after that!"

TWO

$\mathcal{S}$he always went into the house by the side door, the one which the housekeeper had told her she must use when taking the child for his afternoon walk, and on this occasion she was just about to mount the stairs when she heard the familiar voice of Betty Carter from along the passage, saying, "The gig's in the yard. She's back." Immediately she felt the urge to turn and confront the speaker, but told herself to get upstairs and continue to ignore that person.

She had hardly reached the landing before the nurse's sitting-room door opened and the old woman said, "Oh, lass, 'tis good to see you again. Like a touch of spring. Come in, come in. He's all ready and waitin' as he has been every day. I told him you'd be here the day, though. Here, give me your hat and coat and let me have your news. Don't worry about him." She thumbed towards the door. "Peggy is with him at the moment. The thing is, we won't have to laugh else he'll be in here like a shot. Sit down a minute . . . Hasn't it been a winter? I thought after that big do we had it was finished, but then, to start again! I hear they've started fencing part of the land in. How's your da taking that?"

Anna gave the old woman a brief account of how her father was taking the latest situation, but went on to say that, otherwise, the family were all fine. But how was she faring? And what was her news?

"Oh, lass, you should have been here yesterday. There was high jinks downstairs. Her ladyship returned the previous night with luggage that would fill a train, so Betty Carter said. And her and Conway took nearly an hour to sort things out. Grayson said he had seen happier faces at a funeral dinner than was around the dining table that night. But that was nothing to yesterday. She must have collared Mr. Raymond on his own and had a screaming match in the library with him. 'Tis said that Mr. Timothy went down to her and she went for him an' all; then Mr. Raymond came upstairs and told his man to pack a case and off he went. And all this, you know, because of his engagement. You would ask what it's got to do with her to get her boiled up. But then you needn't ask, if you know what I mean, lass."

Anna knew what she meant, but she made no remark and the old woman went on, "When Mr. Simon came in later—he had been in Newcastle—he had word to go to madam straightaway. Well, from there he apparently went looking for his wife, and this led to another shindy, and then another black dinner, so Walters said, with poor Mr. Timothy talking first to one and then the other about this, that, and nothin'. Eeh! by lass, this is a house, and all since that one came into it . . ." Here the door burst open unceremoniously and the child darted in, crying, "Oh, Missanna! Missanna! I knew it was you. I told Peggy it was you. And she said it wasn't. Oh, Missanna, have you come to stay now the snow has gone forever?"

Anna looked down into the face gazing up at her. The boy had his arms around her thighs and his head was back on his shoulders and he looked so appealing that she wanted to bend and kiss him.

But all she did was stroke his hair back and ask him, "Have you been a good boy and kept reading your books?"

"Oh yes, Missanna. And I have teached Peggy."

" 'Taught' Peggy."

He gave a gurgle of a laugh and repeated, "Taught Peggy." Then added, "But she is stupid."

"Now, now, Andrew; that is very naughty. You must not say that anyone is stupid."

"Well, she does not know the alphabet."

"She may not, but that doesn't mean that if Peggy doesn't know the alphabet she is stupid. Now turn and tell Peggy you are sorry."

Peggy was standing at the open doorway leading into the classroom and she smiled broadly as the child now walked towards her and, looking up at her, said, "I am sorry I called you stupid, Peggy. But you still don't know the alphabet, do you?"

The girl laughed, the nurse laughed, and Anna said, "Go on with you! Get inside there. You are a wily young man. When you apologise, you apologise; you don't end up by throwing a brickbat."

"What is a brickbat?"

Laughing now, Anna said, "It is what I'm going to take to your bottom if you are not careful." And at this she slapped him playfully on the buttocks, causing him to squeal gleefully and run madly round the table. And as she brought him to a stop she thought to herself that her welcome in all ways at this end of the house made up for a lot. And she would miss it, because soon the fencing would cut off the road to the gate and that would mean she would have to walk, and through the village, before she could reach McBride and the gig. The walking itself wouldn't matter, but having to walk through the village would. However, it would provide her with an excuse for leaving here.

It was as the child was having his morning milk and she was about to take her cup of coffee in company with the nurse that Betty Carter appeared in the classroom; no knocking, just an abrupt opening of the door and that broad, thick twang saying, "She wants you downstairs."

Anna immediately paused in her walk towards the nurse's sitting-room door and looked hard towards the girl; and now she said, "Who wants me downstairs?"

The girl wagged her head before she answered, "The mistress."

"And where does she wish to see me?"

"Where d'you think?" And with this the girl turned abruptly about and went out, banging the door after her.

Anna drew in a long breath before tapping on the nurse's door, and at the, "Come away in, lass," she said, "I'm wanted downstairs, nurse . . . the mistress wishes to see me."

"Oh, dear, dear. Well, all I can hope for is she's in a better temper. But now, lass"—she put her hand on Anna's shoulder—"just let her get on with it. D'you hear me? Just stand there and take it. The others do; so learn a lesson. It's a backward one for you, I know, an' it'll take some doing, but don't answer her back. And keep that chin of yours down a bit. The cut of your jib, you know, says a lot of how you're thinkin'."

"Oh! nurse." Anna smiled now. "The cut of me jib! The first time I heard that was from Bobby, you know, I've told you about him, the pit lad, when he said some of the men down the pit didn't like the cut of his jib. Dada had to translate it for me. Anyway, I'll remember. I'll try." She poked her face forward now. "That's all I can tell you, I'll try. I'm not promising, but I'll try."

"Go on with you!" The old woman pushed her, and a voice from behind them said, "Can I come with you, Missanna, and see Mama?"

"Not now, dear," she said; "perhaps later. You come and sit with nurse, and—" she bent to him and in a stage whisper said, "see if nurse can recite the alphabet? I don't think she can, not as well as you." And she now pressed the boy towards the old woman, then went out. But at the top of the stairs she hesitated. That girl hadn't said where she would find the mistress. Perhaps she was in the library . . . or in that room next door. But why would she be there? Well, where else? She couldn't go to her private apartments. Oh! that girl. She should go and find her; but that would mean keeping that woman waiting, and that in itself could cause an eruption. And there was no-one else at this end of the house she could ask. And so she made for the library, only to find no one in the big room, or the smaller one. She stood in the corridor, thinking. She'd likely have an office down here where she would see the housekeeper and give her her orders for the day. But where would that be? The only other place she might be was in the studio. So, it was to the studio that she made her way.

She tapped on the door but heard no reply, so she waited, then knocked again, and when she wasn't bidden to enter she gently turned the handle, pushed the door open and went into the room and in one sweeping glance she took in the chaotic scene. The canvasses that she had noticed on her previous visit, stacked against the wall, were strewn over half the floor. Some just had holes in them, others were ripped across; but there on an easel near the window was a full-length canvas and on it the startling picture of a naked man. What was more startling still was that he was dripping with paint. His face was almost obliterated by it, and it had run down his chest and onto his loins. But although the face was hardly recognisable, she knew it to be that of Mr. Raymond.

Looking about her at the chaos the room presented, realisation came, and it was frightening, and she told herself that she must get out of here and quick before . . .

But she was too late, for through the open door now strode the enraged figure of the mistress, and Anna, swinging round and facing her, had a fleeting thought that told her she had never seen this woman other than mad, but never as mad as at this moment.

"*You! You! How dare you!* You were sent for to my office."

She was beginning, "I . . . I didn't get any directions, mistress, so . . ."

"Shut up! Shut that yapping, slimy mouth of yours!" She was advancing now, each step deliberate, and Anna steeled herself for the coming blow which she was sure was intended. But a yard or so from her the woman stopped, the words spewing out of her mouth: "Legal separation and . . . and then divorce, so your bastards would be recognised. That's it, isn't it? But I'll see you in hell first! D'you hear? You brazen, black-haired bastard, you."

The hand wasn't extended towards Anna but to the table to the side, and in a flash it slipped beneath a palette thick with an assortment of still-wet paints and although she knew what was about to happen, she wasn't quick enough in jumping aside. But the palette, missing her face, still came flat against her shoulder and chest. Then, as she screamed and thrust out her hands towards the woman, a heavy object hit her on the side of the head and she felt the liquid flowing over her face. She knew that the woman was screaming, and she was screaming too, but she was also sliding down into somewhere and the scream inside her head was telling her she mustn't let herself faint, because that woman might kill her.

As she felt her body hit the floor it seemed such a long time since she had first begun to fall; she knew that now there were more people screaming.

Unaware that she'd had her eyes shut, she now opened them to see the tall figure of Simon Brodrick pushing his wife against the wall. They were the ones who were screaming. She couldn't make out what either of them was yelling; but then she felt her own body jerk as she saw him lift a hand and catch his wife a blow across one side of her face, then lift it again and bring the back of it across her other cheek. She actually felt the impact when the woman seemed to bounce from the wall, and when next she saw him grip her by the shoulders and throw her onto the floor amid the torn canvasses, she again closed her eyes tightly.

A voice was crying, "Oh my God!" Then, "Anna! Anna! Wake up! Wake up! Are you all right? No, no; of course you're not all right. Oh, my dear."

She opened her eyes to look into Timothy's face now; and she became aware that there was another man bending towards her and Timothy saying to him, "Help me to get her up, Mulroy."

Then the housekeeper's voice came to her as if from a distance saying, "The blood's coming from just above her ear, I think, sir."

They were leading her from the room now. There were more people in the corridor. She couldn't make out who they were: there was something spilling over her face. She seemed to be floating. She *was* floating: she felt herself rising in the air; then someone pulled her down and thrust her into some dark place . . .

She became aware that she was lying on a bed. She knew the sun was shining because it was hitting her eyelids. There was someone standing near her, speaking. She recognised the voice as Mr. Timothy's. Dear Mr. Timothy. She liked that man. He was saying, "When did you tell her that?" and the answer came, "Last night. I'd had enough. To make a show of herself like that with Raymond, and almost in front of my face . . . man, it was impossible to bear. It's been under cover too long; it was bound to come out. So I told her, a legal separation and then divorce."

"What about the child?"

"I said she could have custody of him, but you'll not believe it, she doesn't want him. She said so openly. It was then I told her that his father should have him."

"Oh, Simon! Simon, you didn't!"

"I did, Tim. And it was about time. I've lain under this since the day she spewed it at me during the first week of our so-called honeymoon, because I knew then I hadn't been the first. And she had the nerve to tell me who had."

The voices were moving away. There was more muttering and then Mr. Timothy's voice came again: "Have you flaunted the girl to her?"

"No. No, definitely not." Then more muttering and now Mr. Timothy's voice, "I am not blind; I know of your feelings towards her. Have you spoken of them to her?"

"No; not as yet, but I mean to."

"You think, or you have the impression that she cares for you?"

Anna, awake now, waited for the answer; and then it came: "I don't know, but I mean to find out, and soon. The fact that she's put up with that insanely jealous bitch's antics for so long gives me hope."

"I . . . I wouldn't bank on it, if I were you. That's your ego talking, as they put it these days. There's the child. She's very fond of the child."

"Yes. Yes, I know. Still, ego or not, we'll see what transpires in the future. In the meantime we must let her rest here. Now I must go to mother. She'll have heard about this already."

There was the sound of a door closing, then footsteps approaching the bed again, and she felt a hand on her brow lifting her hair gently to the side and a whispering voice, saying, "Oh, my dear. My dear."

There was such feeling in the words that she wanted to cry and also to put her hand up and stroke the cheek of this kind, thoughtful man whose life was so marred.

When she slowly opened her eyes and looked at him, he said, "How are you feeling?"

"Tired."

"Yes, my dear. But just rest."

"I want to go home."

"You will later on. The housekeeper is going to prepare a bath so you can wash your hair and she is finding a gown for you."

She opened her eyes wider now and put a hand up to her hair, then looked at the hand and asked, "What is it?"

"It was oil, my dear, linseed oil. Fortunately nothing stronger." He did not say it could have been turpentine.

"I shall never come back into this house again."

"I know that, my dear, I know that."

"She is mad."

"Partly, partly."

"No"—she shook her head slowly—"not partly; all mad."

He sighed then said, "I told you once before she's a very unhappy woman. Spoilt women are often unhappy, I have found."

"I would rather go home and wash there. If you could get the gig."

"No, my dear; you're in no condition to go home yet. Do this to please me because, may I say it, we are friends, aren't we?"

She stared at him for a moment before saying, "If you say we're friends, Mr. Timothy, then we are friends."

"Do you think you could say Tim? That would please me so much. And as you won't be in this house much longer there'll be no one to hear you . . . taking liberties." He smiled over the last words.

She made no answer to this but found that her lids were closing again. She did feel sleepy, and weary; no, as he said, she couldn't go home like this. Perhaps later.

It was three o'clock in the afternoon. Mrs. Hewitt had helped her wash her hair, and had then supplied her with a plain smock-like dress, and had also put a bandage round her head to cover the cut behind her ear; and she was now sitting in a room off the hall, her coat and hat on, and Simon Brodrick was standing in front of her. He was saying, "I know that this is the end of your service here. The child is going to miss you, you know, miss you desperately." Then he added softly, "And I, more than he, will miss you. I'm sure you know that." She looked up into his face but didn't answer him. And he said, "If you feel strong enough, my mother would like to have a word with you before you leave. Do you think you could see her?"

He was asking if she thought she could see his mother. It wasn't an order, it was a request. She said simply, "Yes."

"I will take you along, then I will see you home."

"There won't be any need; I . . . I would rather go on my own."

They were facing each other now, and he said, "We must talk, Anna. You know that, don't you?"

She stepped back from him and in a tone as harsh as she could make it at that moment, she said, "No! No, I don't!"

"Oh, Anna, please don't say that. Look, we won't talk about it now, but I will come over and see you in a day or two, for you must know, you must have guessed."

"Please, please, don't say any more." And she again stepped back from him. "You wish me to see your mother?"

He bowed his head for a moment, then went to the door, opened it and walked slightly ahead of her until they reached the grey door, through which he ushered her; then tapping on his mother's bedroom door, he entered, saying, "Miss Dagshaw, Mother," and turning back to her, he added, "I'll be waiting in the hall."

As she had done once before, she walked across the large room and to the foot of the bed, and again she was looking into the bright eyes, which were so like Mr. Timothy's.

It must have been quite a full minute before Mrs. Brodrick said, "I am deeply sorry you have had to be subjected to such awful treatment in this house, Miss Dagshaw."

Anna could not think of a reply, so she just remained still, her eyes fixed on the white face.

"You require an apology at least and . . . and I'm sorry it must come from me alone, as my daughter-in-law stresses the fact that you were asked to go and see her in her office, but instead you went into her studio, where she was disposing of private . . ."

"Madam, I am sorry to interrupt you, but I had no message to the effect that I was to see your daughter-in-law in her office. I was just told I had to come down and see the mistress. There was no explanation of where I must see her. I had never been to her office before. She had spoken to me once in the library and once in her studio. I went to the library first. When she wasn't there, I naturally went to the studio."

Again there was a long pause before Mrs. Brodrick said, "I understand that the message was given to the upper housemaid and that she passed it on to you."

"I'm sorry, madam, but you have been misinformed. Had I known I had to see your daughter-in-law in the office, I should not have gone to the library."

"No, of course you wouldn't . . . Nurse!"

When the nurse appeared at her side, she said, "Tell them to send the upper housemaid to me. And place a chair for Miss Dagshaw, please."

The chair was brought, and Anna found she was thankful to sit down. And now Mrs. Brodrick said, "I am sorry that my grandson will be deprived of your teaching, because he has got on so well under your tuition."

Again Anna remained silent.

"What will you do now?"

"I don't know, madam. I may find employment in the city."

"I do hope so. And then perhaps you . . . you will marry?"

The blue gaze held hers until she said, "I have no intention of doing so yet, madam."

"I don't think the intention will be left with you for very long." The face moved into a tight smile.

The door opened and the nurse brought in Betty Carter, leading her right to the foot of the bed.

The girl was definitely nervous and she dipped her knee towards the face that was looking at her. And then Mrs. Brodrick said, "Tell me exactly, girl, what order your mistress gave you when she wished to speak to Miss Dagshaw."

The girl wetted her lips, her head moved slightly, and then she said, "Go and tell the teacher to come to my office. I wish to speak to her."

"And what did you say to Miss Dagshaw?"

"I . . . I told her that, madam."

Anna had already turned her head towards the girl, and now she couldn't stop herself from saying, "You did not. You did not mention the office."

"I did so. But your nose was too high in the . . ." She stopped and her head drooped.

"Look at me, girl!" Mrs. Brodrick's head was raised. "I am saying to you that you are lying, that you never gave Miss Dagshaw that message. You merely told her that your mistress wanted to see her. Isn't that so?"

"No. No, it isn't, madam. No, it isn't. She's lying, not me. I told her. I said, go to the office."

"You did not, girl. You did not." Anna almost hissed the words under her breath, and Mrs. Brodrick called, "Shh!" Then addressing the girl again, she went on, "If you told Miss Dagshaw to go to your mistress's office, why did she first go to the library then to the studio, and during this time your mistress would have been waiting for her in her office?"

The girl's head was down again and she muttered, "I did. I did tell her. I did."

"You are lying, aren't you?"

The girl was looking into the cold blue eyes now and her own lids were blinking rapidly. Then she burst out, "Well! madam, she's so hoity-toity. She never listens. She acts like . . ."

"Be quiet! girl. Nurse!"

"Yes, madam?" The nurse was standing near the head of the couch. "Send for Mrs. Hewitt immediately."

Mrs. Brodrick turned to the girl again, and now she said, "You were aware that your mistress didn't want anyone to go near her studio this morning, weren't you? Answer me, girl."

"No, madam."

"Lift your head and look at me."

The girl now lifted her head slowly and Mrs. Brodrick repeated, "You were aware that your mistress didn't want anyone to go near her studio this morning, I say to you again, weren't you?"

And now the mutter came, "I . . . I knew she was in a temper, that's . . . that's all."

The door opened again and Mrs. Hewitt almost scurried into the room. She seemed to take no notice of anyone as she went and stood beside Betty Carter, then dipped her knee to the old lady, saying as she did so, "Madam?"

Mrs. Brodrick addressed her: "Hewitt," she said, "you will take this girl and dismiss her. Give her a week's wage in lieu of notice but no reference, for she has been the means of causing a disturbance in my house."

"Oh." It was a small sound coming from Anna: she wished to protest, Oh, don't do that. It'll only make things worse for us in the village. You don't know what it's like, how they feel about us . . .

"You were about to say something, Miss Dagshaw?"

The words were forming in her mind: perhaps I misunderstood her. Perhaps she did tell me where to go, but looking into those blue eyes, she knew she would not be believed. And so she remained silent and Mrs. Brodrick, addressing the housekeeper, said, "That will be all, Hewitt."

Mrs. Hewitt went to take Betty Carter's arm, but she dragged herself away and, rounding on Anna, she cried, "I don't care, I can get a job anywhere, but you watch out; our lads will have you for this."

"Get her out of here." The voice was small now, the blue eyes were closed.

The nurse was standing by the bed holding a glass to her mistress's lips. Anna had risen to her feet and now she was following a motion of the man-servant's hand as he beckoned to her. She gave one last look at the woman on the bed before following him, and as she came abreast of him he bent and whispered, "Madam gets easily tired. You understand?"

She nodded, then went out and across the grey hall and through the grey door; then through the corridors until she entered the main hall, where Simon was standing.

Moving towards her, he said, "Are you all right? You are so white." And she answered, "Yes, I'm all right; but I think it has been a trying time for madam, I . . . I think she may need you."

"I'll see you to the carriage first."

"Please"—her voice was low—"there's no need."

"Need or no need, I will see you to the carriage." His voice was as low as hers but firmer.

When the footman opened first the glass doors and then the main front doors, she thought ironically, I have never been allowed to come in through these doors but I may go out through them.

He helped her into the covered carriage, then reached over and took a rug from the opposite seat and placed it over her knees, before saying, "I will call tomorrow and see you."

"Please don't. I beg you."

"Someone must deliver your dress when it is laundered, and if they cannot get it clean, you must be compensated for it."

She turned her head away, and he withdrew his and closed the door, then gave a signal to the coachman, and the horses walked sedately forward.

Anna leant back against the padded leather head of the seat. She felt ill and tired. Her head was aching, as was the cut behind her ear where the stone bowl had struck her. Fortunately, it had only grazed the skin, so they had told her, yet at the same time, if she were to believe the valet's words, if the mistress's aim had been true it could have killed her, for the vessel that had held the oil had been a stone mortar used for pounding colour ingredients.

Well, she was free . . . But was she? He would come tomorrow, and the scene would be painful. But now she asked herself: would it have been so painful this time last week? and received from her mind the answer, no. Then why the change?

Behind her closed lids the motion of the coach rocked the picture of a man, a gentleman taking his hand and, bringing it with force against one side of his wife's face, then the back of the same hand against the other side, before knocking her on to the floor. Yet, had he not suffered at that woman's hands by deceit . . . and worse? But then, had not her Dada suffered at *his wife's* hands too. Moreover, he'd had to work and scrape for years to keep her at bay.

She looked down the years stretching ahead and she knew that her life would indeed be barren if she waited until she found a man whom she could compare with her Dada.

THREE

The following morning Anna was sitting in the big chair to the side of the fire, her feet on a raised cracket and a rug over her knees.

Earlier, her mother had said, "A day in bed won't do you any harm after that experience," and she had looked from her to her father and said, "I'm half expecting a visitor and please, Ma and Dada, I'd be grateful if you didn't leave me alone during the time he is here."

They both looked hard at her, and Nathaniel had answered for them both, "As you wish, my dear, as you wish . . ."

It was around half-past eleven when Simon arrived. After politely greeting Maria and Nathaniel, he said to Anna, "I have come empty-handed. I'm very sorry, but they can't get your dress clean. The turpentine with which they tried to clean it has itself left a stain, and I'm afraid I must replace it in some way." Then after a pause, he asked quietly, "How are you feeling?"

"Almost quite well, thank you."

"Almost?" He turned and looked at Maria, but she refrained from commenting, saying only, "Will you take a seat, sir?"

"Thank you."

"Can I get you something to drink?"

"No, no; but thank you all the same. I'm on my way to town, but . . . . but I thought I might call in and not only see your daughter"—he glanced at Anna—"but express my regrets and concern for what happened to her yesterday."

When neither of her parents spoke, he turned to Anna again and said, "We have a very unruly boy on our hands this morning. I think I must see about a tutor for him straight away else he's going to get out of hand altogether."

Anna asked quietly, "You told him that . . . that I wouldn't be coming back?"

"Yes, I did. I thought it would be better to do so, but then regretted it at once, because we had tears and stamping of feet." He turned again towards Nathaniel and Maria, adding now, "I have never known him throw a tantrum like it, nor has his old nurse."

"Children soon adjust," said Maria now; "with love and kindness they soon forget."

"Well, in his case, I hope so."

He got to his feet and, looking from Anna to Maria, he said, "Would it be in order if, when I'm in the city, I make arrangements for a dress to be sent, or one or two from which to . . . ?"

"No, sir." It was Nathaniel speaking. "My daughter is not short of dresses, as my wife is very clever with her needle."

"Oh yes, I'm sure she is." Simon smiled at Maria. "I was only thinking, that as her dress was ruined . . ."

"It is very kind of you, sir, and I understand that you might feel obliged to make good what has been spoilt, but I can assure you there's no need." Nathaniel stepped to the side now, and it would seem it was an invitation for the guest to take his leave.

After a moment's pause Simon again looked at Anna, saying, "I will call soon, if I may, to see how you are faring." She simply inclined her head towards him and he turned and went out, followed by Nathaniel. But immediately outside the door, he stopped and, facing Nathaniel, he said, "I'm sorry if you took my suggestion in the wrong way, sir. I only wish to . . ."

"I knew how your suggestion was meant, Mr. Brodrick, but you are a man of the world and my daughter is a young and vulnerable girl. So I ask you to imagine the tale that would be woven if it became known, as is everything we do in the surrounding countryside, that Mr. Brodrick from the Manor is buying clothes for one of Nathaniel Martell's daughters."

Their gaze held for a long moment before Simon, his head nodding in small jerks said, "Yes, you are quite right, sir, quite right. However, I hope you will have no objections to my calling again?" There was a further pause before Nathaniel replied, "It will all depend upon the purpose of your visit, sir."

"Well, Mr. Martell, I hope to make that plain within a short while, or at least when I am lawfully free to do so. You understand?"

Nathaniel stared at this very presentable man who was almost putting into words his determination to come courting his daughter, for that's what he would be doing, while still married. And if he won her heart would he even bother to get his freedom? And then would his dear, dear Anna do what her mother had done . . . God in heaven! No! That must not happen to his Anna.

He still made no comment as Simon bowed towards him and said, "Good day to you, sir." Nor did he wait to see him ride away. Instead he returned indoors and stood for a moment, his hand on the latch of the door, while he looked up the room to where Anna, wide-eyed, was waiting for him. Her mother was no longer with her and so he went straight to her and catching up her hand, he said, "Do you like that man?"

Her gaze was unflinching as she looked back at him and said, "Yes, Dada, I like him."

"But do you love him?"

Now she looked away and towards the fire, and in a low voice she said, "A few days ago I would have said yes, but now I am far from sure."

"Why is that?"

She was again looking at him, but she couldn't bring herself to say, because I saw him striking his wife and knocking her to the floor.

The second visitor from the house was given a different welcome. Timothy came in carrying four beautiful orchids and a very daintily wrapped box. And as he handed her the flowers he said in broad dialect, "Aal grown be me own 'and, ma'am."

"Oh, Mr. Timothy."

"Ah! ah! ah! What did we say about prefixes? You should know all about prefixes; your father here must have knocked them into you." He turned his smiling face towards Nathaniel, saying, "I want the mister knocked off, sir."

"Well, that is easily done . . . sir. But let me first say what extremely beautiful blooms. And you grew these?"

"Yes; it's my only talent," he replied. "I seem to be able to grow orchids. I suppose it's because I like them and I tell them so, being the silly fellow that I am," only to have his attention diverted by the noise of Ben's running into the room, and he called to him, "Ah, there you are, Ben. Guess what's in that box? It's really for your sister, but I'm sure she wouldn't mind you opening it. And I wouldn't either, because I can eat nougat at any time of the day."

"Tim—" Anna stressed his name now, and she added, "Will you please sit down; and my mother here, I am sure is dying to ask you if you would like a drink."

He turned to Maria, now, saying quickly, "Well, before you do, Mrs. Martell, I'm going to say, I would indeed like a drink; you make tea better than anyone else I know."

"Look! Look! Anna." Ben cried out now as he exposed a variety of chocolates and nougat in the top layer of the box.

"Aren't they lovely! May I have one?"

"Of course, my dear, but first of all offer one to Mr. Barrington."

After Timothy had dutifully taken a nougat sweet, Ben pondered over which one he should choose; then, picking up a gold-paper-wrapped sweet, he said, "I like things in pretty paper; they always give you a nice surprise."

They watched the boy unwrap the chocolate and put it in his mouth, and when he cried, "Oh! it's running," Timothy said, "You've got a liqueur. My! aren't you lucky. I love liqueurs. Now what about you, Anna?" and at this she said, "Yes, I do, too," although she couldn't remember ever having tasted one.

It was then that Anna asked, "Did you come in the gig?" and when he answered, "Yes, I did," she looked towards her mother, saying, "Number two will be outside, Ma. Will you give him a cup of tea?" only to be interrupted by Timothy saying, "Number two isn't outside; I came on my own."

Anna did not immediately take up this unexpected statement, but Nathaniel, turning to the window, remarked, "Well, in that case I'll put it and the horse into the shelter of the barn for a while; it's spitting on to rain. Come on you, big fellow!"—he tapped his son on the shoulder—"come help me."

As Maria, too, left the room to go to the kitchen, Anna thought somewhat ironically, well, they didn't think she needed guarding against this man.

The room to themselves, she looked at him and said, "Was that wise? I mean, to drive the gig yourself?" And he, all merriment now gone from his face and his voice, replied, "I had a slight turn after yesterday's do and seeing you in that state. And, you know, it often happens that I have a free period after experiencing something that I really don't experience at all, as I'm not aware of it. Strange, isn't it? And isn't it strange, too, that I can talk to you like this about it? You're the only one to whom I speak of it. Do you know that?"

She took hold of his hand and said, "Thank you for your trust, Tim. It . . . it means a lot to me."

He stared into her face for a while before he said, "And you'll never know what your friendship means to me." Then turning his head away, he looked towards the fire as he said, "You've had a visit from Simon already, I suppose?" And she answered "Yes. Yes, he called." And again there was silence until he said, "Are you aware of his intentions?"

"Yes. Yes, I'm aware of them."

His head jerked round towards her and he said one word, "And?"

And Anna repeated the word, "And?"

"Well, what I mean is, are you . . . well, there's a long way to go. He intends to divorce her. But that'll take time, even a matter of years, because he has to have proof; and the only proof he could offer at the moment is his intention of marrying someone else, and exposure might then wreck other lives. You understand that?"

"Yes, Tim, I understand that, and much more. And please, you needn't fear for me." Then very quietly, she said, "I am not going to do what my mother did. For one reason, I am not strong enough. Even should my feelings direct me, I wouldn't be strong enough. We are a very happy family. We always have been, but there has been a shadow over us from our birth. It breeds hate and disdain. We have all, in a way, suffered from it, and still do. I know Oswald does; and, lately, I myself probably do most of all. And I wouldn't ever bring that on anyone else. Now do you understand?"

He had turned towards her again and was holding both her hands as he said, "Yes, my dear, I understand."

There was the sound of voices coming from the kitchen, and so, releasing his hold of her, he said in a clear voice, "I have news for you now. I . . . I am leaving the Manor and setting up my own establishment."

"No! Really? Where? Far away?"

"No, not all that far. It's at this end of Fellburn. You've probably seen it on your way in; you can just glimpse the house from the road. It's Colonel Nesbitt's old place. Briar Close."

"Oh, Briar Close. Yes. Yes, I've heard it's a nice house."

"Very nice indeed, but very small, at least in comparison with what I'm leaving. So it will only need a small staff. I've always wanted a place of my own. Strange, but I used to visit that house when I was young. My stepfather's cousin lived there then. I would love you to come and see it and perhaps advise me on drapes and such because those that have been left are rather dull; at least, I find them so. The Colonel lived there by himself for some years and the whole place will need decorating. But I am taking on most of the furniture because he had some nice pieces. I . . . I'm looking forward to the change. I'll be able to work there in peace. And there's a small conservatory where I can natter to my orchids when I have no-one else to talk to."

"Is this a new idea?" she asked quietly.

"No, not really; but one gets tired of being a buffer. I'm . . . I'm very fond of my half-sister, you know . . . madam, but she understands and agrees with me. In any case, there's going to be changes in the house. Whether Penella goes or stays, there'll be changes. I've always been very fond of Simon, and I like Raymond too, but the brothers never cared much for each other. So there was always buffering needed. I am their uncle, but really, I never felt old enough for the position, there being only seven years between Raymond and myself. I could have been their brother. Anyway, now that Raymond is top man in the family, things have already changed. It's amazing what a little power will do."

At this point, Maria entered the room with a tray on which were two cups of tea, and when Anna said, "Aren't you having one, Ma?" Maria replied, "Yes; but I'll wait until your father and Ben come back; they've gone out again. Once they get into that barn and with a new horse to fondle they forget about everything else."

She went out smiling, and Anna, taking a cup of tea and saucer from the tray, handed them to Tim, saying, "Drink this while it's hot."

After sipping on the tea Tim remarked, "It really is always good tea your mother makes." Then putting his cup back on to the tray, he said quietly, "I suppose by now you know that Simon is not the father of the child?"

"Yes; I gathered that some time ago. So may I ask you why she married one brother while she loved the other?"

"Oh, she married the one she loved; that was after she had made him jealous enough. Yet I shouldn't say that because he loved her too. She must have been in a panic when she persuaded Simon to elope with her. It caused quite a sensation, especially coming, as it did, only eighteen months after the accident had happened to my half-sister and me. I think if she had been mobile at the time she might have managed to prevent the marriage. But you know how she's placed, and only at that time was she beginning to accept what sort of life lay before her."

He sighed now as he went on, "It's been a sad union, more so because she's continued to love him the while flaunting her association with Raymond, hoping, I suppose, that jealousy once again would stir him to prove his love for her. But it hasn't worked. And then there's the boy. She doesn't care for him because she sees him as the cause of all her misery. And Raymond, I'm sorry to say, couldn't care less about his parenthood. And until recently, too, Simon, the supposed father, had resented the child. Naturally. There again I've acted as a buffer, but no more. In law, the child is Simon's responsibility and he must see to his future."

He took another sip from his cup; then smiled wryly as he said, "Life is a strange affair, isn't it, Anna, for all peoples, rich and poor alike? The poor think if only they had money they would be happy and all their troubles would be at an end; the rich think if only they were free from responsibilities, if they hadn't to spend so much money on the upkeep of big houses and large staffs, if they hadn't to keep up appearances with their neighbours, how simple life would be. Then there are people like me who say, why have I been afflicted like this? Why should it have happened to me? But of late, I have come to think there is a pattern in life, a certain plan. You know, Anna"—his face brightened now—"if I had never had the seizure in that field, and you hadn't been sawing wood at that particular time, we would never have met and I wouldn't be sitting here with you now. Instead, I should have gone on being aware of the emptiness in my life. But since you've come into it, my dear, and have become my friend, the whole aspect has changed."

"Oh, my dear Tim." She smiled at him now, and there was a little quirk to her lips as she said, "You talk just like my father."

"Well, I could have been."

"Don't be silly."

"There's nothing silly about it. There are seventeen-year-old fathers. You, I think I am right in saying, are nineteen, aren't you?"

"Yes, well, just about. And you?"

"Well, I am thirty-six, thirty-seven . . . just about"—and he laughed—"so I am in a position to have been your father."

She looked into his kind, attractive face, the wide mouth showing a row of white teeth, two of which, she knew, were detachable, the deep blue eyes, the thick brown hair, and she repeated to herself the feeling he had recently expressed: why had he been afflicted like this?

He was saying now, "You will marry some day, and likely soon, but I would like to think, Anna, that whoever he is he will accept . . ." His voice was cut off here by Nathaniel coming into the room, followed by Ben who, running up to Timothy, cried "It's a beautiful horse, sir. I like horses. He let me stroke him."

"Did he? Well, you are indeed favoured because he's an old aristocrat, that one. He'll never see twenty again but he is very particular as to whom he allows to take liberties with him, such as stroke him."

The boy smiled at him, then looked up at his father and his smile widened.

With Maria's entry into the room the conversation became general and after a short while Timothy, rising to his feet, said, "I always outstay my welcome when I come to this house. It is unpardonable of me, yet you are all to blame. But I must away now."

Goodbyes were said and Anna's last words to him were, "And come back soon." To which he replied, "I will. Have no fear of that," then went out accompanied by Nathaniel and the boy.

Maria went to the window and, looking out, said, "There he goes. God help him! What an affliction to have and he such a gentleman. A life ruined and no prospect."

"Oh, Ma, I don't think he needs to be so pitied. He writes, and he grows his orchids, and he reads a great deal."

"What's that for a man of his standing"—she turned—"when he'll never have a woman in his life?"

As Anna watched her pick up the tray and make her way towards the kitchen, her mind confirmed that her mother's words were true: he would never have a woman in his life . . .

* * *

Two days later, the sun was shining, the air was warm, and Maria said, "There's a turn in the weather. If it keeps like this tomorrow we'll wash the bedding. There's nothing like it being dried in the sun." Then she added, "Why don't you go for a little stroll, you look peaky. Take Ben and go along the quarry road. See how far they've got with their railing us in. I wonder how your dada is faring in Fellburn, and what advice he'll get from Parson Mason. Oh, I do wish Miss Netherton was here. She has friends in the legal world. She would see to it. They expected her home last week."

"Well, Farmer Billings might be able to do something, because if they bring the fencing any further he won't be able to get his cattle from one field to another. Jimmy said he was blazing mad yesterday."

"Blazing mad won't help much. It's a law man we should have to see to this business. Anyway, go for a stroll. Ben's out digging his patch; call him. But I'd put a coat on, the wind can be keen along there, coming from over the moor."

Anna made no protest. She took an old coat from behind the door, put it on and went out. Her mother, she knew, was uneasy, worried about what was going to happen when the fencing was finally completed. She wondered why Simon Brodrick, knowing how it would curtail their liberty, had not spoken of it. But of course, it was his brother who was in charge and so he would likely have no say in the matter. Cherry said Praggett was acting as if he were building the Roman wall all over again. He was a spiteful man, that Mr. Praggett.

"Ben! Ben!" she called. "Are you coming for a walk?"

The boy stopped digging and looked towards her. "Where?" he asked.

"Oh, as far as we can go along the quarry top." She walked over to him, adding, "They can't take that away from us."

The boy stuck his spade into the ground, rubbed his hands on the back of his corduroy pants, then, looking up at her, he said, "Must you?"

"Must I what?"

"Well, go for a walk?"

"No, I mustn't; but I would like to." She smiled at him. "But go on with your digging if you don't want to come."

"Oh, I want to be with you, Anna. I'll come."

As they walked towards the gate she said to him, "You're always the one for walks; what's the matter? Aren't you feeling well?"

"I'm all right, but I was turning the ground over to set my potatoes; but it doesn't matter, they'll be set."

"I think if you were setting them in June you would still have a better crop than Dada's. Everything you set grows. You have green fingers."

He held out his hands towards her, saying, "Green fingers! My nails are in mourning."

She smiled now, saying, "Before you were born Ma always examined our nails before a meal, and if they were dirty she would say just that: 'Your poor hands are in mourning. Go and lift the blinds.'"

They walked side by side along the quarry top, past the narrow way and on to where the quarry itself petered out with only a four-foot drop from the path, which a little further on merged into the moor.

"Look! They've stopped the fencing by the side of the beet field," said

Ben, pointing. Then suddenly he cried out, "Look! Anna," and when she followed his pointing finger she couldn't believe what she was seeing: "Can't be!" she said. "Can't be! Oh no!"

They ran now to the actual end of the path and she shouted, "Andrew! Andrew!"

The little figure in the far distance stopped for a moment, then came scrambling towards her, and as she herself ran to meet him her mind was exclaiming, Oh my God! How has he got this far?

"Oh! Missanna. Missanna." He was clinging to her, his face awash with tears. "I've been looking for you, but this wasn't the way the carriage came. Oh! Missanna. Missanna. Come back. Please come back."

"Oh my dear!" She lifted the child up in her arms and stumbled back across the uneven ground to the path. There she put him down, and said to Ben, "We'll have to get word to the house. They'll be looking for him."

"No; I don't want the house, Missanna. I hid from Peggy; I want to stay with you."

"I could run to Miss Netherton's; Mr. Stoddart will still be looking after the horse and trap."

"All right. Well, let's go back, and you do that. Come on, Andrew. Come on."

They had started out, almost at a run, when again it was Ben who stopped them, saying, "Listen!" Then turning round he said, "Look!" And there galloping across the moor came two riders, and it was the child who gave name to the first one: "It is Mama, Missanna. 'Tis Mama. I don't want to go back. May I . . . may I stay with you?"

"Be quiet, Andrew. Be quiet."

As the two horses drew almost to a skidding stop within a few feet of them, Anna had to grab the two children and jump back, and her arms around them, she glared up at the woman who now glared down at her, hissing, but almost under her breath, "How dare you! How dare you! You steal my husband and now you have taken my child."

"I have only this moment found the boy; he was wandering!" Anna yelled back at her.

"You told him when to come, and how to come." Her voice had risen; then jerking her head to the side, she cried, "Pick the boy up! McBride."

As Anna watched the man jump from his horse she realised it wasn't the McBride she knew. And when he put his hands on the boy's shoulders the child kicked out at him, crying, "No! No! I want to stay with Missanna. Please, please, Mama, I want to stay with Missanna."

It was as the child broke free from the man and made to run to the side which would have taken him under the horse's head that Ben, quickly thrusting out his hand, pulled him away.

What took place next was hard to define: whether it was the woman cracking her whip or pulling on the horse, or the two children together startling the horse, it reared, and instinctively Anna pulled the child clear. But what happened to Ben occurred so quickly that at the time she had no comprehension of it; only later did the picture come into her mind: it seemed that Ben had remained just where he was and when the hoof came down on the side of his head and lifted him in the air and over the edge into the shallow dip of the quarry, she felt she had witnessed it all before; even to what took place next, when she sprang at the woman, aiming to tear her from the saddle and the whip came down across the side of her face, blinding her for a moment. Then she heard her own voice screaming and she was struggling to get away from the man's hold. She saw the woman dismount, go to the edge of the dip and say, "He's moving. He's only stunned." She was still screaming when the woman remounted and the man let go of her and lifted the crying and thrashing child into his mother's arms.

When she looked over the edge of the quarry to see the still form of her brother lying crumpled among the stones, she cried, "Oh my God!" And the man pulled his horse to a halt and looked back at her as if he were going to dismount again, then changed his mind and rode after his mistress.

She scrambled down the bank now and lifted Ben's head onto her arm, crying, "Ben! Ben! Come on! Come on! Wake up!" She patted his cheek, beseeching him, "Wake up! Wake up!" But when his head fell limply to the side she cried aloud, "No, God! No!" Then standing up, she bent over and lifted the boy into her arms; but then found she was unable to climb the short bank with him. So she leant her body forward against the bank and placed him on the footpath above; then drew herself up beside him and picked him up again. And now, staggering like someone drunk, for he was no light weight, she carried him back along the path, through the gate, and there she started yelling, "Ma! Ma!"

Maria met her half-way across the open ground. "God Almighty! What's happened? What's happened?"

"*She did it! She did it!* With her horse. And she's taken the child. *She did it! She did it!*"

Maria lifted her son into her arms now and ran back into the house and laid him on the mat. And she felt all over him before looking up at Anna where she was leaning against the side of a chair, still gasping, and in a low agonised voice, she said, "My lad is dead. He's dead, Anna. Ben is dead." And when Anna screamed and continued doing so, Maria had to lay back her son on the mat and then shake her daughter by the shoulders, while yelling at her: "Stop it! Stop it! girl. Go and get help," only to say in further distress, "Oh my God! Oh my God!" for the red weal on Anna's face was oozing blood. But she pushed her towards the door, appealing to her now, "Miss Netherton's. Go to Miss Netherton's. Go and get help. Tell Bob Stoddart to get the doctor."

"But he's dead, Ma."

"Go on! Go on!" Maria, half-crazy now, screamed, "Run! Run!"

Anna didn't remember running to Miss Netherton's house. She didn't remember the doctor's coming; nor did she remember both Simon and Timothy standing before her father with bowed heads.

It wasn't until the fourth day when she rose from her drugged sleep and went into the long room and saw the coffin lying on the trestle table and looked down on Ben's face, which even in death still looked alive and beautiful, did she finally realise that he was dead.

But she remembered the following day, when she stood in the midst of her family by his grave, and Parson Mason said kind words over him. It was

being allowed that he be buried in Fellburn because they had all been christened in that town, and because of the latter the parson had once laughingly
said they were eligible for poor-law sustenance, as well as, it now turned out,
the right of burial.

The family had come in two cabs: the carriage from the Manor holding
Simon and Timothy followed, and beyond that had come another carriage in
which sat Miss Netherton. It was also noted that there were half a dozen
people from the village, who must have taken the trouble to come in by cart,
waiting in the cemetery, only that same night to be censured by the clients in
The Swan.

The bar was packed, the counter aflood with spilt beer, which took Lily
Morgan all her time to keep sopped up between exchanging gossip with the
customers. And there was plenty to gossip about on this particular night.

Willie Melton, the painter and decorator, and his son Neil, who was an
apprentice to the wheelwright, stood together at the end of the counter. And
the older man looked across to where the blacksmith was seated on a settle at
right angles to the open fireplace, and he said, "Well, I can understand old
Miss Smythe following them, and Roland Watts, 'cos he was thick with 'em
long afore he left here, but for John Fenton and his Gladys to go to the
cemetery . . . well, that beats me. I thought they were just goin' into town
to put in his order as one or t'other do every week, not both. But there they
left the shop open an' his mother seeing to it and the old snipe wouldn't
open her mouth to my lass at first when she asked her, just skittish like, never
thinkin', would they be going to the funeral, like? No business of anybody's
where they were going, she answered her, but not until she was walkin' out
the shop . . . well!"

Before the blacksmith had time to add his own remarks a voice came
from the other end of the bar-room, shouting, "You'll come to me next,
won't you, Willie?" And Willie Melton, his head wagging, shouted back,
"Aye, I might an' all, Dan, 'cos that was a surprise."

"It should have been no surprise to you or anybody else. I've always said,
they've kept themselves to themselves. Asked us in the village for nowt, neither bread, beer, nor baccy; nor for me to make any of them a pair of shoes.
But I still maintain that no matter what name stuck to them, he and she
brought them up decent and weathered some bad times. An' we could name
names, couldn't we, who helped with those bad times? So I think it beholds
everybody to live and let live."

Robert Lennon took a long draught from his pewter mug, then, turning
and looking at Dan Wallace, he said, "You should talk like that to Parson."

"I could an' all."

"Aye, well, I'd like to be there an' hear you. An' you being made
sidesman of late, strikes me you've turned your coat. What's happened to
make you do that?"

"I've turned no coat. If you think back, I'm one of the few who kept me
own opinion about them."

"Well, does your opinion cover the mischief that one's done? All right, all
right, the bairn was killed but accidentally, an' that's what'll come out in the
court, if it comes up. But what happened up at the Manor when Mr. Simon
found out that the bairn was dead? He goes back and nearly tries to do his

wife in, didn't he? Made a holy show of himself, if all tales be true. Yellin' at his wife, 'You've killed the child! You've killed the child! Now are you satisfied? You hussy.' He called her that, an' in front of the servants. And then Mr. Timothy tried to separate them, so we are told, and he couldn't manage it; it took two men to get him off her. Now that isn't hearsay, it came straight from the Manor. And why did all that happen, eh? It happened 'cos that hussy, not satisfied with tempting the husband, had tempted the bairn. It was a natural thing for the mother to go after it. And if that one went for her it was a natural thing an' all to raise the whip. I would have done it meself."

"Oh aye, you would. There's no doubt about that," said the shoemaker. "Strikes me you've wanted to do it for years."

"Now, now! gentlemen. Now, now!" Reg Morgan intervened from behind the counter. "We all know who's right and who's wrong in this business. As Lily here was sayin' "—he nodded towards his wife—"you can't light a fire without a spark. And that hoity-toity miss certainly caused the spark that killed the child, because don't forget what Betty Carter said and what happened to her. Thrown out on her face she was and blamed for the teacher being covered in paint, or such. Well, as I see it, the mistress must have had cause to throw that stuff. And as Michael Carter and his lad said when Betty came back cryin', if it was left to them they would have tarred and feathered her, not just covered her with paint."

"Aye, 'tis a pity duckin' stools and stocks have gone out of fashion. Morris Bergen was saying the other night that he remembers his dad being put in the stocks when he was a lad. It was to try and stop him drinkin' but he only got more drunk when they lifted him out."

"Oh, so Morris said that, did he?" The innkeeper now nodded towards Dave Cole the butcher. "Transferrin' your custom are you, Dave?"

"No, no. I just happened to drop in; I had a bit of business to do. You know, Reg, I sell meat to everybody. I'd sell it to the corpses in the graveyard if they could pay their way."

This last brought forth guffaws of laughter, but not from the blacksmith's youngest son Arthur who, during all the talk, had said nothing but had looked from one to the other as if studying some deep point, and when he muttered something his father said, "What's that you say?" and he replied, "Nowt; I was just thinkin'."

FOUR

$\mathcal{T}$hey were sitting round the fire as they had done each night since the day they had buried Ben. Nathaniel sat close to Maria, the two girls sat close together, the twins, with Jimmy between them, sat close too.

The sound of laughter had not been heard in the house for weeks. It would seem they were unable to throw off their loss. When they talked it would be in low tones; and after the day of the funeral Ben's name had never been mentioned among them. Sometimes they cried together, but generally they cried in private, that was until this particular night, the evening of the day of the inquest that had looked into the circumstances leading to Ben's death.

Nathaniel had not allowed Anna to go to the court. As he had said that morning, he would tell the justice that she was still very unwell, and that was no lie. Oswald and Olan had accompanied him to the courthouse but Maria had stayed at home with Anna, together with Cherry and Jimmy, for they both refused to go to work this morning.

They had scarcely eaten a bite all day, and when they talked it had been about everything but the matter foremost in their minds. But now here was Nathaniel sitting before the fire holding tightly onto Maria's hand, and the others were gathered round him. The table behind them was laid for a meal but it could wait; they wanted to know what had transpired in the court. It seemed at first that Nathaniel was reluctant to speak, and it was Anna, bending towards him, who said, "Tell us, Dada, what happened, or let the boys."

Nathaniel looked at his sons, and it was Oswald who, looking from one to the other, said, "She got off."

A quiet stunned period of some seconds followed Oswald's words; then he went on: "The court was packed; and there she stood, that woman, looking as if she wouldn't say boo to a goose. And when she was questioned you could hardly hear her answer, her voice was so low. I couldn't hear half of what she said. But when one of the solicitor men had the stable man McBride in the box and he said to him, 'Explain what you saw,' well, the man seemed hesitant; but then he said, 'The young master was about to run under the horse's head and the boy pulled him aside out of harm's way. It was then the horse reared and the offside front hoof caught him on the head and sent him flying.' "

Oswald drew in a long breath and looked at his father as if Nathaniel would take up where he had left off, but Nathaniel remained silent, and so he continued: "The solicitor man then asked him what happened next? And he again seemed hesitant to speak; but then he said, from what he could see the young lady went to grab the mistress and the mistress brought her riding crop down on her. Then the solicitor man suggested again that it was after the young lady tried to grab his mistress.

"And the man said, yes. And then he was asked what happened when he came on the scene with his mistress, and he said, 'Well, sir, the child was clinging to the young girl, and . . .' He hesitated again, and was prompted by the solicitor man who said, 'Yes; go on.' And then he said, 'The child was yelling he didn't want to go home with the mistress but wanted to stay with the teacher.'

" 'But that is not all you heard, is it?' the solicitor asked him, but McBride said, 'I think it is, sir.' Then the solicitor man came back at him again: 'Did you not hear your mistress accuse the teacher of something?' he said. And I could see the man was upset, and he bowed his head now and wagged it a bit as he said, 'There was a lot of confusion and yelling. She said something but I couldn't make out what it was.' And you know"—Oswald was now looking from his mother to Anna—"that woman had been sitting with her head bowed, and now she turned and looked towards the man and that painful look went off her face and for a moment she looked devilish. I'm telling you, she looked devilish. But no matter how the solicitor man kept on, the stable lad wouldn't say any more and he was told to stand down. Then it was the doctor's turn, and he said—" Oswald paused here and wetted his lips before going on. "He said Ben was dead when he examined him, and Anna, Miss Dagshaw, he said, her face was bleeding from what had been a whip lash. What was more, she was demented and had to be put to sleep, and she still wasn't herself. After that the two solicitor men went up to the bench and there was a lot of talk with the justice. And the justice said it was a pity the young teacher was unable to be present as she could have thrown more light on the matter. And then he spoke to the jury. He told them that it would seem there had been no intent to harm the boy, whose action in trying to save the younger child must have startled the horse; then unfortunately he had been struck by the hoof and, according to the doctor, had suffered no pain but must have died immediately.

"It would be for them to decide. Or words to the effect. You know how they go on. The jury wasn't out very long and when they came back they said, it was . . . accidental death."

Oswald now turned and looked at his father. Nathaniel was sitting with his head bowed, and Oswald's voice was very soft as he said, "It was then that Dada sprang up and cried, 'She killed my child! She killed my child!' And there was an uproar in the court and the justice said if Dada couldn't be quiet he would have to leave the courtroom. But he wouldn't. He shouted at them how that woman had tried before to run his daughter down and had attacked her and split her head open with a bowl and covered her with oil. But by this time the policemen were pulling Dada outside. And then the justice man started speaking again and he said that the woman of course was not entirely without blame but it wasn't within his province to judge her, but her reactions had led to a tragedy and it would remain with her how she viewed her conduct in the future."

There followed a long silence until Olan broke it by remarking, "There was nobody from the Manor there, I mean, none of the men, not her husband, or Mr. Raymond, or Mr. Timothy. I looked round and couldn't see one of them. But I saw her come out with the solicitor man. Anyway they said she's been left the Manor for weeks; in fact he put her out."

"Oh, Dada." Anna was kneeling in front of her father now, holding his hand, and he, looking down on her, said, "It's all right. It's all right, my dear. But it was a sorry day when you went to that house."

Then raising his head he glanced around his family, saying, "We have never spoken of death, but I know now we must because he is still here, he is still among us. I also know that he was due to die. Ever since he was a baby and so beautiful I have felt that the saying, Those whom the gods love die young, could be applied to him. I can tell you now that I always had this fear that I would never see him grow up. And you know something, my dear family?"—he paused here before adding—"He knew that. From the things that I remember him saying, he knew that his time was short. So from now on we will speak about him. You know, I saw him last night as plain as I'm looking at you now. You had all gone to bed. I came down the room to lock the door, and he was sitting on the mat there, in front of the fire, where he always sat, his legs tucked under him, and he turned and looked at me and his smile was so serene."

His voice now broke and the tears, welling in his eyes, rolled down his cheeks and he turned and laid his head on Maria's shoulders. She, patting his head with one hand, held up the other and warded her family off, and, her own voice breaking, she said, "Enough. Enough. The weeks of mourning have passed. We must go on living. As Dada says, he is still here. We will talk about him as if he hadn't gone from us in the flesh. Now, not one of us has eaten today and I'm sure you boys and Dada, here too, could do with a meal. So, come on, and rest assured that nothing that can happen in life from now on can hurt us more than Ben's going."

As Anna rose to go to the table she thought, Strange, the things people say. Rest assured that nothing that can happen in life from now can hurt us more than Ben's going. That was assuredly tempting providence and her Dada had said Ben had known his time was short, yet he had insinuated that it was she who had brought his end about by going to that house. Yes, yes, he had. He had voiced what she knew had been in his mind for weeks now, and she wasn't mistaken when she imagined she had caught a look of censure in his eyes.

FIVE

$\mathcal{I}$t was a full fortnight later and Anna was at the wood-pile when she saw the rider coming across the moor, and she would have turned and hurried towards the house except that she knew, were he to follow her, her father would order him away, and in no small voice. She had wondered over the last few weeks how she would have taken her father's attitude to Simon if her own feelings hadn't changed towards him.

She went on sawing until he dismounted and came towards the railings, and only then she looked at him when he said, "How are you?"

"I'm quite well, thank you."

"Come here; I want to talk to you."

To this she answered, "I'd rather you didn't. We have nothing to say to each other."

"I don't agree with you; we have a lot to say to each other. I will tether the horse here and come in by the gate."

She saw there was no way of stopping him, and so she resumed her sawing until he reached her side, when his voice had a curt note to it as he said, "Stop that for a moment, for goodness sake!"

She stopped, took out the saw from its cut and laid it against the wood-pile; then turned to him, saying harshly, "What do you want of me?"

He smiled now as he said, "That's a silly question for an intelligent young woman to ask. You know what I want of you, Anna, what I've wanted of you from the first time I saw you. You remember? The day you lost your position through the Songs of Solomon. I knew that morning that something had happened to me. You must have, too."

"I did not." Her words were emphatic. "Even if you had not been married I would not have thought what you suggest."

"Well, all I can say, my dear, is, you are much stronger than I am."

When he put his hand out towards her she stepped back from him, saying, "You are still as you were that morning, a married man with a child"; then she paused before adding, "Whether he is your son or not, he is your responsibility."

When she saw the dull red colour flood over his face like a blush, she turned her head away, saying, "I am sorry. I am sorry, but I've got to make things plain to you."

It was some seconds before, so it seemed, he could speak, and then he said in a low voice, "All I'm asking is that you give me some hope, and that in the meantime until . . . until I can get a divorce we can be friends. You have no hesitation in being friends with Timothy, so why not with me?"

"There's all the difference in the world: Timothy is not asking for a closer association."

"Oh, isn't he!"

Her eyes widened, and after a moment she said, "How can you suggest such a thing? He is an . . . an invalid, he is . . ."

"He's a man and he's not an invalid, he is subject to fits, but so was Caesar and many other men in the past, and they had their women. And why do you think he is never off your doorstep? The least excuse and he is over here. Oh, I know what I know."

Slowly, she said, "I'm sorry to hear you have such a low opinion of him."

"I have no low opinion of him. You take me up wrongly. I've a very high opinion of Tim. I am very fond of him. I'm only pointing out to you that he is a man and he sees you as a beautiful girl."

"He is seventeen years my senior."

He closed his eyes for a moment, then said, "I want to say to you again, don't be silly, but I won't. I will only point out to you that there's a very large number of the male population of forty or more who marry young women, many still in their teens. Why is it that a female in her mid-twenties is beginning to be looked upon as an old maid? It is because girls marry young and many seem to prefer much older men."

Her answer was: "Well, by my next birthday I shall have reached twenty and so I'll then be bordering on the age for old maids, and I can tell you I would prefer that state to marrying a man in his fifties."

"Oh! Anna." He was laughing at her again. "I know one thing for sure, I could never lose my temper with you, I just have to laugh at you."

She had a flashing mental picture again of his hand coming up first to one side of his wife's face then to the other, and also the tale that Cherry had brought back from Mrs. Praggett's, that he would have throttled his wife on the day that Ben died if the menservants and Mr. Timothy hadn't intervened.

He had taken a step towards her and she couldn't move backwards now because the sawing cradle was in the way, and his voice was very low as he said, "I somehow got the impression some time ago that you didn't dislike me, even that we were both of a similar way of thinking, because, in spite of my wife being there, you came back, and I hoped it wasn't only because of the child. Then quite suddenly you changed. I felt it. Why? It wasn't as if the fact of my marriage had suddenly been sprung on you. You had known that all along and although no word of endearment had passed between us, I felt you knew that I'd come to care for you, and that you were aware of the obstacles but were ignoring them. What made you change towards me, Anna? Tell me."

She stared into his face for a full minute before she said, "When I saw you strike your wife and knock her to the ground."

He stepped back from her, his face screwed up in disbelief. "You mean to say, because I was outraged at the way she had treated you and perhaps could have killed you if that mortar pestle had struck you fully on the temple, and because I was angry for you and so therefore struck her *that turned you against me?*"

"No; it didn't turn me against you. I still think kindly of you, but if you were free tomorrow, I wouldn't marry you."

There was utter disbelief in his voice as he said, "Just because of that incident?"

"I don't know for sure, but yes, I think so. I only knew that my father, under any provocation, would never have done that. He'd had a wife, whom I am sure you have heard about, who drank and showed him up in public, so much so that she threatened his livelihood, and for years he had to work to keep her at bay. And I'm sure he had more provocation to strike her than you had your wife, at least as fiercely as you did."

As he shook his head while muttering, "My God!" she went on, her voice rising, "You say you did it because you were angry at her treatment of me. That wasn't the reason. You did it because you had wanted to do it for a long time, because she had deceived you, because she had made you father of a child that wasn't yours. *That was it, wasn't it?* You had never struck her before; you had just ignored her. And that's what turned her into the fiend that I knew, and made her jealous of anyone you looked at."

There was a look of amazement on his face, but he made no effort to call a halt to her tirade, and she went on, "I've never hated anyone in my life although I've had reason to, especially among the villagers, but I hate your wife because she killed my brother. That was no accident; the horse didn't rear because the child was near it; it reared because she pulled on the reins and dug her heels into its sides. And I know now that she had meant to turn that horse on me, not on my brother. Yet, feeling as I do towards her, I understand her reactions towards me, and in a way I feel sorry I was the cause of them." Her voice sank at this stage and she ended, "So now you must see that it would be foolish on your part to go on hoping that there could be anything between us, even friendship. What is more, my father could not bear it . . ."

"*Oh, your father!*" The words came out in a loud, indignant burst. "It is always *your father*. Have you ever thought what that man has done to you? What he and your mother have done to you all? He has scarred you all for life. He has made you all the butt of the village. You are afraid to walk through it. He prides himself on educating you all, but you are only partly educated because his knowledge is limited. But the fact that he has made you all think and aware of what you are, to my mind has added insult to injury, for you know you are carrying a stigma, whereas, if he had left you like the rest of the clodhoppers in the village and round about, they would have accepted you, and laughed at you, and with you, and joked about your bastardy; no, he had to go and pump his bit of knowledge into you, which aroused your sense of awareness, and all the while priding himself that he was doing the right thing by you. Oh! don't talk to me about your father."

She sidled along by the wood cradle until she was standing a good arm's length from him and, gasping as if out of breath, she said, "No. I won't talk to you about my father, nor anything else. You have made yourself and your feelings quite plain, and I hope I have too. I'll only say this, then I'll never want to talk to you again: you would have been quite willing to act as my father did and take me as a mistress until you got your divorce, by which time, and not having the strength of my father, you would likely have become tired of me. Goodbye, Mr. Brodrick. I won't expect to see you this way again."

He didn't move away, but just remained staring at her, his jaws so tight that the muscles of his face stood out white against his skin. Then suddenly swinging about, he strode from her.

She did not wait to see him unloosen the horse from the other side of the wood-pile, but she hurried down through the trees, across the garden and into the house. And Maria, meeting her, said, "What is it? What's the matter, girl?" And she shook her head and pressed her mother aside as she made for her bedroom. There she threw herself on the bed and burst into tears.

Back in the living-room Maria turned as Nathaniel entered from the kitchen and said to him, "She's in a state. She's gone into her room." And he, nodding at her, said, "He's been. I saw him come, and I saw him go, and I saw her cross the yard. And by the look on her face, I don't think we'll see him again."

To this Maria answered, "Well, thank God for that"; then added, "What did Miss Netherton say about the fencing? Has she heard any news?"

"I didn't go to her, my dear. Let them get on with it. If we are fenced in then they are fenced out. It doesn't matter any more."

"But!" she protested now, "what if we have to go through the village all the time?"

"Well, we'll have to do that, dear. They can only kill us." He smiled wanly at her now, then went towards the fireplace and sat in his big chair, while she stood looking at him and shaking her head. He had become a lost man. He might think Ben was still here, but because he couldn't touch him, he had become a lost man.

SIX

$\mathcal{I}$t was on her visit during the following week that Miss Netherton once more came to the rescue, and in two ways. First, she said she would see to it that their horse-fodder and groceries were brought from the town in her trap and put over the fence at a point where they could easily be picked up.

But in the meantime she was going into the matter of the law concerning the enclosure of land. Secondly she raised a more important issue. She was touching the fading scar on Anna's cheek, saying, "It'll disappear gradually, except where it bled, and you might have two or three little spots there. But that'll be nothing," when, turning to Maria, she asked, "Does she know about the business of the cross?" And when Maria shook her head and said, "No; none of them does," Miss Netherton said, "Well, it's about time they did. So, come, Nathaniel, and sit down; we have a little business to discuss."

Anna saw the glance exchanged between her parents before they looked at her and walked slowly to the table.

When they were all seated Miss Netherton turned to Maria and said, "I needn't remind you of the contract we made: I was to buy the cross from you for the sum of five-hundred pounds. Remember?"

Nathaniel nodded, and Maria said, "Only too well, Miss Netherton, only too well. We are still grateful . . ."

"Oh, well, you might be more grateful still. Now listen." At this point she turned and looked at Anna and said to her, "I won't go into how all this started but your parents can enlighten you later on." Then turning back to Maria, she added, "I've thought: there it is, lying in my box in the bank. I had it recorded in my will what was to become of it; but on thinking further, I came to the conclusion that, being who I am and also a stubborn individual, I could go on for years, and it's now that you need more help. So, having a friend in the jewellery business in Newcastle, and he *is* a friend, and an honest man, as far as a jeweller can be, dealing with gems—" She smiled here, then went on, "I told him part of the story as to how I had bought the cross, but not from whom, yet how it had been found, and he was more than interested to see it. So, I got it from the bank and there"—she put her hand on the table—"I laid it in front of him and I've never before seen a man struck dumb in such admiration. He said he had seen many beautiful pieces of jewellery of all shapes and sizes but nothing like that. I then told him I wanted to sell it and to the highest bidder. And to this he said there should be no bidding in this case; that would bring it into the open. It must go to one man, someone who bought precious things like this just to possess them, and there were a number of such about, but not in this end of the country. He would have to take it to London, where he had a friend in the business who was a frequent visitor to Amsterdam and many other cities in the world looking for rare jewels. Apparently they are becoming scarcer, the real ones, so are more valuable. He asked if I would trust him with this precious and ancient thing, and I said, yes. He went to London last week, and I saw him yesterday, and he told me, in his turn, that he had never seen his friend so excited in his life, and that he was a man who always kept a poker face and usually gave nothing away."

She now looked from one to the other, but when no-one spoke she went on, "I then told him to get on with it and let me know how much it was worth . . . No; not how much it was worth, because we will never handle the worth of that item, but I thought I might be offered as much as a couple of thousand pounds. Then he staggered me by saying that his friend knew of someone who would be very interested in an article like that and that he might get as much as six thousand for it." She now wagged her finger at each of them in turn. "He's my friend, I'm telling you; but if he said six thousand, being a business man, I bet the deal would be eight." Here she pursed her lips. "You see I know a bit about bargaining. However, I did not show any excitement at this point but said, well, he must do his best, and he said he most certainly would and that I should hear sometime this week. Now, my dear"—she placed her hand on top of Maria's, where they were gripped tightly together on the table—"whatever the mysterious big man gives, we will share. Mind again, whatever the mysterious man offers, my friend in London will take his cut; then my friend in Newcastle will also want a cut. You understand?" She didn't wait for an answer, but went on, "However, five per cent or ten per cent, I've worked out we should get at least two thousand pounds each."

Both Maria and Anna made gasping sounds and sat back in their chairs, but Nathaniel did not move, and Miss Netherton said to him, "Well, Nathaniel, aren't you impressed?"

"Miss Netherton, I am amazed, but more so at your kindness and your concern for us."

"Well, I've always been concerned for you because I like you. I like you all, and whatever I've done for you, this girl"—she now put her hand across the table in Anna's direction—"has repaid me with her company over the years. Without her, at times, I should have been very lonely, and there's no money that can pay for good companionship. And anyway, after I knew that those devils had cut off the entry to your own place, which, don't you worry"—she again wagged her finger from one to the other—"I am seeing to. Oh, definitely. I have a solicitor working on it; and I know what you earn as a tutor has naturally been brought to a halt because you cannot use the cart now. So I would like to think that when you get the money you will consider moving from here and all the turmoil you have had to suffer. You'll be able then to buy a nice little place in the town, or wherever you like. Should this happen, and I hope it does, I shall miss you; but then, I've always got my own transport and I can visit you frequently."

Maria's head was already slowly shaking when she brought out slowly, "I would hate to leave this house, Miss Netherton. We have put up with a great deal over the years in order to stay here. And the fact that you were near and championed us has been of such help that I cannot put a name to it. I don't know what Nathaniel will say about it all, but since you let us have this house I've always imagined living here until I died. And . . . and we have brought the family up here and within these four walls and our bit of ground we have been happy; that is"—she bowed her head—"up till lately. But," she sighed, "we are still a united family, so close. As Nathaniel says, only death can separate us."

"Well, my dear, it will be up to you. No, of course not, I wouldn't want you to leave, but I was just thinking of your welfare and that tribe in the village. But . . . but there is hope there; you have friends, more than you know; people who have the courage now to defend you openly in the public bars . . . Oh"—she wagged her head—"you wouldn't believe what I hear. A poor old lady sitting in her house alone . . ."

They all smiled at this, and she joined them, then she said, "Well, I must be off and go and see how Timothy is getting on. He hasn't been well these last few days." She nodded again. "He had a strong exchange with Raymond over the fencing, I may tell you. But I understand that Raymond pointed out that he isn't entirely in control now, but he agrees, and yes, yes, I'm giving it to you straight"—she was nodding again—"that you, Nathaniel, are mostly responsible for what has happened, for you *will* house the men from the pits."

"Would you rather I saw them die, the old people and the children on the moor?"

"No. No, I wouldn't. I would have housed them myself rather than that. But then"—her head drooped—"I was never as brave as you, Nathaniel, or you, Maria. I knew there were many, at times, on the moor but I couldn't bring myself to defy convention. I work mostly with my tongue."

Anna now put in quietly, "And it is a sword, and you've always used it in our defence."

"Well, that's as may be." Miss Netherton rose from the chair, saying, "Now, I've got to walk back and manoeuvre that bank . . ."

"Oh, you don't go down the bank!" said Maria.

"Well, how do I get out, unless I jump the fence and trudge across the turnip fields to the nearest part of the main road, where Stoddart will have the trap? But don't you worry, my dear: I do go down the bank, but Stoddart has made a little four-rung ladder that he places there. They'll not beat us. But come along, Anna, and walk some of the way with me. The sun is shining, the May blossom is about to burst. There are things to look forward to even now." She spread her glance quietly over the three of them, but neither Nathaniel nor Maria made any response to this.

Anna had gone down the room and picked up a shawl from the back of the settle; now she put it around her shoulders and followed Miss Netherton out.

It was as they were walking along the path that led to the stile that Miss Netherton said, "Are you cold, girl?"

"Yes. Well . . . not cold; I . . . I always seem to feel a little shivery."

"I know that feeling; it's from heartache. It'll pass. It'll pass, my dear." They walked on for a moment in silence, then Miss Netherton said, "Did you know that Timothy has left the Manor?"

"No. No, I didn't. I understood he was going to, but that he had to have the new place made ready."

"Yes, that was his idea; but it would have taken another three months or more. The decorators have been in and done some work, but apparently he got himself so worked up that he ordered all his things to be moved into the new place and came and asked my assistance in choosing a small staff. And so there he has been for the last week or so. He has had a really bad turn but that hasn't deterred him. I've got him a cook, a kitchen maid and a housemaid, and a butler-cum-valet, and I vetted them all very carefully before I let him engage them. He's had to buy a carriage and horse, and Stoddart's cousin has taken on that job. Stoddart also recommended a gardener; and so, in a way, Timothy is set up. But oh dear, those turns. Poor fellow; it seems that any sort of conflict brings them on. He can apparently go months at a time, though; even forget about them. I have to ask myself why the nice people in this world have to be so afflicted. Ah, here we are; and there's

Stoddart with my stepladder to heaven, or is it the other place?" She chuckled now, and as she neared the stile she pointed to the left, saying, "If I'd
only been a few years younger, I'm sure I could have slid down that bank.
I've always thought what a stupid place to set a stile. But then I must remember that the road below was dug out of a field. Why, I don't know. I suppose
it was to skirt the village."

Anna helped her over the stile and then held on to the top of the short
ladder until she reached the road. And from there Miss Netherton laughed
up at her, saying, "There's life in the old dog yet."

As he was lifting the ladder from the bank, Stoddart looked up at Anna
and said, "She'll break her neck one of these days, miss, the games she gets
up to."

"What you've got to do, you old fool, is to get up on to your seat and
get that horse moving."

Anna watched the trap bowl away, before turning to walk back to the
house. On reaching the small gate that led through their own fencing she
stopped and looked over the landscape to where, in the distance, the hills
rose. The sun was glinting through clouds, casting their shadows on the hill-
sides and making it appear as if they were running with rivulets of silver. Of a
sudden she longed to be there on those hills and beyond, away, away, anywhere but here.

She drew the edges of the shawl tight about her throat before hurrying
on, telling herself now that this was one feeling she must get rid of. They had
lost Ben, so how would they take to letting her try to find a post some place
far away?

Her mother had said to Miss Netherton that she wanted to die here, and
during the past weeks she had seen herself going on year after year, until she
too died here after a wasted life: digging in the garden, sawing wood, carrying their fodder and groceries from wherever Stoddart would drop them;
sitting round the fire at night in the winter or a table in the summer, reading.
As the years went on the family would assuredly disperse. The boys would
marry: Oswald and Olan were forever talking about the virtues of their employer and her daughter. And Jimmy would marry. Yes, Jimmy would marry.
And Cherry? Oh, Cherry's heart was already placed. Anna had guessed this
some time ago, for whenever she and Bobby could be together, they were.
Her father must have noticed, too, but he wouldn't be displeased with that
association. That left herself.

And what was her future? What had she to look forward to here? Had she
been over-critical in holding up her father as a model to Simon? She could
have become Simon's mistress. Oh yes, she could have become his mistress.
And what would that have mattered? At least to the surrounding countryside
she was a bastard already and she would just be acting out the part again, as
her mother had done. After all, a gilly was a loose woman and the vor was her
offspring. If it hadn't been for her father, would she have succumbed to
Simon's pleas? At this moment she didn't know; she only knew that she was
lonely; she felt lost, and she couldn't help but wonder what was happening to
the child. By now he would certainly have been taken in hand by the male
tutor.

Her father met her at the gate, saying, "Billy got out. He's cleared the remains of the cabbage and has taken the young carrot tops. You mustn't have put the latch on the door."

"Oh, I'm sorry, Dada."

"You should be more careful and pay attention."

She stood and looked after him as he walked away. Her Dada was telling her she must take more care and pay attention. She was a little girl again, being told how to see to the animals; to put false clay eggs under the broody hens; shown how to lift the hens from the barks without them fluttering; told always to be careful how she walked in the low grass near the pond because some of the ducks laid away; how to mix crowdie, hot in the winter with boiled cabbage leaves, and plain in the summer; how never to tether the goats near the bottom field because that is where the yew tree grew, and a stomach full of their leaves could kill them.

Just now he had used the same tone to her as when he had taught her those things, the same tone as when dealing with the book learning: he would say the brain had to be fed as well as the body.

Her father would never be the same again, nor would she.

She went into the house. It seemed as if her mother was waiting for her.

"Sit down," she said; "I must tell you the beginning of what Miss Netherton was on about. I mean, the cross."

As Anna listened to her mother, she was made to wonder why her Dada hadn't told all this in the form of a fairy story as they sat around the fire at night, and this made her say, "Will you tell the others as well, tonight, Ma?"

Maria looked away towards the end of the room, then down at her hand to the fingers that were tapping the table, and she said, "Your Dada and me had a talk about that, and we thought it best not to say anything because you never know how a word might slip out unintentionally."

"But when you get the money, they'll want to know; you can't hide . . ."

"We've thought of that. It'll supposedly have come from my mother's people in yon end of the country. We're going to put it to Miss Netherton and she'll fix it . . . I mean explain it. But then, I don't think there'll be any need; they'll take Dada's word. And we trust you not to say anything either, because, you know, if anything of this ever did leak out, there'd be a lot of trouble. Oh yes, and we've had enough trouble, haven't we?"

Her mother was staring into her face in silence now, and it was as if she were saying, "Whether you admit it or not, you're to blame. You know it, I know it, and your Dada knows it. Oh, yes, your Dada knows it."

It was almost three weeks later when Timothy called. He had walked from the coach road, and after knocking on the door he had shouted, "Anyone in?" And she had opened the door and said, "Oh, hello. Oh, I am pleased to see you." And she was; for, during the past fortnight at least, she had often wondered why he hadn't called and had realised that she was missing him, his talk, his voice, his parleying of words with her. He seemed to be the only one she could smile at, or with.

"I'll tell Father," she said immediately. "He's in the barn with Mother. They are cutting up chaff."

"Oh, I wouldn't disturb them for a moment. Let me have a look at you. How many years is it since I last saw you?"

She said, "I hear you've moved."

"Oh, yes, yes, I'm established, and that's what I've come to see you about. We have been living in chaos for the past few weeks but although the furniture is now in place I am stuck about the colour of drapes. I want a suite covered and I suppose the curtains should match; in fact, I intend to get rid of all the curtains in the house. Wait till you see them. As I told you before, they are very drab, and I was wondering if you would come over and give me some advice?"

"Oh." She shook her head now. "I've never had any experience in choosing materials or matching colours, except for a dress or a blouse that mother would be making for me or Cherry."

"Oh, I'm sure you've got perfect taste. Anyway, they have sent a great assortment of materials from Newcastle. I knew I could have asked Miss Netherton's advice, but you know"—he poked his face towards her now— "her house is still dressed in the style of the fifties and I feel I want something more up to date, more modern, bright, cheerful . . . Oh, the adjectives I use! Anyway, will you come?"

"I should love to, and also to see your home. Do you feel you're settled in it?"

"Oh, yes, yes. I feel different altogether." A sombre look came over his face as he added, "Life became unbearable up there, really unbearable. I went up yesterday to see my sister and she tells me there's going to be further changes. She doesn't know whether Raymond will bring his wife there. But between you and me, I don't think that young lady fancies being mistress of that house. Perhaps it's from what she has already heard. Anyway, her father is a widower and they have taken quite a big place outside Newcastle, and it's my opinion that Raymond will end up there. That, of course, would leave Simon in charge of the house." He stopped abruptly, wetted his lips, then said, "Did I tell you I've acquired a carriage? Nothing elaborate. Also a trap. I enjoy the trap so much. I've brought it today. I've tied her up at yon end of the fence on the west side. Would you like to take a jaunt back with me and see my little hut?"

"Yes. Oh yes." She found herself smiling widely at him, for he appeared at the moment like a bright light suddenly illuminating her dull existence. And she added excitedly, "Would you mind waiting until I change my dress? Perhaps you would like to go and have a word with Dada and Ma in the barn?"

"I'll do that. Yes, I'll do that."

She hurried to her bedroom and after a moment of standing before the small mirror, which reflected her black dress and showed up her face as utterly colourless, she turned swiftly as if making a decision and went to the cupboard in the corner of the room. Two dresses were hanging there. She took down the saxe-blue one with a white collar attached, and after changing into it she again looked in the mirror, then turned the white collar inwards. Next, she took down a paper bag from the top of the cupboard and drew out a black straw hat, which she put on. She then opened the top drawer of a chest of drawers and took out a pair of black gloves and a white handkerchief. Lastly, she donned her black cloak. Now she was ready.

In the yard, where her mother and father were now standing with Timothy, she could see immediately that her parents had noticed she had changed her dress, and their surprise showed. But they did not comment on it, yet she knew there was censure in their eyes that after only a matter of weeks, she could shed her outward sign of mourning.

"I shall bring her safely back." Timothy was smiling from one to the other, but Nathaniel's answer was brief: "Drive carefully, then," he said.

"I certainly shall."

"Don't stay too long," said Maria now. "The twilight still comes early."

"I won't." She looked from one to the other, then turned and walked away, leaving Timothy to say goodbye to them.

As they drove away she lifted her hand in farewell to them, but received no response.

She admired the horse and she admired the trap, and she told him so as he sat on the opposite narrow seat, and she laughed at him as he said, "Get up there! Daisy."

"You call her Daisy."

"Well, it is instead of lazy, because she is the laziest animal I've ever come across. Look at her stomach. She's too full of oats to work. Edward, that's the new coachman, he says we've got to cut down half her feed and stop giving her tid-bits. But I can't resist giving her tid-bits. She loves sugar and sweeties."

"Well, in that case you mustn't grumble if she won't gallop."

"Gallop! I don't think she's ever galloped in her life. She wouldn't know how to. She belonged to my doctor's children. They are grown up now and he didn't know what to do with her. So that's how I came by her."

On entering the village, Anna was immediately aware that there were people standing outside the forge where a horse was being shod. Timothy was sitting sideways and so he merely glimpsed them; but she was sitting facing them and she saw the blacksmith drop the horse's hoof, then straighten his back and stare towards her. She heard him distinctly shout a name, and then, glancing sideways, she saw one of his sons come out of the forge, and although she didn't move her head any further round, she knew that they were both looking in her direction.

Next, a woman about to enter the grocer's shop turned and stared, and was joined by a man coming out. And he stared. Then two faces seemed to pop up over the rim of bottled glass that formed half of the window in the King's Head. Lastly, where the road narrowed as it left the village, two farm workers stepped from the middle of the road onto the verge to allow them to pass. One of them touched his forelock, saying, " 'Day, Mr. Timothy." And Timothy called back, "Good day, Roberts." But the other man just looked at them steadily, at least at her.

After driving some distance further on Timothy said, "It'll be all over the village tonight. Will you mind?"

"Why should I?"

"Yes, why should you? And anyway"—he glanced at her—"they know I'm harmless, at least they consider me so . . . Poor Mr. Timothy. I get annoyed, not just annoyed but angry when I hear that, because I am not poor in their sense of the word."

She put her hand out and touched his knee, saying, "You shouldn't let that trouble you. They are ignorant. I . . . we have all suffered from their ignorance for years, so, in a way, I know how you feel. But they would do you no harm ever, whereas us, they would like to burn us alive."

"*Oh! Oh!* Don't say a thing like that, Anna. As you said, it's ignorance, just ignorance because in the main they're not cruel, just stupid."

"I don't agree with you there, Tim. To me they are ignorant, cruel, *and* stupid. Do you know that my mother never came back from the town for years but that she had to wash her skirt?"

He turned his head quickly towards her, "Wash her skirt?"

"Yes, wash her skirt, because they would spit on her. Was she not living in sin?—and this was the rub which annoyed them, being comfortably under the patronage of Miss Netherton, their landlady, at least of a number of them. Yet they didn't spit on the widow of a certain farmer who had died eight years before but whose place had been taken over by the wife's own brother, and she produced a child each year."

"Oh, yes, yes." He was nodding his head now. "I know who you mean. But two of that family are idiots."

"Idiots or not, they're accepted. So why should we have been tormented all these years? Can you tell me the reason? Those children on the farm are not only bastards . . . yes, I can use that word, at least to you, Tim, but they are the result of incest. But I think at the bottom of it the main reason, or one of them, is that my father educated my mother, and then they educated us as far as it was possible. We were outcasts, yet we acted as superior outcasts, and they couldn't bear that. They still can't. I . . . I"—she bowed her head now—"I'm still afraid of the village, Tim."

"Oh, my dear, you mustn't be; they can do nothing more. And as you said, you're under the patronage of Miss Netherton, and also, may I say so, of me, for what my patronage is worth. But that is the wrong word to use. It is my feeling of friendliness towards your entire family and knowing that I have in you a very, very, special friend. Anyway, come along, smile; you cannot live with the dead, Anna. You are alive and your life is before you. Ah . . . here we are! And look." He pointed to the horse's head. "She knows the gate already, as she knows where the manger is and what's in it. Oh, she's a knowing girl. Get up! there with you."

The drive was short but it opened into a large gravel square, and there stood the house. It was creeper-covered and large flower-heads of wistaria were hanging over the upper windows. He pointed to them as he drew up the horse, saying, "That's growing on to the roof. Fletcher, our gardener, tells me we'll have to get it down if we don't want the gutters to be blocked and water to come through the ceilings. Oh, my goodness, the things that have got to be looked to when you take on a house."

He held out his hand and helped her down from the step; then looking at the man now standing to his side, he said, "Oh, Edward, see to her, will you? But I think you had better cut down her feed tonight."

"Yes, sir." The man grinned now. "So you can give her more tid-bits, sir."

Timothy said nothing to this but exchanged a knowing look with Anna; then, taking her elbow, he led her onto the pillared porch, through an open oak double door and into a hall. It was quite a large hall for such a moderate-sized house, and the broad stairs that went up from it were of plain oak and were uncarpeted and, pointing to them, Timothy said, "I nearly broke my neck on them yesterday. I must get them covered; in spite of Miss Netherton. She thinks it would be a sin to cover up that old wood. Well, my dear, let me have your cloak and hat."

He led her into a room at the far end of the hall and with a theatrical gesture he said, "The drawing-room, ma'am." Then added, "It's hardly bigger than the housekeeper's room in the Manor. But it looks comfortable, don't you think?"

She stood in the middle of the room and looked around, turning her body as she did so. She did this twice before answering, "I think it's lovely, Tim; more than that, beautiful. And I don't know why you want to replace the curtains."

"You don't?"

"No." She went over to one of the two deep-bay windows and, feeling the curtain material, she said, "It's beautiful brocade."

"But it's faded. It should be a deep rose. Look; pull open the pleats and you will see."

"Yes. Yes, I can see from the pelmet and the fringe, but it goes with this room. I don't think you will ever improve on it."

"But if I had new ones made in the same colour?"

"They would be new, unworn, untempered, and shouting at everything else in this room."

He now turned slowly and looked about him before saying, "You know, I think you're right. Yes, you're right. I never thought about it that way; one thing shouting at another. Well, well, I'm so glad you came, Miss Dagshaw. You have saved me quite a bit of money."

They laughed together now; then he said, "Come and see the dining-room."

They were in the hall again when a thick-set middle-aged man approached him, saying, "Would you care for some tea now, sir?"

"Yes. Yes, I think we would, Walters. By the way, this is Miss Dagshaw, a very dear friend of mine, and she's come to help me choose curtains. At least that was the idea, but she tells me now that I would be wrong to change the drawing-room ones."

The man smiled at Anna now. He had a pleasant broad face as he said, "I'm sure the young lady is right; they are magnificent curtains, sir."

"But as I've said, Walters, they're faded."

"A lot of faded things are magnificent, sir."

"Ah. Ah." Timothy now pointed to his butler-cum-valet with his thumb. "I'll have to watch out for him; I've already discovered we've got a philosopher here." And at that he left the man still smiling broadly and led her into the dining-room, saying immediately, "Now don't tell me you like these curtains."

She looked around the room at the mahogany table, chairs, and sideboard, and the two glass cabinets of china; then up at the glass chandelier hanging from the painted decorated circle in the middle of the ceiling, and she said, "Yes, I like them, but this room is not so light as your drawing-room and so I think you could have a less heavy curtain at the window."

"Ah, well, new curtains for the dining-room. Now come along and see what I would like to call the library but daren't. It is a glorified study."

The room was about fifteen feet long and twelve feet wide and two walls had shelves from floor to ceiling and these were filled with books. The table was littered with more books, but in the middle of it was a large writing-pad. And when she looked at it he dismissed it saying, "Scribbles, scribbles. I keep scribbling words in the hope that I may astound myself. You see, the Renaissance interests me, particularly the influence of Florence. You could say, one way and another, I waste a lot of time." And saying so, he pointed to the French window and said, "That leads out into a little conservatory."

A few minutes later she was standing under the covered glass dome, and she turned to him, saying, "Little? Why do you call it little? It must run the length of the side of the house."

"It does, but I suggest at present I'm comparing the rooms with those in the Manor. But I'm not belittling it, oh no, because this is mine. The conservatory up there didn't belong to me, it was only loaned, and then again much against the grain of the head gardener. We didn't see eye to eye; we didn't get on together."

Showing her surprise, she said, "I couldn't imagine you not getting on with anyone."

His face unsmiling, he stared at her as he said, "Under my 'be pleasant on any account' façade, if I don't think a thing is right, I'm almost like you, yes I am, I speak out. I may tell you, I wasn't loved by all the staff in the Manor. You see, as though I were an idiot, a dear idiot, I was allowed to walk and wander where I would, until some people realised that nothing escaped me, and that if you were subject to epileptic fits it didn't mean that you were mental. It took quite a time for some people to realise this; but when they did, their attitude towards me changed: I knew too much about them and their pilfering. And it was on a big scale, too, the top hierarchy working in conjunction with the outside farm staff, and the suppliers all making hay when the sun shone, and even when it didn't.

"I stopped their game; and they were afraid I would split on them. And this I told them I would do if they tried it again. For some, it must have been a gold-mine in which they had been digging for years, even before my sister was confined to her chair. I came across it, of course, when she became ill; and it angered me to know that, even in her state, she was being swindled, and by the Estate steward too. So you see, Anna, everybody doesn't love me."

"I'm glad of that."

"You are?" His eyebrows moved up.

"Yes. It makes us more on a level, say."

"Oh, I see. Oh"—his chin jerked—"I don't know whether I do or not. That's one we will have to talk out. But come, come on upstairs."

The bedrooms were airy and well furnished, but when they came to two steps going off on to another landing, he stopped and said, "That is the staff's private quarters. Cook has a room, and the girls have another which they share. Walters has a room at the far side of the hall near the kitchen; but he is in communication with me upstairs if I should need him, which"—he made a slight face at her now—"I don't intend to for a long time, because the tranquillity of this house will act as a balm on me. Come along, now we'll go down and visit cook, and the girls, then we'll have some tea."

The cook, Mrs. Ada Sprigman, dipped her knee at the introduction and Anna thought how, at one time, she would have made the boys roll on the floor by imitating anyone dipping their knee to her. But not any more, never any more.

The kitchen maid was Lena Cassidy, trim, broad Irish, and she too dipped her knee. The housemaid was Mary Bowles and she addressed her as "ma'am".

What a difference from her reception at the Manor. And she couldn't help but think that these people knew who she was, and therefore all about her.

Walters brought tea into the sitting-room on a trolley. There was a choice of China or Indian tea, dainty sandwiches and small cakes, and she ate of them because she was feeling suddenly hungry and she hadn't felt so for weeks, or months, for that matter . . .

Tea over, she chose from the samples certain materials that might do for the bedroom curtains, and he made notes of her choice. When, later, they sat by the window in the drawing-room, he looked across the small space that divided them and said, "I cannot tell you when I've enjoyed an afternoon more. Anna"—he leant towards her and took her hand—"promise me you'll be kind and come and see me often."

"The kindness will be on your part, Tim, because I wouldn't like anything better. You see"—she looked down at their joined hands—"I cannot any longer talk to Dada; something died in him when Ben went. Ma is good and kind, but we never have a discussion together; she's always been only too pleased to leave that to Dada. At one time, he and I would talk for hours and he would go into a particular period of history when perhaps new thinking, new ideas were developing. Given the opportunity, you know, Tim, my father could have been a great speaker; he is so lucid and everything he talked about he made interesting. I'll never forget one conversation we had. It was many years ago, but at the time it seemed to set the pattern of my thinking. What happened today, he said, didn't really happen today, nor yesterday, nor the day before; it was born as a thought in someone's mind, then passed on by word of mouth, then word of mouth was written down and the writing was read. Another brain picked up these thoughts and worked on them. And so it went on until the effect is seen in what happens today. It may have been the declaration of a war; it may have been an assassination; it may have been the fruition of some great love; but it never really happened today, it happened days gone, perhaps weeks gone, perhaps years gone, hundreds of years gone when someone had a particular thought. All there is, he said, is thought. Without thought, what is there? Nothing, for without thought we cannot conceive anything." She blinked, then muttered, "Oh dear! Fancy me recalling that! Yet, that is how he used to talk. But . . . but not any more. No, not any more."

Now he was shaking her hand up and down, saying, "My dear, you once told me that you scribbled poetry in bits and pieces. I would say to you now, forget about your poetry, put your thoughts down. Put down what you have just said to me, and go on from there."

Slowly she shook her head as she said, "That would be merely simplifying things: I mean, writing simple things, because at bottom, I think simply."

"Oh, my dear, how the world wants to read something that has been simplified. The verbiage that the so-called great minds pen is read through struggle and only by a few. A man gets a name for being a great writer and why? because to the ordinary people he is difficult to understand: he has enjoyed himself spewing out words, words, words, beautiful words, perhaps, but when analysed they are to be found mostly out of context with his subject. I have begun so many books in my time, my dear, and I have thrown them down with irritation, knowing that I was reading the outpourings of a man's idea of himself, as I can only call it, especially when he is so certain that he is right. Science has begun to move fast, and so many scientists depart from their principles to make things known; some are worse than religious fanatics.

"They fight each other for the right to be right. They stand up in lecture rooms and expound their theories, theories that within ten years might be deemed to be out of date, but at the time they are so certain that they are right in what they think, that they convince others, too; just as Catholic or Protestant will do when asserting there is only one God and He is theirs; not only will they kill others but they kill each other in the name of that God; He will be on their dying lips. Have you ever thought, Anna, of the number who have died because of God? Christ was crucified because of God, and His adherents have crucified each other down the ages, burnt each other at the stake, hanged, drawn, and quartered each other. Where is the reason in man that allows him to do this? or believe in such a God? How can anyone be sure that there is any God at all? And have you ever thought, Anna, of Christians who are strong in their faith but who are terrified of dying, and should one of their own die they mourn him, whereas, if they were following their faith they would know he was in these so-called mansions in heaven. So why mourn? Oh, my dear"—he put his hand across his eyes now—"I'm so sorry. I'm on my egg-box; I'm indulging in my pet hate of all dogmatic individuals, when I should be remembering that I am talking to someone who has just suffered a loss."

"Please. Please, Tim"—she drew his hand from his brow—"I understand perfectly. And I'm with you in thought every step of the way. And don't worry about my feelings for Ben; like Dada, I don't think he's gone anywhere yet; his body's in the graveyard but his spirit's still in the house. But"—she looked to the side—"I sometimes wish, for Dada's peace of mind, that he would move on and go wherever spirits go, for, as long as he remains or as Dada thinks he remains, he will be in a daze. And that's all I can call his present state, a daze."

She now looked quickly towards the window, saying, "The sun's going down; I must get home. But oh, Tim, I have enjoyed my visit, and our talk. It's wonderful to be able to talk like this again, and to listen. You say I should write, and I say you should write, but I know you do and I would love to read some of your work, some of your poems."

"Oh, my dear, I'll have to be either very very drunk or very very ill before I let you or anyone else read my poems."

"Well, I'll come some evening on the quiet when you're very very drunk."

"Do that. Oh please, do that."

They went out laughing.

As he drove her home she thought of Simon's words when standing near the sawing block: "He's a man, and some of the greatest men have been epileptics."

Be that as it may, she could never see this dear friend of hers asking any woman to marry him. He was too sensitive of his disability and the knowledge that people shied from even a child in fits, let alone from a thrashing-arms man.

Part Five

The Cross

ONE

*I*t was a strange summer. Towards the end of May the heat became intense; then on the seventh of June people imagined that the world must have gone topsy-turvy or that it was coming to an end, for on this day there was a heavy fall of snow, three and four inches in some places, to be followed directly by muggy and then hot weather again.

It was very noticeable that tempers became frayed. There had been other hot summers or cold winters but these hadn't seemed to affect the family. But since Ben's death so many things had happened, the latest being that Oswald and Olan hadn't returned home until well after nine o'clock the previous night. They were both very tired; they had been working up till half-past eight. It had been too hot for many people to bother cooking, and so the shop had been packed all day, as, in fact, it had been all week. And Oswald had tentatively put a proposal to his parents. Mrs. Simpson had suggested that they make the rooms above the sitting-down shop comfortable where they could both sleep during the week, then come home at the week-ends. Oswald had looked from his mother to his father, then said, "It's a long trail, Dada, when you've had a day on your feet in the heat, and the bustle! And she's doing us so well and is such a kind woman."

Nathaniel had looked at Maria, and she had looked at the floor before she had conceded: "Well, if you want it that way, Oswald, so be it. You're both men now and have to live your own lives. But as long as you come home and see us at the week-end . . ."

"Oh—" Oswald had put out a hand to each of them, saying, "Of course we will, Ma; and bring our money with us."

It was now that Nathaniel put in, "If you are living away, son, we won't expect any money from you; at least, not what you have been giving. And I'm sure Mrs. Simpson will look after you. She seemed a very respectable woman, and sensible."

"She is, Dada; and her daughter, too; and the business is going ahead fine. Both Olan and me think there are prospects there."

At this Maria lifted her head and said, "What kind of prospects?" and looked straight at her son, so that he, a bit flustered, answered, "Well, Ma, she'll give us a good rise at the end of the year; we feel sure on that. And because she's in business, she gets a discount on clothes and things and said if we ever wanted anything . . . well, we could have a ticket."

"Very kind of her, I'm sure," Maria said; then turned away . . .

But it was settled that the boys were to leave home, and Maria had packed up a preliminary bundle of clothes for each of them and which they would take with them the following morning, the rest to be taken on their next return journey.

From then on, for most of the week only Anna herself, Cherry, and Jimmy were at home, at least during the evenings. And then it would seem that there was a lot for Cherry to do outside, especially where Bobby Crane was concerned. However, there was no objection from either her mother or her father.

Anna now often found herself walking with Jimmy. Since Ben's going, he, too, had changed. He seemed to have lost his impishness; in fact, at times, in his talk one would think he was quite as old as the twins.

On this particular night, walking by her side through the wood, he proffered the remark, "The house is breaking up, isn't it, Anna?"

"What do you mean by breaking up, Jimmy?"—she had stopped—"The boys had to go into town."

"Oh, I know that. I know that. But the next to leave will be Cherry. She'll marry Bobby."

"How can she do that? He's still apprenticed: they'll have nothing to live on."

"Oh, I don't think that will matter very much. They'll get through. Dada would help them. Anyway, if she doesn't get married soon there'll be trouble."

"Oh! Jimmy." She again stopped abruptly; and he did so, too, and, looking at her, he said, "She's ready for marrying."

This was her young brother, not yet eighteen. Had it been Oswald talking, she would have understood. Yet, Jimmy was a farmer, living with raw nature every day . . . But, oh dear me.

She walked on now, thinking: He said Dada would help them. Did he know anything about the money that would be coming, supposedly from her mother's people? Her parents hadn't mentioned anything further about what Miss Netherton might get for the cross or if she had already got it; and she hadn't asked them, because there seemed to be a wall growing between them. Of course, she must remember that Miss Netherton had been away for the past three weeks on holiday. She had gone down to a place on the South coast called Brighton.

They had been walking on, but once again she was brought to a stop by Jimmy's saying, "I want to get away, Anna."

Dumfounded for a moment, she could only gaze at him. Then when she managed to speak, her voice was a little above a whisper: "Why, Jimmy? Where to? What do you mean?" she said.

He smiled at her now as he repeated, "Why? Where to? What do you mean? Why? Because what is there here for me? You know something? I'd like to go to sea."

"You would?"

"Yes. Yes, I would. That's where to, to sea."

"They'd be upset if you were to leave."

"Well, they'd still have each other, and that's the main thing in their life, isn't it? And, of course, they'll still have you. Oh! Anna"—he now put his hand on her sleeve—"why didn't you take the chance that was open to you? That fellow would have stood on his head for you: Mr. Simon."

"Jimmy!"

"Oh, you can say 'Jimmy' like that, but we're all bastards, aren't we? And you wouldn't have been any worse thought of; in fact, there are some who would have looked up to you, let me tell you."

She almost pushed him on his back, so fiercely did she thrust him aside as she said, "Well! let me tell you, as I see it, I didn't give myself the name of bastard, it was passed on to me. And I'll tell you this much an' all, I'm never going to earn it, no matter what happens. Now is that clear?"

"Oh, Anna, I'm sorry. I'm sorry. But oh, lass, the thought of you ending your days stuck back there with the pair of them. They see nobody else but themselves. You must face it; I did a long time ago. Oh, aye; they brought us up well, but drugged like with tales around the fire; the happy routine. Nothing was ever going to change. But we're no longer children, we're grown-up men and women, and the older we've grown the more they've grown back into their early days. Night after night I've sat on that mat and watched them. At one time I used to like to watch them, but not any more. They're not two people, they're just one. They could lose the lot of us as long as they have each other."

"Jimmy! Dada's been distraught over Ben. Really! I've never imagined you thinking like this."

"We were all distraught over Ben; and as for how I think, it shows that you haven't given much thought to me."

"I have. I have. But I didn't think you looked on them like that."

"Well, how do *you* look on them?"

She turned from him without answering, and walked slowly towards the chopping block, and there, placing a hand on it, she looked over the railings to the moor, and in her mind she saw riding across it a man who would have taken her for a mistress; and she also saw a man writhing on the ground in an epileptic fit.

When she felt Jimmy's hand on her shoulder she turned and looked at him, asking quietly now, "Do you intend to go soon?"

"Aye, yes; before the winter sets in. But it's strange, because the only one I'm going to miss is you; and wherever I go I'll be thinking of you, and seeing your face, because you've got a beautiful face, you know, Anna. You're beautiful altogether."

"Oh!"—she closed her eyes—"don't, Jimmy. Don't."

"Why shouldn't I say it? Right from a child I used to like looking at you, more so than at Cherry. Cherry's pretty, but you're beautiful. And where's it going to get you? Wasting away in that long room and in this square of ground from which you can't even drive out on the cart. Oh, my God! Anna, it makes me sick when I think of it."

She stared at this brother of hers, this young boy: he was still a young boy but he talked like a man, he thought like a man, he was a man, as much, or even more than the twins. He was a man as Ben would never have been. He was even now a man as his father had never been. She put out her arms towards him and they clung tightly together for a moment and then he swung away from her and, as if he were aiming to leave her and them all at this very moment, he leapt the wall behind the wood-pile and ran across the open moor, leaving her with her head bowed over the wood block and moaning as if she had lost another brother, or someone, someone even closer . . . which she had.

Twice of late she had walked to Timothy's house. It was exactly a mile and a half away, if she went over the stile and dropped down the bank into the road, so avoiding the village. She had enjoyed the walk; and had met only one person, a man driving a farm-cart. And she had not encountered a carriage.

It was towards the middle of July, about four o'clock in the afternoon, when she said to her mother, "I think I'll take a walk along to Mr. Timothy's, Ma; I've got these books I would like to change."

"But it's still so hot."

"There's a breeze coming up and the road's in partial shade for most of the way. Anyway, Ma, I feel I want to stretch my legs."

"You'll feel better tomorrow when Miss Netherton comes back; you'll have something to do then. Fancy her going all the way to Holland! She's been gone more than five weeks now. I . . . I think it might be about . . . about the other thing."

It was the first time her mother had alluded to the cross, and she said, "You think so, Ma?"

"Yes. Your Dada was saying a lot of such trading goes on in Amsterdam."

"She'll have a great deal to tell us when she comes back, I'm sure. Anyway, that's one thing."

"Oh, yes, she will, she will; and it'll likely be settled. But, money or no money, I still wouldn't like to leave here. Would you?"

She drew in a long breath and looked downwards before she said, "Sometimes I feel hemmed in."

"Yes. Yes, you're bound to, lass." Maria put in quickly. "You're bound to. And I understand. Don't think I don't. I understand. But something'll turn up, you'll see, something'll turn up."

Anna didn't ask what her mother thought might turn up, she just said, "Will I have to put a hat on?" and Maria smiled, saying, "I don't see why. We've never conformed to style, have we? No; go as you are; your dress looks cool. It certainly won't rain today." Then she added, "We haven't seen him for a week or so. Perhaps he's had another turn."

"Oh, I wouldn't think so. He goes to Newcastle quite a bit. I know he's researching some old books in the archives of the Literary Library; no, the Literary and Philosophical Society Library, he calls it."

"Well, it's a good thing he's got something to pass his time with, the way he is."

As she left the house and walked towards the stile, Anna wondered why her mother always alluded to his infirmity. She seemed forever to be pressing the point. Yet there was no one more sane and normal than Timothy, and the more often she saw him the more she would forget he was ever ill in any way.

She climbed the stile; then put down her two books on the ground and, preparatory to negotiating the bank, turned her back to the roadway and felt carefully with her right foot for one of the footholds she had made, and placed her left foot in a similar one further down; then let out a scream when a hand gripped her calf and a voice said, "Want a helpin' 'and, miss?"

When the hand pulled her feet to the lower ground, she swung round and fell against the bank, and looked into the face of Arthur Lennon, the blacksmith's son. He was a man of twenty. His hair grew long over his brow and down his cheeks, and he had a moustache trailing down each side of his mouth. His face showed one wide grin.

For a moment she couldn't speak, but looked beyond him to where another man had stepped from behind the hedge that bordered the other side of the road. There was a gap in the hedge wide enough to let a farm-cart through, and the man was holding a large tin by its handle and a brush in the other hand, and to his side stood a younger boy.

"Get out of my way!" She pressed her hands against the bank in order to rise, but the grinning face was hanging over her now, saying, "Ask civilly." And when next his hand came on to her breast and, half turning his head to his companion, he said, "There's nowt in them; flat paps for a gillyvor," she screamed, "Take your filthy hands off me, you dirty-mouthed individual! Get out of my way, you lout!"

"Lout, am I? Who you callin' a lout, you whorin' bastard? Not satisfied with breakin' up one family, you have to go for the fitty one. How does he manage? Does he have a fit when he's at you?"

When her knee came up and caught him in the groin he jumped back, holding himself; and she was about to turn and grab her books from the top of the bank when his arms came about her and, spewing obscenities at her, he dragged her screaming through the opening and into the field. When his hand came across her mouth and her teeth bit into it, he pulled it back, bawling, then brought her a blow on the face that sent her head spinning for a moment and seemed to knock the breath out of her body. The next minute she was on her back and he had one knee across her legs and was now tearing at the front of her dress while he shouted to the man, "Drop the can here, an' go and fetch your Betty. Tell her to bring a pilla."

"A pilla? You don't mean the tar . . . ?"

"Aye, I do. Me da said it should have been done a long time ago. An' look! stop that bugger from scarperin'."

The man put down the tin of tar saying, "My God! Arthur, they'll have you up;" but he was laughing while he said it; and Arthur Lennon said, "Just let them try. Lucky you had the job of doin' the railings. Look! get after him, quick! or he'll be at the village afore you know where you are. Bring him back here; I'll settle him."

The man caught up with the boy and, hauling him by the collar, brought him back and thrust him to the ground beyond Anna, and her assailant grabbed him by his shirt-front now and threatened: "You open your mouth about this and I'll cut your tongue out. D'you hear me? One word an' you know what'll happen to yer. If not that, down below something'll happen there, you understand?"

The boy made no sound but trembled visibly, as he now watched Arthur Lennon trying to pin Anna's clawing hands to her side.

"Untie the york on me legs," Lennon growled at the boy, "an' put it across her mouth. Go on! Untie it."

With shaking hands the boy untied the rope from beneath the man's knee, where it had been used to hold up the trouser leg, and when he leaned over her his eyes were looking straight down into hers, and he shook his head as if to say, I can't help it. I can't help it. Then he put the rope across her gaping mouth.

The man, now taking his knee from her legs, stood up; then bending over, he put one arm between her legs and the other under her waist and with a flick, turned her on to her face as if she had been a sheared sheep. Then, pulling her arms together, he held them with one hand while he loosened the piece of rope from his other leg, and with this he tied her wrists. He then dragged off his thin necktie, with which he tied her ankles together. This done, he now turned her on to her side, and with one pull he split her dress from top to bottom, then her underskirt, then her thin summer camisole. She was now naked to the waist.

It was when Anna felt his hands on her drawers that her whole body writhed. She was screaming inside her head, praying to die now. She next felt the sleeves being torn from her shoulders, then her dress being ripped at the back; but it was after the smell of the tar filled her nostrils and the first full brush of it was slapped on her breasts, then dragged over her stomach and downwards that she knew no more. She did not hear Lennon growl at the boy, "Stop your whimperin' else I'll strip you and lay you aside her."

He had finished tarring her when the other man returned, accompanied by his sister, Betty Carter. She was carrying a pillow and she stood looking down on the black-streaked body with the clothes lying in strips from it, and she said, "You did it, then, Arthur. Uncle Rob said you should an' that you would one day. An' she's only gettin' what she deserves, the bitch."

Looking down on the black nakedness, her brother said, "Didn't ya try her afore you tarred her? In for a penny in for a pound."

"Split that pilla!"

When Betty Carter tried to split the pillow-case the ticking was too strong, and she said, "Give me your knife," and with it, she split the pillow down the middle and then puffed as the feathers floated over her. But she didn't hand it to Lennon; instead, she said, "Let me do it."

And so she stood over the prostrate form and shook the feathers down on to the wet tar.

"Turn her on to the other side," she said, and both men, now using their feet, turned the unrecognisable form on to its other side, and as Betty Carter emptied the pillow-case she cried, "You didn't put any on her hair! Have you any left?" She now took the brush from the can. "Hardly a scrape," she said, "but it'll do." And with this she drew it a number of times over the shining dark hair, then, gathering up some loose feathers that were lying round about, she finished her job. And now they all turned and looked at the boy, who was vomiting.

"He'll split," Davey Carter said.

"My God! he won't."

He now pulled the boy up by the hair of his head and with his doubled fist hit him in the groin, bringing him doubled up again; then warned, "One squeak out of you, just one, an' like I do with the cattle. Understand?"

The boy gasped and made a motion with his head. "Who's gona find her?" Betty Carter said.

"Oh, they'll find her right enough. She was likely goin' on a jaunt to the fitty one an' he was likely expectin' her. Oh aye, he would be. I wonder how much he pays her? Somethin's keepin' that lot in clover up there. Oh, they'll find her all right. Afore the night's out there'll be a hue and cry."

"But what about when she comes round?"

"Oh, well, by that time we'll have had a drink and be givin' them a bit of entertainment in the bar, and then we'll be off. We were goin' in any case. I was due for the sack the morrow, anyroad, 'cos then old Peterson will have found out that he's a pig short. An' Davey here, he's fed up, so we had made wor plans. It was just honest luck that we came across her. By! I've been wantin' to do that to the stinkin' whore for years. She'll not stick her nose in the air so much now."

"What about me? He knows that it was me." She pointed to the boy.

"Don't worry about that." And taking the boy by the collar again, Lennon pulled him towards Betty Carter, pushing his face close to hers as he said, "Look! you've never seen her in your life afore, except in the village, understand? 'Cos if you don't we'll get you. I'll get you. We're not goin' all that far away, we're just goin' to lie low for a time. But if you squeak, one of these nights I'll pick you up and I'll do what I said. Oh, an' I'd like doin' that. I've always liked doin' it and I'll like doin' it to you. Oh yes! You get me?"

The boy was so sick he could neither say anything nor make any movement, but Lennon said to Betty Carter, "He understands all right. Don't you worry, Betty, don't you worry. But let's get some of this off wor boots. Anyway, that's what we've been workin' at, tarrin'; expect to get dabbed up a bit at this job. Oh, an' aye. Bring her books off the bank; she may want to have a read." He laughed.

A minute later he threw the books into the hedge, then with his foot he eased her body towards them; and saying, "Goodbye, Miss Gillyvor," he turned to the others and thumbed towards the village, and they followed him out of the field.

The sun still shone and birds in the thicket still sang.

$THREE$

$\mathcal{M}$rs. Bella Lennon stood at the bedroom window and looked down on the unusually busy village street. There was something up.

Hurrying down the narrow stairs, she went out of her front door and into the smithy, where her husband was standing in the opening talking to their eldest son, Jack.

"What's up?" she said. "What's all the bustle?"

Her son turned to her and said on a laugh, "The gillyvor's lost, the whorin' one. It seems that Mr. Tim called in at her dear Papa's—that was around six o'clock, so they say. So, they've been runnin' like scalded cats ever since. Damn fools, them. I bet she's laid up with somebody else."

"It wouldn't be our Arthur," said the blacksmith on a deep guffaw, then added, "By the way, where is he?"

"He's gone into Fellburn with Davey."

"Fellburn? What for?"

"Well, apparently he was fed up and wanted a night out, so he says. Didn't you see him go in? Didn't he call in?"

"No, he didn't. What time was this?"

"Oh"—she shook her head—"some time ago. He came in the back way and had a sluice under the pump. He had been down with Davey who was tarring the new railin's for Dobson; then he got changed and went out, saying as usual, 'I'll be back when you see me.' "

The smith now looked at his son. "You didn't see him pass this way, did yer?" he said.

"No; and I've been outside here most of the time. Aye! Look!" He pointed. "Here's a carriage, an' comin' hell for leather."

As the carriage passed them, Mrs. Lennon said, "That's Mr. Timothy in there and somebody else." Then turning to her son, her eyes screwed up and her whole face one of enquiry, she said, "You must have seen our Arthur come out of the house?"

"Ma, I'm neither drunk nor daft at this hour of the day and I tell yer he hasn't passed me."

"Well, he surely wouldn't go out the garden and jump the wall."

The three of them looked at each other. Then hurrying from them, Mrs. Lennon went upstairs again and opened a door off a narrow landing and surveyed her son's room. It looked as it always did. But going to the cupboard, she saw his working clothes thrown into the bottom of it, together with his boots. Well, that was nothing new. But looking on the shelf above she saw that something was missing. After opening the top drawer in an old chest, she stood biting on her lip. The two shirts she had ironed and put in there just this morning, after yesterday's wash, were gone, as also were his long pants and two pairs of socks. Then, lifting the lid of a wooden box that took up the space between the chest and the wall, she saw it was empty. The oddments usually in it were no longer there, the two woollen guernseys, his other cap, a good Sunday waistcoat, and a muffler.

She took the stairs almost two at a time and, bursting into the smithy, where her husband and son were now working, she cried, "Stop it! Stop it! He's gone."

The hammering ceased and her husband looked at her and said, "What d'you mean, he's gone?"

"He's done a bunk for good. He's taken his back-pack and his clothes. He must have pushed them all in there and dropped them out of the back window. That's the way he went."

The men looked at each other; then the smith, turning to his son, said, "Finish that. We've got to get that order out; they're waitin'; an' they don't come easy."

And then, pushing his wife before him, they went into the house and at the foot of the stairs he said, "The box?"

"The box? What d'you mean the box?"

"Don't be so bloody stupid, woman! The box under the bed. Have you seen to it?"

"No. No. But he wouldn't, not Arthur."

Without a word the smith bounded up the stairs into their bedroom, pulled out a tin trunk from under the high bed, lifted the lid, put his hand down through oddments of clothes and felt the tin box. Pulling it out, he looked up at her as if in relief. Then he opened it, and as he did so his expression changed. And when they were both looking down into the empty cash box he said, "The bugger! I'll have him. I'll get him. All twenty-seven of them!"

"You should have put it into the bank. I've told you an' told you."

"Aye, and let the buggers know what we've got. They know too much down there already. Gold-mine, they'd be sayin' it is. But my God!" He stood up, his teeth grinding as he said, "I'll get him! I'll find him!"

"You'll do nowt of the sort." She pushed at his big frame. "An' you'd better not let on to our Jack, either. You're always pulling a long face about the bills not bein' paid. He knows nowt about this, an' if his Lena got to know, we wouldn't have a minute's peace, ever. An' you expectin' him to work overtime, like the night. So stick it back!" And she thrust her foot against the big box.

"By God!" Lennon said; "if I could get me hands on him this minute! Anyway, why the rush? He was set to finish the domino game the night. He could have wiped Willie Melton off the board and raked up a nice little pile after fourteen games at sixpence a go."

"Never mind that. Get downstairs and put a face on to our Jack. And from now on that'll larn you. By God! it will. Twenty-seven pounds in that wild young sod's pocket." She paused as though thinking, then said, "D'you think he'll sign on some boat?"

"Likely; an' Davey with him, 'cos whatever he does that dumb head'll follow. An' think on, woman, what's goin' to happen when his mother finds out. She'll be along here, saying, as usual, our Arthur's leading her dear lad astray."

"God! He went astray when he was born that one . . ."

It was about two hours later. The village street was still abuzz, with small groups here and there gossiping, when Dan Wallace came to the forge opening and asked, "Seen anything of our Art, Rob?"

"Young Art? No. Is he lost an' all?"

"Well, he hasn't come in for his tea. And it's now goin' on eight. His mother's goin' up the pole."

"Perhaps he's run off with the gillyvor."

"Don't be so daft! He was helpin' Davey Carter the day, an' I can't see hilt nor hair of Davey, either."

The blacksmith, who was now dressed in his second best suit, came out of the forge and closed the doors, and he had his back to Dan Wallace as he said, "An' you won't. He's . . . he's gone into Fellburn with our Arthur for the night."

"Oh. Oh, I see. Well, I wonder where the young kite has got to . . . ?"

The young kite was now sneaking in the back door of his home. And when his mother saw him she said, "Where d'you think you've been?" then stopped and said, "My God! What's the matter with you, boy? You sick?"

The boy opened his mouth, took in a deep gulp of air and said, "Dad. Where's Dad?"

"Out looking for you, of course. Past eight; where've you been?"

"Get Dad. Get Dad, Mam."

"You bad? Caught somethin'?"

"Get Dad, Mam! Get Dad."

The woman now pushed the boy into a chair; then she turned and ran out of the house, up the village street, past the King's Head, and on past the cottages, shouting to one after another, "Have you see Dan?" And one woman, rising from a chair where she had been sitting trying to keep cool, pointed and said, "Just this minute turned up the alley."

The alley led to Willie Melton's stint, where he kept his pigs, and there she saw her husband talking to Willie, who had a bucket in his hand and a crowd of pigs around him, and she called, "Dan! Dan! He's in. Dan! come on."

When her husband came up to her, she said, "He's bad. Something's wrong with him, he can hardly speak . . ."

When they entered the house the boy straightaway got up from his chair and, going to his father, gripped his hand as he said, "Dad. Dad, they said what they'd . . . he said what he would do, Arthur Lennon, but . . . but you won't let them will you, Dad? You won't let them, will you?"

"What in the name of God! are you talkin' about, boy? What did he say he would do?"

The boy looked at his mother, then put his hand down between his legs and said, "Cut 'em off. Cut 'em off."

The husband and wife exchanged looks, and his father said gently, "Sit down, lad. Sit down and tell me."

"No, Dad, no. You've got to go and get her."

"Get who?"

"The young lass, the young lass. She's lyin' in the hedge."

"Oh my God! My God!" His mother now put her hand up through her hair and let out a cry, and her husband said, "Shut up! Shut up! Tell me. Tell me. Where's the girl? What have they done?"

"Tarred . . . tarred and feathered her, he did, he did. Tied her up. Said . . . said what they would . . . would do, an' . . . an' he will, Dad, he will."

"*He will?*" Dan Wallace stood up now. "He'll swing if I get my hands on him. Come on, lad; show me where she is?"

"No, Dad, no. I can't . . . I can't go. At the stile."

"Come on, come on. Be a brave lad. Nobody'll do anythin' to you."

"They will. They will; I was there. I was there. And Davey Carter an' his sister an' all. Aye . . . aye, she . . . she was awful, Betty . . . she was awful."

"Come on. Come on." Dan Wallace now led his son out into the street, but he had to keep a firm arm round him and keep pressing him forward. Then his wife, who was at the other side of him, turned and said, "Here's the carriage comin'! It's Mr. Timothy's. Stop it! Stop it! Tell 'em!"

Dan Wallace waved his hand, and when Edward pulled up the carriage Timothy put his head out of the window in enquiry and Dan said to him, "My boy here, sir, my boy says he knows where the girl is." He looked beyond Timothy now to the strained face of the girl's father, and Nathaniel cried, "He does? He does? Where?"

"Sir, I think both of you . . . I think you'd better prepare yourself for somethin'. I don't know, but my boy here seems to know all about it. They threatened him."

"Who, man? Who?"

"I'll tell you later, sir, but I think we'd better get there, wherever it is. Come on, sir." He now took his son's arm and ran him down the street, the carriage following, and this brought people out of their houses, out of the gardens, and out of both inns, all asking questions.

Beyond the village, when they came to the gap in the hedge, the boy shrank against his father, but his father dragged him into the field and when the boy pointed, Dan Wallace muttered, "Almighty God! Oh, Almighty God!" And a minute later, when Nathaniel and Timothy stood looking down on the tarred and feathered naked body, with its torn clothes spread like broken wings at each side of her, both, for a moment, had to hold on to each other for support. And then Nathaniel was kneeling on one side of her and Timothy on the other; and Timothy, taking her smeared face between his hands, said not a word, for his mind was screaming against the obscene cruelty that had been inflicted on this innocent girl, on his beloved Anna.

Nathaniel raised his head and looked at him and whispered, "She's . . . she's breathing."

They both stood up and looked about them. It seemed that a crowd of people had gathered from nowhere and were standing awestruck.

Dan Wallace said, "She'll have to be lifted on to a cart or something."

But Timothy's coachman said quietly, "I . . . I wouldn't touch her, sir, until a doctor comes, and the polis."

Nathaniel looked at the man; then he looked at Timothy; and after a slight hesitation Timothy said, "Get into Fellburn at top speed and bring them both."

"We . . . we can't leave her like this. We must loosen her arms and legs," said Nathaniel, kneeling beside Anna.

Timothy too knelt and tugged at the knots, then looking around he muttered, "A knife? Has anyone got a knife?"

At least three knives were handed towards him; then, as he cut the rope around Anna's wrist, Dan Wallace said, "I wouldn't move her arms, sir, not for a bit. She'll be in cramp."

When Timothy had finished there were feathers sticking to his tarred hands and somebody offered him a handkerchief; then another.

The crowd had grown now, but it was silent: it was definitely a group of frightened people, for they could surely see the outcome of this dreadful deed.

The boy was clinging to his mother now and crying openly. And when a thin voice near them said, "Did he do it?" Mrs. Wallace startled everybody by screaming, "No! he didn't. Your bosom drinking mates did it. Arthur Lennon and Davey Carter. And aye, aye, where's his sister? Where's his sister, dear little Betty?"

Her husband turned on her fiercely now, saying, "Shut up! Shut up! woman. That'll be seen to later."

It was noticeable now that here and there a person moved out of the crowd and went quietly away, and one of these was the blacksmith . . .

It was exactly twenty-five minutes later when the doctor and the policeman arrived in the carriage, and after pressing through the crowd they both stood and looked down, first with amazement, then with horror at the sight of the tarred and feathered girl.

The doctor now took off his coat and rolled up his sleeves before kneeling on the ground. Putting his ear to the discoloured mouth and then roughly rubbing the sticking feathers to one side, he felt the flesh below the breast. Standing up, he said, "We must get her to hospital."

"Hospital?" It was a whispered word from Nathaniel, and the doctor said, "Yes. You won't be able to get her clean with soap and water, and I'm afraid she'll be ill for some time, if only with shock." The doctor now looked at the policeman who had already taken out a notebook, and he said grimly, "I hope you get your details right." And the policeman said, "I will that, sir, I will that. Never in me life have I seen anything like it. Whoever did this should swing."

And Timothy's mind yelled at him, "And they might yet. Oh, yes, they might yet. Oh! Anna. Anna. Oh, my dearest Anna."

The doctor was saying, "It's a question of how we're going to get her in. She should be laid out on something flat."

"Can you put her in the carriage?"

The doctor looked at Timothy now and said, "That would be very awkward, sir, especially with the mess she's in."

"Never mind about the mess."

A voice from the crowd shouted, "Me flat cart an' horse is in the road, sir. It's high with hay but that can be dumped. You're welcome."

"Thank you," the doctor called. "Can you back it in here?"

"Aye, if the people'll move."

The people moved and the horse and cart was backed almost up to Anna's side, and she was lifted on to it by Nathaniel and Timothy. And when Timothy said, "I'll sit beside her, Nathaniel," Nathaniel raised his hand and answered quietly, "No; you get in the carriage, sir, I'll sit beside her." And Timothy, admitting to the prerogative of the father, went to the carriage now with the doctor and the policeman, and the carriage followed the flat cart in the long twilight as they took the road to Fellburn and the hospital, leaving a subdued and not a little fearful village behind them.

FOUR

*T*he following day the police arrested Arthur Lennon and Davey Carter as they were about to board a boat they had signed on at South Shields. The boat was bound for Bergen.

Later in the day a cab arrived in the village, holding two policemen and an inspector, to arrest one Betty Carter for her being implicated in a most atrocious attack on a young girl.

The village was quiet, people spoke in undertones. The King's Head was full that night but The Swan was practically empty. The blacksmith and his son, the painter Willie Melton and his son, and a number of others were all conspicuous by their absence from The Swan. There was recalled in the village the conversation that had taken place one evening in the inn about tarring and feathering, and those who laughed about it.

In the King's Head the conversation was quiet as the events of the day were gone over. It was said that all the lass's family had remained at the hospital most of the night; the younger girl hadn't been to work that day nor the boy to the farm; and Mr. Timothy had been at the hospital too. It was also said that Mr. Simon from the Manor had been to the hospital. It was surmised that it was touch and go for the lass. If she didn't come round it would be a hanging job for two, that was sure. As for Betty Carter, well, she only put the feathers on her so it could be just a long stretch. But whichever way it went, this village would never be the same again. Why couldn't they have left them in the Hollow, alone? They had done nobody any harm; in fact, in some ways they had done good. Look how they had taken those families off the moor. It was only four years ago that two old people and some bairns died out there. And did anybody really believe the lass had broken up the couple in the Manor? It was known as loud as the headlines in a newspaper that those two had been at each other's throats ever since returning from their honeymoon. Betty Carter herself used to bring news in on her days off. As for the lass being free an' all with Mr. Timothy, was it likely, seeing he had those fits? Everybody knew he was a book-learned man and her being a teacher like her dad, well they would have something in common, wouldn't they? But young Lennon had always been a vicious type. His father and Jack . . . well, they did the talking, but give them their due, they weren't vicious. No, a voice had put in, they were just the ones that passed on the tinder to set the fire alight, and he had actually done it to their barn, hadn't he? And yes, they all agreed that was right, that was right.

And so it went on, and from day to day now, while everyone waited.

When, a week later, the news spread through the village that the lass had sort of woken up and it was thought she might live, the majority drew in long breaths and said quietly, "Well, thank God for that! There'll be no swingin' job, no matter what else." It only took a swingin' job to get a village a very bad name; and there were families in this village that went back to the last century, such as the Wattses . . . But then, of course, they had to leave. But Miss Penelope Smythe, her people went back a longer way, as did Dan Wallace's. And yes, the grocer's, John Fenton. Oh yes, the grocer; his wife Gladys was always yapping about ancestry. You would think they had made the village. One thing they had done, they had rooked it with their grocery charges. You could buy some of the stuff at only half the price in Fellburn. Gladys was crafty: she knew only too well you had to get to Fellburn and back, and if you hadn't a gig or a trap, that was tuppence on the carrier cart and extra if you had livestock. Oh, the Fentons knew what they were about. Still, all those in the King's Head were glad to know that the lass had woken up.

Timothy's carriage drew up outside his house, with Simon following on horseback. After alighting, they went inside together, and the first words the butler said were, "How is she, sir?"

"She's still very low but she's holding her own."

"That's good news, sir." Then looking from one to the other, he enquired, "Is it something hot or a glass of wine you'll be taking, sir?"

Timothy now looked at Simon, and Simon said, "A brandy would be acceptable."

"And for me, too."

A little while later they were settled in the sitting-room and after no words had passed between them for some minutes, Simon, suddenly getting to his feet, walked to the window, saying, "I know how you are going to respond, but I must say it: she's suffered this indignity and terror for things she hasn't done; so she wouldn't have suffered any worse if she had done them. In fact, it wouldn't have happened."

"You mean, if she had fallen in with your wishes and become your mistress?"

Simon swung round now, saying, "Yes. Yes, I do, Tim. That's exactly what I mean."

"Well, she refused you, didn't she? And she'll always refuse you."

"We'll see about that."

"You won't! You won't, Simon. You won't."

"Who's to stop me? You."

"Yes, if I can."

"You would ask her to marry you?"

Timothy's mouth went into a hard line now as he looked at the other man. "No," he said; "because I wouldn't ask anyone to marry me. But she trusts me. I am her friend. She listens to what I say. And if it's the last thing I do I'll prevent her from following the pattern of her mother. However, there will be no need; she won't have you. At one time she might have had some feelings for you, in the way you imagine she still has, but I'm sure it's no more. What happened to kill it, for I think it is dead, I don't know. But something did happen: perhaps you know what, apart from your having a wife."

Slowly Simon turned away and looked out of the window again, and Timothy now asked, "Have you heard anything from Penella?"

"No; only that she's living in Newcastle as near Raymond as possible. Not that that's going to do her much good."

"I've always thought you were wrong in that direction, Simon. If she had thought so much of Raymond she would have married him when he gave her the child. It was you she wanted and has always wanted. Her chasing Raymond was to stir you up. And it did, but in the wrong way. She wasn't prepared for that. And I must say this: if you had been of a more forgiving nature from the beginning, your life together would have been quite different from what it has turned out to be. The very fact that you could forgive her would have proved your love for her."

"Oh, shut up!" Simon now reached out, took up his half-empty glass from the table, threw off the remainder of the brandy, and said, "I must be on my way. But thank you, dear uncle, for your kind advice."

"You are very welcome, nephew," Timothy answered in the same vein; then added, "You can see yourself out."

But on nearing the door, Simon turned and, looking at Timothy, then round the room, he said, "I envy you this place, you know."

"I know you do; and not only that but my liberty, too."

"Huh! You're a clever old stick, aren't you?"

"Oh, yes. Perhaps not so much clever as old, being nine years your senior."

Simon went out on a harsh laugh and Timothy walked to the window, to see him emerge from the house and mount his horse, and the sight of the smart, lithe figure riding down the drive swept away the assurance he had assumed just a few minutes ago. Will she? he thought; and he answered himself, Yes, she might. Having suffered this indignity, this terrible indignity, she might think, What does anything matter any more? But whatever she should decide to do, life would never be the same for her again.

Anna was in hospital for three weeks and in a convalescent home for two further weeks, the latter having been arranged by Miss Netherton. Then, on the day they brought her home it was into a house full of flowers and with the long table covered with gifts, in the middle of which was a large arrangement of fruit in a high-handled decorative basket trimmed with ribbon.

There were even presents from some of the villagers, as Maria pointed out: ginger cake, jam preserve, a box of homemade toffees; then the large boxes all tied up with ribbon: some, her mother pointed out, were from Mr. Simon and Mr. Timothy and others from the boys and Miss Netherton. And placed among all these were pretty cards wishing her well.

Anna had expressed her thanks quietly and in just a few words.

This was what was troubling the family: she didn't talk any more like she used to do. It was now more than five weeks since that awful time, but as the doctor said, it could be further weeks or perhaps months before she would really be herself again. Again and again he would say she was a lucky girl to be alive at all. And if she hadn't been taken to hospital and treated straightaway she would never have survived.

Unfortunately, they'd had to cut off some of her hair; it had been impossible to get it clear of the tar. And now the ends reached only to her shoulders. Yet, if anything, it seemed to enhance her face. In a strange way, though, it didn't seem to make her any younger as such a crop usually did, for her features appeared to have aged. She could have been a woman in her thirties.

She listened to the buzz of conversation around her, but didn't appear to hear any particular thing that was being said. Her mind seemed to have undergone a change: it no longer picked up and dealt with present issues, but would wander back into the past when she was young, when she was a girl sitting in the barn learning her lessons in the summer-time; or in the winter, hurriedly clearing the long table of the breakfast dishes and spreading the books out and looking across at her dada's bright face as he would laughingly say, "We will now call the register. Benjamin Dagshaw."

"Pesent, sir."

And her father would say yet again, "As I have informed you, Benjamin Dagshaw, you may be a peasant but that 'pesent' is *present.*" And there would be laughter. Then: "James Dagshaw."

"Present, sir, all of me."

More laughter.

"Cherry Dagshaw."

"I am not all here, sir; my heart's in the highlands."

"Your heart will be in your mouth, madam, in a moment."

"Annabel Dagshaw."

"I am all yours, sir."

Often such remarks would come later, but always they brought laughter with the lesson . . .

"What are you smiling at, dear?"

She looked up at Maria. "Was I smiling, Ma?" she said.

"Yes, you were. You must have been thinking something nice. What was it?"

"Oh, I don't know . . . Ma?"

"Yes, dear?"

"I would like to go to bed."

"Then you shall go to bed. It's been a very trying day."

Timothy had left earlier, feeling that she would want to spend a quiet time with her family. Miss Netherton, too, had left with him, having said in an aside to Maria, "I'll come over tomorrow morning. I have news for you."

Now there were only Cherry, Jimmy, and Olan. Oswald had had to remain in the shop for, as he had said, someone must keep things going. But he had sent Anna a book by the poet Tennyson, entitled *Ballads and other Poems.*

So Maria and Cherry had helped to undress her and tuck her up in bed. And when, later, Nathaniel came in, he stood by her side and, taking hold of her limp hand, he said, "You are home, my dear, and I hope never to leave it."

And at this Anna closed her eyes and her mind left her childhood dreaming and leapt ahead into the everlasting future, during which time she would never again leave this house.

FIVE

$\mathscr{I}$t was at the end of August when Arthur Lennon and David Carter, together with Beatrice Carter, were brought before the Justice in Newcastle to answer to the heinous crime that Arthur had committed against a young girl, which could have led to his being tried for the capital crime of murder had she not recovered.

His Lordship, John Makepeace Preston, sentenced Arthur Lennon to five years' hard labour, and David Carter, he who had aided and abetted him, to four years' hard labour, and Beatrice Carter, who had put the final touches on the outrageous and indecent act, three years in the House of Correction. And Arthur John Wallace, the boy who had been subjected to such fearful threats, which had now left him with defective speech not previously apparent, referred to as a stammer, the Justice commended for coming forward and speaking in detail about that which he had witnessed was being carried out by these three vicious people; and also for how he had related, albeit most painfully, the threat made to his person by the prisoner, Arthur Lennon.

There had been no response from anyone in the courtroom when the sentence was passed on Lennon, but when the Justice sentenced both David Carter and his sister, their mother had stood up and screamed, "They didn't do it! They didn't do it! He made them. You can't send her along the line."

After she was evicted from the courtroom, it was noted that her son stood with bowed head and shoulders, while Arthur Lennon stood white-faced and with his eyes glaring, yet his body was trembling as if he were under shock. As for Betty Carter, it would have been expected of her that her face would have been awash with tears, but she remained dry-eyed and tight-lipped. And when the wardress held her shoulder, it was seen that she tried to shrug off her hand.

All the proceedings were related to Maria in various ways by Miss

Netherton, Timothy, and Oswald. Nathaniel, Maria noted, said very little except, "Justice has been done. For once, justice has been done . . ."

Miss Netherton hadn't come the following morning, as promised, to give them her news because her house had been stormed by the blacksmith, his son, and Mr. and Mrs. Carter; also by Willie Melton and his son Dirk and the landlord of The Swan, Reg Morgan, and his wife Lily, for they had all that day been given notice to quit their premises. "Why," had demanded Reg Morgan and Willie Melton, "are we being made to suffer for what the Lennons have done, and the Carters an' all?"

This had caused an argument between the two groups outside the house, and when she appeared at her door with Stoddart on one side of her and Peter Tollis on the other, Miss Netherton told the Meltons that they had been included in the evictions on good authority: they had been inciters in what had happened, together with the innkeeper and his wife. And at this Reg Morgan yelled, "You can't put us out. We were engaged by the brewery."

"Then let the brewery find you other premises. That inn belongs to me, as do the other houses. If you feel you have been wronged, there is always the law. Go and take it up and see how far you will get."

When Willie Melton began to plead and say he was sorry that he had opened his mouth, she stared at him, then stepped back and said to Stoddart, "Come in and close the door."

So the village was once more up in arms, at least in part. However, the four families found they were getting little sympathy from the rest of the inhabitants. But this did not stop the blacksmith from going into the inn that night and saying he wasn't going to lie down under this; he would go to a newspaper and get them to print why all this had happened. And why had it happened? Because, as the parson had said, those two had lived in sin and had bred a family in sin and one of them had followed in the footsteps of her mother, and it was she who had brought tragedy on the village with her antics.

But it was Dan Wallace who stood up to him again and boldly asked who had set fire to the barn all those years ago? Who had crippled the goat? Who had got together a mob to try to scare the wits out of them? And who had set the man-trap? As for him going to a newspaper, the newspapers had had a field day about the case already. What had the headlines said? "Innocent girl near death through the spite of villagers. The first case ever to have been heard in this part of the country of a female being tarred and feathered." And what did they predict? It could be a hanging case if she died. And it was lucky for him and his son and the other two that she had survived. And to his mind the sentences were light.

When this counter-attack brought no support for the blacksmith he had stormed out of the bar and made for the vicarage. But there his reception was cool, and this enraged the man further. He reminded the parson that last Sunday he had preached that the sins of the fathers were passed on to the children even to the third and fourth generation . . .

It was ten days later when Miss Netherton visited the house in the afternoon. The weather had changed: there were squally showers and it had turned cold. And when she entered the room where Anna was sitting in the big chair before the blazing fire, her first words were, "Oh, isn't that a welcome sight! There's a lot to be said for the winter." Then taking Anna's hand, she said, "How are you feeling, my dear?"

"All right, thank you; much better."

"That's good. That's good." Then turning to where both Nathaniel and Maria were standing, she said, "Sit down. Please sit down and I'll sit here next to Anna and tell you my news. At last, at last, it is settled." And as she took her seat she added, "Well, it was settled some time ago, but I never believe in any business deal until it is in writing, stamped with a red seal or the money is in the bank. And in this case the money is almost in the bank." And at this she opened her beaded bag and took out an envelope from which she withdrew a letter and a cheque, which she passed to Maria, saying, "Read that." And when Maria had read it, she said, "Oh, my goodness! Oh! Miss Netherton," before passing it to Nathaniel, who gazed at it, then looked at the spruce, neat figure of his benefactress, murmuring in amazement, "I can't believe it." Then bending towards Anna, he said, "Look at that, my dear." And when Anna read the amount she slowly lifted her eyes and looked at Miss Netherton, and in almost a whisper said, "Seven thousand, two hundred and fifty pounds! Oh, Miss Netherton."

"Well—" Miss Netherton took the cheque from her fingers, put it back into the sheet of writing paper, tapping it as she did so and saying, "This is the amount after all their bits and pieces have been taken off. I told you they would all get their cuts." And again looking at Maria, she said, "The cross was sold to a private dealer in Amsterdam, so I'm told, for ten thousand pounds. You can guess what it's really worth."

"I can't believe it. I just can't believe it."

"Well, my dear, you can, you can. Now the agreement was we would share this. That means we should have three thousand, six hundred and twenty-five pounds each. But let me be practical. I have already given you five hundred pounds, and this deducted from your share leaves you with three thousand, one hundred and twenty-five pounds. Isn't that right? Oh, Maria, Maria, don't cry so. This is a happy event."

"I can't believe it. And . . . and you are so good. You really needn't have done anything about it. We needn't have heard another word, yet you go to all this trouble."

"It was no trouble. You have no idea how I've enjoyed myself over this transaction. Why, when I was in Holland I went about and saw and met people I never imagined I would meet up with in my life, and they were all gentlemen. Oh, yes, the Dutch are very courteous and so wonderfully interesting. And they nearly all spoke English, which was just as well. So, I've got a lot to thank you for because *I* didn't come across that exquisite piece of work, did I? And you, too, Nathaniel, smile please. Come on. We've had enough sorrow about lately, let us rejoice in this piece of good fortune. And you know something?" She was now wagging her finger at Maria, who was wiping her face with the hem of her white apron. "I have never yet come in this house without within five minutes of my arrival being offered a drink of some sort, nearly always a cup of tea. And here I am bearing gifts"—she pulled a face at herself now—"and not a drop am I offered." The last was said in an Irish twang. And when Maria rose hastily to her feet, saying, "Oh,

Miss Netherton, Miss Netherton," and then bent quickly towards her and kissed her on the cheek, the older woman kept swallowing for a moment before she said, "Go on with you! Go on, I want a strong cup of tea. And Nathaniel, look, it is raining and heavily, so would you mind telling Stoddart to take the contraption into your barn, and then bring him into the kitchen for a drink. Will you?"

When they had the room to themselves, Miss Netherton, now taking hold of Anna's hand, said, "I wish my news could have altered the look in your eyes, my dear. But no money in the world will do that. The only person who can do that is yourself. And now I want you to promise to try and put the past behind you, because never again will you be treated as you have been. I can assure you of that. And then there is your future. We shall have to think about that. Is there anything you want to do?"

Anna shook her head slowly, then said, "I cannot think ahead. I don't seem able to think at all."

"Oh, my dear, that feeling will pass. But we must find something for you to do. Timothy was saying that you might like to go and study in some ladies' college?"

The faintest of smiles came on Anna's face as she said, "He said that?"

"Yes, and much more. Oh, he is indeed worried about you. You are so dear to him. Anna—" She now took hold of Anna's hand and, looking into her face, she said, "Tim is a very special person. Do you know that? Have you yet found that out?"

After a pause Anna said, "Yes. Yes, I have. I've never met anyone as kind as him in my life, except yourself."

The answer seemed to make Miss Netherton impatient for a moment, for she dropped Anna's hands, sat back in her chair and said, "Oh, dear me." And Anna said, "Why do you say, Oh dear me, like that?"

"Oh, it doesn't matter just at the moment. I'll talk about it later when you're feeling stronger. And you know, you're not going to get strong sitting in that chair. I know the weather is inclement but there'll be some nice days ahead and you must get out and walk."

In answer to this Anna said, "I haven't seen Timothy since shortly after I returned home."

"Well, you wouldn't, because he's gone to London."

"London? He didn't say."

"Well, he didn't tell you because you weren't in any fit state to listen to him or to anybody else when you first came home. But you see, his book's been accepted."

"His book?" Anna pulled herself up straighter in the chair. "I didn't know he had written a book; he said he just scribbled."

"Oh, yes, he always says he just scribbles. But he's written a book on the Renaissance period. He's very interested in that period of history, and it's going to be published."

"Really?" Anna turned her head away now, saying, "He's never mentioned it."

"He's a very humble person, is Tim, too humble for his own good . . . too thoughtful for his own good. He deprecates himself just because of the one little handicap he's got. And, after all, it is a little handicap. The unfortunate thing about it is he doesn't know when it's going to hit him. But to my mind, otherwise it is of no great importance. So, my dear, yes, he is going to have a book published. He will likely tell you all about it when he returns. It's been in the publisher's hands for some weeks now and, reading between the lines of what he's saying, they seem to think highly of it. Not that I got much out of him about it."

Half dreamily now, Anna said, "Strange that he never mentioned it to me. We talked such a lot about books and authors and the Renaissance period. He used to speak of Dante, and then of the influence of Machiavelli and of the return to Classical learning. 'Tis strange."

"Ah, here's that cup of tea." Miss Netherton turned towards Maria, who was carrying in a tray holding four cups of tea, and as she put the tray down, she said, "Nathaniel has taken a cup out to Stoddart, Miss Netherton. He said he'd better stay with the horse; it seemed rather uneasy being put in a strange place."

After sipping from the cup, Miss Netherton said, "I've always said, Maria, you make a very good cup of tea." Then she added, "Ah! there you are, Nathaniel," as he entered the room. "I know what I wanted to say to both of you. It's this: I don't know what you intend to do with the money, but one of the first things I would suggest is you get yourselves a horse and trap now that the fences are down. And by the way, I can tell you that both Raymond Brodrick and his future father-in-law, Albert Morgansen, have been pulled over the coals for that piece of law-breaking. John Preston got his solicitors to rake from the archives old laws and those two had to pull their horns in when they were confronted with them. There are land-enclosure laws and land-enclosure laws, and those two didn't do their homework. Of course, it was mostly Praggett's doing, I suppose. Anyway, what about the horse and trap?"

Nathaniel looked at Maria and she at him, and they both smiled and Nathaniel said, "Yes, that is a marvellous suggestion. It will certainly be one of the first things we do."

"And secondly, what about you both taking a holiday, away by yourselves? I can see to this young lady here, and the rest of the family are quite able to see to themselves. Of course, I know you'll have to mull over that one, but think about it. And, of course, what I must ask you is, have you any choice of bank into which you'd like to put your money? If you decide it should go into mine, then I will take you both down and introduce you to the manager. He will then explain where best it would be to invest whatever part of it you would like to earn a little interest. Anyway, that will all be explained to you. So, will tomorrow be convenient for you?"

"Oh, Miss Netherton, any time, any time you care to take us in," said Nathaniel now. "And I can say this, neither of us will live long enough to thank you for all you have done for us."

Miss Netherton looked to the side now and upwards as she said, "It's odd what money can do. It's odd what locks it can oil, what doors it can open. If only everybody used it for the good. But there, it's not time for preaching and I must away." She rose to her feet; then turning to Anna, she said, "Remember what I told you. Get out in the air as soon as the weather changes, and walk. Walk over to my place every day. Yes, that's a good idea. I'll expect you every day."

"I will. I will in a short while."

Anna didn't get up from her seat but she watched her parents escort her dear friend out of the house. Then, her head dropping back, she closed her eyes as she said to herself, "Get out and walk. Get out and walk." She didn't care if she never walked again. She just wanted to sit still in this limbo into which she had been thrust. She couldn't see that anything which might happen in the future could arouse her interest ever again. She was dead inside. She had died when that tar brush swept down the front of her body and he had pushed it between her legs.

SIX

It had rained for days; then had come a muggy period: there were mists in the morning, with the sun trying to get through a haze, followed by damp, cold nights. Anna could not often take a walk of any length, but she spent quite a bit of her time now in the barn or the tack-room or in the new stable that had been erected to house the nine-year-old horse they had acquired, whose spruceness had made Neddy look a very poor relation indeed, and whose harness had to be kept burnished. The advantage of doing these chores was that in the main she could be on her own.

Twice during short spells Timothy had brought the carriage over and taken her back to the house, and she had enjoyed these breaks in the monotonous routine. But even so, he had done much of the talking, telling her about London and the publisher and making light and fun of what the critics might say about his book, which was to be published in the coming spring. On the last occasion he had driven her home, and just before they alighted, he had taken her hand and said, "Oh, Anna, Anna, come back." She didn't need to ask, Come back from where? she knew what he meant.

Today she was sitting in the tack-room rubbing a wax mixture into the harness when the door opened and Jimmy appeared, which made her say immediately, "You're back early. Anything wrong?"

"I . . . I asked if I could come away. I've . . . I've had the runs all day and I'm not feeling too good . . . You shouldn't be doing that; it's hard work, that."

"A little bit of hard work won't hurt me."

"Dada or Ma always does it."

"Yes, but they're busy."

He sat down on an upturned box, then asked quietly, "Have they given you any of the cash they came into from our unknown grandmother? I thought she had died years ago; and then our grandfather married again, which was why Ma couldn't lay claim to Low Meadow after he died."

She looked at him in surprise: "No. No," she said. "Why do you ask?"

"Just thinkin'. We've been kept in the dark about lots of things, while the fact of our beginnings has been thumped into us. And now this money business that they are being close about."

"Well, you have your wage, and they take only half of it now."

"Aye. Aye, that's right. But I must tell you, Anna, I'm leaving for sure."

"Oh, Jimmy! Please."

"I've got to, Anna. There's something inside of me raging to be away. Anyway, I've shot me bolt: I gave him me notice, I'm not bonded. A month, I said. He doesn't believe I've got the bellyache; thinks I'm gettin' a bit uppish because I asked to come off early."

"They're going to be upset." She motioned with her hand towards the door.

"Oh, I don't know. You know, I once said to you, as long as they've got themselves, that's all they need. And I'm more convinced of that than ever. You could have died. Any of us could have died and they would have missed us and mourned us, but if one of them were to go the other would go an' all."

"Why do you think like this, Jimmy?"

"Don't you?"

She allowed her gaze to fall on to the harness, then said, "You're bitter about something. You didn't used to be."

"Aye, perhaps I am, but I can see nothing ahead here. I want to get away, escape. And there's another one that'll be escaping shortly, and that's Oswald. He's sweet on the daughter." He laughed, but then put his hand to his stomach, saying, "Here I go again," and turned to leave, and she said, "How long have you been feeling like this?"

"Oh, since the day afore yesterday."

"You could have picked something up in the market."

He halted at the door and turned and looked at her, and she said, "What is it?" But he shook his head and went out.

Jimmy couldn't go to work the next day. He had bad diarrhoea and headache, and Anna said to Maria in the afternoon, "You should call the doctor." But Maria said, "It's only a bout of diarrhoea; he will eat apples before they're ripe."

"Ma, I think Jimmy should have the doctor. He's bad."

"All right, all right, girl. You've all had diarrhoea at one time or another. It's the season of the year."

"I thought the season for a loose bowel was in the Spring."

"Oh, it could come any time; it all depends on what you eat, but if it will ease your mind, dear, I'll get your dada to go for the doctor . . ."

Nathaniel was lucky. He caught the doctor actually coming out of a house in the village and when he told him his boy had diarrhoea the doctor had looked at him hard and said immediately, "Well, let's get away."

He was now standing in the kitchen, his two hands on his black bag which he had placed on the table, and he was saying, "I'm sorry to tell you the lad's got cholera. There's one case in the village and a number in the town. And more in Gateshead Fell. It started there again. It's the water. They've built a blooming hospital for the cases, when what they should be doing is preventing anybody going into it. It's clean water everybody wants. Now, you get your water from the pump, don't you?"

No one answered him.

"Well, boil every drop of it, every drop. And let's hope the lad's a light case. Who have you got coming home?"

After a short intake of breath Nathaniel said, "My daughter. She works for the Praggetts."

"Well, get word to her. Tell her to stay there."

"And tomorrow my two eldest sons come in from Gateshead. And there's a young man sleeps in the barn."

"Oh, you must put a stop to that. Get word to them." He now bit on his lower lip, saying, "Well, you'd better all stay put. I myself will call at Praggett's on my way back home. Where do you say your sons work?"

When Nathaniel told him, Anna put in, "Mr. Barrington, he knows where the shop is; he would get word to them if you asked him."

"I'll do that. I have to pass his house so I'll call in on my way. Now do what I tell you: boil the water, then wash everything that comes in contact with him. There's no need to worry; he's a strong fellow. They can get through better than some. Well, I'm away. We're probably in for another bad patch, as this has spread from the towns. I thought we had seen the last of it years ago. They've hardly got over the smallpox scare, and now this. Well, I must away. I'll call in tomorrow or the next day if possible. But you can't do very much, only what I've told you." And as he was going out of the door he asked, "Where do you bury your slops?"

"In the cesspool at the far end of the land."

"Any running water near it?"

They exchanged glances, and then Nathaniel said, "There's a tinkle of a stream goes by. It comes out of a boulder."

"Do you use that often?"

Maria now put in, "For washing the clothes. Yes, I often do; it seems fresh."

"Where do you take it from? Where it's running along the ground? or where it's coming out of the stone?"

She paused before she said, "Well, some way from the boulder, where it's about three feet wide; at times it's a good foot deep."

"Well, from now on, take it from the boulder. But boil it, always boil it. It's likely picked up less infection from its source than it will have done in passing the cesspool."

"Oh, it isn't all that near."

"Doesn't matter, be on the safe side. Good day to you now. And the best of luck with the lad."

They all looked stunned, yet Anna was asking herself, Why? because she had guessed what was wrong with Jimmy when he had turned and looked at her in the doorway of the tack-room, after she had asked when he had been to the market.

"Cholera. Cholera, that's all we need now. Another affliction. Why?"

Both Anna and Maria looked at Nathaniel and he, looking at Anna, said, "Fate never lets up, does it?"

Four days later, it looked as if Jimmy might be about to take a turn for the better: his diarrhoea had eased, he hadn't been sick once during the day. And now it was one o'clock in the morning.

Anna sat by his bedside. A candle was burning under the cover of a red glass globe, giving a warm glow to the room, which was hers and Cherry's room. For the last three nights she had sat here, sleeping some part of the day, during which time Nathaniel and Maria took over. But the strain was now showing on them, especially on Maria, for Jimmy had to be changed every two hours or so and his nightshirt and the sheets washed. There was a perpetual mist of steam in the long room, where the linen was hung round the fire which Nathaniel kept going.

The only one any of them had been in contact with, and then at a distance, was Timothy. He brought food, medical supplies and extra linen. These he put over the fence, for when he called on that first evening after the doctor had given him the news, Anna had raised her voice for the first time in weeks and yelled at him, "Stay where you are! Don't come in! Please! Please!" And so each day he had come to the railings and left milk and oddments of food, such as jars of calf's foot jelly, a cooked chicken and fresh bread.

When Jimmy stirred, she picked up a wet cloth from a number piled on a plate to her side and placed it across his sweating brow. When his lids lifted and he looked at her she said, "Try to sleep, dear. You'll feel better in the morning. It'll soon be over."

"Yes, Anna, 'twill soon be over."

"Now, now! Jimmy."

"Anna."

"Yes, my dear."

"I . . . I'm going to be free."

She said nothing but stared down into the rose-coloured palor of his face, which at the moment looked like that of an old man.

"I am."

"Now, now! Jimmy. Be quiet."

He gasped before he said, "No time, Anna." Then again he repeated her name, "Anna."

"Yes? Yes, my dear?"

"Escape. You escape, soon, or else . . . else they'll not let . . . you . . . go. They'll . . . they'll cling on."

"Oh Jimmy, Jimmy."

"Go . . . escape. Escape . . . they'll want someone . . . to . . . to look after them. 'Twill be you. Selfish, yes . . . yes, selfish. Get away . . . Anna."

"Jimmy, please! You don't know really what you're saying, dear. Now go to sleep."

"Love you, Anna. Love you."

"Yes, and I love you, too, Jimmy. You'll be better in the morning. Doctor said you're on the turn."

He closed his eyes and made a sound like a sigh, and she said, "That's it. Go to sleep."

She sat now gently stroking his square hand. The hand that had been calloused and hard up till a few days ago now seemed as soft as a child's. It lay limp in hers, and she kept her eyes on it as her own hand moved over it. For how long she sat like this she couldn't remember, but something in the hand seemed to change and caused her to look at her brother's face. It seemed unchanged, just as if he was sleeping. Yet no; his eyes were half open. She gave a gasp, then let out a low moan: "Oh! Jimmy. Jimmy. *No! No! No!* The doctor said you were . . . Oh! Jimmy, Jimmy. Oh, my God!" She now took his face between her hands, and when she released her hold the head lolled to the side. She covered her eyes, then dropped forward over the slim, depleted body under the sheets, murmuring all the time, "Oh! Jimmy. Jimmy."

When finally she stood up she was amazed at the feeling of calmness in herself and, looking down on him, she said, "You did it. You did what you wanted to do, you escaped. Oh, my dear, dear."

Turning now, she lifted up the candlestick with the red glass shade attached and left the room to go to her parents" door. But she didn't knock. Walking straight into the room, she held the light above her head and looked down on them. They were lying face to face, and her father's hand was on the coverlet and resting on her mother's shoulder. She said quietly, "Dada."

She had to say his name three times before he turned on his back, looked at her, then pulled himself upwards, saying, "What is it? What is it?"

"Jimmy has gone," she said simply.

On hearing these words, it seemed that her mother sprang out of the bed, that they both sprang out of the bed. She watched them rush from the room, and slowly she followed them. At the door of the bedroom she put the candle on top of the chest of drawers and it showed up them both lying over their son's body.

She turned and went out and down the long room and blew the fire embers into a blaze.

"Get away," he had said. "Escape. Get away. Or they'll keep you here to look after them." Well, would that be such a bad thing?

Yes. Yes! The cry in her head startled her; but she turned to see her father come staggering down the room. He was in his nightshirt and he too looked an old man. She watched him drop into a chair by the table and rest his head on his hands, and then she heard him say, "The sins of the father indeed shall be visited on the children and the children's children even to the third and fourth generations." Then turning his head slowly towards her, he said, "I always knew we should have to pay. Which one will He take next?"

SEVEN

𝒯here was no formal funeral for Jimmy. They came in a black hearse and took him away, as they also did Stan Cole, the butcher's son from the village.

Two days later Maria went down with it and Nathaniel seemed to enter a period of madness. For four nights and days he hardly left her side. And Anna seemed to spend her whole life running between the bedroom and the cesspool. The doctor said to her, "Let up, girl. Let up." And his voice was harsh when he spoke to Nathaniel, saying, "There's other things to be done besides sitting beside the bed. Your daughter will be next if she doesn't get help." And Nathaniel, after apparently coming out of a daze, said, "I'm sorry, I'm sorry; but I can't lose Maria. I can't lose her."

And to this the doctor replied, "You'll lose them both if you're not careful, and yourself an' all."

"That would make no odds, because if she goes I go."

It was the evening of the fourth night that he left the bedroom and came into the long room and sat at the little desk and began to write.

As Anna passed him for the countless time with the emptied pail, he stopped her and said, "I hadn't made a will but I've written it down here. If we should go"—he didn't say, If your mother should go, or, If I should go, but, If we should go—"the house and the money in the bank will go to Oswald and Olan. They'll look after you. Cherry will be all right; Bobby will take care of her."

She put the pail down on the floor and stared at him, and he turned to her and said, "What is it?"

She couldn't tell him. She couldn't say to him, "You're leaving me in care of the boys; you're not saying to me, there is fifty pounds, or a hundred pounds, or two hundred pounds, you're leaving me in care of the boys. I am to grow old here in this house . . . in care of the boys. They could get married and come and live here. You have even thought of Cherry's future. Bobby will take care of her, you said. So you know what's been going on. But me, your beloved daughter, so I thought, you have left in care of the boys." With a quick jerk she lifted the pail and hurried from him. And he went after her, and at the bedroom door he stopped her, saying, "I could not live without your mother. Don't you understand?"

Yes. Yes, she understood. She understood that an intelligent, caring father could have quite another side to him. Intelligent he was, naturally, but caring was because he wanted them all around him as protection from the outer world and its condemnation. As he had bred each one he hadn't thought of their future, only of his needs of the moment. She had thought him advanced in his thinking, on a par with Timothy, but now, females still had their place, and it was subordinate to men's. She passed him and went in to her mother. On this occasion he did not follow her, but went back down the room again.

As she sat by the bed, Maria turned her head and looked at her. "Look after your father," she said. "Promise me you'll look after your father. He'll need you. Stay with him."

When Anna made no reply, Maria said, "Promise me?"

Still she made no answer; and then Maria, her hand coming out and groping for hers, said between gasps. "Don't . . . don't marry . . . that man. Don't . . . don't saddle yourself. Far better . . . take what . . . the other . . . one offers."

Anna couldn't really believe her ears. She withdrew her hand from her mother's grasp and stood up. Her mother was saying, "Do what I did. Don't marry a good man because he has fits." She had the most awful desire to shout, "I'd marry him tomorrow if he asked me, but he never will, and I know it. And I'll tell you something else. I love him and if he asked me to live with him, I'd do it. But not the other one. Never!"

Nathaniel came into the room now and, looking at her, he said, "What's wrong? Is she worse?"

Anna stepped aside but said nothing, and Maria put her hand out to Nathaniel, and he gripped it and sat down by her side. Anna left the room and went outside into the fresh morning air. The mugginess had gone and there had been a frost in the night and she took in great gulps of air while telling herself not to let go, for she knew there was something in her head on the point of snapping.

EIGHT

Maria did not die. From that night on, she slowly recovered. Perhaps, Anna thought later, it was because she had refused to conform to her mother's wishes and she couldn't bear the thought of her beloved husband being left without someone to take care of him. Although her father had always been handy in making odd things with wood, he was more proficient in directing others to do the chores. He had never made a meal for himself, nor washed a crock nor swept a floor. And she hadn't seen him even set a fire. Either her mother had done it, or she, or one of the boys.

The first day it was considered safe for the others to return to the house was one she tried to forget, for the boys cried and Cherry cried and Bobby Crane cried, and her mother cried and her father cried, all over Jimmy's going. But *she* didn't cry, for all the while she looked at them hugging each other, she could hear Jimmy's voice saying, "Get yourself away. Escape." Odd, when she came to think back. Jimmy knew his parents, the other side of them, the selfish side, the side she had never guessed at. But what she tried to tell herself, and kindly, was, it was all part of one's human nature. Yet she had to force herself to feel sympathetically towards them now.

When one after another asked her how she was, she knew they were referring to her long convalescence, not to when she had been dragged up out of it and forced to be run off her feet these last weeks.

Their mother was better, their father was here. Oswald and Olan had been out of harm's way, going about their business, as had Bobby, living in the room above the boathouse; and, of course, Cherry, in the Praggett fortress. But what she was to remember about the family reunion was her father, standing at the door of the house, looking first up into the sky, then across into the far distance as he cried dramatically. "Why had my second son to be taken when that woman over there who killed my last born is spared?" And Oswald had said, "What Dada. She got it too?"

"Yes, I understood she got it too, and so bad she landed up in Gateshead cholera hospital. Yet she is spared and brought back to live in comfort. There's no justice."

This had been news to Anna, which brought home the fact that there had hardly been any exchange of words, except those necessary for daily contact between her and her father, since the night he had written his will. It was as if, by her reactions, he knew he had failed her in some way.

The next visitor was Miss Netherton. She had commiserated with Nathaniel and Maria over Jimmy's loss, then when she was leaving, she said to Anna, "Come; walk with me to the trap, I've left it at the field gate." But once outside, she said, "What on earth has happened to you, girl? A ghost could have more substance. Tim said he was worried to death by the look of you. He's . . . he's in London again, you know."

"Yes. Yes, I know."

"He's . . . he's been simply marvellous during this dreadful time, not only in keeping you going, which I know he has, but seeing to Penella."

"Penella? Mrs. Brodrick?"

"Yes. Apparently she had written to him from Newcastle; she wanted to see him. And when he got there he was told she had already been taken to the Gateshead cholera hospital. Well, he went there and found she was in a room by herself, but he wasn't allowed in; he could see her through a glass door. She happened to catch sight of him, so he tells me, and she put out her hand towards him. I saw him shortly after this and he was upset. As he himself said, there was nothing of the grand imperious lady left. She was a very ill woman and looked a frightened one. So what does he do? He goes to Simon and tells him. I don't know what passed between them, but I guessed it was something pretty strong. I do know, through Tim, from what he said, the doctor didn't think there was much chance of her surviving. Apparently she had lain too long without attention. So Simon went. This was over a fortnight ago, and the result was she didn't die. However, and again from what Tim says, she must have got the fright of her life, because she's a very changed individual. Oh, by the way, I must tell you, the child's got a tutor and he seems to have taken to him. He's a youngish man and, as Simon said, the first words the child always utters to him are, "When are you going to bring Missanna back?" Apparently when he couldn't be consoled after you left, Simon told him you had gone to look after Uncle Tim."

"That was rather a silly thing to say, wasn't it?"

"Not so silly, when you think about it. The boy was very fond of Tim and likely it was more acceptable to the child that Tim should be the reason for your not coming. Anyway, we've got to forget about other people and concentrate on yourself. Now, what I suggest is that you come over to me and stay for a week or so, and Ethel will fatten you up."

Anna smiled softly on the elderly woman and in a low voice, she said, "You're always so kind to me, always so good and thoughtful, but . . . but on this occasion would you mind if I left your invitation open for a while? There is something at the back of my mind that I'd like to get straight."

"Such as?"

"Oh, well, I can't explain it yet."

"You could if you talked about it."

"Yes, but I want to be sure in my own mind that I can do this."

"You're thinking about taking up a course in a college?"

"No. No, not that."

"Then what?"

Anna's smile widened now as she said, "If I make up my mind to do this, you'll be the first one to know about it. I can assure you of that."

"Ah, there's a mystery here. I like mysteries. Life can be very dull without mysteries. I realised how different life could be when I was in Holland; the excitement, the meeting up with a different breed of men . . . Oh, I know. Thinking about Holland. Let me guess. Tell me if I'm right or wrong. Just give me a nod. Your father is going to provide you with enough money to start a school of your own. That's it, isn't it?"

The smile disappeared from Anna's face and her voice sounded rather cool as she said, "No, Miss Netherton. My father has never even thought along those lines, not in any way."

"What do you mean, not in any way? Has he not settled something on you?"

"No. No; not a penny; in fact I can speak to you about it, because you are my friend. But when he thought my mother was dying, he knew he would go, too. And I'm sure he would have, even if it meant taking his own life, because he couldn't live without her. He made out a rough will"—she turned her head away—"I can see him doing it now. I was going up the room with an empty slop bucket—at that period I seemed to have spent my whole life emptying nauseating slop buckets—and he turned to me and said, 'I am leaving the house and what money there is to the boys. They will look after you. Cherry will be all right; Bobby will see to her.' "

There was silence between them now. Anna watched the older woman pull the fur collar of her coat tighter under her chin and nip on her bottom lip before she said, "I am very disappointed in Nathaniel, and in Maria, too, I must say. The boys are in good positions, by all accounts. That house should be yours and enough money with which to keep it up." She turned and looked to the side and muttered, "Men! Men! Nothing really belongs to women. That cross was originally Maria's. The money that I first gave them was originally Maria's. In those days everything a woman had belonged to her man; but now, as far as I can gather, they are trying to get a law passed which will allow a married woman control of her own money or property. It's to be called the Married Woman's Property Act. Anyway, I think she should have been consulted as to how it was going to be left if anything happened to them. But then"—she shrugged her shoulders—"nobody wants to imagine that there'll come a time when they won't need what they've got; death is something that's not going to happen to them." She put out her hands now and gripped Anna's wrists, saying, "Don't worry, my dear. I'll see you won't be left in care of the boys, you know that."

"Thank you, that is comforting. And I'll always remember that offer, always, on top of remembering all you have been to me over the years. I often wonder what I would have done without you."

"My dear, that, as I am always saying, works both ways. The giver and the receiver nearly always benefit if what passes from one to the other is good. Now I will away, but"—she poked her head forward—"I'll be racking my brains to find out what is in that top storey of yours." She now tapped Anna on the brow. "And I won't rest until I find out. You know me." They parted smiling.

Anna did not return immediately to the house, but she walked through the wood and, as always, to its far end, as far as the sawing block. There she stood as she often did and looked over the moor. But today she nodded to herself as she muttered aloud, "Wait and see what happens when Oswald breaks his news, which he will do shortly. Jimmy wasn't wrong. Propriety will go to the wind now. There'll be no waiting a year in honour of the dead. He's as ready as Cherry is for marriage." Then turning swiftly about, she placed her hands on the block and bowed her head as if in shame at her thoughts. Yet, more and more these days they were facing her with facts, and facts, she had found out only too well over this past year, could be disturbing.

She had expected Timothy to return at the end of the week, but a letter arrived instead, saying that he had a little more business to do, but in the meantime he was enjoying himself and he had found that Walters was a very intelligent companion; and since at one time he had lived in London for five years, he was acting as a splendid guide, especially with regard to theatres. Only one thing could have added to his pleasure and that was her company. He hoped to see her soon, and he signed himself, "Ever your friend, Tim."

When her mother had asked whom the letter was from, she had felt like retorting, "Why ask the road you know?" but she had answered, "Mr. Barrington." Not Mr. Tim or Mr. Timothy as she usually said, but Mr. Barrington, and she had stressed the name.

It was significant that her father made no enquiries with regard to the letter, although it was he who had handed it to her, having taken it from the postman . . .

The daylight was short. They were in winter now and the long evenings became a time of excruciating tension for Anna. After the evening meal, which was often passed in silence, the depleted family would sit round the fire: Nathaniel, Maria, Cherry, and herself. Often now, Bobby would be there, too, and she noticed more and more her father welcomed Bobby's presence and he would talk more to him than to anyone else. And Bobby was very forthcoming with his news. The boatbuilder had apparently appreciated his work and had promised to keep him on as a full-time hand after he had completed his two years' apprenticeship. He had also said there were prospects for him. What they were, the boatbuilder hadn't actually said, but Bobby indicated that he had his own idea of what they might be.

As Anna sat looking from one to the other she tried to thrust her mind back to the times when most of the family were rolling on the mat with laughter as Cherry imitated the antics of Mr. Praggett; or when Jimmy had been describing the incidents on the farm, such as the day the bull butted the herdsman and he himself had to lead it into the ring. And then she, too, reading some of her funny rhymes while acting to them, and the quiet times, when her father would be reading aloud.

Where had they gone? What had happened? This house was now weighed down with misery.

Tonight she felt she couldn't stand any more, and so, rising, she said to her mother, "Would you mind if I went to bed, Ma?" And Maria said, "No. No, not at all, if you're feeling like that." And Nathaniel, looking at her, said, "Go, my dear. You need to rest."

She nodded towards Bobby, saying, "Good-night." And he said, "Good-night, Anna."

It was a good hour later when Cherry came into the bed. She was shivering and she said, "Are you asleep, Anna?" And she answered, "No, Cherry."

"Isn't it awful down there at nights?"

"Yes. Yes, it is."

"I dread coming home."

"I'm home all day, Cherry."

"Oh, yes, I know, Anna, yes, I know. And you've had a rough time of it. In all ways you've had a rough time of it. I said so to Bobby, and he said he doesn't know how you got through looking after them; I mean, Jimmy and then Ma, because Dada wouldn't be much use. Well, I mean, slops and all that."

Anna said nothing, and so they lay in silence for some time until Cherry said, "You don't talk like you used to, Anna. You're miles away most of the time, and"—her voice broke now—"and I've wanted to talk to you. I need to talk to you. Anna . . . Anna."

"Yes? What is it?"

When Anna turned round in the bed, Cherry put her arms about her and laid her head on her shoulder and she muttered something, which Anna could not make out.

"What did you say?" she said.

Then when Cherry repeated it, Anna felt herself stiffen for a moment; and yet in a way she wasn't surprised. And so, all she said was, "When did this happen?" and Cherry said, "One Sunday when I went down to see him. It was a nice room above the . . ."

Anna pulled herself away from her sister's hold, hissing now, "I don't want to know details; I mean, how long have you gone?"

"Nearly three months."

"Oh, my God! And they don't know? I mean, Ma?"

"No, no. I've wanted to tell you. Well, we didn't seem like we used to be, but I can understand, I can understand with what you've been through. But . . . but I . . . I love Bobby, and he loves me."

"He's so young."

"That doesn't matter. There's only about a year between us. And he'll get on. Oh, he means to get on. And I can always work."

"Having a baby? Who's going to look after the baby?"

Anna closed her eyes tightly and the blackness of the room was shut out for a moment by a bright light that showed herself nursing a baby, Cherry's baby, for Cherry would have to work, because they'd never be able to live on what Bobby earned. And there came again Jimmy's voice, urging, "Escape. Escape."

"What am I to do, Anna?"

"You know what you've got to do. You've got to tell them, and soon, and let them work it out for you. Now stop crying and try to go to sleep. You've got one comfort. Dada is very fond of Bobby, and Ma is, too. You'll have their approval, up to that point."

"Anna."

"Yes, dear?"

"You . . . you wouldn't break it to them, would you?"

"No, I wouldn't."

"Oh, Anna, I'm . . . I'm frightened. I'm . . . I'm the only one that . . . well, has gone wrong and they'll be ashamed."

"They can't be ashamed of you for doing what they did. Just look at it like that."

"The people in the village."

"Damn the people in the village. I've paid the people in the village for all of us. It wasn't for me alone, the degradation I was put to, it was against Ma and Dada, paying them out for their daring to flaunt society, especially in a narrow village filled with narrow minds. Dada used to be always bragging that we were the happiest family in the county. That was because he had us all in this little nest; he knew that because of the stigma he had laid on us, we would never be able to fly far."

"Oh, Anna, Anna, fancy you thinking like that. I never thought you would turn against Dada. They did what they did because they were in love, and I understand now exactly how they felt."

"Shut up! Shut up! They only knew one kind of love. The same kind as you do. There are other kinds of love: sacrificing love; love that is shrivelled up through convention and the dirty tricks of fate and—" She stopped suddenly and muttered, "I'm sorry. I'm sorry." Then she turned on her side, only to turn quickly back again when Cherry said, "It's a shame. I know you wanted to go with Mr. Simon, and you should have. And you wouldn't have been any the worse."

"Cherry"—it was a deep whisper—"if you don't shut up, you know what I'll do? I'll slap you across the face. I won't be able to stop myself. I had no intention of ever being Simon Brodrick's mistress. *Never! Never!* Do you hear me? Even if I'd loved him desperately, I still wouldn't have become his mistress."

"All right then; all right, you wouldn't, but I don't see now why you are blaming Ma and Dada for doing what they did. Anyway, if you want to know, people are saying the same thing about you and Mr. Timothy. There! now you have it. And whether you are or not . . ."

Anna sprang from the bed, and yelled now at the top of her voice, "I am not sleeping with Mr. Timothy! or with anyone else. *Do you hear me? Do you hear me?*"

In the deep silence that followed she heard the quick steps on the floorboards. Her parents, as usual, would have been sitting by the fire, hand in hand, before going to bed. And now the door burst open and her father, holding the lamp high, and from behind their mother, said, "What is it? What is it?"

Cherry was now sitting up in bed, her arms hugging her waist and rocking herself backwards and forwards as if she already had a baby in her arms.

"What were you yelling at? What was the matter?"

It was her mother that Anna now addressed. Still in a loud voice, she cried, "I am not sleeping with Mr. Timothy. Do you hear, Ma? I'm not sleeping with Mr. Timothy. I am not his mistress."

"No one said you were, daughter. No one said you were." Maria's voice was quiet. But Nathaniel seemed to ignore Anna's outburst for, after putting down the lamp on the wash-hand stand, he put his arm around Cherry's shoulder, saying, "What is it, dear? What is it? What's the matter?"

When Cherry shook her head, Anna cried. "Tell them! This is your opportunity. Tell them!"

"Tell us what?"

When Cherry still continued to shake her head, Maria came to Anna's side and said, "What is the matter? What has she to tell us?"

"Only that she's going to have a baby. Now, is that any surprise to you, Ma?"

Anna watched her father straighten his back; she watched her mother move slowly and stand beside him, and it was she who said, "Is this true, girl?"

And Cherry, falling back on to the pillow, said, "Yes, Ma. Yes, it's true."

"Well, well!" Nathaniel looked at Maria and she at him. And now Maria, putting her hand out, said, "Come on. Get up, and tell us about it."

Their reception of the news seemed to deflate Anna completely. She suddenly sat down on the wooden chair to the side of the bed, and her mother turned to her and said, "Put a coat round you, dear, and come along; we must talk about this."

A few minutes later the four of them were seated round the fire again, but now Cherry's head was resting on her father's shoulder and his arm was around her and what he was saying was, "Don't worry, dear. The first thing we must do is get you married. There's only one problem. He's a good boy, and I like him. But you can't, as you said, go down there and live above that boathouse. What you must do is to come home. After all, this has been his home for many months now. So that's what I think you must do. Isn't that so, Maria?"

And Maria agreed. "Yes, dear, yes," she said; then added, "It'll be good to have a child about the house again."

Anna closed her eyes and there was the white light: there she was, nursing the baby, but added to the scene now was her mother talking to Cherry, and her father in deep conversation with Bobby. Of a sudden she was so tired that she couldn't even hear the voice of Jimmy's urging, "Escape. Escape."

But she heard Jimmy's voice loud and clear on the Saturday evening when the boys came home. She could see immediately that they were excited, and when Oswald began with, "I know, Ma and Dada, it's not so long ago since we lost Jimmy, but you see I had me news before that to tell you. Well, it's just this; I'm engaged to Carrie; you know, Mrs. Simpson's daughter, and you'll never guess what. Mrs. Simpson's taken me into partnership, and Olan an' all."

"But . . . but I thought she was much older than you, Oswald?" This was Maria speaking.

"Yes, Ma, she's . . . she's all of five years. But I care deeply for her and she me, and she doesn't look her age and she's young in her ways. Anyway, there it is. What d'you think?"

It was his father who answered, "I think it's very good news, excellent news, Oswald, and I'm delighted for you. And it's a marvellous opportunity you're being offered, because from what I saw of that place it should prosper."

"It is, Dada, it is already prospering, but it will do more so. We can open up another place; we've got it all planned."

Nathaniel now looked from one to the other as he said, "The saying is, never one door closes but another opens. And it's true in this case. The house will know a family again, and children. Cherry's and Bobby's will be brought up here and yours when they come, Oswald, will make our week-ends bright. It's something to look forward to. Don't you think so, Maria?"

"Yes. Yes, I do, Nathaniel. "'Tis something to look forward to."

"Well, let's drink to it. Go and bring out the elderberry, Anna."

Anna went into the kitchen and from the floor in the stone pantry she picked up a bottle of elderberry wine and, taking it into the kitchen, she placed it on the draining board where also stood a tallow candle in a tin holder. And she stared at it for a long while before she spoke to it, saying, "I hear you, Jimmy, my dear, I hear you. I'll wait till Monday."

NINE

𝒯he sun was shining, but weakly. There had been a heavy frost and there was the smell of snow in the air. She had milked the goats, and then cleaned out the goat house and the chickens; she had tidied the hay bales in the barn; she had brushed Neddy; and finally had swept down the whole yard.

At twelve o'clock she joined her parents for the mid-day bite, when her father said, "I shouldn't be a bit surprised to see it snow before the day's out, so I think there'd better be some more logs cut. Eh?" He had looked at her, and she had returned his look and said, "I'm sorry, Dada, but I'm going visiting this afternoon."

Maria was all attention now, but she didn't speak; it was her father who asked, "Is he back then?"

"Yes, he was due back yesterday."

Now Maria did speak. With her head lowered, she said, "Wouldn't it be better if you waited for him to call?"

"Not in this case, Ma."

"What case, daughter?" Nathaniel was looking hard at her and his voice was curt; and after a moment she said, "There is something on my mind. I have a question to ask him."

"Well, I've always answered your questions up to now. Can't you ask me?"

"No." She smiled a tight smile. "Not in this case, Dada." As she rose from the bench at the end of the table Nathaniel said, as if to no-one in particular, "The log-pile's going down fast. It always does in this weather, and when they come in from their work it's comforting to see a big glow."

"Yes, it is." She nodded at him and only just stopped herself from adding, "So you should spend more time down on the block instead of reading."

In her room, she stood against the closed door for a moment and muttered aloud, "How blind one can be!" She had never realised, all these years, that her father was lazy where actual work was concerned. Of course, it was different when he was dealing with book-work, for that to him was important.

It was a full twenty minutes later when she emerged from the room, to be greeted by a gasp from Maria and her saying, "Oh, no! Anna; you're not flaunting convention to that extent, going into grey."

"My cloak is dark, Ma."

"Your cloak reaches only just below your knees, girl."

"Ma." She walked up to her mother and, standing close to her, she looked straight into her face as she said, "Has it ever dawned upon you that I ceased to be a girl some time ago, and only a matter of days ago stepped into my twenty-first year."

"You are twenty, not twenty-one."

"I said I had stepped into my twenty-first year, Ma. And one is considered to have left girlhood at twenty. I would have thought you, above all people, would be aware of that."

"What's come over you?"

"Nothing's come over me, Ma, that hasn't come over you and Dada."

"Oh, girl, you used to be so pleasant to have in the house, but not any more. Anyway, let's hope that when the baby comes you'll feel different."

Anna's face actually stretched, and then she laughed and the sound finished on a "Huh!" before she turned about and, saying, "I certainly shall," went out.

She avoided the stile road, for she felt she would never again be able to face that way. She crossed the edge of the moor, then followed the bridle path that led on to the coach road. This way put two thirds of a mile on to her journey, but she didn't mind that. Moreover, there was less chance of meeting anyone, especially at this time of the day.

When she finally turned into the drive it was to see the carriage standing in front of the house. And when Walters answered her ringing of the door-bell he exclaimed, "Why! Miss. How d'you do? You're just in time; the master was for visiting you."

"Oh! Anna. Anna."

She turned quickly to look up the stairs to see Timothy descending, his hands outstretched. "I was just about to drive to see you. Come in. Come in. Oh"—he turned to Walters—"bring my case in from the coach, will you,

Walters, please?" Then helping Anna off with her cloak, he said, "Oh, it is wonderful to see you again. It seems years, but it's just over a fortnight. Give me your hat."

He took the hat from her as she was about to press the hatpin back into it, and he said, "Where do you stick this?"

"Where do you think?" She was laughing at him. "In the hat, of course."

"Yes. Yes, I know, but it's a felt one, madam, and it'll make holes in it, all over. Is it the back or the front? It's the back, isn't it?"

Then he turned to the maid, who was approaching across the hall and said, "Oh, Mary, go and ask cook if she would please let us have some tea, and a cake or two."

The girl laughed at his request for cakes, dipped her knee to Anna, then turned about. And Walters, coming back into the hall, pointed to the case he was carrying and said, "I'll put it in the sitting-room, sir."

As Timothy led Anna into the sitting-room she said to Walters, "Are you glad to be home?" and he answered, "Oh, yes, miss, though I must say I enjoyed our trip to London."

"He would have had me there till Christmas and after." Timothy was now thumbing towards his valet. "Talk about night-life. Oh, I have so much to tell you. Come and sit down, dear." He pressed her into the upholstered chair to the side of the fire; then pulling up a foot-stool, he sat down and, taking her hand and looking into her face, he said, "Oh dear me; you . . . you still look pale. But is it any wonder! Do you know something?"

"No; tell me."

"I think it was simply a miracle that you survived, with you in that weak condition and having to cope with that dreadful plague, and not only with one but two. I know your father was there, but men are not of much use in cases like that unless they're doctors, and then they only do the talking. But here and there during that time, I saw for myself what had to be done for those poor souls, and I've wondered at the bravery of many people, but mostly of yourself."

"There was no bravery attached to my efforts, Tim, just necessity."

"Did . . . did you ever think you would catch it?"

"Yes. Yes, every day."

"That makes your efforts the more praiseworthy. Oh! my dear. My dear. When I used to look at you over those railings my heart ached for you. They are saying in the papers now it was only a light epidemic. As if any epidemic could be light! I suppose they mean in comparison with the do they had in 1853, when I was rather young."

She laid her head back into the wing of the chair and let out a long slow breath and looked at him for some seconds before she said, "Tell me what you did in London."

"Oh, I shall have to write a book about all we did in London. With regard to books though, my business could have been seen to in two days . . . well, two and a bit. I could have been back here over a week ago, but Walters took me to a theatre, and afterwards recommended another, and another. And we did the galleries. He's a very intelligent fellow, is Walters. I'm very lucky to have him. And what is even better, he is of a kindly disposition. And I knew that if at any time I had been in need of his ministrations he would have coped admirably. But do you know, Anna? Time and again, when I was going round the galleries and such, I thought of you and how I'd have loved you to be there. You must go to London some time. Or, come to London; I will take you to London. Yes, yes, I will."

He shook her hand up and down now as if she had refused his invitation. And she laughed at him and said, "All right, all right. Yes, I will go to London with you, sir, any time, any time."

"You're laughing at me."

"Yes. Yes, I am, and it's so good to laugh at you and with you. I haven't laughed for a long time . . . I . . . I have missed you."

He stared into her face before he said, "You really have, Anna?"

"Yes. Yes, very much. Oh, very much of late. Have you ever thought, Tim, how changeable human nature is? Do you think a character can change, really change?"

His voice was slow and thoughtful as he gave his opinion: "Not fundamentally," he said. "You see, there are ingredients of good and bad, and the middling, in all of us and it depends on circumstances which bits, as it were, come out on top and dominate. Yes, it's all to do with circumstance. If life went smoothly for each of us I think our characters would remain the same: I mean the predominant facets in our characters would remain the same. But then we are often hit by circumstance. There's that word again, circumstance. To give an example. You've had your share of Penella, haven't you?" When she didn't answer he said, "I suppose you heard that she caught the cholera. Well, it's a great wonder she didn't die. She was very ill, and so ill that I really thought she was dying and everyone else in the hospital thought so, too. This prompted me to go and see Simon. Well, what transpired between us wasn't pleasant, and not for the first time, either. Anyway, I told him it was his duty at least to go and see her. Well, by the time he went, she had taken a slight turn for the better. And I don't know what transpired between them, either, but I know when I next saw her she was a different creature from the one I had known, and who had held me in very poor esteem. She hadn't been able to bear sickness of any kind. Well, there she was, thrown in at the deep end, so to speak, and she had undoubtedly been terrified by what had befallen her. But the only way I can put it is, the experience must have acted on her like a cleansing balm, because she said to me, 'Do you think he will ever forgive me?' You know, Anna, her attitude in everything she did was because she was still in love with him, and always had been. And I know at bottom he was still in love with her, while being deeply hurt and mad at her, and at his brother at the deception they had played on him. Anyway, I wasn't surprised that, when she was able to be removed, he took her home: but I must say my sister certainly wasn't pleased, nor were any of them in the house. And she was aware of this. Oh, yes, she said as much to me when I saw her just before I went away. She even mentioned you."

"Really?"

"Yes; and, my dear, don't say it like that. 'That girl,' she said, 'must hate my very name.' Of course, you cannot imagine her saying it. And I couldn't have done either at one time, but I heard her say it. And she added, 'I've been insane, Tim, haven't I?' Then her next words to me told me that she thought more deeply than I had imagined, for she said, 'Love is a facet of insanity, you know, Tim. I am still insane with it, but I'm harmless now. Cholera is a potent drug.' "

Quietly though not subdued Anna asked now, "Will they remain together?"

"Yes. Yes, I think so. After visiting her out of a form of duty only, the first time, I think his next visits were out of pity. And, you know, that is another facet of love. Pity is akin to love, it breeds it . . . Ah! here's Mary and Walters with the tea. And look! a cream sponge cake with preserved cherries on the top. Oh Mary, tell cook that I love her, will you?"

"Yes, sir. Yes, sir. I'll do that." The girl grinned widely, bobbed and went out. Walters had wheeled the trolley up to the end of the couch and, looking at Anna, he said, "Will I leave you to officiate, miss?"

"Yes; thank you."

When the door had closed on them Timothy laughed, saying, "Will I leave you to officiate. He's nothing if not correct, is Walters. Anyway, would you kindly pour out, madam?"

She poured out the tea; then handed him the thin, rolled bread and butter, followed by the dainty cucumber sandwiches, and lastly she cut into the sponge cake and he, leaning towards her in order to take it, said, "It's fatal to tell anyone, especially a cook, that you are fond of a speciality of hers. When she first made me a sponge cake I praised it to the skies because it was lovely, but when there's company, high, low, or middling, or she's out to tempt me from my work which, I understand from Walters, she says makes me dour, I'm presented with a cream sponge, and it puts weight on one. Still, it keeps her happy. You know, I learned from my mother years ago that the essence of a happy household starts at the oven in the kitchen. I think she was right."

"Yes, I think so too."

The tea over, he pushed the trolley away and was about to resume his seat on the footstool at her side when she said, "Wouldn't you be more comfortable on the couch?"

"Yes. Yes, I would," he said, looking towards it, "if you would join me there."

She sat at one end of the couch, her back in the corner, and when he sat down next to her he took her hand, but made no remark for some time; he just stared into the fire until, seeming to bestir himself out of a reverie, he said, "It's odd, you know, the dreams one conjures up by looking into the flames. I see pictures there, but the print, so to speak, is in my mind." And after a pause he added, "You always have nice fires up at the cottage."

She did not answer, and presently he turned and looked at her, saying, "Well, don't you?" which did stir her to say, "As you've just remarked, the prints are in your mind. Fires are only nice when the prints are nice, and the prints are only nice when people are in accord, otherwise flames can arouse anger."

"*Oh! Anna.*" He twisted round and, looking into her face, said, "What is it? You're unhappy. Well, I know you have been for some time, but this is different. What's happened?"

"The simple answer, Tim, would be to say I've been left out in the cold and I don't like it. But it's more than that, it's a great unrest and it's been in me for a long time. I've been hurt of late, Tim, taken for granted."

When her head drooped and she couldn't go on, he said, "Tell me. We're friends, close friends; you can tell me anything."

She now looked into his kindly eyes, and so she began, hesitantly at first, to tell him how she had felt over the last two years. She even mentioned the fact that she had thought she might be in love with Simon but had found she wasn't. Then she came to Jimmy, and his views on the family which had surprised her, and how he had been intending to make his escape by going to sea, and how he had almost begged her to get away. He seemed to understand their parents more than any of them did, she told him; and her voice broke when she spoke of his dying words. Then she talked of her father and of how he had changed towards her since the death of Ben, that he seemed to hold her, in a way, responsible for it because of her association with the Manor House.

What she next told him she had to tell only in part, that her mother had been left some money, a considerable sum, and at this he raised his eyebrows and he, too, said, "Really?"

Yes, in the region of three thousand pounds, she said; and that this had come about some time before. But they had never offered her a farthing. And when she came to the night when her father had made his will, he put in, "Oh! Anna, Anna. I want to say how I like your father. I've admired him for his mental ability, but his short-sightedness with regard to you is unforgiveable. But your mother, what was her attitude?"

She then related her mother's words when she thought she was going to die, of the promise she wanted from her and which would have tied her to the house and her father until he, too, went. But then she came to Cherry's predicament and, looking at him now, she could not keep the hurt from her voice as she said, "They welcomed it, Tim. They welcomed it because it would mean starting another family in the house. And only today my mother said that she couldn't understand the change that had come about in me of late, but when the baby came I would feel better. You see, I am to be the handmaid, the baby-minder, while Cherry keeps on her work. She and Bobby will, of course, live in the house, and as there are only two bedrooms on the ground floor they will occupy the one that is mine and I shall be relegated to one of the boys' beds in the roof. This all sounds as if I'm feeling sorry for myself. I'm not, I'm just stating facts. And one after another, the facts, of late, have been thrown at me. The latest is that my father is welcoming Oswald's engagement to the daughter of the Pie and Peas Shop owner, and who is five years older than he is, but he is welcoming this too because he is hoping for more children, as he said, to visit at week-ends. He can see the house coming alive again, and him instructing, teaching . . . teaching. Oh, I know what's in his mind. And what's more, my brothers are going to be offered partnerships. So everybody is settled and accounted for except me. Well, Tim, I'm escaping."

"What do you mean, dear?"

"I have decided to leave."

"Oh! my dear. Have . . . have you talked this over with Miss Netherton?"

"No; Miss Netherton wants me to go and stay with her so she can fatten me up, et cetera. But I have other ideas."

He turned from her and leaned forward and, placing his elbows on his knees, he joined his hands together, and when he again seemed to be in a reverie, she said, "Don't you want to know what I'm going to do?"

"Oh yes, my dear, of course." He had turned to her again. "Is it about entering a college? Miss Netherton and I discussed this some time ago."

"No; it's nothing to do with that."

"No?"

"No. I don't want to enter any college. I don't want to be taught any more except through my own reading and discussions with . . ."

She did not finish the sentence but shook her head. Then drawing herself to the edge of the couch, she pulled herself upwards and walked towards the tea trolley and there she arranged the dirty cups and saucers, moving them about as if on a chess board, while he sat in silence watching her. But when the cups and saucers began to rattle he got to his feet and walked over to her and said, "What is it, Anna? You can tell me."

At this she gave the trolley a push that would have sent it half-way across the room had he not grabbed it and steadied it; then taking her hand, he drew her onto the rug in front of the fire, and now they were facing each other as she said, "I've . . . I've got a proposition to put to you."

"Yes? Yes, well go ahead and put it."

"Well—" She hesitated, then said, "First of all, I must tell you one thing and I'm very, very sure of this, and have been for a long time, whether you have known it or not, and it's got nothing to do with friendship . . . I love you."

She watched the colour seep from his cheeks. She saw his lips tremble, then mouth her name, yet no sound came from them. And so she went on, "The proposition is this. You can either marry me or I can become your mistress."

When he fell back from her, dropped on to the couch, put his elbows on his knees and covered his face with his hands she silently mouthed the words, Oh, my God! She had embarrassed him beyond pardon. She had thought . . . What had she thought? She was mad, for now gone, too, would be the friendship. What had she done? She was about to say, I'm sorry. Oh, I'm sorry, when his arms shot out and around her thighs and his head was buried against her stomach, and the next minute he had swung her round so that she fell on to the couch with a thump, and then they were lying on their sides looking at each other. And his words came out between gasps, "Oh! Anna, my love. What have you said? Only what I've longed to hear, for years and years I've longed to hear those words, I love you, because I couldn't say them to you, not in the state I am in. I've always thought it would be unfair. Most women almost faint at the mention of a fit. I knew you wouldn't do that, but to offer to join yourself to me for life . . . and you said"—he was laughing now—"you said you would be my mistress. Oh, Anna, Anna, that in a way is a great compliment; but I don't want a mistress, I want a wife. I've always wanted a wife and you as my wife . . . Don't cry, my love. Don't cry. Oh, look"—he pointed to the fire now—"you have no idea of the pictures I have seen in those flames. Oh, my dear, dearest Anna, let me dry your eyes. And this, this is what I've seen myself doing in those flames." And now his arms went about her and he laid his lips on hers, and the kiss was long and tender. When their lips parted they still lay and looked at each other in silence, until he said, "There may be happier days for us but not one that I shall remember as I shall this: these last few moments. Oh! Anna. You know, I want to sing, I want to take you by the hand and run with you to some place. Oh, I don't know what I want. I think Byron's words, 'Let joy be unconfined' fit how I'm feeling, although"—he laughed now—"that had to do with the Battle of Waterloo, hadn't it?" And she, laughing too, completed his quotation: "On with the dance, let joy be unconfined." Their foreheads came together for a moment, then taking her face between his hands he asked quietly, "How soon can we be married?"

"As soon as you like, my dear."

"So be it, as soon as I like," and when she whispered, "Well, let it be that soon or sooner," they fell together and laughed and rocked each other until he cried, "Oh! I forgot. I brought you a present. Let me get my case."

When he brought a leather case to the couch he took from it a long, narrow box tied up with a gold cord and he handed it to her, saying, "That'll be the first of many, my dear, because I'll be at liberty now to buy you what I will."

Inside the box were three long strands of twisted gold and she gasped as she said, "Oh! it's beautiful, beautiful. Oh! Tim."

"Stand up, my darling."

She stood up, and he fastened the clasp at the back of her neck, then said, "Come and look in the mirror," and led her to a wall mirror in which she looked at her reflection and that of the three-strand gold necklace hanging down below her collarbone, one strand falling behind the other. Then raising her eyes to his through the mirror, she said, "Oh, my dear, what can I say?"

Turning her towards him, he said, "You can say those three words again that almost brought on my collapse."

"Oh! Tim, my dear, dear Tim, they were true. I do love you and I have for a long, long time. Looking back, I think the seed was sown the day you looked at me from the mat and spoke one word; angel."

"Well, my love, that's how I've thought of you ever since. But now"—he lifted her hand—"you should have a ring. I have some odd bits of jewellery in the safe, but one thing I haven't got is a ring. We will go into town tomorrow and you'll have one with the biggest stone I can find . . ."

"I won't! I'll have a ring, but not one with the biggest stone you can find. I don't care for flashy jewellery."

"You will have one, madam, with the biggest stone I can find, or else."

"What does that mean. None at all?"

"That's right, none at all." He bent forward and kissed her gently again; then he laughed, saying, "I want to shout this out to someone. Shall we tell the staff?"

"You would like that?"

"Wouldn't you? Would it upset you?"

"Upset me? Oh! Tim, no, no. You are doing me an honour, and I am well aware of it because you know my history. It isn't everyone who would . . ."

He clapped his hand over her mouth, saying, "Don't you ever refer to that. You are worth the love of any man, any man, however great he might be, and *I am honoured*. I am the one who is honoured and so very, very grateful. Oh! Anna, you don't know how grateful. You said you had felt rejected, well, I have felt rejected ever since this cursed thing struck me. I have laughed and talked and chattered aimlessly, all the while being aware of how people were even afraid to be in my company in case I had . . . one of those." He nodded his head now. "They were even afraid to put the word fit to it. Many a time I have left a company to prevent myself crying in front of them, because I knew they couldn't differentiate between someone who had fits and a mental defective or an idiot. No, my dear, till the day I die there will be a portion of my heart that will be indebted to you. But before we leave this dire subject I shall tell you this. When I was in London I saw the specialist who has delved into this sickness and although he said he couldn't cure me, he has come up with a pill that, although it cannot prevent the attacks, it can decrease their severity. Well"—he now spread one hand out—"so far so good. Now, let's go and tell them."

He led her out of the drawing-room and, seeing Walters about to mount the stairs, he called, "Would you be kind enough, Walters, to bring in Edward and Fletcher. I have some news I would like you all to share."

"Yes. Yes, of course, sir." He stared from one to the other and smiled widely at them before hurrying out. And now, Tim, still holding her hand, led her into the kitchen, saying, "Where is that woman who stuffs me with cream sponge cake? Oh, there you are, cook!"

Mrs. Ada Sprigman turned from the table, her face beaming. "Oh, sir, you know you are a tease," she said. And the kitchen maid, Lena Cassidy, turned from the sink, a wide grin on her face and, bobbing from one to the other, giggled. And Mary Bowles, who was quickly wiping her mouth, likely after having had her share of another sponge cake, said, "Is there anything you want, sir?"

"Yes, I want all your attention; Walters has gone for Edward and Fletcher. I have some news for you."

The three women now stood side by side against the edge of the table. "'Tis good news, I can see, sir, or you wouldn't be looking so bright."

"Besides being a very good cook you are a very discerning woman, Mrs. Sprigman." And at this the three women laughed. Then the back door opened and the gardener and the coachman entered, both doffing their caps. But it was noticeable that Walters didn't come in the back way, but entered the kitchen from the hallway and approached his master's side, just as Timothy, looking round his small staff, said, "It is with the greatest pleasure in the world I am able to tell you that Miss Dagshaw has consented to be my wife."

There was a slight gasp or two, then a chorus of "Oh! sir. Oh! miss."

"Oh! congratulations, sir. Congratulations, miss. We wish you every happiness, sir."

"If anybody deserves to be happy, it's you, sir."

"And you, miss. Oh yes, and you, miss."

"When is it to be, sir?"

This was from Edward, and Timothy answered him, "Well, it would be tonight if I had my way, but it will be by special licence some time within the next week or so."

"Oh, I'll make you a spread like you've never seen afore, sir, that's if you're having it in the house."

Timothy now turned to Anna and said, "Well, this will be for discussion," and Anna, looking at the cook, said, "That would be lovely, Mrs. Sprigman, to have it in this house. Yes"—she nodded now towards Timothy —"we'll have it in the house." And he, nodding back to her said, "Very good, ma'am," which, in the emotional circumstances, caused loud laughter all round. And now he said, "I think a drink would be in order. What do you think, Walters?"

"I think you're right, sir. What would you like?"

"Well, toasts are usually made in champagne but I don't think we have any in our little cellar, have we?"

"No, sir. But there's a very good claret and a port, and, if the ladies would prefer it, a sherry."

"Well, bring the three choices into the sitting room and we'll drink there. So, come along . . ."

His hold on Anna's hand was only released when, in the sitting-room, they all held a glass and in different ways the staff drank to their health. And when Tim's glass of claret touched Anna's glass and he said, "May you know nothing but happiness, my dear, from now on," there was a concerted chorus of, "Hear-hear! sir. Hear! hear!"

Just before the staff left the room the cook, looking at Timothy, said, "Would you like me to knock you up a nice dinner, sir? I had two pheasants come in this mornin'."

Timothy now turned to Anna, saying, "You'll stay to dinner, won't you?" And she, without hesitation, said, "Yes. Yes, I'd be delighted to."

"Well, that's settled, ma'am, that's settled."

As Mrs. Sprigman bobbed to her, Anna noticed that she had suddenly become ma'am and she felt an added warmth seep through her. She had entered a new world, and she'd be free in it. Oh, so lovingly free . . .

It was turned seven o'clock when they finished their dinner in the dining-room.

Anna had never sat down to such a table, nor had she ever eaten such a meal or drunk so much wine. And so, when Walters said to Timothy, "It's snowing heavily, sir," Timothy said, "Oh, dear me. The carriage is going to have a job. Is it lying?"

"It's a good inch, sir, and there's a wind blowing, so there'll be drifts already."

"Oh go out and see what Edward thinks," Timothy said to him, "and we'll go by that, eh?"

With the room to themselves, he murmured, "Well now, milady, what's to happen if you can't get home?"

She smiled back at him across the table as she answered, "I'll take great pleasure in staying the night here, sir." And at this he laughed, and said loudly, "Will you indeed, madam?" And she answered as playfully, "Yes, sir, if it is your pleasure."

"Oh! Anna, Anna. What a day! What a beautiful, delightful day! And how lovely you are! To think I shall see you every day for the rest of my life sitting across from me at our table. But seriously, would you stay the night?"

"Why not?"

And again he laughed as he said, "Why not indeed! I shall get Mary to put a warming pan into the spare room bed. But I do feel your people should be told, so I'll ask Edward to go over on horseback. If it's only an inch or so the horse will get through all right, whereas the carriage . . . well, that's a different thing. Excuse me, my dear."

After he had gone from the room she sat back and closed her eyes and said to herself, "Oh, Jimmy, Jimmy, what a beautiful escape! And what will they say when they hear the news that I'm staying the night here; that, like Cherry, I've succumbed at last to pattern? Yes, yes; that's what they'll think. And they'll be happy in a way now that I won't be able to hold my head up so high. They'll say, Why him? Why couldn't she have taken this step with the other one? Look what she's saddled herself with, a man who has fits . . . a wonderful man, a thinking man, a kind and generous man, a lovely man. Oh yes, a lovely man . . ."

Timothy came back into the room saying, "It's all been taken care of." Then taking her hand, he said, "Come, my dear, we'll have coffee in the drawing-room."

They were crossing the hall when he suddenly stopped and exclaimed, "Christmas! We'll have a big tree in the corner there, aglow with candles, and holly and mistletoe and flowers everywhere."

When they entered the drawing-room she said, "How old did you say you were?" And he replied, "You've put me into my second childhood, dear."

When, a moment later, they stood facing each other on the rug before the fire, he placed his hands on her shoulders and asked quietly, "Would you like children?" and as quietly she answered, "I'd love children, Tim. Do . . . do you want children?"

"Oh, yes, yes, Anna."

"How many would you like?" Now she was smiling at him, and he pushed his mouth from one side to the other before he said, "Let me think. Well, ten's a round number. I like round numbers, but, all right, I'll be satisfied with five. How's that?"

"Oh! Tim." She put her arms about him, and when they now kissed it wasn't gentle but gave evidence of the hunger in both of them. And when at last they stood apart he said, "It must be soon, mustn't it?" And she answered, "Yes, it must be soon."

It was nine days later when they were married by Parson Mason in the little church at Fellburn. All her family were present, as, of course, was Miss Netherton, and also Timothy's own staff, but his two nephews were conspicuous by their absence. Nor had they received a wedding present from them. There were also present in the church Dan Wallace and his wife and son Art, Miss Penelope Smythe, the dressmaker, and Roland Watts, the carpenter, who had once lived in the village, and his wife.

It would seem that with this representation from the village, the inhabitants were wishing her well. But the village was still the village and in the

King's Head there were those who reminded others that it was through her that there were two men and a girl languishing in jail and also that four families had been turfed out of their homes. Anyway, she had always lived up to her name: in fact, both lasses had, for there was one with her belly full and not married yet. And this one had stayed the night with him, hadn't she? Supposedly because the snow was too thick to drive her home. They could send a fellow on a horse, though, couldn't they? Oh, once a gillyvor always a gillyvor. And they were having the reception at the house and no honeymoon. But, you wouldn't expect them to have a honeymoon now, would you? Well, anyway, just wait and see when she sprouted the next little gillyvor, for that would give the game away. Wait till August or September; we'll see.

And there's another thing: he must have been paying for her on the side for a long time, because where did the old 'uns up in the Hollow get the money for a new horse and trap? It was also being said now that they were buying that pit lad a share in the boatyard, and he not being apprenticed to it for a year yet. Who said the wicked didn't prosper, especially when the devil took a hand in moulding them, like the new Mrs. Barrington, driving here and there in her carriage and pair. Aye, the trouble that one had caused in high and low quarters alike!

It was certainly true what Parson Fawcett said: the evil that men do lives after them; but the evil that women do goes on for countless generations through their breeding.

EPILOGUE

here was an announcement in the "Births" column of *The Times* and also in the local papers, which read as follows:

"On the 1st December, 1884, a daughter to Mr. and Mrs. Timothy Barrington of Briar Close, Maple Road, Fellburn. Joy unconfined.

THE END

The Maltese Angel

THE MALTESE ANGEL

Book One
1886-1888

Part One

ONE

It had taken him only half an hour from leaving Newcastle to reach the first gate of his farm. He had ridden faster than usual, yet all the while asking himself why, because once he got into the house, what would he do? He'd sit down at the table, put his elbows on it, droop his head into his hands and ask himself, and for the countless time, what his reaction would have been had the company at The Empire not been engaged for another week; and the answer he would give would be: he didn't know.

Things had moved too fast: he had never been in a situation like this in his life; he had never felt like this in his life; he had never even known what love was. He had known what need was. Oh, aye. And that had been a kind of torment. And so was this present feeling; but a different kind of torment . . . No, no; he couldn't call it torment, not this feeling of elation, of being taken out of himself; it was like being lifted on to some high hill . . . mountain; yes, mountain; and experiencing an exhilarating emotion flooding through him, more cleansing than frost-filled air in the early dawn.

He would then ask himself if he had gone out of his mind. Four times only had he seen the girl . . . no, the young woman . . . no, the beautiful creature that appeared to him as someone not quite human.

It couldn't be because he was unused to looking at turns on the stage: at least once a month over the past two years he had sat through a performance at The Empire or at one of the other theatres in the city; he had even sat through a play by Shakespeare, which, and he had to admit it, wasn't much to his taste; the twang and the rigmarole were hard to get into . . .

He pulled up at the second gate and, leaning from the saddle, unlatched the iron hoop from the stanchion; but his hand became still for a moment when he looked across the dark field towards the outbuildings of his farm and saw the movement of a lantern, not coming from the direction of the cow byres or the piggeries, or yet from the hen crees in the field, which might have denoted a fox on his rounds and Billy Compton after him, for there was no sound of barking from the dogs; nor was it coming from the floor of the old barn, but from the loft.

Having urged his mount through the gate, he turned in the saddle and replaced the hoop, then put the animal into a gallop towards the mud yard. There, dismounting, he patted its rump, and pushed it towards its stable, saying, "Be with you in a minute, Betty," before hurrying down the yard and entering an open-fronted barn.

Approaching the ladder that rose to the loft, he shouted, "You up there, Billy?"

In answer, a head appeared above him, saying, "Aye, Master Ward. 'Tis I up here all right; and a visitor. Better you come up and make his acquaintance like."

When Ward Gibson reached the loft floor his eyes were drawn to a small figure hunched against the old timbers of the sloping roof, and he walked slowly towards it, saying, "Aye! Aye! And who's this when he's out?"

"Can't get a word out of him, master. But he's in one hell of a state for a bairn."

"What do you mean, hell of a state?" Ward's voice was low; and so was the old man's as he replied, "He's been thrashed, an' badly; scourged, I would say. An' he doesn't seem to have any wits left him, he's so full of fear. Shook like an aspen when I first spoke to him."

Ward dropped on to his hunkers before the very small figure and, kindly, he said, "Hello there! What's your name?"

Two round eyes stared back at him. The lids blinked rapidly, but the boy's lips did not move.

"Come along, now; you've got a name. There's nobody here goin' to touch you."

The old man, too, was now on his hunkers, and he held his hand out gently towards the boy, saying, "Let the master look at your back, laddie. Just let him see your back. Come on, now. Come on."

After a moment the boy slowly hitched himself round, and as slowly Billy lifted up the dirty grey shirt and so exposed in the light of the lantern the scarlet weals criss-crossing each other from the small shoulders down to the equally small buttocks, and that these overlaid older scars.

The elder man now spoke in a whisper: "That whip had a number of tails, don't you think, master? An' take a look at his wrists," and so saying he gently pulled the shirt down and turned the boy round again, and, taking up the small dirt-grimed hands, pointed to the wrists. "Tarry rope, I would say. But look at the ankle! That's definitely a chain mark."

The old man now looked at his master, waiting for him to speak; but it was some seconds before Ward, holding out his hand, said, "Come along, son. Nobody's going to hurt you here. Come on."

The boy did not at first move, but when he attempted to stand up he almost toppled; and instinctively Ward went to pick him up; but the child, as he proved to be from his stature, shunned back from him. And again Ward said, "There's no-one going to hurt you here. Come on; walk if you can; otherwise, I'll carry you."

The boy now walked unsteadily down the loft; but when he came to the edge of the platform and seemed as if he might be about to fall, without any hesitation now, Ward lifted him up and, holding him in one arm, made his way down the ladder.

Outside, and about to cross the yard, he said to Billy, "Is Annie in the cottage?"

"Aye; she is, master; in bed this half hour. But there's your supper in the oven, and plenty of cold victuals. But if you think I should get her up . . ."

"No. We'll do what is necessary . . . How did you find him?"

" 'Twas the dogs. Flo was uneasy; even Cap kept runnin' back and for'ard. An' when Flo barked at the bottom of the ladder, well, I knew somebody was up there. When I shouted twice an' got no answer, I yelled I had me gun with me, and I pushed Flo up afront like. But as soon as she discovered the boy she stopped her yappin'. Funny, but he didn't seem to be feared of her."

"Well, that's about the only thing in life, if you ask me, he isn't afraid of."

It was nearly half an hour later. Billy had washed the boy's face and hands, and Ward himself had cleaned the boy's back as much as he could without causing him more pain than he was apparently already suffering, before applying an ointment that his mother had used on both humans and beasts for bruises and boils and every known skin ailment. Afterwards, they had watched the waif gulp at food like a ravenous animal, and when he had drunk a half pint of milk almost at one swallow, they had exchanged glances. But it wasn't until the lad was seated on the low cracket before the fire, a blanket about him, that the stiffness seemed to go out of his body and his tongue became loose for the first time.

When Ward again asked his name, he said, "Carl Bennett."

The name seemed ordinary enough to them both; but the tone of the voice was not one they would have termed local, nor would it have been recognisable for miles around.

When Ward asked how old he was, the boy at first said, "Eight"; but then his head jerked and he had added, "No; nine."

Where had he come from? At this he had bowed his head before muttering, "Farm."

"Whose farm?" asked Ward. "Which farm?"

The look the boy gave Ward was furtive before he muttered, "A long way off, beyond Durham."

"Beyond Durham?"

The old man and Ward seemed to repeat the words together.

"When did you leave?"

"Yesterday. No . . ." The tousled dark head shook again. "The day before. Not sure."

"Why?"

There was no answer to this, only the look in the boy's eyes seemed to say, "Need you ask?"

"What was the name of the farm . . . or the farmer?"

The boy now looked down to the wide hearth and seemed to focus his gaze on the huge black iron dog that supported the set of equally huge fire-irons; and he didn't raise his head again until Ward said, "Well, don't worry; you're not going back. My man, here"—he nodded towards Billy—"was saying only last week he could do with some help; that he's not getting any younger and was looking for a youngster to do the odds and ends. Weren't you?"

"Oh aye. Oh, yes. Aye, I was that, master. I was that. Definitely I was lookin' out for a youngster."

The boy stared from one to the other and his voice held a note of natural eagerness when he said, "I can work . . . work hard."

"How long were you on the farm?"

"Two years."

"Where did you live before that?"

The head made a movement as if about to droop again, but the thin bony chin jerked slightly as the words came: "The workhouse."

"Had you been there long?"

"Since being four . . . I mean, since I was four."

Again they both noted the boy's strange way of speaking.

"How did you get there?"

"I am told that my parents were set upon on their journey. My mother had the sickness; she died, and my father, too."

"What was the sickness?"

"Her chest. But I don't know how my father died. Joe said he knew, but he wouldn't tell me."

"Who was Joe?"

"He was a boy in the workhouse, but he was taken to a farm before I was. He was older."

"Is he still on the farm?"

"No, he ran away twice. He didn't come back the second time."

"Is this the first time you've run away?"

Again the boy's head drooped and the voice was low as he replied, "No; three times."

"And you were whipped when you got back, and tied up?"

"Yes."

"Well, why didn't you go back to the workhouse and tell them of the treatment?"

Both the boy and Billy stared at Ward now, and it was to Billy that Ward made the sharp retort: "Well, there's laws, you know. They send inspectors to the farms; at least, they're supposed to do. Arthur Meyer has a workhouse boy. I think he's got two and the Masons have one. And as far as I understand they've got to be signed for and reports given as to progress."

"Aye, well"—Billy's head wagged—"there are workhouses an' workhouses, an' some folks would cut your throat for a back-hander. Anyway, master, where is he gona sleep the night?"

After a moment's thought Ward said, "Put him in the boiler-house; it's nice and warm there; and we'll see about rigging up a room for him above the stables tomorrow." He turned now to the boy and smiled at him, saying, "How does that suit you?"

The boy did not immediately answer; when he did, his voice came as a thin mutter: "You are not just speaking like this, sir, then tomorrow you will change?"

"No, son; I am not just speaking like this. And you will find that I don't say one thing at night and another in the morning. Go with Billy now, and he'll bed you down, and tomorrow we will talk. But I think, for the time being and for your own safety, you must not be seen abroad too much because, as the law stands, you could be sent back. You understand?"

"Oh yes. Yes, I understand, sir. And . . . and thank you."

He stood up now. He was not more than four feet tall, and apparently he was a child of eight or nine—he had seemed uncertain of his own age—yet from the set look on his face and the expression in his eyes at this moment he could be taken for an adult; and this disturbed both men.

It was Billy who now said briskly, "Well, come along, young man. If you're goin' to be any use to me you must get your sleep. Aye, you must that." And with this he hitched up the blanket around the boy, put his hand on his shoulder and pressed him towards the door. But there he stopped and, turning towards Ward, he said, "By the way, master, did you see to Betty?"

"No; but I'm going to do that now. Anyway"—Ward smiled—"she's likely stuffed herself full of oats by now and taken her own harness off. I'm sure she's quite capable of it. So get yourself away to bed; the morning will soon be here."

" 'Twill that, master. 'Twill that. That's one of the things you can be sure of: whether we're here or not, the mornin' will be."

Ward did not immediately follow his man out and see to the horse, but he sat down with a heavy plop on one of the high-backed, wooden kitchen chairs; and now he did place his elbows on the table, but he did not droop his head into his hands. What he said to himself was, Funny, but this little business has knocked it clean out of my head. It's there though, and I've got to do something about it.

But what? Tomorrow is Sunday. I can do nothing till Monday night, when I can sit there again and face her. And how many nights after that am I going to be there without having a word with her? She knows I'm there; I'm sure of that. She looked at me tonight, and she smiled . . . she smiled at me, not the rest of them, she didn't lift her eyes over the stalls or raise them to the gallery. I'm not imagining it. No, no; I'm not. One thing, she isn't married. The doorman said she wasn't. His thoughts now took him back to the doorman, and he gritted his teeth as he said to himself, By, it's a wonder I didn't let go at him when he said, "What d'you want to know for? And if she was, it wouldn't be to a yokel from the country." A yokel from the country! And he was in his good suit, made of the best home-spun cloth. Of course, he'd had it these five years, and the neck was high. But surely that wouldn't have stamped him as being from the country. He was lucky, that chap, that he left him still standing on his feet.

He went to rise from the chair; then he stopped himself, saying half aloud, "What about tomorrow?" He had promised Parson Tracey that he would turn up for the choir . . . at least he had made the promise through

Frank Noble, the curate, when he had called here only two days ago, and Frank, in his "Hail fellow, well met" voice had exclaimed loudly how they all missed him; that the choir wasn't the same without him: all tenors and tremors, not a bass among them. "You're being missed, you know, Ward," he had added. "You're being missed by everybody . . . everybody." What he had meant by the second everybody was that he was being missed by one in particular.

Well, what had he to be afraid of? Daisy understood all right, by now, how things stood. She had been a pal since schooldays; she had been more of a pal to him than had either of her brothers, Sep or Pete. That was all she had been, a pal.

His rising from the chair was in the form of a jerk and as he made hastily for the door an inner voice checked his step. "Stop kidding yourself, man," it said. "Face up to it. You know what she's always been after. Remember what Dad said to you the day before he died: 'She'd make a good wife and she'd give you a family. Aye, a big one. But what else you'll get from her, you alone know. Just remember, lad: there's more in marriage than the bed, which you've got to get out of most times at five in the morning. And days are long, especially in the winter.' "

His dad had been a wise man, a quiet, thinking, wise man; and he had picked right for himself. Which was why he had been unable to go on living without his partner, because she had given him more than was called upon as her duty.

Well, tomorrow morning he would go and sing in the choir, and leave the rest to God and common sense.

TWO

*P*art of St. Stephen's Church dated from the early sixteenth century; surprisingly, not the chancel and sanctuary section, but the part of the nave containing the font.

Eight rows of pews were contained in this old part, the rest, ten rows, were within the newer walls built earlier in the century.

And, again surprisingly, a gallery was built to overhang the font, and it was here the organ was housed and the choir sang.

A huge wrought-iron screen stretched across the front of the chancel, thereby cutting off the view of the altar and sanctuary from the congregation, apart from those favoured with the direct view allowed through the necessary central opening in the screen.

However, the pulpit to the right side of the screen was in view of all the congregation.

The screen had been given by a member of the Ramsmore family in honour of his father, a general who had died in battle.

Its immediate effect on the villagers had been one of muted protest, muted because, for most of them, a man's daily bread depended either directly upon the Ramsmores or on their patronage. In those days, most of the village and the surrounding countryside was owned by them.

However, nowadays, things were changed in all ways up at the Hall. At one time, as many as sixty people would have been employed in the house or on the estate, but, now, the fingers of two hands would have numbered them. Three farms had gone, as well as most of the immediate estate. Yet, they were still generally looked upon as Lords of the Manor, for the Colonel was a class man, and his second wife, Lady Lydia, was a lady in her own right, and she had given him a new son two years ago. Moreover, she was a woman who received respect without it being demanded, for she spoke her mind. It had even been whispered here and there that if she'd had anything to do with it, the screen would have come down, and without delay, and this might have encouraged a more open objection to it by the villagers, except that anyone daring to suggest such a thing would have had to face the wrath of Parson Tracey, and Parson Tracey was a power in the village. In fact, it was laughingly said he thought he had created the village, the church, and God.

From where he sat in the gallery, Ward gazed fixedly at the minister in the pulpit, and he asked himself for the hundredth time how much longer the man was going to keep yammering on about Job and his wrongs: poor Job had been stung by everything but a horsefly, but apparently God was now rewarding him in abundance with thousands of sheep, she-asses, and camels. My! My! He had heard it all before. How many times over the years? From when he was a boy he had pictured the sheep being chased by the she-asses, and the lot of them being chased by the camels. He had even made it his business to look out a picture of a camel. They were big and he had early come to the conclusion that thousands of them would soon have put paid to the sheep and the she-asses.

Parson Tracey had no imagination. He had six sermons, which he would vary from time to time. Even when they were boys, Ward would lay a bet with Fred Newberry, who was sitting next to him now, that he could repeat at least two of the sermons. The bet had always been his wind-up engine against Fred's pinching two meat and onion pies from his dad's bakery. The engine was still lying amongst the oddments up in the attic.

Fred dug him gently in the ribs now, and a whisper came from the corner of his mouth, saying, "Bet you a tanner Old Smythe goes to assist Miss Alice from the pew, eh?"

Ward made an almost audible sound that could have been Huh! as he thought, Fred gets dafter. Of course the verger would go and offer Miss Alice his hand to assist her out of the pew as if she were an old woman instead of an eighteen-year-old buxom miss. The verger was a dirty-minded old swine. Perhaps he ogled the young ones because he had no children of his own.

Ah! There, it was over, the end being signalled, first by the scraping of feet as the four men on the choir bench and the three boys seated in front of them rose to their feet, and by the rising, almost as one, of those in the bare wooden pews just slightly before the more favoured ones in the three pews where the seats were padded, and the rustling of gowns seeming to accentuate further the difference of favour.

Sometimes as many as six gentry families would attend at the main service, but this morning the pews were occupied by only three: the Ramsmores, the Hopkins from Border Manor, and the Bentfords, who lived in the old Wearside Grange. They were a nice family, the Bentfords, so Ward thought; but they were under suspicion in the village as their daughter had married one of the Franklins who owned The Mill, and they were Methodists.

Ward drew in a deep breath, and looked towards the organ, which was now beginning to get under way as two young boys put all their strength into pumping its wooden handle. Then he glanced back along the row to where Ben Oldman, the shoemaker, who was honoured by the title of choirmaster, was now bending forward with his hand at shoulder height and seeming to pat the air.

They were away: Fred's voice in full flood, and Jimmy Conroy, the butcher's son, mouthing the words while thinking, so Ward was sure, not of his soul but of Susan Beaker down there at the end of the sixth row, her straw hat bobbing with the tune, and then, there at the end of the row Charlie Dempsey the blacksmith, as usual a note higher and a note in front of everyone else. But Charlie was a nice fellow, as were his sons John and Harry an' all. But they shunned church, the pair of them, as he himself had been doing for some time.

> Jesus, Lover of my soul,
> Let me to Thy bosom fly . . .

Now why should he be looking at Daisy down there, because there was one thing sure, especially now, he didn't want to fly to her bosom. But had he ever wanted to fly to her bosom? No; no, definitely not. Not like that.

> While the nearer waters roll,
> While the tempest still is high;
> Hide me, O my Saviour, hide,
> Till the storm of life is past:
> Safe into the haven guide,
> O, receive my soul at last.

The hymn finished on the Amen being dragged out, the congregation sat back and with impatient patience, the outcome of practice, waited while the Reverend Bertram Tracey slowly made his way, followed by his two servers, from the altar, down the two steps, through the arch in the screen, and after turning right, disappeared into the vestry.

Ward did not hurry from the gallery; nor did Fred; and once they were alone, Fred said, "Like to drop in home for a minute or so?" And leaning towards Ward, exclaimed, "Home brew going. As good as what you'll get in The Running Hare or The Crown Head. I can vouch for it, 'cos this mornin' I had a head on me as big as the bell tower, with the bell in it goin' hell for leather." He spluttered, adding, "Eeh! let's get out of this."

At the foot of the spiral staircase he nudged Ward, saying, "Bet yer Daisy'll be at the gate . . . What d'you say?"

Ward made no answer: from experience he knew that Fred didn't require answers.

Outside, it was evident that they must be among the last to leave, for there was the Reverend making his way across the graveyard towards his extra large Sunday dinner and the following nap that could go on till four in the afternoon, or at least until his wife returned from taking the Sunday school.

Everything in the village had a pattern; and there was part of it standing outside the lych-gate. The Mason family had mounted the trap, the father John, and Gladys his wife and Pete and Sep, their manly sons.

The occupants of the trap waved and called to him as they moved off, and Fred, too, bade him a jovial farewell, saying, "You're not comin' then? Well, if I don't see you at the Harvest Festival, I'll see you on the Christmas tree," and as if he hadn't been aware of her before, he now added, "Hello there, Daisy. You get bigger and bonnier every week."

"You're a fool, Fred Newberry. Always were and always will be."

"Very likely you're right, Daisy. Very likely you're right. Ta-ra. Ta-ra, Ward. Happy days."

"He talks the same as he did at school." She was looking at Ward now, and he answered, "Yes, I suppose so; but he's harmless, and I've never known him to come out with anything that would hurt another."

"Huh! You got religion all of a sudden?"

He gave her no answer, but as she made to walk on and towards the village street, he stopped and said, "I've got to get back; there's a lot to do."

They were standing at the end of the cemetery wall, in the shade of a beech tree, and now, almost glaring at him, she said, "What's up with you?"

"Up with me? Nothing."

"You've never been to church for over a month."

"Well, Daisy, if you keep count, you'll know that, for a time before that, I hadn't been for over a year. I have fits and starts in that way."

"And in other ways an' all," she put in quickly; "and I say again, what's the matter with you?"

"Nothing's the matter with me," he snarled back at her. "What's the matter with *you?*"

"Now, don't you come the simpleton with me, Ward Gibson; you're not Fred Newberry. I've only seen you once in a fortnight."

"Well, if you're reckoning on time, there's times when you've only seen me once in a month. And, if you recall, I've got a farm to see to, and I've only got one man to help out. Your dad has the two lads and you, and your mother, besides the hired boy."

As soon as he mentioned the hired boy his mind recalled the happenings at breakfast concerning their young visitor; he shelved it, the present issue being much more important, for she was saying, "You've been four times to Newcastle in the week."

"Ohoo!" He moved his head slowly up and down, then repeated, "Ohoo! I'm being watched, am I? And everybody wants to know what I'm doing in Newcastle, I suppose?"

"I know what you did one night. You went to The Empire."

"Yes. Yes, Daisy, I went to The Empire. But what did I do on the other nights? Haven't you found out?"

When she didn't answer, he said, "Oh, that would surprise you. It would give you and your spies something to talk about, where I went the other nights."

Her full-lipped mouth pouted before she said, and softly now, "You're playin' fast and loose with me, Ward, and we're as good as engaged."

He gaped at her. *"What! Engaged?* What are you talking about? I've never even mentioned marriage to you."

"No; you've been crafty'—her voice was no longer soft—"you've never mentioned it, but you've acted it. I mean, you've had me on a string, you've played about with me."

"My God! Daisy. Played about with you? I've danced with you at the barn dances; I've taken you to the Hoppings, twice, if I remember rightly, and I've kissed you once or twice. But God in heaven! that doesn't signify I've asked you to marry me." Even as he said this he was wishing he was like Fred and never hurt anybody by what he said; but then he must go on and say it, and for more reasons than one. Oh yes, for more reasons than one. And now he said it: "I've never had any thoughts of marrying you, Daisy. I've known you since we were nippers, sat at school with you, ran the fields with you; we've climbed trees together. You were like one of the lads."

He wished he could stop talking, for he couldn't stand the look on her face. And now he added in a subdued tone, "Oh, Daisy, I'm sorry. I really am. We were pals . . . I mean friends."

"Friends! Friends! I could have been married twice over but didn't because of you. *Do you hear?* Arthur Steel wanted me, him over in Chester-le-Street. He has a farm, a big 'un, he could use yours for pig sties. He . . . he asked me twice."

His voice was very low now and soothing as he said, "Well, then, Daisy, he could ask you again."

He watched her lips move into a snarl, which issued through her clenched teeth as she hissed, "He's married! You . . . you pig of a man! He's married." She was audibly crying now, the sound coming from deep in her throat. Then gulping, she seemed to steady herself before pleading now, "Don't do this to me, Ward. The lads expect it. Me dad and mum expect it; everybody expects it. They have for years while we've been walking out."

He shook his head. "Daisy, we've never been walking out, not in that sense. Listen to me." He now put his hand on her shoulder and drew her along the side of the cemetery wall into a narrow lane; and there he leaned towards her as he said thickly, "Have . . . have I ever tried to touch you? You know . . . you know what I mean. Answer me truly: have I ever?"

"That makes no difference."

"But it does. I'm a man. You know all about mating; that's farming life.

If I'd had marriage in mind I would have tried something on. So there you have it. But well, I . . . I went elsewhere, because I wouldn't insult you, or spoil what was between us, which was a good friendship. We could laugh together, joke together, make fun of them all . . . at least up till the last year or so."

She seemed not to have heard his last words, for she muttered, "You went elsewhere." It was a statement, not a question. Shamefaced, he looked away from her and said, "Aye; yes, I had to. But it was nothing. She was married. She wasn't a whore or . . . or anything like that, she was . . . well . . ."

How could he find words to explain that a chance meeting at an inn on the road to Durham with a woman who could, at a pinch, have been his mother, could not lead to anything? She must have been in her forties. But she had been nice, kind and understanding. His mother had just died, and it was as if, besides a lover, he had gained another mother. He had known her only a short time, and then she had said it must stop because her husband would soon be coming back from sea. At their parting, she had spoken words to him that he would always remember: "It's been the most beautiful time in my life," she had said; "and I'll remember it till I die. But this is the time to end it, for even the most beautiful flowers fade."

He had never known anyone talk as she did, and he had missed her. Even up till this last week he had wondered if he had loved her; and he knew he had in a way, but the feeling was something different; it could never happen again; it had been the birth of his manhood, and you can't be born twice, not in that way.

"What?"

"*You! You!* You heard. She's in Newcastle, isn't she?"

He couldn't answer this, not really; and so he remained silent. The next instant he sprang back in surprise and pain as her fingernails tore down each side of his face.

Instinctively, his fist came out and, catching her on the shoulder, knocked her back against the wall. But she didn't slide down to the ground; she just stood, pressed tight against the rough stone, her large breasts heaving, her face contorted.

As he put one hand to his face and felt it wet, he backed from her; and at this she pulled herself from the wall, and she stood there, staring at him.

There was no movement of any part of her body now; even her lips seemed not to part as she said, "I'll have my own back on you, Ward Gibson. I swear before God I will; you and all yours. D'you hear me?"

He made no rejoinder; but now watched as her hands slowly went to her hat and straightened it, then down to her coat to button it over her heaving breasts, before she turned slowly away to walk back along by the side of the cemetery wall.

Now he, too, moved, but only as far as the wall; in fact, to the very spot where she had been standing; and he laid his head against it and, taking a handkerchief from his pocket, gently drew it over his left cheek; then looked at it. It was covered with blood. He felt his other cheek. It was sore, but it was dry. He closed his eyes, and his body slumped.

How long he stayed like this against the wall, he didn't know; he only knew that for the first time in his life he was experiencing fear, for he could still see her face. He doubted if he would ever forget the look on it. He imagined it to be how a real mad woman might look.

After pulling himself up straight, he didn't make for the village street, but went down the narrow path that skirted the west wall of the cemetery, to lead into open pasture, then Morgan's wood. This way would take him twice as long to reach home; but he needed time to compose himself and to think.

Yet all he could think about throughout the whole journey was the look on her face and her threat, and the surprise, too, that the Daisy he had played with as a child, romped with during his boyhood years, teased, laughed and danced with, and kissed occasionally, should have in her what now appeared to him as an evil spirit, such as you read about in the Bible but never took any notice of, or, if you did, you thought of it as a fable. But Daisy Mason represented no fable. *No! No!*

"In the name of God!" said Annie. "Where've you been? An' what's done that to your face? I thought you were at church."

"Get me a drink, Annie."

"Aye. Aye." Her head wagged. "Is it ale you want, or a drop of the hard?"

"A drop of the hard."

She was only a minute gone from the kitchen before she returned with a glass in her hand, one third full of whisky; and after he had thrown it back without pausing she took the glass from him; then, her hand going out, she gently touched the two weals that were now covered in dried blood, and she asked quietly, "An animal?"

For a moment he gazed up at her as if he were thinking. "Well, it was like the act of one," he said.

She now stood back from him, her face screwed up in enquiry; then, as if a light were dawning on her, she muttered, "Not Daisy Mason?"

"The very same, Annie."

She emitted a slow breath before commenting, the while nodding her head, "I shouldn't be surprised. No, I shouldn't, because I've always thought of her as an untamed bitch in that great bulk of hers. But you've asked for it, you know."

"I've never asked for it, Annie."

"Oh yes, you have. There's half a dozen lasses round about you could have taken on jaunts, but who did you take? Daisy Mason. Now that must have made her think. But tell me what's made her think otherwise?"

"I told her I wasn't for marrying."

"What brought it about?"

"Oh, she implied . . . No, she didn't imply, she said right out that we were as good as engaged."

"And you said you weren't, and then she went for you?"

"There was more to it than that. I had to speak plainly. I'm sorry I had to do so, but there was nothing else for it."

Annie turned from him and walked towards the oven as she said, "Would there have been nothing else for it up till this last week?"

He stared at her bent back as she opened the oven door and took out a large dripping tin holding a sizzling joint, and she had placed it on the end of the table before he answered, "Yes, Annie, it would have been the same. And what do you mean by . . . this last week?"

"Oh, lad; you're talking to an old woman." She grinned now, and then said, "Well, if not old, getting on, and as far as I can remember in this house, since the day you could toddle you've never made four journeys into Newcastle in a week, and I shouldn't imagine it was to the Haymarket, or to your solicitor man, nor anything else like that, an' going by the programme I found on your dressing table, I think I've got the answer." She now pushed the hot roasting tin away from her, laid the coarse towel with which she had been holding it over the back of a chair, which she then pulled towards her and sat down on. Her knees now almost touching his, she leaned towards him, asking, "Is it the young lass on the front of the programme that's caught your eye?"

He stared back at her, his face and neck suffused red with embarrassment. "It isn't just a fancy, Annie," he said; "I can't explain it. I'm drawn there, you know, like the saying is, as if by a magnet."

"Well, lad, you know your own road best, but from what I understand and it might only be hearsay, but it's been said over the years that those bits of lasses on the stage are of light character."

"Yes, Annie; I've heard all that."

"But you think this one's different. What has she to say for herself? Is she well spoken? Is she . . . ?"

"I wouldn't know, Annie; I haven't met her."

"*Oh! lad.*" She gave a chuckle now. "If you had told me you'd jumped off one of the Newcastle bridges because you thought you could fly, I would have said, well, these things happen to daft individuals who haven't been well brought up and who haven't heads on their shoulders, but not to you, never to somebody like you. Ah, Master Ward"—she put her hand out and patted his shoulder—"it's a sad dream. We all have 'em, you know. Women an' all. For meself, I never thought I'd marry a man like Bill; the fellow I was goin' to give me hand to wasn't goin' to do farm work. No, by gum. I was above that; I'd seen enough of it in this house, although there was nobody better as a master or mistress than your folks. But, in a way, I had taken a pattern from them and I wanted somebody better, somebody who wore a collar an' tie when he went to work, an' didn't smell of cow byres or pig muck." Her whole body began to shake now as she went on, "But then something hit me. I don't know what it is to this day; I only know if I hadn't him, life wouldn't be worth living; and he's a grumpy, impatient sod at the best of times."

"Oh, Annie!" He closed his eyes and flapped his hand towards her, saying, "Don't make me laugh. Please don't make me laugh; my face is sore; and at the moment my heart is sore, an' all. I've hurt somebody deeply, and what's more I've seen her character change so much that it frightened me."

She stared at him and, seriously now, she said, "She must have gone a bit wild to do that to you."

"More than a bit, Annie; I would never have believed it of her. Anyway, I must go and clean this up."

As he lifted his hand towards his face, she said, "Sit where you are. I'll go and get some witch hazel and rose water, and wash it for you, then put the salve on. But I can see you're goin' to have a couple of marks there for some time. The other side'll fade . . . By! she did a job on you." As she rose to her feet she added, "It's been a funny morning all round. I got a surprise when I looked at that youngster's back; and then there was that salt business. That was funny, wasn't it?"

He nodded at her. "Yes; yes it was funny."

"I'll say it was. Fancy being frightened to touch salt! When I pushed it towards him, do you remember, and me saying, "Put salt on your egg now," he almost threw the cellar across the table, and at the same time shrank back in his chair as if it was going to bite him? Most odd, wasn't it?"

"It was, Annie. Yes, it was."

As she once again hurried from the room he recalled to mind the incident of the salt and the look on the boy's face. It was full of fear, as it had been last night when he had first seen him. It was as if the salt had been a live snake.

The thought of the boy's fear recalled his own of a short while ago, because for a time he had been swamped with fear. It was a new emotion, almost as strong as the one he felt for the beautiful figure flitting from one side of the stage to the other, as light as he imagined a fairy would be; and when, at the end, turning into a bird by lifting her arms head high to expose wings of fine ribbed silk, before she was lifted and, the wings rippling like water, she flew from the stage to loud cheers and clapping from the audience, the feeling she left him with was so strong as to be painful, for she appeared more angelic than any angel his imagination had ever been able to conjure up.

But then, Daisy had expressed a fierce hate of him such as again his imagination had never been able to conjure up. Of a sudden he felt weak and fearful with the force of both.

THREE

*I*t was a drizzling rain, and Annie remarked on it: "It's in for the night," she said; "you'll get sodden." She now raised her eyebrows, so stretching her longish features even further as she said, "Have you got to go in?"

"Yes, Annie; I've got to go in. But as for asking me what I've got to go in for, well, I'll tell you shortly; and I might do it with a pleasant grin on my face or, on the other hand, looking at me, you'll know it's better to keep your tongue quiet and not ask questions."

"Like that, is it?"

"It's like that, Annie. Yes, it's like that."

"Well, I only hope she's worth it." She was standing at the wooden sink and looking out of the kitchen window, and she exclaimed, "You won't be goin' this minute, you've got company."

"Who is it?" He went quickly across the room to stand by her side, and when he saw John Mason step down from his trap he bit on his lower lip, and before turning away, he said quietly, "Show him into the sitting-room, Annie."

"The sitting-room?" Her face stretched again. "Well, all right, I'll do that; but he's always come straight into the kitchen afore; all of them have. But as you say . . ."

She went from him, leaving him again nipping on his lip, this time whilst waiting for Annie's welcome: "Oh; good evenin', Mr. Mason. Can I have your coat; you're a bit wet."

"Is Ward anywhere about?"

"Yes; yes, he is. If you'll just take a seat in the parlour, I'll go fetch him for you."

By the silence that followed Ward could imagine the man hesitating on the invitation to go into the parlour as if he were a stranger.

A minute or so later, on Annie's entering the kitchen, Ward held up his hand to silence anything she might say, then walked past her across the stone-flagged hall and into the parlour.

John Mason was standing with his back to the empty grate, and his greeting was, "Hello there, Ward. Oh . . . oh, I see you're ready for going on the road. Well, I won't keep you long."

When Ward stood before him, the older man stared at his face, then turned his head to the side before saying softly, "I'm sorry she did that to you. But she was upset. Oh, yes, she was upset . . . What's come over you, Ward?"

He didn't answer for quite some time, for what could he say to this decent man, a man he had always liked, because he was a fair man in all his dealings. Not so his two sons, at least not so Sep. He had never liked Sep; he was a big-mouth. And Pete . . . well, Pete didn't talk as much, but there had always been a slyness about Pete. Yet the father and mother were the nicest couple you could meet in a day's walk; and so, could he say to this man that he had become obsessed, because that word somehow fitted his feelings, and to a girl to whom he had never spoken and knew nothing whatever about except that she danced beautifully and was beautiful to look at, yet so fragile?

What he did say was, "I never mentioned marriage to Daisy, Mr. Mason."

"No, lad; no. Perhaps you didn't mention the word, but all your actions over the past years have sort of implied that was your intention. To tell you the truth, me and her mother took it for granted that you would one day match up, because she would have made you a good wife. She knows everything about a farm that is to know; besides which she's a fine cook . . . Not much good with her needle." A faint smile came on his face now. "Not like her mother in that way; but you can't have everything. I thought, though, she had everything that you needed, Ward. Oh yes. And I still do."

"I'm sorry, Mr. Mason. I am indeed. I'm sorry to the heart to upset you and your wife, because you've both always been very kind to me; and I shall never forget the help you were when both Mam and Dad died. But look at it from my point of view if you can. I've known Daisy all me life. We were like friends. She was . . . well, it's a funny way to put it, but she was like a mate to me, as neither Sep nor Pete were."

"Well, if that was the case, Ward, why did you continue to keep company with her and not take up with some other girl in the village or hereabouts? No . . . no." Mr. Mason moved his head slowly now. "Be fair, Ward, there only seemed to be Daisy for you. You took her to the barn dances, you took her to the Hoppings, Sunday after Sunday you used to drop in to tea. Well, that was some time back, I admit, before your people went; but, nevertheless, our house was like your second home."

"That's it, Mr. Mason," Ward put in quickly, "it was like my second home; you were all too close; too familiar; there was no . . . well, excitement. Oh—" He half turned away now, saying, "I'm sorry about all this. I keep saying that, but I really am."

"Tell me truthfully, Ward. Just answer me a simple question: have you found somebody else?"

Ward turned now and, facing Mr. Mason again, he said, "You could put it like that, Mr. Mason; yes, you could put it like that."

Mr. Mason now walked slowly past Ward and towards the door, saying as he went, "One could say, this is life, and these things happen; but that's from people standing apart. They are the onlookers, not the ones it's actually happening to. And it's happening to my Daisy, and she's hurt to the core." He stopped, and he opened the parlour door before turning and saying to Ward, "I haven't it in me to wish you harm because I've always imagined you becoming another son, but I would be lying if I said I wish you luck and happiness in your choice, because, in a way, you've ruined my lass's life. Yes; yes, you have, Ward."

When the door had closed on him, Ward turned to the mantelshelf and, laying his arm along it, he drooped his head on to it, and as he muttered, "God in heaven!" his fist thumped the wood.

After a moment he straightened up; and now he was looking into the iron-framed mirror above the fireplace, and his reflection was telling him Mr. Mason was right: he *had* acted as if he had intended to marry Daisy. He had been utterly thoughtless, at least until a year or so ago when he guessed how things were with her. But still, in the end, perhaps he would have married her if this other thing hadn't hit him, for there would have been this same strong need in him; and it wasn't possible he would ever again come across such an obliging and understanding woman as Mrs. Oswald.

And now he was in a fix, all because he had dropped into The Empire a week ago.

Was he mad? He must be. He had seen the creature only four times. God above! Why was he thinking of her as a creature now? Because she could be a creature: on closer acquaintance she could prove to be just a painted doll. Those bright lights bamboozled people. She could be a slut; most of them were; a lot of them sold themselves to men . . . old men, for money and big houses . . . or titles.

He turned from the mirror, and his gaze now focussed on the horse-hair sofa that fronted the hand-made rug set before the hearth, and he seemed to address it as his galloping thoughts said, Well the only thing to do to find out what she is really like is to wait till after the show's over and speak to her.

He had only once joined the crowd outside, and that had been on Saturday night. But she hadn't put in an appearance. The leading lady had come out, and made her way to the waiting cab; and the comedian and the juggler and six chorus girls had come out of the stage door; but she hadn't put in an appearance, and so, left alone on the pavement, he had surmised there must be another way out at the back of the theatre.

But tonight, stage door or back door, he must speak to her—and he would, so what was he standing here for?

When he reached the yard, Billy was coming out of the open barn and, seeing him, called, "I'm having trouble with the youngster."

"Trouble? Why?"

"As soon as he saw Mr. Mason come into the yard he scooted up into the loft, and there he is up against the timbers again as if he was glued. An' I can't talk him down. And another thing: I think his back should be seen to; one of those weals is running matter. Would you think about callin' the doctor on your way to Newcastle?"

"No, I wouldn't think about calling the doctor; unless you want the child to be whipped back to wherever he came from. What's the matter with your head, Billy? You should know Old Wheatley by this time, for, either drunk or sober, he's always for the law, especially where lads are concerned. Spare the whip and spoil the child. He wouldn't give youngsters the light of day until they were ready for work, of one kind or another, if he had his way. You know him. Anyway, I'll have a look at it when I come back . . . He seemed all right earlier on."

"Oh, I think he was trying his best to show us he could work. But now he's a bundle of fear again. Could you give him a shout, do you think?"

Ward drew in a long breath. Already he'd be too late for the opening; and so he'd have to stay at the back. Anyway, it wasn't the show he wanted to see, it was her. But it was impatiently he marched into the barn and stood at the foot of the ladder shouting, "Boy! Come down this minute!"

When there was no response, his voice louder and angry sounding, he cried, "I am dressed for the road, and I am not coming up this ladder. If you don't put in an appearance before I count five you'll be on your way back tomorrow to where you came from. Do you hear me?"

He couldn't have reached three when the small head looked down on him; then the thin shanks stepped down slowly from one rung of the ladder to another.

Having reached the floor, he stood with his head down, and Ward, speaking slowly now, said, "You know what I promised you last night: that you could be here for good, but I want a worker." He now glanced sharply towards Billy before going on, "And not a lad that skitters into the barn every time a trap comes into the yard."

The small head came up, and the boy's voice became a stutter as he said, "I . . . I th . . . th . . . thought he had come for me. He s . . . s . . . said he would."

"Who's he? What's his name?"

Again the head drooped.

Ward became impatient, saying, "I'm not going through all this again tonight. Now, listen to me, and finally: nobody's going to take you back to that place. I promised you. Now go to the house and get your supper."

As the boy now hurried from them, Billy put in flatly, "He was right to skitter, for you could have the authorities round here if anybody gets wind of him. Well, I mean they would want to know where we got him, and all the rest of it. You know yourself you can't keep anything quiet for long, not round here. In the village your business is their business, at least, so it seems. So, in a way, the youngster was wise to make himself scarce. They all seem to know about what they call the Poor Law Contract; they know they'll be sent back, no matter where they're found, either to the same farm or to the same workhouse. You know yourself what the so-called guardians are like. Remember the business over at Burnley's farm a few years back?"

"Those boys were mental."

"Aye. If I remember rightly they had escaped an' all; but Burnley kept them on. Then what happened when he was taken up for it? He said if the lads were mental then he was mental an' all; and they should never have been put away as children . . . They fined him. Oh, heavy."

Impatient to be gone, Ward hurried from the barn and into the stables; and when presently he led the saddled horse into the yard, Billy called, "She hates the rain. You'll get her under cover, I suppose?" And at this, Ward turned a look of disdain on the man for whom he had a deep affection, before putting the horse into a trot that turned into a gallop as soon as they left the farm yard; and Billy's remark to the wind and rain was, "He's caught something a poultice won't help."

He couldn't understand it. He was on the pavement outside the theatre looking at the rain-soaked poster on the wall. It was the same as last week's, except for one thing: there was no flying angel across the middle, but over it had been stuck a bill that read: Laugh With The Lorenzoes, the three side-splitting maniac acrobats from Spain. Above them and central was the picture of the soprano, with, to one side of her, the big fat woman and the little fat man with their four poodles, and, to the other side, the juggler. Below were the names of the "lesser turns," the print getting smaller towards the end of the bill.

But where was the Maltese Angel? Gone too was her picture from the sandwich board that was positioned further along the pavement.

He did not go into the booking hall but hurried towards the stage door at the side; and when he saw the doorman standing in the passage-way, he gabbled, "What's happened? I mean to the Maltese Angel? To . . . well, the dancer?"

The doorman looked him up and down, and grinned as he said, "Oh! You here again? Not a night to come out and have your journey for nowt."

"What's happened to her?"

"Oh, she had a bit of an accident. She won't be tripping the light fantastic for a few weeks, I would say. The wire gave way and she hurt her foot."

"Where is she now?"

"Oh; back at her lodgings, I suppose. Yes, that's where she is."

As the spout above him overflowed, Ward stepped quickly into the doorway, and from there into the hallway to where the doorman had retreated, only to be surprised by being sharply admonished by the man: "Here! There's no entrance this way," which succeeded in bringing forth an equally sharp reply from Ward: "I'm not thinking about going in this way, but I'm not going to stand out in that while I'm asking you a question."

The change of note in Ward's voice caused the man to back from him and again to look him up and down, then say, "Well, the answer you'll get to your question will be no; I'm not at liberty to tell you where she's staying. An' you're not the only one this week who would have liked to know that."

"I can understand your position; but I must tell you, I mean the lady no harm . . . none at all."

"Aye; an' I can tell you, mister, that's what they all say, whether they're from the town or the country. An' you're from the country, aren't you?"

Before Ward could get over his indignation in order to make an appropriate reply to this observant man and demand how the devil he knew he was from the country, the man told him: "Oh . . . Oh you needn't get on your high horse, mister," he said; "I've seen 'em all. But none of your townees would come four times in a week an' sit in the front row. No; by the second night they would have had a cab at the door an' flowers sent to her dressing-room. Oh, they're all the same, London, Manchester, or here. I've seen 'em all," he boasted again; but then his tone changing, he said, "Anyway, I'm sorry I can't let on where she's stayin', not even for a backhander."

"I wasn't thinking about giving you a backhander. And seeing that you've weighed me up, and everybody else apparently—" His words were cut off by the opening of the swing door to his right and, through it the appearance of an enormous woman and a very small man, each of them carrying two dogs and each dog enveloped in a red flannel coat.

The woman, ignoring Ward, spoke directly to the doorman, "That bugger won't do that to us again. Put us on in the first half. We know our place. We should be third from last by now. I'll have something to say to him at the end of the week. A year now since we first hit Newcastle, and it'll be ten before we hit it again."

When one of the dogs in her arms moved uneasily and turned its head towards Ward while giving a sharp bark, she turned her attention to him, saying, "It's all right, mister; as long as you don't touch her she won't bite you."

But Ward had already put his hand out and was scratching the immaculate white topknot of the poodle, and the poodle, instead of biting him, was licking his wrist, the sight of which brought an exclamation from the small man in a voice that was so high as to seem to be issuing from the mouth of a young boy: "Flora! Flora! Did you ever! Do you see what Sophia's doing?"

The large woman, looking straight at Ward now, said, "You used to animals, mister? Trainer or something?"

He was forced to smile as he answered, "No; no; but I have two dogs of my own."

"Poodles?"

"No. Sheep dogs. I'm . . . I'm a farmer."

"Oh. Oh." She now said pointedly, "Bitches?"

He was still smiling as he answered her: "One of each."

"Well, all I can say she must have got a sniff of something that pleased her, because she's very particular, is Sophia."

Ward looked at Sophia. He recognised her as the clever one that pulled the little bottle out of the man's coat, withdrew the cork with her teeth, and then, standing on her hindlegs, put the bottle to her mouth; after which she staggered across the stage to the uproarious laughter of the audience, fell on her back and kicked her legs in the air, to be chastised by this woman, who picked her up, smacked her bottom and sent her off the stage, only for the dog to come slinking in the other side, supposedly unknown to anyone.

The woman was addressing him now: "Have you seen the show, sir?"

"Yes; I've seen the show."

She now leaned towards him, to peer in the dim light of the passage. Then, her mouth opening into a big gape and the smile spreading across her face, she exclaimed, "Oh yes! The front row. The front row."

Rather shamefacedly now, Ward nodded and said, "Yes; the front row."

"To see Stephanie."

Before he had time to acknowledge this, the doorman put in, "This . . . this gentleman . . . This gentleman came to see Miss McQueen the night, but was very disappointed that she wasn't on."

"Oh. Oh." The woman's head was now bobbing up and down. "Well, I'm sorry you've had your journey for nothing, sir; but she had an accident, you see. Saturday night just gone. He let her down too quickly." She now turned her head and addressed the doorman: "He's a bloody maniac, that Watson," she said. "He's never sober. I'm not against a drink, you know that, Harry, but there's a time an' a place for it. And she's as light on her feet as a feather. But he bounced her down. She stotted off that foot like a rubber ball."

"Is she in a bad way?" Ward's voice held an anxious note.

"Well"—the woman shrugged her shoulders and the flesh on her body seemed to ripple—"not in a bad way, really; no life or death business. Yet, what am I talking about? It's her livelihood. Her feet are her fortune, you could say, and it'll be a week or two before she's able to go on the boards again. Yet she keeps rubbing it and declares she'll be all right for Sunderland next week. But she won't, will she, Ken?" She turned to the little man, who answered accordingly, "No, Flora; 'cause she won't. But she's got pluck. Oh yes, she's got pluck."

"Do . . . do you think . . . I mean, do you think I might see her? Sort of be introduced to her? I . . . I would like to make her acquaintance."

The woman and the man looked at each other, their glances holding for some time before she, as if having come to a great decision, said with emphasis, "I don't see any reason, sir, why you shouldn't make her acquaintance.

Sophia here seemed to have a good opinion of you, so, animals having much more sense than humans, I've always said so, and I would trust them any day in the week to give me the right answer, I would say, no, I don't see any obstacle that need be put in the way. Have you got a conveyance?"

The word conveyance came out on a high note and with a change of tone; and when he had to confess that he was sorry he hadn't, only his horse, the woman laughed and her ah-la changed as she said, "Well, we can't all get on that, can we? And so, as it's only a stone's throw from here, where we are residing, we could all walk the distance, couldn't we? Good night, Harry."

She was nodding towards the doorman, who replied, "Good night, Mrs. Killjoy. Good night, Mr. Killjoy." And the little man answered, "Good night, Harry."

They were now in the street, Ward walking between the woman and the man, with the rain pelting down on them, and Mrs. Killjoy wiped it from her face as she enquired of him, "And what is your name, sir?"

"I'm Hayward Gibson, but I'm usually called Ward."

"Ward. It's an unusual Christian name . . . Ward. Well, Mr. Gibson, you know our occupation, so may I enquire if your farm is a large farm or a small one. You see, we are town folk, and the only thing we seem to know is that farms belong to estates where smallholdings don't."

Ward smiled to himself at this diplomatic grilling, and he pursed his lip before he explained, "Well, my farm isn't held on lease to one of the land-owners, by which I mean it isn't rented; it is a freehold farm, much bigger than a smallholding, but much smaller than some other farms in the country."

"Well, that is a fair answer." She now turned towards him and smiled broadly as she said, "We cross over here, and then we are almost there. But to get back to the farmers: you see, we are very ignorant of the country, we people who live by the boards, for entertainments such as ours are performed in the town, you know, aren't they?"

They were in the middle of the road now, and, halting suddenly, she held up a hand, as a constable might, to stop the approaching traffic. The astonished driver of a cab to one side of her and two boys pushing a flat cart to the other pulled up sharply, causing further astonishment from the drivers of the following vehicles dimly seen through the rain and gathering twilight as she led her company across the other half of the road and to the pavement, to the accompaniment of highly seasoned language from the cab driver and others and the ribald laughter of the boys. But as if this incident had not happened, she continued where she had left off, saying, "So we must always enquire into the work, station, and habits of those who wish to make our acquaintance."

He wanted to laugh aloud, he wanted to roar: here he was, walking between these two oddities and their four dogs and being questioned as to his character as if he were in a courtroom, and all the while there was racing through him a feeling of anticipation and excitement; he was going to meet her . . . not as the actress coming out of the stage door, whom he would not really have known how to approach, but he was going to face her in her lodgings.

For a moment the anticipation and elation were chilled by the thought: what if he didn't take to her? What if she were a hoity-toity piece and thought too much of herself; or, on the other hand, just plain common; but oh dear! what if she didn't take to him? Yes, that was the main point: what if she didn't take to him?

"Ah! Here we are. Home from home."

He was standing in a street where every house appeared to be approached by three steps, guarded on each side by sloping iron railings. They were quite large houses. He wouldn't say this was the best end of the city, but it was no cheap street.

The front door to the house looked heavy and strong and was graced with a brass letter-box and door-knob, and when it was opened, the woman sailed in; and the man pressed Ward forward. And now he was being introduced to a woman who was apparently the owner of the house, for Mrs. Killjoy was saying, "This is a friend of ours, Connie. We have met him by chance this evening." She turned towards Ward now, saying, "Mr. Hayward Gibson." Then extending her hand to the flat bosomed middle-aged woman, she added, "Mrs. Borman, our landlady and the kindest you will find in a day's walk." And now, with fingers wagging, she exclaimed, "And I mean that, Connie. You know I mean that."

Mrs. Borman did not spread her gaze over his entire body as Mrs. Killjoy had done; but she looked him straight in the face and in a pleasant voice said, "Good evening, Mr. Gibson. Any friend of Mrs. Killjoy is welcome to my house."

Nodding and smiling, Mrs. Killjoy put down her small charges, as did her husband, and informed the landlady in the most polite terms, "They have already done their number ones and twos, and Ken will give them their dinner as usual and put them to bed . . . Go along, my darlings. Go along with your papa."

During this little scene Ward had been standing apart, holding his wide-brimmed hat level so that the rain wouldn't drip on to the polished linoleum of the hall floor, and not really believing what he was hearing and witnessing. It was as if he himself had been lifted on to a stage and was taking part in a play; and then more so when Mrs. Killjoy asked in her assumed refined tone, "And how is our patient faring? Has she behaved herself?"

"Yes," replied Mrs. Borman; "I would say she has, as always, behaved herself. She is now in the parlour."

"Oh, she has managed to get there! That is wonderful. And it has eased what might have been an embarrassing question, which I would have had to phrase very diplomatically in asking if our friend here would have been allowed to visit her privately. Oh, the parlour is very suitable. Would you come this way?" She inclined a hand towards Ward. "But, ah"—she stopped again —"before doing so, let me divest you of your coat and take that hat."

He had to close his eyes for a moment whilst being divested of his coat. But then he was following Mrs. Killjoy, a person, he considered, most definitely misnamed, into a room that seemed to be furnished entirely with chairs of all shapes and sizes, and there, sitting on one to the side of the fireplace, was a slim young girl.

As he walked slowly towards her, Mrs. Killjoy was exclaiming loudly, "I've brought a gentleman to see you, dear. He was so disappointed that you weren't on stage tonight. He was enquiring of your health. He is a Mr. Hay

. . . ward Gibson." She split the name. "He is from the country . . . How is your ankle, dear?"

As the girl answered, "Much better, thank you," she did not look at Mrs. Killjoy, but at the tall man staring down at her, and she was recognising him, much more than at the moment he was recognising her, because he was looking down on a girl he imagined to be not more than sixteen, with her abundant brown hair lying in a loose bun at the back of her head. Her face was oval-shaped; her eyes large, and they were brown, too, but of a deeper brown than her hair. She had a wide full mouth and a small nose, and her skin appeared to be slightly tanned. In no way did she fit the picture of the Maltese Angel.

"Good evening."

"Good evening." He bowed slightly; then he added, "I . . . I was sorry to hear of your accident."

"Oh, it was nothing. It will soon be better." She put her hand towards where her foot was resting on the low stool. "I'll be dancing again next week."

"That you won't. I've never been a betting woman but I'll take a bet on that. Three weeks at the least. That's what the doctor said. And, by the way" —Mrs. Killjoy now indicated Ward with a quite gracious wave of her hand— "Mr. Gibson is a farmer. And Sophia took to him, so that's a good reference, don't you think." She smiled now from one to the other; then hitching up her large bosom, she added, "Now, I'm away to tidy myself up and get ready for supper, although we'll have a good hour or more to wait, seeing that we're early in. He put us on in the first half." She now bent forward, her finger wagging as if at the culprit who had done this thing. "Would you believe that, Stephanie? The effrontery of it! Still, I'll tell you all about it later."

At this, she turned about and sailed from the room, for, in spite of her bulk, her step was light.

Ward searched in his mind for something to say, but the only words it prompted were, "It is still raining," to which inane remark the girl quietly invited him to sit down.

He looked around as to which chair he would take, and her voice full of laughter now, prompted him, saying, "Don't sit in the big leather one. It looks very comfortable, but the springs have gone. I think the safest would be the Bentwood arm." She pointed to a chair a little to the left of her.

He returned her smile and, nodding, walked around her outstretched leg and seated himself in the chair which stood within a few feet of her own; and she turned to face him fully and said, "It was very kind of you to come to the show." She did not add, "so often."

He knew his colour had risen as he replied, "You noticed me, then?"

"Yes. Yes, I noticed you."

"I . . . I enjoyed your dancing."

"Thank you."

He sat looking at her in silence now. She had a nice voice, different from any he had heard, except perhaps that of Colonel Ramsmore's wife or of Mrs. Hopkins, when either the one or the other opened the fair. Yet there was nothing high-falutin about it, like theirs; but it was different. Oh yes, it was different. She was different all round: different from her stage appearance; different from what he had expected her to be off stage; but she looked so young. He was slightly surprised to hear himself voicing his thoughts: "You looked young on the stage, but pardon my saying, you look much younger off."

She now leant back against the padded head of the high-backed chair, and she laughed as she said, "I'm a very deceptive person. I shall be nineteen on my next birthday."

He found he was so relieved that he, too, laughed back as he said brightly, "My! no-one would ever guess it," a remark which made her neither blush nor become coy, but divert any further allusion by asserting, "Mrs. Killjoy is a wonderful woman, a wonderful friend, but she is very bad at betting and I have proved her wrong so many times, for by next week I shall certainly be dancing again. But in Sunderland. That is our next booking."

He did not wonder why she said this, but he repeated, "Sunderland?" then nodded at her, saying, "I often pop down to Sunderland. How long are you likely to be there?"

"Just a week, I think."

"Oh. Only a week." Another inane remark, he thought; then he asked, "Where do you live . . . I mean your home?"

She turned her gaze away from him and looked towards her foot, and she seemed to sigh before she said, "Wherever we are playing: I have no settled home."

"No?" The syllable held a note of surprise, and she answered, "My parents were on the stage too. My mother was a dancer, and my father sang. And so I've always been on the move. I think it was a year after my father brought my mother from Malta that we settled in Bristol, because I wasn't born until the following year. And that was in York, and two days after Christmas Day."

He did not remark on her Christmas birth, but asked, "Your parents . . . they are . . . ?"

Her answer was without false sentiment: "They are dead," she said. "My mother died of smallpox, and a year later my father was drowned. But that was almost six years ago. Since then Mr. and Mrs. Killjoy have been almost like parents to me."

"I'm sure. I'm sure." His head was nodding, but he could find no more to say; he felt utterly tongue-tied, all he could do was listen to his thoughts: she was beautiful, but of a different beauty to that which she showed from the stage. The word that suited her there, he supposed, would be ethereal, not quite of this world. But this girl was of this world. And she seemed at ease in it. There was a quietness about her. And yet her eyes were merry, and she smiled often. He wished he could see her standing up; he didn't know how tall she would be. She was very slim. Well, she would have to be very slim, wouldn't she, and of no weight to be hanging from that wire?

"Now you've heard all about my life, so may I ask about yours? Mrs. Killjoy says you're a farmer. That sounds so interesting. It must be wonderful dealing with animals. I love the poodles." She indicated a door at the end of the room as if that was where the dogs were.

He could answer her now: he gave a short laugh as he said, "Not so wonderful when you have to get up on a winter morning around five, because you know, cows wear watches." He actually pulled a face at her. "And they don't like it if you're a bit late; they kick up a row."

She was laughing outright now, as she repeated his words: "Cows wear watches. Have you many?"

"Eighteen milkers and six youngsters coming on . . . heifers, you know; and three horses, one for the trap or riding. Her name is Betsy. And two Shires . . . you know, the big horses. I am sure you've seen them pulling the beer drays; well, mine pull the plough and many other things."

"Oh, yes. Yes. And they are lovely. Have you got ducks?"

"Oh, yes; ducks, chickens, a few geese. And pigs, of course. All that you expect to find on a farm."

"Have you always lived on a farm?"

"Always. And my father, and his father, and his father before him."

She was staring at him again. Her face had been smiling; but now the smile slid away and her hand came out tentatively as if she were about to touch him; but she withdrew it quickly as she said, "I . . . I noticed you've had an injury to your face."

"Oh that." He fingered the two thin lines of dried scab. "I had a sort of accident."

"With . . . with an animal?"

He could have replied, "Yes, a bitch;" instead, he said, "A wild cat got into the barn. I must have surprised her, frightened her. She sprang down from . . . a sort of platform that's found in some barns"—his hand wavered over his brow—"and her claws caught me."

"Oh dear! It must have been very frightening, and painful."

His manner was offhand now as he said, "The only thing is, it's a nuisance. I find it difficult to shave."

"Yes. Yes, of course."

At this point the far door opened and Mr. and Mrs. Killjoy entered the room. On Ward's rising to his feet, the woman exclaimed loudly, at the same time wagging her finger at the young girl, "Now that's the action of a gentleman. You can always tell a gentleman if he'll get off his backside . . . I mean . . . er"—she slanted her gaze at him—"rises from his seat when a woman enters the room."

"Oh, Mrs. Killjoy."

The finger wagged again. "Well, you know me by now, Stephanie: I say what's in my mind, and I can't stop it, because there's a leak there." The large body shook with laughter, in which her husband joined. Then turning to Ward, she said, "Would you like to stop and have a bite of supper? Mrs. Borman says there's enough for all, and plenty of it."

He did not immediately answer; then he said, "I'm sorry; but I'll have to be going. Another time, though, if I am allowed to call"—he glanced towards the girl—"I'd be very pleased to accept."

"Oh, you'd be quite welcome to call again, 'cos there she is—" Mrs. Killjoy turned to the now embarrassed girl, crying, "Well, you're sitting there all day by yourself; you'll be glad of company." Then to Ward, she ended, "Yes, you'd be welcome. She's too shy to say so, but I'm asking it for her."

It was to the girl he spoke again; "Well, if I may, it would be in the evening," he said.

She merely inclined her head towards him; and at this, he swung about and hurried from the room, with Mrs. Killjoy endeavouring to keep pace behind him.

As she helped him into his coat she remarked in an undertone, "You weren't mistaken in your opinion, were you?"

He turned and looked at this surprising woman, and he said soberly, "No, Mrs. Killjoy, you're right, I wasn't. And I will call again at the first opportunity."

"I'm sure, you will, son. I'm sure you will." She patted him on the shoulder now; then handing him his hat and coat she opened the door and, with a wave of her hand, ushered him out.

It was still pouring, and he had the inclination to run, not from the rain, but just to relieve his feelings. She was right. She was right: he hadn't been wrong in his opinion. But the girl wasn't an angel. No, she wasn't an angel; she was a girl of nineteen, and she was sweet, lovely, beautiful . . . very beautiful. God send tomorrow soon.

Back in the parlour of the boarding house, Mrs. Killjoy was sitting facing Stephanie McQueen, and she was addressing her as Fanny. "Fanny," she was saying, "look . . . look at us . . . Ken and me. We're nearly on our last legs. I'm getting past falling flat on my face on those boards every night, sometimes twice nightly. Even without Charlie and Rose attacking me in the backside I could fall down many a night, for me legs an' me back are killin' me. Now, you know, we've got a little bit put by: and we're on the look-out for that little cottage with a patch of garden. It's been the dream of our life. It's forty-three years since I took over from my dad, and I'm nearing the end of the road. As for Ken, I don't know how he keeps going. Now! now!" She held up her hand. "Hear me out. You've been like a daughter to us since your folks went. And I promised your mum I'd always keep an eye on you. And I've done that, haven't I?"

Stephanie's hands came out and gripped the podgy ones, and, her voice breaking and with tears in her eyes, she said, "Oh! Mrs. Killjoy. You know what I think about you, what I think about you both. I would never have got along without you. And I don't think I ever could . . ."

"Oh yes, you could, 'cos you've got an excellent turn. But how long is it going to last? That's what I'm worried about. Look at that." She pointed to the foot resting on the stool. "That can happen again at any time. And anywhere. And that's the point: if you're on your own, what's to become of you, with all the sharks about? And . . . and"—now she was wagging her hand—"it's no use saying you can take care of yourself. No girl can take care of herself when she looks like you and she's in this racket. You've had some experience already, haven't you? But there hasn't been anyone like him before. Now, I'm going to talk plainly. He's a country fella. That's evident. And he's not of the upper class. That's also evident. But what is fully evident is he's certainly not of the clodhopper or farmworker class either. He's what I would call a respectable young country fella; and he owns his own farm . . ."

"Mrs. Killjoy, dear"—the girl sighed—"I've just met him for the first time. Yes, I'm aware I noticed him on the second night, and on the third and the fourth; but nevertheless, I've actually met him only a moment ago: I couldn't possibly think of him as . . ."

"Now listen to me. I don't expect you to think of him in any way yet; but he's going to call, and if he's come four times to the show he'll come four times here next week."

"I could be back at work next week."

Mrs. Killjoy looked towards the slim ankle and she nodded as she said, "Yes. Yes; I know you've been using those hands of yours, and I'm not saying you couldn't be back at work next week, because I also know the power you have in them—you got Beattie on to her feet when I never expected her to be on the boards again—but I'm asking you a favour, and it is a favour: let your hands alone for the next day or so until you get better acquainted with him, then say what you think. Will you do that for me, Fanny?"

Stephanie hesitated for a moment; then she smiled and said, "Yes. You know I will; I'll do anything for you; but don't count on the result, please. And stop worrying about me and think of yourself and Mr. Ken more, and get into that cottage soon."

"Well, let's put it this way: we'll think of the cottage once we've got you settled."

"Oh! Mrs. Killjoy."

"Oh! Miss Stephanie McQueen." And now the woman, shaking with laughter, hugged the slim body to her, whilst she asked, "If you had to choose between Mr. Harry Henley, that loud-mouth juggler, or the Honourable James Wilson Carter, so called, with his mimes, rhymes, and readings . . . educated idiot that he is, and our farmer, who would you choose?"

"No-one of them, at the moment, Mrs. Killjoy. No-one of them."

FOUR

"*A*nnie, I would like you to make something suitable for a tea in the parlour tomorrow."

"Oh aye?" Annie took up a canister and sprinkled flour liberally over a large wooden board resting on the kitchen table before adding, "And what would you have in mind?"

"As I said, something suitable for tea in the parlour, like you used to make years gone by for Sunday tea: scones, griddles, and little fancies."

"Oh aye?" Annie lifted a large lump of dough out of a brown earthenware bowl and dropped it on to the floured board; and not until she started to knead it did she say further, "And how many company are to be expected?"

"Only three."

"Only three?"

"That's what I said, only three. But accompanied by four dogs."

This last remark turned Annie from the board, flapping her flour-covered hands together, then wiping them on her apron, as she cried, "Four dogs! People don't bring dogs to afternoon tea."

"This company does." He was smiling at her now, knowing he had her full attention. "Don't worry; they're only little dogs . . . poodles."

"Poodles?" She screwed up her face. "Like Pekingese? Them like Pekingese?"

"No; larger; they're performing dogs."

"Oo . . . h." Her lips described the word, and she went on, "Now I get it. Performing dogs. The guests are from the stage, aren't they?"

"Yes, you're right, Annie, they're from the stage. But you should have guessed that long before now."

"I hope you know what you're doin'."

"I know what I'm doing." The banter had gone from his voice. "And I would like you to be civil to them, because I might as well tell you, Annie, if I have my way one of them will soon be mistress of this house."

Annie stared at him for fully five seconds before she turned back to her baking board, saying quietly, "Well, it's your house and you're the master; but I've had concern for you since you were born, and so I can only say I hope your choice is the right one. But we'll have to wait and see, won't we?"

"Yes, Annie, just as you say. Anyway, they'll be here around three o'clock. I hope the table will look nice."

He had reached the door leading into the boot-room, which gave way on to the yard, when he was stopped by her voice crying again, "It's all over the place, you know, about your jaunting; and it's known to one an' all."

"Oh. Is it really?"

"Aye, an' you needn't put that tone on with me, Master Ward. I'm just tellin' you for your own good: if anybody goes night after night to a theatre he goes for a purpose."

"Well, Annie, I'll give you something to tell them, I haven't been once to the theatre this week. Now what do you think about that?" On which he closed the door none too quietly.

He made his way to the coachhouse, and there he saw the boy rubbing an oily rag around the hub of the trap wheel, and after making a point of inspecting the whole trap, he said to him, "You've done a good job. Leave it now and go and clean yourself up; your meal will be ready soon."

"Yes, sir."

He stood watching the boy cleaning his hands at the pump at the end of the yard. He liked him: there was something about him, sort of appealing, fetching. Then his gaze returned to the trap and he told himself that for two pins he would put the horse into the shafts and ride in comfort to Newcastle, but Billy already had Betty harnessed.

He owned up to himself that he was feeling tired: he had come into the yard at half-past four this morning, as he had done every morning this week, in order to get through his share of the work well before evening, and to forestall any possible comment from Billy; although, and he gave him his due, it wasn't likely he would openly protest, which wasn't saying he wouldn't have his own thoughts about the matter, as assuredly as Annie had hers. Oh yes; she had made up her mind to be awkward. He could see that. Well, awkward or not, she would have to put up with it, because there was one thing sure, he'd have to speak to Fanny within the next day or so; if not she'd be on the road again.

He thought of her as Fanny because it was she herself who had stopped him addressing her as Miss Stephanie. "Call me Fanny," she had said. And so he did and he thought of her as Fanny now, even the while thinking that the name didn't suit her: it was too ordinary, too common, and in sound too near to Annie.

Billy was standing by the horse teasing its mane with his gnarled fingers as he said, "Be all right, Master Ward, if I don't wait up for you the night?"

Ward stared at him. "Of course it'll be all right," he answered. "Is anything the matter? Are you feeling off colour?"

"Me back's playin' me up lately."

"Then why the devil didn't you say so? You don't want to find yourself flat out again, do you?"

"Oh, don't you worry. I won't be flat out; I'll still do me work."

"Oh! you madden me sometimes, man." Ward was mounting the horse, and the old man was on his way back to the stable, and he yelled at him, "And don't you take me up the wrong way, Billy Compton. I'm having enough of it from indoors so, don't you start."

He didn't wait for a response, but with a "Gee up!" set the horse forward, but at a walk. And later, he defiantly brought it back to a walk as he passed through the village, where he answered one or two desultory hails from patrons making their way to The Crown Head.

He had passed the blacksmith's shop and was riding into the open country when he was hailed from the rising ground to his right, and there he saw Fred Newberry lolloping towards him.

Ward pulled up his horse and, as Fred slid down the grass bank to the road, he remarked, "So you've been in the river again? They'll find you floating in there one day."

"Oh! man; it's hot in the bakehouse." Fred ran a hand over his wet hair; then, swinging the wet towel he was carrying in a circle about his head, he laughed as he said, "Good job I kept me underpants on the day: two lasses came round the bend. Swimming like fish, they were. Never seen anything like it, 'cos none of the village ones goes in the river, do they? Well, not that I've seen. Have you?"

"No, I haven't, Fred."

"They were cheeky pieces in all ways. By! they were. One of them waved to me. Out of the water, mind, she waved. They were on bicycles, of all things . . . Bicycles. I saw them lying in the grass, with their clothes . . ."

"Well," Ward laughed, "you read about the new-fangled lasses in the papers, don't you? You should have had a crack with them, man." He laughed now and he was about to jerk the reins again when Fred spoke, and this time without the perpetual grin on his face. "I'm on your side, Ward," he said, "no matter what they say. If you want to take a lass from the town, it's your business, nobody else's. It's as our John said, it's about time somebody brought fresh blood into the place. Of course, Will didn't like it, 'cos he's after Susan Beaker. So is Jimmy Conroy. There'll be hell to pay shortly. But anyway, Ward, you do what you want to do; there's bound to be some nice lasses among actresses. I only wish I had your spunk. I'm frightened of lasses, really. I always make me tongue go, but that's as far as it gets." The smile slowly returned to his face now as he added, "Me dad says I'll be hanging on me ma's apron strings when I'm sixty, 'cos she still thinks she's got me in the pram." He covered up his self-conscious acceptance with an outburst of laughter, in which Ward could not help but join while affectionately pushing the flat of his hand against his friend's wet head and saying, "It'll hit you one of these days, never you fear, Fred; and you'll wonder which cuddy's kicked you." Then he urged his horse into a walk as Fred said, "Do you think so, Ward? Well, you show me the cuddy and it can kick me with both back legs, and I'll welcome it . . . Will you be in church the morrow?" he now called.

And Ward, turning in his saddle, called back, "No, not tomorrow, Fred. Tomorrow I'm going to give the village something to think about."

"Aye? What's that?"

"Wait and see, Fred. You wait and see. So long."

"So long, Ward."

Some distance along the road, he muttered to himself: "I'm on your side, Ward, no matter what they say." So they must be saying a lot, then? and all in sympathy with her. And the words conjured up the face looming before him as he'd last seen it, and no will or strength in him could check an involuntary shudder. But then he attacked it with: to the devil with her! and them all. Gee up! there . . . As John had said, there was need for fresh blood in the place.

It was three o'clock on the Sunday afternoon when he drove the heavily laden trap through the last farm gate. He had skirted the village. He had not, at first, intended to, but when he saw Mrs. Killjoy perched on one side of the trap, with the small man by her side, he who must appear to all who saw him, at least from his stature, like a fat boy with an old face, and each of them holding two be-ribboned and powdered white poodles, he knew that he had to save them the ridicule they would have evoked if he had driven through the village. Now, if he had been alone with Fanny . . . oh, yes, that would have been a different matter altogether.

They were in the yard and he was helping them down from the trap, having taken the dogs in turn from them and carefully put them on the ground, being thankful as he did so that the weather had been dry for days so that there were no muddy puddles: he gave a hand first to Mrs. Killjoy; then to her husband; and lastly, he held out both hands to the beautiful girl wearing a long blue summer dress and a large leghorn hat, the rim trimmed with a blue veil, so casting a shadow over her face.

Billy had looked on in astonishment throughout these proceedings, understanding fully now why he had been told to lock up Flo and Captain; for it was more than likely they would have swallowed these four yapping so-called dogs.

Ward was now apologising loudly as he led the party out of the yard and round by the side of the house, saying, "This is a very odd house: the front door was put on the wrong side of it, and the hedge stops us driving up to it." He pointed to the low box hedge that bordered the square of newly cut grass fronting the house. "My father planted the hedge or I would have dug it up a long time ago. Anyway, here we are."

The front door was open, and much to Ward's amazement, which he skilfully hid, there was Annie standing in the middle of the hall, wearing a clean white bibbed apron, and a tiny cap, which he had never seen before, resting on the top of her grey hair, and for a moment he felt qualms, thinking that she was about to bend her knee and turn the whole thing into a farce. But no: she stood waiting, as a housekeeper might have done, and he said, pointing first to the beaming woman, "Annie, this is Mrs. Killjoy. Mrs. Killjoy, this is Mrs. Compton, who has been with the family for years; in fact, she is one of the family, and she has looked after this house and me since my parents died."

"How do you do, Mrs. Compton?" Mrs. Killjoy was at her theatrical best; she held out her hand, and, with a slight hesitation, Annie took it. Then Mr. Killjoy was introduced, and, as Annie said to Billy later that night, "How I kept me face straight, God only knows. Her like a house end and him only as big as a pea on a drum. And when he bowed over my hand . . . it was like a play."

And now, Ward's voice was level as he said, "This is Miss Stephanie McQueen, Annie."

"I am very pleased to meet you, Mrs. Compton."

And what Annie said, as she took the thin hand in hers, was, "And you, miss. And you." And as she also remarked to Billy later, "Well, I admit I was staggered, for anything unlike a stage piece I never did see or imagine."

There were no outer clothes to be taken off, and as one wouldn't dream of taking off one's hat to partake of tea, they allowed themselves, accompanied by the four dogs, to be led by Ward to the parlour where, at a round table placed near the window, was set, on a lace hand-worked cloth, a tea surpassing anything that Ward had expected to see served to his guests.

Then a diversion was caused by Mrs. Killjoy's directing her family to the hearth and informing them to be seated on the rug before the empty fire grate; admonishing them, meanwhile, to behave; and one after the other they lowered themselves, head on front paws, eyes directed towards their mistress, or their mother, as she termed herself, as whom, in their doggy world, they accepted apparently gladly.

Amid laughter the company were now seated at the table, and while Ward did his duty in handing round the plates of eatables, Annie stood at the side-table and poured tea.

What was surprising Ward more than anything at this moment was Annie's attitude towards the whole affair: she was acting as he imagined she might if in service in a big house as the housekeeper, or even the butler, and this, he knew was certainly not in her character. Was she determined to show the future mistress of this house where she stood? Ah yes, that was likely what was in her mind, for even during his parents' time she had never been relegated completely to the kitchen . . .

The tea over, and the dogs having been given their titbits, Ward now enquired if they would like to walk around the farm; and at this, Mrs. Killjoy exclaimed in her unique way, "No offence meant, Mr. Ward, but if you were asking me what I would enjoy, I would say a nice sit-down and talk with the good lady housekeeper here, as would my husband. Wouldn't you, Ken?" and obediently Ken answered, "I would."

Ward slanted his gaze downwards: one up to Mrs. Killjoy. She was a diplomat of diplomats, was this lady: she wasn't only getting into Annie's good books, but was leaving open the opportunity for him to have Fanny to himself. And this he took immediately by turning to her and saying, "Well, would you like to see around my farm, Miss McQueen?" He stressed her name. And she answered in the same vein, "Yes, Mr. Gibson, I'd be delighted to." And with exaggerated ceremony, he offered her his arm, and together, amid laughter, they walked from the room.

Ward showed her, first, the cow byres which, at the moment, were empty and pointed out the cow-stands, each bearing the name of an individual cow: Dolly, Mary, Agnes, Jessie, Beatrice, Flora, and so on; and she laughed gaily, saying, "I can't believe it! Cows being named. It's so nice, though." She shook her head, unable to find further words to describe the apparent treatment of his cows.

Then they visited the stables, the tack room, the boiler house, and the barn; and so to the round of the animals, from the sow and its litter to the two shires in the meadow; then he pointed out the cut hay that had been turned and was just about ready for gathering in.

Her amazement grew as they walked and he described the routine that went to the making of a farm year, season by season.

When they reached the stone wall bordering his land, he pointed beyond it, saying, "Here begins the Ramsmore's estate, and over there, to the right lies the village church. You see the church belfry sticking up above those trees? It has one of the oldest bells in the country, so it is said. Old Crack, they call it."

With her elbows resting on the top of the wall, she stood looking down over the slope, and her voice was low as she said, "It's all very lovely, but not quite real."

"What do you mean? Not quite real."

"Well, all this." She spread out her hand before turning to him and looking up into his face. "And you, too, Ward," she said, "you're not quite real."

"I am real enough, Fanny. Oh yes, I'm real enough. And you're real enough to me; and have been from the first time I clapped eyes on you and felt something stirring here." He tapped his breast with his doubled fist. "It was as if I'd known you from my beginnings, and I was just waiting for you to come to life. I can't believe this is only the sixth time I have spoken to you, although I have looked on your beautiful face nine times. You . . . you know what I feel for you, Fanny?"

"Yes, Ward. But I . . ."

"Don't finish it. Don't finish it; just hear me out. I love you. Dear God! How I love you. It surprises even meself. I wake up in the night and wonder what's hit me. I never thought to feel like this, never in me life. And now I ask you, do you like me?"

"Oh yes. Yes." Her head went back and she gazed up into his face and she repeated, "Oh, yes, Ward. I like you. I like you very much; but . . . but I must be fair, my feelings aren't the same as yours. You see, I've known you such a short time. Yet I am well aware you are a man of the finest character, and it wouldn't be fair to accept what you are offering . . ."

"Don't say any more, dear. Don't say any more. Just listen. I'll wait. I'll wait as long as ever you like, until your feelings change. That's if you want it that way. But—" Slowly he shook his head. "What am I saying? I say I'll wait as long as you like. But who will I be waiting for? The week after next you'll be gone . . . where? I don't know. Travelling from one town to another; and you'll meet all kinds of men who will make you offers. And you've likely had them afore now."

She now put her hand out and gently placed it on his shoulder as she said, "Yes, Ward. I've had all kinds of offers but not one such as you are making me now, for I assume it is marriage you are suggesting?"

"Of course! Of course; nothing else. Why! who would dare . . . ?" He clutched at her hand.

"Oh"—she smiled gently at him—"many would dare; they would call such an offer "protection." I have had offers to be protected since my people died. But the only protection I wanted was that of Mr. and Mrs. Killjoy. Now they are worried for me because they hope to retire soon and the thought of me being on my own troubles them. But I love to dance. You see, Ward, I cannot remember when I first walked, but I can remember when I first danced. My mother was a dancer, a beautiful dancer. She taught me all I know. As she said, she never, what they called, bounced me on her knee, I stood up and danced from my earliest days; and this being so I could never imagine not dancing again. Yet, having said that, at times I get tired of the routine, I mean of travelling, of boarding houses and back-stage conditions, and, I must confess, of some types of audience, especially the Friday and Saturday ones."

He now took her face between his hands as he said, "I can understand that. Oh my dear, yes, I can understand that. To me, you are too fragile, too beautiful, too nice for that type of life; and if you want to dance, well, I'll take you to a dance every week. There's the Assembly Rooms in Newcastle; there's the . . ."

She laughed and, taking his hands from her face, said, "I don't think I would care for that kind of dancing. I don't need people, you know, to enable me to dance. Oh . . . I am not expressing myself well. But look—" She turned and pointed to the field where the hay was spread and she said, "I could very easily dance through your hay. But, of course, I should have to have slightly thicker shoes on than when on the stage."

He laughed with her now, saying, "Aye, that would be a sight; I would love to see it. But . . . but, Fanny"—again he had hold of her hands—"if it's just dancing you want for your own pleasure I'd build some place.

"Look . . ." He didn't continue, but quickly taking her hand, ran her along by the wall, round a copse of trees, and through a piece of woodland; and then, pulling her to a breathless stop, he pointed into the distance, saying, "Look yonder. That's the back of the barns; but look there!" He now threw his arm out to the right and towards a strip of high stone wall as he said, "That could be the very thing." Still holding her hand, he drew her towards what she now made out to be some kind of glass-fronted lean-to. The wall was all of ten feet high and forty feet long. Fronting it was an eight-foot structure still holding, here and there, panes of glass.

"That," he said, pointing to it, "could be your own theatre. I'd have it done up. It used to be a vinery. My great-grandfather built it. Some say the wall was the end of a house that once stood there; but there's nothing in the deeds about it. Anyway, with the price of milk and meat changing so much in his early days, my father had to cut down on labour, and it was let go until it is as you see now. But the structure's fine. Come and look into it."

He now beat a way with his boots through the tangled grass; and when they both stood in the doorless aperture, looking along the length of the building, the floor padded with the rotted foliage of years and yet still sprouting new growth, some of it reaching almost to the top of the wall, he said, "It's a mess now, I admit, but I can see it being a fine place. There's a sketch of it somewhere in the house that my great-grandfather did when the vines were still covering the whole place, the grapes on it as big as plonkers." He now laughed down on her, saying, "You don't know what plonkers are?"

"No, I don't."

"Well, they're what the lads call large marbles, the outsize ones."

Her smile was soft as she stood gazing up at him without speaking, yet her mind was racing over the words Mrs. Killjoy had spoken to her just before he had arrived to bring them on the journey here. "Don't let him slip through your hands, me dear," she had said. "You're so young; you know really nothing of life. You've been on the boards practically since you could walk, but still you know nothing of life . . . and men, and I'm telling you, it is my opinion you'll not find a better. He's too . . . I won't say simple, because there's nothing simple about him; but he's too straightforward to be bad. His tongue is not false; nor is his face; and there are those, you know, who appear to be gentlemen, whose words are coated with butter; only something in the eyes gives them away. This I have learnt. And there's nothing in that countryman's eyes that warns me of any treachery one way or the other. What's more, he's no boy, he's a man of twenty-five, and looks older than his years. All right. All right." Mrs. Killjoy's voice was ringing in Fanny's ears now, repeating the words she herself had spoken. "You say you don't love him, not as you would expect to about the man you intend to marry. But that comes, dear, that comes. It's amazing how it springs on you, often brought to life by some little action or word. But it comes."

Would it come to her with regard to this man? At the moment she couldn't say; what she did say was, "I am not being swayed, Ward, by the promise of a long room in which I can dance, but rather because your sincere offer of marriage has made me hope that you could be right, that my tender feelings for you will grow into something stronger, and so with the hope that you will never regret having asked me, I promise you now to become your wife, whenever you wish it."

She gasped as she was lifted from her feet and held so that she looked down at him, and as he slowly returned her to the ground, his hands, like his whole body, trembling the while, he muttered, "I'm sorry. I'm sorry. That was enough to frighten you off altogether. I'm like a bear. But, oh Fanny! Fanny! You'll never regret those words ever, not as long as either you and I live." And taking her face once more into his hands, he bent down and kissed her gently on the lips.

The action was restrained, and she was aware of this; and impulsively she reached up her arms and put them around his neck; and when her lips touched his cheek he remained still. His own arms about her, he held her as gently as if she were some ethereal creature; which in reality is how he saw her.

It was she who now said brightly as she straightened her hat, "Let us go and tell them."

"Oh aye . . . yes. But I don't think it will be any surprise. Well, it may be a surprise that you are going to take me on, but not that I've been breaking me neck for you over the past days. I know what Annie will say."

"What?"

"Tell me something I wasn't expecting."

Hand in hand now, they ran back up the field; then through another, and skirted the back of the barns and so into the yard. But in the kitchen they came to a stop: there was laughter coming from the hall; and she whispered to him, "I know what's happening: the children are doing their turn. I . . . I mean the dogs. But that's how Mrs. Killjoy sees them."

When he opened the door into the hall, it was to see the surprising sight of Annie with her hand pressed tightly over her mouth, her body shaking with laughter, and Billy at her side, his head wagging like a golliwog; but more surprising still was the sight of the boy. He was smiling for the first time since he had come into the place; but more than smiling, he was gurgling as he watched the pretty white dog stagger down the hallway as if it were drunk; then fall on its back, its legs in the air, doing its turns as if on the stage; and when the little man bent over it, gently smacking its hindquarters as he scolded it, it rolled over twice before getting on its hind legs, its front paws wagging as it staggered down the room to where Mrs. Killjoy was waiting.

Instinctively, Annie clapped; and so did little Billy; but the boy walked straight-faced across the hall to Mrs. Killjoy, and said, "May I pat him, ma'am?"

"You can that, son. You can not only pat him, you can put your arms around him. But 'he' is a she. She's a drunken little no-good. Come here with you!"

She drew the dog towards her and, lifting it, put it in the boy's arms. And when the dog's tongue came out and licked his cheek, the boy actually laughed. But it was a strange sound, not like a laugh at all. But the sound changed quickly into a moan when Mrs. Killjoy clapped her hand on to his back; and when his arms opened and the dog slid from him, she said, "What is it, laddie? What is it?"

"He's got a sore back, Mrs. Killjoy," Ward explained, walking up the room. "He's just new to us, but where he was last he was badly treated."

"Never! Never! And him but a spelk of a child with no flesh on his bones."

"True, Mrs. Killjoy. But come into the parlour and I'll show you something," Ward said, gently pushing the dog forward; and the company followed him, dogs and all.

There, saying to Carl, "Lift up your shirt," the boy did as he was bidden and exposed the rough bandage around his back; and when Annie took out the two safety pins holding it in place and so further exposed the suppurating weal, both Mr. and Mrs. Killjoy stood dumbfounded for a moment. Then the woman demanded, "Who did that to him? He should be in gaol. He should that. If I knew . . ."

"Only the boy knows, Mrs. Killjoy, and he doesn't want to say; nor does he want this to go any further because, as he'll tell you, he's afraid of being sent back. And so I know you won't mention this matter."

Mrs. Killjoy now turned to Fanny, saying, "Did you ever see anything like it."

Fanny made no reply, but she went to the boy and laid a hand on his head and murmured something to him that caused his face to brighten and for him to say, "Italiano?"

"No." She shook her head. "From Malta . . . And you? You are Italian?"

The brightness faded from the small face; and his answer was again muttered: "I don't know. My mother was, I think. I can remember only odd words she said. It was long time ago. But my father, he spoke different, like everyone else. I did, too."

She bent down to him and said slowly, "I am going to touch your back; but you won't feel any pain."

It was at this point Annie made a movement of protest, only to be stopped by Mrs. Killjoy saying quietly, "She knows what she's doing. Just leave her. She is like her own mother, she has power in her hands." And she turned to Ward and nodded; and he looked from her to the slip of a girl who had promised to be his wife. He had hurried her here to bring the wonderful news, but now it seemed secondary to the needs of the boy, as he watched her place her hands across the suppurating sore. He watched her press hard on it, and the boy make no movement that might indicate he felt pain of any kind.

He now watched this beautiful girl, who had driven him half crazy over these past few days, close her eyes, bow her head, and talk as if to herself for a minute; then quickly taking her hand from the boy's back, she took out a handkerchief from her dress pocket and wiped it whilst smiling widely at the boy and assuring him: "It will soon be better. Did . . . did you feel anything?"

He was smiling up into her face now. "My back was warm, very warm, but nice. I mean comfort . . . comforting."

She now asked him, "Did you used to speak Italian?"

He shook his head. "I don't know. As I said, my mother used some words. I can remember 'bambino.'"

She touched his cheek, then asked, "What is your name?"

"Carl, ma'am."

"Well, be happy, Carl. Be happy."

"Yes, ma'am." He turned now to look at Ward who, assuming now a stiff, almost angry front, exclaimed, "You know what you have done, boy?" and the lad, somewhat apprehensively now, answered, "No, no, sir."

"You have stolen my thunder, that's all." And Ward's hand went out and ruffled the boy's thick hair, while addressing the others, saying, "And I mean that. I came tearing back to tell you my splendid news . . . our splendid news—" He held out a hand towards Fanny, and when she took it he drew her to his side and, placing an arm about her narrow shoulders, as he spread his gaze round from one to the other he said, "This beautiful lady here has promised to be my wife."

They all stared at him, and with the exception of the boy, it would appear from their expressions that they were dumbfounded. Then the exclamations came pouring out: and while Fanny was becoming breathless in being hugged to Mrs. Killjoy's overflowing flesh, Ward's hand was being shaken, first by Mr. Killjoy, then by Billy, and lastly, Annie stood there before him. She did not shake his hand, but smiling at him, she said jokingly, "What a surprise! What a surprise!" and in answer he gave her a playful push in the shoulder. And then she pleased him by saying quietly, "She's different from what I expected. You could travel far and fare worse. In fact, later on, when I come to think over it, I might even consider she's a bit too good for you," and before he had time to reply, she added, "Anyway, this calls for a drink, doesn't it?"

"Yes, Annie; I think it does."

"Well, get them all into the dining-room and I'll see to it. But"—she paused—"by the way, how about taking the little 'un in with you?"

He turned to look towards the boy whose face was bright and eager looking, only for his attention to be diverted to Billy who was now shaking the hand of his future mistress. However, he quickly turned back to answer Annie: "Why not? Why not indeed! There's ginger beer there, isn't there?" And at this he thrust out an arm towards the child, saying, "Come along, scallywag. Come and experience your first celebration. And remember, you'll never in your life be at a happier one."

He now caught hold of the boy's hand and with his other arm he drew Fanny to his side and linked thus, like a family, it seemed to foretell their future.

FIVE

The vicar's plump figure swelled with indignation: "I never thought I should say this to you, Ward Gibson, but I find your suggestion utterly insensitive. You come here asking me to call the banns of your marriage to a person who has spent her life on the stage, and that would be questionable even if it were depicted in a higher form such as the noble prose of Shakespeare, or in the works of Mr. Dickens; but not a dancer of the lowest type . . ."

"Be careful, parson! And let me tell you something: if it wasn't for your cloth you would now be stretched out on your vestry floor . . . Yes; you may well step back, for, let me tell you, I'm marrying a lady."

"So you think. So you think. But what about the lady you've courted for years and have left desolate, slighted, and with a weight of disgrace lying not only on her but on her people, so much so that they cannot bear to come to church."

"Oh. And you'll find that a great pity, won't you, parson? There'll be no more comforts handed out to you to fill that swollen belly of yours. You'll miss the suckling pigs, and the lamb carcass now and again, not forgetting your daily milk that you get free while your curate is called on to pay for his. Isn't that so, parson?"

The vicar's face was showing not only a purple hue but also an expression that revealed he was consumed with a blazing anger now as he cried, "You're a wicked man, Ward Gibson. And you are bringing disgrace on the village. This is a family community. And let me tell you, the general opinion of you is the same as mine."

Ward's lips spread out from his teeth and his whole expression was one of disdain. "That may be so, Parson," he said, "but have you any idea of what the general opinion is of you, and has been for as far back as I can remember? Well, if you don't know I'll tell you now. You're a sucker-up to those that have and you ignore those that haven't. It's left to your curate and others to help them. Aye, those who dare to be Methodists or Baptists, even those who belong to no church or chapel. What about the Regan family down in Bracken Hollow: they wouldn't turn their coats, would they, and go to St.

Matthew's down there, so you disputed whether the old man should be buried in the graveyard. You'd have left him on the moor if you'd had your way, 'cos there was a taint on them, wasn't there? They were Catholics. It was the same with the McNabs. But John McNab put you in your place, didn't he? He kicked your backside out of the door. And it's odd, isn't it, when others were getting poor law assistance a few years back, they would have starved if it hadn't been for a few unchristian people living in this village. Oh, Parson, you would know how you are thought of in this place and beyond if it wasn't that half of your congregation are afraid of opening their mouths, for fear that what they might say would go back to their employers when you are sitting stuffing your kite at their tables. Well, here's a member of the community, if not of the village, who's going to tell you how you appear to him, and that's as an overblown, unintelligent crawler . . . crawler, always crawling. So now you've got it." And on this he turned from the infuriated countenance and strode out of the vestry and into the church, and there, standing by the pulpit, he yelled back towards the vestry, "The next time I put my foot inside your church it will have to be for some very, very good reason. Aye, a very good reason."

"I'll talk him round, Ward. Well, what I mean is, I'll tell him that I'll marry you down at St. Matthew's. It's just about big enough to hold a wedding party. For myself, I prefer it to St. Stephen's: more homely and . . . holy, I dare add. And it was built with love by the Ramsmore forebears. It was a better idea than that grotesque lump of iron cutting off the altar. Oh, that screen gets on my nerves."

Ward looked kindly on the young curate, who called in at the farm the following day. "Thanks all the same, Frank," he said, "but I've made up me mind, and Fanny is with me in this, it'll be a civil ceremony in Newcastle. Candidly, it doesn't matter a damn to me where it takes place, so long as it does and we are married."

"She's a charming girl; I can understand your feelings for her. Anyway, what I've come to say is, Jane would like you to pop in for a meal. It'll be nothing special, for, as yet, I'm the recipient only of new potatoes. And these only at intervals. But I can have as many turnips as I care to store."

"I heard just a few days ago that you were having to buy your milk from Hannah Beaton's shop in the village."

"Yes; that is so. And Jane prefers it that way, unlike me, holding my hands out gratefully for scraps; but she wants no charity, she says. It irks her that our living itself is a charity."

"Your living? What d'you mean, Frank?"

"Oh well; Lady Lydia, you know, happens to have a cousin, who happened to go to school with Jane's mother, and through the beating of the tom-toms it was discovered that dear Jane had married an impecunious and ailing curate, and that they were living in the most awful conditions, almost under the river itself in the lowest part of Newcastle. It simply could not go on. And as there happened to be a small church, and a so-called vicarage next to it, occupied by a very aged pastor who was incapable of even taking the service, and who was allowed to remain there only through the clemency of Colonel Ramsmore, the suggestion was to transfer the old fellow to a cottage and let the poor curate take over. His wife and child would at least have fresh air, if nothing else. And so that's how it came about."

"What did you mean, Frank, ailing? Are you ill? You've never looked it to me, never spoken of it."

Frank Noble now patted the left side of his chest, saying, "A touch of tuberculosis. Just a little bit. I don't even cough any more; I'm really fit. But, and this I'll confess to you, Ward, as I wouldn't even to Jane, I'd rather be back on that river front among many more who are in the same boat, some coughing their lungs out because, you see, the people are different there. I've always detested villages. I was brought up on the outskirts of one, very like the one here." He inclined his head to the side. "And there were so many irritations, apart from the marked division in class. There has got to be this division, I know; there always has been and always will be; but narrowness in both sets used to prey on my mind at times, and I had no sympathy with either lot. You know, I still haven't." And now he bent towards Ward and whispered, "I don't know why I'm in this garb . . . in this job, so to speak. I've asked God a number of times, but He never gives me a straight answer. But Jane, now, she's on much better terms with Him and gets a straight answer every time. You've made the biggest mistake of your life in your choice of a career, she tells me at least once a week. And you know something, Ward? If of a sudden I were to decide to leave and go and look for a job in a shipyard or a factory, or down a mine, she would jump for joy. I know she would." He laughed before adding, "Perhaps not as much now as she would have done three years ago, before the children came. Anyway, you're coming to supper. Which night?"

"Any night you choose."

"Say Thursday. A quiet day all round, Thursday, don't you think? By Wednesday, the locals have chalked up so much on the slate in the inns that Thursday is a comparatively dry night. Friday, everybody's very busy getting ready for Saturday's market, to be followed by a swilling at night in the inn to finish off the week. Of course, that doesn't include our small band of Methodists. Decent lot, the Methodists. Always thought that."

He was backing away now, laughing and waving at the same time, and Ward stood shaking his head and smiling broadly. Frank was a man after his own heart, and to his mind he certainly wasn't in the wrong profession: he should be in the parish; and he wouldn't be afraid to speak his mind from the pulpit; and he'd have more than six sermons a year to work on. It was good to feel he had one friend . . . What was he talking about? He had a number. There was Fred, over the moon about being asked to be best man. And his father, his brothers, John and Will, and Mr. Newberry, who had promised to bake a wedding cake. It was supposed to be a surprise, but as Fred wasn't good at keeping secrets, he already knew it was to have two tiers and the best egg-white icing above an almond topping.

He stood and watched until the young parson had disappeared along the road, when he turned and hurried into the house.

In the hall he shouted, "Where are you?" And Annie calling from upstairs, cried back at him, "Where do you think?"

He bounded up the stairs two at a time, shouting as he went, "What are you doing up there?"

Again he was given the answer, "What d'you think?" And her voice led him to the room that had been his parents'; and there, Annie, standing on a chair, was taking down the curtains from the window.

"What are you up to? Get off that chair. With your weight, you'll go through it and break your legs. Get down, woman!"

"Don't rock me unless you want me to fall on top of you. And wait a minute until I get this pin out of the ring."

When she had accomplished that task, she dropped the heavy curtain, half of it falling across his head. And now on the floor once more, she exclaimed, "These should have been down years ago. Your mother liked tapestries. She picked these up at least . . . oh, twenty-five years ago; in fact, just before you were born, when they were selling off the things at Quayle Manor. It was beautiful stuff then; but now, I bet, it won't bear the look of water; it'll drop to bits."

"What do you propose putting up then?"

"That depends on you and what stuff you buy. I think something nice and light; something that will tone in with the new carpet. Aye, aye." Now she was poking her finger at him. "Just look down at your feet. That's been down ever since I was in this house, and it must be claggy with sweat from your father's bare feet, for, you know, once in the house he would never go round in slippers if he could help it."

He stood back from her, saying, "Well, that's a carpet and curtains. Now what about the furniture, Annie? You want all that removed?"

"You know, what I don't want now is any of your sarky remarks. And in taking this on meself I'm only pointing out your dimwittedness, for if you'd had any sense you would have had Miss Fanny up here and asked her what colour drapes she would like. And that's what you can do now. Are you going in the night?"

"Of course I'm going in the night."

"Then I suggest you also go in first thing in the morning and bring her back, for what it must be like sitting in those lodgings all day, I don't know."

He stared at her now as she gathered up the heavy dust-dispersing curtains, but said nothing, until she staggered past him, her arms full, when he suggested, "How would it be if I brought her back tomorrow and let her stay in the house for the next three weeks?"

She stopped and, her chin stretching over the material towards him, she said, "Wouldn't shock me."

"No, I don't suppose it would, Annie. For two pins I would do it, too, for you know what? Old Tracey has refused to marry us in church."

"*No!*"

"But yes. Frank though, he's offered to do it along at St. Matthew's. But I said no, we'd have it done at the registrar's."

"He's an old bugger, that, if ever there was one." She humped the curtains further up into her arms, then said soberly, "But perhaps it'll work out for the best, because whether you know it or not there's a civil war goin' on down in the village. Some are backing you, but others are backing Daisy Mason; in fact, things, I understand, have hotted up in that direction, stirred by the two Mason lads. What they're goin' to do, or what they would like to do to you is nobody's business, but like and actin' are two different things.

That Pete is a big mouth. But Sep, he couldn't knock the stuffin' out of a feather pillow. Anyway, we'll only have to wait an' see which side comes off best, won't we? And by the way, I've made an egg custard for her; take it in with you. She needs feeding up, and you don't want to marry a clothes prop with a frock on it, do you?"

Ward nodded his head, which then seemed to be in answer to her previous comment when he muttered, "Yes, we'll just have to wait and see," before he turned and moved towards the brass and iron bed, and he stood looking at it. He had been born in that bed; and his father had been born in it. But it had a different mattress on it then; two feather ticks, they said, and you sank through one into the other.

He looked about him. It was a large room. The furniture was good solid mahogany, but the walls could do with new wallpaper. Annie was right; it needed brightening up. The whole house needed brightening up; and yes, she must have a hand in it, so he would go in early morning and bring her here every day, and take her back in the evening, and they would plan the house together.

He stood holding the bed rail, in one part of him a feeling of joy wanting to lift him from his feet in a great leap, while in the other was a mixture of bitterness and regret, regret that he couldn't be married in the same church as his father and mother had been, regret that the whole village couldn't be one with him on the day, as he understood they had been on his parents' wedding day, regret that the barn down below would not ring to the sound of Harry Bates's and Jake Mulberry's fiddles, and Amos Laker's accordion, with laughter, merriment and high jinks rising as the spirits flowed.

His head shook as a dog does when throwing off water. What did the village lot matter? He still had friends there. The only thing that really mattered was, she would soon be here . . . and—his thoughts had rushed ahead —"in that bed." He warned himself now not to forget what he had learned from Nell: it was not as if it was Daisy Mason coming to that bed, oh no, but a young girl, fragile, like an angel. Yes, like an angel; but a laughing, kind, wonderful angel, and a different being from anyone he had ever known.

Yes—he paused in his thinking—different, so different. There was that business of Carl's back. The morning following the day she had laid her hand on him there was no puss on the lint; in fact, although the strike marks all remained, the scars looked different, paler, as if in time they might disappear. He had been shaken by that, but when he mentioned it to Annie, he was surprised that she should accept it. She had heard of such things, she had said: people with healing hands. Oh yes, she had gone on to explain, at one time they used to burn them for witches. Thank God all that was in the past. At least, most of it, she had added.

He walked slowly towards the head of the bed and touched one of the pillows lying on top of the bolster, and he spoke aloud at it: "I will never hurt you in any way," he said. "And may God forgive me if I should."

SIX

*I*t was done. She was his. And now the wedding party were piling into the brake. As Ward's farm only harboured vehicles such as the farm cart, the hay wagon, and the trap, Annie had voiced to Ward in Fred's hearing that he must hire a brake. It was following this that Mr. Newberry had offered the use of his brake, which not only held ten people but also had a detachable cover.

There were nine guests in the vehicle, four of whom were connected with the theatre; and Billy in his Sunday suit and bowler was now shaking the reins and calling, "Get up! there," which set off Betsy into a dignified walk, because it was a heavy load she was pulling.

The journey back to the farm seemed long but merry. This was brought about by the cross talk between Fred and the juggler, and Mr. Carter interposing the scraps of monologues; so no-one noticed that the newly married couple had little to say; nothing in fact, as they sat hand in hand, and it wasn't until the brake entered the farmyard that Ward gave vent to a surprised exclamation: "Good gracious!" he cried. "Look!" for there, awaiting them, was an unexpected number of people, and the next ten minutes were taken up with congratulations, handshakes and introductions.

Ward's heart was warm: here were people who weren't cutting him dead, who hadn't refused to take his milk. The cutting had started when the news of his forthcoming marriage was brought to the village. Billy was delivering the churn to Hannah Beaton's shop, as he had done for countless years, only to be bawled out by Hannah: "You can save yourself the trouble, Billy Compton, an' tell him we won't be sellin' his milk any more. An' that goes for his eggs an' all."

And she hadn't been the only one in the village to refuse his milk that day, for four others had done the same, and Annie's comment had been, "Well, what d'you expect? Old Mother Beaton and Mrs. Mason are cousins."

But now, here was the whole blacksmith's family, not only Charlie Dempsey himself, but also their two young sons, John and Henry, and Phyllis, one of their married daughters from Fellburn; and there was Fred Conroy, the butcher, a quiet fellow, Fred, and a widower these ten years; but he had

brought their Jimmy with him, he who was courting Susie Beaton; and surprisingly, there was Ben Holman the cobbler, go-between man or undertaker,
which occupation he was following at this particular time. And lastly, which
was no surprise to Ward, there was the Reverend Frank Noble and his wife
Jane, and one of their two young children . . . and the boy Carl, smiling
widely now as he gazed at the new mistress.

Ward stopped, and he turned and looked at Fanny. She was gazing at
him, but not smiling: her eyes were large and moist.

As those from outside pressed in behind him, he gently guided her towards the top of the table, where Annie was standing beaming as if she had
just conjured up all this out of thin air; and, impulsively, Fanny threw her
arms about her and kissed her on the cheek.

For a moment Annie returned the hug, but then exclaimed loudly, her
voice above the hubbub, "I didn't do all this, ma'am; everybody pigged in.
And there's a table full of presents next door an' all. Anyway, sit yourself
down, ma'am; they're all dying to get started, 'cos they've never had a bite or
sup across their lips since this morning."

This caused a great roar of laughter, setting the pattern for the enjoyment
of the meal which, between eating and toasting, and amid cries of goodwill,
went on for the next hour or more.

Following this, the whole company crowded into the parlour where, to
his regret, the juggler found there was no room to perform his act; but Mr.
Carter's talents didn't take up any space, and so he entertained the company
with monologues, and to the surprise of those who knew him well, he never
touched either on Shakespeare or on Mr. Dickens. Nor did he mention the
Cornhill Magazine, or any other erudite publication from where he had
gleaned his knowledge, but he continually had them in gales of laughter
when proving to be an admirable mimic of dialects from Geordie to Cockney.

And so the afternoon wore on, until it was time for the Newcastle party
to take their leave. This they did amidst cheers and invitations to come again,
not only to the farm but to the blacksmith's and the baker's; and, lastly, a
somewhat macabre invitation from Ben Holman, who said, "You can come
any time to me and I'll fit you out with a nice box, brass handles thrown in
free." And so they departed in further laughter.

Others now began to make their departure, again amidst hilarious chaf-
fing from Rob Newberry when he exclaimed in mock indignation, "It's come
to something, hasn't it, when me family's got to walk back home because I've
been daft enough to lend me brake to those barmy actors."

When the last trap rolled out of the yard with the young vicar and his
wife waving their goodbyes, no-one remarked about the bride standing close
to her husband and having her arm around the young lad, who was wearing a
new knickerbocker suit and sporting a white shirt, for it had been whispered
here and there that he was some relation to the bride: and had he not come
on the scene at the same time as she? No-one had mentioned anything to
Ward about the assumed relationship because Ward had been very touchy,
and he would more than likely have told them to mind their own business.
But that was before he had taken a wife . . . well, a man was always more
approachable then, and the relationship to the boy would likely come
out . . .

Fanny insisted on helping Annie clear the table and put things to rights, and although Annie objected, Ward did not, because what might have been a stumbling block for the harmony of the house between Annie and his wife did not after all exist. And so he walked out into his farmyard; but there was no-one to talk to now except the boy, and he said to him, "Well, Carl, have you enjoyed your first wedding?"

And the boy, looking up at him, did not answer his question, but what he said was, "She is so beautiful . . . bella, bella."

At this Ward laughed and, affectionately rumpling the boy's hair, said, "Yes, you're right. Oh, so right; she is bella, bella."

At nine o'clock the house was back to normal, and Annie bade them a smiling but lower-lidded good night; after which Ward bolted the door. Then he carried his wife upstairs to bed.

He had definitely slept in, for the sun was up and shining through the new curtains. He turned hastily on to his side; and there she was, wide awake and smiling at him; and it was she who spoke first. Putting out her hand, she ran her fingers through the thick hair that was tousled on his brow as she said very softly, "I still like you, Mr. Gibson; but I must confess the feeling I have for you now is so strange that it might come under the heading of . . . love."

"Fanny . . . Oh, Fanny. Fanny," was all he was able to say.

Part Two

ONE

The first six months of their marriage was, for both of them, like a fairy tale. To Ward, each day was a joy to wake up to, and each night was a joy to go to their bed. To Fanny it was different types of joy: Ward had been as good as his word and had the vinery re-built and every now and again when she felt like it she would run down to it and dance, at times to an audience consisting only of her husband; at others she would be aware of Billy being in the background, but more often of the boy watching her.

As she had found her love for Ward, so she came to have most tender feelings for the boy. It was strange, she would tell herself, it was as if they were related; and perhaps they were, because he didn't really know who his people were. He had, though, definitely hailed from the same part of the world as her mother, for every now and again, spontaneously, he would come out with an Italian word that would surprise himself. But what troubled her about the boy was his nightmares, for Ward had often heard him yelling out from his bed in the loft.

But her joy wasn't only in her own dancing, for hardly a week passed but Ward took her into Newcastle. She had visited the theatre there, and had spent an hilarious evening at Balhambras, noted for its variety, much of it bawdy, and whose audience, Fanny felt, would not have received her type of act very well; and nor would Mr. and Mrs. Killjoy and their family have been as much appreciated as they had been at The Empire. But the occasion she had enjoyed most was the dance at the Assembly Rooms. Yet Ward had said that was their first and last visit there, because she had attracted too much attention.

He had laughed when saying this, but she wasn't displeased that he had meant it.

Ward's consuming love seemed to have touched everything he owned, for his crops were blooming and his cows had never yielded so much milk; yet all the happiness seemed to be contained within the precincts of his land. It was a different story when he went into the village.

Within a few days of his marriage he knew where he stood there. He wasn't in favour in The Running Hare, because Sam Longstaffe and his little wife Linda were church-going. However, at The Crown Head he had been made more than welcome by Michael Holding and members of his family; not that he frequented the inn often, but on his return from Fellburn or Gateshead, he might step in for a pint of ale. He had laughingly said to Annie that as long as he had the barman, the baker and the blacksmith, and the shoemaker and the undertaker on his side, he would get by. Nevertheless, it annoyed him that most of the church folk could hardly bring themselves to give him the time of day. And yet it was because of this that it seemed he had found favour with Pastor Wainwright of the Methodist Chapel: he and his four sons would nod to him and bid him good-day. The two younger lads even raised their caps to him.

It was now the beginning of March 1887, and the month was living up to its reputation, with the wind raging and sending sprays of iced rain against the windows on the day when Fanny told him she was carrying his child.

The farmyard was a sea of mud and Annie was once again yelling at him, "Will you take your boots off! I'm not getting down on me hands an' knees today again and scrubbin' this kitchen or that hall, so I'm telling you, Master Ward. And anyway, if you could lay a concrete floor in that dancing room for the missis, you could put one in that yard. They tell me that Bainbridge's farm is as clean as a whistle now that he's had the whole place laid with slabs cemented together."

To this, he had said, "Annie, if you say another word to me about mud or boots or wet clothes, either to get them off, or not put me boots on your floor, I'll take up the first thing to hand and I'll let you have it."

After a moment of silence between them, he asked, and quietly, "Where's the missis?"

"The last time I saw her she was up in the attics. She's taken it into her head to scour them out. I can't stop her, so see if you can. See if you get the same answer as I get. She must keep busy. If it isn't her feet going it's her hands," saying which, she herself continued to be about her own business, whilst he padded across the kitchen floor in his stockinged feet, went into the hall and up the stairs, and on the first landing he called, "Where are you?"

After a moment, her voice came faintly to him: "I'm up among the gods, sir. I've got a good seat, and it's free."

He took the steep stairs to the attics two at a time, and when he saw her on her knees before an open trunk and scattered around her, pieces of material and old albums, he said harshly, "Now what are you up to? You're not thinking about washing out the trunks now, are you?"

"Yes; that's just what I am thinking about doing, sir." She laughed at him, then added, "Come and sit down."

"I'm not going to sit down. You get up." He pulled her to her feet; then held her at arm's length, saying, "Look at you! Your skirt's covered with dust and . . ."

"Well, that shows that this place has never had a clean out for a long, long time, and"—she looked about her—"you know, a lot of use could have been made of these rooms. There're three good size ones besides the small one along the passage."

"I know the number of rooms that are up here, but we've got enough downstairs to see to."

She now pulled herself from his arms and, going to an old basket chair that was propped against the wall, she sat down on it, then beckoned him to her, saying, "Bring that box and sit down; I want to talk to you."

When with a loud sigh he carried out her bidding, she caught hold of his hands, then began to rub them, saying, "You're cold." To which he answered, "Of course, I'm cold: it's freezing up here, it's raining outside, the wind's howling. I've been wet through; Billy's in a temper; the boy's got a cough and has been in bed all day. As for Annie, no . . . no, don't let me talk about Annie. And now here's you."

"Yes, here's me." She nodded at him. "And I, sir, I must confess, am . . . well, I think the word is devious, I'm a devious woman."

"What are you talking about? What's the matter with you? Come on downstairs."

"Ward—" Her voice checked him, because there was no banter in it now as she said, "Not knowing about these things and having no-one to talk to, even Mrs. Killjoy didn't discuss her personal matters, I . . . I had to be sure, and now I am. I am going to have a baby, Ward."

He sat motionless; but when eventually he moved it was not to thrust out his arms and pull her roughly to him, but slowly to lean forward and to rest his head on her lap and as slowly to place his hand gently upon her stomach. There was no way he could speak, for at this moment it was impossible for him to express what he was feeling: he had been married six months and he had felt that his loving would surely have created a child long before now, and there had been times when she had lain asleep in his arms and he had wondered if there might be something lacking in his make-up: he himself had been the only offspring of his mother and father, and they themselves had each been an only child. And so he had asked himself, was the line running out? Did these things happen? But now she was carrying his child, this beautiful, beautiful girl, as he still thought of her, because sometimes he just couldn't believe that she was his wife, a young woman of twenty now. She was so slight, even ethereal. At times, when he watched her from a distance it looked as if a puff of wind would blow her away. All her movements, too, were quick and light. Often he was surprised by the way she spoke: her voice didn't match her body, or her face, and there was a surprising and unaccustomed depth to her mind.

As she stroked his hair, there was a strong desire in him to cry as any woman might. She didn't ask the silly question, "Are you pleased?" but rather, with that practical side of her, she said, "You *are* cold. Let us go down. I . . . I want to tell Annie, too."

He rose from the box; and now he picked her up in his arms as he often did; but at the top of the attic stairs she began to laugh and shake in his hold, saying, "You had better not try to go down there, because we'll get stuck."

At this, he joined his laughter to hers and put her on to her feet. Still he hadn't spoken, not a word, and not until they were opposite the bedroom door did he push her slightly away from him, saying, "Well, go down now and tell Annie." And with this, he turned from her and went into the bedroom; and wisely and without murmur she went down the stairs to the kitchen.

The door shut, he stood with his back to it, his hand pressed tight across his eyes, and there was, at this moment, a deep shame in him, for he had never cried in his life; nor had he seen his father cry, not even when his wife died. He'd have to take a hold of himself, because this was an event that occurred every day to some man somewhere, and surely few men would react to such news as he wanted to do, and cry like a woman.

He must have a drink, and a strong one . . .

It seemed that from this glorious day the outside world began to impinge on Ward's happiness. On the day she broke the news to him, Fanny must have been two months pregnant. And it should also happen that a few days later Annie was seized with a pain in her side, and Ward called the doctor to her. While he was there, he spoke to him about his wife's happy condition and asked if he would see to her health.

Doctor Wheatley not only saw to her health and advised her cheerily to carry on as if nothing had happened, but he apparently informed someone in the village, and in his usual coarse way, that Ward Gibson had got results at last; he was beginning to think the young fellow had taken on a dud. When this was repeated in The Running Hare there was great laughter, except from the Mason brothers . . .

The first worrying incident occurred towards the end of March. The routine of the farm had been changed, though not to everyone's satisfaction, no. As Billy stated bluntly, he could neither read nor write, but the cows didn't take it out on him for that, nor did it interfere with his ploughing, or the gathering in of the crops, so he reckoned he had all the skills necessary for a farmhand, and that's what the young lad was going to be, wasn't he? And so he didn't see where readin' and writin' was going to help him. Besides which, it was taking an hour out in the morning, and another in late afternoon at that; and count that up for five days, and that was ten hours work lost a week. And hadn't he, the master, said himself that the lad was almost as good as a paid hand; better, in fact, than either one of the Regans or the McNabbs from the Hollow that could be called upon at times, for "them two Irish lumps" liked work so much they could lie down beside it. But if it was the mistress's wish, well, he supposed he must put up with it. But to his mind, book learning was for them who hadn't the sense to use their hands.

Frankly, Ward himself had been a little surprised and taken aback by Fanny's request, which at first was that the boy should be sent mornings to the village school. And he had quickly pooh-poohed this, reasoning that they would want to know his particulars. But to this, Fanny had laughingly reminded him that if they were to believe the gossip brought to their notice through Annie, Carl was a relation of hers, for hadn't he appeared on the scene at the same time as herself?

No, no; Ward wouldn't hear of the village school, for that would have meant having to tell the boy he would have to pose as a relation, and that would be going too far. But all right, she could have him for a working hour at the beginning of the day and at any slack hour in the late evening. At this, she had rewarded him with some spontaneous kisses, and this openly in the hall with Annie passing, trying to look the other way. And then he was being told that she would need some books, one on arithmetic, another on history, and another on geography.

Privately, he was amazed that she was so learned when she had openly confessed that she had never been to school; but it appeared that her schooling had been very much of the same pattern as she was planning for the boy, for both her father and mother had taken a hand in her tutoring. They had not always been on the road, and had themselves both received some sort of education.

Fanny had fitted up a small room at the back of the house. It was sparsely furnished, and it had been used mostly for storing lumber. It now housed two wooden chairs, a small table, a shelf to hold the books she had requested, and two slates and lead pencils. But to her mind there was one book missing, and as yet she couldn't ask Ward to get it for her, because he would want to know what she meant to do with a book on learning Italian.

Her own knowledge of the Italian language was sketchy indeed because her mother had spoken the language only when they were alone together; apparently her father did not like the language, or, as she had come to suspect later, he was jealous of it, fearing that his wife might, in spite of all her protestations, be secretly homesick.

She was leaning across the table now and smiling at her young pupil while admonishing him: "You must pay attention, Carl. Look at your book, look at your slate, you are doing a sum."

The boy returned her smile as he answered, "I've done the sum, mistress. The answer is twenty-two sheep."

"Ah. Ah." The smile went from her face now. "That is where you are wrong, sir. The answer is twenty-four sheep."

"Oh. I've missed something out?"

The boy looked from his slate to his book. Then said, "Yes. Yes; I can see . . . twenty-four sheep. You are right."

Fanny covered her eyes with a hand for a moment, before leaning across the table again, and now her voice held an earnest note as she said, "Carl, you must pay attention to your school work. Or would you rather not have lessons? Would you prefer to work outside?"

Before she had finished the last word his head was wagging: "Oh no, no, mistress. Oh n'n'no. I promise I will pay attention. I will look at the book more." He could have added here, "But I can't stop looking at you," for this lady sitting across the table appeared to him really as an angel; no-one had ever been so kind; no-one had ever spoken to him as she did; no-one he had ever seen in his short life looked as she did. He would die for her; which is what he often told himself at night as he buried his face in the straw tick in the dark room above the stable.

"I . . . I promise, and I promise also to repeat the words I read at night. I can do it now: The cat sat on the mat. The dog barked at the cat. The cows give milk."

She held up her hand, saying, "That's splendid. That's splendid. Now you've got that far I will read you this little story. And then you will read it, eh?"

"Oh yes, mistress. Yes, mistress."

She was checked as she took up the book to begin the story, for the door swung open and there stood Ward. His face looked grave. He spoke to her direct, saying, "I want you a moment. Put your coat on, it's cold. I want you over in the shed. And you, boy, get about your work."

As the boy scampered from the room, Fanny went hastily to Ward, saying, "What is it? Something wrong?"

He pushed the door half closed as he looked at her, and speaking slowly, he said, "Yes; very wrong, to my mind; and to any decent person's. Somebody's set two traps in the pasture. A cow . . . Maisie got her foot caught. She was bellowing; and there they were all standing round her. Billy heard the commotion, even in the yard here. I've never seen him run for years. I was in the bottom field."

"A trap? What kind of trap? A man-trap? They've been abolished. It's punishable."

"No; not a man-trap. These are home-made ones, on the lines of rabbit ones. You know—" He moved his hands as if to explain them. "Some are just so big, enough to catch a rabbit's paw, but others are bigger." His fingers spread. "To get its neck. I've made them myself when I was a lad. We were swarmed with rabbits at times. But these were big enough to take a cow's hoof. Somebody knew what they were about. Anyway, come and see what you can do."

For some time now, ever since she had healed the boy's back, he had accepted that she was one of these people who had healing in their hands. His mother used to talk about an old woman who had lived in the Hollow; and of the farmers who had come from far and wide for her services. Yet she was feared and held at arm's length by the majority of the villagers. However, she had never been known to cure any humans; it was just animals that responded to her touch.

As they hurried through the kitchen Annie, who was scrubbing the seat of a wooden chair, did not straighten her back, but commented to no-one in particular. "It's started."

As Fanny turned questioningly towards the woman, who now was not only the servant in the house, but a friend, meaning to ask the reason for the statement, she was actually pulled towards the kitchen door, then pushed through it.

The cow was in her stall. Billy was holding the animal's injured foot, and there was a large bowl of hot water placed on the box to the side of him.

Fanny did not immediately go to the back of the animal, but she touched its face and said, "Hello, Maisie! That's a good girl. You're going to be all right. Do you hear me? You're going to be all right."

Ward, standing to the side, turned his head away for a moment, for he did not like this side of the proceedings. It was all right her dressing a wound or holding it, but she had a way of talking to the creatures before she did anything. It was a bit off-putting . . . he did not use the word "weird." Still, she had marvellous hands. She was marvellous altogether; but . . . His voice was slightly terse as he said, "Have a look at it."

She stroked the cow's face twice before she turned away and joined Billy. Then looking about her, she said, "Where's the stool?"

Almost instantly it was handed to her by Ward; and as she sat down on it, Billy straightened up, saying, "Do you want to bathe it, mistress?"

For answer, she lifted the cow's hoof and looked at the cut made by the wire. It was deep, likely caused by the animal's struggles to release its limb. Her hands around the heel and without looking at Billy, she said, "Would you please go and ask Annie for the bandage box?"

When Billy left her side Ward said, "It's almost to the bone. She was nearly going mad; she could have snapped her hoof off."

"Why should people do this to animals?"

He looked down on her head and found it impossible to say, "I don't know;" and more so to answer, "Because I married you." He had never told her about Daisy Mason, but he knew that at times she must have felt something wasn't right between him and the village, such as when she expressed a desire to go to a service, he'd had to counter it with, "Well, not in St. Stephen's; we'll go to St. Matthew's, Frank's place, one of these Sundays, when he has time to take a service there, when old Tracey's done with him. If ever there was a false minister of God it's that man, for to me he expresses the two main sins, gluttony and sloth." What he said now was, "Do you think you can do anything with it?"

She turned and glanced up at him, her hands still holding the animal's heel: "I don't know; it'll be as God wills, not me."

He felt his shoulders stiffening, his head going back on them. Why was the tone of her voice different when she was treating animals? At such times she was different altogether; she was like someone he didn't know, not his wonderful, warm, loving Fanny, his beautiful, beautiful Fanny. Sometimes he wished she hadn't this . . . whatever it was, for it was like a part of her that didn't belong to him; and he knew she was all his, entirely all his. Yet, no, not when she was doing what she was doing now.

Billy had returned with the box, and she now took from it a piece of linen and soaked it in the warm water before using it to clean the jagged ring of flesh and skin. Following this, she took some strips of linen, thickened one with ointment from the jar in the corner of the box, and placed it tenderly round the wound; then with more strips, she bandaged the heel and part of the leg, tying it top and bottom in place with a narrow strip of linen; after which she again took the now bandaged limb in her hands, bowed her head for a moment, then quite smartly got to her feet and, passing Ward, went to the cow's head, saying, "It'll be all right, Maisie. Be a good girl, and I'll see you in the morning."

She turned to look up at Ward, and he looked down on her. She was his Fanny once more: she was smiling tenderly at him, and she asked, "Are you going to make sure there are not any more of them . . . I mean in any other pastures?"

He shook his head. "I don't think there'll be any in the other pastures; this was the one that runs by the bridle path and leads into the wood on Ramsmore's estate. But the path starts in the village, and it's quite easy for anyone to pop over the wall alongside. But my God! I'll see they don't pop over again."

"What are you going to do?"

"Shoot the first bugger I see standing where he shouldn't belong."

It was the first time she had heard him swear; it was the first time she had heard him use this tone, especially so when he turned to Billy, who was standing to the side and said, "I mean that, Billy. By God! I mean that."

"And I don't blame you, master. Here's one that wouldn't blame you or anybody else. Anyway, if they were given over to the authorities, they would go along the line. It's punishable now; in any form, they're punishable . . . traps. Except, of course, when you set them on your own land for rabbits."

As Ward marched out of the cow byre, Billy, after glancing at Fanny and nodding towards her, followed him. But she remained where she was for quite some moments. Shoot them, he had said. Yes, and perhaps he would. He had every reason in the world to be angry, but the man who had just gone out of the byres was a different man from the one she had come to love. She looked back at the cow who was now standing docilely looking towards her, and in her mind she spoke to it: There is more in this than meets the eye, Maisie, she said. There's something behind it. Why would anyone want to do him an injury through his animals? And why, when I go to the village, do some people pass me without speaking, while others are cheery? Why?

She went from the byres, across the yard and into the kitchen. Annie had finished her scrubbing, and had donned a clean apron. She had just banged the oven door closed, while exclaiming again as if she were talking to the air: "This flue'll have to be swept; I'm not gettin' the heat I should. That piecrust in there is as pale as a reluctant bride."

"Annie."

"Yes, mistress?" Annie straightened up, dusted her hands and waited.

"Come and sit down."

"There's no time to sit down; it's half past eleven in the mornin', ma'am."

"Sit down, Annie. I want to talk to you."

Reluctantly, Annie lowered her plump body down on to a chair she had recently scrubbed, and Fanny went on, "At least I want you to talk to me. I want you to explain something, tell me something."

"What do I know, ma'am, that I could tell you, you who are educated enough to learn the lad his letters an' such?"

"Listen to me, Annie. I am going to ask you a question, and it's this: what is it that makes some people in the village ignore me and others speak quite kindly to me? Is it because War . . . the master married me?"

Annie turned slightly and looked towards her oven, then lifted up the corner of the large white apron and rubbed it around her mouth before returning her gaze to Fanny and saying, "He's never told you anything?"

"Told me about what?"

"Daisy Mason."

When Fanny made no reply Annie gave an impatient jerk of her head; then casting her eyes upwards a moment, she explained, "Men! Men! The silly buggers. They think they can hide behind their own shadows." Then bringing her eyes back to Fanny, she said bluntly, "Daisy Mason is a lass . . . oh, a woman, who expected to find herself in your place. Now that's the top an' the bottom of it. And don't look like that; these things happen. You hit him like a bull on the rampage. But anything further from a bull I'd like to find." Her lips now moved into the semblance of a smile.

"You mean . . . he jilted her for . . . ?"

"Oh no, no!" Annie's head was being almost violently shaken. "There was no jilting on his part, because the thickhead had imagined there was nobody to jilt. It's like this, ma'am. He and Daisy Mason went to school together in the village; an' with her and her two brothers, he romped about when they weren't working, as youngsters will; and as they grew, they still kept company . . . No, that's wrong, not company, because keeping company means courtship. And as far as I can gather I doubt if he has as much as kissed her over the years. I don't know, but I shouldn't expect so because, like most of his kind, he was blind, at least where a lass's feelings range from she's sixteen onwards. You know what I mean, ma'am. And he took her to one or two barn dances, set her home from church; an' sometimes he went and had tea with her people. Well, he had always dropped in there for a bite to eat at odd times—the two families were friends—that is, until about two years ago, when I think he must have smelt a rat, because he stopped going to church. I realise now it was really because he would have to set her home after. It was the rule to do so. And he started to visit Newcastle more; and Gateshead and the like towns, where there were good turns on. I'm sure he did it because he had seen the signal in Daisy's eyes; and he wasn't for marrying her, or anybody else at the time. Then, one night, he goes to The Empire, and there you were, the Maltese Angel, they called you. You were flying all over the stage, and dancing like a fairy, so he told me. And you were just the opposite in every way that God could think of to Daisy Mason. And you know the rest."

It was a full minute before Fanny said, "And that's what they're holding against him . . . and me?"

"Aye, in a way, you could say that. But it would have been the same whoever he had married . . . I mean the effect on Daisy and her family, because, you see, give them an' people their due, everybody expected it. To all intents an' purposes they had been courtin'. Well, I tell you, when you went about courtin' you kept to the same lass. And he had never bothered with anybody else over the years. And you know somethin', ma'am? If he had lived in a town it would have been different . . . Oh! different altogether," and she expressed the difference with a great wave of her hand. "Nobody would have noticed unless the lass had taken him to the justices for breach of promise, which a lot of them are doin' these days, brazen hussies that they are. But in a village it's different. Well, in this one it is, anyway, 'cos it's like one big family: it is as if everybody was related to everybody else. And some are, you know, some are. They have intermarried for generations, some of them; and the results . . ."—her eyebrows went up—"the results have left a lot to be wished for here and there. And the village isn't only the main street, lass; it spreads out . . . aye, even to the gentry, because you can keep nothing secret: everybody knows everything about everybody else. And if they think anything's been kept back they get the mud rakes out . . . That's a village, ma'am. They're nearly all alike; there's not a pin to choose atween them. But don't worry yourself. Just think of what you're carryin' and let them get on with it . . . But having said that, it's not saying that your man will, because once this kind of thing starts you don't know where it's gona stop. But one last thing, please don't let on that I've told you all this. There'll come a time when it's right for him to enlighten you about the whole matter. Until then, my advice, ma'am, is to plead dumb. You understand?"

"Yes. Yes, Annie, I understand. And thank you for making things plain to me. But nevertheless, I am saddened to think that I have been the cause of the division in the village."

"Well"—Annie now rose from the chair—"if it wasn't you doin' something, ma'am, it would be somebody else, because there's nothin' lies faller hereabouts. If it isn't some farmer knocking on the door in the dark, or high jinks at harvest time, it's somebody goin' off with the Christmas money from The Running Hare, like Sep Newton did three years ago. And he's never turned up since. Yet his mother still shows her face at church on a Sunday, I understand. And them's only scraping the surface of things. So don't worry, ma'am, just carry on with your life, and continue to be a nine-day wonder to your man." She now grinned widely as she added, "And that's what you are, you know. He still can't get over having you."

"Oh, Annie." Fanny moved impulsively forward and put her arms around the sturdy body, and for a moment she rested her head on Annie's shoulder, saying, "What would I have done without you? I thought when I parted from the friendship of Mrs. Killjoy I would be alone here, but from the moment I stepped in the front door you took me under your wing. I shall always remember that, Annie. And I thank you."

"Oh, go on with you, ma'am. Go on with you. Besides having dancing feet you've got a dancing tongue," and at this she pushed Fanny gently from her and turned her attention quickly to the oven, saying again, "They've got to sweep this chimney, and soon, unless they want cold porridge set afore them on the table."

Before the day was out the village was made aware of Ward Gibson's reaction to the planting of the trap. The term "tearing mad" was putting it mildly. First, he visited the blacksmith's shop, and there, showing the trap to the blacksmith, he said, "What d'you make of that, Charlie?"

Charlie Dempsey grasped the iron spike to which was attached a piece of wire with a loop on the end, and he fingered it for a time, pushing one end of the loop backwards and forwards; then looking at Ward, he said, "Crude job, Ward, I'd say, but very effective. It's on the lines of a rabbit snare, but bigger. I don't know what they'd hope to catch with it. Nothing like a man-trap, 'cos as I see it, you would have to step into this. And it's a pretty big loop."

"Big enough to take a heifer's foot?"

Charlie looked at Ward before he said, "Aye. Aye, yes. It could step into it, but being silly bitches they wouldn't step out, they would just pull it and it would tighten. Aye." He now pulled on the main piece of wire and repeated, "Aye. Aye. What's it about?"

"It's about crippling my herd, Charlie. That's what it's about."

The blacksmith made a gesture of almost throwing the contraption away from him, saying, "No! No, man. Who'd do a blasted thing like that? I mean, it's never been heard of. Rabbits, foxes, badgers, aye, but never cows . . . Is it badly seared?"

"Almost to the bone in one part."

"Good God! Well, I'll be damned! This is something I've never known afore."

"But you've likely seen those spikes; they're all of nine inches, and it takes some knocking into the ground."

"Yes, I've seen those spikes, because I made them; and I think I've supplied them to every farmer in the district, and to every farmer for miles around; an' you yourself. But they would have had to be knocked fully into the ground else they could have been spotted."

"Yes, if they were on bare ground; but they were placed cunningly in some lush grass, near one end of the field. And there's another thing: bairns cross that field, those that come from the school. The lads, in particular, climb the wall. Amos Laker's two young 'uns often do. I've yelled at them more than once because the little devils go scattering the cows and disturbing the milk. What if one of them had been caught in that, because their clogs would have dropped off and some damage would have been done before they could have got their foot out of the infernal thing."

The blacksmith now picked up a pair of tongs, took a piece of iron from the glowing forge and hammered the end of it flat before he spoke again, saying, "You've got to face up to it, Ward; there's them round about that's got it in for you. It's like a lot of bloody fools in this world, going fighting other people's battles, because, you know, I don't think the Masons themselves would do anything. There's not a nicer couple than him and her; and I've had a drink with the lads now and again, and they never utter a word against you. No; it's some of them like the Conway lot, or Ted Read and his pal Jock MacIntosh. Oh, he gets under my skin, that fella. Why doesn't he go back to Scotland among all his brave countrymen, those who he shoots his mouth off about? Likely one of that ilk. Of course, we mustn't forget them down in the Hollow. There's good and bad among all kinds, but there's one or two that smell down there; like Riley, for instance. I know where I'd like to stick a hot rod in that one . . . sly, smooth-tongued . . . crawler. He'd spit on his Pope for a tanner."

This tirade had been going on between bangs of the hammer; and now, dipping the piece of bent iron into a bucket of water, Charlie Dempsey waited until the sound of the sizzling had died away before he said, quietly now, "Anyway, there's another side to it: you've got good friends among us; and I can tell you this, the more I see of your little wife the more I understand your situation."

The leather apron around his stomach now began to wobble, and he bent his head and rubbed his sweat-covered face with his blackened hand as he muttered, "You should have heard my missis the other night when I was talking about your young lass. And you know what I said? I said, we all had regrets in life, and it was a pity that I hadn't clapped eyes on that dainty piece before Ward had, because he wouldn't have had a look in. And do you know what? She brought her hand across me ear; and her hand's not delicate, it's a mitt, I can tell you."

Ward did not smile. At this moment he couldn't appreciate his friend's trend, which was an effort to lighten his humour, so that when he turned slowly and went towards the open door of the forge, Charlie said, "Where you off to?"

And Ward's reply was short: "To both of them: The Hare and The Head; and I won't be drinking in either. But I'll tell Sam Longstaffe of The Hare and Michael Holden of The Head in no small voice so that their customers can hear me, that I'll not rest until I find out who did this." He now shook the trap that was hanging from his hand. "Then God help them." And with this, he walked down the street in the direction of the two inns.

In bed that night, holding Fanny in his arms, he said to her, "Don't go walking round the fields by yourself. Do you hear me? And don't go into the village again, unless Annie goes with you."

"But Ward, my dear, that won't happen again . . . I mean what's happened today."

"No, it mightn't happen again; and yet it might. But other things could happen; and don't say 'Why?' just do as I ask. Do you hear?"

"Yes, Ward, I hear."

"I love you."

"And I love you, too, Ward, so very much."

TWO

𝒯he weeks wore on; the months wore on; the weather remained favourable, the crops were good; the prices in the market were moderate, but healthy enough to allow Ward to make improvements. Not only did he have the yard stone-paved from the open barn right to the yard gates but he had the house painted and, what was more, he didn't engage Arthur Wilberforce, cousin to the verger, but a Mr. Percy Connor, painter and decorator, who had a business in Fellburn. The village didn't like this at all: even his friends felt he was going too far, because everybody knew the village tried to be self-sufficient, and likes and dislikes were forgotten when they touched on a man's livelihood; even the gentry round about rarely went farther afield than the village for either victuals or inside and outside work. As Hannah Beaton confided to one of her customers, "That little dancer up there has wrought havoc in this place."

As for the little dancer herself, she no longer felt little: she was carrying inside her a weight that grew heavier each day. She was almost on her time. Annie told her she had carried well: she hadn't been sick at all, and she had been blithe in herself, which wasn't always the way with the first one.

It was now nearing the end of August. During the months past they'd harvested two crops of hay; and now they were stooking the last of the corn. Ward, Billy and the boy had been working from early morning, and during the day Annie and Fanny had brought out three meals to them; and to eat the last one they had not sat propped up against the hay cart, or seated in the shadow of the hedge. Instead, Fanny had laid a check cloth on the stubble, and they had all sat round and drunk of the cool beer and ate shives of bread and cheese and veal pie, and a great deal of laughter had ensued, mainly over Annie's chatter.

However, as soon as the meal was over, Ward and Billy rose and were away to resume work; but Carl, his mouth still wide with laughter, continued to stare at Annie, and she shouted at him, "Don't you laugh at me, young man, else I'll come over there and skite the hunger off you," and at this, Carl, still laughing, enquired, "What does that mean, Mrs. Annie, skite the hunger off you?"

Annie paused before replying, "Well, I don't really know, lad. Me mother used to use it. I suppose it's sort of saying, 'look out or I'll box your ears.' " Then she cried, "Mind where you're going!" and thrust out her hand as Fanny stumbled a little on the rough ground and, grabbing the basket from her, she said, "Give me that here! You've got enough to carry with that lump of yours. Have you been having any pains?"

"Not pains exactly, no; just a feeling."

"Well, from what I gather, you've got another week to go. But then I might have gathered wrong."

"Oh, I'll go another week. I mean to"—she nodded at Annie—"because I'd love Mr. and Mrs. Killjoy to be here . . . You won't mind them staying for a few days, will you, Annie?"

"Oh, my goodness me! girl," and Annie let out a long slow breath. "It isn't my house. I've told you afore, you've got to know your place, like I know mine. You can have who you like: the old Queen if you like, or that juggler friend of yours and his pal; you can do what you like in your own . . ."

"Annie, I know, I know; I am well aware of that, but I hold you in such regard that I don't want to put on you with more work, or displease you."

They had now reached the yard and Annie walked on without answering. She pushed the door open so that her mistress could precede her through the boot room and into the kitchen; and there, dropping the basket of crockery on to the table, she bent over it before she said, "You know, sometimes, ma'am, I think you're too good to be true, and it's just as well I am who I am else you'd be taken advantage of up to the hilt."

"Oh, no, I wouldn't Annie! I'm not as simple as it might appear."

"Oh, ma'am; there's nothing simple about you. Funny thing is, you've got a head on your shoulders; but you get too soft about people, you could be taken in."

"Annie."

"Yes, ma'am?"

"I am now going to say to you what I have heard my husband say so often in his way of appreciation . . . Shut up!"

She now lumbered round the table and walked out of the kitchen, leaving Annie biting on her lip to stop herself from laughing; but as she saw the door close on her mistress, she said to herself, "Just think what this house would have been like if he had taken that big hulk. Dear God in heaven! I should go on me knees and thank God for big mercies, not little ones."

She was on the point of scooping up the dishes from the table to take them to the sink when she heard her name being called, but in a way she hadn't heard before, for this time it was in the nature of a cry.

Within seconds she was in the hall, there to see Fanny clinging to the stanchion of the parlour door.

"Lord above!" Annie almost carried the bent form towards the couch, and there she exclaimed, "It's coming?"

Lying back, and her eyes closed, Fanny made a slight movement with her head as she muttered, "Bad pain."

"Lordy!" Annie straightened up, looked about the room as if waiting to be directed what to do, then said, "Not a soul in the yard. Now, do I go for them? or do I get you upstairs?"

The answer came from Fanny who, sitting forward, said, "It's eased off; but if you would help me upstairs, and then . . . get Ward."

"Yes. Yes, that's the best thing. Come on now."

A few minutes later, in the middle of undressing, Fanny was again brought double with pain; and with this, Annie exclaimed, "You're not going to wait for Mrs. Killjoy then?"

The spasm passed, and Fanny breathing heavily muttered, "Go and get Ward, please Annie . . . now."

And to this Annie replied, "I think it's Billy who's more necessary than your lord and master at this minute, lass. He'll have to get the midwife an' Doctor Wheatley, that's if the old sod's sober enough, yet I hope he isn't, so the young 'un can come. Will you be all right?"

"I'll be all right." Left alone, Fanny finished her undressing and climbed into bed; and there, lying back amidst the pillows, she closed her eyes, and now, as if appealing to an unseen but present force, she said, "Help me through this and bring my child into life," then lay quiet.

Presently she nodded her head twice and, as if in reply to a suggestion, she let her body sink into the depths of the feather tick.

"It isn't seemly; you can't go in."

"Seemly bedamned! I could do something. It's gone on too long."

"You're not talking about a cow. What d'you think you could do? Put your arm in up to the elbow? I tell you it'll come in its own time, as Doctor Wheatley said."

"Doctor Wheatley. Where is he now? He should be back here."

"Master Ward"—Annie put out her hand and rested it on Ward's shoulder—"I know how you feel. It seems it's always the same with the first, the man gives birth an' all; but it eases off with the second and third and fourth . . . at least so they tell me."

He stared down into her face, then muttered, "Oh! Annie, I'm fright-ened. It's been going on since seven last night; now it's half-past two in the morning. And . . . and she's not the heifer type, is she?"

"No. No, she's not, lad. But it's amazing how calm she keeps in between times. But you go on downstairs and get Billy to make another pot of tea."

"It's no time since the last."

"I know. I know. But it's hot work in there; and Kate must have lost a couple of pounds already in sweat, I should think." She made an attempt at smiling as she pushed him away.

When he entered the kitchen he realised, by the way he pulled himself to his feet, that Billy had been nodding in the chair; but even so the question he would ask of Ward was plain enough in his eyes, and for answer Ward shook his head; it was the boy, who had been sitting on the low cracket at the other side of the fireplace, his arm around Pip, the poodle Mrs. Killjoy had brought as a present for Fanny, who spoke. "I . . . I rubbed Delia's stomach. I kept rubbing it and she stopped whingeing," he said.

Both men now looked at the boy, and it was Billy who said, "What d'you mean, you kept rubbin' her stomach? She must have had it in the middle of the night, around two o'clock?"

Carl hung his head now, saying, "Aye, I know. But . . . but Delia . . . she knows me." He now glanced at Ward. "And so . . . and so I came down and sat with her."

Three days previously, one of the cows had calved somewhat before its time. She hadn't been too well and they had been dosing her. She had been placed in the rest box, as they called the section that was railed off at the end of the byre.

The two men exchanged glances, but it was Billy who said, "No wonder you were dozy an' asleep on your feet t'other day. The beasts know what to do without your help, young man." But the chastising words did not carry any harshness, rather a note of kindness and understanding. Ward now walked slowly to the window through which the moonlight was streaming.

It was like daylight outside. A wind was blowing and he could see wisps of straw being lifted here and there as if they were dancing . . . Dancing. He drew his lower lip tightly between his teeth. If anything happened to her he would go mad. Yes; surely he would. He wanted a child, but not at her expense. Last night, while holding her as the pains increased, he had thought, I shall soon have a son, and he had felt elated. But no longer.

He turned towards the boy. The dog was making that thin whining sound as he strained from the boy's arms to go towards the door. That dog loved her. It had never willingly left her side since the day it had arrived. And that boy loved her, too. And he was a good boy; a boy who would stay up half the night to comfort an animal was a good boy. He could hope if he did have a son he would grow up like this youngster. There he was again: it didn't matter whether it was a son or a daughter; the only thing that mattered was that she should come through this alive.

He turned from the window, remembering why he had come downstairs, and said to Billy, "They want more tea up there."

Almost before he had finished speaking Annie's voice came to them from a distance, and at the sound they all three dashed to the kitchen door and into the lamplit hall, to come to a stop at the foot of the stairs and look up to Annie who was shouting down to them, "It's come! the bairn. It's a girl."

There was a split second of disappointment before Ward leapt to the stairs, only to be checked by Annie's strong arms and her saying, "Now look! Hold your hand a minute. Hold your hand. You can't go in there yet. She's in a bit of a mess, and she'll want to be cleaned up. But I'll bring the bairn out in a minute. She's big and bonny." She laughed outright and pushed him none too gently in the chest, crying, "She's like you. Got your hair already."

He made no further protest, but stood now with his back against the landing wall, his head dropped almost on to his chest. She had come through and he had a daughter. Well, he had a daughter . . .

It was almost a half hour later when he saw his daughter; but it was to his wife he went first. And after standing for a moment looking down on her almost deadly white face, he dropped on to his knees by the side of the bed and laid his head on her shoulder while his hand stroked her face; and as Kate Holden said later to Hannah Beaton in the grocery store, "You never did see anything like it: on his knees he was, as if she was the Queen of England who had just delivered. Although that would have been a miracle at her age, wouldn't it? Still, talk about excess and palaver. Not like a man at all, he wasn't, but like some daft lad. And what he gets out of her two pennorth of nothing beats me, because she's hardly a bit of flesh on her bones. Talk about being bewitched."

And at this moment, Ward felt bewitched: his angel, as he thought of her privately, had come through and given him offspring.

Presently, he lifted his head, rose from the bed, and walked round the foot of it to where a wooden cradle stood, draped in white lace. And he looked down on his daughter for the first time.

The face was wrinkled; the eyelids were opening and shutting; the lips were moving in and out; and there was a tuft of hair, almost black, like his own.

Well, well! So this was his daughter. But he hoped she wouldn't grow up to look like him, like her mother, yes. Oh, yes, she must look like her mother.

"Satisfied?"

He turned and looked at the midwife. As he put it to himself, he had no room for her; besides being a blowsy piece, she had a very slack tongue. Nevertheless, she was good at her job, so he understood; and although it had taken a long time, she had been good at this one. And so he answered her, "Yes, you could say I'm satisfied."

"Not disappointed because it wasn't a lad?"

He was quick to reply, "No; oh no; as long as my wife is all right, that's all that matters to me."

"Aye, well, she's come through; and not many squeaks out of her, which"—she now turned and looked towards the bed—"when you come to think of it is odd, because she's not as big as two penn'orth of copper. Still, she's done it. It doesn't really surprise me, though, because I meet all kinds in this line of business."

Then with a sly grin, she said, "Seeing how you've suffered in this lot, are you for trying again?"

His countenance darkened, and she did not wait for what would have been a brusque reply, but went out laughing.

He returned to the bed, and sitting down on the edge of it, he leant over and placed his lips gently on hers. Then, his face hanging over hers, he whispered, "This must never happen again. It has been torment."

She closed her eyes while saying, "Oh, Ward. You can be very funny at times."

"I'm not being funny, Granny Shipton," he said and gently tweaked her nose; but when she smiled and sighed, then closed her eyes, he said, "You're tired, my love. Go to sleep."

Without opening her eyes, she said softly, "I have been thinking of names, and I wonder if you would mind Flora, because, as you know, Mr. and Mrs. Killjoy have, in a way, become as dear as parents to me. If it had been a boy, I should have liked Kenneth, Mr. Killjoy's name."

He, too, had been thinking of names, but those of his father and mother, John and Jessie. He liked the name Jessie. He simply said, "Whatever you wish, my dear; I only know if it had been a boy, I would have been dead against Hayward."

He watched her smile widen; yet her eyes still remained closed.

Slowly he rose from the bed; then quietly he walked around it again and looked on the child.

Flora Gibson. It was a nondescript name somehow. Flora Gibson. He'd much rather have Jessie . . . He'd put it to her later.

Only the very necessary work was done on the farm that day. The weather was still very dry: the stooks could remain for a day or two before being gathered in. What was more, Ward was definitely needed at the house to receive the number of visitors. The first was Fred Newberry; and he took hold of Ward's hands and shook them up and down, much to the new father's embarrassment, for it happened in the yard, and not only Billy and the boy were there looking on, but Annie was, too, from the kitchen door; and they all listened to Fred gabbling, "Oh, I am pleased, man. I am pleased. And the lass . . . a girl. Mam said straight away you'd be calling it Jessie; and Dad's got a great idea for a christening cake. Mam's coming over later. She's bringing some sugar dollies. Dad's baking them now. Eeh! I am glad you've got it over."

At this Ward was forced to let out a bellow of laughter in which Billy joined, and the boy too; but Annie from the kitchen door cried, "You're a fool, Fred Newberry. Always were and always will be. Why aren't you surprised that the father isn't in bed with a binder on?"

At this, it was her husband who let out a bellow of a laugh, in which Fred joined as he answered Annie back, saying, "Well, I only know that Dad says he suffered twice as much during Mam's carrying the three of us than she did. And he had to get drunk each time to help him get over it."

"Oh you're an idiot, all right." Ward thumped Fred on the back, then urged him towards the kitchen door, saying, "Come in and have a drink."

Maisie Dempster was the next visitor; and she cooed over the mother and baby. Then Jane Oldham, the shoemaker's wife, called. But she wouldn't accept the invitation to go upstairs to see the mother and baby: she had been unable to have children of her own, and it was known that this brought on dark bouts in which she might weep a lot. However, she called to pay her respects and to leave a basket of fruit, all picked from their garden.

Frank and Jane Noble were the last to call; and Frank was already talking about the christening. But it was as they were leaving and he was helping his wife up into the trap that he saw Carl. The boy was carrying a bucket of swill from the boiler house towards the pig sty, and he called to him, "Would you like to come to the magic lantern show this evening, Carl?"

The boy stopped, put down the bucket, and he was on the point of expressing his delight, but he looked towards Ward, who was standing near the curate; and Ward answered for him, saying, "Get your work done, and you may go."

The boy picked up the bucket again, and without having said a word, hurried away, and Frank Noble, turning to Ward, said, "You've got a good boy there. And Fanny has done a wonderful job on him. He can read whole passages of the Bible, as good as myself."

At this, Ward put on a mock serious expression as he replied, "I'm not interested in what he can do with the Bible, but how quick he can carry that swill."

"Go on with you!" Frank thrust him aside; then mounted the trap, and Jane, from her seat, called to the boy, "We start at seven, Carl," and Carl answered, "Yes, ma'am." Then stood still while watching the trap leave the yard; that is until Ward's voice caused him to jump: "You'll get your work done standing there gaping, won't you?"

Carl did not immediately turn and run; but he stared at Ward, saying, "Would . . . would you let me have a look at the baby, master?"

Ward pulled a long face as if he were listening to an impossible request; then shaking his head as if addressing company, he said, "And he's going out to a magic lantern show? It doesn't matter to him about the evening chores. Oh no. And now he's asking for more time off in order to see the baby." He adopted a false glare as he stared down on the boy; but then quickly he thrust out his hand and, laughing, grabbed the thin veined arm as he said, "Come on. Come on. You'll see the baby."

However, their hurried progress was checked by Annie emerging from the bedroom and demanding, "Where do you think you're going?" And she looked from one to the other, then ended, "Eh?"

"I am taking this young gentleman to see my daughter. Is there any harm in that?"

"Could be. Could be," said Annie. "Stay there till I see if they're ready to receive you."

She pushed open the bedroom door, put her head round, saying, "You've got more visitors; are you up to it?"

If there was an answer it was inaudible, but Annie stood aside and allowed them to pass her, Ward still holding the boy by the hand.

"Oh! Hello, Carl."

"Hello, ma'am. Are you better?"

"Yes. Yes, Carl. Thank you. You've come to see the baby?"

"Yes, ma'am. Please."

"Well, there she is, in the cradle."

They both watched the boy now walk towards the cradle and stand looking down on the child. Then his hand, in the act of moving downwards, wavered, and he looked across the bed towards them, saying, "Me hand's clean," and immediately returned his attention to the child, resting his forefinger on the tiny fist, and when it was grabbed his face became alight and he actually gurgled; and turning to them again, he whispered, "She's got my finger."

Ward glanced at Fanny, and she at him, and the look they exchanged was soft with understanding: the boy was experiencing, next to suckling, one of the first natural instincts of a baby, but the impression on Carl's face was as if it could never have happened before; and it hadn't, not in his world.

When his finger was released, he lifted his hand and looked at it; then his lips were drawn in between his teeth as if to suppress some inner emotion connected with either tears or laughter, but with something new and strange springing from the depths of his growing and groping mind.

He now left the cradle and, walking to the side of the bed, he said, "She is beautiful . . . lovely, ma'am. Thank you."

He did not look at his master, but turned and went from the room, across the landing, down the stairs, and into the kitchen where Annie said, "Well, what d'you think?" But he gave her no reply; he did not even stop, leaving her gaping after him and saying aloud, "Well, I'll be jiggered! That was a response and a half."

The boy now made his way across to the stables, but not into the cowshed or into the barn, but up the ladder and into his room. And there he sat on the side of his shakedown bed, his eyes fixed on the sloping rafters above as he questioned his feelings: he had felt wonderful when the baby was holding his finger; then of a sudden when he had looked at his mistress that nightmare feeling had attacked him again, not of being flailed, or screaming out when the salt was thrown on to his back and hearing Mr. Zedmond's drunken, insane laughter. No; it wasn't that feeling, but another, not unlinked with the past. Of the fearful dread of Mr. Brown, the workhouse master? No, it wasn't that either, but a fear of some sort. He couldn't understand it because it had come upon him in that happy room, and in that happy house. Perhaps something was going to happen to himself that would make them get rid of him, send him away? Oh, that was silly thinking. He would never do anything to upset either the master or mistress, or Mr. Billy, or Mrs. Annie. They had all been so kind to him. And he knew that the master liked him. Well, otherwise he wouldn't have kept him from the beginning, would he? Sometimes he bawled at him; but it was mostly in fun; and he could always tell.

Why was he sitting here? The master wouldn't be joking if he found him up here at this time of the day. What was the matter with him? Was he going wrong in the head?

He sprang from the pallet; but paused a moment to stick out his forefinger and to look at it. He started to smile: she had gripped it, hadn't she? and really tight.

Then in a rush he made for the ladder.

THREE

There were only ten children at the magic lantern show. Apart from Carl, they were the children of the families from the Hollow. If the show had taken place in the schoolroom most of the village would have been there, but not those from the Hollow, and Frank Noble had purposely set up the apparatus in the little church to give the Hollow children a treat. It did not matter to him that the parents seldom attended his services, and he understood: in any case, a number of them were Catholics in whom the feeling of hellfire was strong, and any Catholic would be bound straight for that place were he to enter a Protestant church. But the children were different, and the parents seemed to think this way too. Perhaps they considered their offspring would only go to Purgatory for committing what would have been for them a mortal sin.

Anyway, the children enjoyed the show immensely. Carl, with the rest, rocked on the form when the donkey kicked the man with the stick into the air. And the following plate was better still, because the donkey was now chasing the man with the stick. Then there was the lovely one of the bird feeding its young. But the one that the Reverend kept on longest was that of Jesus sitting among a group of children. He had a lovely face. He hadn't a beard, and his hair was fair and fell on his shoulders, and he was dressed in a white gown.

But Carl wasn't exactly familiar with this particular picture. In the workhouse, he had heard a lot about Jesus and how kind he was, especially to children. This was from the preacher, yet none of the staff or the master seemed to have heard of him. They knew a lot about the devil, though, and what he could do; and when he was farmed out he was to find that there was no doubt about the power of the devil.

The Reverend had made the show last for more than an hour, for he had given a commentary on each slide, his remarks being amusing enough to keep the children laughing heartily.

After the show, sweetmeats were distributed by Mrs. Noble, then the children quickly dispersed to their so-called homes, which were little more than hovels.

Carl was the last to leave; and as Frank and Jane stood with him at the church door, Frank said, "You're going to be blown about on your walk home, Carl," and pointed to where the tops of the trees were swaying. "The moon's on a wild rampage tonight. She doesn't know whether to stay in or come out. But you know your way back, don't you?"

"Oh yes, sir."

"Well"—Frank Noble pointed again to where the scudding clouds were blocking out the moonlight—"I would run when she's out and walk when she's in."

Carl laughed and said, "I'll do that, sir. 'Tis good advice."

"Oh, I always give good advice, Carl."

"Yes, you do, sir." Carl was still laughing; then he added, "Good night, sir. And good night to you, ma'am. And thank you for the evening. It has been wonderful." Then with a touch of humour, he added, "I hope the donkey caught that man and kicked him hard." And with this he hurried away, Frank and Jane Noble's laughter following him.

He was feeling pleased with himself: he had made the parson and his wife laugh.

The moon was riding through a clear patch of sky now. It was a lovely night, in spite of the wind. Well, it had been dry and warm for ages. Tomorrow, they'd get the last of the corn in. They would have had it in today if the baby hadn't come.

He skirted the woodland, for although the moon was bright, he did not know how long it would stay that way and he didn't want to be caught in the dark among all the trees. He didn't like the dark. The cellar on that farm had been black, pitch black. Two whole days . . . No, he mustn't start thinking about that again . . . He would take the bridle path that led to the village, and half-way along he would climb the wall with the help of the old oak whose roots went under the wall and the lower branches over it. This way he would drop into the corn field where they had finished stacking the stooks yesterday.

It was as he reached the bridle path that once more the clouds obscured the moon; but he was on a path he knew, and it was only a short way to the tree. The wind seemed to be getting stronger, for it was bending the hedge growth almost into the middle of the path; at one time a branch whipped his cheek.

When he reached the oak the clouds were clearing just the slightest. He lifted his arms and gripped the lowest branch and pulled himself up to the top of the wall. Astride it, the position was very uncomfortable, for the top stones were angled. But instead of lifting his right leg over and dropping into the field he became perfectly still as, further along on the field side of the wall, he watched the dark bulk of a figure swinging a can. He knew it to be a can, for he caught the glint of it. When the can stopped swinging the widening of his mouth and the intake of breath were but the precursors to the loud yell he emitted when the flames shot up from the grass and rivulets licked their way towards the stooks.

When he was gripped by the shoulders and hoisted upwards he was still screaming, until his face was bashed against the tree trunk, when all went quiet.

How long he lay on the edge of the field he didn't know, but he was brought into startling life by the realisation that his hair was on fire; also his coat. His reaction was to stagger to his feet and to break into the war-dance of a dervish. With one hand he frantically tore at his hair the while dancing on his coat in an endeavour to put out the flames.

As yet he wasn't aware of what was happening in the field; but when with startled and unbelieving eyes he saw the flames licking hungrily at the dry stubble and climbing one stook after another, he was again screaming, but running drunkenly as well.

The moon was again clear of the curtain of clouds; and his throat was sore and his step almost flagging when he reached the yard. But his screaming penetrated the bedroom and brought Ward down the stairs and into the yard, to see the boy grabbing at Annie's apron and yelling, "It's the field. It's afire! Afire! All of it."

"What are you talking about, boy?"

Before the lad could answer Ward, Annie cried, "Look! His hair's all singed, and his coat, look! Dear God in heaven!"

"Buckets! Buckets! master." The boy was staggering towards the boiler house.

Ward himself was now running frantically after Carl and yelling, "Get Billy! Get Billy! He's in the cottage."

Carl was running again, but so muddled was he in his mind that he hammered on the door of the empty cottage next to Billy's. But this brought Billy out of his own door, crying, "What's up, lad?" He was dressed only in singlet and trousers, and when Carl yelled at him, "The cornfield! It's afire . . . blazin'," Billy paused only a second before leaping forward, Carl behind him now.

From the boiler house door Annie threw two pails at her husband's feet, while she cried to the boy, "Run to the Hollow an' get the men! Look at that sky!"

The moonlight was now tinted by the delicate flame flush that seemed to be borne on the wind; and as Carl went stumbling off behind Billy, she screamed at him, "Don't go empty-handed!" and a milk pail came rolling to his feet, and her voice hit him again, crying, "And put a move on!"

When he reached the field, he brought himself to a sudden halt: at the sight before him, Billy himself too had become stock-still, and he was whispering in dismay, "Oh my God! My God!" But then a cry from Ward brought them both running again, and he yelled to Carl what Annie had said, "Go to the Hollow! Fetch the men." He hadn't said the village, but the Hollow. And to Billy he cried, "Get to the rill, Billy. Hand me the buckets, I'll douche the hedge, else it'll get into the bottom field."

Carl had jumped the tiny stream that ran between the two fields, and when he reached the hill which formed one side of the Hollow he stotted down it like a ball, crying, "Mr. Riley! Mr. Read! Mr. Mackintosh!"

As he banged on the first cottage door, others along the row opened and voices cried through the darkness. "What's it? Is it a fire or something?"

And in answer to this usual first reaction, Carl yelled, "It's master's cornfield. All ablaze. He wants you."

More doors opened to cries and statements such as:

"My God!"

"Jesus in heaven!"

"Can you believe it?"

Then someone cried, "Look at that sky! God, it's a fire all right. Let's away! Eeh! let's away."

Eight men and seven young boys, not one older than twelve, scampered along the Hollow, then up the hill; but strangely, Carl made no move to follow the yelling mass that had disappeared into the darkness, for the moon had momentarily hidden itself again. There was something wrong with him: he couldn't make his legs move, yet they felt light. All his body felt light. It was as if he were about to fly. But of a sudden it wasn't into the air he went but deep into the ground.

"The lad's collapsed. Well, I never did! An' look at his hair! It's been on fire. And his shirt's singed an' all. Poor young 'un," said a large woman.

"Will I throw some water over him, Ma?"

"I'd throw a barrel full over yersel if I'd one near at this minute. An' don't hang over him, you lot." She pushed the children and two other women aside. "Move your hides till I lift him." She gave a wiggle of her wide hips, and two children suddenly sat down on the mud road; then she stooped and picked up Carl in her arms and, stepping over her youngest, she went sideways through the door into the cottage, and laid her burden down on a wooden bench covered with a straw tick, saying to her daughter in an aside, "Bring the lamp nearer. Then wet the small coarse towel in the bucket and let's have it." The nine-year-old girl did not run immediately to do her mother's bidding, but muttered under her breath, "You always bring me da round by douching him."

"As sure as God's in heaven this night, Patsy Riley, I'll douche you with your own blood if you don't do this minute what I'm askin' of you. An' you lot back there! Settle down, else I'll scud your hides one after t'other. An' you know me, I waste neither spit nor words."

Five small but interested spectators, three boys and two girls, scuttled away towards the open hearth where a fire, built up with slack coal, was endeavouring to show a glow. They sat all close together and watched their mother wrap coarse towels round the visitor's head; and they listened to their sister Patsy saying, "He's Mr. Gibson's lad. He's got a cushy job there, an' he knows it, 'cos he never gives you the time o' day when he passes you. You'd think his nose was smellin' a midden. He's comin' round. He's blinkin'. An' I bet when he wakes up he won't thank you for landin' him in here."

The children hunched their shoulders when their mother yelled, "Will you shut that wobblin' gob of yours, Patsy Riley, or else I'll shut it for you, an' with such a bang you'll think a cuddy's kicked yer."

During the short silence that followed this exchange, Mrs. Riley looked down at the blood-stained face: the nose was caked with dried blood, and blood had been running from a cut in the lad's brow. Someone had given him a right bashing. And for why? she would like to know. But all in good time.

"Hello there," she said. "Are you feelin' better then?"

Carl lifted his heavy eyelids but he couldn't really make out the face hanging over him, yet he knew who it was; at least he knew it was one of the

Irish women from the Hollow . . . He had come to the Hollow for the men.

He tried to rise, saying, "The fire."

"Lie yersel back, lad. Lie yersel back for a minute. They've all gone. 'Twill likely be out by now." She again spoke in an aside to her daughter, saying, "Go and get me the bairn's flannel."

"The bairn's flannel? His face'll mucky it up. You won't let any of us use it."

Mrs. Maggie Riley's voice was still low as she said, "One of these days, Patsy Riley, I'll use a hammer on you, as sure as God's me judge, I will that, I'll use a hammer on you." With a swift movement, she now turned and barked, "Get me the flannel!"

The sound of her raised voice startled Carl, and he made another effort to get up; but Mrs. Riley's voice was once again calm and soothing: "Lie still, lad. Take no notice. The storms are always risin' an' fallin' in this house. But would you like to tell me who did that to your face?" She stretched out her hand to the side now and took the piece of wet flannel from her daughter; and when she applied it, and gently, to Carl's cheeks, he winced and whimpered, "No! No!"

"All right. All right; we'll leave it."

"I must get back to . . . to help."

He now managed to pull himself upright from the bench, and after slowly sliding his feet to the floor he put his hand to his head and held it there for a moment, saying, "Thank you very much, ma'am, for your kindness."

"Oh, 'tis nothin', lad. 'Tis nothin' at all. But I don't think you're goin' to make it on your own back to the farm."

The suggested inability of his walking back to the farm brought him to his feet, and for the first time he took in his surroundings. Although the image was hazy he made out the group of children by the fire, the kale pot hanging on a chain over smouldering coals, the clutter in the room of boxes and bedding. There seemed to be only two chairs. The table was littered with pots and pans.

At the door, he held on to the stanchion for a moment; and it was then that Mrs. Riley said to her daughter, "Go along of him, Patsy, an' see that he gets there."

The girl having made no objection to this command, and Carl none to her accompanying him, they had nevertheless walked in silence until, having emerged from the wood and on to the bridle path, Carl stopped and, putting a hand out, supported himself against a tree for a moment. It was then that Patsy, her voice as soft as her mother's could be, said, "Let me give you a hand."

And so for the first time, Patsy touched him, and they were both to remember this.

When they reached that part of the wall which, with the help of the oak tree, he had climbed a short time before, he now leant against it and peered over the top. To him, a haze of smoke seemed to be still covering the field with a red patch here and there breaking through; and he could just make out a dim line of dark figures. They seemed to be standing still looking towards him. Then he imagined them to be all running towards him, and he was rising from the ground once more and about to fly.

As he slid down by the wall Patsy Riley shook him by the shoulders, crying, "Come on, man! Come on!" But when he made no attempt to move, she did what he had done earlier: she pulled herself up and on to the wall with the help of the long branch and, with its support, she stood on the coping and yelled, "Somebody come! Hi! there. Hi! there. Somebody come! He's passed out again." Then finally, she screamed, "Da! This is Patsy. The lad's conked out!"

There was a break in the dim line of figures, and when three of them reached her, she pointed down to the other side of the wall, saying, "It's Mr. Gibson's lad. He's been battered, and he's conked out."

It was Ward, hardly recognisable from his two companions, one of them being Fred, who clambered over the wall and dropped to his knee beside Carl.

Lifting him, he handed him back to Fred, saying, "God above! Look at his face." Then looking wildly beyond Fred at the men, all of whom were now gathered together, he cried, "I swear to you on my oath, when I find out who has done this, not only to my field, but to the lad, I'll kill him, even if I have to swing for it."

The men remained silent, for each knew that if Ward Gibson were to find the perpetrator within the next few hours he would likely do what he said, and swing for him. But they also knew that the one who should swing was he who was so low he would set fire to a man's field, the work of a year, his livelihood; for one of the worst crimes against a farmer was to set fire to his barns or his fields. And no man standing there this night could recall it ever having happened, not around here, anyway. Accidents, yes, would happen; and there had been fires of sorts; but nothing ever deliberate.

They all knew that this had been a deliberate act, and all because he had married someone other than Daisy Mason; and here and there the thought passed through a man's mind: God help those two Mason lads if it could be laid at their door.

Ward clambered back over the wall, and taking the boy from Fred Newberry's arms, he paused a moment to look at the smoke-blackened faces of the men who had helped him; then he said quietly, "Thank you all. Thank you very much. Without your help, the hedge would have gone and the other field an' all. I'm grateful."

There were grunts and murmurs, but no-one made any rational reply as Ward stumbled away, the boy hugged to him.

The men dispersed, some making their way along the bridle path towards the village; while those from the Hollow moved away in the opposite direction.

As Patsy's father held her by the hand, he did not ask why she had come to be there with the boy, the one she would often speak about as being the stuck-up skit from Gibson's farm. He loved his daughter and he knew why she talked about that particular lad; it was because she was wise enough to know that from where she was placed now she could never hope to link up with someone like him . . . even the farmer's boy that he was.

* * *

You could have said that the field had looked almost pretty in the moonlight, with a flame here and there spitting through the haze of smoke. Everything last night had looked pink or silver grey, only the men had looked black. But as Ward gazed on the devastation of his land in the early morning light, the dirty blackened sight of the charred stooks that yesterday had been golden pyramids fanned the rage that was still boiling in him.

When he first saw the licking flames the name that had sprung immediately to mind was the Masons; and while battering the ground with a sack between grabbing the buckets of water and drenching the hedge, his mind had dwelt on the name. And it did so until Fred, who came back later, happened to say, "I don't know who did it, Ward, but you can count the Mason lads out," at which Ward had swung round, growling, "Why count them out?"

"Because from six o'clock onwards, they were in The Crown Head. I saw them go in meself. And when I dropped in later, they were still there. And they were playing dominoes when I left. And it was only ten minutes later when I came out of the bakery and saw the weird light in the sky from over here. At first, I didn't take it for a fire, but me dad did. He was just coming out of the house an' we both took to our heels . . . And as for Daisy. Well, she went into Fellburn this afternoon to stay with her cousin. Now you'll ask how I know that. Well, she dropped into the shop. She wanted half a dozen rice dollies, because she said her cousin liked them. She was chatting to me mam for a time. So you've got to look elsewhere, Ward. And in a way I'm glad of that, 'cos you know, there's not a nicer couple than John and Gladys Mason, and they wouldn't let their lads do anything like that. He would die of shame, would John Mason, if people thought that way."

It was then that Rob Newberry, who had also come back after cleaning up, put in, "You'll likely get your best lead from the lad later, because by the looks of him he must have come across whoever it was actually doing it, and they battered him. The poor lad's face is in a state, and I wouldn't be a bit surprised if his head's been hurt an' all. You've said yourself he's asleep again."

Well, if it wasn't the Masons, who was it? The family had many friends in the village. But would friends feel a bitterness as members of the family would feel; and if they did, enough to do a thing like this? Kids might start a fire, but no kid had started this fire. This one had been paraffin fed. The quart can lying against the wall proved that. Whoever was carrying out the work must have retreated in a hurry.

And now there was the worry of Fanny. When Annie had gone back into the house it was to find her sitting slumped on a chair near the landing window from where she could see, if not the actual field, the smoke and the flames at their height. And she had hardly stopped crying since, blaming herself that this had happened. And in a way it had. Yes, in a way it had. But he wouldn't change things, not for one minute. That didn't mean, though, that when he found the culprit he wouldn't throttle him with his own hands. Last night he had been stupid enough to say those very words to her, and it had made her worse.

He turned about and hurried quickly back towards the house. That boy must start talking.

* * *

They had had to call the doctor to Carl, for he had been unable to keep awake. Doctor Patten was a young man who was now noted for looking at and listening to patients, but had little to say himself, which made the villagers wonder if he actually knew anything about medicine, for he was altogether different from Doctor Wheatley. After examining Carl he had said simply that he was badly concussed and needed rest.

But Ward could not wait until the boy was fully rested, because he meant to go and put the matter in the hands of the justices; and besides the evidence of the fire itself, he wanted to know from the boy what he had seen before he had been attacked.

Carl was now lying in the storeroom beyond the kitchen, because Annie had stated flatly she wasn't going to climb that ladder in order to see to him. And so his pallet bed had been brought down and a space found for it. And it was to there that Ward now made his way.

The pallet bed was headed by an old chest, against which was placed a sack full of some commodity, and two pillows; and Ward had to drop on to his hunkers in order to come face to face with the boy. As he looked at him he gritted his teeth, for the lad could not possibly see out of his eyes. The flesh around them was purple and his nose was swollen. He did not say to him, "How are you feeling?" but, "You feeling bad?" and at this Carl muttered, "Sore."

"Oh aye, yes, you would be sore. Now listen, Carl. Try to tell me what happened."

Try to tell the master what happened? Between sleeping and waking he could still see the flames licking at the stubble, and then the great black thing springing on him. But the master wanted to know what happened. He said slowly, "He was a big man . . . very big. Cap on." He lifted a hand to his brow to indicate the peak; then muttered, "Big cap . . . He had a big cap I . . . I think."

"Didn't you see his face?"

"No. No; 'twas dark. 'Twas dark . . . well, nearly."

"And you think it was a big man?"

"Oh yes. Yes . . . strong. He lifted me by . . ." He now patted his shoulder before saying, "Up, and crashed me against the tree."

"He didn't hit you with his fists then?"

"No. No . . . just the tree . . . I'm tired, master."

"All right. All right, Carl." Ward now put his hand upon the boy's head where the thick hair was standing up in tufts; then he straightened his back. He did not, however, immediately leave the room but stood looking down on the boy's face. He had said "a big man"; and it would need a big strong man to lift that boy up by the shoulders and bang his head against the tree, because the boy, although thin, was no lightweight, and, too, the bole of the tree was only visible above the wall. Of course, there was that low branch, but that came over at an angle. A big man. A big man. Who were the big men in the village? The blacksmith, or his lads John and Henry? No, they were more broad than tall. But they were his friends; as were the Newberrys. Hannah Beaton wasn't; but then she had no man behind her. The verger? Aye, there was a big man. But pot-bellied and bloated, and he doubted that he had lifted anything heavier than the Bible in his life.

He went through others in the village. They were all men of medium height, from the shoemaker up to Parson Tracey. But there were some big men in the Hollow. Some of those Irish Paddys could lift a horse; but all of them had, at some time or other during the year, done jobs for him, and they all seemed to like working for him—they had told him so, more than once— for when times were hard he had taken one or other of them on when he could easily have done without them. No; it had not been anyone from the Hollow.

Then who? His mind swung back to the Masons. As Fred had vouched, the brothers had been in the inn; and Daisy was away from the place. That left only Mr. Mason.

Well, he would just as easily blame God for setting light to his fields as he would have John Mason.

But he wasn't going to let this matter rest, for likely the same one who had caused the fire had set the trap for the cattle; and once having started, God knew what he would do next. So he was going to the Justice.

In the kitchen he said as much to Annie; and she agreed with him, saying, "Aye, well somebody wants bringin' to boot. Apart from the field, there's that lad's face. To my mind, somebody got a big gliff when they were doing their handiwork, and thought to finish him off. And they could have, an' all. By the way, I've had to burn his clothes; and the bit of hair he's got left was running with them."

"Running with what?"

"Dickies, of course. He had lain in that hovel of the Rileys, hadn't he? Well, you only need to put your nose in the door of one of those shanties and the dickies, lice and bugs come out to meet you. You'll have to buy him a new rig-out, at least coat and pants. But when you're at it, you could throw in a couple of shirts, 'cos as he stood he had only one on his back and one off it."

"Anything else you can think of?"

"No, not at the minute, but you owe him that."

"Huh!"

He walked from her, out of the kitchen and up to the bedroom.

Fanny had the child at her breast; and he pulled a chair to the side of the bed and watched his daughter feed; and he didn't speak until Fanny, laying the child to her side, said, "What do you intend to do?"

"I told you. I'm going to the polis. Let them deal with it, because I've racked my brains and I can't think of anyone I can lay it on, not round about, anyway."

"Have you thought of the boy?"

"Yes; yes, I have; and that's why I'm doing it."

"When you mention his name they will likely question him."

"Of course."

"What if it should reach the papers, Ward, and that man from whom he ran sees it? The local papers probably get as far as Durham, and it was from some farm near there that he ran away."

"I see what you mean."

"You could change his name, and instil into him why you're doing it. It's for his good. And yet he once said to me that that was all he had, his name."

"Well, what shall I say it is?"

"You could give him mine . . . McQueen. Anyway, from what I understand, Annie tells me that some people think we are related, because we came on the scene at the same time." She did not smile when making this statement; and he, taking her hand, patted it as he said, "I'll say it's Carl McQueen. Sounds a good name, one he shouldn't object to."

When her eyes moistened, he said quickly, "Now stop it. You are not to cry any more. Think of her"—he pointed to the child lying on the patchwork quilt—"and remember, the more you worry the longer you will have to stay in bed."

She now brought the hand that covered hers up to her breast and, pressing it tight, she said, almost in a whimper, "I'm afraid, not for myself, but for you. What will they do next?"

"Nothing. Nothing, my dear. Once they know it's in the hands of the polis, that will scare them. You know, in a way they are sort of proud of the village and its good name, and so they don't like intruders, and for them the polis are intruders. Probably we all have something to hide."

There was a pause before she said, "No; no, they certainly don't like intruders, not of any sort."

He could give no answer to this, but he bent forward and kissed her; then he went hastily from the room, thinking, Yes, she is right. They don't like intruders of any sort. Someone was determined to make him pay for the one he had brought in.

Two days later there was a report in the *Newcastle Journal*. It was headed: Outrage on farmer. And the journalist went on to prove his powers of imagination in describing the blazing cornfield and the intruder who must have been intent on killing Farmer Gibson's young farmhand, Carl McQueen, who was now suffering from severe concussion and with his face utterly distorted, having been banged repeatedly against a tree trunk. And this wasn't the first time that Farmer Gibson had been the recipient of village spite: not so long ago his cattle had been nobbled. There must have been a reason for these actions, the journalist went on; but as yet he had not been able to fathom it, as the villagers themselves were all tight-lipped.

The villagers were not tight-lipped in the inns, nor in the grocery shop, the butcher's, the cobbler's, nor the baker's. Even Fred said it was a mistake to call in the polis; in the end they would have found out who it was. As for neighbouring gentry, Colonel Ramsmore had suggested it was the outcome of a lad tampering with matches and tobacco, having a sly smoke behind the wall. When the state of the boy's face had been pointed out to him, he had blithely come back with, Oh, that could be explained by the young fellow's climbing the tree; then slipping and falling on to the top of the stone wall. Those copings were pretty sharp. Perhaps it was indeed Gibson's own boy who was the arsonist.

When this version was spoken by the man who was in all senses Lord of the Manor, well, said the villagers here and there, there could be something in it. And wasn't Ward Gibson's wife called McQueen before he married her? Now that was funny, wasn't it?

However, the overall version was, let them wait and see what the polis did. But those friendly towards Ward Gibson hoped that the polis would get the fellow before Ward did, for if they didn't, then the village would definitely be in the papers; and not only the local ones, because they remembered what Ward had said on the night of the fire.

As it happened, nothing emerged from the enquiries, and Ward soon found he had other problems to deal with.

FOUR

$\mathcal{F}$anny was slow in regaining her physical strength, and so it was two months later when the baby was christened Jessie Flora Gibson: Jessie, after Ward's mother, and Flora, after Mrs. Killjoy. Frank Noble had taken the service in the little chapel in the Hollow; and the children of the Hollow had waited outside to receive the christening piece. The contents of the christening piece, so named, held whatever the family could afford, be it sweetmeats, a piece of silver, or even just a copper. It should happen that Patsy Riley had placed herself determinedly at the head of the queue and so received the bag from Ward. And, as primed, she said, "Health an' wealth an' all things good fortune bring to it."

Present at the christening tea were, except for the actors and Mrs. Boorman, those who had sat round the table at the wedding feast. Mr. and Mrs. Killjoy were present, and of course their family who, on this occasion, had been relegated to the barn under the care of Carl, and following the tea, they weren't brought back into the house to show off their tricks. There were two reasons for this: first, Mr. Killjoy was not at all well; and secondly, an unusual altercation took place at the end of the tea between Charlie Dempster and the Reverend Frank Noble. It came about when Jane Noble happened to remark that she was glad to see Patsy Riley get the christening piece, and Charlie came back promptly with, "Well, here's one that wasn't glad to see her get it, missis, for she's a scamp, that one, leading the others rampaging around, picking up things they oughtn't to. Been round my backway. If I'd caught her I'd have wrung her neck. She should be where her dad is at this minute, doing time," which caused Frank to come back at him with: "Now, now, Charlie, be fair. Riley got into a fight, and, after all, he was just defending his own."

"Got into a fight, you say, Parson? Are you for them? Those Feenians comin' over here blastin' an' bombin' an' murderin' the gentry; all under orders from that man Parnell. Scum he is, lowest of the low. Riot-rousers."

"Now! now! Charlie; you've got your facts wrong." He didn't add, "again," but went on, "Parnell, let me tell you, is of the gentry, born and bred; all he is doing is fighting for the Irish poor, and if he was an Englishman fighting for the English poor, such as the factory workers, the miners and such, he'd be praised as a hero." Frank was tactful at this point not to mention farm labourers.

"You're damn well on his side; and on theirs an' all, that lot in the Hollow. Of course, you live next to 'em, that's why, likely."

"It isn't because I live next to them," said Frank quietly now; "it's simply because I read history: I see two sides of this question. Have you asked yourself why so many Irish come over to this country? It's because they're starving; and they were brought low through the rents and taxes of the English landlords over in their country. And I would add this," said Frank, getting a little heated now, "if this was just a matter of politics it would soon be settled, but the main trouble is religion and bigotry. Yes, bigotry, believing that, there being only one God, He is for you, and you alone. Bigotry, I say again. And you needn't go any further than your own village, which is rife with bigotry."

Seeing the look on Fanny's face, Ward put in quickly and on a false laugh, "I'll always remember this day, and we'll talk about it to Jessie when she's grown up, won't we?" He reached out and took hold of Fanny's hand. "We'll tell her that our two friends, the parson and the blacksmith, almost came to blows, and it was a good job the argument didn't take place in the forge, else you, Frank, would have been a gonner."

This caused general laughter around the table, and Frank, looking now at Charlie, said, "I'm sorry, Charlie. I lost my head. And as Ward's just said, I could, couldn't I, literally have lost my head had I been in the forge."

But Charlie wasn't to be placated so easily and, his big head wagging from side to side, he said, "I still don't know, Parson, how you can be on their side after Mike Riley busting that fellow's jaw."

"Well," said Frank, with a broad smile on his face now, "what would you do if someone called you a pig-nose Paddy? and to that added, 'Do you push the pigs out of your bed to let your wife in?' I can tell you what, Charlie, I'd have had a go meself if that had been said to me."

"Sticks and stones may break me bones, but words won't hurt me."

At this childish retort, Fred and his father and other men at the table laughingly shouted him down.

Mr. and Mrs. Killjoy were the last to leave; and it was while Mr. Killjoy was outside gathering up his family ready for the journey back to Newcastle in the brake that Mrs. Killjoy, already dressed in hat and cape, suddenly took Fanny by the hand and led her unhurriedly back into the sitting-room, and there in a mumbling whisper she said, "I must tell you. I promised him I wouldn't, but I must. He's not long for the top. We did our last turn a fortnight ago. My heart is heavy, Fanny, so heavy.''

"Oh my dear. My dear." Fanny was now embracing her friend as far as her arms would go around her, and exclaiming rapidly, "Why didn't you tell me before? Oh, you must stay, you mustn't go. We can look after him. There's plenty of room. There's . . ."

"Quiet, dear. Quiet. Now we've been through all this, Mr. Killjoy and I, and it is his wish that we stay with Mrs. Boorman. She has been good to us all over the years, and she understands us. And, of course, our family. We had intended to stay there in any case while we were looking around for the cottage. But he'll never live in a cottage now. Don't . . . don't cry, my dear, else he'll be angry. No. No, I mustn't say that; he has never been angry with me; nor even vexed. Everything I have done has been right in his eyes, for he was so grateful that I chose him, and I was more than grateful that he chose me, because we were two oddities, despised in different ways for our bulk, or lack of it; but no two people have been happier than we have. And for this I thank God; and now we both say His will be done . . . Oh, please, my dear, don't . . . don't. As he said, when he goes I will still have the consolation of the family and you, though Biddy and Rose are getting on, and their death, too, has to be faced. But from the moment we are born a day is regularly knocked off our life, whether the number is written long or short. Oh, there he is now." She gently pushed Fanny away from her, saying briskly now, "Dry your face. Come, dry your face. Oh dear! If he sees you like that he'll know in a moment. Go on, fetch the baby down; and you can hide your face in hers. Quickly now."

She had already turned and was walking towards the door, calling loudly, "I can hear you, Mr. Killjoy. I can hear you. And my family too."

In the yard, Billy was in the driving seat of the brake, and behind him the dogs were barking their heads off while jumping up at the door of the brake to receive Carl's last patting.

When a strict word came from Mr. Killjoy, they scrambled on to the seat and sat quivering with pleasure as Ward helped their mistress up beside them.

Annie now called to Mrs. Killjoy, "Come back soon, please," to which Mrs. Killjoy replied, "I will. I will, me dear . . . with pleasure."

As for Mr. Killjoy, he looked towards Fanny, who was slowly approaching him across the yard and, hurrying towards her, he kissed her on the cheek as he said, "Bye-bye, my love. Be seeing you soon."

She could not answer him, but she took one hand from holding the child, and gripped his; then she stayed where she was, not joining with Ward, Annie and the boy in waving goodbye; but as soon as the brake had disappeared from sight, she turned hurriedly to go into the house; and there, Ward and Annie found her sitting in the kitchen on a straight-back chair, rocking the child back and forth, the tears once again running down her face.

"What is it? What is it?" Ward was on his hunkers before her, and Annie to the side of her.

After a moment, haltingly, she told them what she had learned about her dear Mr. Killjoy.

When she had finished, neither of them made any immediate remark; but presently Annie said, "When he goes you must have her here, 'cos as you've always said, ma'am, she's been like a mother to you."

When Ward made no comment on this suggestion, Annie looked at him, and she said, "She needn't stay in the house. Well, you wouldn't want that tribe of dogs in the house; but there's always the cottage next door to us. It's been empty these many years, but it's still dry; just wants airing. It's got a good flue. I remember that much about it: it doesn't smoke like ours. Well, what do you say?" She was looking straight at Ward; and his non-committal answer was, "We'll see." Then taking Fanny's arm, he said, "Come on, dear, and put the child down and rest a while. It's been a busy day." And as he left the kitchen he would not have been surprised had Annie called after him, "I can read your thoughts," because he was recalling the look on her face when she had put it to him with the words, "Well, what do you say?"

He liked Mrs. Killjoy; he'd always feel indebted to her, for if it hadn't been for her, Fanny wouldn't be his now. But that was not the point: Fanny was his, and his only, and the thought of her sharing her affection at close quarters with anyone else was at the moment unbearable to him. He knew that she loved him, but how could he measure her love against his own? His feeling for her was more than just love, it was a burning passion that he had to control. And there were times when he was even jealous of the attention she gave to the child, which, he knew, was a kind of madness. But there it was, he wanted her for himself, for himself only: he wanted her every thought, every feeling to be directed towards him; and even then it wouldn't be enough.

There were times when he questioned his feelings for her. Was this possessiveness normal? He could give himself no answer, because he had no-one or nothing with whom or with which to compare it; he only felt sure that for as long as he lived the feeling would not lessen; nor would it increase, for he couldn't see any other form that it could take: she was the centre of his life and the pivot around which he revolved. Yet never, never, not once did he wish that this thing had not happened to him. Even when they had maimed his cattle and burned his crops, no thought of his had touched her with blame for having come into his life. But now that she was in it, there was in him something that demanded her entire devotion. Her attention to Carl had more than once annoyed him and had made him sorry he had ever taken on the boy. But when the same feeling had been directed against his own child he had said to himself, Steady on! But the command was equivalent to trying to curb a stallion with a donkey rein, for the stallion in him was out of control, except in one way: he never roughly overrode her body, for in his arms she appeared a fragile thing. Yet he was constantly aware there was a strength in her beyond his control. It was a spiritual strength that at times made him fearful, because he could never understand it. Nor could he face up to the fact that what he lacked was sensitivity.

After he had made her comfortable on the couch, she said, "What do you think about Annie's suggestion?" to which he could, or would, only answer: "Well, we'll have to leave it to Mrs. Killjoy, won't we?"

It happened that, after all, Ward had no need to worry about Mrs. Killjoy's coming to live with them, or near them. Mr. Killjoy died on January 2, 1888, and was buried three days later amid a storm of sleet, snow and piercing wind.

It was the custom that no woman should attend a funeral; therefore, besides Ward and Billy, only Harry Bates the fiddler and Mr. James Wilson Carter the Shakespearian actor, who happened to be engaged in the town at the time, were in attendance, Mrs. Killjoy and Fanny meanwhile awaiting their return with Mrs. Boorman in this lady's sitting-room.

From the moment the coffin left the house, Fanny had been unable to suppress her tears, and Mrs. Boorman, too, had cried, but Mrs. Killjoy's face remained quite dry. As Mrs. Boorman later remarked on the quiet to Fanny, how strange, indeed very strange, it was that she had never shed one tear since Mr. Killjoy had breathed his last breath, not one sign of it; but very likely, she had added, she had cried inside.

It was some time after the four men had returned and been warmed with glasses of whisky, and had sat down to a hot meal of beef stew and dumplings, that Ward found himself alone in the sitting-room with Mrs. Killjoy and Fanny, and Mrs. Killjoy was saying quietly but firmly in answer to Fanny's statement that she must come and live with them, that everything was already arranged: the idea of a cottage now was out of the question; nor had she any intention of imposing herself on her two good friends; but there had been an arrangement struck between her third friend, Mrs. Boorman and herself. Mrs. Boorman was alone in the world, except for her fleeting visitors, and over the years an understanding friendship had grown between them, and she had now offered to share her home with her, and of course her family. And she had added, "Where would I get anyone else who would understand my family as Mrs. Boorman has done?" And when Fanny put in, "Oh, my dear Mrs. Killjoy, we would. You know we would."

"Yes, I know you would, my dear," Mrs. Killjoy hastened to assure them, "but have you consulted your cows and your own dogs, not forgetting your sheep?"

At any other time this would have been the cue for loud laughter, but neither Ward nor Fanny smiled; but Ward, looking at Fanny, said, "She's right, you know; she's right." Then turning to Mrs. Killjoy, he added, "But that won't stop you visiting us often, will it?"

"Oh no, my dear. I shall make it my business to come and see you as often as possible."

As Fanny again embraced the bulk of her dear Mrs. Killjoy, Ward gave vent to a long slow breath of relief, the while feeling satisfied with himself for having told Fanny only a few hours earlier that he would fall in with whatever plans she had for Mrs. Killjoy's future.

It was as if, for him, a giant pair of arms were about to release their hold on his wife, that from now on she would continue to be all his. He conveniently forgot, as if it had never existed, the jealousy he felt for her attention to his own child, and, too, the irritation caused by the interest she showed in Carl.

Life would be plain sailing from now on, he told himself.

FIVE

It was in March 1888 that their second child was conceived, and Fanny told Ward in May; but his reception of the news was not as she had expected.

"I'm sorry," he said. "You're not fit yet; you were just getting on your feet."

"Don't be silly. And as for fitness, don't go by my height or weight; I feel strong inside." She could have added, "Spiritually," but she didn't, because she knew that Ward did not understand that part of her; in fact, she was aware he was a little afraid of that in her which he couldn't reach. And so, smiling now and holding his face between her hands, she said, "This time it will be a boy. And that will be a good thing, because Billy is getting on, you know, and you'll soon need another hand."

"Shut up!" He held her to him. "I don't care what it is, but what I care about is your health. And what is more, you have your hands full with that bouncer along the corridor there." He nodded towards the bedroom door. "She's going to be a whopper; she must put on a pound nearly every day."

"Well, I said from the beginning she looks like you and takes after you."

"God forbid!"

"Oh Ward. She's beautiful now, and she'll grow more so. You'll see."

"What if it *is* a boy," he said, "and takes after you and isn't able to lift a pitchfork, never mind carry a bale of hay?"

"Well, in that case I'll send Jessie out on the farm and I'll keep the young Master Gibson in petticoats for as long as I can."

They fell together, laughing; then, when softly he laid his lips on hers the kiss was broken by Annie's voice outside the door, saying, "You've got a visitor, ma'am."

When Ward opened the door, Annie said, " 'Tisn't for you, 'tis for the missis."

"Who is it?"

Annie was suppressing a broad grin as she said, "She says to me her name is Miss Patsy Riley and she wants to speak to the missis. That's what she says.

But she said it outside the back door, because I wouldn't let her in; I want to walk home to me cottage the night, not to be carried there by livestock."

Fanny had now come on to the landing and she looked at Ward and said, "Patsy Riley? The girl from the Hollow? What would she want?"

"I'll come down with you. We'll soon see."

But just before they arrived at the back door, Fanny put her hand to stay Ward, and in a whisper said, "Let me talk to her. Stay back." And this was meant, too, for Annie.

When Fanny opened the back door, both amusement and pity rose in her at the sight of the young girl: the heart-shaped face with the deep black eyes had been washed in a style; the hands joined in front of her, they too had been washed in a style, for the nails were showing rims as black as her eyes; the hair beneath the grey straw hat that had once been cream-coloured and had likely adorned some prim miss showed the ends of her straight black hair. She was wearing a coat which also, originally, had been made for some child of a bigger stature and better class. The skirt of the dress, which fell just below her knees, had evidently seen many rough washes, and her thin bare legs disappeared into a pair of heavy boots which, from their size, indicated they must be cramping her toes.

Fanny leaned forward towards her, saying softly, "Yes, my dear? You wanted to see me?"

"Do ya want any help, missis?"

"Help?"

"Aye. Mindin' the bairn, an' such. I'm good at mindin' bairns. I've seen to our squad. But me da cannot get set on; an' me ma's tried the fields, but they've got their own crews. An' so I thought, you see, missis . . ."

"But aren't you going to school?"

"Oh . . . Only half days now and then. Johnny, Mike and Shane go to keep the school-board man quiet; but Rob, he's stone pickin'. Not that that brings in much. You couldn't wipe your nose on what he earns."

Fanny's lids were shading her eyes; her head was slightly drooped; she said softly, "My baby is very young, and as yet I see to it myself."

"I'm not nitty now. I've cleaned me hair. Look." The hat was lifted with both hands from her head as far as the elastic band under her chin would allow. "I did it with a small toothcomb an' washed it in the stream. It's not alive."

What Fanny was saying inside herself now was, Dear Lord. Dear Lord. That a child has to come to this. She swallowed deeply, then asked, "How old are you?"

"Nine. I'm the eldest now. There was three others, but they went with the cholera; an' there was another atween Rob 'n me. She hadn't the cholera; she was just puny."

When a voice behind her said, "Fanny," she thrust a hand backwards and flapped it at Ward; then she said to the girl, "Stay there a moment now." She did not close the door on her, but, hurrying past both Ward and Annie, she went into the kitchen, and there, turning, she confronted them saying, "I know what you're both going to say, but I'm going to say this: I mean to do something for that child. I don't know what, so you tell me."

"I don't want her in this kitchen, ma'am."

"Oh, Annie. She's desperate; she's in need of help, she's trying her best to be decent. You heard what she said."

"Yes, ma'am, I heard what she said; but I know that lot. Let her in here in the daytime and she'll go back to that mucky kip at night, and she won't be able to keep herself clean. Don't you see, ma'am? she won't be able to keep herself clean."

Fanny looked from Annie's straight face to Ward. "Is there anything she can do outside; anything?"

"Oh, Fanny. What can she do outside, a lass like that?"

"Scrub. Sweep up. Help feed the animals . . . anything."

"There's Carl to do that, and do you think he would put up with a lass in the yard?"

All of a sudden it was as if Fanny had put on inches: her back stiffened, her chin went up, and, looking straight at Annie, she said, "You've been on for some time, Annie, about the old dairy. When it's been hard to place the milk, you said that if a hand could be engaged they could make their pay, and more, through butter and cheese."

"Oh my God!" Ward turned from her, shaking his head. "A dairy is the cleanest place on a farm, or should be, and you're proposing to put that lass in there? It's madness. No! No!"

"Yes, it's madness, ma'am. As he says, it's madness. Another thing: that churn needs some handling; it would take a young ox to turn it at times."

"Well, let me tell you both"—Fanny looked from one to the other now—"need makes people as strong as oxen. And she wouldn't go in there dirty; I would see to that myself: I'd strip her and clean her and dress her."

"No, by God! you won't do any such thing, Fanny. You're forgetting what you told me not fifteen minutes ago, you're carrying another within you."

"No. No." It was Annie now who was shaking her head as she looked towards Fanny. "You're carryin' again, ma'am, and you're proposin' to take on that thing outside? Oh, you must be mad indeed."

Fanny's voice was low now, and even had a sad note in it when she said, "Yes. Yes, there's part of me quite mad. But it's a madness I mean to carry through. Ward, I've never asked anything of you for myself; but now I'm asking this: I'm begging you to let me do this for that child."

For answer, Ward went towards the fire, put his hand up and gripped the mantelshelf, then lowered his head, and all he muttered was, "Oh, Fanny. Fanny." And through the tone of his voice she knew she had won.

Turning now to address her other opponent, a much harder nut to crack, she said, "Help me, Annie. I won't be able to carry it right through without your help, for I know nothing about a dairy, or butter or cheese-making. But you do. And so that I can promise you she won't go home every night and come back lousy, I'll tell you what you could do. It's like this: you were willing that Mrs. Killjoy should have the cottage next to you, so why not let Carl go into there; there's enough odds and ends in the attic to furnish a room. The girl could then sleep in the loft."

"Dear Lord in heaven! I've never seen anything happen so quickly, not even a miracle. You've got it all cut and dried, ma'am, haven't you? Talk about a quick thinker."

"When you want something very badly, Annie, and you know it's right, you know inside yourself that you've got to help that person, then God helps you to think quickly." She glanced towards her husband's back; then back to Annie, before turning and almost running out of the kitchen.

In the yard, the girl was still standing as she had left her, and saying, "Come with me," Fanny led the way across the yard.

She pushed open a weather-beaten door next to the cowshed, and stood aside, indicating to the girl to enter, which she did with some caution, looking around her in a half-fearful, half-defiant manner.

It was a square room, with a long stone slab attached to one wall; along another was a table holding buckets and bowls and platters, and from their lack of brightness the utensils showed that it was some time since they had been used.

But in the middle of the room stood a large wooden churn, its wheel as big as that of a small dog-cart.

"This is a dairy," said Fanny, "where butter and cheese are made. Now, my dear, I cannot offer you a position inside the house, but I would like this room cleaned up and made very bright again." She pointed to the utensils. "Then we might start making butter and cheese. But, you see, to achieve this, everything must be very clean, spanking clean, and the person who will work in here must also be clean." She paused, and looking down into the dark staring eyes and unsmiling face, she emphasised this: "Very clean. You understand me, dear?"

"Yes, ma'am, I understand. An' I said me hair's clean, an' I'll wash."

Fanny turned her head away for a moment before looking back at the girl and saying, "I must be truthful to you: the persons who would do such work as required must be scrupulously clean . . . very, very clean, and must not be in contact with anyone who is . . . well, not so clean. If my husband employed you, I would have to see to your well-being and clothes and such; but the main thing would be you would have to sleep on the farm."

The girl's voice came brisk now, saying, "Not go back at night?"

"Yes, my dear, that's what I mean: you would have to stay here and only visit your people on leave days."

"No, no. I couldn't do that, missis. Me ma wants me at night; the bairns are fractious. Nights? No, no, I couldn't." The head was shaking violently now. "An' me da. Well . . . well, we go rabbit . . . in'." The word trailed off.

"In that case," said Fanny, "I'm sorry, my dear. But you go home and talk it over with your mother."

At this, the girl looked round the room, and it seemed for a moment that she might be about to change her mind. But turning, she darted out of the door, leaving Fanny standing with her head bowed for the moment. When she did go into the yard it was to see the girl running into the distance beyond the farm gate . . .

"Well, that's a good job," said Annie. "You must have been mad, ma'am. I can tell you, if you had taken her on she wouldn't have got into my kitchen, 'cos if she had, I would've walked out. Have you ever seen those hovels they live in, ma'am?"

"Yes, I have seen them, Annie, and that is why I felt I must do something for that child."

Ward's relief was the same as Annie's, although he didn't express it so plainly: "And there was the school, you know. They have been on her to go to school. And yet from what I hear, they keep the whole tribe from the Hollow to one side of the class, and the other bairns are told not to play with them. There's been mothers up there complaining before today."

As Fanny tugged at some straw poking out from a bale Ward had just stacked, she muttered, "I could have seen to that, the same as Carl." Then she almost jumped at the sound of her husband's voice, for he barked at her, "By God! no; you wouldn't have seen to that. I put up with the lad and the time wasted; but I'll draw the line at another, and such another. If you had your way you'd have a school running in here shortly."

As they stared at each other, his mouth opened and shut twice before he turned from her and beat his fist against the stanchion of the barn, saying, "I'm sorry, dear. I'm sorry."

She did not answer for a moment; but then going to him, she placed her head on his shoulder, saying, "It's all right. I understand. And it's not the first time I must have tested your temper with my silly ideas."

He turned towards her and, taking her by the shoulders, he repeated, "*I am sorry,* my love. I am. I never imagined anything could make me bark at you."

She was smiling at him now, saying, "Well, you have been proved wrong, and you were right." But although she thought them, she did not add the words, "I suppose."

At this he bent his head over her until his brow touched hers and he whispered, "I would do anything in the world for you, anything." To which she answered, "I know, dear. I know."

It was his statement that was put to the test the following morning . . .

Ward, Billy, and the boy had been up since before five o'clock lambing, and Annie had left her cottage shortly after five to get the fire blazing and to attend two orphaned lambs that had been dumped into her kitchen. And she had just finished serving a number of long thick rashers of bacon, six eggs, dabs of white pudding and slices of fried bread on to the three plates which she now laid before her master, her husband and the boy, when Ward asked, "Has she had her cup of tea?"

"Had her cup of tea!" Annie shook her head. "This hour gone. And what's more, she's had her bite. But I wish she ate like you lot." She now flicked her hand across the table. "Anyway, for the last hour she's been at her books, preparing stuff, I suppose, to knock into that one." And with her thumb she indicated Carl, and he, his mouth full, turned and grinned at her.

There was no more conversation until they had almost cleared their plates, when Billy said, "Another night like this 'un and we'll need an extra hand. What do you say, master?"

"Oh, I don't know. And yet . . . aye, perhaps yes. We'll see."

At this moment came a knock on the back door. They all looked towards Annie, who spoke for them, saying, "And who's this at this time in the mornin'?"

"Well, until you go to the door you won't find out, will you?" Ward said to her. And she flounced out of the kitchen, only within seconds to flounce back again and to go and stand close to Ward, her face almost near his ear, and to say, "You've got two visitors instead of one, an' they'll both be alive."

He stared at her for a moment before rising; then he turned his gaze on Billy as if to confirm his thinking, before slowly walking from the kitchen and through the boot-room, where stood Mike Riley and his daughter Patsy.

"Mornin', master."

Ward's voice was a low mutter as he answered, "Morning." But then in a clearer tone he asked, "What can I do for you?"

"Well 'tis like this, master: your good missis, she gave this one here"—he nudged his daughter with his hip—"the chance of a lifetime yesterda', an' the silly little bugger, what did she do now but turn it down 'cos she thought her ma couldn't do without her. Well, her ma's of the same mind as meself, she could do without her fine if it means a new life for her." His voice now dropping to a low tone as if his daughter wasn't present, he said, "Just for one of 'em to be given a chance, master, just one of 'em, 'twas like as if the good God hadn't forgotten us after all, for it seems to have been empty bellies an' cold nights ever since we settled here. But as I said to her, me missis, 'twas as if God was relentin' an' pullin' open a door in hell an' lettin' one of 'em out. I'm an ignorant man, master, like most of us down there, an' that life suits some of 'em, but not all. Nothin' can alter for us elders, but for the youngsters, well, as I said, master . . ." He now hunched his shoulders and spread his hands out, and as Ward stared at him, for a moment he saw the whole situation through Fanny's eyes, but only for a moment. He had a farm to run; he had two good servants who were more like faithful friends; taking on this strip of a girl who looked all bones and eyes would surely bring discord into the place, and hadn't he enough discord flooding in from the village?

"Good morning, Mr. Riley."

"Good morning, Patsy."

Mike Riley looked at the slight form of the woman standing beside her husband and he smiled widely at her, saying, "Good mornin' to you, mistress. A very good mornin' to you. I've just brought this 'un." Again he indicated his daughter by a movement of his hip. "She sees now that you are right, she should stay on the job. And, ma'am, it's up to you how often you let her home. If it's once in a month for an hour or so, or once in six, I'll understand. An' I'll say this, ma'am, you've got me thanks from the bottom of me heart. An' there'll come the day when she'll bless you an' all, won't you?" His hand went out and was placed gently on his daughter's shoulder, but she made no response, she just continued to stare at Fanny, and not without defiance in her look. Then her father, putting on his cap and pulling the peak to the side, addressed a definitely bewildered Ward, saying, "If there's anyt'in in this world I can do for you, sir, I'm your man. 'Tis at liberty I am at the moment, so if you should need a helpin' hand, just call on me, sir. Anytime, night or day, call on me." And with that he took three steps backwards before turning his glance on his daughter and in a soft voice saying to her: "Ta-ra, girlo. Behave yoursel'. Remember the crack we had." He stared at her one moment longer and it was evident that his lips were trembling before he turned and walked smartly away, leaving the girl looking after him, and Fanny and Ward looking at each other.

It was a week later and there was tension in the house, and it had touched every member of it, not least Carl.

The boy had been delighted with the news that he was going to have a cottage to himself; at least he was until the reason for it was put to him, which had been immediately after Mike Riley's departure.

"But she's dirty, mistress. They're lousy, all of them. They could keep themselves clean, but they don't, they're lousy."

"It isn't their fault, it's the conditions. It's those awful hovels that they live in, and they haven't any money."

"There's a stream; they could still be clean."

She had taken his hand, saying, "Carl, do this for me. Be kind to her. She needs the work: her family are in desperate straits; they go hungry."

"The master gives them turnips, and he sent two sacks of taties."

"People cannot live just on turnips and potatoes. And what your master sent them wouldn't have lasted long."

"They all gang up down there and they steal."

"Well, Carl, you've never been in a position where you had to steal. I don't want to remind you but I must now. If it hadn't been for the master's kindness when you were in dire need, where do you think you would have been now? So, I'm asking you to extend the same kindness to the girl by way of repayment in part. Because, you know, we can never repay a good deed, but we must keep trying."

"Is . . . is she coming into the kitchen?"

"Oh, no, no. Her meals will be sent out to her. She'll eat them in the boiler room, where it is warm or in the barn or up in the loft, wherever she chooses. But no, she won't be coming into the kitchen." She said this emphatically as if Annie were prodding her.

When she had told him what work she intended to give her, he was amazed and he brought out, with a wrinkled nose, "She smells."

"She won't smell when I'm finished cleaning her. And"—she had smiled—"I'm not much bigger than her, am I? So she will adjust to my clothes."

That was the first battle over. However, that had left two still to be won. One concerned the newcomer's wage. Ward had said a shilling a week.

Couldn't he make it two?

No, he could not. And it had been only by a great deal of self-control that he had not bellowed at her once more.

Even so, they had both known that the heated discussion with regard to the wage was but a small matter; it was the presence of the girl herself and the reason why she was there. This butter and cheese business; hadn't he enough to contend with?

But the third battle had been the hardest—this time coming in the form of a verbal attack from Annie, who made her feelings plain, not to Fanny but to Carl.

"I've told the mistress I'll not go near that girl to learn her anything: I'll pass on what I know to her herself, and then she can please herself how she instructs that one. In any case, by the time any butter comes out of that dairy it'll be rancid. An' to think of the mistress cleansin' that one, stripping her bare. I can tell you this for nothin', 'cos afterwards she'll have to do some cleansin' of herself on the quiet. She's tried to keep it dark, but different fuels give off different smells an' that what came from the boiler house was singed cloth, if I know anything. Oh, I've never in all me born days experienced anything like this; an' it all goes back to Parson Noble's door, if you ask me, because they would have been hounded out of that Hollow years gone if he hadn't come an' put his nose in, with his live an' let live patter. I'm all for live an' let live meself, but where is another question. And you, young Carl, keep your arm's distance from her. Her clothes might be clean and her body too, but you can't get nits out of her head in one, two, or three goes. They are stickers, are nits. Oh, I never thought I'd see the day when the mistress of this house got mixed up with that lot down there. Now the master's mother was the kindest body you'd ever come across, but would she have done a thing like that? No; no way. Send them down taties and such, but that would have been the limit. I don't know where it's gona end. I really don't."

It didn't end, but it began for Annie two further weeks later. The dairy now spotless, she showed Fanny how long the milk should be left in the big trays for the cream to rise to the top; how to use the skimmer; then how the handle of the churn should be used, not jerked, but in a steady swing. And she had immediately exclaimed, "But *you're* not turning it. It'll have you dead in a day. If that 'un's here to be a dairymaid, then let her be a dairymaid an' get at it."

The progress made by the new dairymaid was related to Annie each evening during the respite between supper and the last round. At least it was brought out of Carl by tactful questioning. At first he did not seem reluctant to tell of . . . that one's progress. Then one evening, having taken her seat at the side of the fireplace, Annie said, "Well lad, what's your news today?" But no answer was forthcoming. Carl simply bowed his head, which made her lean towards him, saying, "Ah-ha! you've got something bad to tell me, haven't you?"

"No, no!" His head jerked up. "Well, not really bad, no."

"What d'you mean, not really bad? 'Tis about her, isn't it?"

"Yes; but . . ."

"Come on, no yes, buts. What's she been up to? I knew she'd get up to something sooner or later, and the mistress would be covered with shame for makin' a stand on her behalf. Oh, I knew it."

"No, no; it isn't like that, Mrs. Annie."

"Well what is it like then?"

"She ain't eating."

"What? Ain't eating? I send her a good heaped plateful out twice a day. I haven't been spiteful like that, no matter what I think. If she's got to turn that churn, she needs somethin' in her belly. I've sent out two good . . ."

"Yes; yes, I know you have, Mrs. Annie. Well, it's like this. I took her dinner over one day during the week and I went back a few minutes after and her plate was clean."

"She gollops, then?"

"No. No. I watched her the next day. The same thing happened. I'd seen her taking bits of paper from the waste heap and I wondered why. But I found out this morning. You know"—he looked down again—"the mistress said she hadn't to be roused before six. And when I shout up the ladder, she generally shouts back, "All right," but this morning I was on me way to the new piggeries. It must have just turned half-past and it wasn't really light, but the moon was still out and I felt sure I saw her going round by the big wall, and when I went to see I made her out running like a hare across the fields. And . . . and I followed her, near as I could, like, without her knowing. She went right over the bottom field an' all, and I stood at the side of the glass house and I could just make her out bending down at the railings. Then the next minute she came flying past. If she had put her arm out she could have touched me. And I waited until she was well away, then I went to the place she had been and I saw the little bundle of newspaper."

He stopped now as if he were thinking, and his voice jerked his head up as he went on rapidly, "I opened it: it was the meat and some of your carrots and taties, that was the day's dinner, and there was some crackling and a bit of pork, that was from yesterday. That's as much as I could make out. I bundled it up quick."

They were now staring at each other in silence, and he watched her lean back in the rocking chair. She didn't rock herself, but her head fell back against the top bar and she bit her lip. Then she again startled him by bending forward and gripping his shoulder as she said, "Now don't you repeat a word of this to the mistress. Do you hear me? Not a word, else she'll be clearing this kitchen to feed the whole tribe. But I've got to think about this. She can't do her work if she doesn't eat. And anyway, have you thought that she must have been in contact with one of them?"

"No"—he shook his head—"I don't think she'd be in contact, I mean, she wouldn't be close. She's likely told one or other of them, likely the brother who's next to her, that if she got any bits she would leave them somewhere. I don't know. But now that she's clean I don't think she'd go near them . . . well, I think she would know better, because if she got dirty again even the mistress would give her up."

"Oh, I don't know about that. The mistress is a very stubborn lady underneath that gentle skin of hers. And look what she's been asking you to do now, 'cos the master won't let her do it herself: pass on your lessons to her, hasn't she?"

"Yes, but I don't mind."

"Well, you should mind; you're not paid to waste your time."

"I don't waste me time, Mrs. Annie. And anyway, the mistress said . . ."

Annie got to her feet now, saying, "I know what the mistress says; she says more than her prayers and she whistles them. Oh, what am I saying? Look, I've got to think. I'll see about this matter later. Now, as I told you, not a word to anybody, else I'll ring your ear for you, both of them, until you think there's two bells in the church steeple."

It was from this time that the discord in the house eased, and no-one other than those directly concerned knew what took place on the day the master drove the mistress into Newcastle and Annie confronted the dairymaid for the first time. The only result of this meeting was made plain to Carl when the slop buckets for the pigs were not so full of table scraps, and the dogs were given fewer meaty bones to chew upon.

The day came when the first ivy-leaved pat of butter was put on the kitchen table and Annie, reluctantly, pronounced it not bad.

So one more strand was worked into the pattern of their lives. And not only one, for on the day Billy took the first few pounds of butter into the market, a round of it was bought by Colonel Ramsmore's housekeeper. A fortnight later a note came from Lady Lydia of Forest Hall to say she would be obliged if they could supply her with two pounds of butter weekly, and also if they were disposing of any suckling pigs, could she be informed.

This benevolent order made even Annie say, "Well, well! We're going up in the world, aren't we? 'Tis the country folk now coming to our door."

But whatever Ward really thought, his only comment to Fanny was, "This is Lady Lydia's doing, not the old fella's. He's of the type, know your place, man, and keep it. But as far as I can understand, she's go-ahead, and a very genial woman. I've glimpsed her a number of times and she looks as pleasant as her character. But there"—he had tweaked her nose—"your butter business, my dear wife, is going to make a name for itself in the end." And to this she had answered, "Thanks to Patsy," only to have him come back scoffingly, "Oh yes, thanks to Patsy;" and then he added, "You know something? That girl has never opened her lips to me in all the weeks she's been here. But her eyes speak for her."

"And what do you think they say?" asked Fanny.

"Oh, I wouldn't know, but one thing I do is, she'll take some mastering when she grows up, that one."

And Fanny, looking away from him, said softly, almost dreamily, "Yes, she will . . . she will."

On the 20th December 1888, Fanny's second child was born. It was a daughter and on looking down on her for the first time Ward exclaimed, "She's the image of you . . . absolute image." And his face bright, he picked up the child and held it to him and repeated, "Just like you, the spitting image. We'll call her Angela. What about that? Angela."

Fanny was too weary to make any comment, but she could see that her husband's reaction was different altogether from that which he had shown at the sight of his first child.

Jessie was now a bouncing and loving, happy child; but she had never seen Ward look on her as he was looking on this, his second daughter. And she was too weak at the moment to reason why she felt pained at the sight.

Book Two
1896–1914

Part One

ONE

$\mathcal{H}$e was six feet tall, well-built and he carried no spare flesh. His hair was fair almost to whiteness and this was emphasised by his weather-tanned skin. His movements were lithe, as he unconsciously demonstrated when he jumped from the high seat fronting the farm wagon.

The farm wagon had built-up detachable sides, and so he bent over the tail-end of the wagon and lifted from it a basket full of shopping, two parcels, each wrapped in thin brown paper, and a slim book which he now pushed into the inner pocket of his coat. Then calling to the horse, "Stay a while; I'll be back in a minute," he hurried across the yard and into the farm kitchen.

And as he went to drop the packages on to the table, Annie's voice came from the scullery, crying, "Don't put them there! I'm just about to bake. Leave them on the saddle." Then she added, as she came into the kitchen, "How did things go?"

"Quite well considering; butter and cheese holding, and the vegetables up quite a bit because of the drought. Where's the master?"

"Down in the lower field, I should imagine, seeing that the two Irishers do a better job on the fencing than they did afore."

"Oh, they were put up all right; it was somebody in the farming business knew how to take them down. That was no kids' work."

"Aye, I'm with you there. An' there's another thing I'll tell you, Carl, if the nigglin' business starts again in any quarter, it'll drive him round the bend. Since Mrs. Killjoy's dog got it, I don't think he's had a complete night's rest. It's affecting the missis an' all. And Jessie's had one of her crying bouts again."

"What for this time?"

"You ask me, I don't know. Oh yes, I do. What am I sayin'? But we won't go into that now. You had better get yourself changed and get your hand in, because I think it's going to be a heavy night for you. Billy's back went again this mornin'. And you know something? I never thought to hear my man say this place needs another hand. But he's right, it does, you know, 'cos you're doin' practically the work of two."

"Oh, don't worry about me, Annie. I could go on for forty-eight hours; you know I have, without sleep." He paused and smiled to himself as he said, "Funny, that. If I have three hours straight off I'm as fresh as a daisy. But give me five and I wake up with a thick head as if I'd been on the beer the night before."

"Did you get my wool?"

"Yes; I got everything you asked for."

"An' I suppose, the lasses' taffy? Well, if I were you, if you can spare a minute, I would find Miss Jessie and give her hers first for a change."

"What d'you mean, give her hers first for a change, Annie?"

"What I say, lad. Because she doesn't get put first much in this house nowadays. Perhaps you haven't noticed. He's not unkind to her. No, no. But he doesn't treat her like he does the young one. Right from the beginnin', from the first moment he saw her there was nobody else, because she took after the missis. He had a full-grown one and a young one and his first born was put aside. What am I talkin' about? Look, lad, you open parts in me that haven't any right to be spoken of."

"I haven't said a word."

"It isn't what you say, it's what you look, an' just standing there. Look, get out of my sight, will you?"

He went out, but not on a laugh. Annie was right about the master and the child, his first born. He himself had never seen him lift her up in his arms, or open his arms wide for her to run into, like he did with Angela. It was hard to believe that Angela was nearly eight years old, for she still had that elfin, babyish way and look about her; whereas Jessie, coming up nine, was sturdy, tall for her age but well built. And although she was quite pretty, she had none of the appeal of her sister. He unharnessed the horse from the wagon and put her in her stable, saying as he did so, "Have a feed. I'll brush you down later."

He now pushed open the door of the dairy and, taking a small paper bag from his coat pocket, he threw it towards the young woman who had turned from the bench, a wooden patter in each hand. Her face was bright and she smiled at him, crying, "Oh, thanks, Carl."

"Houghhound candy. It was a new batch, just made. She sells it out so quick. 'Tis a month since I managed to get any."

Again she said, "Thanks."

"All right?"

There was a hesitation before she said, "Yes; yes, all right."

He stared at her over the distance, then hurriedly closing the door, he walked towards her.

"Something wrong?"

She turned her head to the side, her dark eyes shadowed as she said, "I've had a do with Miss Jessie. I found her crying an' went to comfort her and she turned on me." She pointed to her chin, saying, "Her claws went in."

Slowly he took her face between his hands and he said softly, "Oh, Patsy. I'm sorry."

She stared into his face, the image of which never left her mind day or night: his kindly eyes, his thin but shapely mouth, his beautiful hair. He was beautiful altogether to her. Never once since she had been in this service had he said a harsh word to her. The mistress was kind, the master was tolerant. Billy, too, was tolerant, even more tolerant, and Mrs. Compton put up with her. But Carl, here, had been kind, understanding and thoughtful; and he had taught her so much, more than any of them in the house knew. The midnight hours with the books and the candle, learning not only how to spell, but where tea came from, and what happened to the coal when it went from the mines hereabouts. And she had even learned the name of the last prime minister, Mr. Gladstone. And she remembered crying over the story of the babes in the Tower of London. She would have known nothing about these things if it hadn't been for Carl.

When he said, "Do you know . . . why she did it, I mean?" she answered, "Oh yes," and nodded her head. "She was splattering that nobody loved her, and I understood how she felt."

"Oh, Patsy." His fingers moved up and down her cheek, but he didn't say, "I love you, Patsy."

Yet she felt that he loved her, but she also felt that she understood why he wouldn't speak: he had his way to make. He was well in with the family: he ate with them; he also sat in their sitting-room and talked to the mistress about what he called books, things that farmer's wives don't usually talk about. But then, the mistress wasn't an ordinary farmer's wife. In no way was she like a farmer's wife. She was delicate and learned and, as her da said, she was fey. Her da said she was the nearest thing to the Irish wee folk he had come across in this country: wasn't it proved when she could heal an animal? Yet she hadn't managed to heal the fat woman's dog last year. But then she hadn't much time, for the woman had whisked it away. Oh, that had been a day.

There was now making itself felt within her that strong feeling, that independent feeling, that feeling that told her at times not to bow her head to anyone. And she didn't, except to Carl. But he was different. Yet the feeling made her step back from him now, causing his hand to fall from her face, and it gave her tone a dignity as she said, "Thank you very much for the candy." Even to him, the feeling told her that she must never cheapen herself.

Carl was aware of this feeling. There were times when a cloud would fall between them, when he could neither understand her nor reason why this should be. So now he turned about and went out of the dairy, saying, "I'd better get changed. I've got a night's work ahead of me."

On opening his cottage door he stopped abruptly, for there, sitting in his one easy chair, was Jessie.

She did not get up as he closed the door behind him, but said, "I know Mammy said I hadn't to come into your house, but I don't care if I'm scolded: I feel awful; I've been awful all day."

"Look, Jessie," he said softly, "I'm in a hurry. I've got to get changed for work. There's a lot to be done. Now if you'll go over to the house and . . ."

She was now on her feet, her voice high, and crying, "Don't be like all the others, telling me to go some place else. Everybody else tells me to go some place else. Nobody loves me. Nobody. Nobody."

"Now that's silly. Of course people love you."

She was standing close to him now, her head back, looking up at him as she demanded, "Do you love me?"

"Of course I love you. I love you both. I've told you all along I love you because you were the first baby I held. Of course I love you."

"Not like you love Patsy Riley though, do you? Not the same as you love her."

"Now, Jessie, stop that. I don't love Patsy Riley, well what I mean is . . ."

"You don't love Patsy Riley? She thinks you love her. I scratched her face, do you know that? I scratched her face. I told her I would do it again if she didn't stop pestering you."

"Patsy doesn't pester me." His voice was harsh now. "You are the one who pesters, Jessie, not Patsy. Now look—" He stopped as her head drooped and the tears flowed down her face, and he watched them drop from the end of her nose. He sighed deeply, then went and put his arm around her shoulders, saying, "There now, there. You must get this silly notion out of your head that nobody loves you. We all love you."

Her shoulders shaking, her head wagging from side to side, she gulped out, "Oh no. No. Daddy doesn't love me. He doesn't know I'm here. The only one he sees is Angela. It's always Angela. He cuddles Angela. He throws her up in the air."

"Well now, well now, he'd have a job to throw you up in the air, because you're a big girl."

She pulled herself away from him and, almost shouting now, she said, "Yes, I'm a big girl, and I'm ugly, and she is dainty and like Mammy. And Daddy loves them both, but he doesn't love . . . me! Do you hear? He doesn't love . . . me!"

Carl was silent. This was no eight-, coming on nine-year-old girl he was looking at; she was no child; her awareness of the lack of parental love had made her into an adult.

He put out his hand towards her, about to lie yet again to her, when she shrank back from him and stepped towards the door, saying, "I know what you're going to say and I don't believe you." And with this, she pulled open the door, only to give vent to her surprise through an audible gasp as she was confronted by her father.

Ward's voice came deep from within his throat, almost as a growl, as he said, "What have I told you about pestering? You're in for a spanking, my girl." And he grabbed her by the shoulder, swung her round and brought his hand across her buttocks in no light slap; in fact her feet almost left the ground; then he thrust her forward, yelling after her: "Get into the house this minute!"

Turning angrily on Carl, he cried, "You've got to stop soft-soaping her. She's not a little child any more. She's getting out of hand." Then, without waiting for any defensive reply, he went on, but in a lower tone, "How did things go?"

"Very well. Prices held, vegetables went up; but that's because of the scarcity."

Ward stepped over the threshold and into the cottage and there he dropped wearily into the chair so recently vacated by Jessie and as though he were having to force his words through his teeth now, he said, "It's starting again."

"More railings down?"

"Worse than that. Mike Riley just told me. He found two rabbits last week. They had been poisoned; their bodies were bloated."

"Where did he come across them?"

"Just on the borders of the Hall grounds, next to our bottom field. But rabbits don't die instantly. And anyway, there's nobody going to do anything against the colonel."

"Oh, I don't know so much. There's a couple of the fellas down in the Hollow could have it in for him, because he's threatened them with the gun."

"Yes; but that lot down there wouldn't go in for poisoning. Don't you see? They'd be killing off their source of meat?"

"Yes. Yes." Carl nodded now. "There's that in it. Do you think we'd better move the flock up?"

Ward rose to his feet now, saying, "I don't know what to think. If it isn't trouble outside, it's trouble inside. I must go now and see to that daughter of mine. She's causing her mother distress, and I won't have it." And he looked straight at Carl while he added, "And don't let her in here again."

"I didn't let her in; she was here when I got back. And . . . and master, I'm going to say this, I feel bound to. She . . . she acts as she does because . . . well, she needs comfort."

"Comfort? She has every comfort in the . . ."

"Not that kind of comfort; she needs loving as . . . as much as Miss Angela does. You see, she's different."

Ward's head was nodding now. "Yes, of course she's different from Angela. She's been a trouble since she was a baby, if she ever has been a baby. Can you recall the time we had with her from she was two years old, crying and slapping out? Oh, don't talk to me about caring and love." He now stamped out of the room; but then called from the road, "Put a move on! Bill's back's gone again. He can't see to the milking."

Carl stared at the open door for a moment; then he went to it and actually banged it closed. It was the first protest in any way he had made against his master . . .

Fanny was sitting on the edge of her elder daughter's bed in the girls' room in the attic. She was holding her close and saying, "There now, there now. He didn't mean it. But you know, you've been told you mustn't pester Carl. Nor be rude to Patsy."

"He . . . he thrashed me."

"Your daddy wouldn't thrash you. He smacked your bottom. I smack your bottom, and Angela's too."

"Oh no, you don't, Mammy." The tear-drenched face was lifted now defiantly. "You smack me harder than you smack Angela. You never smack Angela, only in play."

Fanny sat staring at her daughter, and thinking much the same as Carl had done a short time earlier, when he had been confronted with someone who should have been a little girl but was a little girl no longer, at least in her mind. But in her own defence Fanny knew that all the love she could give this child would not compensate for that lost through her father and the complete absorption which he shared between herself and her young daughter. Oh, how she had wished over the years that Angela hadn't been born a replica of herself, not only in looks but in disposition, too. And in her mind, she still wondered in amazement at Ward's constancy towards her, and for which he'd had to pay dearly over the years; just as she herself had paid, too, in the loss of the deep friendship and love of her dear Mrs. Killjoy. The scene in the yard would never be erased from her mind. Mrs. Killjoy had lost two of her family, Beatty and Rose, one of them through advanced age, the other through no known reason except that it had been while on a visit here. And she had mourned them as much as she had Mr. Killjoy, perhaps more, because they were her children. On this particular day, she had brought Charlie and Sophia on a visit, and when they were ready to go only Charlie could be found. Everyone joined in the search and it was Patsy Riley who found her. Her pitiful whining had attracted her to a shallow ditch out of which the little creature was trying to climb on three legs.

When Patsy had carried her back into the yard it was found she had two pellet shots in her thigh, and, in the words of one of the Hollow men, "The fat woman howled like any banshee at the sight of her wee creature."

Fanny still remembered holding the soft little body of Sophia, aiming to alleviate her pain, which she apparently succeeded in doing, for the little dog ceased whining as Ward extracted the pellet from its leg. Then to her amazement, when the dog's leg was bandaged and it once again lay in the arms of its mistress, Mrs. Killjoy not only ceased her wailing but addressed her in a voice that all could hear, crying, "I rue the day I was the means of bringing you to this house, for there's evil in it, and all about it. And I might tell you that Mr. Killjoy said the same thing. He prophesied to me that Ward would have to pay for you till the day he died. That was after you found your dear Pip missing. And what had happened to him? Shot dead. Yes, there is evil about this house." And in the ensuing shocked silence she had mounted the trap. And so she had gone out of their lives.

She recalled now the scene when they had found Pip. He, too, had been shot with an airgun, but in the head. However, what was worse, he had been found by Phil Steel, one of the colonel's yardsmen. And Ward's reaction had been to tear over to the Hall and accuse the colonel of shooting his wife's dog. The colonel, of course, always peppery, said he hadn't been out shooting for days; but if Ward didn't get off his land he would start immediately.

This altercation had resulted in a surprise, for the following day Fanny had a visit from Lady Lydia herself. She had called to say she was so sorry that the little dog had died and also to assure Mrs. Gibson that neither the colonel nor any member of the staff had been out shooting for days. She had gone on to praise Mrs. Gibson's two fine daughters, and how like her mother the younger one was. And wasn't it strange, the characteristics of children? There was her own son whose features were like those of his father, but whose character was more like her own: he didn't like shooting of any kind. And confidentially, she had added with a smile, this angered the colonel, for being an army man, shooting was his business, so to speak. But having a son who didn't enjoy killing of any kind caused a clash of temperaments.

Fanny recalled how she had agreed on the last point with Lady Lydia. And after she had thanked her Ladyship for being kind enough to call, that lady had assured her she had been desirous of making her acquaintance for a long time, and she hoped that now she would be permitted to call, and they had drunk a cup of tea together in the sitting-room.

And so it might have been thought that when the news got through the village that Lady Lydia was visiting Ward Gibson's wife, it would have been the signal for all further petty irritations to cease. The reverse, however, was the case. If anything, they increased: gates were opened, cattle strayed, stays were pulled up, even gaps were made in drystone walls, the incidents always being perpetrated at night time. It was impossible to keep watch on every yard of fencing or walling all round the place. And when Ward exploded his chagrin to Fred or to his father, or to the blacksmith, demanding almost if one or the other could give him an inkling who was at the bottom of this, he would be answered simply by a silent shaking of the head. It was as if they were tired of his ranting, or, as he put it to Billy, they knew who it was and they wouldn't let on. And to this, Billy had replied quietly, "Aye, likely."

At times Fanny had great difficulty in hiding her concern from Ward, for not only was she physically weak, but also her spiritual resistance seemed to have lessened. Especially since the episode with her dear friend, because Mrs. Killjoy's last words were forever in her mind. She, too, was being made to wonder if it would have been better for all concerned had she never come to this house, had never met Ward, and so had never experienced a man's over-powering love, and for some time now she had faced up to the fact that it *was* overpowering. Her returning love, measured against it, was as something minute; and she knew it wasn't good or healthy to be held in such high esteem and made to feel that she was incapable of any mean thought or action. To be put on such a plane caused her to feel less than human. However, she knew she could never make her husband understand this, for he saw her as being apart from all others.

"Daddy doesn't love me, not even a little bit."

Fanny's voice was stern now as, wagging her finger at her daughter, she said, "You must not say that, Jessie. It isn't true."

"Oh, Mammy." The girl now rose from the bed and, standing with her face on a level with her mother's, she leant towards her and asked pointedly, "Why do you lie like Carl? He lies all the time. He says he loves me but he loves Patsy better. Although he says he doesn't love her, he does."

"Be quiet, Jessie. Be quiet this minute. All this silly talk about love. Now it has got to stop. Let me tell you something." She now reached out and gripped her daughter's arm. "If Carl loves Patsy and Patsy loves him, it is quite a natural thing, because they are grown up. This happens when people are grown up. But you are not grown up and you shouldn't be talking like you do."

"He said he didn't love her."

"What did you say?"

"Carl, he said he didn't love her. I asked him."

"You had no right to ask him. I am finding you a naughty girl today, Jessie, and it is upsetting me. How do you expect people to love you when you are so naughty?"

"I am naughty because nobody loves me and never has."

Fanny closed her eyes. That the child should be thinking like this, talking of love in this way, was worrying. It was as if she were grabbing at it, wanting to tear it out of people. She herself had always shown her love. But then it wasn't her love she needed, it was her father's love, or Carl's, a male love. She would have wished to refute any such thought connected with her daughter; yet, she knew that, deep within her mind, it had been born some time ago.

TWO

𝒥t was a week later and there was no sign of the irate, love-starved girl as Jessie forked some of the last hay upwards to her father, near the top of the haystack at the end of the yard. She didn't even seem to notice that Patsy was working near Carl, straightening out the ropes attached to the tarpaulin that would eventually cover the stack. The change had come on Thursday evening after her father had said to her, "How would you like to stay off school tomorrow and help me get the last of the hay in?" He had not said, "Help us," but "Help *me*."

For a moment she had been unable to answer, but then she had said, "Oh yes, Daddy. That would be lovely."

And so on the following morning there was no need for either Billy or Carl to drive the sisters to school, or later in the day, to meet them coming out, which had been the protective procedure since they had started at the village school. So, all day yesterday Jessie had raked and carried hay. Angela had been there, too, but not accomplishing half the work her sister was showing she could do. And later, it had been a merry evening meal.

This morning she would have gone out before breakfast if Fanny hadn't insisted that she eat a good meal, reminding her that there was a hard day's work before her, the while thinking how simple the solution had been with regard to her daughter's state of mind: her appealing to Ward to show his daughter a little personal attention, which he could do unobtrusively by suggesting the girl should have a day off school in order to help in the hay field.

She knew he would not immediately see the point of it all, but he complied with her wishes, even acting the part he didn't feel. Yet, last night, he had to admit the effort he had made had brought results, for it was a long time since he had seen his daughter so merry and talkative, at least in his company.

It was when the work was completed that Annie came into the yard, saying, "You all look like dustbins and it'll be another half hour, I should imagine, afore you get yourselves cleaned up an' ready for a bite to eat, so why not have it like you are, outside, eh?"

It was the two girls who cried at once, "Oh, yes! Annie. Yes. We can have it in the meadow."

"Oh, that's too far to carry the stuff," said Annie. And at this Ward shouted back to her, "Well, you don't expect us to sit on the yard or in the stubble fields, do you?"

"That's up to you," she said cheerfully. "And it'll be all hands to the pumps. I'll pack the baskets; but you're not getting me across there, for me legs are worn off to the knees as it is."

"Aye, poor soul, it's her age," and this coming from Billy caused a gale of laughter.

And there was more laughter when the girls went through the unusual procedure for them of washing under the pump; at least, sluicing their faces and hands.

In the kitchen the baskets were handed out to Carl and Patsy and the girls carried the cans of cold milk and equally cold beer; Ward brought the rugs from the blanket-box in the hall and a large cushion from the sitting-room, the latter for Fanny's benefit.

As he was passing through the kitchen, Annie said, "Here! they forgot the cloth," and loaded him further with a large check tablecloth.

"Sure you'll not join us?" he asked her, and when she answered, "Me head would like to but me feet are contrary," he said, "Well, that's your fault; you should put them up more. And don't tell me you haven't got the time. All right. All right." He shrugged away what remark she was about to make and went out and followed the small cavalcade along by the side of the barn, down by the field that had been turned into a vegetable garden, past the glass house that Fanny had not used for the past two years and which he had now turned into a forcing shed for plants, and into the field that had lain fallow for a year and now should have been covered with lush green grass. But the heat had yellowed it, except where it was shaded by the wood that marked the beginning of Colonel Ramsmore's estate on this side of the Hall.

When Jessie's voice came to him over the distance, calling, "Shall we lay it in the shade, Daddy?" he shouted back, "Yes, of course, unless you want to cook. But wait, I've got the cloth."

It was Patsy who, kneeling, spread the cloth and emptied the victuals from the basket; Fanny filled the mugs with either milk or beer, all but the last when, looking at Patsy, she asked, on a laugh, "Milk or mild for you, Patsy?" And Patsy, smiling back at her, said, "Mild, mistress, please; I've seen all the milk I want to today."

"Oh, sour milk and rancid butter we'll be having from now on," put in Billy, "now she's taken to ale." And with this he pushed Patsy none too gently so that she toppled on to her side, and Jessie, laughing, helped to pull her upright again, so that Carl was made to wonder at the change in the girl. What a difference from this time last week, for she looked so happy; it was like a small miracle.

After they had eaten bacon and egg pie, hard boiled eggs, crusty bread thickened with their own butter, and all had quenched their thirsts, in their separate ways they lounged in the cool shade of the trees: Ward lying stretched out alongside Fanny, who was sitting on her cushion, her hands joined round her knees and looking almost as young as her daughters who, too, were lying flat out on the grass; Billy had his back supported by a stake of the boundary fence, while Carl was resting on his elbow looking towards Patsy, who was sitting upright, her feet tucked under her. She was pulling a round stemmed grass between her teeth, her tongue licking at the white sap, looking to Carl like a picture he had seen hanging in one of the galleries in Newcastle. It was of a young Spanish girl in a red flowing gown. Patsy had no red flowing gown, but she was beautiful.

It was an idyllic scene. It was one of those moments they were all to remember, broken not by a human voice only by the sound of nature, a rustling of leaves from the wood and a drone of bees, with the "zimming" of midges high up, portending still further fine weather. Then came a sound as if a small line of bees were parting the air and which ended on a cry from Fanny as something struck her temple and caused her to fall across Ward.

"What is it? What is it?" He was holding her as the others were rising to their feet.

She did not speak for a moment; then on a gasp, she said, "Something . . . something struck me." Her fingers were pressing at her temple, and Ward, on his knees now, raised her into a sitting position again.

It was Patsy who said, " 'Tis a stone. Look!" She pointed to Fanny's skirt where, lying near the hem, was what appeared to be a large pebble.

Ward examined it as it lay on his palm. It was pointed at one end, flat at the other.

" 'Tis a catapult stone." It was a whisper from Billy.

"What? God!" Ward thrust the stone into the pocket of his breeches, then looked along the fence that bordered the wood. And Carl was doing the same as he cried, "They must be in the wood."

"Get your mistress back to the house, Patsy. Help her, girls!" ordered Ward; then he was racing alongside the fence, with Carl running in the opposite direction, each looking for a place where he might get over the barrier of wired palings that fenced the boundary of the Hall, for in many parts the wire had become entwined between the many saplings, so forming an almost impregnable tangle.

Ward had to go to the very end of the field before he found a place over which he could climb. Then he was running through trees, zig-zagging here and there and stopping now and again to listen for running footsteps.

The woodland opened out abruptly into a narrow field, crossing which was the path leading, in one direction, to the village and to the Hollow in the other, and bordering it on the far side was Morgan's Wood. Presently, while he was standing still, two running figures appeared on the path. One was swinging a can, the other had something dangling from his hand, something he could not make out from this distance. But they were the culprits, he'd bet, Michael Holden's grandsons. He'd had trouble with the young scamps before, jumping the walls and crossing right through the middle of his corn. By! when he got his hands on them. But he checked his thinking at this moment; surely, they couldn't have got that far in this short time; they would have had to cut through the Hall's private grounds. Well, they could have done that, and come out on to the path before it turned to the Hollow. Just wait till he got his hands on them.

He now turned as Carl's voice hailed him: "Seen anybody?"

He returned to the fence, shouting, "The two Holden youngsters."

As Carl put his hand out to help Ward over the fence, he said, "Oh, those two! They can use a catapult all right."

Billy now arrived on the scene, saying, "You said the Holden youngsters? Where did you see them?"

"Running down the path near Morgan's Wood."

"That far? They'd have to be goin' some to have got from here to there in that short space of time, don't you think?"

"Those two rips have got wings on their heels. But by God! they'll need them if I get hold of them; another half inch and that stone could have put her eye out."

The thought seemed to act as a spur for he now started to run, with Carl at his side . . .

Fanny was sitting in the kitchen holding a damp cloth to her temple and the girls and Patsy and Annie were standing around her. But she said immediately to Ward as he entered the kitchen, "Now, now, it's all right. Don't make a fuss. Only," she smiled now, "I'll likely have a black eye in the morning."

"You could have lost your eye."

After a pause, she said, "Well I didn't, and don't take it so seriously. It was someone's prank."

"Someone's prank, be damned! And look, don't sit there. I think you should get upstairs and rest."

"Oh, Ward."

"Never mind 'Oh Ward.' Come on." He pushed the others aside and drew her up, and as he led her from the room, Annie said, "Nice end to a picnic party, if you ask me." Then turning to Patsy, she went on, "Does your lot down there use catapults?"

"No, our lot down there doesn't use *catapults.*" And the word was emphasised as if it had been fired from the instrument itself.

"Don't you speak to me like that, miss."

At this, Patsy tossed her head and went from the kitchen with Annie's voice following her, saying, "It's coming to something. By! that it is." Then she, too, went from the kitchen and up the stairs and, after tapping on the bedroom door, she opened it, to be greeted by Fanny saying, "Will you stop this silly man from making such a fuss, Annie?"

"If you can't stop him, ma'am, how d'you expect me to."

"Shall we send for the doctor, Daddy?"

Ward turned to answer his daughter, but any derisive remark was checked by Fanny, saying, "No, my dear. I don't need a doctor. Look, you and Angela go downstairs and see if there is any way in which you can help Patsy and

Carl. You could get the chickens in; being so hot, they won't want to roost inside and who knows but Mr. Fox may be passing by."

Reluctantly, it would seem, the girls left the room, and as Annie followed them Ward pulled a chair up to the bed and sat down, saying, "First thing in the morning I'm going into that pub, not for ale, but to tell Mike Holden to take his hand to those two devils of his."

"But it may not have been them; surely, all boys use catapults."

"Not with pointed flints as ammunition."

"Well, tomorrow's Sunday, so leave it to the beginning of the week . . . Please."

The look he gave her and his silence told her he would comply.

But at seven on Monday morning, well before he would have made his way to The Crown Head, he was shouting down from the landing window into the yard, "Carl! Billy! Carl!" and when they appeared, from different buildings, in the stockyard and peered up at him through the early morning light it was Billy who shouted back, "What is it, master?"

"This . . . my . . . it's the mistress. I cannot waken her. When I left her at half past five I thought she was still asleep. You, Carl, ride in for Doctor Wheatley as fast as you can go. Now!"

Carl made no comment but immediately ran to the stables, and Patsy, who had appeared outside the dairy, ran with him and helped to saddle the horse. And it was significant to their understanding that neither of them spoke a word.

Doctor Wheatley's house lay at yon side of the village, and the shortest way to it was through the village. Carl had galloped the horse as far as the cemetery wall, and was just pulling her into a trot when from a side road there appeared a small gig, which he recognised immediately and he pulled up to the side of it, crying, "Oh! Doctor Patten. 'Tis well met. I'm on my way to fetch Doctor Wheatley to the mistress; the master can't get her wakened."

Philip Patten leant from the seat, saying, "Can't get her wakened? What d'you mean, Carl?"

"Well, she was hit by a catapult—'twas a sharp stone—on Saturday when we were all eating in the meadow, and she's been in bed since. And now 'tis as I said."

Hit by a catapult stone and now can't wake up? The Gibsons were the old man's patients and he was very touchy about trespassing, as he termed it, unless one was invited for consultation, and then who dare express an opinion that went against his. But what young Carl was describing was very like a coma, and by the time his superior could manage to get to the farm after the load he had on him last night, it might be too late to do anything that would be of help. After four hours at The Grange, he wanted nothing but his bed at this moment, having endeavoured to bring Drayton's grandson into the world, which he had done, although without thanks, for the poor mite was a mongol.

"Ride on. I'll follow."

As soon as Philip Patten looked down on Fanny he gnawed at his bottom lip before he asked Ward, "Has she been moved at all?"

"No."

He now gently pulled back the bedclothes and began to examine her while Ward stood at the other side of the bed, staring at him as if to extract from his expression the reason why his beloved Fanny was in this state. He watched the doctor go to his bag, open it, then close it again before turning to him, saying, "Go and tell Carl to ride for Doctor Wheatley and request him to bring some leeches with him and make it as quick as possible."

"What is it? What's wrong with her?"

"I don't really know yet, Ward," Philip Patten lied. "I would like another opinion. Go now and get him away."

Ward didn't respond straightaway to the command, but remained for some seconds looking down on Fanny, his lower jaw moving as if he was grinding his teeth.

A few minutes later Annie entered the room and was surprised to hear the young doctor talking away to the mistress, which she thought was silly, because if the poor thing could hear him she would have made some sign, wouldn't she? Tommy Taylor went like that, but he tapped a finger.

It was only half an hour later when Doctor Wheatley entered the room, which indicated he had indeed answered the call promptly; not so much, perhaps, because of the patient's need, but because the young snipe was not only on his preserve but had sent him an order, a veiled order maybe, but nevertheless an order, to bring leeches, which suggested he had already diagnosed the trouble. So it wasn't unusual that he should ignore the young know-all and go straight to the inert figure in the bed.

"Well! Well! What have we here, Mrs. Gibson, eh?" He took the limp hand and wagged it; then let it go so that it dropped back on to the coverlet, and he turned to Ward and said, "How did this come about?"

"She was hit on the temple by a stone from a catapult on Saturday."

"Saturday! It's now Monday. Why didn't you inform me before?"

"She seemed all right until this morning."

The old man now pursed his lips, looked down on Fanny, then again lifted his head sharply towards Ward, and as if he had made a decision he said, "Go down and get them to bring up a bowl of very hot water and towels." Then he took off his coat as if he meant business.

As soon as Ward had left the room, however, the urgency went out of his actions, and now addressing his partner, he said simply, "Coma? What do you think?" and Philip Patten replied, "Yes; through a clot on the brain, I would say."

"Would you?"

They stared at each other; then Doctor Wheatley said, "She should go to hospital."

"I doubt if she would make it."

"Would you now? Well, perhaps for once you're right and so we will try your other notion with the leeches, for what it may be worth in this case. And you know something, Patten? She is one problem, but there's a bigger one looming up in him, should she go."

"Yes, I'm aware of that."

The old man again stared at his younger associate; that's what he couldn't stand about the fellow, that bloody cocksure manner of his.

They had bled her. They had wrapped her in hot, then cold towels, but to no avail; and so the day wore on and it came to six-thirty on the Tuesday morning. Annie was dozing in a chair at one side of the bed while Ward sat close to it at the other side. He was resting on his elbow, his back half bent as he held the limp hand. When his head nodded he gave a slight start and blinked rapidly. Then, his eyes wide, he stared down at the face on the pillow. It had changed. There was no colour in it; it had changed into that of a wax doll. He was now on his feet, muttering, "Annie. Annie; come here."

When Annie reached his side she muttered, "Oh my God! No!" and he echoed her last word, but as a yell: "No! No! Fanny! Fanny!"

When the door was thrust open and Jessie's frightened face appeared, Annie cried at her, "Tell Carl to ride for Doctor Patten. He's nearest." Then she almost fell on her back as Ward thrust her aside and, throwing back the bedclothes, lifted Fanny bodily into his arms and rocked her as he would have a child, the while moaning, "Love. Love. No, you can't! You can't leave me. No! Fanny, don't go. No! No! I can't go on. Wake up! Wake up!"

He was still walking the floor bearing her limp body in his arms when Philip Patten hurried into the room and exclaimed, "Oh, dear God!" Then putting out his hands, he checked Ward's flagging steps and said softly, "Come; lay her down . . . Come."

As if in a daze, Ward allowed himself to be led towards the bed and to let his beloved slip from his arms, but remained looking down on her, and Annie whimpered, "All through a catapult."

"Catapult," Ward took up the word; then he repeated the word: "Catapult! That's it! That's what killed her! They killed her!" And with his arm thrust out towards the doctor, the fingers stretched accusingly, he cried, "Bear witness, you! she's dead! They killed her, and, by God! I'll finish them."

The sudden movement of his body as he sprang towards the door startled them all and motivated Philip to run on to the landing crying out to him, "Wait! Hold your hand a moment. Wait!" and then to step quickly back into the room and to address Annie: "Who does he mean, they? Who was he referring to?"

As Annie shook her head it was Patsy who answered him: "He thinks it was the young Holden lads."

"The Holdens? Dear God!" And on this he dashed from the room; and on reaching the yard, he shouted to where Billy and Carl were standing on the road outside the gate, "Go after him! He's making for the Holdens and their lads, and the state he's in anything could happen. I'll follow on." Then he rushed back into the house and up to the bedroom again . . .

Ward entered the village from the church end, and as he ran alongside the cemetery wall and so into the street, William Smythe, the verger, paused while putting a large key into the vestry door, which he then left in the lock and hurried down the gravel path and into the street to watch Ward Gibson in his shirt sleeves racing along it. And he wasn't the only one to be surprised by the sight: Fred was loading the van with the early baking and he could not at first believe his eyes. Instead of running after Ward, however, he rushed into the house, shouting his news.

Jimmy Conway was heaving a carcass from the back of the cart. He, too, stopped in amazement; then he shouted across to Hannah Beaton, who was humping a sackload of potatoes up the two steps into the shop: "Did you see what I've seen? Or am I seeing things? Where's he bound for?"

Ward soon reached where he was bound for, and it wasn't for the front of The Crown Head but round to the back of it.

At the kitchen door he stopped for a moment, his chest heaving, and he gulped in his throat before banging on the door, and which he continued to do until the voice from behind it cried, "All right! All right! What is it?"

The door was pulled open; and he stood staring at Holden for a full ten seconds before bringing out on a growl, "You satisfied then? You've let your breed act for the village, eh? You meant to do her in one way or another, didn't you?"

"In the name of God! What are you talking about, Ward? Are you drunk or daft? What's up with you?"

"Don't tell me you don't know. They came running in, didn't they, after they had shot their bolt? Well, it's the last catapult they'll use. By God! they'll pay for this, or you will through them."

But as Ward's hands came out to grab him Holden struck out at him, the while he yelled, "You're mad! That's what you are."

"What is it? What's the matter?" Winnie Holden was now standing beside her husband, and Ward answered her: "The matter is, you've spawned two murderers, missis. Your devils have killed my wife," he cried at her.

"Oh my God!"

He watched the big woman put her hand over her mouth, and then turn and look back into the room before saying, and quickly now, "Come in. Come in, Ward."

He seemed to need no second bidding: he almost thrust them aside because he had caught sight of the two lads who had been sitting at the table but who were now standing against the far wall of the room and close together, and he was himself now thrust aside by the Holdens and held against the wall, all the while hearing the older man shouting, "They never hurt your wife! Listen to me, Ward! but I know who did."

"Shut up! Mike. Shut up!" It was his big brawny wife yelling at him now.

"I won't, woman, I won't. It's our lads he's trying to get at, as if you didn't know."

They were talking now as if they were alone in the room together and not struggling with a man who was behaving like a maniac.

Again Holden cried at Ward, "Stop it, man! Stop it! Quiet! Listen to me, and I'll tell you who it was. The same one as set fire to your crops, and crippled your cattle, the one you threw over for your wife."

Suddenly Ward became still. His face was close to Holden's and he whispered a name: "Daisy? No."

"Aye; Daisy Mason. Well, what did you expect, lad? What did you expect? Haven't you ever given it a thought?"

Slowly Ward pushed their arms from him and straightened up; but a doubt still remained and he continued to stare at the two boys who were crouched close together, until their father said, "Sit down, lads, and finish your breakfast."

As Ward watched them come slowly, even furtively to the table, some part of him was saying, "I'm sorry. I'm sorry." Then he muttered as if to himself, "It couldn't have been her, not the fire. She was away at the time in Fellburn."

It was Winnie Holden who now spoke, and quietly: "She was wily," she said. "She had it all planned out, like everything else. She's been goin' mad these last years, but nobody would let on 'cos John and Gladys are a decent couple, and they've had enough on their plate trying to keep her under lock and key most of the time. But everybody in the place seemed to know who was the culprit for your misfortunes, except you, and we've often wondered why it hasn't dawned on you. And on Saturday gone the lads were in the Hall wood. They shouldn't have been there, but there's some good bleeberry bushes and that's what they were doing, gatherin'. They saw her. She had a catapult, they said, and through the bushes they saw her fire it. She caught sight of them and whether she meant to chase them or not, they were so scared they took to their heels and didn't stop running until they reached this kitchen."

There was silence for a matter of thirty seconds, and it was broken by George Holden saying in a fear-filled voice, "Don't tell me, Ward, that your wife's dead!"

Ward didn't answer him, but he moved from the wall, then turned and looked towards the fire. There was a pot on the hob with porridge bubbling in it, but he wasn't seeing it: he was back near the cemetery wall and her hands were coming out and clawing his face. Why hadn't his suspicions touched on her? They had on one family after another in the village: the Longstaff twins, Mike and Adam. He had never frequented The Running Hare, which seemed, in his state of mind, reason enough to feel they had it in for him. Or it could have been one of Kate Holden's lot? His suspicions had even touched on the McNabs in the Hollow. Then there were the Wain-wrights. They were Methodists, and they had four sons, all married and scattered round about the countryside. No; that was daft thinking: just because he was the Methodist pastor. Why! he had always spoken to him, he had even bought his milk. No; he had been blind, stupid, not to put his finger on Daisy, after her parting shot. He remembered her actual words.

"I'll have my own back on you, Ward Gibson. I swear before God I will. You and yours. Do you hear me?"

And she had carried out her threat. She had killed Fanny, his beloved Fanny. Oh! Fanny, Fanny. There was a strange feeling in his head. For a moment he felt as though he might burst into tears like a woman, or howl like some animal, such was the pain of her loss. And he realised that this was only the beginning . . .

He turned his gaze from the fire towards George Holden, who had caught his attention with the words, "You and yours will never be safe, Ward, as long as she's about. She should be put away where she cannot do any more harm."

You and yours. These were her words again. He had two girls, he had two daughters . . . you and yours will never be safe as long as she's about.

He swung round as if he were going to leave the room, but, turning again, he said simply, "I'm sorry."

"That's all right, Ward. That's all right. We understand." And they moved to the door with him, and on its being opened they were as surprised as Ward to see, standing in the long dray yard, Philip Patten, Carl, Fred and his father, and a number of other villagers.

It was the doctor who moved towards him, saying, "Come on home, Ward."

Ward looked at the doctor and around the small crowd and when he spoke to Philip Patten his voice gave no indication of the rage that was rising in him, as he said, "I'm going home, Doctor; just leave me alone for the time being . . . Come, Carl." And with that he walked through the villagers, seeming not to notice Fred's outstretched hand.

Ward did not now run back through the village, but his step was quick and firm, as was Carl's. Once past the church and well out of sight of any of the villagers, however, Ward stopped and, looking at Carl, said, "Go back home and see to things." And before Carl had time to put any kind of question to him, such as, "Can't I come with you, master?" Ward had jumped a ditch to the side of the road and was once more running across his field of stubble . . .

The work so far at Beacon Farm had been carried out according to the usual daily routine: the first milking had been done, the byres swilled out, and Seth Mason had just finished harnessing the two shires and was leading one from the stable, when the sight of Ward Gibson stopped him in his tracks. And after glancing swiftly about him as if looking for someone, he left the horse and began to run to where Ward was nearing the kitchen door, crying as he ran, "Here! Wait a minute. Don't go in there. What d'you want, anyway?"

And to this Ward answered grimly, "You know what I want," which impelled Seth to spring forward and confront him, the while yelling, "Pete! Pete! Here!"

As Ward's forearm thrust Seth staggering back against the wall of the house, Pete Mason came racing across the yard, and as he barred Ward's way to the kitchen door, he cried at him, "Get yourself to hell out of here, and quick!"

Again Ward's arm came out, straight this time, but the blow just grazed Pete Mason's cheek, and now he retaliated with his own fists, only to be stopped by the kitchen door being dragged open and his father's hands on his shoulders pulling him back, as he yelled above the mêlée, "Stop it! For God's sake! What's come over you all?"

The two combatants were now glaring at each other when Mr. Mason again spoke. "What brings you here, Ward?" he demanded. "You're not welcome; you know that."

"Huh! In the name of God! listen to the man: I'm not welcome. And what brings me here, you ask? Well, I'll tell you, Mr. Mason, what brings me here. Just a small matter of having your daughter put away for murdering my wife. That's all. That's all." The last words seemed to rattle in his throat, and the three men looked at him aghast and in silence. Then Pete and Seth Mason turned to look at their father, who first put one hand to his head, then with the other felt, as if for support, for the stanchion of the door, and there was a note of both fear and disbelief in his voice as he said, "No! No! What d'you mean? What d'you mean?"

"Just what I say. My wife died this morning from a catapult shot that carried a flint."

It was a thin voice that seemed to pipe in as Seth Mason said, "People don't die from catapult shots."

"No?" The bark made Seth Mason retreat a step and he muttered, "Well . . . well, I mean . . ."

"She . . . she wouldn't do that. Mischief, yes, mischief: she gets up to mischief, but not that, not that."

"Mr. Mason—" Ward's voice seemed strangely calm as he now went on, "that flint burst a blood vessel in my wife's brain. And I have only this morning been awakened to the fact that all my ill-fortune over the past years: fires, maiming of my animals, shooting innocent little dogs, and all other irritations I've had to put up with, have come from the hand of your daughter. Everybody seems to have known this, but they have been protecting you. Well now, murder cannot be protected. If I had my hands on her this minute, there would be another one. This I promise you. But that would be letting her off lightly. What I've come to tell you is, I'll have her certified before this day's out."

"No, no. Oh Ward, no, no."

The voice caused them all to turn and look at the frail figure of Gladys Mason; and when her husband gripped her shoulders crying, "Go back! Go back!" she answered him, "Leave me be, John. I must speak to Ward." And she pressed herself from his hands and, moving to the threshold of the door, she looked at Ward and pleaded, "Please, don't do that, Ward. I beg of you. I'll . . . I'll see that she causes you no more trouble."

"What more trouble can she cause me, Mrs. Mason? She has killed my wife. Didn't you hear? She has killed my wife. Your mad daughter has killed my wife. You say she can cause me no more trouble. I have two girls, remember, and she'll not rest until she gets them an' all, if not me before that. Can't you take it in, woman? She's mad; and she won't stop at one."

"Don't you speak to my mother like that."

Before Ward had time to respond, John Mason cried at his son, "Shut up! you. Shut up! If you had kept your eyes open and done what you were . . ." He again put his hand to his head; then, as if a surprising thought had struck him, he said sharply, "What proof have you got, Ward, that Daisy has done this thing? There's hardly a lad in the village that hasn't got a catapult."

"Granted. But George Holden's sons, young Peter and Alan, saw her."

"Oh, those two." It was the thin voice of Seth Mason piping in again. "They are noted liars, and thieves into the bargain. We caught them raiding our chicken run only a few weeks ago. Didn't we, Pete?"

"Aye, we did that. And either of them would say anything to save their own skin."

"She was in the wood. They saw her. She chased them."

"Aye, she could have, likely because they were using the catapult. Ward" —John Mason's bent shoulders seemed to straighten—"she's been up to mischief, I admit, and there's something to be said on her side, as you only too well know. What you did turned her brain. But murder? No. No. I won't have it. Anyway, she hardly ever leaves the room up above, except to go for a short ramble now and again. And then one or two of us keep an eye on her as much as—" He stopped . . . then he pointed to Seth, saying, "Go up and tell her she's wanted downstairs."

As Seth was about to pass his father to enter the house, he paused for a moment, saying, "What if she won't . . . ?" Only to be cut short by his father's voice crying at him, "Bring her down!" Then turning to Ward, he said, "Come indoors a minute, will you, and we'll clear this thing up one way or another. There's one thing I'm sure of, she won't lie to me." And he stepped back, at the same time pressing his wife aside to allow Ward to enter before them.

It seemed to Ward that the kitchen hadn't changed in any way since the last time he had sat at the long, white kitchen table and had eaten a good meal amid laughter and joking about different members of the church community. The breakfast crockery was there on the table now.

He stood some distance from the end of it, waiting, as were Mr. and Mrs. Mason and their son, their gaze directed towards the door at the far end of the room. No-one spoke and the silence became eerie until it was suddenly pierced by a high female voice, crying, "Leave me be! will you? Leave me be!"

When the far door opened it seemed that the bulky figure had been thrust into the room and that it was about to turn round again in protest, when it stiffened. Ward saw the head slowly turn to look at him, and the expression on the face seemed to be no different from the one he had looked on at their last meeting all those years ago, except, as the body had, so it had swollen to almost twice its size: for the figure now walking heavily towards the end of the table was enormous.

Her father checked her, saying, "Sit down, Daisy. I want to talk to you."

It was as if she hadn't heard her father speak, for she took no notice of him. Instead, putting her two hands flat on the table, her fingers began to tap out a regular beat.

When her mother said sharply, "Don't do that, dear. Sit down. Do what Dad said," she again made no response; nor did she when her brother Pete barked at her, "Do what you're told and listen to Dad, or you'll find yourself in hot water."

When his father reprimanded sternly, "Pete!" his son cried back at him, "Well, get on with it. Ask her the question you brought her down for."

Putting a hand on his daughter's shoulder, John Mason said, "Look at me, Daisy. Did you take a catapult and fire it at Mrs. Gibson? I want the truth."

She glanced towards Ward, then looking back at her father and a sly smile coming over her face, she answered him with, "You never let her out, do you?"

Mr. Mason's head dropped on to his chest for a moment before again looking at his daughter and demanding, "Did you fire a catapult? Did you take a catapult out?" then attempting to shake the large solid body as he demanded further of her: "Answer me truthfully! You know what can happen to you if you don't behave. Now, have you been out these last few days and taken a catapult and fired it at Mrs. Gibson, causing her to die?"

The bulky body seemed suddenly to come to life, normal life, and in a voice of enquiry, she said, "She died?"

"Yes. Yes she did, Daisy. Mrs. Gibson has died from a catapult shot."

Mr. and Mrs. Mason and their two sons watched Daisy turn and look fully at Ward; and a thread of despair ran through each of them as the habitually dull expression on her face turned to one of glee, her voice then expressing this feeling as she cried, "I got her, then. I knew I would one day. Payment. Payment. I said I'd make you pay."

"Oh, dear God!" As Mrs. Mason dropped on to a chair and John Mason turned away for the moment from the sight of his daughter, she cried at Ward: "By way of payment, eh? By way of payment."

It was at this that Ward found his voice, and he cried at her: "And you'll pay, too, you mad hussy, for I'll have you in the asylum before the day's out."

"Asylum? Asylum?" and she shook her head. Then again she was shouting at Ward and in a voice that sounded normal now, "Oh no! you won't. Oh no! you won't."

What happened next came so swiftly that not one of the three men could have prevented it: grabbing up the bread knife that was lying across a wooden platter on which lay half a loaf of bread, and with the artistry of a knife thrower, she levelled it at Ward's face.

Whether or not he saw it coming, he never knew; but his body instinctively stretched upwards and to the side which took his face and neck away from her blade, to be conscious that it had found a target when he realised he was pinned to the side of the delph rack against which he was now leaning. In the confusion he was aware that the long wooden handle was weighting the blade down. Then, as his body bent forward, the knife slid to the floor, leaving him standing in a daze, watching the blood soak into his shirt sleeve where it was rolled up above the elbow, then stream down his forearm.

There was a queasy feeling in his stomach; then he became aware that the kitchen was empty except for Mrs. Mason and himself and that the yelling and squealing were coming from a distance.

Mrs. Mason's words came out on a trembling stutter: "It . . . it isn't deep, Ward; it . . . it's ju . . . just gone through the top." She had torn his shirt sleeve apart, and now she was wrapping a towel around the wound, saying, "Ke . . . keep the end under your oxter, Ward, and . . . and the lads will ge . . . get you to the doctor."

He pressed her away from him, and as he turned towards the door to go out, she muttered, "Oh, Ward. Ward. I'm sorry. I . . . I'm s . . . sorry for us all."

His left arm pressed tight to his side and his right hand holding the towel on to the top of his shoulder, he walked across the farmyard. And he wasn't surprised at all as he was about to enter the first field to see Carl standing in the shadow of a hedge. And Carl's greeting to him was, "Oh! master. Good God! What's happened?"

And the strange reply he received was, "Run on home. Harness the trap. I want it straightaway."

"You . . . you're sure you can manage? I mean . . ."

"Do what I say."

As Carl sprinted from him Ward told himself that it was as well this last incident had happened, for it would help to put her where she should have been a long time ago.

Twice he leant against a drystone wall, not because there was a weakness in him, but because he was pondering as to why he himself hadn't suspected the source of his misfortunes: everybody had seemed to know the culprit but himself. One thing he could have understood was that his friends had kept quiet because they feared the result of his knowing.

He reached the farm gate to see Carl leading a horse and trap into the yard, with Billy tightening the horse's girth as he moved. Annie was there, too, with the girls one on each side of her, and Patsy standing apart, her forefinger nipped tight between her teeth.

On seeing her master, Annie pushed the girls to one side and, hurrying towards him, said, "Dear Lord in heaven! Come away in and let me see to that. Oh, this is surely a day that God didn't make."

As she made to take Ward's free arm, he pressed her aside, but he did not speak; nor did he look at his daughters as they cried to him, "Oh, Daddy! Daddy!" But with a heave he pulled himself up on to the trap, where Carl was already seated, the reins in his hands, and with a muttered, "Get going," they rode out of the yard.

It wasn't until they had gone some distance that he again muttered, "Make for Doctor Patten's"; and within five minutes the trotting horse brought them to the doctor's cottage, which lay just outside the village at the church and cemetery end.

When Carl jumped down and ran up the path towards the door, it was pulled open before he got there by the doctor's old housekeeper, who exclaimed, "Oh; I thought it was himself. He's out. But he should be back at any time. He hadn't sat down to his meal when he was called again. With one thing and another, he's done a day's work already. What is it you will be wanting?" Then she looked beyond him, and after a pause said, "Oh. Oh, yes; I see," only to exclaim louder now as she looked along the road, "Speak of the devil! Here he comes, and it looks like he won't be sitting down to his meal again."

When Philip Patten drew his horse to a stop alongside Ward's trap, he stared at the blood-soaked arm before asking quietly, "How did that come about?"

"A knife. She aimed at my throat. I want you to come back to Doctor Wheatley's with me; I'm having her put away if it's the last thing I do this day."

Philip Patten made no comment, but he held Ward's gaze for some seconds before he jerked his horse forward and turned it in the road, by which time Carl had taken his seat again and set the horse at a trot in the direction of the village.

Again many of the villagers stood and gaped as Ward Gibson, his arm

covered with blood, was driven through the village, followed by the young
doctor on horseback.

It was evident that Doctor Wheatley had not gone without his breakfast,
which never varied: no matter what he had imbibed the night before, he was
ready for his steak topped with two fried eggs and also for a mug of tea into
which a raw egg had been beaten. It was said in the village that it was his
plain diet that had prevented his indulgence in raw spirits from eating away
his innards.

One of the rooms of his well-equipped house he used as a surgery, and
there he was confronted by the three men, towards not one of whom he had
any kindly feelings.

"Well! What's this? Been getting yourself shot?"

When Ward made no reply but just stared at the bloated face and figure
before him, the doctor bawled, "Come on! Come on! Out with it!"

And Ward did come out with it, and right to the point: "I want you to
come back to the Masons' farm and certify the Masons' daughter," he said.

"What!" The doctor looked towards Philip Patten, then back to Ward,
before he said, and very quickly now, "You do, do you? And on what
grounds?"

Philip Patten came out with one word that seemed to speak volumes:
staring at his superior, he said simply, *"Doctor!"* And in return, the older man
yelled at him, "Yes? Doctor! What were you going to say?"

"You know what I was going to say, what Mr. Gibson here is going to
say: she should have been seen to some time ago. You knew the way things
were going."

"I knew nothing of the kind, fellow! The girl . . . woman was under
stress. Do you lock people up because of that?"

It was now Ward who answered: "Stress that killed my wife, sir!"
he cried. "That maniac laughed when she knew that her catapult had done
the trick. She gloried in it. Then she did this." He pointed to his shoulder
and went to pull the towel away, but winced as it brought the torn skin
with it.

They all stood for a moment staring at the bared arm with the blood
oozing down both the back and front of his body. Then Ward muttered:
"She aimed for my throat. And she'll do it again. And remember, I have two
daughters. She won't rest until she finishes them. She's raving mad."

"And who's to blame for that, Mr. Gibson? Do you ask yourself who's to
blame for that? You turned her brain when you threw her over."

"I did not throw her over. There had been no talk of marriage."

"No; not talk, but action."

"Do you intend to do what I ask, or have I to go for the police to assist
you?"

The older man now stood glaring at Ward. Then, his voice muffled and
sounding ominous, he said, "You brought distress on this good and respected family the minute you married your cheap dancing piece."

Philip Patten and Carl reacted simultaneously by stretching out their arms
to prevent Ward from attacking the doctor, who had fearfully stepped back

towards the open door, but was nevertheless determined Ward Gibson should take heed of his words: for they were, "I may not live long enough to see it, but what you are forcing me to do will have its repercussions on you a thousandfold, for the family that you have destroyed will eventually destroy you."

Part Two

ONE

Carl watched Patsy coming down the side of the stubble field. She was walking in the shadow of a short line of trees, where the March sun had not been strong enough to thaw the heavy frost of the night, so that her feet seemed to be treading a silver path; but even as his thought presented the image to him he discarded it, for Patsy's life had always been devoid of silver paths.

As she emerged into the light it was as if he were seeing her for the first time as a young woman, a young beautiful woman who carried herself straight, head bowing to no-one, while still having to be subservient.

When she reached him, where he was standing by the stile, she took his outstretched hand and before he had time to greet her she said, "Will you kindly tell me, Mr. Carl, why you never come up this field to meet me?" to which he answered, "For the simple fact, Miss Riley, that I like to see you walk. You walk proud, a different walk altogether from what you walk inside the farm."

The smile left her face as she said, somewhat soulfully, "Yes, yes; it's a different walk, for there I am running or scurrying to someone's bidding."

He helped her over the stile, saying, "It won't always be like that, Patsy. Believe me."

"No?" It was a question; and now, she leant against the wooden stanchion as she said, "I am twenty-five years old, Carl. Ma reminded me of it the day. 'Breeding time will soon be past,' she said. She does not mince words, does Ma. And she was right, Carl: I want a family; but most of all, I want you."

He put his arms about her and pulled her tightly to him, saying, "Not more than I want you, Patsy. Oh, no; not more than I want you. I ache for you."

"Then why can't we just go to him and put it to him? It should be so simple. You have the cottage; I've just got to move from the loft. Oh my dear." She put up her hand and touched his cheek. "I know the situation; that was a silly thing to say. But on the surface, it seems as simple as that. The truth is, he looks upon you as a son; but me, I'm still Patsy Riley from the Hollow. Oh . . . oh, I know." She patted his lips. "I know he's been good in other ways; in letting Da take Billy's place; and taking Rob on too. Oh, I know I said it was good, but, in a way, it makes matters worse for me. There's Da, a feckless Irishman, and Rob following in his footsteps. They're good workers when they're being governed, but like all the Irish, except perhaps me"—she twisted his nose—"who will work without being overlooked. But what they are besides this is, they're loyal. And of course"—she now drew herself slightly from him, yet not out of his embrace, as she added, "There is Miss . . . there is Miss Jessie."

"Oh dear me! Patsy, as I've told you before, time and again, for my part she's like a sister. I've told you: I held her as a tiny baby; and I'm ten years older than her. She's just a silly girl."

"Oh no." Patsy shook her head, and a knowing look came into her eyes as she said, "Miss Jessie's no silly girl. When I first came into that yard sixteen years ago she made it plain who owns you."

He now actually thrust her from him and angrily he said, "Nobody owns me, neither her nor her father, nor anyone else. But I owe them a debt; at least, her father. He took me in and saw to me when I could have died. He could have sent me back to that farm. He took a risk in keeping me. He's been good to me."

Patsy closed her eyes and slowly turned from him, saying, "It's like an old fairy tale, Carl: I've heard it so many times; you keep repeating it." And now she swung round to him. "I'm going to ask you something. Is your debt so great that you're going to repay him with your life? You're not bonded; nor am I. We could up tomorrow and go and get work elsewhere."

"Where? Where? Tell me."

Her head to the side now, she kicked the toe of her boot into a stiff tuft of grass. But he was holding her again, and both his eyes and his voice held a plea as he said, "Believe me, Patsy, there is no other in my life but you. The master had a feeling for his wife which, at one time, I couldn't understand. I used to think it was a mania. She was a lovable creature, but his feelings for her were more like adoration. Well, I've come to understand a little how he must have felt, for, Patsy, the very sight of you warms me and wakes such a stirring in me that I want to throw everything to the wind and do as you say, get away . . . run with you into a life that is entirely ours, free from duty or guilt or being ungrateful. And so I ask you, Patsy, to wait just a little longer. I've got the feeling that things are coming to a head in one way or another. Yes, believe me, I have. A strong feeling tells me that I shall be forced to come into the open. And so then, if we can't marry, we'll leave. That's all."

She stared at him again, but softly now; and then in a quiet voice, she said, "He'll never let you leave, Carl. Apart from any feeling he has for you, you run that place. He's never taken a real hand in it since the missis went.

He makes decisions, oh yes, but only when you put them to him. Oh no, he'll never let you go."

"Well"—he nodded at her—"if he wants me to stay so badly he'll let me take the wife I want to have. So that's all about it. Come on!" And with his arm around her shoulders now, they walked down the narrow field path that would give on to the bridle path about a quarter of a mile distant. But before they reached it, he pulled her to a stop again and, putting his arms about her, he kissed her long and hard; and her returning the pressure of his body caused them to sway together for a moment before she withdrew herself from him. But as they walked on, it wasn't with her head held high, it was with it leaning against his shoulder . . .

And that is how Ward saw them as he entered the field path. He had sat on his horse on a bank some distance from the path, and had kept them in sight ever since they left the stile. He had known there was a liking between them, but he had never thought it would come to anything: surely the boy, as he still named Carl in his mind, would have more sense; had he not, over the years, imbued in him a feeling of class through his treating him as a member of his household? No; but he had thought he would never let himself down to the level of any member of the Hollow tribe. They were workers of the lowest class, all of them. The fact that Patsy's father was the cowman and her brother the yard boy should have emphasised the plane to which he was stooping.

His Fanny had always maintained that the boy was well bred; and his growing had seemed to prove it, for in voice and manner and intelligence, he was far above the ordinary. He had become a great reader, a talent with which he had been imbued by his dear Fanny and which, he thought, should have helped.

Well, he wasn't going to let any little Irish chit from the Hollow alter the plans he'd had in mind for some time now. He had always looked upon Carl as a son, and a son he determined he should now become . . .

But what if he left? He was a free man.

He wouldn't dare; he owed him too much to walk out.

But the question persisted: what if he did? How would he ever replace him? He realised he had left almost the entire running of the farm in the boy's hands for this long time. Eight years? Was it eight years since he had lost his beloved? What had he done in that time? His eyelids blinked rapidly as he thought back. It seemed that he had spent the time erecting fences around his land and keeping a watch on the girls. He had taken them to school and brought them back. He had trusted no-one else to do this; and when the time had come for Jessie to leave he made Angela leave too for, as he told himself, he couldn't be in two places at once. And now he would allow them to leave the farm only on a Saturday, when he would take them into town. Carl always accompanied them and saw to the delivery of the produce to the wholesale trader. On the odd occasion he had allowed Patsy to accompany them. But not during this past year.

His daughters had never been to Newcastle. As for attending a play or a variety show, they never knew about such things. And what was more, he had stopped them dancing.

One day he had found them, with their hands joined, doing the steps their mother had taught them. Perhaps it was because, compared with her, their actions looked cumbersome. Yet, had that been the truth it would have applied only to Jessie, not to Angela, who was so much like her mother that, at times, even now, he found it painful to look on her; at others he would hold her close, hugging her tightly to him, trying to recover the essence of his beloved Fanny.

He pressed a heel against the horse's flank, and it began to move down the hill. By the time he reached the farmyard there was no sight of either Carl or Patsy; but coming from the direction of the front door and accompanied by Jessie and Angela was Frank Noble, and the curate hailed him in his usual smiling way, calling, "Oh, I'm glad I've caught you. I just dropped in to say I'm looking for an audience for tomorrow night: I'm putting on a real good show. A friend in Newcastle has brought me two dozen . . . mark you, two dozen new slides; with what I've got, they'll run for an hour and a half, or more." He now looked from one girl to the other, saying, "I think I'll have to charge an entrance fee, don't you?"

Laughing, Jessie answered him: "Well, I can promise you I'll pay with left-over pies from Annie's last baking." Then bending forward to look round the curate at her sister standing now by his side, she said, "What'll you pay with, Angela?"

"Acorns."

"Do you hear that?" said Frank Noble.

Ward had dismounted and his reply was, "It's far too much, to my mind."

"May we go, Daddy?" Angela had now taken her father's arm, and as he answered her he looked at Frank Noble. "I don't see why not," he said, "although the man's whole show is so inane I'm surprised you waste your time looking at it."

"It's the way of the world"—Frank was nodding seriously towards Jessie now—"ingratitude. Ingratitude. I'm so used to it that I no longer retaliate. I only hope the good Lord chalks it up in my favour."

"Have you had anything to eat?"

"Oh yes. I've had two shives of Annie's treacle tart; I've had a slice of her currant bun cake, lathered with butter as thick as the cake, and I've had three cups of tea with real cream in it. To tell you the truth, that's all I come for."

"Oh, I've known that for some time," said Ward. "And by the way, hasn't Annie given you anything to take back for the children?"

"She offered, but I refused."

"You had no right to."

"I have every right to; my children are being spoilt. Every time they come here they go back laden, and when they know I've been here they expect me to come back with my pockets stuffed. Well, I've put a stop to it. Speaking seriously now, Ward, I just had to: there is a limit to receiving as there is to giving. Well, now"—his voice changed—"after that little sermon, I must be off; but I'll see you ladies tomorrow night, eh?"

"Yes. Oh, yes, we'd love to come."

"I'm going over now to Forest Hall to see if I can persuade Lady Lydia to come; or failing that, get the young master to persuade her. He's a great ally, is Mr. Gerald . . . Well, see you tomorrow night."

Ward now looked round the farmyard, then said, "You haven't walked? Where's your horse?"

"He's slightly lame. Anyway, it's Sunday and he needs a rest; and the walk does me good."

Ward shook his head, then stood beside his daughters watching the ailing parson stride out of the gate, and as he wondered how long was left to him, he experienced a tinge of envy for the serenity that emanated from this proven friend . . .

The girls had gone to the sitting-room: Angela was seated in the corner of the couch, her feet tucked under her, and looking like an outsize doll, her shining, straight black hair drawn back into two thick plaits, emphasising the alabaster tint of her skin. She could really have been a replica of her mother, except that her eyes were a clear grey, not a dark brown.

Jessie was placing some pieces of coal on the fire with a large pair of tongs, and Angela was saying, "I wonder if the Lord of the Manor has grown out of making sheep's eyes. It must be over a year since we saw him."

"Don't be silly." Jessie dusted her hands one against the other; then took a handkerchief from her dress pocket and proceeded to wipe her fingers, before taking a round tapestry frame from a nearby table. Then she sat down at the other end of the couch, saying, "That's a silly term . . . sheep's eyes."

"No sillier than you saying, 'Don't be silly.' You're always saying that to me, you know, Jessie, 'Don't be silly.' " But then she laid her head back into the cushions before adding, "Perhaps I am silly after all, because I think silly things, fairy-tale things, things that could never happen, and things that might happen, frightening things. Do you think frightening things, Jessie?"

There was a pause before Jessie answered quietly, "Yes, sometimes. I mostly dream them."

"What about?"

"Oh, I couldn't tell you." Jessie now thrust the needle into the canvas, pulled it through, then thrust it back again before going on, "Dreams never really enter into reality; dreams are outrageous things, fantastic, impossible things." Her hands slowly laid the frame on her knee, and she sat staring towards the fire until she was jerked back into an awareness of her sister by Angela saying, "Don't you think we lead a very restricted life here, Jessie? I sometimes feel that the walls of the farm and all those fences are like bars."

Jessie's mouth was agape. She could not have been more startled if her sister had used obscene language, and she was only fifteen and a bit: to her mind, she was feather-brained; yet here she was daring to put into words the thoughts that had for some time been tormenting herself. Then she was more amazed as Angela went on, "Daddy is too caring for us, don't you think? Do you think that he is still afraid that that woman will break out of the asylum and do us an injury?"

Angela turned her head now and must have seen the startled expression on her sister's face, but she still went on: "We never go anywhere. You remember the girls at school? Well, we never invited them here, did we? And do you remember Bella Scott? She used to talk about the family going to the pantomime at Christmas; and she once went to a play and saw a famous actress in Newcastle. You remember . . . ? We never go anywhere, do we, Jessie? Only to the dear Reverend Noble's magic lantern show."

When she stopped speaking, they continued to stare at each other. Then in a mere whisper and with a tremble in her voice, she said, "I feel lost at times, Jessie . . . lonely. And I want to do things which I know I mustn't, such as dance. Oh, I do want to dance. You remember, Mummy danced so beautifully? Sometimes I think I'm her: in my dreams I dance. Oh, Jessie."

Almost with a spring, Jessie hitched herself along the couch and enfolded her sister and, as if she were the mother, she was patting Angela's head, saying, "There, there. Don't cry, dear. I know what you mean. I, too, feel it. We must talk to Daddy; at least, I will. I shall ask him if he will take us to the city, and let us buy some clothes from the shop. Mrs. Ranshaw has a poor idea of dress. All our clothes look home-made. Yes; yes, I shall talk to him."

Angela raised her head. Her face was running with tears. "Oh, if only you would, Jessie," she said. "Anyway, if he says no, it won't matter so much, for now you understand me."

"Yes; yes, my dear; I understand." And again Jessie's arms went around her sister; and again she comforted her and felt a strange feeling as she did so; she could almost say she felt happy, until Angela whispered, "I feel so guilty, Jessie, because—I want to get away. I dream of, of . . . someone coming and, and"—the words became fainter—"taking me away and into a wonderful life . . . different."

It was around ten o'clock the next morning when Ward entered the kitchen and, looking at his daughter where she was rolling out some pastry on the floured board, said to her, "Leave that, and go and tell Carl I want a word with him in my office. You'll find him likely in the second paddock."

Jessie paused a moment and looked across the table towards Annie, who was sitting peeling the last of the apples from the previous year's crop. And she, noticing Jessie's hesitation, said, "Well, leave that; it won't walk away."

It wasn't until Jessie had left the kitchen, after washing her hands in the wooden sink, then drying them whilst looking out of the window, that Ward's voice came at her harshly, saying, "You don't need to titivate yourself to walk to the fields, Jessie; and I haven't got time to waste."

After the girl had left the kitchen through the back door and Ward was about to leave by the far door, Annie spoke again, saying, "She has a light hand with pastry, has Miss Jessie."

He turned and looked at her, saying, "What?"

"I said she has a light hand with pastry. She'll make a good house-keeper."

Ward stared at her over the length of the room before going out hastily and closing the door none too gently after him. And Annie, continuing to peel the apples without snapping the rind, muttered, "He'll appreciate her one day. But then, perhaps, it'll be too late; you can't keep birds caged if you leave the gate open."

Meanwhile, Jessie had reached the bottom of the second field where Mick Riley and Rob, with the assistance of Carl, were patching a drystone wall bordering the bridle path on that side of the land.

Mick and his son greeted her as they always did with exaggerated Irish courtesy: "Mornin' to you, Miss Jessie," with Rob's voice just a little behind that of his father, but he left the rest to Mike as his father said, " 'Tis a grand day, isn't it, miss? Can't ya hear it singin' 'Spring's on its way?' "

Jessie did not answer, but she smiled, then turned to Carl who was now saying, "You want me, Miss Jessie?"

Jessie looked at him. His blond hair looked to be almost silver; his face, as always, appeared beautiful to her; and his straight body was something on which she must not let her thoughts dwell; and she could have answered, "Yes, I want you, Carl. I always have; but you don't want me; you want the daughter of this rough man, don't you? I wish I hated Patsy, like I used to, but she won't let me, for she, more than any other, has understood how I have felt, and in her own way she has been kind to me. She it was who would put her arms around me after Mother died, not Annie, and oh, not Daddy. No, the only one who's ever felt his arms since then has been Angela. Yet his love doesn't satisfy Angela. Angela would fly away tomorrow and forget him if her fairy prince were to come riding along, whereas I, who have never had his love, could never forget him."

Carl was saying, "Is anything the matter, Miss Jessie?"

"What? . . . No. I'm sorry." And she gave a little laugh. "I was thinking of something else for the moment; as Mike says, it's a bit of a Spring day . . . . Father would like to see you in his study."

"Now?"

"Well"—she shrugged her shoulder—"he sent me for you."

Looking at Mike, Carl said, "I won't be long," the words implying, And so you had better keep going; no sliding down against the wall and lighting your clay pipe . . .

They were walking side by side across the field when she said, "Will you be going to the magic lantern show tonight?"

He laughed as he replied, "No; I don't think so. In fact, I've seen it so many times I could give you the show without the slides."

"But the parson tells us he has twelve new slides."

"Oh well, I suppose that's something to look forward to. And he's always obliged to you when you go. It makes his efforts worthwhile. He's a good man."

"Yes. Yes"—she nodded—"he's a good man. It's a pity he's so sick. But I feel he'd improve somewhat if he'd only move out of the Hollow. It's a damp place at the best of times."

"Yes, you're right there. But those down there are his flock; although half of them"—he refrained from saying, the Irish—"don't pass over the church steps; but nevertheless he treats them all alike. They would all have known even harder times if it hadn't been for him."

"But Daddy's been kind to them." Her voice sounded on the defensive now, and he confirmed quickly that he recognised this by saying, "Yes; yes, of course. No-one kinder. With his taties and turnips, and all the odd bits, and giving Mike half a pig at Christmas. Yes, you're right." But again he had to stop himself from saying, It's easy to give when you've got plenty, but when you've got as little as Parson Noble, it's like his name: it's a noble deed he does every time he shares the little he's got. Instead he said, "You say your father's in his study?"

"Yes. Yes, Father's in his study."

When they reached the yard, she left him to go into the kitchen alone, and there, looking at Annie, he said, "I'm wanted in the study. What's afoot? Do you know?"

"Now, why ask me that? What would I know of the inner workings of the master's mind?"

He smiled and pushed her gently in the shoulder, saying, "More than the next, Annie."

"Are your boots clean?"

He looked down at them, saying, "Yes; yes, they're clean; the ground is as hard as flint."

A minute later he was knocking on the study door, and when Ward's voice called, "Come in!" he entered the room, which was small, although it was lined with bookshelves, the only other pieces of furniture being a desk and two chairs, in one of which Ward was sitting, the other one being placed near the window.

Pointing to it, Ward said, "Draw it up; I want to talk to you."

They sat for a moment looking at each other; then Ward, running his fingers through the front of his greying hair, said, "I've asked you here because this is a private talk. It will be the one and only, I suppose, we'll ever have along these lines. How old are you now?"

"Oh . . . Oh. Well, you know, master, I wasn't sure whether I was nine or ten when I came to you, but I reckon I am now twenty-seven." And he was in such a position in this household that he could add, "I wouldn't have thought you would have to ask that."

"Oh, perhaps not. But I just wanted it to be emphasised that you are twenty-seven; you are no longer a youth, not even a young man, you are a fully-fledged man. And now I am going to ask you if you have thought of your future."

"Oh yes; many a time."

"Have you ever thought that one day you could own this house and farm?"

Carl moved slightly on the chair, which caused the legs to squeak on the polished boards; then emphatically he said, "No! No, never!"

"Well, well; you surprise me, because any onlooker, any close onlooker, that is, would have said you have been running this farm for a good few years now."

"Oh no . . . no."

Carl was shaking his head, when Ward put in, "But yes; I don't want to hear any false modesty: you know you've been carrying the weight of it since I lost my"—he had to gulp in his throat before he could bring out—"wife. I haven't been the farmer I was before. My mind has been centered on protecting my daughters; and yes . . . and yes, myself, too. I have enemies in that village, strong enemies. I'm only too well aware of it; and because of this, I've left you to carry on, for you've not only helped to grow the produce, you've seen to the marketing of most of it. I've taken the profit and paid out the bills and wages, and in a way, I am still master here, but I haven't been running my farm. You have. So, what would you say if I offered to make you my heir? But wait!" He lifted a hand. "There is a condition. And the condition has weighed heavily on me for some time. I am going to ask you a straight question: do you like Jessie?"

Carl sat perfectly still for at least ten seconds; then he closed his eyes and bit on his lower lip before he said quietly, "Yes; yes, of course, master, I like Jessie. Apart from yourself and Annie, I was the first to hold her. She is like . . ."

"Don't . . . don't say she is like a sister to you, because she is not your sister; and she has never felt that she was your sister. Jessie is very fond of you."

Carl drew in a deep breath before he said, "Yes . . . yes, I know that, master; and I am fond of her . . ."

"But what you are going to say is, fondness isn't love; you don't love her."

"Yes; that's about it, master."

"But let me tell you, Carl, that after marriage fondness very often grows to love, a lasting love. There's more to marriage than a burning flame that attacks you."

It was at this point that Ward sat back in his chair and closed his eyes. What was he saying? More to marriage than a burning flame. Had *he* not been consumed with the flame? Were not its embers still burning within him? It wasn't only protection of his daughters that had filled his mind all these years, it was the constant ache for his loss, for his love had been a mania; there was nothing reasonable or logical about it. And here he was telling this young fellow, whom he already thought of as a son, that love grew out of fondness.

He was actually startled when Carl said, "I'm afraid I can't agree with you, sir. And anyway, now that we're speaking openly, I love someone else, and I am sure you know who that is. And I've often felt, sir, that as you loved your dear wife so I, in a similar way, love . . ."

"Don't say it! Don't speak of Patsy Riley in the same breath as my wife, or of my feelings for her. What is she? She is not even a village girl, but springs from that Hollow where pigs are cleaner than some of their owners. And don't say to me that she is different, for breeding will out. Just look at her father and her brother. Do you want to link yourself with that lot? You will either marry Jessie or you will no longer remain here."

Carl was now on his feet looking down on the man whom he had loved as a father, and his heart was sore for him as he said, "I would do anything in the world for you, sir, because I owe you a great debt, but if I did what you ask I would make two people very unhappy, not to mention a third, for I don't love Miss Jessie as a man should love a woman, and she would suffer for that. Then the woman I love would suffer, too. And yes, she is from the Hollow, but she is an intelligent woman; she is a fine woman. You, sir, have never spoken more than half a dozen words to her in all the years she's been in your employ. And now I am going to say this: your wife valued her; she lent her books, and she talked with her on the side when you were out of the way so it wouldn't annoy you, because she realised that the little Irish girl who came to your door, pointing out that she had washed her hands and her hair in the river, was worthy of better treatment than that meted out to a pigswiller or dairymaid."

They were again looking at each other, each in deep sorrow now.

When Carl stepped back, he asked one question: "Do you want me to leave now, sir?"

It was noticeable to them both that he was no longer using the word master; and with averted gaze Ward answered, "You may work your month."

When Carl passed through the kitchen, Annie turned from her seat and, looking at him, asked, "What is it, lad? Something wrong?"

"Yes, Annie. Yes, you could say that, something's wrong. I'll . . . I'll talk to you in a short while." And with this, he hurried out into the yard, where he stood as if in a daze, until he saw Patsy coming from the open barn.

He ran towards her and, taking her arm, drew her back into the barn, into the corner where some bales of hay were stacked but where the sunlight streaming in through the shrunken old oak slats dappled them both in light and shade as they stood looking at each other.

Patsy did not question, "What's the matter? What's happened?" for from the look on Carl's face she guessed something vital to them must have taken place; and when he suddenly moved from her to lean back against a supporting beam, his head touching the wood as he muttered, "We're free!" she sprang towards him, her hands on his shoulders now, her voice rapid as she said, "You've told him? You've told him? And he said we can? Oh Carl! Carl!"

He brought his head down to the level of her own now, and quietly he said, "No, he didn't say we can, he gave me the option: he offered me the house and the farm if I married Jessie."

"No." Her voice was a whisper. "He made it as plain as that?"

"Yes, my dear; he made it as plain as that. But I told him I couldn't make her unhappy and myself at the same time because I loved you."

When she fell against him, her head on his shoulder, he placed his arms gently about her; and as he held her he said, "It was awful, Patsy, really awful. Although I felt I owed him so much, the price he was asking was too much for me to pay."

"It's my fault."

And to her almost inaudible mutter, he replied, "No, it isn't your fault; it's nobody's fault. Anyway, we've got a month to find another place. And we'll be together, in the open. That's the main thing, because it's been a long time"—he raised her face to his now—"overlong. It's odd, you know, but I was thinking about it this morning, that it was overlong already. Now we're going to be like Jimmy Conway and Susan Beaker. By what is said in the village they had been going together since he was nineteen and she eighteen, but he had to stay with his father until he died, and she had to stay with her mother until she died. And there they are now: she's thirty-six and he's thirty-eight, almost twenty years' courtship; and I could see ours being the same, because we've known each other for nearly sixteen years. Anyway, they are being married today. That's what made me think of it."

She turned from him, yet retained a hold of his hand as she said, "Strange that you should mention them; that was the first thing I thought of, too, this morning. I thought it was because Ma said yesterday that there would be high jinks in the village tonight, for both inns were stocking up, and Da said there would be free drinks all round because the butcher's business has been thriving and he had been the closest of men, and so Jimmy would be very warm. And he said the Beakers would be, too. Strangely, though, I didn't think about their wedding, I just wondered if we would have to wait almost twenty years, and if so could we last out."

They turned together to look at each other.

He bowed his head and, his lips in her hair, he said, "For my part, I doubt it." Again they were in each other's arms; and now tightly holding, he added, "We can make it as soon as you like."

"Oh, Carl; as soon as ever you like."

After they had kissed again a gentle, warm gesture now, they separated from each other and walked side by side into the yard.

But beyond the farther side of the barn, Jessie did not move, only, just as Carl had done, to lean her head back against the wood as she pressed her lips into an indrawn thin line in order to prevent the tears from spurting from her eyes. She hadn't meant to listen. It was as she walked along the back of the barn towards the hen pens to gather the morning eggs that she heard their voices, and stopped for a second to look through a cleft in the wood. And so she saw and heard almost all they had to say to each other.

Now she was saying to herself, "Oh, Daddy! Daddy, why had you to do it? I could have borne it. But never to see him again. I might have been able to change my feeling into that for . . . a beloved brother. Yes. Yes, I could, because I am not a silly girl; I never have been; I have been made old by my feeling for both of you, you and him; and soon there will be only you, and you don't know I exist."

TWO

"Look, Mummy! You promised. And you know it gives old Noble a kick if you're there. You're always saying he's a saint and should be supported."

"Yes, I know, Gerald; but I made that promise before your father came in an hour ago and said Percy and Catherine would be popping in, and so I can't possibly leave the house. And Alice and Nell will be with them, and so you should be here, too"—she now wagged her finger at him—"you should stay and *support me*."

"The very sight of Nell terrifies me, Mummy; you know that. I shouldn't be surprised if she were to bring her horse into the drawing-room one of these days. She smells of the stables."

Lady Lydia Ramsmore gave a girlish giggle, then put a hand over her mouth as she said, "She does rather reek a little of the horseflesh, I admit; but Alice is nice, different."

"Not different enough, Mummy. Anyway, I'd rather sit through a night with Captain and Mrs. Hopkins and their *two* eligible daughters."

"Your father will be annoyed."

"I can't help that, Mummy; it'll only add one more annoyance to the list I create."

"You're still of the same mind, dear?"

"Yes, Mummy, I'm still of the same mind. And always will be."

"But literature, dear, is all very well; and you know how I like reading. As far as I can judge it will be very difficult to make a career out of writing poetry and such. And another thing, dear: I just cannot understand why you are so against entering the Army, because you know you must have inherited something from both sides. You know, my ancestors, too, were involved in the battling business, oh, far back. And you know, dear, your father can't help getting annoyed when he hears Percy Hopkins rattling on about his boys fighting in the Boer War, and who will be sailing for India shortly. Don't you feel any remorse? I mean . . . well, not actually remorse, but . . . Oh, I don't know what the word is."

"The word is guilt, Mummy. No, I don't feel any guilt in not going to shoot someone I have never seen in my life before. And let us state plain facts, Mummy: they are men who are trying to protect their own way of life and that of their families." He bent over her now, where she was sitting on the couch, and his face close to hers, he said, "I'm a changeling, dear; and at times I feel that you've had a hand in it. Now tell me, just between ourselves, did you not, in your gay days, fall in love with somebody like me, a literary man? A classics scholar, perhaps?" he teased.

"Oh, you are impossible." She slapped him lightly on his cheek; but she was laughing as she pushed him away, saying, "No, I didn't! But I have an idea from where you might have sprung, and from your father's side, too, for there was one of them more than a bit odd: he would eat nothing but green-stuff, and he lived for the last twenty years of his life in the end of the hall here, the part that was first built, and he never left it. I understand he sewed himself into his clothes." She laughed outright now as she said, "What he must have smelt like would certainly have put Nell in the shade. Anyway, he didn't waste his time, it must be admitted, and apparently he translated things from the ancient Greek language; but what it was he translated nobody seems to know. I think it's quite possible that the following generation wanted to forget him."

"Where did you hear that, Mummy?"

"I didn't hear it; I read it one day when I was browsing among the tomes in the library. I came across a sort of diary in which there were a few sentences about him, and when I mentioned it to your father his response was, "Oh, him!""

"Well, Mummy, I can promise you that there's a chance I might follow the old fellow, and within the next forty, fifty, sixty years translate something from Latin or Greek, but I can also promise you I shall never do anything that will make me smell. By the way, you said he ate only greenstuff. I suppose that means vegetables. Odd that, don't you think? Because I'm not very fond of meat, am I? I'll have to look up that old fellow and get to know more about him. But now to the present. You won't come to the show?"

"We've been through it, dear. I can't come to the show. I have to live with your father, remember, while you can jaunt off, to Oxford or London or wherever your fancy takes you. Where's your fancy going to take you for the remainder of the vacation?"

"I've been invited to Roger Newton's in Shropshire."

"Oh well. I'll miss you, dear. I always do."

He now dropped down on to the couch beside her and, putting an arm around her shoulders, he said, "I needn't go to Roger's; it was to be for only a short spell. They're having a hunt ball, and you know how I love hunting and shooting."

"Then why are you friendly with him at all if he loves hunting and shooting?"

"Simply because we have like ideas. And fortunately for him he isn't plagued to take up arms. His people are in law . . . Oh, look at the time!" He pointed to the gilt clock on the mantelpiece. "I must be off."

He bent down and kissed his mother's cheek, and then, pulling a face at her, he said, "Give my love to the girls, won't you? Have a nice evening."

She again laughed at him, then said, "Are you riding in?"

"No; I'm going to walk; it'll be a lovely evening, for there'll be a full moon."

She watched him striding down the room, but before he reached the door she called to him, "Your father will have something to say to you, remember."

He paused and looked over his shoulder at her, and his voice was flat now as he said, "Yes, I suppose he will, dear." And with this, he went out, and she lay back on the couch and sighed. He was such a lovely boy. No; not a boy any more, a young man. But she wished, oh how she wished he didn't annoy his father.

The magic lantern show was over and Frank Noble was showing the children of the Hollow out of the door. One by one he spoke to them as he handed to each child a square of barley sugar, and they, in turn and each in his own way, assured him it had been the best show ever.

It had been a poor audience tonight. In the past, there had been as many as twenty children, but tonight there had been only four from the outlying farms apart from the children from the Hollow: a wedding tea had been held in Farmer Green's barn earlier on, and at this very moment a dance was being held there which would likely continue into the small hours if the patrons from the inn should decide to join them. There would be some sore heads tomorrow and, as Jane had said in her forthright way, other results, too, if she knew anything about barn weddings.

He turned now to his last three guests. His young friend Gerald was gathering up the slides while Jessie and Angela seemed to be wiping their eyes. "Oh, I'm sorry," he called to them; "it does give off a fug, doesn't it, that coke stove." He coughed, then said, "It gets me, too; but I wouldn't have an audience without the stove, now, would I?"

When they smiled at him, he said, "Carl should be here shortly. But we did finish earlier than I expected."

"It was the dogs running, I suppose," said Angela. "It made the time go quicker."

He laughed at her joke, saying, "I shouldn't be surprised. It was a funny bit, that, wasn't it?"

"Yes. Yes." Angela nodded at him. "You would actually think the dogs were running. You made them go so quickly; and it was so funny when the little one hung on to the policeman's trousers." She paused before ending, "I like the funny ones."

"Then I'll have to see if I can get some more . . . Do you like the funny ones?" He looked at Jessie, who answered, "Yes, I do. But I also like the ones showing the black children. They all look so merry."

"Yes. Yes, they do." He did not add, "some of them," but turned to speak to Gerald who had joined them, saying, "I am not going to ask you if you enjoyed the show, for I am sure it must be a penance to be behind the screen."

"No, no; not at all. I think I get more fun watching the reactions of your audience, because, you know, I think some of them must groan, for they've seen the old ones so often."

"No, they don't. Now! now! You can't get too much of a good thing. What do you say, girls?"

The girls said nothing, and there was a moment's embarrassed silence before Gerald said quietly, "You're waiting for Carl to fetch you? But there is an awful fug in here; it's getting in my eyes, too. May I escort you along the road, until you meet him?"

As if she had been stung, Jessie took a quick step to the side, and taking hold of Angela's arm she turned her about, saying, "No, thank you. You're very kind, but no thank you. And it's bright moonlight outside. Carl should be here any minute. We'll just walk along to meet him."

As the girls made their way towards the door, Frank Noble looked at the face of the young man who had definitely been snubbed and whose expression was showing it; then he hurried outside, and there he stopped for a moment and drew in a deep breath of the cold air, as the girls were also doing.

Another time, knowing the feelings of their father, so protective as to amount almost to a mania and which to his mind was cramping their lives, Frank would have said to them, "I do think you had better wait"; but tonight, the moon was giving out a light almost as bright as daylight, and although the show had finished early it was almost time for Carl to appear, being a few minutes off eight o'clock, so he said, "You're bound to meet him within a very short distance; he's always on time, isn't he?"

"Yes; yes." It was Angela who answered him. "And I did enjoy the show. Thank you so much."

As they were walking away he called to them, "Oh, and don't forget to thank your father for that parcel: he is too kind."

No answer came to him, but he watched until they were beyond the bend in the path and should be mounting the hill out of the Hollow.

The girls didn't speak to each other until they reached the brow of the hill and were on the path leading to the junction where one branch led off to the valley; and it was Angela again who spoke, saying, "Why didn't you let him escort us? He's very nice."

But when she received no answer, she added, "And yet it's nice, too, to be able to walk alone, isn't it, Jessie?"

"Yes; yes, it is." Jessie now caught hold of her sister's hand, and as she did so, they both turned their heads towards the sound of laughter and shouting that was reaching them from the village.

"That must be some of the wedding . . . party, and by the sound of them, they appear to be drunk."

Their steps seemed instinctively to slow until Jessie said, "They're likely on their way from the barn to the village inn."

The laughter died away, and they resumed their normal pace until they were within a few yards of the junction; and here, emerging from the village path they saw three men, and over the distance they could see that the men were laughing, but silently. Angela pressed herself close to Jessie's side, and they stopped.

The men, too, stopped within a short distance of them, and one of them exclaimed, "Good God! See who we've met up with?" And another one called out, "Aye. Aye. An' we thought it was Mary Ellen and Cissie. But it's the Angel's daughters; he's let them out, and unprotected. Do you see, lads? Unprotected."

Neither of the girls knew the man who stepped towards them and who, bowing low, said, "Good evenin', missis. Are you lost?"

For a moment Jessie stared at the man she didn't know; then she appealed to the one she did know. He was the verger. "We are waiting for C . . . C . . . Carl," she stammered.

The verger's fat belly began to shake, and he turned to his companion on to whom he was hanging, and in a thick and fuddled voice he said, "Did you hear that, Pete? She's waiting for Carl."

Without answering the verger, Pete Mason pushed him aside and, swaying, stepped towards the girls; and looking from one frightened face to the other, he muttered something under his breath; although his next words were just audible. "The time has come," he said. "I knew it would one day." And with this, he thrust out an arm and grabbed Angela, meaning to drag her towards him. But Jessie's hands tore at him, her screams joining Angela's, but only for a moment for Angela's were now being smothered: with an arm around her neck and the hand across her mouth, Pete Mason's other hand tore at the front of her cloak.

Meanwhile Jessie had been clawed away from Mason by the third man and was being thrust against a tree. There was a mighty scream within her which couldn't escape through the hand over her mouth; but it activated her limbs, as did the cold air that hit her chest when her blouse was ripped down the front.

Clawing at the man's face, she lifted a knee and brought it upwards; then she was free, with the man staggering back before doubling up. When she forced herself to move, she too staggered and not until her feet left the grass verge and hit the rough path again did she regain her bearings; and then she was screaming, "Angela! Angela!" But there was no answering cry from Angela, only a rustling in the thicket to the side of the road telling her that the men were there; and her fear gave wings to her feet as she flew back towards the Hollow.

At the top of the bank she almost fell into Gerald Ramsmore's arms. Her hands gripping the lapels of his coat, she gasped, "The men! They've got Angela."

For a moment he was unable to take in what she was saying, for her whole appearance staggered him: her hair, which must have been piled up under her hat, was now hanging down her back and part of her bosom was bare.

"It was the verger," she was saying. "They are drunk. They . . ." She screwed up her face. "He . . . one tried. Oh, please! Come! Come now!" She was pulling at him, and he was running by her side.

When they reached the place where Angela had been dragged from her, she pointed, crying, "Look! There they are," and he was able to make out three figures reeling drunkenly across the open field.

"Where is she? Where is she? Have they taken her? It was here! It was here! It was here!"

Gerald jumped across a shallow ditch and rounded a small group of bushes, only to come to a stop when he saw something that was to impinge on his mind for the rest of his life. This delicate, fairy-like girl whose beauty alone had always touched on his artistic sense and drawn his eyes towards her, lay sprawled, her arms outstretched, her hands at each side gripping the earth, the bottom of her skirt half covering her face, her lower limbs exposed; and he shut his eyes against the sight, and gripped his face tightly with one hand while he groaned. Then he spun around as he heard Jessie stepping over the ditch; and he cried to her, "No! No! She's here; but she needs help. Get Carl. Go to your people quickly! Go and get help!"

"I must see . . ."

"Please, she's in distress. Go and get help."

As she turned from him and leapt the ditch again, calling out as she ran, "Carl! Carl!" he walked slowly to the side of the prone figure and, pulling the skirt down from her face, he slid an arm under her head, saying, "It's all right. It's all right," even though his mind was yelling at him that it would never again be all right for this child, never; and he went on, "Your people are coming. Dear Miss Angela. Oh, dear Miss Angela."

When she made no movement whatever, he thought, Dear God! She's dead. Then he dared to put a hand where he thought her heart was, and after a second or two he heaved a deep sigh. And now his hand was stroking the hair, that beautiful, seal-shiny black hair, from her face.

He was not aware of Carl's approach until the bending body over him blocked out the moonlight and the exclamation, "O . . . oh!" preceding words which could have been said to be blasphemous, and then the loud and despairing, *"No! No!* This can't have happened. *No! No!"*

Gerald looked up at Carl and said quietly, "But it has. We must get her home."

Carl, too, was now kneeling by Angela, patting her face and saying, "Come on, love. Come on. This is Carl here. Come on. Don't be frightened any more. Come on, love. Come on."

But receiving no response, he muttered, "Oh dear God!" Then looking across at Gerald, he said, "He'll kill them for this; there'll be murder done. He'll kill them surely."

"Do you think we could carry her between us?"

"Aye. Yes. But I can carry her myself."

"There's some way to go; I'd better help you."

After gently pulling up her ripped drawers and straightening her limbs, Carl picked her up bodily; and Gerald said again, "Let me help," and laid her legs across his arm, and together they started towards home.

They were about a quarter of a mile from the farmhouse when they were aware of Ward tearing towards them; and when he met up with them he stopped for barely a moment to look down on the white face of his child. Then thrusting out his arms, he relieved them of their burden; and without uttering a word he turned and hurried back to the farm.

Gerald followed on with Carl, and as they entered the yard, he said, "If I could use your horse I could ride for the doctor."

Carl turned to him. "Yes. Yes, by all means, yes. But wait! I should see what the master says." But then shaking his head, he said, "No. She'll need a doctor. Oh yes, she'll need a doctor."

Patsy could be seen standing in the light from the open door. Her hands were joined at her throat, and Ward called to her, "Go and get Annie!"

After the evening meal, because of the condition of her legs, Annie usually returned to her cottage, leaving the washing-up and the preparation for the following morning's breakfast to Patsy. And Patsy had been attending to these duties when Jessie, like a wild woman, had dashed through the kitchen, calling for her father.

She now took to her heels and ran to Annie's cottage and, banging on the door, she cried, "Are you in bed?"

Annie's answer came back to her, "I'm getting ready for it. What's the matter with you now?"

When the door was pulled open, Patsy gasped, "The master . . . he's just carried Miss Angela in. She looks dead. And Miss Jessie's been attacked, the clothes torn from her back."

"Dear God! What are you saying, girl?" Annie demanded, at the same time reaching out to lift her shawl from the back of the door and putting it around her shoulders. Then she was shambling as fast as her legs would carry her towards the house . . .

Fifteen minutes later she and Patsy gently drew the last of the clothes from Angela's bruised body. They were both crying, and it could be said they were both frightened of the master, and for him. Ward had not spoken a word until he saw that they had been about to wash his daughter's limbs; and then he said, "Leave them until I get the doctor."

Patsy now muttered quietly, "He's been sent for, master. Mr. Gerald from the Hall, he's gone for him."

At this, Ward stood back and waited for them to put her into a night-dress, when he said simply, "Leave her," which they did. Annie went down into the kitchen where Carl was waiting; Patsy went to the bathroom where she knew Jessie would be. However, receiving no answer to her knock, she gently pushed open the door, to see the girl sitting on a stool. She was in her nightdress, her clothes lying in a heap on the floor; she turned her white and scared face towards Patsy, and her lips trembled as she muttered, "Oh, Patsy, Patsy."

Kneeling by the girl's side, Patsy put her arms about her and brought her head on to her shoulder, and as a mother would, she comforted her, saying, "There, there, dear. There, there. It's all over." And when Jessie murmured, "No, no; never will be, never will be," she countered, "Yes; yes, it will. It'll fade away with time. I know. These things do."

When Jessie's sobs shook them both, Patsy didn't say, "Don't cry, my dear," she murmured softly, "That's it. That's it: get it out of you," at the same time hoping that the death-like figure in the bedroom along the landing would soon wake up and that she, too, would cry. Perhaps, too, she would have something more to cry about. God help her. Oh, yes, God help her. Three of them! Oh Jesus in heaven! For such a thing to happen, and to a child such as Angela, so fragile, so light and airy as was her mother. As Annie had said, it would seem she was a twin fairy. Oh, this house. She'd be glad when she got out of it . . . when they both got out of it. But what was she talking about? Would Carl leave the master now, being able only to guess what his reactions would be to this outrage? And could she leave this girl, leave the pair of them with Annie, who could hardly trot now? Oh, and she had thought . . . she shook her head . . . enough of her own wants at the moment, for there would be more tragedies afore another day was out, if she knew anything about it.

"Come," she said now; "dry your eyes. There you are. And lie yourself down in the spare room. If Doctor Patten comes, he'll likely see you and give you a draught."

Jessie pulled herself up from the stool, saying, "I want no draught. I must go to Angela."

"No. No, dear; your father's with her, and he sent us out. Leave him be until after the doctor's been. Come; do as I say now, and lie yourself down. I'll get you a hot drink, hot milk with nutmeg in it, the way you like it. It's very soothing."

Jessie allowed herself to be led out of the bathroom and to the end of the landing; and in the spare room, Patsy said, "The bed'll be still aired: you both slept in it not two weeks ago when I turned your room out. You lie down now, and I'll be back directly."

As Patsy made to move away Jessie stretched out her hand and, gripping her wrist, spoke in a voice that held a plea and a question. "What'll happen? What'll happen to her?"

"I don't know yet, my dear. I don't know yet."

"Men are dreadful, aren't they, Patsy? Dreadful, dreadful."

"Not all, dear. Not all. Lie down now. Lie down." And Patsy unwound the fingers from her wrist; then went quickly out of the room and stood on the landing for a moment, her hands gripped tightly against her neck as she was wont to do when agitated or worried.

As she went to go down the stairs, so the doctor was about to come up;

and on sight of her, he stepped back and bade her descend; then without a word he passed her, and she continued to the kitchen, there to see the young master from the Hall talking to Carl; and she was surprised to hear his voice almost breaking as if he were on the verge of tears as he said, "I'll never forget this night. I'll call in the morning to see how she's faring."

"Yes; do that." Carl was nodding at him.

The young man inclined his head towards Annie, saying now, "Good night," and she answered, "Good night, sir. And whatever happens, you are to be thanked for your help."

He made no response, but stared straight at her for a moment before turning and going out.

Looking at Annie now, the while pulling a chair forward, Carl said, "Here, get off your feet," and she obediently sat down. Then he asked of Patsy, "How's Miss Jessie?"

"In a state. I'm going to make her a hot drink. I think the doctor should see her and give her a draught," which brought the immediate response from Annie, "Oh, I'd better go up and tell him then. And he might need assistance."

"Stay where you are," said Carl; "Patsy can go and wait outside until he finishes what he has to do. She can tell him what is needed. And he'll have something to tell too. My God! he will at that. But speaking of draughts, I think it's the master who needs one; I'm fearful for him. . . ."

It was a full half hour before Philip Patten finished what he had to do. Even before he began his examination he had been aghast, and when, in a small voice, he had ventured to say, "I think I should have Annie here," Ward had come back with, "What help you need, I'm here." And so it had been.

Now that it was completed, Ward asked him in what appeared a deceptively calm voice, "Will she live?" And Philip answered, "I hope so: her heart is strong; but this will depend upon her will."

"Her will?"

"Yes. Yes, I said her will."

"Why doesn't she open her eyes? Is she unconscious?"

"She's in shock; and she might be like this for . . . well, two or three days. I can't tell you how long. On the other hand she might awaken tomorrow morning after the draught I have given her has worn off."

Philip Patten watched Ward look down on his daughter, and what the man said next and how he said it sent a shiver through him. "She is fifteen. Her woman time began last year; there could be results," he said; then turning slowly to confront Philip, he stated rather than questioned, "Even with the damage that's been done, there could still be results, couldn't there?"

Philip Patten gulped in his throat, and he had to look away from the eyes that were staring into his before he could say, "That's to be seen; only . . . only the future can say yes or no to that." And on Ward's next words, he had to turn his back on both the bed and the man, for Ward said, "Three of them couldn't miss, could they?"

Philip made no reply, but then almost jumped when the voice barked at him, "Could they?" and he swung round to face the distraught man, saying,

"We don't know if there were three. I mean, there were three men there, so I understand, but . . ."

"Then I ask you, doctor, could one man have done that damage?"

"Yes. Yes, he could." Philip Patten's head was bobbing now and his voice was loud.

"But three could do more harm, couldn't they?"

"Ward. Ward." Philip's head was drooped almost on to his chest, and there was a plea in his voice as he said, "We don't know."

"You don't know? You didn't see Jessie when she came in, half mad, the clothes torn off her back. She managed to escape; so, would that one be satisfied? No; he would take his turn."

"Oh, for God's sake! Ward. You've got to stop this way of thinking, else it will drive you to do something that can only bring disaster. You must let it be dealt with by the authorities. I will contact the police myself."

"Oh no! O . . . oh! no; you'll do no such thing, doctor!" And besides shaking his head, allowed his body, too, to follow the movement as if to emphasise his request: "I'm asking as a favour, don't go to the police."

"What! But those men must be punished. *And you mustn't, Ward. No, you must not* take it into your own hands. That will mean murder; and what will happen? You'll swing. Putting it plainly, you'll swing. And how will your girls be left then? What protection will they have?"

"Who's speaking of murder? I am not going to murder them. After what I intend to do, their own consciences, and the village, will murder them in their own way; just as they have murdered me over the years."

Definitely puzzled now, Philip said, "What . . . ? Well, I mean, what do you mean to do?"

"What do I mean to do?" Ward looked to the side. He had seen what he meant to do from the moment he had looked down on his daughter's ravished body. Although the method of its accomplishment was not wholly formed in his mind, in one part it was indeed very clear; but he had as yet to work out how to bring it about, and so he said, "Just leave things for a few days, will you, doctor? I'll come back to you in, say, a week."

"A week! But they'll think they've got off with it. And what about Doctor Wheatley, when he gets wind of it?"

"I would think that if I don't make any move your superior won't. What do you think?"

What Philip thought was: Ward is right, for if a scandal such as this were to break it would scar his village, for just as it was usual for the parson never to think otherwise, he too considered it to be his, and far beyond the village. "My patients," he would say. "Do not interfere with *my* patients."

He said now, "All right, I'll do as you wish. But don't forget that the young man from the Hall was the first on the scene, so I understand, and by now I should imagine he has informed his parents; he was greatly affected, you know."

"Well, we shall have to take that chance. Being the gentleman he is, he will likely call tomorrow to see what has transpired; if so I shall ask him what I have asked you, to remain silent for a few days more."

"Oh, Ward." The doctor put out his hand and placed it on Ward's shoulder, saying, "Don't do anything that's going to bring retribution on you. I beg of you."

"If there's any justice in the world, it won't; but is there any justice in the world?" Ward said vehemently and through his clenched teeth; but then added more calmly, "Has any justice been dealt out to me and mine over the years because, as a young man, I was silly enough to be pleasant to a young woman whom I had no intention of marrying? Justice is blind, Doctor. I thought you would have become aware of that in your profession. The young and innocent die, while the no good, Godless, wrecking, raping villagers survive. But how they'll survive after this is another question . . . oh yes."

Philip could find no way to refute Ward's original request, but the implied intent in the last words, spoken with such a look in the man's eyes, made him shiver, and so without further words, and not even a nod of assent or goodbye, he picked up his bag from the table, glanced once more at the bed and left the room.

In the kitchen, he looked from one to the other and said, "He'll likely sit up all night with her, but I think somebody should be on the alert." And Carl said, "Don't worry about that, Doctor. I'll be up, and Patsy, too."

"Good night then," he said; and as an afterthought added, "I imagine the running of the place will now have to be shared between you for a long time to come."

THREE

The village was uneasy. A strange tale was being circulated. Some believed there was some truth in it, others denied it flatly, saying it had originated from Rob Riley in the Hollow, who with his father worked for Ward Gibson. Part of the rumour was that the young daughter had been frightened by some drunks from Jimmy Conroy's wedding. Some said that the young girl had been interfered with. But how could that happen? She was never let out without a guard. A disgrace, it was, the way the lasses were hemmed in. But there was something wrong, and Fred Newberry said so to his parents. It was the first time he had been in that house, he said, and had not been offered a cup of tea or some such; and when he asked of Ward's whereabouts, he was told that he was busy upstairs. And that was that. He had come away thinking they were all close-mouthed about something, and it must be to do with the rumour that was going round the village. It wasn't like Ward not to have a word with him, although as everybody knew he had been acting strange ever since he had lost his wife. All he now seemed to think about was building his walls and his fences higher and not letting the girls out of his sight.

It was Fred's mother who had said, "Perhaps he's afraid of Daisy escaping again, because she has become sly enough, you know that. By! she was sly. I was always thankful she didn't pass her spleen on to us for being friendly with Ward."

The patrons of the two inns were asking similar questions. Was there any truth in the rumour? And who were the three fellows who were supposed to have shocked the girls? It would be hard, it was said, to pick them out of all those who danced in the barn and had drunk deeply from the barrels that night, for it had been classed as one of the best wedding receptions that had been held in the village for many a year, if you could rate it on the liquor drunk and the food eaten. Nevertheless, it was generally agreed there was something afoot. But what? And look what had happened to Parson Noble from the Hollow when he called at the house: he had collapsed and had been taken home to bed. Oh yes, there was something fishy about the whole business.

It was on the Wednesday morning that Angela opened her eyes; and the first face she saw was Jessie's, and she made a moaning sound as she lifted her hand towards her. Gripping her sister's hand, Jessie cried almost joyfully, "Oh! Angela. Angela. You're better. Oh, that's wonderful. How are you feeling?"

Even as she said it she knew it to be a silly thing to ask; but she waited for the answer.

When her sister's mouth opened and shut and no words came, she said, "All right, dear. Just rest. Don't trouble yourself. I'll go and get Daddy," and she ran from the room and to the landing window that looked on to the yard, and shouted down, "Patsy! Patsy! Carl!"

When Patsy came running from the dairy and looked up at her, Jessie called, "Get Daddy! Angela has come round."

"Oh, good! miss. Good!" And Patsy ran the length of the yard and round by the woodstack and into what was called the box-house, used for stacking timber and cutting staves, where the master had been for the past two days doing things with binding twine and shaving poles as long as clothes-props. What he intended to use them for, she didn't know; and neither did Carl, who had said they were much too long for fencing. He had also cut yards and yards of binding twine into strips. In a way, it was frightening. She did not enter the place, but stretched her arms across the opening to grasp the stanchions and leaned forward, crying at him, "She's come round, master! She's come round!"

Almost before she had time to move aside he had rushed past her and was in the house and up the stairs.

When he thrust open the bedroom door and saw his beloved child looking towards him, he hurried to her; then stood aghast when her mouth widened as if she were about to scream; then shrank back from him, her hands spread wide against her shoulders as if pushing him away. And at this, Jessie cried, "It's Daddy! Angela. It's Daddy!" And she stepped aside so that he could come further up the bedside.

Bending over her, he said softly, "It's me, my love . . . Daddy."

When he took hold of her hand, she tried to withdraw it; which elicited from him the plea, "Look at me, dear. See? It's your daddy, who loves you. Angela, look at me."

Her eyes were now tightly closed, and as if in despair he turned to look at Jessie, and she said, "It's all right, Daddy. It's as the doctor said, she's still in shock. She'll know you shortly."

He straightened up and turned slowly from the bed, and he whimpered, "Oh, my God." He had seen a look of horror in her eyes because she was looking at a man. What if she didn't recover? The thought was so unbearable that he turned quickly again and, taking hold of Jessie's hand, pulled her towards the door, and there, bending down to her, he whispered, "Keep telling her, will you, Jessie? Keep telling her that I'm her daddy, I'm not the —" He jerked his head to one side, breaking off what he was about to say.

And she, holding his hand in both of hers, pressed it tightly as she said, "It's all right, Daddy. It's all right. I'll make her understand. Don't worry. Please don't worry."

He nodded at her, and said, "Yes, you do that, Jessie. You do that."

"I will, Daddy; so please, don't worry. Try not to."

The fact that he did not withdraw his hand from hers, that she was the one who let it go, caused her to experience a feeling of warmth. For the first time in her life she felt needed, and by the one who mattered most to her. But oh, if only it hadn't happened this way. Her hand went to the front of her dress and gathered the material into a bunch as if she were once again being exposed and that not one, but two, three men were tearing at her. Last night she had woken up screaming, and Patsy who had been sitting with Angela had hurried into her room and comforted her. Patsy was like a mother to her. What would happen to her when she left? She didn't mind any more her having Carl because what she really wanted now was a mother to comfort her. As Angela did. Oh yes, Angela needed a comforter.

She went hurriedly to the bed now, and bending over her sister, she said softly, "It's me, dear. It's me. Open your eyes." And obediently Angela raised her lids and her mouth opened again as if she wanted to speak. But no sound came; and Jessie said, "It's all right, dear. Don't try to speak yet. But that was Daddy. And Daddy loves you. You know Daddy loves you. He is not one of those wicked men. Try to understand, darling. Do try to understand he is not one of those wicked men. And don't close your eyes again. Look at me."

When Angela's eyes opened wide again, Jessie went on talking to her: "You know what I was thinking, dear? That when you are better I am going to ask Daddy to take us on a holiday to the seaside. You would like that, wouldn't you? We have never been on a holiday, have we?"

When the head on the pillow was slowly turned to the side and towards her, she reached out and pulled her chair closer to the bed and in such a position that she herself could lay her head on the pillow and in much the same position as they had done since they were children, except for the times when one or the other would flounce about after some petty upset.

However, now Jessie knew that never again would there be petty upsets between them; nor ever again would she be jealous of her sister's beauty or of her father's love for her. Life had changed for them both, for good and all.

FOUR

*P*hilip Patten called every day. When, by Thursday, Angela still had made no effort to speak, and when Ward asked tersely, "How long do you think this will go on?" he was given the blunt answer: "It could go on for ever, as long as she lives, as could her fear of men. Such cases have been known. She's afraid of me, and of you; but I don't know how you are going to break that down. You'll have to be very, very gentle with her. That's all I can say. But of one thing I must warn you with regard to the future, unless something untoward happens, enough to overcome her present condition, and I really can't see that coming about, well, in that case, there is little hope of her leading a normal life. But"—he let out a long slow breath—"you never know; we are not masters of our destinies. God, if you believe in Him, seems to take a hand now and again."

"*Be quiet! man.* What are you saying?" Ward's words were not tersely spoken now, they were growled out.

Philip did not come back with any sharp retort, but in softly spoken words, he said, "Yes, I'll be quiet, for I know so little; my training has left great gaps; I can only follow my books and common sense. And so, at times, you have to leave it to the Deity. That's all one can do. Well, I'll be off now; but"—he hesitated—"before I go I will dare to say one more thing to you. It's a piece of advice: I think you must remember you have two daughters, and that Jessie, too, is in a state of shock. I think she's coping admirably, but only because of the potions she is taking."

Without further words, he turned towards the stairs, leaving Ward to stand looking after him, his teeth gripping his lower lip; then he turned to glance towards the bedroom door: leave the rest to the Deity, he had said. Well, some things had been in the hands of the Deity too long; from now on he would play God, and see what came of that.

On this thought Ward hurried down the stairs. He did not, however, pass through the kitchen, where he would no doubt have to re-encounter the doctor, who would assuredly have been plied with a hot drink; instead, he opened the glass door that led into a small flower garden; then skirted the back of the house and made for the grain store where, just a short while ago, he had seen Mike Riley enter, two large scoops in his hand. He knew from experience that, being on his own, Mike would take his time to fill them; and he wouldn't be surprised to find him sitting at rest among the sacks.

In this case he was wrong, for Mike was about to emerge from the store weighed down with the two large heavy scoops. On seeing Ward, he put them down on the ground, saying, "You looking for me, master?"

"Yes, Mike, I was looking for you." And he pointed to the two skips, saying, "Pull them to one side, I want to shut the door."

Mike did as he was bidden and in the dim light afforded by one narrow window he watched his master close the door, then walk between the racks of the narrow room, before seating himself on a box a little distance from the window. As he followed Ward he had to wonder at such unusual behaviour, but he was indeed surprised at the question now put to him: "Can I trust you, Mike Riley?"

Mike's eyes narrowed, and his big, broad face screwed up for a moment before he said, "If you were to ask me, master, what I think of that question, I would say it was unnecessary, for you should know if you could trust me or not. I've nivvor taken a grain of corn from this place, although I have chickens of me own. I've nivvor asked Pattie for a bit of butter or cheese . . ."

Shaking his head impatiently, Ward said, "I'm not meaning that kind of trust, Mike; I'm meaning, would you stand by me in trouble?"

"Trouble! Oh aye, aye if you're in trouble, master, I'm your man. Aye, I'm with you there." The tall middle-aged Irishman now nodded as he repeated, "Trouble? You'll have no better beside you, if it's trouble you're in, than meself."

"That's good enough for me. What about Rob?"

"Well now, Rob's from me own bone an' breed, an' being as big as meself, an' only half me age, he'd be on the other side of you."

"How many Irish families are there in the Hollow?"

"Seven of us. But that's not the lot of 'em down there. Counting them of a different colour, bein' Protestants, there'd be sixteen families all told."

"Are there any among your lot . . . I mean the Catholics, that I could rely on as much as I can on you . . . I mean, who wouldn't shirk me in a tight corner or in taking a risk?"

"Oh, well now, there's Tim Regan an' Johnnie Mullins; there's a pair of them that I'd bet me life on. An' there's another; but he's a Scot, an' not of our colour; but he's a grand fella. That's Hamish McNabb. He's a great talker, a bit of an agitator, I'd say, but there's nothing wrong in that."

"Which one of the lot has been along the line for break-in and entry?"

"Oh . . ." Mike now tossed his head slightly as if throwing off any aspersion on his friend as he said, "Oh, that was Johnnie, master, but it was some long time ago . . . five years or more, an' he's nivvor had to look a polis in the eye since."

"Do you think he could still pick a lock?"

Mike's face stretched, his eyes widened, and he said, "You want somebody to pick a lock, master?"

"It's one of the things I want."

"Oh well, now. Well, now"—Mike's face spread into a beam—"Johnnie's the boy for you. He could pick the teeth out of your head, an' you wouldn't know they'd gone. He makes locks, you know; a sort of pastime. He makes 'em out of any old bits of iron and tin. An' keys. Give him a bit of wire and a file an' the Bank of England would be open to you. But"—and the smile went from his face now—"he looks after his family, he does. And he's a hard worker, he is, when he can get it. You've had him around here, master, when you've needed more in the fields, an' he's not like some that only go when they're pushed."

Ward passed over this comment, and what he said now was, "You have a gun?"

Again Mike's expression changed; but this time he didn't speak, and Ward said, "It's all right. It's all right, I know you're not licensed; but you shoot, don't you?"

"A rabbit now an' then. Not so much lately; it was when things were tough."

"But you can still shoot?" The words came out with force now.

"Oh aye . . . yes, master, I can still shoot."

"And straight?"

"Aye, master, an' straight."

"What about Rob?"

"Oh, Rob. He could shoot the pom-pom off a Scot's glengarry an' the fella wouldn't know it was gone. Oh, Rob's a . . ." He stopped, knowing he had said too much; but then he added offhandedly, "Well, I put him in the way of it from he was a lad. An' it was only rabbits or rooks and crows; an' the Colonel's keeper turned a blind eye 'cos he was glad to get rid of the vermin. You see, they haven't got the staff up there to see to things as they used to . . ."

Ward's upraised hand stopped the flow; and now he put a hand to his brow and squeezed his temples tightly for a moment before saying, "The main thing about this business, Mike, is a closed mouth. Can you count on your friends keeping their mouths shut for forty-eight hours?"

"Aye, master; I'll stand for them. It all depends upon how many you want; but however many, they'll go along with what I say."

"Besides yourself and Rob I'll want another two, perhaps three. How many guns are there in the Hollow altogether?"

Mike looked a little sheepish now as he said, "Well, Rob's got one, but it's an old shot-gun. The pellets fly all over the place. But when he uses mine his aim's as straight as a die. There's only the two; but now an' again I lend Tim mine 'cos he's like family. As for Johnnie Mullins, well, he seems to manage without guns. He doesn't need suchlike implements, he says. 'Tis the locks that . . ." he was stopped again, this time by the look on Ward's face; and now Ward said, "Listen to me carefully. Bring the men you choose here to me tomorrow night round eight o'clock, and I will tell them what's required of them; at least, some part of it. But now bear this in mind, Mike: if one of them opens his mouth that they've been here, or even gives a hint that something's afoot, there'll be nothing afoot, and what is more neither you nor Rob will put a foot in this place again. D'you get my meaning?"

"I do that, master. Yes, I do that. An' let me tell you as man to man, so to speak, you have no need to tell me to keep me mouth shut." He did not add, "Nor that of my son," for what he had done to his son on Tuesday after he found he had opened his mouth about the happenings to the lasses would be nothing to what would happen to him if he dared to let his tongue pass between his teeth about this new business, whatever it was.

Ward rose from the box, saying, "One last thing: don't mention any of this to Carl"; and in some surprise, Mike said, "He's not in on it? Carl?"

"No; he's not in on it."

Mike thought it best at this point not to ask why; he simply followed his master to the door and picked up the scoops and went about his work, his mind in a questioning whirl as to what the master was up to. Whatever it was it was some funny business that required guns, and somehow he felt shy of guns himself.

It was early evening on the Friday that Ward spoke to Patsy, who was now helping in the house. "Go and tell Carl to come to my study."

Although he knew that the house, in a way, was now depending on her services, for Jessie hardly ever left her sister, he could not bring himself to be civil to her, for he still saw her as the one who had frustrated his plans for the future, which concerned this house and the lives of those in it.

When for the second time within days Carl stood at the other side of the desk, he was not this time bidden to sit. Ward addressed him immediately, saying, "You haven't changed your mind?"

Looking pityingly at the man before him, Carl did not pause before he said, "In one way, sir"—there it was again, the sir instead of the master—"I am very much of the same mind. I mean to marry Patsy. After you dismissed me I made it my business to have a word with Parson Noble. He is putting our first banns up on Sunday. But having said that, sir, I must tell you that right from"—he paused a moment—"this terrible thing happened, we knew we couldn't leave you as long as you needed us: Patsy, too, is strong on this point and . . ."

Ward cut him off here saying, abruptly, "Later on this evening some men from the Hollow will be coming to see me. I am using them for something I have in mind, and you are not involved in it."

Carl's voice was stiff now when he said, "And may I ask why?"

"Yes, you may. And the answer is, I may return here after the event, or I may not be long at liberty . . . Whichever way it goes, I may not remain long at liberty. And in that case, I"—he wetted his lips now—"I would need you to carry on, as you always have done, and to see to my daughters until such time as I return." He looked down at his desk now, and asked himself on what counts would they be able to take him? And the answer was, on two. But there were extenuating circumstances, surely? Here, however, his line of thinking was sharply interrupted by Carl's action of leaning across the desk, his hands flat on it, and himself appealing to him. "Sir, for God's sake! don't do anything rash. I mean, anything that might have you put away. They need you. The two girls, they need you. And what's done's done: retribution is not going to help them."

"If you were in my place, would you let those men go free?"

Carl drew back slightly. His head was drooping now, and he thought, No. Oh no, for he, too, would have sought revenge.

Slowly he straightened up, then quietly he said, "Whatever happens I am with you for as long as you need me; and no matter how long or short you might be away, we"—he did not say "I," but "we will see to your house and land and family as long as it is necessary."

Ward did not say, "Thank you," but his head drooped and he looked down on his desk again; and on this, Carl went slowly from the room . . .

The men were assembled in the barn. Besides Mike Riley and Rob, there were Tim Regan, Johnnie Mullins, and the Scotsman, Hamish McNabb. Of them all, this last man stood out, for he was the tallest, standing about six feet, but of bony frame and with a long unsmiling face, whereas Tim Regan was of the same sturdy build as Mike and Rob; but the one who seemed not to belong to either the Irish or the Scots clan was the one called Johnnie Mullins. He was small and thin, but was wiry.

They had all risen to their feet when Ward entered the barn; and he now stood surveying them. All except Rob were middle-aged; but he knew from experience that at least four of them were strong; of the small thin one, he knew nothing.

Ward looked at him now, saying, "Your name?"

"Johnnie Mullins, sir."

He stared at the small man for a moment. Then he glanced towards Mike before addressing him again, saying, "Could you open a vestry door?"

Now Johnnie Mullins narrowed his gaze and peered along the line of men as if to say, That's a damn silly question, isn't it? Then looking straight up at Ward, he said, "I could that, sir, any time you like."

"You're sure?"

"Oh, I'm sure." The thin face was unsmiling now. "But to prove it to you, sir, I could take you back there this minute; in fact, I'll do it as we're passin' the church, and Mike there can give you the verdict in the mornin'."

Ward, now looking towards Tim Regan and the Scotsman, said, "You're both used to guns?"

Tim Regan looked slightly sheepish, but Hamish McNabb answered, "If I had the pleasure, sir, of havin' one in me hand, then I could use it. No man better. 'Twas in the Army I spent my early life; an' travelled I am. There's nothin' I wouldn't do, sir, to help a man in trouble."

He was about to go on when Ward put in, "Yes. Yes." He hadn't met up with this man before, but from the sound of his voice and volubility of his talk he was surprised he was still living in the Hollow. But then he recalled something: he hadn't actually met up with him personally, but he had seen him. Yes, he it was who had led a pit strike and was now likely blacklisted. He had been in the Army, and had come into the mines later in life and so did not possess the miners' inbred tenacity to put up with such unremitting toil. He said briefly, "You will have a gun. But there's one thing I would like to know first. There was a third man in the assault—" He wetted his lips before he added, "on my daughter. I don't know his name. The verger was one." And now he had difficulty in uttering the second name, "Pete Mason was the second. But I would like one of you to find out who accompanied these two when they reached the barn on . . . that particular night."

It was the Scot who spoke up again, and quickly. "Oh, I can name him for you, sir, right away. If he was with Will Smythe and the farmer Mason, then 'twas Smythe's relative. His name's Wilberforce. He lives on Walker's Bank, not five minutes from the inn. He left along with the others. I was there that night. Free drinks there were." He turned to look from one to the other now and smiled. "They were all very merry. I can say that for them. Not blind, nor mortallious, they could stand on their feet; but they were on their way to finish up the night at the barn dance. Oh, it was Wilberforce. There you have it, sir."

In the ensuing silence, the five men looked at Ward, who was staring down towards the straw-strewn floor; then they watched him put his hand to his inner pocket and bring out a four-folded piece of paper, and after looking round as if for some place on which to lay it, he went towards a broad standing beam that supported the roof; and here, unfolding the sheet, he said to Mike, "Bring the lantern." When he seemed satisfied with its position, he called to the others, "Come here!" Then to Rob, "Put your hands on the top and bottom of this sheet," and after Rob complied, he began his explanation: "This is a drawing of the screen in the church," he said. "I am giving you instructions what to do in order that I can fulfil my intentions, at least, in part. And this is what I wish you to do. But before going into detail I must ask you to be prepared to be here at six o'clock on Sunday morning, and everything done as quietly . . ." and he repeated, "as quietly as possible." He paused now, then said, "Who of you has a young son who could run an errand?"

It was Tim Regan who answered: "My youngest is ten. He's a good lad an' he's quick on his feet."

"Then I'll want him to run two errands. Don't tell him anything beforehand. Bring him with you on the morning. Now these are your positions." He indicated a position to each man in turn. "And this is what you must do."

As the men listened, their eyes, without exception, widened; and when the expression "Holy Mother of God!" escaped the lips of Tim Regan, Ward turned on him sharply, saying, "You're not getting cold feet?"

"No . . . No, no, no, sir. I've never had cold feet in me life."

"Well, you might all have when I tell you that if you're recognised you could be in trouble. *I'm* prepared for that; but as for you, I think you should cover your faces in some way."

"Oh, master." It was Mike now, laughing as he spoke. "We could cover our faces till the cows come home, but once we open our mouths they would know; if not us individually like, then from where we hail. The trouble you refer to, sir, means the polis; we could be run in?"

"Just that," said Ward briefly.

"Well, here's me; I'm for me plain face. I don't know about the rest." He looked from one to the other of his neighbours, and it was the Scot who said, "I've never covered up in the face of any foe, an' I'm not goin' to start now, sir. In for a penny, in for a pound. That's what I say."

"An' . . . an' so say I." Tim Regan was nodding now.

"Thank you. Well, in that case I will leave it in writing that should any of you be detained with me for a long or short time your families will be seen to."

"Well, you can't say any fairer than that. Englishman that you are, you can't say any fairer than that."

Ward turned a sharp glance on the Scot. He knew he was dealing here with a man who would neither bow his head nor touch his forelock to any master, and although he knew it stemmed from the same pride as was in himself, nevertheless, he didn't like it. He said now, "Anything more I want you to know I shall pass on through Mike."

He had actually stepped out of the barn and into the dimly lit yard when he turned back and, facing the men, who were now gathered in a bunch, he said, "As for yourselves, you will be well paid when this is over, whichever way it goes."

They replied in chorus, "Thank you. Thank you, sir."

Once in the house, Ward went straight upstairs and to his own bedroom, and there, taking a chair, he sat by the head of the bed and put his hand on the pillow where once her head had lain, and he spoke to her, as he did every day.

"Am I mad, Fanny?" he said. "Am I mad? What put this idea into my head?" And it was as though he did receive an answer from her, for he said, "Yes. Yes. The minute I saw her, I knew what I intended to do, but didn't know how to accomplish it. But now I know." He stared at his hand on the pillow for quite some time, and then he said, "You are not for it. I know . . . I know you are not for it, my love, as you are not for Carl going. What's done's done, you say, as he said too, but I am me, Fanny; I am still me. Even your soft tongue and guiding hand could not keep me from dealing out this retribution."

Again he waited; and then he said, "Well, Carl will be here; and he's going to marry that girl. And you understand that, too, don't you? You have always said she is for him; but I don't see it like that, my love. Anyway, come what may, he will look after the girls . . . What do you think will be the outcome, my love? Oh, don't fade away. Please don't fade away." He now leaned over and laid his face on the pillow. "And don't ask why I can't let you go. I've told you I thought I could, because Angela was you re-born; but now, you see what's happened: she shrinks from me. I can't stand the agony of it, Fanny. Fanny, don't go. Don't go."

When there was a tap on the door he sprang up, straightened his neckerchief, stroked his hair back, and said, "Yes?"

Jessie entered, saying, "The doctor has come. He's sorry he couldn't get here earlier."

"I'll be there in a minute." He made small movements with his hands as if waving her away. And he stood now staring towards the door before turning slowly again and looking at the bed and the dent in the pillow where his head had lain; and he asked himself again if he was mad, while appearing sane on the surface, and the answer he gave was: well, if he was he had been mad for some time, and he couldn't see himself returning to normality, because she was with him in this room. He knew she was. She was always waiting, because he willed her to be here. But at times he was made to wonder if it was the sane patches in his mind that made her cry out, "Let me go!"

Where was it going to end? In a like place as the mad bitch who had willed disaster on him? Yes, there was the word "willed." You could will things to happen. He had willed Fanny's spirit from the grave, and now he was willing infamy on the village. What he would make happen would cause that village to stink for generations to come. The pride of the hypocrites would be ground into the dust. As he saw it, in justice he owed it to himself.

FIVE

$\mathcal{A}$s soon as the first two members of the congregation, Mr. and Mrs. Napier from The Lodden, entered St. Stephen's on this Sunday morning, they not only sensed, they knew something was wrong. Miss Steel, the new assistant teacher at the village school, who had taken over as organist when John Silburn had given it up because of cramp in his hands, was not doing her weekly duty, and they knew that playing the organ was in her contract, for the school was under the patronage of the church. And then, what was the matter with the screen? Had something happened to it? The left hand side was completely covered over with what seemed to be a hayrick sheet held away from the top of the screen by poles, but kept in place at the bottom by three large stones.

But why? They hadn't heard that there was anything wrong with the screen. If some idiot had defaced it, it would soon have been made known around the village.

So too thought the rest of the congregation as they took their seats. And there were murmurs here and there as people leaned forward or back over the pew and whispered, "What do you think's happened to the screen? And there's no-one in the organ gallery, I notice."

The tolling of the bell seemed to be the only sign of normality in the church.

As was usual, the gentry were the last to file into their pews. There were six of the Hopkins' from Border Manor, an indication that they must have someone staying for the week-end. These days, there were only two of the Bedfords, for their daughter had gone over to the Methodists years ago.

Then there were the Arkwrights. They were comparative newcomers to the village, having been here only six years. They had moved into Whiteberg Farm; Mr. Arkwright was what was called a gentleman farmer. And lastly this morning, there were the Ramsmores.

The colonel, it was noted, really was getting doddery, and his son just managed to prevent him from falling as his foot caught the end of the pew.

After the bell stopped tolling there was an eerie silence in the church. At this point it was usual for the vicar, followed by his servers, to emerge from the vestry, the choir having already assembled in the gallery; but this morning there was no emergence, no swishing of surplices; the only procession being that of the Youngston family entering the church and being quickly ushered into a back pew, the mother and father admonishing, as usual, the four children to be quiet.

But then a series of very unusual events began to occur.

First: the church door was closed with a bang; and when heads turned towards it, they saw a strange man standing there grasping something by his side. Here and there, those near enough to him thought it to be a gun; but that was surely not the case.

Secondly: the congregation's attention was swung to the opening between the screens and to the two men who had appeared. One of these was certainly carrying a gun. This man walked down the steps and to the far side of the covered screen. *His* gun, however, wasn't being held by his side, but in a position that left no doubt as to what he meant to do with it.

The astonishment of the whole congregation had so far kept them silent, but now there was a concerted gasp as the first man made his way towards the pulpit, for even those at the back of the church, as well as those straining their necks to see beyond the pillars at the left side of the main aisle, immediately recognised him as being the farmer, Ward Gibson.

All through his young days and well into his twenties, Ward had watched Parson Tracey climb the steps of this pulpit, and now here he was, standing in it, gazing on the sea of faces and gaping mouths. All the week he had known what he was going to do, and at times he had wondered whether he would falter in his purpose; of how he might react when he was forced to speak of his daughter and of her ordeal. But now, he found he was possessed of a strange calmness, albeit a smouldering calmness, for he must go beyond telling them, he must drive home into the minds of these staring faces something they would never in their lives forget.

For a while he allowed his gaze to roam over them; then he spoke, and quietly. "Some of you may not know why I am standing in this pulpit, here in place of your hypocrite of a vicar. Well, I shall tell you. I am standing here because there are three men, all church-going, God-fearing citizens, who are so vile that they do not deserve to live.

"As you all know, I have two daughters, and I have tried to protect them since that mad woman, Daisy Mason, killed my wife; but although she was put away, the threat hanging over myself and the children did not abate. Your opinion, as a whole, was that I deserved all I had got because I dared to marry someone other than that mad bitch, to whom I had never offered marriage in the first place. The girl I married . . . the woman I married was superior in all ways to anyone I am looking on now. She was an intelligent, cultured woman. Yes, she was a dancer; but that was her career, as it had been that of her parents before her. They were artists, of which profession you, neither the high nor the low among you, would know anything."

He now passed his glance over the front rows as he went on, "It should happen that last Monday night I allowed my daughters to attend Parson Noble's lantern show. I had them escorted there, and my man was on his way to fetch them, but it being a bright moonlight night, they did not wait for him, they dared"—and now he leaned over the pulpit—"they dared to walk alone on the outskirts of this village. Do you hear me? They *dared* to walk alone. And the first time they walked alone they were confronted by three men." He drew himself up now and took in a deep breath before going on. "My daughter, Angela, a replica of her mother, but even smaller—" his voice now faltered a little as he said, "has just turned fifteen, and therefore had already reached her womanhood." Now he again bent over the pulpit, but further this time and, his head swinging from side to side, he allowed his gaze to rest on different women, and he repeated, "She had just come into her womanhood. Well . . . she was torn from her elder sister and dragged into a field while her sister was also being attacked and the clothes torn off her back. She, thankfully, managed to escape. *But what of my little Angela?* Many of you in fact, all of you, have seen her at some time or other. She is tiny, fragile, no semblance of a fifteen-year-old village girl about her. She was from another sphere, as was her mother." He stopped now, and there wasn't a murmur in the church, not a cough, nor a movement. And then, his voice became so loud, so high-pitched, almost a scream, so that many of the faces were screwed up against it as he cried, "She was raped by three men! Not one . . . not two, but *three!*" His head was now bowed and he was gripping each side of the pulpit. When he raised his head he wasn't a little surprised to hear women crying. But it did not touch him in the least; and he went on. "She was found by a young man who was so shocked at the sight of her that he said he will never forget it to his dying day. And this young man helped to carry her home." He now looked down to where Gerald, his face white, his lower lip drawn tight between his teeth, was staring at him. And he went on, "She did not open her eyes for two days, and from the moment she was laid on the bed until this very morning she has not spoken a word, and Doctor Patten can give me no hope that she will ever recover normality. What is more, she is terrified to death of the sight of a man . . . even of me"—he now thrust his finger into his chest—"I who love her as I did her mother daren't go near her."

Again bending forward, and in a rising voice he said, "But this is not the end, is it, ladies? This is not the end. We will not know for two, or perhaps three months, will we, what her body holds, if anything but the feeling of torture."

A man now stood up and cried at him, "Enough! Enough!" then looked down on his wife who was bent double: and Ward answered him, "No, not yet," and when after a moment he added, "I have only just begun," an actual shiver passed through all those present.

He now took one step back as if he were about to leave the pulpit, but then stopped and said, "I would advise you, every one of you, not to make any move at all," and he pointed now to the man at the church door, then to the one standing by the screen. And then he did turn and descend the steps of the pulpit.

Having walked across the front of the screens, he knocked on the vestry door, all eyes having followed him. When it opened and there stepped out another man with a gun and, following him and almost tottering on his feet, there came Parson Tracey, the whole congregation gasped when it could be seen that his hands were bound behind his back and that he was gagged. Behind him came four servers. They were all young boys, and they cast pleading glances towards their parents in the congregation, bringing forth cries of, "Oh! Oh!" from here and there. Then followed seven members of the choir, and the lady organist.

The men looked sheepish, but it was noted that she held herself straight and looked defiant. Lastly came the bell-ringer. He was an oldish man and he was actually smiling as if he considered the whole thing a joke; that was until a few minutes later, after they had been lined up along the steps at the foot of the uncovered right-hand side of the screen when, as did everyone else, he watched two of the men go behind the screen.

It soon became evident that they had loosened something, for the great heavy sheet began to slip, together with the poles that had prevented it from hanging straight down and close to the front of the screen. The men quickly reappeared and were just in time to gather up the sheet and the poles as they fell. These they laid aside in a tumbled heap . . .

What was revealed now caused, first of all, a horrified, blank, utter silence, then a great combined gasp, followed by cries of loud protest; and here and there a moan. Some women actually collapsed in their seats or on to the floor, *for there,* strapped to the screen by their ankles, their arms, waists and their necks, and their mouths gagged, were three naked men. Their heads could not hang in shame, so tight were they held against the ornamental ironwork, but their eyes roamed, wild with fear.

Great shouts and cries now came from different parts of the church, some calling on God, others, mostly from men, shouting that enough was enough. But when the latter cries came to Ward's ears he yelled back at them, "Not yet! Not quite," and with this he leapt up the steps and put his hand behind the screen, and when he brought it forth he was holding a splay tailed whip, and on the sight of which a great roar came from the colonel. But when he stepped into the aisle with the intention of making for Ward, Mike Riley's voice rose into a shout above the mêlée, crying, "Stay where you are!" He too had stepped forward, with his gun at shoulder level; and fixing his gaze on the colonel, he said, "Another step, Colonel, an' I'll splatter your knees with so many pellets you'll be pickin' 'em out for months."

Whether or not he was deterred by this, or by Lady Lydia preventing his further movement by putting her arms around him and pulling his wavering body back into the pew, it did not prevent him from yelling at Ward, "You'll pay for this, my man! I'll see to that."

"No doubt. No doubt, Colonel. As I always have done, I'll pay for this but I'll do it gladly."

He now motioned towards Mike, indicating he should step back; then he went and stood before the verger; and he looked into the man's fear-filled and cringing face for a number of seconds before he brought the whip viciously twice across the bloated loins, and the fat repulsive-looking body jerked within its tight bounds, and the screen seemed to shudder.

Seemingly taking no heed of the cries of the women and screaming children, he now stood in front of Pete Mason, and his gaze remained longer on the hate-filled eyes before he meted out the medicine again, with three lashes this time.

He did not hesitate when he came to the third man, for this one had offered no fight when he was trapped: he was a cringing individual, trying to put the blame on the other two; and so he did what he had to do. Then he walked to the opening in the screen again, before turning and looking at the congregation, some crying, some shouting, others just standing utterly mute. He went now to where a man and woman were undoing the vicar's bonds. They had taken the gag from his mouth, and he was gasping for breath as Ward addressed him, saying, "It's all in your hands now, Vicar. When the police come they know where to find me; so we'll take it from there, shall we?"

The vicar's response was to cry out: "You'll . . . you'll pay for this day, Ward Gibson. God . . . God's house will not be mocked."

Ward's reaction to this was to motion to the man standing at the back of the church, and to the one who was still holding the gun at the ready. Two other men then emerged from behind the screen and rolled up the sheet that had covered it. And then they all followed Ward into the vestry.

When the door had banged closed behind the men the hubbub in the church died away for a moment, but there was no immediate rush to release the men from the screen. But then, as if of one mind, a number of men rushed forward, some to stand in front of the trussed figures in order to hide their nakedness, while others went behind the screen and endeavoured to undo the knots of the ropes binding the men firmly to the framework.

When a lone voice cried, "They'd better have a doctor," another drowned it by screaming, "It's the polis we want, and now, for it's no use trying to explain what has happened; they'll want to see it for themselves. I'll ride in this minute."

"No. No."

It was the vicar now, clinging to the lectern for support, and he repeated loudly now, "*No! No! I say*. Listen . . . listen, all of you. *That is what he wants.* Don't you see? He wants the polis brought here. He wants this to be taken to court and blazoned in every paper in the country, because he's out to defame this village. Don't you see? Don't you see?" His arms stretched wide, he was swinging his body from one side to the other in an endeavour to influence them all.

It had its effect, for, apart from the continued moaning of some women and the crying of children, the commotion died down, and the vicar again shouted his warning: "If this is blazoned in the papers, this village will never again be able to lift up its head; but what will happen? It will become notorious: people will even come from a distance to see the screen that has been defiled by these men, who themselves have defiled nature. God forgive them, because I never can. My . . . your church, God's house, will become a peep-show. I can see it all as clearly as if it is happening now. This place would attract young hooligans from the city because a maniac of a man has taken justice into his own hands and tied three naked men on a holy screen before scourging them. *Can't you see? Can't you see the headlines?"* He paused again; then, dropping his arms and joining his hands together, he pressed them outwards, beseeching his congregation now, "Let us suffer this together. Let us not even discuss it among ourselves. The three men who have committed this outrage will suffer from it for the rest of their lives; they will be ostracised by all good folk." And now his voice rose as he ended, "As will the perpetrator who has dared to commit sacrilege in the house of God this day. That man has been a bane on this village for years, and has wrought havoc on a good-living family; he has been the means of incarcerating one of that household, and through sorrow causing the early death of the mother. Ward Gibson is an evil man and . . ."

Suddenly, not only the minister was now startled but also the occupants of the first rows of the select pews, as young Gerald Ramsmore almost sprang into the aisle and, facing the parson, cried, "He is not an evil man; he is a man who has been wronged. Your narrow-mindedness, sir, has helped to turn the villagers against him. Yes, you're afraid of bringing in the police because it would show up your hypocrisy and that of many more who attend this church. And why do they attend? Let me tell you: not for the love of God, but for the fear of where you might place them in the so-called society of this community."

A voice suddenly barked, "Be quiet! Hold your tongue, sir! I order you. Come here this minute!"

Gerald Ramsmore turned and looked at his father's florid face, and to him he said, "I am going to speak my mind. Remember, Father, I was the one who came across that child after she had been savaged by those three evil individuals." He pointed towards the men now being led into the vestry, and then flinging wide an arm, went on, "If anyone here had seen the state they left her in, they would never . . . as I shall never forget the sight till the day I die."

He looked at his father again and cried, "I'll tell you this, sir: I only wish I had been asked to take a hand in what has transpired this morning. Yes, right up to the use of the whip."

Gerald was drawn now to look at his mother, whose eyes and voice were beseeching him; her arms were about his father, steadying him, and for a moment he lowered his head. He knew he had gone too far: his father was an old man. But anyway, he had said what in justice had to be said; and now, bringing up his head again, he marched past his people and up the aisle and out of the church, leaving behind him another kind of amazement.

Those of the congregation who were now moving out of the pews, many women being helped by their menfolk, turned once more as the vicar addressed them.

In a shaken voice, he said, "There is confirmation of my words for you: evil has the power to bring discord into the best of families. And you know from where this particular evil springs."

SIX

"How could you do such a thing, Gerald! And to your father. And in front of the whole village—to defy him like that! Oh, I know, I know that poor man has had a lot to put up with; and now his poor little girl. And those men deserved to be punished. Oh, yes. Oh, yes. And I would have gone along with him, all the way, no matter what your father said; but I would have had the sense to keep it to myself. What came over you?"

Gerald looked at this woman whom he loved, she whom he could never understand having married his father. What on earth had she seen in this stiff-necked, narrow, ageing, opinionated man who thought that the Army was the beginning and the middle and the end of life. Although they had been married for twenty years, he couldn't imagine he had ever been much different from what he was now.

He said gently, "I'm sorry if I upset him so much, but it had to be said. Mr. Gibson is a good man—you yourself have always said so—also that he had been misjudged from the time he married his pretty little wife."

"Oh yes, I know . . . I know." She flapped her hands at him. "Personally, I like the man, but you cannot get away from the fact that it was because he married that pretty little wife, and having rejected a young woman with whom he had been friendly for years; and really, the truth is he must have deceived not only her but her parents into thinking his attentions were other than serious, and that was very wrong of him, and consequently he has wrought havoc in the Mason household. And now, Gerald, whether you want to believe it or not, he is causing havoc in this house. And your career is at stake now, for your father says he will no longer support you at Oxford, and you must know, in any case, he has found this difficult, for our finances are stretched to the very limit. He has already had to sell a cottage and another stretch of land in order to meet your expenses. Just think, too, how I have had to cut down on the household, and in the yard also."

She turned from him now, saying tearfully, "It was inexcusable of you, Gerald, inexcusable." And with this, she turned from him and hurried out of the breakfast-room, along the corridor and into the small drawing-room. And after closing the door, she stood just within the room and put her hands over her face.

Her whole body was shivering, not only from the coldness of the room, but also with anxiety and fear of what was now going to happen to her son, for she knew that unless he went into the Army his father would wash his hands of him. And she also knew in her heart that there was no threat strong enough to drive her son into the Army.

She now walked further into the room and sat on the edge of a chair, asking herself just what was the matter with her son? her beloved son, her only son, her only child. Why was he so different?

She would never forget the night, which was the forerunner of what had happened in the church today. She had left her husband in the billiard-room. She liked a game of billiards; but having been brought up in the diplomatic world, she knew it was policy to give way to the other side more often than one would normally do, and she did this often when playing her husband at billiards, for now neither his hand nor his eye were as steady as they once were. She had found out very early in their married life that he *had* to win in most everything he undertook: if battles were lost it must never be his fault; and that evening she had left him happy again as he knocked the balls here and there on the table, and as she entered the hall she had said to Roberts, "Has Mr. Gerald come in yet?" And he, looking up the broad staircase, had answered, "Yes, madam. Just a few minutes ago. And—" he paused before adding, "he seemed in some distress, madam."

At this she had hurried up the stairs and, after knocking on his door and receiving no reply, she had pushed it gently open, there to see her son sprawled across the bed, his shoulders heaving.

She had hurried to him, saying, "What is it, Gerald?"

When she placed her hands on him and he did not turn to her, she couldn't believe, for she did not want to believe, that her son was crying, actually crying. And it shocked her, and in that moment she thanked God that his father was not present.

She had been brought up in a family of four brothers and three sisters. Now and again the sisters would cry, as Ann had when she received news of her young husband having been killed in battle; but when her brother Harry had lost the girl he was going to marry just two days before the wedding when her horse had rolled on her, he had remained dry-eyed, even at her burial. Men didn't cry. No; men didn't cry. *No, men . . . did . . . not . . . cry.*

Her voice had been curt as she pulled him around, saying, "What on earth's the matter with you, Gerald? What has happened? Why are you in this state, crying like . . ." She did not add, "a girl?" nor "a woman?" because he had now swung himself around to the edge of the bed and, his head bowed, he had taken a handkerchief from his pocket and dried his eyes before looking up at her and saying, "I am crying, Mama and, as you were going to add, like a woman, because tonight I have witnessed something that will be imprinted on my mind for ever: I have looked on the ravished limbs of Mr. Gibson's young daughter, the small one who was the image of her mother, after she had been raped, Mama. *Raped, Mama, raped,* and by three men! Yes, apparently, three men. I don't imagine just one could have wreaked the havoc on her body as I saw it. She was unconscious when I found her; but at what stage her mind closed up will never be known. The elder sister, too, had the clothes torn from her breasts. When she came running to me she was like a mad thing; she had just escaped from one of the fiends. I had seen both girls just a few minutes earlier. It was a moonlight night, so they wouldn't accept my company because Carl was to meet them."

He had then leant forward and gripped her arm and, his voice choking, he had said, "You know how I hate shooting, shooting anything, but I have longed to go after those men, at least the two that Miss Jessie recognised, and blast them to hell."

When she had muttered, "Oh, Gerald, Gerald . . . How awful!" she didn't know whether her horror was against the crime that had been committed on the girl, or the fact that her son had been so affected by it that he would actually have done what he said, or because he was crying his eyes out.

And then she had been further shocked a few minutes ago when he had said, "I have waited all the week wondering why her father was making no move; but the retribution he must have been planning was more effective than anything I could have thought up. And I was elated. Do you hear, Mama? I was elated by the outcome of his plan and, as I made clear, my only regret was that I couldn't join him in the infliction of the punishment he was dealing out."

It was from that first painful scene that she knew she had, in some way, lost her son, for the man that had been born in him that night was of a stronger and more determined nature than any military training could have achieved.

Yet he had cried. She would never be able to forget that he had cried; and in such an abandoned way.

SEVEN

*T*hey waited for the coming of the police, those in the farmhouse and those in the Hollow. And when by Monday evening neither a police constable nor a reporter acting on rumours had made his appearance, Annie said to Carl, "It couldn't be they are going to let such a thing as this drop; you know, besides the flailing they could be had up for levelling guns.

"And then there were the fights they'd had afore they could get them stripped. They say it was Pete Mason who left his bootmarks on Johnnie Mullins. His shin was split. But both he and the Wilberforce fellow must have been scared in the first place when they assumed that the notes were from the verger; as Mike said, they came skittering into the vestry like rabbits. But whereas Mason put up a fight, the other one was as cringing as a beggar. Well, they got their deserts. The only thing I'm sorry about is I wasn't there to see it."

Raising his eyes to look up at the ceiling, Carl said, "Patsy says there's no improvement whatsoever," and to this Annie replied, "And if you ask me, there never will be; she's gone far away into another self, and it's filled with terror. One thing I do know, if her fear of a man doesn't soften a little, himself will wither away inside. You mark my words. And God knows, there might be still more torment for him to come. But this we won't know for a time, will we?" She looked at Carl, who was sitting at the end of the table, and she added, "There's one good thing has come out of all this: he can't do without you; in fact, he can't do without you both, for Miss Jessie must have somebody to relieve her or shortly she herself will end up in bed. But 'tis odd"—Annie nodded her head now and repeated, " 'Tis odd, really it is, for that young lass has come into her own with this business, an' there's no gettin' away from the fact that himself, though he be her father, didn't even seem to notice she was there. It was Angela, Angela, all the time; but of course, being so much like her mother, you could understand that. Still, now that he's got no solace in that direction, he's havin' to look at his first-born. Although he's seeing her without any real feelin' for her, he will, nevertheless for the future, I should imagine, have to rely on her."

Annie now turned to the stove, her voice trailing away as she said, "Funny that. And all she ever wanted from him was a kind word, a loving word, which she never got."

It was on the following day that Fred paid a tentative visit to the farm. Their boyhood friendship and that of their early youth had been strained somewhat over the last few years as Ward had grown more and more into himself. But now he was knocking on the kitchen door, and when Patsy opened it, he said, "Hello there," and she answered simply, "Hello," and looked back to where Annie was at the table cutting raw meat away from a bone, and she said, "It's Mr. Newberry," and Annie called, "Come away in, Fred. Come away in." And then she added, " 'Tis some time since we've seen you."

"Aye, Annie, aye. Business has been brisk. How are you?"

"Fine, Fred, fine; at least down to me waist, the rest of me is rotten."

He grinned at her; then straight-faced again, he said, "Me mother . . . I mean, we all were upset about the latest business, Annie. And poor little Angela . . . Is he about?" And to this she answered, "No. He's along the corridor, in his office, where he seems to spend more than half his days. He's in a state. You can understand."

"Oh aye. Oh aye. D'you think I should pop along and have a word?"

"Yes, I would do that, Fred; an' I'll have a drink ready for you when you come back."

"Ta, Annie. Thanks." He walked around her cautiously as if he were unused to being in this kitchen, and he smiled at Patsy before going out.

When he tapped on the study door, there was no answering voice calling, "Come in," but the door was pulled open, and Ward stood there, looking surprised for a moment, and when Fred said, "I thought I would just pop in, Ward. Hope you don't . . . you don't mind," Ward stood aside, saying, "No; come in, Fred." And after Fred had passed him, he closed the door, then pointed to a seat, before again seating himself behind his desk. "I suppose you're surprised at finding me here?" he said gruffly.

"No; no, man, no. I'd have been surprised if I hadn't found you here. That would have meant that all had gone against him."

"Gone against him! What d'you mean, gone against him? Who do you mean? What are you talking about?"

"Well . . . well, you know, Sunday. Me meself, I've never set foot in the church for years. You know that. But it seems some of them wanted to get the authorities straightaway. It was then the young master from the Hall jumped up and what he didn't say wasn't worth listenin' to, so they tell me. And the old man, the Colonel, yelled at him, an' he yelled back. He said he'd stand up in court and tell . . . well"—Fred now lowered his eyes—"just how he came across poor, dear Angela . . ." Then looking directly at Ward again, he went on, "That seemed to put the seal on it. Anyway, they have all taken heed of what Tracey said, that the village would attract hordes of all kinds, so they had to keep their mouths shut." He now leant forward towards Ward, adding in a low voice, "And I know this: almost everybody in the county would have been with you."

Ward made no comment, and there followed a silence for a few moments, before Fred, his tone changing, said, "Charlie and his lads were a bit peeved, you know, Ward, that you hadn't let him and us in on it. He said he would have liked nothin' better than puttin' some iron into his fire an' shaping body-belts for the three of 'em; and similar things have been said in the village here and there. You won't believe it, Ward; you never would; but there's a lot over there that are for you. Always have been. And they've always objected to old Tracey making out that the village was his. And you know somethin' else, Ward?" Fred's voice dropped a tone: "Yesterday, me dad had me drive over two big baskets of stuff to the Hollow, and it wasn't all week-end stuff, stale. No; some was freshly baked yesterday morning. But it was just to show that if they went along the line their womenfolk would be seen to."

Ward lay back in his chair and looked at this kindly simple man, this innately shy man, one who was never likely to marry and so experience the heights and the depths of such a state, but who could only find his happiness through supporting and being supported by his close friends. And at this moment he felt a tinge of guilt at never having appreciated Fred; in fact, he had despised him for his simplicity. But now he said quietly, "Thank you. Thank your dad and your mother, too. Tell them . . . that I appreciate what they did, and their support." And he added, "And yours, too, Fred. Yes, and yours."

"Oh"—Fred's head now wagged from one side to the other—" 'Tis nothin', man. 'Tis nothin'; we just want you to know we're with you, always have been. And my mum told me to say if there's anythin' she can do, you know where she is. Night or day. An' she says she could put her hand out to half a dozen others who would say the same. Women are handy at these times, you know, Ward."

It was too much. Ward could stand no more at the moment, not of this kind of emotion, such sympathy tore at him.

He now rose so quickly to his feet, saying, "Have you had a drink?" that Fred almost fell backwards with his chair as Ward passed him, and he laughed as he stumbled and said, "You'd think I'd had one of the hard stuff already, wouldn't you? But Annie said she would have a drink ready for me."

"Good. Anyway, thanks for coming, Fred. And, as I said, thank your dad and mother, and—" He nipped on his lip before he could add, "Charlie and the rest."

"I will. I will, Ward. I'll tell them."

In the hall, Ward placed a hand on Fred's shoulder and gave him a gentle thrust towards the kitchen, saying, "I'll be seeing you."

"Aye, Ward, aye. So long then."

Ward stood for a moment watching this friend making his way to the kitchen. Then he hurried up the stairs to his daughter's bedroom. But after entering the room, he stood looking towards where his beautiful little Angela was sitting propped up in a chair to the side of the bed, her eyes wide and staring. To her side sat Jessie, the book she had been reading aloud from now lying on her lap, and she turned to look at her father and said one word that was hardly above a whisper: "Slowly."

And he obeyed. Walking almost on tiptoe, he crept towards the chair. And he looked at his daughter, and she looked at him; but this time she did not shrink back into her pillows. And Jessie now smiled at him and nodded her head, and he nodded back at her, and when she made a small flicking motion with her hand he stepped back from the bed and walked softly towards the door again.

When it had closed on him, Jessie, leaning towards the still figure, said, "That was Daddy, dear. He came to see how you are. Do you understand?"

The face was turned towards her; the lips opened slightly but no sound came from them, and Jessie said, "You're not afraid of Daddy; he loves you very dearly. Never, never be afraid of Daddy. You see, I'm not afraid of him."

It seemed that the slight chest heaved as if a long breath were being drawn into it; and Jessie said, "You liked this story, didn't you? It's about the little match-girl. At one time it used to make you cry, didn't it?"

As Jessie now lifted the book to begin reading again, she thought, Oh, if only it could make her cry again. But they were making progress. Oh, yes; they were making progress because she no longer shrank into her pillows when their daddy came into the room. His next step must be to sit at the very foot of the bed. A thought now crossed her mind, which was startling: she was giving her father orders, and he was obeying them. It was like being imbued with a strange power, and she recognised that it was this feeling that was keeping her going and enabling her to see to her sister, for at times she felt strangely ill: her nightmares were not abating, and whenever she fastened her bodice she could feel that man's hands on her.

But her father had avenged her, avenged them both; Angela more so, of

course. Oh yes, Angela especially. If it had happened to her alone, would he
have gone to such lengths as she had heard had transpired in the church on
the Sunday morning, when naked men were strung on to the screen and
lashed? When her mind aimed to conceive the picture of its happening she
brought the book nearer her face and began to read, her voice over-loud as if
to drown her thoughts.

EIGHT

*I*t was six weeks later when Angela indicated that she was about to
be sick. Patsy happened to be sitting with her at the time. She had, by now,
persuaded the young girl to sit in a chair by the window. There were two
windows in the bedroom, one overlooking the yard; the other, at the back of
the house, had a view of the garden.

It was to the latter that they would lead her, Jessie and Patsy between
them, as if the small slight girl were an old, enfeebled woman.

The routine repeated itself day after day. First, they would wash her, then
place the breakfast before her, which by this time she would manage to eat, at
least in part, although never quite finishing it. They would then wrap her in a
warm dressing-gown and sit her before the window. She was, however, never
left on her own. And this was tiring for the two girls, although Annie, when
her swollen limbs would allow her to climb the stairs, would occasionally give
them relief.

Patsy no longer had time for the yard work, and so another dairymaid
had been engaged by Carl. She came from Fellburn on the carrier's cart,
arriving at nine in the morning, leaving at six in the evening. It was soon
apparent that she knew her work well; and this lessened any objection Ward
might have felt, for the dairy produce supplied a good portion of the profits.

But this morning the daily routine was to be altered, for Angela, for the
first time, was sick.

When Patsy saw this, she did not exclaim as Annie might have done,
"God in heaven!" or call on the deity in any way, for her feelings were too
deep, in fact, too frozen with the horror that this sign portended.

The effect on Jessie, however, was different: she exclaimed loudly, "Oh
no! No! Please, Angela, no! No!" Then she turned to Patsy beseeching her

now to deny what she was saying, "Is this a sign? It is said that . . . Oh Patsy! Patsy!"

"Hush! Hush! What will be, will be, miss. Yet she ate more than usual last night; and fish has a tendency that way."

"Oh please! Please say it is the fish."

"I can't, miss, not yet; we'll have to wait a day or two to see if it is repeated."

"But Daddy . . ."

"Say nothing to the master, miss, nothing at all. Do you hear? For we don't know, not for sure." Yet in her heart she *was* sure; but she could only hope that the child would be born dead . . .

Two weeks later Ward learned that his daughter was carrying a child, but it was days before he reached a state of acceptance such that he could sit opposite his beloved daughter as she gazed out of the window, for straight-away he had again felt the urge to take drastic action. In any case, he could have done nothing more to the perpetrators of this evil, for they all had left the village; even Pete Mason, so he understood. The desire for vengeance was however more than ever terrible for it was becoming centred on his own child. For two nights running, while pacing his room, sleep being beyond him, he had thought she would be better off dead than bringing into the world a being bred of one or other of those beasts. Which of them was responsible would never be known. What lay ahead for the offspring? How would it face life when the knowledge of its creation was one day thrown at it, as undoubtedly it would be, either through tormentors or someone deciding it was time the creature should know why it was isolated, for isolated it would remain all its life in this place.

So yes, she would be better off dead, also the creature that was inside of her. But how to bring this about?

His mind grappled with the means. There were weeds and herbs that could kill cattle and were known to be dangerous to humans: there were the seeds of the laburnum; there was monkshood. These could be administered in her dinner drink; her fear of him had by now so lessened that she would take something from his hand.

When Annie had put him in the picture, for neither Patsy nor Jessie dared break the news to him, and had dared to say, "It's God's will," he had screamed at her, "Don't be so bloody stupid, woman!" And when she hadn't retaliated, as she usually dared to do, but said quietly, "I'll say it again, if it has to be it has to be, 'tis God's will; and 'tis said He works in mysterious ways. And I'm goin' to say this to you, whether it vexes you or pleases you, it has taken this happenin' to make you realise you yourself have a first-born, and it's only now she's come into her own when you need her," her words had angered him further, and he had banged out of the room. But from then on he was honest enough to ask himself what he would have done over these past weeks if it hadn't been for Jessie, for she had not only comforted her sister, but in a way she had aimed to comfort him. But what of the future? Would she be able to cope with two children, for surely Angela would go on needing the constant attention of a child?

And it was at this point there came into his mind the thought that she must not be put to the test . . .

It was almost a week later when he forced himself to enter his daughter's bedroom. It was mid-morning and she was sitting by the window; and as he slowly approached her, she turned her head towards him and the expression on her face seemed to alter slightly. And when he took the seat opposite her, she actually leant a little towards him, and a strange sound issued from her opening mouth.

Jessie, who had been straightening the coverlets on the bed, rushed towards them now, saying, "Daddy, did you hear that? She was trying to say your name."

He shook his head. "It was merely a sound."

"But she has never . . . never made that sound before." And she bent close to her sister now and said, "Say it again, Angela. Say 'Daddy.' "

Angela looked at her, and her stare became blank for a moment. Then her eyelids blinking, she again made the sound, and now it was distinct: "Dad . . . dy." The word was drawn out, but it was certainly "Daddy."

Ward lowered his chin on to his chest and bit hard on his lip; then, his hands reaching out blindly, he picked up Angela's fragile one from where it was lying limp on her dressing-gown and pressed it between his palms, before laying it gently back on her knee; then rising from the chair, he made to go out of the room, only for Jessie to step in front of him before he reached the door.

Looking up into his face and with a sob in her voice, she said, "It's a start. She'll come back now; and she'll be your Angela again. She will . . . she will. And she'll need you more than ever now, Daddy."

Then her father made a gesture that brought the tears streaming from her eyes, for he put out his hand and gently stroked her cheek as he said, "You're a good girl, Jessie, such a good girl." And with this he left the room, and Jessie moved to the other window, where she pressed her mouth against the wooden casement in order to stifle the sound of her sobbing and in an effort to subdue her emotion . . . Her daddy had caressed her cheek; her daddy had spoken to her like that; her daddy had looked at her as he had never done before, with a deep kindness in his eyes. She was overcome. Whatever happened in the future, even though his whole devotion be again centred on Angela, she wouldn't mind; in fact, she would pray that it would happen, because from now on he would be aware that she was there: he had touched her; he had caressed her cheek, and looked at her as he had never done before.

Patsy stood in the little sitting-cum-living-room-cum-kitchen of Carl's cottage. She had just put the new print cover she had made on the biscuit pad of the two-seat settle that flanked the wall between the open range and the scullery door. The cover matched the pad on the seat of the armchair at the other side of the fireplace; the small wooden table in the middle of the room was covered with a chenille cloth much too large for it so that the ends almost reached the floor; although, as Patsy thought, it gave a tone to the room, for it wasn't everybody who had a chenille table cover, and she'd always treasure it, for it was the combined wedding present from those in the Hollow; even the Protestants, her mother had said, had tipped up their coppers. On the wall opposite the fireplace was a small delph rack, and it held a full tea-set, besides four fine dinner plates with matching side plates. All this was a present from Annie: it had been her own wedding present many years earlier, but she had always felt that the tea service was too good to use, and so it had remained stacked away in a cupboard. But on a Sunday she had used the other two plates belonging to the dinner service. But when they were accidentally broken she had replaced them with cheap white ones from the market stall.

Patsy had been very touched by this gift, and she had dared to kiss the giver, being more than surprised when Annie had taken her into her arms and hugged her for a moment before roughly pushing her aside, saying, "Now then, that's enough of that kind of palaver."

She was now waiting for Carl to return after breaking the news to the master of tomorrow morning's event.

A few minutes later, when she heard his step on the path, she flew to the door and pulled it open, and when he stepped in he put his arms about her and hugged her tightly. Then when they were seated on the settle, still enfolded, she said, "Well, how did it go? What did he say?"

Carl turned his head away and looked towards the fire. "I'm so sorry for him, Patsy," he said; "he makes my heart ache, so much so that at times I think I could cry. I do. I do really."

"Yes. Yes, I know. In a way I feel the same. But what did he say to you when you told him?"

"Well, he stared at me for some time without saying a word, and I didn't know what his response was going to be; and then it was surprising, for his voice was quiet and he said, 'I can only wish you to be happy. I've always wished that for you. I think you know that.' That's what he said. And when I said, 'We'll just have the morning off; we'll be back about twelve,' he said, 'There's no hurry. There's no hurry. Annie will help, and I'll be there.' And then, what d'you think? He went to a drawer and took out this." He put his hand into his pocket and brought out a chamois-leather bag, and opening it, he poured ten golden sovereigns on to her hand.

As she looked at him, her mouth agape, he said, "And that's not all: he's putting up my wage by five shillings a week, and yours by three."

"*Never!*"

"Well, what am I telling you? Eight shillings a week in all. That's what he said."

"And that means he's got no intention of letting us go then?"

"I shouldn't think so, my dear, because he needs you more inside than he does me outside."

"Oh no, no. You're runnin' the place, as you have done for years. It would gallop downhill if you weren't here, and he knows it. But oh, I never expected him to be so kind."

"Nor me; but at the same time, if anybody's worked for a raise, it's been you. Because who would want your job inside there? Fourteen hours a day, seven days a week, because you've never had your full time off for weeks."

"Oh, that doesn't matter." She now put her arms around his neck and said, "Where else would I want to be but where my heart is? An' tomorrow my heart will be right in this house." She moved her head and looked around the small room. "This is my palace . . . our palace, an' I'll keep it as bright as such, even if I've got to take hours from the night."

"That you won't." He pulled her to him now, laughing down into her face. "You'll do it some time in the day, but not in the night."

Her laughter now joined his; but presently she said, "Never in me life, Carl, did I think it would ever happen. I've dreamt of it a long time, while tellin' meself it wouldn't be my luck, me from the Hollow and you from here."

"Oh Patsy. Patsy. Never look down on yourself like that."

"I don't . . . not really, but others do. An' you know they do. And there's families down there, I know, who have already said I've got above meself. And there are others from the village who will think you're stoopin' very low in takin' Gibson's dairymaid, and her from the Hollow. I know what people think; I've been wide awake to it for years."

"Now look here!" He had her by the shoulders, shaking her now. "There's no real difference atween you an' me. I don't even know who my people were, brought up in a workhouse, then farmed out to a villain of a man. You know who your parents are, and your father's a decent fellow." He made no reference to her mother, but went on, "Tomorrow you'll be my wife, and that's all that matters to me—" then seriously, he added, "If poor Parson Noble can stand up to it. You know, I'm worried about that man: he looks as though he'll not last much longer; he's never been the same since that night, for he blames himself and the lantern show. But"—he smiled now—"he'll be there, never fear, to make you the mother of my children, and I want at least six, oh yes, and I want them mostly boys because they can claim better wages than the girls. And we'll start them off early in the fields . . ."

Her body shaking with laughter, she beat her closed fists on his chest: and then they were holding tight again, until of a sudden he almost thrust her from him, saying, "Only one more night. Come, you'd better go back to the house." And silent now, she let him lead her out of the cottage.

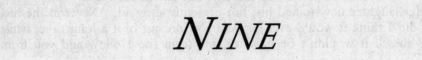

Carl and Patsy were married in the first week of June, and the following weeks were taken up with long hours and hard work, but no matter how tired they might be some part of the night was given over to their love for each other; and so they were content and happy, at least between themselves. But the atmosphere in the house could not help but impinge on their lives, as more and more work fell to Patsy's lot within the house, and more responsibility, besides the actual work, had to be taken on by Carl on the farm, for the master seemed to have forgotten that he owned the place and therefore had decisions to make. Carl was forever asking him if it would be permissible to take this or that step with regard to the rotation of the crops; or about the price to be charged for what they might be sending to market on a Saturday, for at the time prices of farm produce were very unstable indeed.

And then there was the feeling emanating from the village. This wasn't pointed so much at Carl, but at the men, the Irishmen from the Hollow, for it had been made plain to them that they were not welcome in either inn and, further, some of them were finding it not only difficult but impossible to get set on as casual labour on two of the other four farms hereabouts.

At one period, Carl felt he had to bring this to the notice of the master, and when he did so, saying, "Can you do anything for them?" Ward had answered, "Leave it with me"; then the following day he had said, "The old barn wants renewing. Give the first choice to Tim Regan, Mullins and Mc-Nabb. I'll be out there to see them myself but, generally, you keep an eye on them."

The only regular visitor to the house was Philip Patten. Sometimes it would be twice a week, although he never missed looking in at least once. Angela had accepted him, but guardedly, for at seven months her belly was prominent and in a way grotesque, for her slight body did not seem strong enough to support it. On one particular day after she had indicated she was in pain by rubbing her sides with her hand, Patsy had spoken to the doctor about it.

Angela was in bed at the time and when Jessie had pulled back the bedcover and the doctor had gone to lay his hands on the mound covered by the lawn nightdress, the girl thrust out her hands like claws and tried to drag the bedclothes back over her, and staring wildly at him and shaking her head, she emitted loud sounds of protest.

He had, of course, been quick to reassure her, saying, "It's all right, Angela. It's all right. I just wanted to find out where your pain is coming from. Don't disturb yourself, my dear." And as he straightened up he looked towards the far window and intimated to her: "It's lovely outside. The autumn leaves are turning. You could sit out today, couldn't you? Will you try?"

However, she made no response, and so he picked up his bag, and from the landing just beyond the open door he beckoned Patsy towards him; then said to her, softly, "If she keeps rubbing her thighs and evinces any sign of further pain, send for me."

"You think the baby might be coming, Doctor?"

"I don't know, but it's a possibility; she's seven months gone. It . . . it was early March, and this is the beginning of October: she's past seven months. But there . . ."

"It's to be hoped she goes the full time, Doctor, 'cos in any case, it's not goin' to be easy for her."

They looked at each other as old acquaintances might, and by now they could be termed such, for he had spoken to her frankly during all his visits, more so than he did to Jessie. And now he asked, "Where is Miss Jessie?"

It was a whispered reply: "I made her take a walk in the fresh air, Doctor. She's never out of the house. The master's gone out this mornin' on his rounds. That's something an' all. He was examining the new barn—that's been made out of the old 'un, you know—an' then I espied him going over the fields. I . . . I told Miss Jessie which way he had gone. Just in passin' like, you know, Doctor? I thought it might be nice for them both if they could walk together in the air."

Philip Patten said nothing for a moment. Then he put a hand on Patsy's shoulder, saying, "You've got a wise and kind head on your shoulders, Patsy. Should everything else fail, these two qualities will always stand you in good stead."

Her colour had risen; and she laughed gently, but then glanced quickly towards the open bedroom door as if to brush the compliment aside and said, "That isn't a general opinion, Doctor. Even me ma's got a name for me."

"What is that?" He was smiling as he leant towards her.

"The Black Vixen."

"Oh . . . never!"

"Oh yes; when I wouldn't do her biddin' as a child, that's what she used to call me."

"But no longer, I hope."

"Oh, I don't know. There are still times when the stour flies."

He flapped his hand at her as he went away smiling, thinking he well knew the reason why the stour flew, for her mother was one of the laziest women he knew of: the house was like the proverbial pigsty. Yet laughter was never far from the woman's face. But here was her daughter, solemn-faced mostly, yet beautifully solemn-faced. Oh yes; she was a bonny piece, and she was as clean as a new pin. That had likely been the result of her training under Annie, those long years ago.

In the kitchen, Annie enquired, "Well, how do you find her, Doctor?"

"I'm not quite sure, Annie," he replied. "Only I've told Patsy if the child continues to have those pains in her side to let me know. I'll be quite close round about for the next couple of days, but on Friday I'm taking two days off. I haven't had any leave for some time. It's to be the equivalent of a cowman's holiday spent helping with the harvest, for I'm going to attend a couple of medical lectures."

"Oh. Well, what'll happen then, Doctor, say she comes on on Friday? Shall I have to send for his nibs?"

"Oh, I hope not. But if it should happen that someone is needed, well, you'll have to."

"He's kept his distance all these months, hasn't he, Doctor?"

"Yes, I suppose he has, Annie."

"Wanted to show the village which side he was on, I suppose."

He could have replied, "Not so much the village, Annie, but the gentry round about, at least those who were present at that special Sunday service." But Annie spoke his thoughts for him by remarking caustically, "He's like the vicar, frightened he'll lose his place at the big tables."

He laughed now as he said, "Perhaps . . . perhaps you're right. Well, I must be off. Something in the oven smells good." He sniffed towards it, and she answered, "Nothing more than usual . . . a bit of pork," then added, "onion sauce and a suet pudding. Workhouse fare, really."

He chuckled as he went out of the room repeating, "Yes, Annie, workhouse fare."

He paid a brief visit on the Thursday afternoon. Jessie was with her sister, and her report was, "Yes, sometimes she does rub her sides; but not all the time," to which Philip said, "Good. Good," and went on to repeat to her what he had said to Annie previously, that he would be away on the morrow and Saturday; but should there be an emergency she must call Doctor Wheatley; and she answered that she too hoped nothing would happen to make her call on Doctor Wheatley, but that she also hoped he would enjoy his little holiday, to which he smilingly replied, "I don't know about enjoy. If I manage to come away a little wiser, that will be satisfactory." Then he pulled a slight face as he said, "He is one of the great men from London, and I am very lucky to have been given a seat," but immediately brought the subject matter back to her: "Where is your father?" he asked. And when Jessie said, "He's out on the farm," he exclaimed, "Oh, that's good. I'm glad he's getting out and about again. I won't trouble to find him, but tell him everything's in order."

"I will, Doctor."

On returning to the bedroom, she said to Angela, "Isn't Doctor Patten nice?"

But to this Angela made no reply; what she did do was to place her hands down her sides again, and her face twisted slightly, causing her to grimace as if she were experiencing pain.

* * *

Jessie peered down into Angela's face to make sure she was asleep before going round to the other side of the bed to turn the lamp down low and then taking her place in the bed beside her sister.

This pattern of childhood and youth had been taken up again some weeks earlier when it became evident that Jessie could no longer spend her nights dozing in a chair by the side of the bed and be expected to keep awake and attend to her sister during the day.

She hadn't slept in the bed from the start of Angela's illness because the girl herself had shunned close proximity with anyone at all, even with her. That Angela was aware of what was being said to her had been made plain one day when Patsy had spoken sternly to her, saying, "You understand me, Miss Angela, don't you? you understand when I say that if you want to have Miss Jessie tend you during the day then you've got to let her sleep at nights, and in bed."

Jessie lay on her side for some time gazing at the indistinct mound in the bedclothes and wondering, as she often did, what would happen when the baby was born. Would Angela act as a mother to it? And how would her father treat it? Would it be a boy or a girl? Whatever it was, she knew it would be strange to have a small baby in the house; and, further, the work shared between her and Patsy would probably be doubled. She wondered if she would be able to approach her father for help in the house. As it was now, but for himself in his room at the far end of the landing, she was alone: Annie was in her cottage, and Carl and Patsy were in theirs. This latter fact did not now disturb her. For the first week or so it had, when she would think of Patsy no longer sleeping above the stables, but in the cottage with Carl, and in bed with Carl. But gradually it registered in her mind that it was an established fact, and it registered, too, that they were both so very necessary inside and outside the house. And so she wisely came round to telling herself it was done. She had her father, and he needed her. Oh yes, he needed her. But when the baby came there would be broken nights, for babies had to be seen to during the night, and if Angela did not fully return to her normal self, then she would never be able to take charge of the child.

But now, she said to herself as her eyelids became heavy, there was enough to worry about without anticipating further trouble; she must wait until the child was born and take it from there . . .

She didn't know what time in the night it was when she was woken from a deep sleep by the sound of a groan. At first it seemed to be coming from some distance; then suddenly it was in her ear, and she sprang into a sitting position and dimly made out through her sleep-filled eyes that Angela was not only sitting up but bent forward, her hands clutching her stomach.

"What is it, dear? Are you in pain?"

For answer Angela just rocked herself from side to side; and Jessie sprang from the bed, turned up the light and was pulling on her dressing-gown as she went round the bed, exclaiming, "It's all right, dear! It's all right." But when her sister flopped back into the pillows and lay gasping, she had the horrified feeling that it wasn't all right and that there would be no time before the responsibility of the baby was indeed upon her.

She now went to the wash-hand stand and brought a wet flannel back to the bed, and with it she began to wipe Angela's sweating face.

When she was almost thrust aside by her sister's outflung arm as Angela again sat upright and began to rock herself, Jessie looked wildly about her for a moment, before she rushed from the room and along the landing to hammer on her father's door. And when she heard a sort of grunting sound, she flung it open, crying, "Daddy! Daddy! Angela's in great pain. Come, please! Come!" Then she was running back to the bedroom again.

A few minutes later, when Ward looked down on his daughter as she cried out aloud, he turned to Jessie, saying, "Go and get Carl. Tell him to ride for the doctor."

"Yes, Daddy."

She was at the bedroom door before she turned, saying, "But Doctor Patten is away."

He looked towards her, then seemed to grind his teeth for a moment before he said, "Well, you'll have to get the other one. And fetch Patsy back."

On reaching the hall she paused a moment before running into the clothes closet, where she pulled off a peg one of her father's coats which she flung around her shoulders.

In the kitchen she put a match to a candle lantern; and then she was out in the yard, the cold night air making her gasp.

At the cottages, she hammered with her fist on Carl's door, and in a loud voice she yelled, "Carl! Carl! Come quickly. Daddy wants you to get a doctor. Come on, Carl! Do you hear?"

It was a full minute before the door was pulled open, and Carl, blinking down on her, said, "What on earth's the matter? What is it?"

"The baby . . . the baby's coming. Daddy wants you to ride for the doctor. Doctor Patten is away; you'll have to get Doctor Wheatley. And . . . and he wants Patsy."

Patsy had appeared at Carl's shoulder and Jessie said to her, "She's going to have the baby. She's crying out."

When Carl said, "Good Lord! It's only seven months gone," Patsy muttered, "I'm not surprised," and dashed back into the room, calling over her shoulder, "I'll be there as soon as I get into me clothes, Miss Jessie."

Carl now said, "Go on back. You'll be frozen."

When the adjoining cottage door opened and Annie appeared, enquiring, "What is it, child? What's the rumpus?" Carl answered, "It's Miss Angela, Annie. I think the baby is about to come." And when Annie answered, "I'll be over directly," Patsy's voice came from their cottage, yelling, "You stay where you are, Annie!"

Annie made no retort to this, but, looking down on Jessie, she said, "Get yourself back, dear, and into your clothes; you'll freeze," and with this she banged her door; and Jessie was running again.

Back in the cottage Carl began to pull on his outdoor clothes as he said, "I hate to go to old Wheatley's. It just would have to happen that Doctor Patten should be away the night." Then hurrying towards the door, he called, "See you, love," and Patsy's answer was brief: "Sure."

Five minutes later he was on his horse, and within a further ten minutes he was banging on Doctor Wheatley's door. But he had to bang for a third time before a window was opened and a female voice called, "Who is it?"

He stepped back and looked at the bulky shoulders of the housekeeper, and he called up to her, "The doctor's wanted. 'Tis an emergency. The baby's coming . . . Gibson's farm."

The head was withdrawn, but within a moment it seemed, the woman cried down to him, "Doctor's in no fit state; he's heavy with cold. He shouldn't be taken out of his bed."

Carl knew what he was heavy with, and it wouldn't be with cold, and so he cried back to her, "You rise him up; I want a word with him."

"He'll be no use to you, I tell you."

"Nevertheless, woman, get him up."

"Who do you think you are talkin' to? Don't you dare call me woman. And he's not this long in bed; he shouldn't have been . . ." There was a pause before she added, "He shouldn't have been out," and these words were practically cut off by the window being banged.

It was some minutes later when the door was pulled open and the housekeeper stood grimly aside to let him enter; and there he saw the doctor shambling down the staircase, and having to aid himself by holding on to the banister.

On reaching the bottom, he stood swaying, a sign giving no satisfaction to Carl that his surmise had been correct: the man had not long been in his bed and had been indulging as usual with some crony or other. The man was a disgrace.

"What time of night . . . is this? What you want?"

"Mr. Gibson's daughter's child is about coming; and she needs attention."

"Well . . . why come to me? Where's your favourite scien . . . tific modern man and . . ."

The housekeeper was standing by him now, and she said something that was not audible to Carl, but the doctor seemingly understood, and he said, "Yes . . . Yes. Playing the big fella." Then looking at Carl, he said, "I've . . . I've got a chill on me. I . . . I couldn't travel." His words were becoming thicker.

Carl watched him turn an ear towards his housekeeper and nod; then he was speaking again: "As . . . as this good woman says, there are two . . . two women there. They should . . . be able to handle it. 'Tis a farm, isn't it? Seen things born before."

When his arm that had been around the stanchion of the stair-post slid slowly from it, and the florid bulk sat down with a plop on the second stair, Carl looked at the man in disgust, and he dared to say, "You're not fit to carry the name of a doctor, sir." And on this he turned and went out, and, having mounted his horse, he rode swiftly back to the farm.

When he reached the house it was to find Annie in the kitchen, the kettle bubbling on the hob and her busily cutting up a linen sheet into squares, and as she did so she greeted him with, "These are things that should have been already prepared, yet even these have been under taboo. But nature will out, and it's shown it will out in this case . . . Is he coming?"

"No; he's as full as a gun, mortallious, I would say."

"Dear God! Well, what's to be done?"

He looked at her in some surprise and said, "Couldn't you see to her, Annie?"

She looked down at her work and did not speak for a moment; then she said, "I've never had any childer of my own; and although I was in the room when the lasses were born, the doctor was there, and he did the necessary. Quite truthfully, lad, I'd be no hand at it. But your Patsy now; she's helped bring calves into the world and a good few sheep, besides what she must have learned in the Hollow. She'll handle it all right."

He looked at her in amazement, the while thinking that there were things about people you never guessed at. Annie, this motherly-looking woman who had spent her life on a farm was afraid of birth. And now she even shocked him by saying, "And in this case, God knows what to expect. It could be a monstrosity, and I wouldn't bear look on it. I just couldn't," and she looked up at Carl again, her expression seeming to plead for understanding; but he could say nothing except, "I'd better go up and tell them."

She nodded at him, then returned to her task of cutting up the sheet.

On reaching the landing, he was surprised to find the master standing there. He seemed to have been leaning against the wall; but now he was facing Carl.

"Well?"

"He won't come. In any case he would have been of no use, sir. He's drunk, heavily so. But I shouldn't worry; Patsy will see to her."

When Ward made no reply, Carl asked, "Will you tell her, sir?" Then after a moment, just when it appeared that Ward was thinking deeply about something, he answered sharply, "Yes. Yes, I'll tell her," and with this he turned about and went towards the bedroom. But as he opened the door there came at him a piercing cry, one which might have been wrenched from an animal in torment. He stopped dead and turned his head away.

When he again looked towards the bed it was to see Patsy endeavouring to pull a sheet over his daughter's knees.

Taking a few steps into the room, he beckoned to her, but before she moved from the bed she spoke to Jessie, and none too quietly, saying, "Don't try to hold her arms down. I've told you, miss." Then she turned to peer at Ward who was standing beyond the rim of light cast by the lamp; he leaned towards her, saying quietly, "Carl couldn't get old Wheatley, he's drunk. Do . . . do you think you could manage?"

She drew in a deep breath before she answered, "I'll have to, won't I? There's nothing else for it. I . . . I've never brought a child afore . . . animals, yes. Yet"—she moved one shoulder in a characteristic gesture—"I've seen some bairns being born." She nodded at him now, more reassuringly: "Yes, aye, I'll manage," she said. "That is if things come straightforwardly. If it gets stuck . . . well, I don't know. We'll just have to wait an' see."

During this exchange she had not once addressed him as master or sir, and it had not passed his notice, and somewhere in his mind was the thought that she was speaking to him in much the same manner as Annie did.

She was about to turn away when she said, "How's the time going—" and now she did add, "master?"

"Nearly one o'clock, I think," he answered, as he watched her walk towards the bed in which his daughter was lying, comparatively quiet now except for her heavy gasping breath. He knew that he himself could bring the child; yet not for the life of him could he even approach the bed at this moment, for whatever she was about to deliver into the world would be obnoxious to him. And if it was a distorted body, well, he had already made up his mind what he would do about that . . . and even if it wasn't.

When Patsy heard the door being closed, she turned to Jessie, saying, "I'd bring the big chair up, miss, and sit yourself down. There's nothing going to happen for a while; it could be a long night."

Jessie's voice came in a startled whisper now as she said, "But she couldn't go on like this all night, Patsy. She'd be worn out. She's tired already. It's dreadful . . . terrible."

"It's natural, miss."

"What!" Jessie screwed up her face. "All that pain? her screaming with it? No, no; don't say it's natural."

"I have to say it, miss: that's birth. That's how you came, and me an' all," to which Jessie's reaction was in words which were long drawn out, spoken as she walked away: "It's unthinkable. Well, I knew there must be some discomfort, having seen the animals; but . . . but not like this."

"Look, miss. Sit yourself down for a time. She'll be all right. Don't worry. The quicker the pains come the quicker it'll be born."

When, by four o'clock in the morning, there was still no sign of Angela's delivering her child, Ward ordered Annie into the room, saying, "Those are both young lasses up there; go and see what you can do."

And so Annie, eyes weary for sleep, her legs heavy with water, mounted the stairs and went into the bedroom. She knew it would be of little use telling the distraught man that she'd had no experience in such matters. And after saying, "There, there, my lovely," and patting the face of the heaving half-demented girl, she willingly sat in the armchair that Patsy indicated, and waited.

Annie was dozing when she heard Patsy's voice exclaiming, "Aye, aye! Here it comes, miss. Another push. Another push. That's a good girl. Come on. Come on," and she struggled to her feet as she watched the tiny body slipping out of the equally small frame, and heard the girl let out a great sigh before sinking deep into the bed.

"She's whole . . . bonny." The tears were in Patsy's eyes and her voice was thick as she dealt with the cord before handing the tiny, yelling infant to Jessie, standing now holding a towel, her face awash with tears.

Patsy pointed to the basin of water on the wash-hand stand: "Clean her eyes first; an' put another towel under her; then lay her on the wash-hand stand. She'll be all right. Go on: you can do it. I must see to Miss."

Annie was now wiping Angela's face, and she turned to Patsy, saying, "Can you deal with the afterbirth?" and Patsy replied, "Yes, if it comes natural like. Otherwise, I don't know. We'll just have to wait and see. Poor little soul." She stretched out her hand and touched Angela's cheek, encouraging her: "That's a good lass. You've made it. You've made it." Then turning to where Jessie was still attending the child, she said softly, "Bring her here, and show it to her."

Jessie gathered up the child in a towel, almost joyfully now, and moved hurriedly towards the bed, both Annie and Patsy stepping aside so that Angela could see her child. And when she did, the response was so loud, so piercing that they both fell back in astonishment. Angela's mouth was wide as the screams issued from it, and her hands were flailing as if to throw the child from her.

"There now! There now! There! my love." Annie was aiming to hold down the flapping hands when Patsy said, "Out of my way! Annie," and she took hold of Angela by the shoulders and shook her gently as she cried, "Stop it! miss. Stop it! All right! All right! You don't have to see it. Only stop it!"

They were all well aware of the opening of the door, but no-one moved towards it until Jessie, who was standing in the corner of the room holding the small bundle to her, suddenly turned about to where the padded basket was standing on a low chair and, placing the child in it, she wrapped the towels well around it before covering it with the small quilt that lay across the bottom of the basket. Then she carried it towards her father; but she passed him and went into the corridor without speaking; but as he muttered, "Wait!" he followed her, closing the door quickly behind him.

"She couldn't bear the sight of it, Daddy. It is dreadful . . . dreadful. And it is so lovely. It's a little girl, and she is quite whole . . . beautiful. And look, she's got quite an abundance of hair already."

He did not look at the child, but at her, and said, "I'll take it down."

"It . . . it has to be kept warm, near the fire."

She did not release her hold on the basket until he said, "Yes. Yes, I know. Give it here."

She stood watching him carrying the basket and holding it away from him until he disappeared down the stairs. Then she returned to the room, only to stand near the door, her hand tightly over her mouth, the tears running over her fingers, before she made her way towards where Patsy was seeing to something on the bed that looked very distasteful.

Becoming aware of Jessie, Patsy stopped what she was doing and turned quickly towards her and asked, "Where's the child?"

Between sobs, Jessie said, "Daddy's taken her down to the kitchen," causing an immediate, unprecedented reaction from Patsy: she dug her elbow sharply into Jessie's arm, saying, "Go down and see to the child. Go on now, quick!"

"But why? Daddy has . . ."

"Do what you're told, Miss Jessie," Annie interrupted her, and the tone of her voice made Jessie turn and stumble from the room; but it wasn't until she was running down the stairs that she asked herself again, Why? and when the horrifying answer came to her she cried out inwardly. No! No! How dreadful of them to think he would do such a thing.

She entered the kitchen in a rush, and Ward turned from where he was standing in front of the fire, demanding, "What do you want?"

She didn't answer but she looked towards the hearth and around the room. There was no sign of the basket holding the child.

"Look, go back upstairs. I'll be with you shortly."

"*Daddy,* where is the baby?" Her tone was harsh now and she was no longer crying.

"Do what I say immediately."

"*No! No! Daddy.* I won't. Not this time I won't. What have you done to the baby?"

"I've done nothing to the baby."

"Well, where is it?"

"I've told you. Go upstairs and stay for a while. When you come back it'll be on the hearth waiting for you."

She shook her head wildly, and then started to yell, "I want the baby, and I want it now. Where . . . ?"

She stopped when she heard a whimper, and she looked towards the cold-store larder at the far end of the kitchen. This was a narrow room, marble-shelved and stone-floored, and cold enough to keep milk fresh for three days, even colder than the dairy. And now she flew towards it, thrust open the door, and there, on the stone floor and lying on the towel, she saw the child quite naked. The basket was on the shelf.

Grabbing up the child, she held it tightly to her breast and pulled her shoulder wrap around it; then she turned and confronted her father, who was standing in the open doorway and the look in her eyes silenced him until, swinging his body around, he went to the table and beat his fist on it, the while growling, "It was the best way."

"*No! No!*" Her voice was as deep as his. "The child is perfectly formed. It isn't a monstrosity."

Swinging about again he cried back at her, "What about its mind? Its mother is half-mad. You've got to face up to that . . . I've had to face up to it. And who can it claim as a father? Which one of the three? And each an evil, lustful, ignorant swine. Tell me, what kind of character is it going to have? What evil will it perpetrate, coming from such loins as those? *Tell me! girl. Tell me!*"

She could make no answer; she could only hold the child more closely to her.

And now he went on, "And who's to care for it? Certainly not its mother. Certainly not Annie, who can hardly stand on her feet. And then there's Patsy, who will soon be creating a brood of her own. And that leaves you. Do you understand that, girl? Are you going to give your life for that thing?"—he was thrusting his finger towards her now—"for she'll have to be guarded from her mother, and from me. *Yes, from me,* for I don't wish to set eyes on it. And then there's her growing. I guarded you both from the village, but there will be no-one to guard her from their tongues and their slurs. What name do you think they will pin on her, a child of three fathers, eh? an offspring of an unholy trinity."

"Stop it, Daddy! Stop it! Please!" Her voice was low now but such was its unusual tone and authority that it silenced him. "I'll never marry," she said. "The only one I wanted and I think I'll ever want is Carl. You offered me to him as a bribe in order to keep his services." When she saw his eyes widen, she nodded her head, saying, "I know all about it; and when he refused to take me the girl in me died. But I was left with one hope. Now that your favourite daughter was rejecting you, simply placing you among men, of whom she had become terrified, you would need me. And sure enough, you did notice me, because you needed me. But, like all second-hand things, it had no freshness: all your thoughts, in fact your whole being, is taken up with the tragedies that life has dealt you. And lately I have realised that your main concern is how things are affecting *you*. Not how they have affected Angela or me, or even Patsy and Carl and Annie. The tragedies that have touched you have rebounded on all of us, yet you can't see it."

He stared open-mouthed at her. She was just eighteen years old but she could have been twenty-eight, in looks, in manner and in her thinking. Oh yes, in her thinking. And at this moment he could find nothing to say in answer to her sudden tirade, no reprimand welled up in him to chastise her for daring to speak to him in such a manner. But he was aware she had saved him from murdering the child, and it was murder he had intended. Oh yes; and if the cold hadn't done it, in the present state of things a hand over its mouth would have.

He continued to stare at her as he wondered what had brought her running in as she did. Some sixth sense? And then it came to him as never before that his first-born had inherited the character of his dear Fanny while her replica inherited only her stature and looks, and further, that she would have become frivolous. Appealing, yes, but wayward and frivolous.

As he turned from her and made for the kitchen door leading into the yard, it seemed to her that his shoulders had taken on a permanent stoop. But without dwelling further on this, she quickly stepped back into the larder, whipped up the basket and brought it to the fireplace and laid it on the end of the fender. Then with one hand she held up the towel before the fire, first one side then the other, before wrapping the child in it.

She was on her knees when the door suddenly opened and Carl entered. "It's come then?" he said.

"Yes. Yes, Carl." She did not look up at him. "It's a girl."

"I . . . I thought it had; the master's gone striding out of the gate."

But she made no reply to this implication; and Carl was already bending over her and looking down into the basket and saying softly, "She looks canny, but small."

"Yes. Yes, she's very small."

"She's whole?"

"Yes. Yes, Carl, she's quite whole."

"Good."

"Carl."

"Yes, Miss Jessie?"

She had her face turned up to his. "How . . . how does one feed a baby when . . . when the mother won't have it?"

"She won't have it?"

"No; she screamed at the sight of it."

"Oh, dear, dear. Well, miss, it's er . . . I think they use pap bags."

"Pap bags?"

"Yes. You just fold some linen"—he demonstrated now as if he was folding the linen round his finger—"into about that thickness, you see, and tie it at one end. Then keep dipping it into the milk."

"Is that all?"

"That's all for a time, until you can get a bottle. You can buy bottles now with, sort of, well, teats on the end, you know."

She didn't know, but she nodded. "How . . . how soon can you get a bottle?"

"Oh, I'd have to go into town, to a chemist's shop."

"Would . . . would you get one today?"

"Aye. Yes. As soon as the chores are underway I'll get meself off."

"Thank you, Carl."

He slowly straightened up but remained looking down on her. A small fist had appeared over the edge of the blanket and was grabbing at the air; and when Jessie put her finger towards it, it was held, and after a moment she turned and looked up at him. Her eyes were bright with tears and her voice breaking: "She's sweet, isn't she?" she said. He nodded at her, saying in a low tone, "Yes. Yes she is," while a wave of pity swept over him, not for the child but strangely for her, and even more strangely still he was wishing at this moment that things could have been different, for she looked so lost. And his feeling deepened as he said, "You're going to have your hands full." And she replied, "I don't mind, Carl. I don't mind in the least. I'll take full responsibility for her. And . . . and she'll give me an interest. Well, I mean" —she glanced up at him—"one must have something in life and she'll be my something."

He nodded, then stepped back from her and went quickly out of the kitchen. And when she turned her head towards the door she closed her eyes tightly for a moment and wondered why the old feeling for him should return at this moment in particular, when before her there stretched a life of service to this child, which would mean rearing her, protecting her, guarding her, not only from outsiders but from this house, where neither her mother nor her grandfather would own her presence.

Part Three

Part Three

ONE

The long cortège that had followed the last remains of Colonel Ramsmore to the cemetery on this bleak November day had dispersed, as too had those close friends of the family who had returned to the Hall for a warm drink and a light meal. And now, in the drawing-room, there remained only the sparse family, consisting of Lady Lydia's eldest step-son, Beverly, a man of sixty who had recently retired from the Army, and her own son Gerald, now twenty-nine years old, who had returned to his family home a week ago after a nine-year absence.

At this moment it was as if Colonel Beverly Ramsmore could contain himself no longer for, after draining his wine glass, he thrust it none too gently on to a side table; then rising to his feet he confronted his half-brother and, using the same tone as he might have done when speaking to a subordinate, he said to him, "Am I to believe what your mother tells me, that if war did break out, and it is looming strongly on the horizon, let me tell you, you would not even enlist? I could never understand you turning down the Army; but not to stand up and fight for your country, should it need you, is to me atrocious, and coming from a member of this family . . . well, it simply astonishes me. We are an army family, have been for generations on both sides until"—he now pulled at his short moustache before ending—"you came on the scene."

"Beverly!" Although Lady Lydia's voice was firm there was a tired note in it, and he turned to her now, saying, "It's no use, Lydia, someone's got to speak out and tell him what we all think."

"Beverly, I have already told you, you can save your breath."

At this point Gerald put in, lightly, "Yes; why don't you take Mama's advice and stop wasting your breath? Because you're getting short of it, you know."

The portly figure swung round to where Gerald was lounging in a deep armchair and looking so utterly relaxed, and this seemed to infuriate the older man for now he blustered, "You delight, don't you, in being different? But I'll put another name to you: you're a coward, a rank coward, have been since you were a little chap," and then was utterly startled by the springing up of the reclining body, for Gerald was now standing within a foot of him and his finger was daring to stab into his chest as he cried, "Yes! I'm cowardly enough not to go and shoot natives; I'm cowardly enough not to play God and laud it over men, those who in many cases have more brains and intelligence than either you or any other of your kind possesses. Yet you treat them as scum of the earth, cannon fodder. And I'll answer your question. Yes, I know there's every sign of a war coming. But do you know why? Do you read history? In fact, have you ever read anything in your life but army rules and regulations?"

When his hand was slapped hard down it did not silence his tongue, for now he went on, "Greed! Greed! That's what makes war: the French and Germans at each other's throats to gain control of coal and iron; and the Russians, their greedy eyes on the Balkans; everybody out to take something from someone else. And what about our dear country? Oh, we only want to gobble up the whole bloody world."

"Gerald!"

"Oh, let him go on, Lydia, let him go on. I've heard it all before from the ranters, the soap box politicians, the shirkers. You should amalgamate with the suffragettes."

"Even your sarcasm is weak, Beverly, and as far back as I can remember, which is from when I was five years old, you've never had an original thought in your head. It's to be hoped, for their sake, that your sons take after their mother, who, I recall, had a lively mind. Do you know something, Beverly? Neil and I are about the same age, I think he is probably a year older, but I know he was about sixteen when he said to me that he didn't want to go into the Army but that he was destined for it, just as Roger was, because Daddy was adamant. Do you know what he wanted to be? A farmer. But, of course, as he said, Daddy was adamant."

He stepped back now and his lip curled when he said quietly, "Daddy will be very proud of them if war comes and they are both shot to smithereens or bayoneted through the belly." And with this he turned and stamped from the room.

With the banging of the door Lady Lydia closed her eyes tightly, and when the irate soldier demanded, "Why on earth have you asked him to stay here?" her eyes opened wide and she exclaimed in a tone so like his own, "Because someone must see to the place, the little that is left of it. And you, my dear Beverly, have made it plain you have no intention of leaving Hampshire and bringing your family to settle in this house. As you pointed out, what prospects would there be here for your grandchildren? And of course, there's your London clubs. And while I'm speaking plainly, I'm going to say that during the last four years you have been stationed at home, you have thought to come and see your father but once, to my knowledge . . . once.

There is an excuse for your brothers, Arthur and William, they being stationed in India. Yet even they, on their leaves, came and went as if there were a plague attached to the house. It wasn't like that in their young days, when the place was running with servants to answer their beck and call. But when money ran out, yes, I will say this: that was helped considerably in seeing to your three careers and your generous allowances. The money flowed over all of you and your new families. But when my son needed an education, a cottage and a piece of land had to be sold, and his meagre allowance ended abruptly when he was barely twenty, as did his university education, for the simple reason he had the courage . . . and I object strongly, Beverly, to your daring to put the name 'coward' to him. I couldn't see you standing up in public defending a man who had been wronged, as my son did, and refuse to be silenced by his father and was therefore made to suffer for it." Her voice now sank as she ended, "There are different kinds of courage, and I may tell you my son has a great store of the right kind. And that's my opinion, and no matter what happens in the future, should he refuse to fight for his country, as he undoubtedly will, I shall stand by him. And you can convey that to your brothers." And at this she pulled herself up from the couch and she, too, marched from the room.

They were walking up the weed-strewn path between the overgrown ornamental borders. They had been walking in silence for some time, seeming to be aware only of their breath visible in the cold air, when suddenly he said, "It's a mess, isn't it?" And she answered, "Yes, and has been for some time. But what can one man do? McNamara achieves miracles in his own way. I'm really amazed at times that he stays on. But he's very loyal. He came into the yard when you were about twelve, remember? He was fourteen at the time. It's a good job he never married else we should surely have lost him. One has to be thankful for his odd eye, in a way." She turned, her chin moving over the rim of her high collar, and smiled at him, and he answered, "He was always a good chap."

She now thrust her arm into his, exclaiming, "Oh! I'm so glad you're going to stay, Gerald. I'm so grateful."

"It works both ways, Mama. Believe me it does."

"But I thought you liked London and being in a publishing house, and . . . ?"

"Yes. Yes, I did; and honestly I'm going to miss it, not so much the work but the atmosphere of the place, those pokey little rooms. Mr. Herbert and Mr. Darrington. I'll always see them at their desks, practically back to back, surrounded by papers. Very odd, you know." He nodded at her. "It never seemed to me that they were actually reading books, checking books."

"Well, that was your job, wasn't it?"

"Yes, I suppose so; but not until I'd been there . . . oh, three years. I was the dogsbody at first and glad, let me tell you, to be any kind of a body in a job where my main work was to read. But oh, some of those manuscripts. It seemed to me at times that the whole country was writing, yet more than half of them had never learned to write." He paused now and said, "And some of their accompanying letters were pathetic: will you please publish my book because I need the money. And it would likely be a love story full of fantasy;

or as sometimes happened, a record of an awful childhood or marriage." He looked down at her as he said, "I received an education there, Mama, that showed me a way of life that we, as a whole, know nothing about. And not only working for those two dear, old-fashioned gentlemen, and Mr. Herbert and Mr. Darrington were indeed gentlemen and very particular about what they published; but at the same time they were from another world. Sometimes, I'm sure, they weren't aware of either Ronald or me . . . you know, Ronald Pearson, whom I told you about; they didn't know we were there. At other times, when they were aware, they would bawl the place down. Poor Ronald. When Mr. Darrington called for him he would shout, "Peasant! here." And they would treat him as a peasant. One day they accidentally heard him referring to them as 'Hell and Damnation.' You see Herbert and Darrington were on their way out to lunch, and I couldn't shut him up for I was holding the door open for them, and I watched them turn away, both their faces showing surprise and amusement. And from then until we left the office at six o'clock I couldn't convince him other than he was in for the sack."

They were now walking through the just-as-tangled flower garden and somewhat dolefully she said, "You'll miss it all; and that funny lodging house where you were." And he answered, "Yes, I suppose so for a time; not the surroundings so much but the people, because they were so different. Especially the Cramps. Oh yes"—he was smiling broadly—"especially the Cramps."

"How on earth did you come to take lodgings in the East End of London? I mean, when you left, you had enough money to go to an hotel or, as I told you, to Beverly's cousin. He didn't like Beverly and I felt he would take to you."

"For how long, Mama? Anyway, with the money you gave me and the bit I had saved I knew I could last out only about a month, and so I had to find cheap lodgings. Thankfully I found Mrs. Cramp, or at least she found me . . . looking in a shop window where there were rooms advertised to rent." He pulled a face. "Erb . . . Mr. Herbert Cramp and our Doug, Mr. Douglas Cramp, and oh yes, little Glad, who was then really little but is now seventeen, and you could say from that day I was, in a way, happy ever after."

"Oh, Gerald, you make the comparison sound as if your life here had been terrible."

"I'm sorry, Mama, but they were such different people from those I'd been used to, so honest, so open and"—he now pulled a face at her—"so wily, so crafty. The men, Mr. Herbert worked in Covent Garden, had done since he was a boy, and Douglas followed in his father's footsteps. They also had a barrow on the side. Oh, the things I learned about commerce, you wouldn't believe. But what I enjoyed most was the house and the evenings spent there. It was a ramshackle place, dropping to bits in parts. It had originally been the home of some businessman or other, I should imagine, just as many others were in that quarter. Anyway, it had four habitable bedrooms and an attic. I had the attic. Oh . . . oh," he emphasised now, "from choice, for the attic space covered half the house and my books could sprawl all over the place and nobody bothered, least of all Mrs. B . . . Bertha was her name. You know, Mama, she had the loudest voice I've ever heard issuing from any human being. You didn't need an alarm clock. Especially when she screamed up those stairs practically in the middle of the night, 'You! Doug, get out of that bed or I'll dig you out with a fork!' " He now began to shake with laughter as he said, "I won't trouble to tell you where the fork was destined for, Mama."

"No, I'm glad you won't, thank you, but I can use my imagination." She, too, now was laughing.

"Erb . . . Herbert didn't need any calling. I think she pushed him out of bed the minute she got up. As for me, she would come to the bottom of those narrow stairs and bawl, 'It'll be on the table in fifteen minutes, Mr. G.' And, oh, I would crawl out of bed, get into my clothes, all except my jacket and collar and tie, and down I would go into the scullery to wash."

"Oh, Gerald, you had to wash in the . . . ?"

"It was very good training, Mama, and I, being a gent, as she openly stated to anyone who would listen, and that was most of the neighbourhood, I was given the privilege of using the large tin bath on a Friday or Saturday night. I had my choice." This brought them both to a stop, and with her arm around her waist, she laughed loudly before she muttered, "You're exaggerating."

"I'm not. I'm quite serious, Mama. They all used the tin bath. And it wasn't too bad; there was a boiler in the corner of the scullery. The only trouble was the time limit given to your ablutions. You weren't allowed to relax in the, very often, almost scalding water she would ladle into the bath by the bucket. Then there was the possibility that either our Doug or our lad would put his head round the door, and more than once a neighbour, female, took the opportunity. Fortunately, I was either deep in the water or enveloped in a towel, which, I may say, seemed to be faced with sand paper. Yet in a way, they were very decorous, especially with regard to their womenfolk, and the women themselves . . . Glad always sang loudly when enjoying her ablutions. This was mostly on a Friday evening before she went to the . . . palais de danse. She was a very good dancer, so I was told. I'd never witnessed her display. Not that I didn't have constant invitations." He now went into an imitation of Glad. "Ah, come, Mister G. Do you the world o' good. Slacken yer knee caps . . . you'd be a wow down there, that's if you opened yer mouth.' "

"Oh, Gerald." Lady Lydia was looking at her son softly now and surprisingly she said, "It might have at that. Am I right in thinking that you have no attachments? Well, I mean, you haven't made acquaintance with anyone . . . of a . . . ?"

He put his arm around her waist and pulled her to him as they walked on, the while saying, "No, Mama, I have not made acquaintance of anyone of that class, which was what you were trying to say, wasn't it?"

"No." She tried to pull herself away. "Not really."

"Yes. Yes, you were. You see, I have learned to study human nature. I've even written about it." He paused now as if he had said too much, and she pulled him to a stop as she said, "You have? I mean, you're writing, actually writing?"

"Yes, Mama, I am actually writing. And now I'll let you into a secret. I have actually been paid money for my writing, stuff that's come out of here."

He tapped his forehead. "Fifteen pounds I got for my last short story. It was about the country."

"Really? About what you garnered when you were . . . ?"

"Yes, what I garnered when I was young and lived here and about the people I knew."

"Such as?"

"Well, the Gibsons."

"You didn't . . . ?"

"Oh, no. No, no; I didn't touch on anything that happened: I wrote about farmers and the way they lived, what they did."

"And you got fifteen pounds for it?"

"I got fifteen pounds for it."

"That was kind of Mr. Herbert and Mr. Darrington."

"Oh, Mama, Mr. Harry and Mr. David would not have given it a second glance. Trite, one would have said. Simple, the other would have added."

"But if they saw your name?"

"They wouldn't see my name, Mama, because I used yours, at least your maiden name, Fordish. James Fordish, that was the name of my maternal grandfather, wasn't it?"

"Well, well." Her face was beaming now. "You are a strange young man, you know. You always have been unaccountable. But it could be a wonderful career."

"Yes. Yes, it could be a career, if I ever get further than writing articles and short stories. It could be a career, but of sorts, a sideline."

"Well, what do you really want to do, dear?"

"To tell the truth, Mama, I'm not quite sure, except—" he poked his face towards her now and whispered, "I'd love to sit in the library, in there" —he pointed back towards the house—"and read and read and read, and have someone to feed me. And I would have a good wash once a week, but it would have to be in a tin bath."

"Oh, Gerald!" She pushed him now. "Be serious. Anyway, did your . . . Mrs. Cramp know you were a writer?"

"Good Lord! no. Oh, no."

"Well what about James Fordish and any correspondence?"

"Oh, I had an understanding with my publisher." He now cocked his chin up in a pose, moving his head from side to side, and saying, "It's got a nice sound that, hasn't it? My publisher. I really saw him only once. It was his editor I generally dealt with. But oh, as for letting the Cramps know I wrote anything and got paid for it, they would have had it out, they would have blazoned it all over the neighbourhood." And he now struck another pose, his arms folded, his head nodding: " 'My gent writes. I told you he was different.' I actually heard her say that one day to her close friend, someone twice her size and that's saying something, but with no wit. 'Win,' she said, 'he's not just a lodger, he's a gent, like them along, you know, the West End.' I won't recall, Mama, how she then described my further connections, not only with the West End, but with further along in the large stone house."

"Oh, my dear, my dear." Her gloved hand was gripping his now. "You are very funny, you know. You could write funny things from the way you say them."

"Mama, I'm going to tell you something. Talking and writing are poles apart. If any writer could write the way he speaks he'd be a millionaire in no time. You see it's getting the stuff from here"—he again pointed to his brow —"down that arm, into the hand and on to the paper. That's the difficult part. It loses something in the journey."

Her face straight now, she said, "I love you dearly, Gerald. You are my only son, my only child, my only offspring. I've never loved anyone like I love you. But I've never been able to understand what goes on in that head of yours, nor from where you inherited it."

"Well, my dear, there was always an odd one in the family. You said so yourself."

"Yes, I know, but your oddness is different. Anyway, what did we come out for on this bitter morning but to see what could be done with the grounds. Isn't that so?"

"Yes, Mama, that is so. And I've been giving it a lot of thought. All told, we have about sixty acres left, and part of this is taken up with two woods and what you've always called the stone field, because of all the rocks in it that border the Gibson farm. Now that leaves, as it is, about thirty acres. Not enough to set up a small farm; and anyway the buildings down at Brook End are in an awful dilapidated state and would take quite a bit of money spent on them before they'd be of any use. So what do you think about a market garden?"

She screwed up her face as she said, "A market garden? You mean, vegetables and . . . ?"

"Yes, Mama, that's what I mean, vegetables and fruit. And you know, if anyone knows anything about growing vegetables it's McNamara. And fruit, too. He's kept the house supplied for years, hasn't he, when there's been very little else? As you've admitted yourself, there's always been plenty of vegetables of every sort. And there's the vinery and the greenhouses. When you were to meet me in London last year, you offered to bring me a basket of grapes, and if you remember I had to refuse because that would have needed some explaining to Mrs. C: her gentleman's people grew grapes. My! my!"

"But would it pay? I mean, you would have to engage another man."

"Mama, there are farms all around us here and farmers are notorious for not bothering with flower gardens or wasting much land on ordinary vegetables. Oh, yes, potato fields, turnip fields, but for the rest it's dairy food and milk and beef they supply. Well, we could supply all kinds of vegetables, fruit and flowers. We have just passed through two large gardens which are now covered with a mat of dead flowers. It's worth a try."

"Yes. Yes, dear, I can see that, but it's . . . it's labour."

"Well, I've worked that out, too: with McNamara, one more hand and myself. By this time next year we could be in business; and this is the time to start clearing the land."

She smiled now, saying, "Have you ever wielded a pick or shovel, Gerald?"

"No, I haven't, Mama; but for experience I have spent a number of mornings in Covent Garden, humping boxes of fruit and flowers with Erb and Doug. And after a few mornings I got used to my aching bones, and when the fortnight was up—it was during my yearly holiday—I was not only paid handsomely for my assistance but I later received ten pounds for an article I wrote about it. So, yes, Mama, I think I would be capable of wielding a shovel and, through practice, could handle a pick." He smiled at her now and patted her cheek as he said, "Well, what d'you think?"

"Oh, I am with you. In fact, I am with anything you wish to do, Gerald, so long as I can have you with me. I . . . I have been so lonely."

"Oh, my dear, my dear. Please, Mama, don't cry. Oh, don't, don't cry. You'll undo me if you cry."

She turned away and they walked on in silence now until she murmured, "I never cried over your father: love dies, and one asks oneself if love had ever been born. The only evidence lies in . . . well, what it produces." She turned now and looked at him, and when she did not continue to speak he took her arm and pressed it close to his side.

They had entered the wood on the east side of the grounds and there, stretching before them, was a long meadow, studded here and there with crops of rock. And the immediate effect of it was to bring them to a standstill. After a moment she said, "You'll never be able to do much here."

"You never know. If we got the business going we could afford to engage a few navvies to uproot that lot. But look!" He pointed. "It seems quite clear near Gibson's border. There's a long stretch there, not a rock to be seen." He now led her forward, skirting the mounds of rock on their way, until they were standing near the five-foot stone wall that Ward had erected, the coping stones set in a serrated style.

They were actually standing close to the wall and looking over the frozen ridges of the ploughed field beyond, when a little girl came running up on the side of the field to their left. She had apparently caught sight of them before they had of her, but now she was coming round the corner and the curving of the high wall hid her from them for a moment. Then, there she was, standing below them, gazing up at them. "Hello," she said.

Gerald answered, "Hello." And he turned to look at his mother, who was already gazing at him questioningly; then they both returned their attention to the child who was saying, "It's a cold day, isn't it?" She was addressing Lady Lydia now, and she, nodding down at the child, answered, "Yes. Yes, it is a cold day, my dear."

"What is your name?" Her attention was on Gerald again.

"My name is Gerald Ramsmore," he said: "and this lady is my mother."

"Oh." The child now took a step backwards before gazing up into Lady Lydia's face which seemed to be just topping the wall. And she kept her eyes fixed on her for a moment before she said, "My mother is sick."

"Is she, dear?"

"Yes; she doesn't walk about."

"Oh. Oh, I'm sorry for that."

The child now turned her gaze on Gerald as she said, "My grandfather walks about, but he isn't well either." And she lowered her head and was looking down into the ruts when there came the sound of a loud cry from the far end of the field: "Janie! Janie!" it called.

But the child did not turn about and run; in fact, she took a step forward and towards the wall as she said, "That is my Auntie Jessie."

"Shouldn't you go to her, dear?"

The child didn't answer but remained with her head back, staring up first at one, and then at the other.

"I think we had better go," Lady Lydia whispered.

"No"—Gerald did not move—"Stay still, Mama. This could be interesting."

"Janie! Janie! Come here at once!"

The woman was now taking a short cut over the ridges, holding her long skirt in both hands. And when she reached the child she was panting so much she could not speak for a moment. But after grabbing the child's hand she stared at the two faces confronting her.

That this woman standing there on the rough ground could be the one and same young girl who had flung herself on him in such frantic despair that night, the night which had seared a mark on his mind that he knew he could never erase and which in a way had stifled his natural emotions, Gerald could not believe. Was it only ten years ago it had happened? Surely not, for this girl . . . no, this woman looked to be in her late thirties, not twenty-six or twenty-seven as she must be now. He heard himself saying, "Good morning, Miss Jessie. Perhaps . . . perhaps you don't remember me? Gerald Ramsmore; and this is my mother, Lady Lydia."

He watched her eyes flicker from one to the other of them; he watched her wet her lips and say, "Yes. Yes. Good morning." Then looking down at the child she was holding firmly by the hand, she said, "I'm sorry . . . I'm sorry if she's troubled you."

"I didn't. I didn't trouble anybody, Auntie Jessie. I only wanted to talk." The child now looked up at them again and added brightly, "I like to talk."

"Come along."

Before the child was tugged away she called to them, "Will you come again?"

Neither of them gave any reply to this, but Lady Lydia muttered, "Oh, dear me. Dear me."

Gerald knew that his mother's head had drooped but he kept his gaze fixed on the woman and the child slipping and scurrying now across the ploughed field. And not until they had gone from his sight did he turn away and walk to where his mother was now standing some distance from the wall, and they looked at each other while she said softly, "That's the child, the girl's child whom they say they keep locked away almost like a prisoner."

Gerald, however, made no comment on this as they walked towards the wood; his jaws were clenched tight: he was seeing again the beautiful girl, her bare blood-covered limbs stretched wide. He could even feel the moan rising up through his own body again. It was nearly ten years ago; he shouldn't still be feeling like this . . .

The child was standing near a stool at the side of the open fire in the cottage that had once housed Annie. Annie had been dead now for eight years. And this cottage and the adjoining one were now linked together through a doorway between the two kitchens, and they had been the home of both the child and Jessie ever since Carl and Patsy had moved into the house.

Jessie was bending over the child, saying in a harsh voice, "I've warned you, haven't I? If your grandfather finds you roaming around there'll be trouble."

"Why?"

"I've . . . I've told you why. He's not well."

"He's quite able to walk about. He won't speak to me. He never looks at me."

"*Child!*"

"I am not a child, Auntie Jessie. I am nine years old. On my next birthday I shall be ten years old and I think things already, and I feel things. And I would like to know why I cannot see my sick mammy, and why she doesn't walk about."

Jessie straightened her back now and sighed as she said, "I've told you, she never leaves her room and . . . and children, or a child like you, would annoy her."

The girl stared up at Jessie before saying quietly, "In the new book you got for my lessons there is a lady sitting with a little girl on her knee and . . . and she's reading to her."

Jessie's whole demeanour now softened as it was wont to do at her child's need, for that's how she thought of her, as her child. Softly now, and putting out her hand to touch the cream-tinted cheek, she said, "Don't I have you on my knee when I'm reading to you?"

"Yes. Yes, you do, Auntie Jessie; but you are not my mammy, are you? You are just my auntie."

Jessie swallowed deeply. "Yes, I may just be your auntie," she said, "but I have cared for you from the moment you were born, because"—again she swallowed—"There was no-one else to care for you."

"Patsy once said she had brought me into the world."

Before she spoke Jessie thought, Oh, did she? That was stupid of her. But she said, "Yes. Yes, she did, but she handed you to me straightaway, and ever since I've looked after you as my little girl."

For a moment longer Janie stared at Jessie; then sitting down abruptly on the stool she looked towards the fire, saying, "I . . . I get frightened at night now, Auntie Jessie. I . . . I have been having strange dreams."

Immediately Jessie was on her knees by the side of the wide-eyed child, saying earnestly, "But you never told me. You seem to sleep soundly."

The little girl brought her gaze round to Jessie's again. "Well, it's only this last few weeks or so, since I cannot help wanting to run, wanting to get out. I . . . I have no-one to play with. In all our books"—she looked towards the table—"children are playing games: 'London Bridge is Falling Down,' 'Ring a Ring o' Roses,' skipping and such."

"Well, you skip. You skip very well. And Carl and Rob and you and I have played ball together in the field."

"Yes. Yes, I know." The child nodded now, adding, "But they are not little. I mean, they are not my size. And, oh yes, Mike remarked that I was growing up too quickly and would outdo my strength. What did he mean by that?"

"Oh, Mike says silly things. It only means that you will be tall when you are a young lady."

"Will I ever be a young lady?"

The thought leapt the years and fashioned a young lady before Jessie's eyes, and the face it presented was not the bright shining countenance of this child, the long-lashed lids, the full-lipped mouth, and the luxuriant brown hair, so strong it had a life of its own and would stay neither in curl nor in plaits.

"Will I, Auntie Jessie, be a young lady some day?"

"Of course you will."

"Will I marry a prince and live happy ever after?"

Jessie pulled herself to her feet, saying briskly now, "That's a silly thing to ask. Where did you read that?"

"In one of the fairy tales, Mr. Grimms."

Oh yes, Mr. Grimms, whose stories to Jessie's mind were either terrifying or silly . . . marry a prince and live happy ever after. She was about to turn away when she paused and, pointing an admonishing finger down at Janie again, she said, "Promise me you'll never run off on your own like you did this morning."

And now to her amazement *her child* stood up and dared to say, "No, Auntie Jessie, I can't promise you that, because all the time I want to run, to run away outside the walls and the gate and the railings, everything that keeps me in. And if you won't take me out some time, one day I will run away and see the market where Carl goes, and the village where the men go and get drunk. And another thing I must say to you, Auntie Jessie: one day I must see Mama. I must, because she has never wanted to see me. I shall never love her as I do you, but I still must see her."

Dear Lord in heaven! Her nine years of incarceration now appeared to be a most senseless thing, for from whomsoever she had inherited her traits, this child had a strength of will and a mind beyond her years. One thing was sure, she did not take after her mother in any way, nor after her grandmother, for she had never shown any inclination to dance as both she herself and Angela had done at a very early age. She had asked if she would ever be a young lady. Well, there was one certainty: she would grow to an age when that term could be applied to her, by which time the truth would assuredly have been revealed in one way or another. And what then would be her reactions? Only God knew. Yes, only God knew.

She turned to her now and said briskly, "No more talk; there's your lesson on the table. I'm just going to slip across to the house. I'll not be more than five minutes."

As she was taking down a shawl from the wooden rack attached to the inside of the door, she was startled when Janie's voice came to her, saying, "Don't lock me in, please."

"I . . . I mu . . ."

"If you do, Auntie Jessie, one day I shall climb out through the window."

Jessie paused for a moment as she fumbled in her pocket for the key to the door with one hand while groping for the latch with the other, realising that Janie had meant what she said. Without answering her, she dropped the key back into her pocket and opened the door. Closing it behind her, she muttered to herself, "Oh, dear Lord."

As she made her way across to the house, she recalled how it had come about that only the kitchen now remained as it had been for years; and how, after Annie had died, alterations had been made to the rest of the house.

Up till then she had kept Janie in her bedroom and shared her time between her and attending to her sister, the latter task being shared by Patsy. But when, later, Patsy had had to take over the kitchen and the housekeeping and had become heavy carrying her own child, naturally she had spent less and less time upstairs. And so the complete burden of Angela's dumb but effective demands had been left to her to cope with. Until one day it had come to her that if her sister were capable of eating by herself and walking across the room to her chair, then she should be able to wash and dress herself.

The response from Angela had been a bout of tantrums, during which she had thumped the bedclothes, then gripped the head of the bed, causing her body to stretch out and to become taut and so provide the impetus for her suddenly to strike out at her and to push her almost on to her back, and with such a strength that denied her weak, apparently fragile condition.

It was then that her own pent-up frustrations had caused her to take her hand and slap her sister across the face, on both sides. And this had had the intended result, for when their father had come bounding into the room she had immediately cried at him, "Now you can take over! I've had enough. She's quite capable of helping herself. She's almost knocked me on my back, all because I suggested she should wash and dress herself. So, there you have it." And on this she had run from the room, leaving Ward looking from the screaming figure on the bed to the open door. But having realised at this moment that she had meant what she said, he had rushed after her and caught her just as she was about to enter her bedroom, and gripping her by the shoulder, he had swung her round, saying, "You can't do this! You can't leave her! She's sick."

"Well, you must help in seeing to her, Daddy, mustn't you? or get help in. And that's final. And another thing I'll tell you: if I have to stand this strain much longer I shall walk out of here and you will have *that* on your hands too."

She had then pointed towards the bedroom door: "And it will be too late to try to murder it this time, won't it?"

He had glanced hurriedly behind him, saying, "Be quiet! girl. You don't know what you're talking about."

"I know what I'm talking about, Daddy, and so do you," she had come back at him. "And I mean what I say. Now, you can go downstairs and get Patsy to see to her for as long as she can, and then engage a cook to take her place. Now there you have it." And she had bustled away from him and into her bedroom, banging the door almost in his face . . .

This fracas had resulted in Ward having to do some quick thinking: Patsy would soon be having her child, and what then? Put his beloved daughter away?

No! No! Never! He couldn't do that. They would say it was retribution for having had the other one put in the asylum.

This had led to further pondering and harassed thinking, until he thought he had found a solution. And in a way he had. The next morning he had again called Carl into his office.

"You know what happened last night," he had said; "and this state of affairs can't go on." And Carl had answered, "I can see that, sir, and I don't know what's going to happen when Patsy is nearing her time."

"I've thought about all that, so I've got a proposal to put to you. If you fall in with it then I will make a statement . . . an addition to my will . . . to the effect that you will become part-owner, complete in half, of this house and farm when I die. Should that happen before my daughter Angela goes you would promise to see to her until her demise. And my terms are these: you and Patsy take up your abode in this house. This room could be turned into a bedroom and next door, the dining-room, could be put to your use as a sitting-room; I myself would eat in my own sitting-room. We have too much furniture in the house anyway, but this would not go to waste, for I would install my elder daughter in the cottages. A communicating door between the two could make it into one. That would be her abode." He did not mention who would go with her to that abode, but it was plain to Carl, whose face was showing no surprise. And when Ward asked, "How do you see this?" he paused for a long time before answering, "It could be done, sir." But he did not add his thanks for the offer of the half-share in the house and farm, for he knew his own worth and that there would have been no farm left if he and Patsy had gone when they had first intended to. What he *did* say was, "If that arrangement is to be made possible, sir, you will have to employ someone in the kitchen for cooking and housework. And someone to look after Miss Angela during Patsy's confinement."

Ward had risen to his feet, but soon made his decision: "I will engage someone for the kitchen and the house," he said; "but with regard to the attention my daughter needs, I shall put it to Jessie that unless she agrees to see to her sister during the necessary time that Patsy will need to be free of her duty, then I will not allow her to continue to live in the cottage, and, if necessary, I myself will do what has to be done."

Carl had nodded his head but said nothing, for he was thinking: Yes. Yes, he would do what had to be done for his daughter rather than let a stranger in and note her condition. As Patsy had continually said during the years since the child was born, Miss Angela had become more and more trying and she felt that her mind was being affected.

"Well, Carl, tell me." Ward's voice had changed now: he was no longer the master putting over his proposals and demands in stilted language; he was like a man seeking support as he had added, "What do you really think? Will it work? And . . . and would you be happy to do as I ask?"

Carl had answered straightaway. "Yes, sir. I'll do anything that will ease the situation, and I'm sure Patsy will see it in this way, too. And I thank you for your kind offer. I . . . I appreciate it, sir. And have I your leave to engage a woman for the kitchen?" And he had paused for some time before finishing: "Of course it will have to be someone from the Hollow. Perhaps McNabb's wife or daughter. They are clean people."

Ward had sighed and agreed. "Yes. Yes, go ahead."

And so it was that things had gone ahead. The house was altered, and just in time for Patsy's baby to be born in the room that had been known as the master's study. But unfortunately it lived only a few hours and this had heralded a further period of child-bearing anxiety, for over the previous years she had experienced three miscarriages. Her bright and kindly nature had strained to accept fate, but now it became somewhat embittered, so that she thought as her father did: had they been still living in the cottages this would not have happened. There was surely a curse on this house and all in it . . .

Patsy turned from the table as Jessie entered the room and said briefly, "You found her?"

"Yes, right down by the far wall. And who do you think she was talking to?"

"I couldn't guess. But it could only be somebody from the village, and they'd likely appear to her as if they were from another country."

"No, it wasn't anyone from the village; it was Mr. Gerald and . . . and his mother, from the Hall."

Now Patsy stopped placing an assortment of cooking utensils on the table as she said, "Oh, aye? Well, me da said he was back for the funeral. So he didn't turn out like all the rest. It must be worse up there than it is here, for they've only got two inside the house now, I understand, the old cook and the maid. My! my! Even I can remember when the place was overrun with servants. But that's life."

"What am I going to do with her, Patsy? I mean to . . . to prevent her roaming?"

"Well, if she really wanted to roam she could walk out the gates, couldn't she? It's the only place that isn't barred or walled. I've wondered she hasn't done it afore."

"She's been warned not to."

"Huh! She's also been warned not to roam."

Patsy dusted her hands one against the other, and now looking on Jessie, as Annie might have done, and not unkindly, she said, "Sit yourself down. There's a cup of tea in the pot."

"I . . . I don't want any tea, Patsy," Jessie said as she sat down. "But what am I going to do with her? She has openly defied me. When I asked her to promise not to roam again she said she couldn't, and . . . and then she told me not to lock the door on her. She's only nine, but the way she's talking now she could be . . . Oh!" She shook her head. "She's so intelligent, far above her age, so alive, so wanting to know."

"Well, it'll get worse not better, you know that. She'll be asking real questions shortly. Oh my!" She turned to the table and picked up the rolling pin, then laid it down again as she said, "You should take her away out of this altogether. He's got enough money . . ." It was noticeable that her reference was to neither "the master" nor "your father," but to "he." "He's got enough money to let you live comfortably somewhere else. You could ask him to advance some of your share in the place."

Jessie was gazing down on her locked hands lying on her lap and she knew what Patsy said was the solution. But as much as the child wanted to roam away from this place, all she herself wanted to do was to stay here. This was her home: it had always encased her, and she wanted it to go on. And then there was Carl. The thought of not seeing him some part of every day was unthinkable to her. The fact that Patsy hadn't provided him with a family seemed, in a strange way, to have left him free. She rose abruptly from the chair, saying, "Daddy would never agree to that. I doubt if he would give me a penny, even if it meant keeping me from starving. I have a feeling that he begrudges me my food because I share it with her."

Patsy did not contradict her; all she said was, "In that case, you'll have to keep a wider eye on her. But you won't do it by locking her up, for she's a determined miss if ever there was one." She didn't add, "I wonder from which one she's got it?" Rather, she thought, God help her.

TWO

*I*t was on the evening of July 28, 1914, that Lady Lydia put down the newspaper and went in search of her son. She found him in the stables rubbing down their latest acquisition of the new venture, which was a horse.

"Gerald! Gerald!"

"Yes? Yes, Mama? What is it?" He turned to her, and when she thrust the paper at him, she said, "You were right. It's come. Austria's declared war on Serbia and Russia is mobilising."

After he had scanned the newspaper headlines, Gerald said, "Well, they've waited a full month, longer than I thought, since they did their dirty work at Sarajevo, when they murdered the heir to the throne. Now we will just have to wait and see what Russia and Germany do. It won't be long; a matter of days, I should imagine."

"Oh, dear me, dear me. What will you do?"

"Mama! Mama! Come along. Stop worrying."

"I can't help it. Oh, Gerald, if you would only see things differently."

"Now, now. You go in the house this minute and I'll join you after attending to my friend here. Betsy is hungry. She's had a hard day."

"I . . . I don't know how you can take things so lightly, Gerald, when . . ."

"Get away, woman! Do you hear me? And take this rag with you." He pushed the newspaper back into her hand.

When, a few minutes later, he returned to the house, she met him in the hall, saying, "A meal is on the table."

"Well, let me get some of this dirt off me and I'll be with you. Five minutes." He held up a hand before her face, the fingers spread.

"That means fifteen to twenty; then it will be stone cold."

"Look; get yours and put mine in the oven. Or I'll do it myself now."

As he made towards the dining-room she caught his arm and said, "No; no. Please! You know how cook can't get over you messing about in the kitchen; and if you start pushing her dinners back in the oven . . . Oh, dear! dear! Go and get your wash, and be quick. I mean it, mind, be quick!"

He was laughing as he ran up the stairs; but there was no laughter on her face as she turned towards the dining-room. The prospect of war meant trouble for him because he was so outspoken in his views. All this would happen, wouldn't it? when he was making such a go with his business ideas with regard to the smallholding. He and McNamara, together with the odd-job helper, had worked wonders in less than a year, aided by the new inhabitant of the stables, a horse, albeit neither a racer nor a hunter, but one that could certainly pull a cart. And it had pulled some carts of fruit to the market this summer. So much so, it had made her wonder what had happened to all the fruit in previous years. Of course, then there had been a much larger staff, and as Gerald had finickally pointed out, the staff at Buckingham Palace could not have gone through half the amount they had managed to sell this year alone. So he would give her two guesses as to what had happened to it. And then he had answered for her. It had likely found its way to the market but through different channels.

Oh, she knew there was always a kind of pecking order in all households such as theirs had been. And often the hierarchy among the servants would have their appropriate pickings from bonuses, depending on the size of orders. She remembered her father saying years ago that whatever was lost in that way was worth it to keep a happy staff. And he had added that the quartermaster's store should be left to the quartermaster, the implication in their case, she knew, meaning the butler. And her thoughts remained with her early days, those days even before she was brought out in London that were so gloriously happy; and she asked herself yet again, as she had done many times over the years, would she have married Bede if she hadn't still been feeling the hurt of breaking off her engagement with Raymond after she found out about his mistress? She doubted it, Bede being twenty years her senior and with a grown-up family. He had spelt security, a shield from a dirty world. She had been very naïve in those days, hadn't she? Yet what was a young girl to think when her future husband showed no intention of giving up his mistress, on the excuse that it was nothing to do with love; he loved *her*, he said, and perhaps after marriage things might alter. But couldn't she understand the situation?

No; she hadn't been able to understand the situation. And she still didn't. So perhaps she had remained naïve.

"You're a silly woman. Why have you not yet started on your meal? I have been seven minutes; I timed myself." ·

When he sat down and took the cover off the plate he sniffed and said, "It smells good. I could eat a horse . . . but never Betsy. You know, I'm very fond of that old girl. She has worked, hasn't she? She's been a godsend. Oh, my dear." He put down his knife and fork and, leaning across the corner of the table, he placed his hand on hers, saying, "Don't look like that. It may never happen. I mean, conscription. And it won't come about rightaway. There'll be dozens, hundreds of them flying to the Colours, all brave fellows dying to be butchered. Oh, I'm sorry." He picked up his knife and fork again, and in a more sober-like voice now he went on, "Anyway, dear, it's nothing new; conscription's been going on, well, practically down the ages in other countries. They used it in America during the Civil War, and it started in France sometime in the seventeen-hundreds, as far back as that. It's nothing new, I tell you."

"I'm not thinking just about the actual conscription, Gerald, and you know I'm not. It's . . . it's what people will think because, knowing the position that your father held and your half-brothers do, it will be expected of you. And . . . and when you don't conform, as I know you won't"—she stressed the last words—"you'll be made to suffer in so many ways. People are cruel."

Again, he laid down his knife and fork before asking her quietly, "What would you have me do, Mama? Deny all my principles and do something that I abhor, such as shooting a man, or whipping off his head with a sword, or stabbing him in the guts?"

He sprang up now and stopped her as she was endeavouring to rise from her chair, and pressing her down again, he said, "Mama, you forced me to talk of this matter, and I can't polish my words. I know your thoughts are with me—war is abhorrent to you as it is to me—so why do you want me to ignore my principles and . . . ?"

She twisted her body now and looked up at him, saying, "Don't you see? Don't you understand I don't want you to suffer? And I feel you will suffer more through your opinions and open attitude than you would if you were taking up arms and, be it against all you think, making yourself fight for the cause of your country."

He slowly moved from her and took his place at the table again, and after a moment he said quietly, "Mama, I don't believe a word of it. But what I do believe is that if I were to do as you say I would lose your respect, and very likely your love. Whatever you say now you would feel deep and grievous disappointment that the one you loved most, and you have impressed this on me, could be swayed to do something that went against every fibre of his being, just because he was afraid of public opinion."

A tap came on the door and Nancy Bellways entered carrying a tray and paused half-way up the room, saying, "Oh, I'm sorry m'lady; I thought you'd be through by now."

Lydia turned to her, saying, "Oh, let us have it here, Nancy. We've wasted our mealtime in talking, but we'll soon be through. Just leave it there; I'll see to it."

"Cook left it in the basin, m'lady, and the custard's in the tureen," Nancy Bellways now added, "in case Master Gerald was late." And he, nodding at her, teased, "You're insinuating, Nancy, that I'm always late."

"Well nearly, Master Gerald, nearly." She was now smiling broadly at him as she added, "And you'll be pleased to know we've reached the hundredth jar of fruit s'afternoon."

"*You have?* Marvellous! But carry on. And tell cook I love her—I love you both. I do. I do. And wait till Christmas when we take some of that lot to market; they'll dive on them."

As Nancy Bellways who, after giving this house forty years' service, was afforded the liberty of what her mistress termed backchat, now said, "Oh well, Master Gerald, cook says she's gona lock half that lot up in the cellar so you can't get your hands on any of it, and that'll see us through the winter."

"Oh, does she? Well you can go and tell her that I'm coming out there shortly to have a word with her. Likely box her ears into the bargain. You tell her that."

When Nancy went from the room laughing, Lady Lydia looked hard at her son as she said, "You have learned a special way of dealing with staff, haven't you?"

"Have I? Well, perhaps it's because I served my time as an underling with Hell and Damnation." He laughed.

"You know, I often think of them and the poor peasant, you know, Ronald Pearson, and wonder how he's getting on. I'd like to go up to town one day and look in on him. And, of course, the Cramps."

"You liked that family, didn't you?"

"Yes. Yes, I did, Mama."

"You never told me you kept in touch with them; I mean, wrote to them, until you got that letter."

"Well, I didn't see the need. I just wanted to let them know how I was getting on in my new business. And you know yourself, you laughed at the letter, especially the end." And he quoted: " 'I hope this finds you as it does me at present, half-stripped to go into the tub when Mam gets out. Dad's got a runny cold and has sewed himself into his vest, camphor block an' all. That'll take care of him for the winter.' " He smiled at his mother now as he said, "And the last bit which expressed their warmth. You remember? 'We'd all like to see you pop in one of these nights, Mr. G.' "

Again Lady Lydia stared at her son, who was now silent and staring down at his plate, and she said in a voice that held a mixture of sadness, and yet criticism, "You always seem happier with that type of person. Don't you, dear?"

He looked at her and moved his head slightly, saying, "It's just that I like people who act naturally. They had nothing to hide, they weren't playing a part: they hadn't to keep up any social class. In fact, they were proud of what they were. And don't think they were all ignorant slobs, as Beverly classes them. There was a bright intelligence running through the majority of them. They only needed the chance to widen it. And then I also enjoyed my days with the publishers; Mr. Herbert and Mr. Darrington were gentlemen, and so was Ronald Pearson. He, too, would have come under the banner of middle-class, upper middle-class. But being the tail-end of a huge family, he had to earn his living. I enjoyed their company. I don't like fakes, Mama."

"Those you would call fakes, Gerald, are sometimes merely diplomats."

"Oh, no, no. Anyway, my dear, let's start on cook's pudding and leave the future until it happens, eh? What about it? And by the way, I'm going to take another look at the woodman's cottage. You know, it could be made habitable again, and we could offer it to someone in return for a few hours of their labour."

"It will take a lot to bring it into order."

"Only the materials. McNamara and I could do it between us."

"It was practically overgrown with scrub the last time I was down there."

"Oh, the clearing of that will be the easiest part. And if I remember rightly, Trotter had a bit of a garden down there, grew his own stuff."

"You couldn't remember Trotter, dear; he left when you were very small."

"Not so small. I must have been about five. Anyway, I can recall what the place looked like, and if we can work another patch down there it'll all help."

She smiled tolerantly at him now, saying, "Given time, I can see you turning all the grounds into a vegetable patch."

"And wouldn't that be good! Just think of the money it would bring in. You could go up to town, do the shows, get yourself seasonable rig-outs."

She answered soberly now, "If there was money to spend, I'd rather put it for help in the house."

And he answered just as soberly now, "Yes. Yes, that would be more sensible. But that's what will happen in the next year or two, you'll see."

He finished his pudding and, rising from the table, asked, "Will you excuse me, dear?" Then went round to her and kissed her cheek before going out.

But she sat on, thinking of the dread of going on living in this mausoleum of a house if anything should happen to him . . .

He was standing on the edge of what had once been a large clearing but which was now padded down with seasons of dank grass, with patches here and there of tall weeds. One such patch was obscuring the small window of the cottage. Then he noticed something odd: a patch of weeds near the door had been pressed to the side. The door, which for some long time, had been hanging half-open on one hinge, was pressed well back. It wasn't likely, he told himself, that a tramp had taken shelter in there, because the cottage was situated in the middle of the grounds and even now, although the acreage had become shrunken over the years, its situation was a good half mile from the nearest public path.

He had almost reached the cottage itself when he was startled by a combined screeching: a black shape just missed his face, cawing angrily as it went, and a small, screeching figure pelted herself at him before springing back and turning a terrified countenance up to him.

"Well! it was the bird. It . . . it jumped at me from the fireplace. I . . . I wasn't doing any harm, I was just looking."

"Yes. Yes," he said soothingly, "I'm sure you weren't doing any harm, you were just looking." He bent down to her now. "You are Mr. Gibson's granddaughter, aren't you? We have met before."

She blinked rapidly before saying, "Oh yes, yes. You were at the wall with your mother."

"Yes, that's it; I was at the wall with my mother. But tell me, why are you roaming around here? How did you manage to find this?" He waved his hand towards the cottage.

"I was upset. I mean . . . Oh! dear me"—she put her hand to her head—"that bird frightened me."

He looked about him and to the side and said, "There's a fallen tree. If we move the weeds we can sit down."

After he had pushed the weeds aside and trampled on them, he pointed, saying, "There you are." And when they were both seated on the lying trunk he said again, "Tell me, how did you manage to get this far? I mean, how did you manage to leave the farm?"

She now turned her face up to his and smiled widely as she said, "It was quite by accident. It was the rabbits, you know. You see, I am not allowed to go out of the gates and I had told Auntie Jessie that I couldn't promise her that I wouldn't go wandering."

"You told her that?"

"Oh yes. Yes. It was no good lying. Well, I mean it was no good telling her that I would do as she asked when I knew I couldn't help wandering. Well, I was at the wall, you know, where I saw you and the lady, your mother. And further along there is a mound and some bushes growing on the top and I saw a family of rabbits, baby ones. They were playing; but when I went near them they scattered. The men shoot the rabbits, you know, because of the crops. I don't like to hear them shooting. Anyway, I pushed between the bushes and the wall to see if I could look in their burrows. They don't have nests, you know, they have burrows."

"Oh." He nodded at her.

"Well, there were lots of holes and they had all disappeared down them. Then when I nearly tripped over a root of a tree, I noticed it had grown into the bottom of the wall and pushed a stone aside. It was quite a large stone; roots must be very strong, don't you think?"

"Yes. Yes, I do. Then what did you do?"

"Well—" A look almost of glee passed over the small face now as she said, "I pulled the stone aside and then another one slipped out from above. I became afraid then in case the wall should topple down. It didn't, but just in case it did, you know what I did next?"

He shook his head.

She now held out her hands to him, saying, "You see my nails?"

"Yes." He nodded at her.

"They're very dirty, aren't they? Well, you see, I did what our dogs do before they bury a bone, and the rabbits do it and the foxes. I scraped the soil away with the help of a piece of wood. But I really couldn't go very deep. Although I kept away from the big root there were smaller ones criss-crossing. Anyway, I must have managed to dig for about three to four inches and it was enough to make the hole large enough for me to crawl through. I had to lie flat, of course. It was quite an adventure. I did think at one time that the wall might suddenly drop on me, but it didn't. The stones are usually placed very firm against each other, I understand from Mike. He is the cowman, he helps to mend the walls. But that big root had certainly oozed them out."

"Won't your aunt be looking for you and be worried again?" he said.

"Yes, I suppose so; but she knows I will come back. I promised her only yesterday that if I roamed round the farm I would always come back."

"But you didn't say anything about roaming outside the farm, I suppose."

She stared at him for a moment, as if thinking, then said, "No. No, I didn't."

"I should imagine she will be very worried, perhaps annoyed."

"No doubt. No doubt."

He had the urge to laugh, for she sounded so old-fashioned. How old would she be now? Yes, he remembered she had said before that she was nearly ten. Dear! Dear! and not allowed to go to school. Not allowed to mix with other children. It was a crime against youth.

He watched her now looking straight ahead, her hands joined tightly between her knees, and this caused her long dress to ride up above her black shoes and white socks. And he was on the point of saying, "Come along; I'll take you back to your rabbit hole," when she turned to him quite suddenly and asked, "What is an unholy trinity?"

"A what?"

"An . . . unholy . . . trinity."

It was a moment or so before he said, "Why do you ask?"

"Because I want to know."

Well yes, of course, that's why she asked. But where had she heard that? "I realise you want to know," he said, "but tell me why and where have you heard that?"

She was looking away from him again; it was a moment or two before she said, "There's the village over there." She pointed in front of her, but then let her arm travel to the right before adding, "It's somewhere in that direction, I think. But I wanted to see it. And there is a school. You see, I don't meet many children. In fact, I don't meet any children at all except in books, and so when I got through the hole the other day I didn't come this way, I walked by the wall on your side and I came to a wood. And when I came to the end of it there was a ditch; but the railings on the far side were broken here and there, and so it was easy to step on to the pathway. And I walked up the pathway and I heard children . . . children's voices. And when I got nearer I saw some buildings and from the end one children were running. They were coming out of a gate in twos and threes and they were running, not towards me but away. I suppose to their homes. But there were three girls: one was just my size and the others were larger." She paused here as if thinking, and he remained silent, looking at her, until she went on, "When I went up to them they stared at me. Then one said, 'Who are you?' And I said, 'I am Janie Gibson. Who are you?' And she laughed at me and giggled, and she looked at the taller girls and now one of them turned to where two ladies were coming out of this building. And when they got to the gate they stood behind the girls and they, too, looked at me. One was, I suppose, young, and the other seemed old. Then one of the girls turned, reached up to the older woman and whispered something. And what she whispered was my name. I have very good hearing, you know. 'Her name is Janie Gibson,' she said; and the older woman stared at me before she said to the girls, 'Go along! Get along home.' And when they didn't obey her at once she raised her voice to them and then they ran off. Then she said to me, 'Go home, dear.' Just like that, very quietly, 'Go home, dear.' And I turned and I had taken some steps when I heard the younger woman saying, 'So that's the result of the unholy trinity.' And then the older woman said something to her that sounded harsh, but I couldn't hear what it was she said. So, that is why I am asking you, sir, what is an unholy trinity?"

He said, "That . . . that wasn't meant for you, it's . . . it's just a saying."

"Then why did she say I was the result of it?"

"People say the oddest things. There's a lot of ignorant people in that village."

"But she was a woman, and perhaps she was a teacher; I think she was. The older woman was, because she sent the girls home. Are you telling me the truth when you say you don't know what it means?"

He drew a deep breath into his chest before he lied, saying, "As far as I can gather it has no meaning, not really. But people make bad meanings out of simple words." And now he took her hand as he added, "I would ask you to forget it; and you know, you do realise that if your aunt knew that you had been outside the perimeter of the farm she would be very upset, especially if she knew you had been talking to people from the village, because many of them in that village are not nice people."

She stared at him wide-eyed until he became almost embarrassed. And he was embarrassed when she said, "You are a very kind man." Then she asked, "How old are you?"

He smiled now at her before answering, "Very old. Twenty-nine come thirty."

She nodded at him. "Yes," she agreed; "that is very old. Auntie Jessie, too, is old. She's nearly twenty-seven, I think."

"Yes"—he was laughing now—"age is a dreadful thing. But one day you will be twenty-seven or even twenty-nine come thirty."

"Yes. Yes, I shall." There was a brightness to her voice and she now sprang up from the tree-trunk and, her face on a level with his, she said, "And then I shall be able to go where I wish, to travel the world. I have a globe of the world. It is very big, and one day I shall go round it." She made a big circle with her finger, ending, "Right round it."

He again took her hand as he said, "Yes, my dear, I'm sure you will. Yes, you will, you will travel the world. But now I think you had better travel to your rabbit hole. Don't you?"

She hunched her shoulders and laughed gently as she answered him conspiratorially, "Yes, I think so. But . . . but may I come again?"

He hesitated; then pulling himself to his full height, which to her made him appear very tall, and gazing over her head, he said in what he imagined to be a stern voice, "I have no say in the matter, miss. I don't know anything about rabbit holes or little girls escaping through farm walls. And if I saw one here again I'm sure I wouldn't recognise her."

She now flapped her hand up at him and actually laughed out aloud. It was a high tinkling sound as might come from a young child, not one with an old head that had been forced on to her shoulders. And then she said, "I like you. I like you a lot, and I shall come again when you can't see me." And at this she tugged at his hand, and he led her through the labyrinth until they came to the wall; and from here she led him to the hole which was hidden by the bushes on the mound. And as he watched her lie flat and crawl through it, he wondered how she was going to explain her soil-dabbed dress as well as her dirty hands.

THREE

*A*part from the front door and the kitchen door, there was another entry to the house: a door from the yard to a back stairway leading up to the attic rooms, but with a door, half-way up, on to the main landing. The attic rooms had at one time been used for winter storing; but the door had been locked for many years now. Janie was very aware of this door for she had more than once tried to open it. But this morning she had a key; at least, she had a bunch of keys, seven in all, most of them rusty.

She had first noticed a very old horse collar hanging in the corner of the harness-room, and on investigation had seen the keys on the nail driven into the wall at the collar's centre. A few days previously she had been passing the front of the house, when her attention was caught by an indistinct figure standing in front of one of the upper windows. One minute it was there, the next it was gone. She knew immediately that the figure could be no other than that of her sick mother. But if she was sick, why wasn't she in bed?

The glimpse she'd had of the person had suggested someone very small. But she had reasoned that having seen only the upper part of her, she might perhaps have been sitting on a chair.

However, that glimpse had been enough to stir her determination to see her mother. Why not? And her mind did not take her further than "why not?"

Shortly after this sighting, the bunch of old keys caused her to plan a way of bringing about the encounter. First, she told herself that even if one of those keys fitted the lock it would not turn because it was rusty. So when the opportunity occurred, she took down the ring and dipped the whole of the keys into the oil bucket, then let them drain for a while before hanging them back on the wall. The oil would need to soak in, she told herself.

However, it was to be some time before she could bring her plan to fruition, for it was on that same day she had met the nice man, and as a result of this meeting she had been confined under lock and key.

After returning home with a soiled dress and dirty hands and refusing to explain how this had come about, her Auntie Jessie had said there was no alternative: she must be kept in. And she was until the day there was great excitement in the yard, all because war had been declared somewhere. Even her Auntie Jessie was excited. And so she was let out and left to her own devices. It was then that she decided there was no better time to try the keys in the lock of that door.

And this she was now doing.

It wasn't until she tried the fourth key that she felt it click as if it had dropped into a socket. And when she turned it half-way round and the door moved under her hand, she was so overcome by trembling excitement that for a moment she didn't push it open. When she did, she saw a flight of stairs with cobwebs hanging from the sloping ceiling. One step at a time she mounted the stairs, to be confronted at the head by another door. But this opened easily. And now she was in a small hallway where more stairs went off to her right. But opposite was a large landing and she stepped cautiously on to it, only to jump back when she heard a door opening. She waited, her head turned to the side, so that she could see part of the landing; but then stiffened when there emerged from a room the figure of Patsy carrying a slop pail.

She held her breath, wondering which way Patsy would go, for were she to pass this way she would certainly see her. And there wasn't time now to scamper down those stairs. But she sighed with relief as Patsy's figure disappeared from her view.

After waiting some minutes, which she gauged would give Patsy time to reach the kitchen, she stepped on to the landing and noticed there were doors on both sides. But she knew now which one she must go to.

At the door, she paused for a long moment before tapping on it. But when there was no response she opened it and, lifting her feet as if she were about to tread on something fragile, she entered her mother's room. And what she saw was a large bed—she did not take in other pieces of furniture, only the bed—and standing at the far side of it was a very small . . . she hesitated to think lady, and woman didn't fit either. The only way to describe the person she was looking at was "a young girl." She was fat; even under a loose dress it could be seen that she was fat. But it was the head that Janie stared at, for this wasn't the face of a girl and her hair was almost white.

Unaware that she had closed the door behind her and that she was standing with her back to it, she knew only that the small person had walked down by the side of the bed and that she could now see all of her where she was clinging to the iron frame of the foot of the bed. And what the complete sight of her conveyed to Janie was that there must be a mistake. This little person could not be her mother, for she was not much bigger than herself. And she didn't look the kind of person to be a mother.

She wanted to get out of this room and with this in mind she stepped away from the door and opened her mouth to say "I am sorry," but instead what issued from it was a high scream as she found herself flung back against the door. And now the room seemed to echo with screams.

The bouncing of her head against the door made her feel dizzy for a moment, although this did not prevent her from letting out another scream when she saw the small woman lift the lamp from the bedside table with a very obvious intention. She sprang to the side, but not quickly enough to evade the splintered lamp-glass splattering the back of the hand she had put up to shield her face.

Still screaming, she groped blindly for the door as more objects were hurled against it. But then she was out on the landing, so terrified that she didn't know which way to run until, looking to the right, she saw her grandfather appearing at the top of the stairhead. He was running, but at the sight of her he paused for a moment, his mouth agape. Then as he came at her, she sprang back towards her exit; and she actually fell down the last three stairs and tumbled through the door into the open again. But once on her feet she began to run.

Philip Patten stood by the bed, looking down on the contorted face which, like the rest of the body, was gradually relaxing. And now he turned towards Ward, who stood at the foot of the bed, and said, "That should keep her under for a few hours. I'll come back later and give her another shot." He bent now and closed his black bag and was making for the door when he stopped and looked back at Ward, saying, "I warned you some time ago, you know, how she would react and matters won't improve. All right, she was provoked this time, but there have been times when she hadn't been provoked . . . well, let us say nothing that would provoke any sane person. Oh, yes, I know, Ward." He put his hand out as if in protest. "You don't like that word, but you've got to face it. Her mind is deranged. It has been from the beginning. She'll have to be put under control—I've said so before—or you must engage someone to do that. I'm warning you; Patsy can't put up with much more. As for Jessie, she's had to cope with more than any human being should be asked to do. She's got her hands full as it is; and this last event has proved that. Now, I'll say no more at the moment; except that she has to be sedated and . . . yes, I'll say it, guarded. Just imagine if this had happened during the evening when that lamp was lit; the whole house would have gone up. From what I see here, even since it's been tidied up"—he looked around the room now—"it must have been a shambles. It seems that not even your presence or Patsy's could stop her wreaking havoc. She should have been tied down. It's no news to you that Patsy has voiced this again and again when she's had to deal with her alone."

"She doesn't often deal with her alone; I'm always on hand."

"You're not always on hand; you can't be. Anyway, you have my opinion, and I don't think, on this occasion, that you want a second one, do you? But I'm telling you, if this is allowed to go on as it is now and you don't have her restrained in some way, there will come a time when there will be a second outburst, and perhaps at night; and I'm putting this plainly to you; it isn't far ahead." But then, his voice softening, he said, "I know this must be affecting you, Ward. But in your heart you've known for years how things were with her. Well, I'll be off, but I'll see you shortly."

When he reached the kitchen and before he had time to say anything to Patsy, she confronted him, saying, "I'm not standing much more of this, Doctor. Not for all the bribes in the world. And I've told Carl, and him an' all"—she thumbed towards the ceiling—"there's got to be more help up there, night and day, and somebody experienced. D'you know, you wouldn't believe it, but she's got more strength when she's in one of them turns than me and Carl and him put together."

Her voice sinking, and with it her whole tense frame, she asked, "What's to be done, Doctor? Things can't go on like this, can they?"

"No, they can't, Patsy; and I've just told him so; it's either one thing or the other. I've put it plainly to him. The first suggestion I know he wouldn't hear of, and that's having her put away. So he'll have to engage more help. But don't forget that'll mean more work for you down here."

"Oh, I don't mind that. I don't mind that. It's the running up and down; and her, she's become more thankless with the years. It's funny; she can't speak, yet she can demand. Oh, aye, she can demand. And scream. Oh, my God! her screaming."

He put in, "What happened to the child? Where is she?"

"Don't ask me, Doctor. Miss Jessie's out hunting for her now, and Carl an' all, 'cos Rob said he saw her flying across the lower field, and he swears there was blood on her. Where's it all going to end? Can you tell me that, Doctor, where's it all going to end?"

"I can no more answer that than you can, Patsy; only time will tell." Then he lifted his hand as she went towards the teapot. "Nothing for me this morning, thank you," he said; "I've got a very busy day ahead of me. I must be off, but I'll see you this evening." And with that he left . . .

It was in the afternoon when, sitting beside the bed on which lay his beloved child, as he still thought of her, Ward came to a decision. The doctor had given him two options. One he would never condone; having her put away would give the village two bells to ring. The first: it was only justice that his daughter should end up in the same place as Daisy Mason; and secondly: God would not be mocked: He was making him pay for His desecration through his daughter. No, that had always been out of the question. And as for the second option, having a day and night warder in this room, the image presented to him was of big strong, hefty women handling his child. Never! Never!

He now put out his hand and stroked her hair back from her brow. Her face was relaxed; she was his little girl again, so like her mother, at least her countenance was, for her inactivity had bloated her body.

He rose now and, gazing down on her, he murmured, "When you join your mother you will be so happy, and then together you will wait for me." Then he bent and kissed her, a long slow kiss, before going out of the room.

Jessie was nearing the farm gates when she saw Carl riding in from the other direction, and when he pulled his horse to a stop she could see by his expression that he had no news. Without her enquiring, he said, "Not hilt nor hair of her." Then she asked, "Did you see the blacksmith?"

"Yes. Yes, and nobody gets past him. I went to the Newberrys too, and to the Holdens, and to Mr. Wainwright's. He's the Methodist minister at the far end of the village, you know, and his wife's ailing and sits in the garden a lot, and she said no-one had passed there. They were very kind in their concern for her. Lastly, I went right through to the other end and made it my business to go to the school, because I've always said she's been starved of her own like and age and"—he nodded down at her now—"I did find out something there, but not touching on today. Apparently, some time ago she turned up at the school gate."

"No! At the school gate?"

"Aye. Yes. That's what Miss Pratt said, and . . . and she apparently told her to go home because there were some children around and she thought it was better that they didn't get to talking, although Janie had already told them her name."

She said now, "There's nothing for it but to tell the polis."

"Not yet." He bent down towards her. "The state that things are in, your . . . well, I mean, your father would be more upset. You know what happens when they arrive on the scene; they're always followed by newspaper men."

"Well, where can she be?"

"She could be hiding somewhere quite close."

"I've been through the wood." She now paused a moment before she asked, "You don't think she could have got in the Hall grounds? I can't see her climbing the walls, and certainly not the fences. And she knows she mustn't go out through the gate."

"After what happened this morning," Carl said tersely now, "I think she would have gone straight through a blank wall."

She was silent for a moment as she looked around her, as if searching for some clue, and then she seemed to get it by saying, "You remember when she came back that day with her dress and hands all soiled and she wouldn't tell me where she had been or what she had been doing? She could have crawled through some place, couldn't she?"

"Yes. Yes, I remember. But you know," and he was shaking his head now, "we went all round those walls. She'd have to be a badger to get underneath that wall, wouldn't she?"

"Yes, but she had been crawling somewhere. Carl"—she put her hand up to him now—"would you go to the Hall, and ask if you could look through the grounds?"

"Yes. Yes." He nodded down at her. "The young master up there is very amenable, I hear, and Lady Lydia always has been pleasant. Yes, I'll do that, although it's a faint hope; if she kept running in the direction that Ron saw her, it wouldn't have led her towards the Hall. She would have to go out of the gate for that. Anyway—" He now turned the horse about, saying, "It's a long shot." Then he galloped off leaving her standing, her arms tight about her waist now as if trying to squeeze out the anxiety that was filling her body. If anything had happened to the child she wouldn't be able to bear it, she just wouldn't. She had done wrong in disobeying her orders, but then, what could you expect? She knew she had a mother, and now what could she think of her mother? Only as a mad woman; for it had to be faced, and her father had to face it, too, his beloved Angela was mad, and craftily mad: what sweetness remained in her she expressed only when her father was present, but her manner towards both herself and Patsy was demanding and aggressive, and it had worsened with time, so much so that she had to make a big effort not to hate her.

What if anything had happened to her child! And Janie *was* her child: she had reared her, cared for her, loved her; and yet in doing so she had imprisoned her; but only for her own safety. With what result? Yes, she knew if anything had happened to Janie she would scream her loathing at her sister, and at her father, too. Oh, yes, at her father, who cared for nothing, nor for no-one but the replica of his wife.

As she turned away she was surprised by the fact that she could think of her mother just as her father's wife . . .

Carl had dismounted from his horse, which was now holding up its head as it answered the neighing of another in a stable along the yard; then he turned to meet Lady Lydia's approach.

Her greeting was warm: "Hello, Carl," she said. "Dear! dear! it's such a long time since we met, but . . . but it's enviable how you carry your years because you don't appear any older than when I last saw you."

"Thank you, Lady Lydia." He nodded at her as he smiled. "I would like to believe that. You're very kind, as always."

She asked now, "Can I help you in any way?"

"We've had a little upset back at the farm, and the child—you know, the young girl, Janie—has been missing since this morning. And Miss Jessie wondered if you would allow me to look through your grounds to see if she might . . . well"—he shrugged his shoulders—"it's a faint hope because I don't know how she could have got into your place. But as I said, Miss Jessie thinks she might be hiding somewhere. It's a sort of last straw before we apply for further help from . . . the polis. And I . . . well, you can understand Mr. Gibson wouldn't take kindly to that."

"Oh no; I can understand. And of course you are very welcome to search where you like. My son is out at the moment. He's on some business in the town and McNamara, our gardener, is with him. They were killing two birds with one stone, so to speak." She smiled before adding, "We run a business now, you know, called a smallholding." She poked her face forward, an amused expression on it, and he said, "Yes. Yes, I've heard, and also, m'lady, that it's doing well."

"Yes. Yes." Her eyes widened now. "Surprisingly well. My son seems to be a genius with a pick and shovel, which, too, is very surprising when he doesn't appear to be . . . well, to have a manual temperament. Books are more in his line."

Carl smiled at her now, saying, "Yes. Yes, I recall that was his line, m'lady. We had a talk now and again when he came home from the university, and he recommended one or two books to me that were good reading. Yes, yes, that was his line."

"Would you like to leave your horse here"—she pointed . . . "there are plenty of empty stables—while you look around?"

"Thank you, thank you. I'll do that." Now his smile widened: "And he won't be lost for company, as he's already made evident," he added.

He turned now and led the horse into a stable towards which Lady Lydia was pointing; then after closing the half-door on his animal he bade her goodbye by saying, "Thank you for your kindness, m'lady." And to this she answered, while shaking her head, "Oh, 'tis nothing. If we can be of help in any way, you must tell us."

It was a full hour later when he returned to the yard, and there being no-one about he knocked on the kitchen door; and when it was opened by a maid, he said briefly to her, "Will you please give her ladyship my thanks?" He did not add, "I haven't found her," for, as he knew only too well, maids' tongues rattled, and not only inside the house. So he turned and retrieved his horse and rode away, leaving Nancy Bellways asking herself, "And what has he got to thank her for, I wonder."

It was not fifteen minutes later when Gerald entered the house and, having been informed by Nancy that his mother was in the sitting-room, he went straight there, making a dramatic gesture as he opened the door: flinging his arms wide, he cried, "Success! Success! Another avenue has opened: fruit, flowers and vegetables, they'll take as much as we can supply."

He allowed his arms to drop, then moved quickly towards her, asking, "What's wrong?"

"Nothing here," she said. "And I'm so glad about the new orders. But Carl from Gibson's farm called in. The child is missing, you know, the daughter of the young girl. Something must have happened at the farm this morning because they've been searching all day, and he came to see if he could look through the grounds. Of course I said yes, but I didn't see him when later he left. He gave only a brief message to Nancy, and didn't say whether or not he had found her. Well, I didn't expect him to. Likely, if the child was running away she would have come here, wouldn't she? She would have made for a house, surely? Yet, I don't know."

"How long ago was this?"

"Oh"—she thought for a moment—"since Nancy told me, I should think some twenty minutes or so. Anyway, our place seemed to be the last resort for them before they went to the police. But come; sit down and tell me all your news. Nancy's just brought the tea in."

"I'll just have a cup, Mama, then I'll go and have a look through the woods and thereabouts."

"But Carl has already done that, dear."

"Yes, I know, but"—he smiled at her—"he doesn't know this place as I know it. Don't forget, I used to hide in the woods when father was on the rampage looking for me when I had yet again refused to play toy soldiers."

"Don't be silly, Gerald. Your father never wanted you to play toy soldiers."

"Well, the equivalent during my vacs: riding hell for leather over the fields as if we were in tournaments, lances pointed—I'm sure he imagined he was doing that half of his time—then yelling at me when I purposely missed shooting the rooks. What was that but soldier practice? Anyway, I knew some good hidey-holes. Now, I won't be long, and I'll tell you all about our latest rise in the business when I come back."

He heard her tut-tutting as he left the room; then he was hurrying through the yard and into the labyrinth of garden beds that still hadn't been cleared. As he approached the near-derelict woodman's cottage his step slowed, and at the door he stopped and called in a low voice, "Are you there? It's only me." Then there being no answer, he went on, "I'm the man that knows about your rabbit hole."

When there was still no answer he pushed past the hanging door and passed through the first room and into the second. And there, about to rise from the mattress that he knew had housed a colony of field mice, he saw her. And he stared at her in amazement and pity for her chin and neck were covered with dried blood, as was one of her hands. She was blinking at him as she said, "I . . . I must have fallen asleep."

"Oh, my dear!" He was sitting on the mattress beside her now. "What on earth's happened?" And when he went to touch her hand, she jerked it back from him, saying, "There's . . . there's pieces of glass still in it."

"What?"

"She . . . she threw the lamp at me."

"Who did?"

"The . . . the—" She had to swallow hard now before she could go on and say, "The woman, or person who they say is my mother."

His eyes stretched, his mouth dropped into a gape, and he asked softly, "But how did it come about?"

"I . . . I wanted to see her. I oiled the rusty keys and got in the back way. When I went into her room—" She now screwed up her eyes tightly, then did a strange thing: she put her tongue right out and brought her teeth down on it as if to stop herself talking. And when he said, "Come, dear; we must get you home," she shrank back from him, saying, "No! No! Auntie Jessie will keep the door locked on me forever now."

"Oh no, she won't. No. No, she won't. I promise you."

"How . . . how can you promise me; you don't live there."

"No, I don't." His voice was stern now. "But I shall see . . . I shall make it my business that no-one locks you up again."

"Will you?"

"Yes, I will. And that is a promise."

"I feel very tired. I . . . I heard Carl calling me."

"Didn't he come in here?"

"I wasn't in here then, I was lying in the thicket, but I didn't let him know. Then I felt very tired and I remembered the bed." She turned her head and looked behind her and said, "The mice all ran away. They were only small. I am not afraid of mice."

He took out a handkerchief now, but when he went to wipe her face she pulled her head back, saying, "I think my neck is cut." And when he looked closer he could detect a long scratch covered with dried blood. He didn't know how deep it might be, but he did know he must get her back to her home, and that she must see a doctor, for there were still pieces of glass in her hand. Good God! It was unbelievable that her mother, who had once been that beautiful, fragile young girl, was capable of wreaking such vengeance on her offspring; but then it was her offspring that had wrecked her life. What a tangle! What a dreadful, dreadful tangle!

"You're a very sensible little girl," he said more gently now, "and you must know that you cannot stay here. It will soon be nightfall and the animals"—he moved his hand as though he knew of their whereabouts—"they'll come roving round here and frighten the life out of you."

"I'm not afraid of animals."

No, she wasn't afraid of animals, it was people she was afraid of, and with good cause. He said, "Now listen, my dear. Nothing bad is going to happen to you when you get back home. I shall make it my business to see that you are in no way punished for—" What word would he give to a child for wanting to see her mother? The only one that came to mind was escapade, and that is what he said—"for your escapade."

She shook her head slowly now, then asked him a question that he could not answer: "Why are things at the farm like they are?" When he made no reply, she went on, "Other children can get out and run about. I saw them, lots of them. Were you ever locked up when you were a boy?"

"Yes"—he could smile at her—"and apart from some water I had nothing to eat or drink for a full day."

"What had you done?"

"Well . . . I had kicked one of the yard men; then I had thrown a bucket of"—again he paused—"not too clean water over him."

"Why did you do that?"

"Because"—he had to think here of his next words—"he was treating some animals as I thought he shouldn't." He couldn't go on to say he was drowning a litter of unwanted puppies.

When she moved her hand and winced, he got up, saying firmly, "Now you must come back with me. I've already told you, haven't I? and I promise you again, you won't be locked in."

"How can you stop me being locked in? You don't live there."

"There are ways and means, my dear, ways and means. Now, come along."

When she stood up she swayed slightly. And when he went to take her hand she said, "Oh, don't touch that hand, please, it's very sore."

"I wasn't going to touch your poor hand; but give me your other hand."

She gave him her hand; but when they were outside the cottage he stopped her and, looking down on her, said, "Now you know you can't crawl back through your rabbit hole because you mustn't get dirt in that hand. If you were to do so, well . . . I don't know what would happen. So we'll go by the road."

To this she made no objection; and so he now led her through the grounds and to the actual ditch she had jumped on the day she visited the school. And after helping her across, he stamped down the broken railings with his feet, making note that this part of the boundary must be seen to. But they hadn't walked very far towards the farm when her step slowed and she said, "Can we sit down for a while? I am feeling very tired."

He looked down at her, then along both sides of the road before saying reluctantly, "There is nowhere to sit here, my dear, except on the verge." But when she suddenly leant her head against his arm he shook his own as though for the moment he was perplexed, but then, bending down to her, he said, "I am going to lift you up and carry you. Now I won't hurt your hand. Just hold it out away from me."

She made no protest. But when she was in his arms and leant her head against his shoulder, it came to him that on their walk here she had not chatted at all and that the child might not only be tired, but ill, and not only from her injuries but from shock. And further, as he approached the farm gate, he was thinking it not only strange but somewhat weird that he had once also helped to carry the child's mother through these gates, and now he was carrying the child herself.

He was greeted with a loud shout: it was from Hamish McNabb, crying, "Mr. Carl! man. Look! Look!" as he dashed, not towards Gerald, but to the kitchen door, from where there now appeared not only Carl but also Jessie and Patsy.

"Where did you find her?" Jessie ran quickly to meet them.

"God! Look at the sight of her." This remark came from Carl and was mixed up with other exclamations.

But it was to Jessie that Gerald addressed himself, saying, "Where does she sleep? And . . . and I think you should get a doctor as soon as possible."

Jessie had stepped quickly ahead of him, one hand stretched out as if to guide him to the cottage, but now turned and called, "Carl! get . . . get Doctor Patten." Then she was pushing open the cottage door; and when they stepped into the room she guided Gerald further, saying, "Through here. Through here, please."

They were in the bedroom now, and gently and thankfully he laid the child down on the bed. And when Jessie exclaimed tearfully, "Oh! the blood. I . . . I'll get a basin," he stopped her, saying, "I would do nothing until the doctor comes. I think there are splinters of glass still in her hand. I don't know about her neck."

"Where . . . where did you find her?"

"In my wood."

"But Carl searched there not long . . ."

"Yes, I know. But Carl belongs to this house, and I must tell you it was to this house she was afraid of returning." He watched her stiffen as he went on, "And, too, I must tell you, Miss Jessie, that her freedom must not be curtailed to the extent of her being locked up."

"Mr. Ramsmore, this . . . this is our business. She is my responsibility."

"I am aware of that, Miss Jessie. But I repeat, she is to be given the freedom due to a child."

"Sir, you are interfering in something that is none of your business."

"It may not have been in the past, but I can inform you that it certainly will be in the future."

"My father is the head of this household and he can do what he likes."

"To my knowledge, your father ignores the child, and if I am to go by rumour, he cursed the day she was born. So your father wouldn't care if she roamed the country and was picked up by the gypsies or run down by a horse."

"Sir! You are taking advantage." She choked on her next words but brought out, "You have no right at all."

"I think I have, Miss Jessie. Remember I found her mother and I helped to carry her back into this house. And it is that very mother who has denied this child her rights to a mother and who, I would imagine, made an attempt to kill her. Look at her." He now turned about and pointed down to the still and apparently sleeping figure of the child, then said, "Whether or not you like it, I have been forced through circumstances to take an interest in the child. Today isn't the first time we've met. And if I don't happen to meet her in the near future then I shall know that you have continued to incarcerate her. That might seem a strong word, but the child is of a very lively nature and to be locked up in this"—he looked from one side to the other, as if encompassing the whole room—"rabbit hutch, can be described as nothing else but incarceration." And almost bouncing his head towards her, he turned about and stamped from the cottage, leaving her gasping, one hand clutching her throat, the other her bodice.

A movement from the bed brought her attention back to the child, who had raised heavy lids to look at her for a moment before she brought out slowly, "I'm sorry, Auntie Jessie." And with only the plight of the child filling her mind now, Jessie said, "It's all right, dear, it's all right. Lie quiet, the doctor's coming."

But when presently Janie said, "Where's the nice man?" Jessie had to force herself to say, "He . . . he has gone home."

"Will he come back?"

"Er . . . perhaps. Go to sleep now."

"Auntie Jessie?"

"Yes, dear?"

"I know now why you didn't want me to see her. She isn't nice, is she?"

Jessie didn't question who wasn't nice, but after biting down on her lip she said, "Lie quiet now, dear." Then bending closer to Janie's face, she asked, "What did you say?" and almost a look of horror came on her own as she heard the child say, "She was in disorder like the bull."

When, last year, they had to shoot the bull that had suddenly gone mad, the child had been a witness to the men's efforts with pitchforks to corner it in the barn, and she herself had explained that it was some disorder in its mind and it would have done serious harm if it hadn't been destroyed. And now she had likened her mother to the bull. She hadn't said mad, just disordered, yet she must have heard the men in the yard discussing the animal as mad. She turned away from the bed, saying to herself, "Hurry up, Doctor, please, so I can get her cleaned and into bed."

It was a good hour later when Doctor Philip Patten arrived. And he stood looking down where the child lay fully dressed and just as Gerald had brought her in. Then turning to Jessie, he remarked, "Well, this should clinch the matter, shouldn't it? whatever your father decides. I shall want a bowl of warm water." Then turning to the bed again, he said softly, "How do you feel, Janie?"

"Very tired, Doctor; and my hand is paining."

"We'll soon put that right, dear. Now this might hurt just a little." He lifted her hand and moved his finger in between the blood stains, and each time she winced so his eyes met hers. And then he said, "Ah, well now, you have four splinters in there, Janie, and I'll have to take them out, won't I?"

"Yes, Doctor."

"Well, now, I'll be as gentle as I possibly can, but in the meantime we will get it nicely cleaned up. Ah, here is your aunt with a dish of nice warm water. Now I want you to put your hand into it and keep it there while I look at your neck. Ah, that's right. Now can you move it backwards and forwards? Oh, that's a clever girl."

After examining her neck, he said, "Just a long scratch, no glass here." Then he turned and pointed to his bag, saying briefly, "Cotton wool." And after Jessie had handed it to him he showed it to Janie, saying, "I'm just going to wipe your hand very gently"; and as he did so she did not wince.

As he extracted the first sliver of glass she cried, "Oh! Oh dear!"

And by the time he had extracted the fourth sliver she was lying gasping, and her face was wet with perspiration.

After he had carried out the cleansing of her neck, he put his hand on her forehead before taking her pulse; then patting her cheek, he said, "The quicker you get into your nightie and into bed the better, eh?"

When, a few minutes later, he was standing in the other room facing Jessie, his tone had an edge to it as he said, "She has a temperature. It is some time since this morning when this incident occurred—I understand Mr. Ramsmore found her lying in his wood. Well, the result of that delay, if not of the shock, will likely result in a fever. I will leave a mild draught to settle her down, but I'll be back first thing in the morning."

He sighed deeply as if he were tired of the happenings that called for his attention in this household; and when he left without bidding her goodbye, she had much the same feeling as when Gerald Ramsmore had departed, and she muttered to herself, "Men! Arrogant men!" And lining up with these two was the figure of her father . . . but not Carl. No; not Carl. Carl was the only male in her life whose tone had never been other than kind.

It was four days later. Janie had developed pneumonia, and Jessie's and Patsy's time was taken up attending her. And every spare moment Carl had would be spent assisting them. A steam tent was erected and this necessitated a continuous supply of kettles full of steaming Friar's Balsam.

Ward was left almost entirely on his own to see to the needs of his daughter, which however were now very simple: the draught the doctor was giving her was keeping her quietly subdued. In fact, she seemed to sleep all the time; only when her father would raise her head and say, "Drink this, dear," which might be milk or tea, did she rouse herself. At first she had protested, but he had put one strong arm around her, so pinning her hands, and forced her to gulp at the liquid. But now on the fourth day she was making no effort to refuse; the only effort she made was when she was sick. And it was on this fourth day that Philip Patten came into the room unannounced and to witness her vomiting.

"How long has she been like this? I mean, is she often sick?"

"No, not often," Ward replied. "I made her eat some dinner. It was cold food as usual, for you can imagine we have no attention from downstairs, and I think that's what she's bringing up."

When Ward took the dish from the bed, Philip Patten noticed the colour of it, and it wasn't, he thought, much like the eruption of cold mutton. It had a dark greeny tinge, which could very well be bile.

After taking hold of her wrist he turned for a moment and looked at Ward as if he was about to say something. Instead, he first laid the hand back on the coverlet and paused for a moment before announcing, "I'm going to stop the draughts. I think she's had enough; she should come round now. And may I ask what you have decided to do?"

"Yes. Yes." Ward was washing his hands in the basin on the wash-hand stand, his back to the doctor, and he repeated, "Yes. Yes, I have decided. We'll get someone in."

"Good. Good. I'm glad of that. Well now"—Philip Patten gave a half smile—"I've no need to open my bag tonight. By the way, there's a good nursing agency in Newcastle. It's just off Northumberland Street. I've forgotten exactly the name of the street."

"Oh, I know it. It's Cranwell Place; at least, so I found out yesterday. I looked it up. It was advertised in the paper. I'll go in today and make arrangements."

The doctor turned and looked at the bed. "She'll still be quiet I think. Yes. Yes. What time did you give her the dose last night?"

"Oh, not till rather late, about eleven, just before I lay down myself."

"Oh well, I suppose that will do it." He did not add, "I must go and see your granddaughter," for he knew what would make this man happy was the thought that the child could die. And so he left the room saying simply, "I'll see you tomorrow."

Half an hour later Ward once again lifted his daughter up from the pillows and, forcing her head back, poured most of a glass of milk down her throat, then put the glass on the side table before he wiped her mouth and arranged her hair. Finally, bending over her, he kissed her twice and, his head deep on his chest, he muttered, "Goodbye, my darling." Then he went out of the room. He entered the kitchen to see Patsy scurrying around. She was throwing roughly-cut vegetables into a pot in which already there was a piece of lamb. As she pushed it on to the hob she remarked, "You'll have a hot meal by dinner time."

"I won't be in to dinner. You'll be pleased to hear I'm going into town to engage help . . . nursing help, for both night and day."

She stood looking at him for some seconds; then she nodded once, saying, "Yes. Yes, master. I'm pleased to hear that."

As he turned to go back into the hall, he remarked, "I'll have a bite in town; and she won't need anything, she's still under the doctor's draught."

"Very good." Patsy nodded towards his back. The kitchen to herself again, she thought, none too pleasantly, that'll mean two of them, night and day I suppose. Well, they won't have me waiting on them. Meals, yes: but that's all. And this decision made, she left the kitchen by the back door that took her into the yard, there to see her master mounting the trap. Carl was standing to the side of it and the master was saying something to him. And she watched her husband wait until the trap had disappeared into the lane beyond the farm gates before he turned towards her, and she to him, and her first words were, "He's going to get help, night and day people."

"Yes." He nodded at her, then enquired, "How's the youngster?"

"Oh, we won't know until tonight, I suppose, but she's holding her own. You know, I think Miss Jessie will go as daft as her sister up there"—she thumbed towards the house—"if anything happens to that child. You know, she looks upon her as if she had given birth to her."

"Well, she might as well have; she's seen to her since the minute she was born."

She looked at him closely now, saying, "What's the matter? Something wrong?"

"No. No, nothing."

"You look more thoughtful than usual."

He smiled at her now, saying, "Do I? Well, I've got a lot to think about."

"Yes," she said somewhat tartly, "about this bloomin' place. It's never about us, ourselves."

"Oh, that isn't fair, Patsy. You know it isn't."

She folded her arms tightly now before saying, "I get tired of it at times, Carl. We have no life of our own. And I'm at the beck and call of that one up there."

"Well, you won't be any longer, will you, if he's getting help?"

"No; but I'll have other work. I'll have more cooking, won't I? And Mrs. McNabb can only do the rough."

"But, you know, dear, we took it on, and we will be half owners of the place . . ."

She turned quickly to interrupt him, saying, "Yes, but when? When? When he dies, the master? He could live for another twenty years. And so could she. But just imagine if he went and we're left with her. I know what I would do with her, and I've heard the doctor say the same on the quiet. Perhaps not in so many words, but I know what he thinks."

"Yes. Yes, you're right, Patsy. But that's the last thing the master would do. He'd never let her be put away, you know that. He'd go to any lengths, yes, any lengths"—he nodded now as he looked to the side—"before he'd put her in an asylum."

"Well, if she has another turn like she had the other morning, that's where she'll end, because she could have killed the child. Her poor little hand is swollen up twice the size, and it was only a scratch on her neck, so Doctor Patten said, but it's going to leave a mark. It started to ooze blood again yesterday. To my mind it should have been stitched."

"Well, I suppose the doctor knew what he was doing," and then as if to dismiss the matter, he said further: "I've got to get on now." But as he went to walk away, she called after him, "Carl, the master said he wouldn't be in for dinner—he's going to have a bite in town—and that she would sleep. But I can't leave her all day up there by herself, can I? And yet, at the same time, I'm not going to go in that room by myself. I've never ventured in, unless the master's been there, for some time now. So will you come on up with me?"

"Yes. Yes, of course. But she'll likely scream the place down when she sees me."

"I don't suppose so; she's been under those sleeping draughts for days now. But I must warn you, you'll see a difference in her. Since you last saw her she's become like an old woman."

"I could never imagine her looking like an old woman."

"Just wait till you see her. She's a vixen of an old woman at that."

"Well, give me a shout when you need me." And with that he went across the yard, and she made her way to the cottage . . .

It was almost three o'clock when she called to him as he was weighing out the meal in the corn room: "I'm going up now," she said.

"Righto." He left what he was doing and walked towards her, clapping his hands and dusting down his clothes. And as he crossed the yard he smiled at her as he said, "I don't suppose she'll notice I'm not spruced up."

"I don't suppose she'll notice you're even there. But, of course, you never know; I haven't seen her for days. I really don't know how the master can stand looking after her day and night. He's even been sleeping on the sofa in the room. But then, he's always been as barmy about her as he was about her mother."

They were in the kitchen when he put an arm around her waist and said, "Aren't you still barmy about me?"

And now she looked at him softly and seriously as she said, "Yes, Carl. I'm still barmy about you, and always will be. But at the same time I'm filled full of guilt, because I can't rear a family for you."

"Now, look . . . look, I've told you, it doesn't matter one jot to me. I want you and not a family. I've told you, dear."

"Aye, you could go on telling me for the rest of your life and I would try to believe it, all the while knowing that I can't. Every man wants a family. But . . . but look, I don't want to start and bubble here; I've done enough crying in me time. Let's get upstairs."

He kissed her before he let her go; then they were climbing the stairs together.

She entered the room first, and he hesitantly followed. She went and stood near the bed and looked down on the still form; then she turned towards him, whispering hoarsely, "Carl! Carl! Come here. Look at her."

Quickly and quietly he went and stood by her side, but said nothing as he looked down on the face that now had a young appearance. The eyes were wide open, the lips apart. He was seeing the young girl again as she was before the night of the magic lantern show.

"Oh, my God! My God!"

"Be quiet!" he said. "Get out of the way."

He moved close to the head of the bed and put his hand tentatively on the white nightdress and left it there for some seconds. Then Patsy's voice expressed the futility of what he was doing as she hissed at him, "She's dead! She's dead! Look at her eyes, she's dead." She backed from the bed now, whimpering, "I should have come up before. I should. Yes, I should."

"No, you shouldn't!" His voice was firm but quiet. "Look; go down and get one of them. It better be Rob, as he can ride the horse. Tell him to go for Doctor Patten as soon as possible. I'll stay here. Go on now." But he had to press her as she walked backwards towards the door.

He looked about him, and presently muttered something to himself, then said aloud, " 'Tis the best way. And he knew what he was doing." And with the thought he went over to the side table on which stood a glass with about half an inch of white liquid left in it. This he lifted and smelt, then held it up to eye level. There was some sediment at the bottom of the glass. His suspicions had been right. Yet, he wouldn't believe it when he had seen him at the tin. It was the dim light of a covered lantern that had attracted him to the store-room. He had been unable to sleep, and he had lain listening to the dogs growling in the yard. It was when they stopped abruptly that he had risen and gone to the window of their bedroom, the room that used to be the master's study and which looked on to the end of the yard. It was from there he had seen the light in the store-room. This had puzzled him. If the light had been next door in the harness-room he could have understood it, for then somebody would have been after a harness or horse's accoutrements of some kind. But who would want to be in the store-room, where only empty sacks, boxes, or tools and such were kept?

He had pulled on a coat and gone quietly outside and made for the window, and there, to his amazement, he had seen the master with a tin in his hand. After watching him put the tin back on the shelf on which were kept rat poisons and such, he had scampered back into the house. But the next morning, early on, he had examined the tins. There was a dust of powder against three of them: one contained rat poison; a second, arsenic; the third a kind of jellied liquid which they diluted for spraying.

He now put his hand tightly across his jaws. But when he heard footsteps running on the landing, he turned towards the door and there was Patsy again. She was breathless, and she said, "Doctor's behind. There was no need to go, he was just coming in the yard to see the child. He's . . . he's here now." Her face was wet with tears, and again she said, "I should have come up earlier. I should, I know I should."

"Be quiet! Be quiet!" He turned and looked towards the glass on the table, but there was no time to remove it, for there stood the doctor.

Philip Patten looked down on the woman whom death had transformed into a girl, and slowly he did what Carl had done earlier; he placed his hand on her chest. Then he felt her wrist. Then, just as slowly, he closed her eyelids and drew the bed-sheet over her, before turning to the two people who were standing staring at him. And now he spoke, saying, "When did it happen? I mean, when did you find her?"

"It was me, Doctor. Just . . . just a few minutes ago. I was scampering downstairs to send for you and . . . and, well, there you were. I know I should have come up earlier. But when he left, I mean the master, he said she would be quiet after the draught you gave her, and that he was going into town to hire some help."

He nodded, then said, "She's had nothing to drink today?"

"No. No. I should have brought something up, but I was afraid of her on me own, the way she's been. Well, he said she would sleep for some time. And then I went and got Carl to come up with me."

"It's all right. It's all right, Patsy. Look, go downstairs and make us a pot of tea."

"Yes. Yes, Doctor." She looked from one to the other, then turned and hurried out.

Philip Patten now looked around the room, taking in the glass on the side table holding a small amount of white liquid; and he resisted the urge to go near it. This room was impregnated with tragedy and sorrow and he asked himself, Was he going to add to it? He knew full well that the sedative he had left to be given to her each day in no way would have caused her demise. Anyway, if more proof than was already in his own mind were needed, he had only to go by her pupils, and the fact that her father had definitely made up his mind what was going to happen to her. He had taken advantage of her being rested under the sedative and then had thought he was being clever in showing that he was apparently agreeing to the lesser evil: either she went into an asylum or he got competent nurses to see to her. Oh, Ward had thought it all out. But what was he himself to do about it? Accuse him? There was that accusing white sediment in that glass. He had slipped up there, hadn't he? He had only to test it himself and find the slightest trace of a poison and that would be proof enough. And what then? The man could hang, or, if compassion came into the judgment, be imprisoned for the rest of his life. And how old was he now? Early fifties?

He went past Carl and stood near the window looking down on the garden, and he asked himself where he stood in this. What was his duty? Oh, he knew what his duty was all right. But could he carry it out? And who was to know if he didn't? Who was to ask questions about the death of one demented woman, when the whole country was at war? Even the village was caught up in the excitement. The fact that Ward Gibson's daughter had died would cause nothing but a flutter.

He turned briskly from the window and, looking towards the bed, he said, "I think I have missed something. I had better examine her again. There are signs that she may have died from a blood clot on the brain. As I recall, her mother went the same way. Look, slip down and bring me a cup of tea up, will you?"

"Yes. Yes, Doctor."

As soon as Carl had left the room Philip Patten picked up the glass, swirled the contents round, dipped his finger in it, then tasted it. As he placed the glass back on the table his jaws met tightly together for a moment. Before grabbing it up again he emptied the contents in the china slop bucket standing beneath the wash-hand stand; then he half-filled the glass with water from a ewer, did some more swilling, then poured this into the bucket, after which he took a handkerchief from his pocket and wiped the glass clean, paying particular attention to the bottom of it. He had only just managed to pull the sheet down from over the still face when the door opened and Carl entered carrying a small tray with cups of tea on it and by its side a bowl of sugar.

As he laid the tray on the side table, Carl noticed the clean glass, and he stared at it for a second. When he looked up the doctor had turned from the bed and their gaze linked and held for some seconds with the unspoken knowledge they both shared . . .

Philip Patten did not return to the house until six o'clock that evening. Ward was sitting in the room that he used also as a dining-room. He rose to his feet as Philip came up the room, and his head was slightly drooped and his eyes cast down as he said, "I came back to a shock."

When there was no response to this he raised his head and looked at Philip, and added, "She was resting peacefully when I left her."

There was a war going on in the doctor's mind. The man's attitude was making him regret that he had washed that glass out: he must think him an idiot. Had Ward's wily brain not taken in the fact that there would be a post-mortem? He hated to be thought the doctor who didn't know his business; but he knew he must go carefully; if the man thought that his doctor was condoning a poisoning, he could hold it over him. Not that he thought Ward would do such a thing. Yet one never knew how a man's mind could be turned, given the circumstances. The next moment he only just prevented himself from speaking the truth, bawling it, when Ward said, naïvely, "How do you think it came about, and . . . and so quickly?"

Philip had to turn away. And it was some seconds before he was able to say, "I . . . I think her heart must have given out, or she had a blood clot on the brain."

"Oh. Well, well!"

Philip swung round to see Ward now walking towards the fireplace, where he put one hand up and gripped the mantelshelf and stood looking down into the fire as he said, "Isn't that strange: her mother went in the same way. Well, she's at peace now. God rest her soul. Yes. Yes." He turned now from the fireplace and looked at Philip, saying again, "She's at peace. But what I must do first thing in the morning is get word to the agency in Newcastle. I'll be able to prevent one of the nurses coming. She was due at the week-end. But the other, the day nurse, she was to start in the morning."

Philip could stand no more. He made his way towards the door, saying, "I must go and see your granddaughter. She's in a very bad way. By the look of her she may not last the night." He was half-way down the room when he swung round and in a loud voice said, "And don't say that you hope she joins the others! Just don't say it!"

And now he witnessed the real man again, not the actor, as Ward yelled back at him, "Don't say that she will join the others, for she never will. She's not of this house. There's none of my daughter in her."

For a matter of seconds they glared at each other across the distance, until Philip turned about and, on leaving the room, banged the oak door so fiercely behind him that it actually shook the architrave.

Janie recovered from the pneumonia. But the illness had so sapped her small strength that it was not until the end of September, seven weeks later, that she was able to walk alone in the farmyard. And there she was greeted by McNabb, who cried, "Well, you're a sight for sore eyes, I'll say that, Miss Janie. And look at the height of you. You've sprouted. You'll soon be as big as meself. Where've you got that height from? You were a little striplin' the last time I saw you."

She smiled at him now as she said, "That must have been many years ago, Mr. McNabb." And at this, his head went back on his shoulders and he laughed as he said, "Well, it's many weeks ago, but it must have been years to you lyin' there. By! it is nice to see you again."

"Thank you, Mr. McNabb. It is nice to be out. I'm . . . I'm tired of sitting."

"Oh." He bent down to her and in a loud whisper he said, "If only they would let me sit a bit. Oh, if only; I'm on me feet mornin' till night. D'you think you could see Mr. Carl and ask him to let me sit?"

She was laughing into his face now, and what she said was, "You are a funny man, Mr. McNabb."

Now she turned to watch Carl approaching across the yard, and to hear McNabb cry at him, "She says I'm a funny man, Mr. Carl. That's what she said, I'm a funny man."

"And you'll look funny, too," Carl admonished him, "if you don't get about your business, and this minute!"

"There you are, miss. You see what I mean about sittin'?" And the tall Scot turned away laughing, and Carl, taking Janie's hand, said, "You going for a walk?"

"Just a little."

"You're looking grand."

"Mr. McNabb says I've sprouted. That's what he said, I've sprouted. Am I much taller than I was?"

"Yes. Yes, you are. My! I would say you have sprouted. I didn't notice it so much when you were in the cottage. But here, now"—he drew away from her and looked her up and down—"you must have put on six inches. Yes, I'd say you've put on six inches."

"Is that a lot?"

"It's a lot at your age," he said, but then quickly asked, "Where're you making for? I wouldn't try the fields; there was a lot of dew in the night."

"No, I wasn't going across the fields. I was going on to the road, nice and flat. Auntie Jessie says I may go through the gate."

"She did?" There was a note of surprise in his voice. And she nodded at him, saying, "Yes. But she also said"—and now she looked up at him—"that I mustn't be a nuisance. And that means, should I meet my grandfather I am not to speak to him. Can you tell me why, Carl? I've asked Auntie Jessie, but what she says is, that he . . . he is still suffering the loss of—" She paused and swallowed: she could not say, "my mother," but tactfully added, "his daughter. But I told her, or I reminded her, that he hadn't spoken to me when she was alive. I cannot understand it, Carl."

Carl asked himself how he could answer this one. However weak the illness had left her, it hadn't weakened her thinking or probing. She would get to the bottom of it one day. But it shouldn't be now. She was too old for her years. But what could you expect? she'd had no ordinary babyhood or childhood. She had been among adults all her life and she had listened to their prattle. And her thinking must have been heightened by her sharp ears and taking in what wasn't meant for her, with the result that things had left her puzzled.

"Can I ask you something, Carl?"

"Anything, Janie."

"Well, did the nice man call when I was ill?"

"The nice man?" He screwed up his face, thought a moment, then said, "Oh, you mean Mr. Gerald from the Hall?"

"Yes, from the Hall."

"Yes. Yes, he came a number of times, and brought you nice big bunches of grapes. Didn't Miss Jessie tell you who the grapes were from?"

"No. She only said a visitor had brought them. She does not like me speaking . . . of him. When I first mentioned him she said she didn't want to hear anything more about him, as he was a very rude man. But I found him very nice."

"I'm sure you did. And he is a nice man. He carried you home, you know, on that particular day."

"Oh, I knew he brought me home, but I don't remember him carrying me."

"Well, he did." He now bent down to her, saying, "You were so drunk you couldn't stand."

She pushed him with her hand, laughing, as she exclaimed now, "Oh, it is nice to be out again, Carl, and to be able to walk. I mean, on my own."

Looking down on her, he thought to himself, Yes, and you've got the nice man to thank for that an' all. He recalled Gerald's second visit and the talk they'd had in the barn there. It had been very open on both sides. And he believed what the young fellow had said he would do if the child was locked up again. Oh yes, he certainly meant business about that, and this was the result. The only obstacle to this new freedom, as he saw it, was a big one: what would happen should she confront the master and in her forthright way ask him why he wouldn't speak to her or recognise her person . . . Well, sufficient unto the day the evil thereof. Today was bright and the child was happy. In fact, it could be said the whole atmosphere of the place had certainly lightened from the day they had buried Miss Angela; yet he knew it hadn't for the master: he had become more morose than ever.

Carl had imagined that now Ward didn't need to give most of his time to his daughter, his old interest in the farm would have returned. But it hadn't. In fact, he walked less, and spent most of his time either in the sitting-room or in his bedroom. Could it be that his mind was affected, too?

However, the work inside the house was definitely lighter, and Patsy was in a better frame of mind. At first, the war had troubled her in case he should be called up: being thirty-six he was still within the age limit. But then he was running a farm and food was wanted, and so it was a special job. He had no fear for himself, but they might take Rob. The first spate of patriotism seemed to have died down somewhat, only to have been re-awakened by rumour of German atrocities, especially that of sticking babies on the end of bayonets. Unfounded, but it had brought a fresh surge to the Colours. It also brought, and soon, three heroes into the village, but they were all dead ones. And Mike had reported the strong village feeling that was growing against Mr. Gerald, because he had openly said that in no way would he take up arms and fight. Apparently he had made no bones about it. This, Carl thought, was a daft thing to have done; he should have kept his mouth shut. He had surely lived long enough in the vicinity before he went away to know how the villagers reacted to individual opposition. Of course, he was well aware of it, for hadn't he had to leave his home because he dared to stand up for the truth that day in the church? Nevertheless, he still thought he was a fool for making his opinions so plain, because as far as he could gather, conscientious objectors were being given hell one way or another.

They were outside the gate now, and he said to Janie, "Which way are you going to walk?" And she pointed along the road: "That way," she said.

He bent down to her and, quietly, he said, "That leads, after a long walk, to the village. But you won't go that far, will you?" And she looked at him and said, "No. No, I won't, Carl. I don't want to go to the village. The people there are not nice. No, I will just walk a little way, then I will come back. I promised Auntie Jessie that, too."

Watching her walking away, he thought: there goes an old head on young shoulders. And he wondered if the old head would be strong enough to face the future and what lay in it, particularly for her.

Book Three
1916–1921

Part One

ONE

*I*t was in February 1916 that War Office form W.3236 came through the post. It stated that the recipient was required to join some section of the armed forces. And that if this was not complied with the recipient would be regarded as a deserter. Also the recipient was expected either to present himself at the local recruiting station or to send documentary evidence entitling him to exemption. But the exemption, it stated, had to be accompanied by a certificate from the local tribunal before which he would have appeared.

In November 1915 Gerald had appeared before a tribunal, made up, he recognised, of local businessmen of supposedly assumed varying standards, from the bank manager down to the butcher. There were women members, too, and their questioning he found virulent when he truthfully owned up to being a conscientious objector. However, he had pointed out that he was supplying a great deal of food to the community. And he felt it was only because of this and the particular sympathy of two members of the tribunal, that it ordered suspension of the verdict for three months.

He knew that his suspension had, in a way, been a matter of luck, for his objections to his conscription had not been pleaded on religious grounds, for there were many doing so solely to save their own skins. It was reasonable to suspect that no conscientious objector was objecting solely on his principles.

And this he had strongly pointed out to his mother, to which she replied, "I don't blame them. And I beg of you, Gerald, do what I ask, please. Do this for me, or else I can see you, too, landing up in prison."

"I fully expect to, Mama."

"Oh, don't say that." She closed her eyes tightly, then swung round. "You've already told me what some of your company, as you call them, are going through in prisons. I couldn't believe it, but since that acting soldier wrote to the papers about it . . . well, you've got to think there's some truth in it."

"There's all truth in it, Mama. Some of the Army and the prison warders are treating these men of conscience much worse than any German would do. They claim that the Germans are barbarians; they haven't got a look-in where our brave Englishmen are concerned. Yes, it *is* true that they are being manacled, beaten into insensibility in some cases, and degraded in such a way that is hardly possible to imagine, because they refuse to do work of any kind to enable this barbarous business to go on. These men, to my mind, Mama, are heroes."

"So you want to be a *hero*, do you?"

"*No, I don't.* I'm not made of such stuff."

"Well, why don't you do what I'm asking? You said yourself, some time back, that you wouldn't mind driving an ambulance and going into the thick of it. So what's the difference in signing up with the Friends' Ambulance Unit? because you said there were Red Cross units that wouldn't look at a conscientious objector."

Gerald emitted a long drawn-out sigh before he flopped down on to a chair, saying, "It . . . it seems too easy a way out."

"Easy? If I'm to go by what Arthur says, they are given the most menial tasks possible and sent to France and all over the place."

"What does Arthur Tollett know about it? and he being in the Army all his life."

"Yes, Arthur's been in the Army all his life, but he's got very broad views. And . . . and although it's like betrayal, I must say that he saw things differently from your father." She went to him now and dropped down on her knees beside him and, gripping his hand, she said, "Do this for me, please. I'm worn out with worry about you."

He leant towards her and took her face into his hands and said softly, "And I'm worn out with worrying about me. And what will you do if I go now? McNamara will never be able to carry on by himself."

"I'll . . . I'll help him. I'm much stronger than I look. As long as I know you aren't in prison and . . ."

He sighed deeply, saying now, "Hush. Hush. All right. Let me have a look at that form again."

She now almost sprang up from the floor, rushed over to a sofa table, and returned with a sheet of paper.

Sitting back now, he read aloud: "I, so and so, and so and so, and so and so, of the so and so, so and so, so and so, in undertaking service with the Friends' Ambulance Unit, hereby agree to comply with the conditions which entitle me to the protection of the Geneva Convention and to observe the rules, regulations and orders issued by the officer commanding or by the committee, provided that I am not called upon to enlist and that my conscientious objection to military service is respected."

He now looked upon his mother, saying, "It's a Friends' Ambulance Unit, yet they go on to say that you must conform to all military etiquette when wearing the uniform, which you're expected to provide yourself, as well as your own kit. Now, I think that's a bit thick. They give you your food and lodgings and travelling expenses. How kind of them." He again looked up at her; then read on, "You are expected to serve for the duration of the war but with the right to leave after six months"—he nodded his head at her now—"which I take to mean I'd be drafted into the armed forces after all . . . Oh, Mama."

She stared at him now and her look was so pitiful that he said, "All right, all right. I've given you my word; I'll do it. And you know something? You're worse than any tribunal. I could face them and defy them, to the last breath, but there's you with that plaintive look on your face." He drew her up and, putting his arms about her shoulders, said, "I'm not worth all your trouble, dear. I really am not. Inside myself I know I'm not worth twopennorth of copper. The only real, strong bit about me is my so-called principles, which just means I don't like sticking a bayonet into another fellow's belly. All right! all right! My conversation tends to be coarse even before I get into the army or corps or whatever."

She smiled at him now, saying, "Unit, dear, friendly unit."

"Friendly unit? My!" He shook his head, then said, "How much time are you giving me before I sign my name on the dotted line?"

"No more than twenty-four hours, dear."

"You're joking!"

"No, I'm not. From what I gathered from Arthur, you could be up before another board, and this time not the local one, and this one wouldn't let you off for three months. And, oh, dear me! The very thought of it makes me . . ."

"All right, all right! dear. I have twenty-four hours. What shall I do with them?" He turned from her, walked over to one of the long windows that overlooked the terrace, and after a moment turned around, saying, "I'll get drunk, simply blind, paralytic drunk."

"There's not enough wine left in the cellar for that, dear."

"Who's talking about the cellar? I'll go out and paint the village red, give them something to remember me by, and likely land up in a cell and you'll have to come and bail me out."

She smiled at him tolerantly, saying, "Do that, dear, but not before dinner; it's Nancy's night off and cook's legs won't carry her back and forth from the dining-room to the kitchen, as you know; so leave it until after we've had dinner."

She now put her hand to his cheek in a gentle gesture and smiled at him before leaving the room. And he turned to the window again and his gaze roamed over the balcony, the drive, and that part of the flower garden they had cleared and which now looked bare, but actually was full of seeds, bulbs and young plants which, come the spring, would have given him a good harvest. And he looked beyond that, over the tall hedge to where lay the work of their main labours, now showing rows and rows of bright green heads of winter cabbages and brussel sprouts. Then on to the store-house where stood boxes of carrots and parsnips and such ready for Saturday market. And he felt a weakness in the bottom of his stomach, and it rose to his chest, then into his throat. Only the feeling that it might spring from his eyes in the form of tears turned him about.

He had never, up till this moment, realised how he was going to miss his work on his land, and this house, and his mother. And yes, the little visitor who came occasionally, not only to the woodman's cottage but also to this house, for she had become a kind of responsibility, a responsibility that worried him; at least her future did.

The calf was motherless. The cow, having died shortly after giving birth, had left a sickly calf which, if she were to survive, had to be fed four-hourly; and Janie had taken on to herself part of this nursing.

The calf was housed in a small partitioned area at the end of the long byre: Carl had told her that it would be comforted there by the sound of the others' voices. It was lying now in a bed of straw and, in order to give it a constant body warmth, two lighted lanterns were hanging close by on the end of the byre wall.

Janie was sitting with her back to the partition, and she talked softly to the small animal, which was lying quite inert: "Come on now, you'll like this," she said.

When it moved its head away from the teat she squeezed some milk out on to her fingers and put one to its mouth and rubbed its lip gently. And slowly now it began to suck; then with a deft movement she inserted the teat into its mouth and, tilting its head a little back, she said, "There now. Drink it all up, then you'll grow up to be a big girl, or"—she smiled down on it—"a big cow."

It was when the bottle was half-empty that she heard Mike come into the byre, and he was talking to someone. "You see," he was saying, "look at the length of this place. There's plenty to do an' this is just half of 'em. So, what we need here is more hands, not to lose any."

And now she heard a voice, one that she didn't recognise, reply, "Well, I should say you're safe enough."

"And so are all the others, mister."

"I understand you have a son working for you."

"Aye, you've been well informed. Me son does work here, but he's on forty. So, I should think it's been a waste of your journey trying to recruit round here."

"Oh, not entirely, not entirely. I got four from the village yesterday."

"Huh! I bet they were half canned."

Janie now heard the stranger's voice turn to laughter as he replied, "Well, not quite, but it helps, it helps. By! that's a funny village of yours down there."

"It isn't my village, mister, never has been."

"No? You don't seem to think much of it."

"You're right there, you're right there."

"Well, if one believes only half of what that lot get talking about in the inn there's no love lost. By! they can spin the yarns like fairy-tales. But I suppose there was something in it, for they say all the mischief started when your boss jilted a lass in the village and went and married a dancing piece from Newcastle. Is there any truth in that?"

"There's truth in part, mister. She was no piece, she was a lady."

"Oh! But did he jilt anybody?"

"I don't know so much about that. I can only repeat what I've said: his wife was a lady."

"Well, is it true that the supposed jilted one set fire to the place?"

"She didn't set fire to the place, just a field."

"Oh, just a field. Well, as I said they spin the yarns down there. They even said she killed the wife, I mean . . . dancing lady, with a catapult. I laughed at that, but they swore it was true."

There was silence in the barn for a moment; then the stranger's voice said again, "They say he had her put away in an asylum, and there she is to this day."

Still Mike made no reply until the stranger said, in a low tone now: "If what they said next is true, I'd put them down as a rotten spiteful lot of buggers, for they said that three of the village blokes raped his daughter, and her but a lass of fifteen. And she had a child and the lass is of an age now . . . Well, I gather by your silence there was some truth in it. By God! All I can say is, I would have helped that lass's father to strip those buggers, as they said he did, an' pin 'em up on the church screen. By! I would. And I would have helped to flail them an' all. They deserve to be shot. And you know something? I didn't like the village when I came into it. I'm a recruiting sergeant, right enough, an' I take all I can get me hands on, because that's me duty, but as I said, I never liked that village from when I first smelt it; and I've been in lots of villages. They're all peculiar in their own ways. Give me the city any time. And it's true what I said, mister, I didn't believe half of it. But I can see now, as I said, by your still tongue, I didn't know the half of it. That child will never find out from where she sprang, will she? And they talk about the atrocities of the bloody Germans and what they did to the Belgian women! Well, I would say you couldn't go much further than this village. Anyway, we'll be leaving it the night and I won't be sorry. But thank you, mate, for showing me around. And I'll take your word the whole place is run by old codgers."

There was the sound of laughter now, then the byre door closed, and the empty bottle dropped out of Janie's hand on to the straw. And she sat staring across the calf at the wall opposite . . .

How long she sat there she never knew, but she didn't seem to come to herself until Jessie's voice said, "Have you gone to sleep, dear?"

She turned to see Jessie standing in the opening to the little byre, and she gave her no answer but tried to stretch out her legs, which had gone into cramp. And when Jessie's hands came under her arms and lifted her up and her voice said, "Did you fall asleep?" she muttered, "Yes. Yes, I must have."

Jessie now stooped and picked up the empty bottle, saying, "It drank it all. And oh, it looks more lively. Come along."

As they walked up the byre Jessie, bending down to her, said, "You must have fallen asleep; you look dozy. Are you all right? You're not feeling tired?"

Janie shook her head slowly. "No," she said; "it . . . it was warm in there."

"Yes. Yes, and you must have dropped off to sleep. Come and have a cup of tea. I've made some of those scones you like."

Janie drank a cup of tea and forced herself to eat a scone. "Must I have my history lesson this morning? I . . . I could do it later on today."

Jessie looked at her closely. "Well, you have done your English and geography," she mused. "Yes, I suppose you could have your history lesson later. But what do you wish to do instead?"

"I . . . I would just like to take a walk."

Jessie remained silent for a moment. She had just checked herself from saying, "You won't go over to the Hall again, will you? I mean, you mustn't trouble them." But she knew if she voiced those words a look would appear on Janie's face that she had come to dread. The only name she could give to it was withdrawal; and oh, she didn't want her child, as she still thought of her, to move away from her again, because lately, through not penning her in any way they had become close. Nevertheless she was worried about the association with that man, who had outrageous ideas and was said to be a conscientious objector. Oh, how she wished they would force him into the services, so that his absence would break his self-imposed responsibility for her.

"You won't go far, will you? You get tired so easily, you know."

"I won't get tired, Auntie Jessie. I'll walk slowly."

"Well then, you must wrap up well. Come and put on your thicker coat and your woollen hat."

She now helped Janie into her outdoor clothes, and lastly she put a woollen muffler around her neck before handing her her gloves. Then stooping, she kissed her cheek, saying, "Don't be long now, dear, because it will soon be dinner time."

Without giving her aunt any response other than a smile, Janie turned and left the cottage, walked across the yard and into the road; then along it until she came to the stile. Having crossed this, she walked half round the perimeter of the field, pulled herself up into a sitting position on top of a low stone wall, then swung her legs over and walked across the meadow and into the wood. Beyond this, she skirted another field before arriving at the edge of the smallholding, and from there she made her way towards the first of the long greenhouses; but seeing Gerald apparently in serious conversation with McNamara, she stopped. But presently McNamara pointed towards her; and then there he was . . . her nice man, standing before her, saying, "Where have you sprung from? This is a coincidence. I was just on my way to visit you."

"You were?"

"Yes. Yes, I was. I . . . I wanted to tell you something. Come along; come into the house."

She did not move, but said, "Could . . . could we go to the cottage first?"

He looked down on her for a moment before saying, "Yes. Yes, of course, if you wish." And so they walked side by side along a roughly hewn path until they came to the cottage. The outside had been cleared of dank grass and weeds and the door was now upright on its hinges. He pushed it open; then when they were both inside and he had closed the door, he shivered and said, "Well there's one thing: we can't remain long in here, it's enough to freeze you. But come and sit down a minute."

They went into the next room, which no longer held the bed. Its window had been mended, and the presence of a number of large wooden crates showed it had been used as a store-room.

She sat down on one of the crates, and he pulled another in order that he could sit opposite to her. And now, bending forward, he said, "Something wrong?"

"I . . . I don't know. What I mean is, yes, there is something wrong. But it must have happened a long time ago. A lot of wrong things happened a long time ago. And that's why I am—" she stopped now and shook her head, then said, "me."

His voice was quiet when he spoke, saying, "You're beating about the bush. What has happened?" He now watched her bend forward and put her joined hands between her knees, and this, as always, indicated her troubled mind. Then she started: "I was in the cow byre," she said, "we've got a sick calf; I was feeding it. No-one could see me; it's partitioned off. Then Mike came in. I recognised his voice but not the man's who was with him. From what I know now, he is one of those men who go around gathering recruits. Well, he was in a public house in the village and he heard things that he didn't believe or only half-believed. And he asked Mike if they were true or not."

She lifted her head and looked at him, and she said, "Now I know what it's all about: why . . . why I am lonely, always have been lonely; and why, when I once asked Auntie Jessie if my mother was upstairs ill, and where my father was, and why wasn't he with her, she screamed at me and yelled, "He's dead. He's dead! Do you hear? He's dead!" And now I wish he *was* dead, because I don't know who my father is, do I?"

The words that were passing through his mind could have been considered blasphemous. He continued staring back into her eyes, when all the while he wanted to turn away from her, or yell in much the same manner as Jessie had done: not "He's dead! He's dead!" but "It doesn't matter who your father was. You are you, yourself, and you are a wonderful little girl, one growing rapidly into a tall big girl." Oh, my God! what was he going to say? This shouldn't be happening to him. That stiff-necked individual should in some way have broken it to her.

Yet, how could anyone break such news to a thinking child? But no; she was no longer a child; she had never been a child. They had never allowed her to be a child. She had a mind and she used it. A mind that had been cultured in an adult school without love, or with such love that was frustrated through fear. He put out his hands now and gathered hers into them. Then, his voice cracking on the words, he said, "It makes no matter who your father was"— he could not say which one was your father—"you are yourself, someone very special; and not only to your aunt, but . . . but to me. Yes, to me." He nodded at her. "Always remember that." And now feeling he had found a way to take her mind off the present situation by enlisting her sympathy for him, he added, "I may not see you for a long, long time after today. I . . . I'm leaving in a few hours."

"*No! No!*" She was on her feet now, her knees touching his, her hands still between his, pressed against his chest; and again she cried, "*No! No!* Oh, please, please don't go. You are the only one I have."

"I've . . . I've got to, my dear. I am not going into the Army because, as I think I told you, I'm against killing people, but . . . but this is a kind of job that others don't like doing, you know."

She closed her eyes and shook her head from side to side in a despairing fashion as she said, "I will have nobody. Nobody."

"Look at me. I shall write to you and you will write to me; and in the meantime you must continue to come over and see my mother. She's very fond of you, and you can keep her company now and again."

"She's not you. I can't talk to her, tell her things like I can to you. You're the only one I can talk to. And now I know this dreadful thing, I won't be able to speak about it to anyone else."

"Well, that's as it should be: it is all past and finished with; you now have only yourself to contend with. By that I mean . . ."

Shaking her head impatiently, she interrupted him; "I know what you mean," she said, "I know what you mean. You mean that I shall never get rid of this . . . well, what I know."

"I mean nothing of the sort. I mean, as you grow older your common sense will tell you that it is something you've got to accept. You cannot change yourself. You are what you are"—he paused—"a very beautiful person."

When she fell against him he put his arms about her, but when he felt her body shudder he pressed her gently from him, saying, "Now, now. No tears. I don't want to remember you with a wet face." When her eyelids blinked rapidly he leaned forward and put his lips gently on her brow. But when her arms came around his neck he bit tightly on his lip and pulled himself to his feet. His own lids moving rapidly now, he looked down on her, saying, "Come along. We'll go and see my mother." But when she said quickly, "No, no. Please not now. And anyway, I promised I wouldn't be long. But I will, I will come and see her soon. Yes, very soon, because she will tell me what you are doing. And . . . and you will write to me?"

"Oh yes, I will write to you. And I will expect long letters back mind."

"I have never written a letter to anyone, but I can write well."

"Then you must practise your letter writing on me."

They were outside the cottage now and when he said, "I will see you to the stile," she answered quickly, "No. No. I'll leave you here. I . . . I would rather. Yes, I would rather I left you here because this is where we first met. I don't count the time by the wall."

He held out a hand now, saying, "Goodbye then, my dear." And she, placing hers in it, said, "Goodbye," then she turned and walked away from him. And he watched her until she had disappeared into the thicket.

Slowly now he made his way back to the Hall, and there, after telling his mother what had transpired, he said, "Keep an eye on her, will you, dear? Make her welcome. Try to get her to talk"—he smiled—"if it's only about me."

As she kissed him she said, "Let her be the least of your worries. I shall see to her. And perhaps we shall comfort each other for your loss." And when she added, "Oh, my dear, what am I going to do without you?" he replied, "As I've told you before, dear, it's more a case of what am I going to do without you?" to which his mind added, "and her."

TWO

❀

*T*he first letter he wrote was neither to his mother nor to Janie, but to Jessie. He wrote it that night, before he left the house. It was brief, stating that her niece had found out the facts of her beginning through overhearing one of the men and a recruiting officer talking while she was attending to a sick calf. And authoritatively, he ended, "If she does not mention this to you herself, it would be very unwise of you, at this stage, to make her aware that you know. No doubt the opportunity will occur some time when she's more able to handle the situation."

He knew that this letter would undoubtedly anger Jessie, but he had little patience with her and condemned her for her treatment in keeping a child segregated for years.

The next letter he wrote was to his mother, and this was from Birmingham, telling her he was stationed in a camp near a village and undergoing training. The letter was quite cheery. He sent a similar, shorter one, to Janie. And this he ended on a light note, saying that the kind people in charge were thinking of sending him to London on a holiday, but that he wouldn't be given any spending money.

The next letter his mother received from him was from a hospital in Richmond, and in it it was evident that he could not contain his feelings, for he was angered at the purposeless suffering of the men there.

Gerald had known well from the beginning that he would go through the mill, even though he was under a certain protection, being a member of the Friends' Ambulance Unit. Yet it wasn't the way he was received and treated, nor the menial tasks imposed on him and the others in the same corps, but the number of mangled bodies filling the wards. He was sickened and horrified by the agony endured by the limbless and mangled remains of men, and rent inside himself by the nameless courage that sustained many of them with the desire to go on living. But there were equally as many who gave up the ghost, and for these he was thankful that their crucifixion was over. Yet, covering all his emotions was an anger at the senseless waste of human life and the feeling of frustration at being unable to do anything about it. Here he was cleaning latrines, his hands burnt with the use of so much chlorine. And he was sickened further with the habits of men *en masse*.

They were camped outside in unheated huts and he had made friends with a couple of like minds in his section. But he had also discovered there were some weak knees within their company when one day he was warned by a young fellow that it would be well for him if he kept his mouth shut and his opinions to himself, else the lot of them would be landed overseas before they knew where they were.

Gerald had asked in mock enquiry, "Do you happen to be a conscientious objector?" And the answer he got was, "Oh, to hell with you!"

One day, when he was on his way to the theatre to wheel out blood-stained sheets and parts of human anatomy to be consigned to the incinerator, and seeing a visitor whom he had noticed once or twice before now making her way towards a ward door, he stepped forward and was about to open it for her when the side of her hand came like a chisel across his wrist, and in a deep throaty voice she said, "Your courtesy doesn't hide your cowardice. My son is back there, his body mangled just to protect the likes of you. I know what I would do with the lot of you if I had my way. But this is what I think of you." And then she spat in his face.

He remained still while the door was opened and then closed on her. He felt as if all the blood had been drained from his body. They called cowards white-livered, and that's what he felt at this moment, white right through. Nothing seemed to be working inside him. Even when he turned away he found that his legs didn't actually obey him; it was as if he were drunk.

This incident attacked the sensitivity in him. Not only did it increase his awareness of who he was, and why he thought as he did, but also the knowledge of how the action of one person, that might cover merely a matter of seconds, could affect the life of another, as it was to do in his case for the next three years.

THREE

*I*t was towards the end of July 1917 that Janie received a letter from Gerald telling her he was in France, and so glad to be there, for now he felt he would be of some real help. And when she next wrote to him to the address he would leave at the bottom of the page, she must tell him how the smallholding was going, because his mother didn't give him many details. And was she really all right and not ill? But he had finished on a light note, saying, "Before I make myself of some use I think I'll just pop over to Paris tonight and have dinner, somewhere along the Champs-Elysées; then perhaps go to the opera. Or on the other hand, I may prefer a lighter entertainment. It all depends upon my mood. Be a good girl, and one day I shall bring you over to France, that is after I've shown you all the beautiful places in London." And he signed himself as always, "The 'nice man' Gerald."

Jessie had watched her reading the letter, the while pushing from her thoughts the hope that they might suddenly cease, for terrible things were happening in this war. As McNabb said, the papers were just one big cover-up. He had proof of it, he said: his grandson, minus a leg and half an arm, had recently been sent home from a hospital where they had endeavoured to make him walk; but the mutilations being on both sides of his body, he found himself unable to balance. And now his life would be spent in a wheelchair, and what pension he got would scarcely feed him.

But Jessie resisted the thought that there was still hope. Yet she knew if that man survived nothing she could do would change her child's attitude towards him. It would be only the man himself who could change it, and he had become her father figure, which he could well have been, having been twenty years old when she was born.

Seeing Janie raise her head from the letter as if about to speak, she put in quickly, "No, you can't miss your lessons this morning, dear. It's becoming a habit."

"Oh, it isn't, Auntie Jessie. I don't often ask in the mornings, I go over in the afternoon. You know I do. And I know what's the matter with Lady Lydia; it's because the house is full of soldiers and she hasn't told Mr. Gerald about it. And they are noisy; some of them are quite rude. Although she's had most of the furniture packed away there are some things she can't move, of course, such as the big bookcases in the library. And one of the men in the last lot pulled out illustrated plates from the big books. And when she went for him he was rude to her. The sergeant said he was sorry and had him moved . . . Some people are very ignorant."

"And you will be one of them if you continue to miss your lessons."

"I don't miss my lessons, Auntie Jessie. You do exaggerate, you know. And when I don't have to do the lessons, I still read."

"Yes, but not the things you should. Poetry won't get you very far in this world."

As Janie looked at the thin, tight-lipped face of her aunt, she thought she knew why her nice man and her aunt didn't like each other. Yet how could she put it into words? Only that one was light and the other was heavy. Yes, she understood the heaviness that was on her Auntie Jessie's shoulders, and that she herself was a big part of that heaviness.

Of a sudden she sprang up and with an unusual display of tenderness put her arm around Jessie's shoulders and kissed her on the cheek.

Jessie was much taken aback by this unexpected gesture, for what kissing had to be done she did herself, and then with a peck on the child's brow or cheeks at night. But as it was now, she had the urge not only to cry but also to hold the child tightly to her, as she used to when she was small and manageable. The embrace, however, ended as quickly as it had begun, with Janie, laughing and saying, "Let's away to the grindstone, for if the corn is not turned to flour, there'll be no bread and then we'll all be surprised when we find ourselves dead."

Jessie had been about to turn away to go into the other room, but now she swung around and looked at the laughing girl, saying, "Where on earth did you hear that?"

Janie seemed to think for a moment, then said, "I've never heard it. I mean, it just came out."

Jessie sighed. Rhyming. Another result of her association with that man, and so she remarked tartly, "Well, in future I think what you let . . . just come out should have a little more sense to it. Come along."

Janie sighed. There was no fun with her Auntie Jessie, whereas Lady Lydia, although she was very worried about Mr. Gerald, could always laugh and see the funny side of some things. Oh, she wished this afternoon was here. She seemed to be always wishing these days: wishing the war was over, wishing her nice man was back again, wishing she wouldn't keep growing so tall, wishing she was older. Oh yes, a lot older, seventeen or eighteen, wishing . . . Here, her wishing came to a full stop and she answered herself, No, she didn't wish any more that her grandfather would speak to her. Her grandfather hated her and she hated him. Oh yes, she hated him.

Well before reaching the main gates she could see that the old lot of soldiers must have gone and a new company had arrived, for behind the line of trees on the right side of the drive, tents had been erected right down to the lodge. But she saw no soldiers until she was about to ascend the steps leading to the balcony and the front door, when she was hailed by a voice behind her, saying, "Ah, now, what 'ave we here? A spritely young miss who 'as come to see the lord of the manor and asked to be taken into his service. Eh?"

Janie turned on the bottom step and so her face was almost on a level with those of the two grinning soldiers; and when one looked at the other and said, "She has lost her tongue," she quickly came back at him, saying, "It's a great pity you haven't lost yours, too, if you can't make it say anything sensible."

The smile slid from the man's face whilst the grin on his companion's widened; and in a very changed tone the first man said, "Now, now! missie! there's no need to be cheeky."

As she went to turn away from him, he added, "And where d'you think you're off to?"

"That's my business."

"Oh, but it isn't, madam. Let me tell you it isn't. This house has been taken over."

"Yes, and it's a great pity."

"Look"—he had quickly placed himself one step above her now—"it's my business to see who goes in and out of here." He pointed to the single stripe on his arm. "And now I'd advise you to get yourself away. There's a notice on the gate that this is private property. Weren't you checked there?"

"No; but you will certainly be checked if you don't let me pass."

"What is it?" The voice brought the man round to see Lady Lydia coming across the balcony to the top of the steps, and he was about to say, "This 'ere girl," when she said, "Is there anything the matter, Janie?"

She was coming down the steps now and the man looked up at her, saying in a tone that could only be called smarmy, "I was just enquiring, m'ladyship, what her business was. We've just come in, as you know, and not used to the run of the place yet."

Lady Lydia stared at the man for a moment, taking in his type; then she held out her hand to Janie as she said to him, "Then the sooner you recognise members of my family, the better, Corporal."

"Yes, ma'am, your ladyship." He stepped aside, then watched the two figures mount the steps, cross the balcony and enter the house through the front door of the hall, before he muttered, "Bloody upstarts! One thing this war'll do will be to put an end to that lot."

"And perhaps your lot an' all." As his companion turned away laughing, the man demanded, "Whose side are you on?"

Still holding Janie by the hand, Lady Lydia crossed the empty hall, passing the uncarpeted stairs, to the broad passage where new notices had been attached to the doors, and so to the far end to a door on which the notice said, "Private. No admittance"; through this and into a further passage that led into a largish room which had been the servants' hall but was now fitted out as a sitting-room. Next to it, what had been the housekeeper's sitting-room was now Lady Lydia's bedroom. The butler's pantry, the silver room, the housekeeper's office and various other small rooms in this quarter, with the exception of one which held a bed for Nancy Bellways, were filled with silver and china and relics of family history, besides small pieces of antique furniture.

In the sitting-room Lady Lydia said, "Come, warm yourself." Then she pointed, "Look at the big lumps of coal. We've got a coal-house half-full."

"Really? Where did you get it?"

"Well there was a soldier in the last lot, they really were a nice crowd altogether . . . well, he and one or two of them went out with a lorry yesterday, apparently, and did some foraging, all in the name of the Army, of course." She bit on her lip now and shrugged her shoulders as a young girl might. "And just before they left, and it was quite early, quite early in the morning, they handed me a great big key. And they said, 'We've left a present for you, ma'am. It's in the coal-house. And hang on to that key. Anyway, that lock'll take some getting off.' I didn't know what to say. Having said it was in the coal-house, I thought it must be wood, because, you know, they've been chopping down a lot of trees. Oh, Gerald would have been so angry if he were here. Anyway, after they left . . . and you know, they waved me good-bye from the lorries—it was as if they were going on holiday. And, oh dear, dear"—her tone changed now—"they're all for France, all of them, and they know it. And some of them don't want to go, from what they said. But anyway, I was telling you"—she shook her head—"when I opened the coal-house door I couldn't believe my eyes. You've never seen our coal-house, have you? It's enormous, like a small room, and there . . . there was a hill going up from it and all beautiful big lumps of coal, what they call roundies here. And another thing—of course we've had to store it in here: we daren't leave it in the kitchen cupboard—but look at that!'' She pulled open the doors of a large Dutch press, and there on one shelf was an array of tea, sugar, butter, bacon, and some eggs. On another shelf was an array of tins, some of jam, others of bully beef. "Isn't that marvellous! The only thing is the butter won't keep. But that doesn't really matter because your aunt is always kind in sending me both butter and cheese. But wasn't that sweet of those men? And you know something? When they brought the stuff in, it was late last night, they said, 'This, ma'am, is with the quartermaster's compliments.' Nancy had let them in, and when she saw all that stuff and heard what they said, she answered, 'Like Jimmy McGregor, it is.' And at that, one of the soldiers burst out laughing and pushed her, and she pushed him back. My dear, I've never seen such goings-on in this house. I couldn't help but laugh.'' She paused now as she closed the door and said, "It's good to laugh at times, isn't it, Janie?''

"Yes, Lady Lydia, I think so, too. But the only ones at the farm who seem to laugh are the men, and mostly the Irishmen. McNabb—he's a Scot, you know—he rarely laughs but he says funny things. And you can laugh at them, although he never really laughs. Yet Mike—you know, Patsy's father— says the most comforting things at times. Some of them may be a bit mixed up. I remember the other day he said to Patsy: 'God helps those who helps themselves,' but then added, 'And God help those who are caught helping themselves; it'll be three months' hard labour.' It was funny, wasn't it? The Irish people talk very mixed up. But other people's talk is nearly always about war, don't you think?''

"Yes, I suppose so, dear. But, come and sit down.'' She drew her towards the fire, and when they were seated, she said, "A lot of warm things happened to me yesterday. There was the coal, and all that food, but most of all there were those words that a soldier spoke to me. He was just a private, and during the weeks they've been here I've noticed him once or twice looking at me as I walked across to the greenhouses. In fact, it was he who, when the unit first came here, said he was sorry that the vinery had been stripped the way it had, before the fruit was really ripe. I was so angry at the time I didn't take much notice of him. But then yesterday he made a point of coming to me and asking me if he could have a word. And he started with, 'We'll be leaving here tomorrow, ma'am, and there's something I want to say to you, and it's just this.' And he went on to say that he was, as he put it, dead nuts against conchies. At least when the war had first started, he was. To him they were simply just a lot of cowards. But after he had joined up, or was enlisted, or, as he put it, was pulled in, and himself now saw how men of conscience were treated, with the lowest type of work being put on them, he had had to change his opinion. He was now seeing for himself. And having recently heard from the village that my son was a conscientious objector, he felt that he wanted to say to me—'' Here she stopped and, taking out her handkerchief, she wiped her mouth hard with it before going on, "He wanted to say to me I should be proud of my son.''

When Janie caught hold of her hand and in a breaking voice said, "You've always been proud of him, and I have, too. I . . . I wish he had been my father,'' Lady Lydia leaned forward to touch her, saying, "Oh, my dear.'' Then she was holding the sobbing body to her and comforting her:

"There, there. And I can tell you something, my dear, he looks upon you as if he were your father. He feels he has a responsibility towards you. If he'd had a daughter he'd have wished for one just like you. There, there now. Dry your eyes; here comes Nancy with some tea. You can hear her feet a mile off. And oh dear me, she's had to be on them such a lot since cook left. But, of course, cook was getting very old. It was the soldiers in her kitchen that she couldn't put up with. But Nancy doesn't seem to mind." She now took her handkerchief and dried Janie's eyes, saying in a whisper, "She gets very skittish with them. They tease her and she loves it. Poor Nancy. But why do I say poor Nancy? She could have been married years ago but she didn't want it. She's of a happy and contented nature. All she wants is to look after me. Don't you think that's wonderful? I should be so thankful, and I am. Oh, I am. Every day I'm thankful for her. And for you, dear. Oh yes, and for you. Ah, here it is."

The far door of the room was now opened by a bump from Nancy's buttocks and she came in carrying a laden tray, saying, "Oh, ma'am, we've got a lot 'ere; I feel as if I want to run after the others and bring 'em back. The sergeant's as snotty as a polis. Wanted to know how many hours I was allowed in the kitchen, and I told him it was more a case of how many hours I was going to allow him in my kitchen." She now put the tray down none too gently on a side table, adding, "The officer came in. He wasn't too bad, but young, ma'am, just out of the cradle. How he'll ever give orders to that lot beats me. But there, it's them pips on the shoulders that does it. Will I pour out, ma'am?"

"No, Nancy; Janie will do it. Thank you."

Nancy approached Janie now and, bending down towards her, she whispered, "Did you see our gold-store?" She jerked her head back towards the cupboard, and Janie whispered back, "Yes, and I won't split."

"You'd better not, you'd better not, 'cos I'd cut off your retreat." And with this she went out, leaving them both smiling now, and Lady Lydia saying, "What she means by that last bit I don't know. But look"—she was pointing to the tray—"she's managed to make some scones and a fruit tart. Come on, let us tuck in. You pour the tea and I'll cut up the tart and butter the scones."

It was an hour later when Janie left the Hall. It was then spitting rain mixed with sleet, but before she was half-way to the farm she was enveloped in a downpour of hailstones. They stotted off her hood and stung her face, causing her to slow her running. But she was still running when she reached the farm gates. She bent forward, and through the hail she thought she saw Patsy going into the dairy, and so, keeping to the shelter of the buildings, she was making for it when someone stepped out of the harness-room, and she bounced into the figure, only to bounce back again and stare up, gasping, into the face of her grandfather. She was standing in such a position that she was blocking his way forward, and when the voice growled at her, *"Out of my way* you!" she screamed at him, "I hate you! Do you hear? I hate you! You're cruel! ugly, horrible! I wish you were *dead. Dead!"*

She did not know that the arm going round her was Patsy's, but she knew it was Patsy's voice, louder than her own had been, that was crying, "Don't you dare hit her!" And then it seemed they were both sent flying into the air as his forearm hit her shoulder, while at the same time Patsy was lifted off her feet.

For the next minute or so all Janie seemed to be aware of was the shouting, everyone shouting in the yard. And then, as someone picked her up from the ground another voice shouted, "You'd better get Carl, Patsy's dead out."

Janie was also aware now of Jessie being on the scene and of her saying, "What happened? What happened?" and a voice answering, "All I know is he knocked them flying. And the slush didn't help."

"Father?"

And the reply in the Scottish accent was curt: "Who else? Now, who else?"

Her head had cleared by the time they reached the cottage; and now Jessie was plying her with questions. And when, for the third time, she said, "Look, tell me what happened," she shouted back at her, "I couldn't see through the hailstones and I bumped into him. He lifted his hand to strike me."

"He would not do that, child."

"He did! He did! It was not to push me away. I know the difference. I am not a baby or a child. No, I am not a child, Auntie Jessie. And I tell you again I am not a child and I know what he meant to do. And so did Patsy, and with his whole forearm. And . . . and I told him what I thought."

"You . . . you mean you went at him?"

"Yes, I went at him. I told him he was cruel and ugly and a beast. And you can close your eyes like that, Auntie Jessie, but he is. He is. He always has been to me. He's never wanted to own me and I don't want to own him. Do you know something?" She now stood up and her voice rose to almost a high scream now: "I would rather have had one of those other men who made me than him for a . . ."

When the hand came across her face and stung her, while knocking her backwards, they both became silent. And when Janie now began to cry, Jessie made no move towards her; instead, turning about, she went towards the door and grabbed up the coat that she had thrown off as she entered.

There was no-one to be seen when she reached the yard, but seeing Rob emerge from the door into the kitchen, she called to him, "Where is Patsy?" And he answered, "On her bed, miss; and Mr. Carl is sending me for the doctor."

"Has she not come round?"

"She's come round all right, miss, but . . . but she's hurt her back."

Straightaway, she hurried to Patsy's room, and there, bending over her, asked, "Where are you hurt, Patsy?"

"I'm . . . I'm not sure, miss. At the present moment I feel I'm hurt all over," and she tried to smile; but then said, "The bottom of me back pains, the more so when I move me legs."

"You can move your legs?"

"Yes. Yes, thank God, I can move me legs."

Jessie raised her eyes to where Carl was standing at the foot of the bed, and when he said, "Your father will be the death of all of us before he finishes, miss," the bitter note in his voice being such as she had never heard him use before, she turned from him and looked again at Patsy, and asked, "How . . . how did it happen?"

"Well, as far as I could see, miss, I had just stepped out from the dairy when I heard her screaming at him. He must have been coming out of the tack-room and she dunched into him. He was about to raise his hand to her and I just got to her in time; at least I thought I was in time to pull her away when his arm knocked us both flying. He really meant to swipe her. Oh yes, he did. But it caught us both. If she had got the full force of it and hit the ground with her head instead of me hitting it first with me backside, her brains would have been knocked out. Because it was no light blow, oh no, not with the forearm. And the force of it! It was like a chop."

"Oh, Patsy, Patsy, where's it going to end?"

"You tell me, miss, just you tell me. But what you've got to face up to, miss, is Janie's no longer a child. She's thirteen years old and an old thirteen at that, and it's this place that's put the age on her. She's never had a child's life. So you shouldn't blame her because her mind thinks beyond her age. And let me tell you some thing, she's not afraid of him, not when she could scream at him, 'I wish you were dead!' "

"She said that . . . ? No. No."

"Oh yes, yes, and more than that, judging by the bits I caught before we were sent flying. Anyway, we must get down to brass tacks, mustn't we, miss? Because I can't get up for a while. As I said, I can move me legs but the pain's hellish when I do that. Anyway, it's about time there was some help in this house again. It was cut off needlessly after Miss Angela went. So, for the time being, if you don't want to have it on your own hands, you should get McNabb's wife in again. She was quite good and she's clean."

"Yes. Yes, Patsy. I'll do that."

She nodded now at Carl, then went out; and he, going to the bed and sitting on its side, bent over Patsy and said, "I've wished it many a time, dear, and not more than I do at this minute, that we had up and left when we had first made up our minds. Even with the circumstances as they were. I could have said to hell with the bribes of a half share. What life have you had here? Working morning, noon and night. And now this, knocked flat on your back, and we don't know yet what damage has been done. Backs are funny things. I feel like going to him this minute and giving him, not a piece of my mind, but the whole bloody lot of it. I no longer feel, as I did years ago, that I owe him my life. He's had more than the best part of it."

When her hand came on his cheek, she said, "As long as I've got you, I'll consider me life all right. And I've given you very little in return for what you've given me. Now, now"—she tapped his cheek smartly—"don't start. I know, I know what you're going to say: as long as you have me you're all right. Well, for once I'm going to make meself believe it and you can believe it when I say, as long as I have you I'm more than all right. And now, you know what I want?"

"No, dear, no."

"A cup of strong tea with four spoonfuls of sugar in it. Really strong, thick enough to keep a knife standing up in it, and helped with a wee drop of the hard."

He smiled, and when he bent and kissed her, she said, "You know something? You're too bonny for your own good."

Now he pushed her face to one side, at the same time clicking his tongue, then left her.

But when she was alone the smile went from her face and she bit tightly on her lip. Her back felt bad; the pain was gripping her waist. She hoped to God there was nothing wrong and she'd be able to get on her feet in a day or so . . .

The doctor's verdict was that she might have cracked a bone at the bottom of her spine: she must lie still for at least two weeks, by which time she would likely be able to get on to her feet again.

Later, not for the first time in his career, Philip Patten had to admit to himself that his diagnosis had been wrong. It was to be many months before Patsy could get on her feet, and then it was with much effort and a great deal of pain and only with the help of crutches.

FOUR

*T*rains, trains, trains. Stretchers, stretchers, stretchers. Bodies, bodies, bodies. Blood, blood, blood. That's what the wheels were saying. That's what all the train wheels said. They never speeded up the rhythm: they slowed it down, they stopped, but they never speeded it up.

He was tired. His body was crying out for rest; but more so, his mind pleading for it.

How many ambulance trains had he travelled on over these past months? When did he come here anyway? May? Yes it was May, when the Arras affair was on. God! God! That was an introduction. They were shovelling them in then, those who got back across the Somme at Abbeville. And many of those that were left were wishing they had never got back.

How many times had he thrown up? If it hadn't been for Jim Anderson and David Mayhew he might have joined the mutineers or the absconders and risked being shot. Jim had said he had suffered from diarrhea for the first three months. "But you get used to it," he had said. David was more laconic, less sensitive. "It's what you asked for," had been his comment. Yet it was

David who had taken him aside and said, "We've been put here because we're needed. I've asked God time and time again, why is this happening? Why is He allowing it? And the answer is, as the answer always is, man's free will. It's a paltry answer and I've told Him that. But He's also reminded me that His Son was crucified for doing good and that we and fellows like us are in the same boat. And then David had added in his usual manner, "And it's no good crying out like His Son did, 'Why hast thou forsaken me?' because we'll get the same answer, 'You asked for it, so you've got to see it through.'"

Yes, it was David that had been his prop really, and still was. But if they should ever have a quiet minute together again, and God only knew when that could possibly be, he'd ask him if he, too, had this whirling repetition in his brain that woke him out of sleep, repeating everything three times.

David's voice came to him now, saying, "Have a word with Geordie at the far end there, will you? because if he starts ranting again he'll wake the whole lot up. And as long as we're stuck here they might as well get a little sleep, those who can."

Gerald repeated to himself, "Those who can," as he looked along a double row of stretchers flanking each side of the long railway carriage. This carriage was supposed to take only twenty-five in some kind of comfort, but there were over forty on this trip. How many had been left behind altogether? He didn't know. What he did know was that by the time the next train arrived, some of them wouldn't need to be lifted up.

He stepped cautiously down the narrow, dimly lit aisle. The place was hazy with breaths that took a little of the chill off the atmosphere. Suddenly the carriage shook violently and a voice to his side said, "A couple of inches more and it would have been goodbye, Blighty."

He looked at the man whose stretcher was on a rack to his shoulder and he uttered a platitude that was beginning to wear thin in his vocabulary: "A miss is as good as a mile." And then he moved on to where the voice could be heard above the mutterings and groans; but before he reached the source at the end of the carriage, the train shuddered again and he had to thrust both hands over a platform stretcher to steady himself against the blacked-out carriage window. The man whom he was leaning over and whose whole face was bandaged, as was one arm, muttered through a slit where his lips were, "Why don't they get their aim right and finish with it?"

He could give no answer, and especially not a quip, and so moved on to the man who was doing the talking. He had pulled himself up over his pillow, with his head now resting against the partition that divided this section from the rest of the train, and he greeted Gerald with, "How much longer are they gona dither here? A sitting bloody duck, that's what we are. Nobody seems to learn a bloody thing in this war. Keep moving. Keep moving. That's the thing to do."

Gerald dropped down on to his hunkers and he said quietly, "Arty, isn't it?"

"Aye, that's me name, Arty Makepeace. And that's a hell of a joke, isn't it? Makepeace."

His voice only just above a whisper now, Gerald said, "There's one or two along the line there not too good. They're trying to sleep it off." And the man's voice now was even lower as he said, "For the last time, you mean."

"Could be. Could be."

"Aye, well, join the band."

"Oh, you'll be all right."

"Think so?"

"Yes, once you get back to base; and after that it won't be long before you're on the boat."

The man's voice had become really quiet now when he said, "Funny thing, you know, this is my third bloody year out here. Aye. Aye, end of '14 I joined. And I'd begun to think nothing could touch me, all because me wife always finished her letters with, 'I'm praying that God will protect you.' And, you know, I had got to believe it up to this." He now pointed down to where the blanket sank below his left knee. "Went through a lot, I did, and not a scratch. Bullets going through me cap, an' the seat of me pants, but not a scratch. Even *this* bloody year, when I was in the counter-attack at Arras. Aye, I was, and we thought we were away. Oh, aye, we did. After having been pushed back across the Somme at Abbeville. Oh, we were all cocking our snooks, when it happened again. You know summat? The lot that they're sendin' over now are like bloody boy scouts. Some of the buggers couldn't tell their arses from their elbows. Trained. Aye. By God! they call it training!"

His voice was rising again, and so Gerald interrupted the threatened flow, whispering, "What's your regiment?" And thankfully a whisper came back to him: "Tyneside Scottish. We were with the Tenth and Eleventh Battalions, you know. Eeh! the commander. He was a bloke. A leader all right; he ferried us across in little boats. But what did we meet, eh? Air attacks, tanks, and their bloody infantry."

"Shh! Shh!"

"Now don't you Shh! me, lad. Anyway, you just sound like me old man. He always used to say, 'Shh! Shh thy gob!' And, you know, it's a funny thing, I'll tell you somethin'. I've been more frightened of the bloody mud than the bullets, crawling in it, being choked by it, gulping it down. If we lose the war, an' it's a penny to a pound that we will, it'll be the mud that's done it. But the funny thing is, I was brought up with mud. You see, me old man always had an allotment, kept our bellies full many a time mind, but workin' on it he would sometimes put the fork through his boot or get a cut in his hand. What did he do? He stuck mud on it. Aye. If the ground wasn't wet he would wet it, you know, then stick mud on it. That was when he was outside the house. Inside he went for salt. So—" He now pointed down towards what was left of his right leg below the knee, and he went on, "When I was lyin' in that bloody shell-hole, half covered in water, I thought of me da an' the mud. And when I came to meself an' saw what'd happened, well, that's what I did. I packed the stinking thing with mud an' I'd like to bet that was why I lived to reach that stinkin' station. How long did we lie on that stinkin' platform eh . . . ? For how long?"

Gerald didn't give him an answer. But he knew some of them had been left there for twenty-four hours and for many it had turned out to be just four hours too long. And the rest of them, those who had been picked up with this lot, would now probably go the same way if this bombardment went on much longer.

The man now lay back on the pillow, but as Gerald was about to move away he found his wrist gripped, and the voice, now quite low and solemn, said, "You have my respects, lad, and all your gang. As that bloke across there said"—he now jerked his head towards a stretcher at the other side of the aisle—"you lot were the heroes of this bloody senseless game. That's what he said after your mate got it just afore we pushed off. By! that was a quicker do: here the day an' gone the morrow. You know, he was an 'ero; he could have been picked up on the last train, but he gave way to a bloke that was in a bad way." He suddenly paused. "I'm sweatin' like a bullock now. I was freezin' a minute ago."

Gerald put his hand on the man's brow. It was wet. Here was the answer to his jabbering; he was in a fever. He now pulled the blanket up under his chin, saying quietly, "Lie still. I'll be back in a moment." Then he exclaimed, "Ah now! Listen! We're moving off, and we haven't got all that far to go." He did not add, just another five hours, that was if they weren't held up again.

He had got only half-way down the carriage when he had to stop and help David Mayhew hold down a burly sergeant. The poor man was back in the trenches giving orders and yelling: "Over! Over! Over! Come on! Lift it! Never mind the bloody moonlight. If they can see you, you can see them. Over! Over! Over! Hell! move it."

As they pressed the man down, David, gasping, said, "This is where we need Arthur and that damn needle of his."

Yes indeed, Gerald thought. Arthur the hero. Arthur Sprite had almost completed his training as a doctor when he had joined their ranks and become such an asset to them. Yet strangely, he hadn't been liked. Perhaps it was because he had aimed to show his superiority from the beginning. That he was brave, there was no doubt; but there had always been the question as to the reason why he was one of them. Was it on religious grounds? Political? Personal morality? Or what? Strangely, he could never be drawn.

Anyway, he was dead now, killed while carrying out an apparently brave act. As David had pointed out, there had been no need for him to dash along the road to the two wounded men supporting each other. Having got that far, they would have made it the other few yards to the station and the Red Cross vans. But no, he had to be spectacular and he had raced along the road and right into the bomb that had not only killed the three of them, but also blew the last van to smithereens. Daily he was asking himself what drove people to do the things they did. What had driven him into this hell-hole? Principles? What were principles but the sparks of one's ego? Variety? No. No. No. Don't start again, he told himself.

It was two-thirty in the morning when the train drew slowly into the base. There was no need for lanterns for the moon was shining, transforming the night almost into daylight. And now there was a scramble to get the wounded from the train and into the field hospital.

He and David had laid the last man of their section in a sort of outpatients' tent, waiting their turn for a doctor's attention, when a nurse, coming by, looked at them and said, "You're late as usual." And they both said together, "Hello there, Susie."

"You've packed some in this time."

"Not one half of what we've left behind," said David. "And we've had to crawl most of the way, so slowly at one period that we picked up some stragglers, six of them, three of them in a bad way. They had become separated from their unit. But who hasn't! Well, here I'm off for something to eat."

"You'll be lucky. Oh, I forgot, you've got a kitchen of your own; half of ours got it." Her voice sank. "And two orderlies with it."

David said nothing to this, but he sighed and turned away. And the nurse, looking at Gerald, said softly, "You look all-in."

"Me, look all-in? I could go for another . . . full ten minutes."

"How long have you been on this trip?"

"Since the beginning of the year."

"Don't be daft." She pushed at him, then added, "But it must feel like that at times. It must be twenty-four hours, at least."

He sighed now and said, "Well, I've got a forty-eight coming. And you know what I'm going to do in it?"

"Yes. Yes. Sleep."

"Right on the dot, Susie. Right on the dot."

"I'd like to take a bet with you."

"Yes?"

"You won't sleep for twenty-four hours; you'll hardly sleep for twelve."

"Perhaps you're right . . ." He knew she was right. You got past sleep. You might be lying on your bed, and there you were, your eyes wide open, staring straight ahead into the past . . . you were on orderly duty, running here and there. Then quite suddenly there was Dunkirk and the ambulance train, and the sickness in his stomach mixed with anger by the sight of more mangled men.

It had been in Dunkirk that he first saw Susie, during the bombardment. The Germans were firing their long-range guns on the town from Dixmude. And he could even hear her now saying, "If you don't want to have to lie on a stretcher, lie on your belly, man."

It was a brief meeting in the mud; he was not to see her again until some three months later, and that was in Rouen.

Then they had met in this medical outpost that seemed to be part of no man's land. That was two months ago. Since then, now and again, they had exchanged a few words, as they were doing now.

"Part of your billet got it, but your kitchens are left. That's the main thing." She smiled her impish smile as she added, "You can sleep standing up as long as your belly's full. And by the way, thank your mother for the cheese; that was real cheese. You're lucky. I hope there's another parcel waiting for you."

All he could manage was a short laugh before he turned from her. But he was thinking, I must put a stop to those parcels. They're really worse off over there than we are here. Janie must be sending the butter and cheese from the farm . . . But then, if he stopped the parcels, he'd miss the fruit-loaf. Good God! Fancy thinking about fruit-loaf after the experiences of the last twenty-four hours. Just let him get into that bunk, that's all he wanted right now. Sleep. Sleep . . .

But he wasn't to get straight into his bunk, for he was stopped by Jim with the order that he was to report to the officer in charge, one William Haslett.

William Haslett told him what he already knew: he would not be on duty for the next twenty-four hours. When, however, he added, "After one more train run you'll be due for seven days' leave. I bet you'll be glad to see home again," the man was not a little amazed when Gerald said, "I won't be going that far."

"You . . . you won't? Why not?"

"For the simple reason that if I got there I'd not come back."

Gerald had delivered this with a wry smile, as one might a joke. But it was no joke, for he knew that once home he would never return to this hell-hole. He also knew that he could not possibly take that risk for he wasn't brave enough to stand the result, a term in gaol. He was sure, too, he would even be unable to face the reception he understood still awaited the conscientious objector in England.

He could not believe that it was just on a year since he left the Hall; and yet all his life beforehand now seemed a hazy dream. Sometimes he could not visualise clearly even his mother's face. As for Janie, her letters were perky enough but did nothing to bring back the real picture of her.

William Haslett had been staring at him and his mouth opened twice as if he were searching for words; and then he said, "It was dreadful about Sprite. He's going to be an awful loss," to which Gerald nodded, saying, "Yes. Yes, indeed."

"But there," said Haslett now, "you're all well acquainted with first aid and I'll get Doctor Blane to have a talk with you and advise you on"—he stopped—"well, anything that you might be able to do . . . further, I mean when it comes to handling drugs."

When there was no comment on this, and taking in the blank look on Gerald's face, he ended quickly, "Ah, well, we'll see about it. All you want now, I suppose, is your bunk."

"Yes, you've said it," said Gerald. "That's all I want now," and turned away, leaving the man thinking: stiff-neck. Odd fellow. Surprise me if he lasts out.

David was waiting for him outside the hut, and his first words were, "Seven days. Think of it laddie, seven days."

But Gerald did not comment on this particular statement; instead, he said, "You talk quite a bit to him"—he jerked his head back—"why don't you suggest he takes a ride along with us on the next trip? And the one after that . . . And the next . . ."

David surveyed Gerald for a moment before he said gravely, "If you had put that question to Jim, him with his kind heart, he would have said, 'Oh, well, he does good work here.' There's a lot of organising to be done one way or another. We're quite a big unit, you know. But since you ask me, I'd say simply it's got something to do with his guts." Then his voice changing, he said, "But anyway, let's forget our dear organiser and think of Blighty."

"I won't be going across, David."

David looked at him for a moment in disbelief before exclaiming, "In the name of God! why not?"

"Well, I must say to you as I said to him"—he now thumbed towards the hut—"once over there I wouldn't come back."

"Oh, you would, lad, you would."

"No, I wouldn't. I wouldn't come back. No! No! I couldn't, and because of that I know I must not go over, for there would be worse in store once they caught up with me. So, I ask myself, why do I criticise old William? Because if the truth was known my guts are in a worse state than his."

"Never! You'd come back because you would know you were needed. That's what keeps you going here. Quite candidly, I've always thought you've got more compassion in your little finger than I've got in both hands. Come on. Come on, lad, make up your mind. I mean . . . you needn't go home. We could have a good time in London. Come to my place. I've a mother who's as skittish as a kitten. She's kicking fifty. The last time I saw her she was holding dances for our "dear boys," together with Lady this and the Honourable that. She'd introduce you to some piece who would assuredly make you forget . . ."

Now Gerald pushed him none too gently, saying, "You're wasting your breath. Anyway, get yourself to bed. I'm telling you, if you keep me standing here talking any longer, you'll have to carry me to my bunk . . . See you in twenty-four hours' time, boy." And with this he went to his bunk. But as Susie had predicted, he did not sleep for the full twenty-four hours.

It had been seven in the morning when he lay down, and he woke up at six in the evening. After a good wash, he had a meal, then returned to his hut and wrote to his mother and also to Janie.

They were not long letters now, just terse notes telling them he was very busy, and that he didn't like moonlight nights. He made a joke about this. And he asked his mother how she was putting up with the soldiers she now had in her house.

In his letter to Janie, he thanked her for being such a companion to his mother. And he ended it, saying, "Don't be as generous with your butter and cheese et cetera. We get enough to tuck in here." Which was far from the truth.

Having made the letters ready for the post, he then put on his greatcoat, his cap and a muffler, and went out for a walk. The air was cold and bracing and the moonlight was hazy.

He went down what had once been a village street but which now, apart from two houses, both roofless, had nothing to indicate anyone had ever lived there. Where the road led beyond the village it was bordered on both sides by fields, which no longer held crops but were pock-marked with craters, black-holed craters. Further along stood a farmhouse, intact except that part of the roof had slates missing, and also seemingly quite untouched was a barn, from which came the sound of cattle mooing.

At the sound, Gerald made a small motion of disbelief with his head, as he had done a number of times before, wondering how they had escaped, not only the bombs but the butcher's knife. There was no sound of cackling hens, which was understandable: hens were easy target for the pot. He recalled that he had once been put on guard at night to protect their meagre stores from a new company of soldiers that had just arrived. What he would have done if a few of them had set about him he didn't know, because, of course, he didn't carry a rifle. Food seemed to be the priority of everyone these days. It didn't matter about the sameness of it as long as it filled you up.

He had walked some distance when the moon appeared again, and he told himself he should turn about and make for the camp: it was the sort of night those fellows over there might make full use of; even so, the influence of the moon set his mind singing:

> The moon has raised her lamp above
> To light the way to thee my love . . .
> To light . . . the way . . . to thee . . . my love.

However, the Dictator, as he thought of that inner voice that was constantly getting at him these days, suddenly said, Enough of that!

He was passing by the farm again when he saw a figure coming out of the farmhouse door he instantly recognised as Susie. She was carrying a can.

Having heard his footsteps, then recognised him, she shook hands with the small round figure of the farmer's wife, before hurrying towards him. He greeted her with: "Been on the scrounge again?"

"She's been very kind. Guess what I've got in my pocket? But don't come too near me."

He said, "A chicken?" well knowing that it couldn't be.

"You're getting warm."

"Never!"

"Well, not a chicken but a couple of eggs."

"I thought they hadn't any fowl left."

"She's a wise woman. She's got half a dozen penned up in the back of the house."

He laughed. "And you found out so she's had to bribe you."

"No, I didn't find out. Well, I mean, after she gave me two eggs and I looked at them in amazement, she took me by the hand and into the back place, and there they were, six females, and very contented, even though their husbands had been polished off some time ago. But nevertheless, they were singing to themselves . . . Have you ever heard a hen sing? They do, you know."

He made no further comment, and they walked on in silence for some moments before she said, "I wish I'd laid some money on my bet. It wasn't even twelve hours, was it?"

"No; but nearly. Anyway, I feel a little more like myself; although that is no credential for saneness."

"You really were all in, weren't you? You've hardly had a full night's sleep in the last three or four trips."

Another silence ensued before he said, "How do you stand it out here, Susie?"

"Oh, well, I stand it the same as the others do: it's got to be done. And anyway, with all the muck, misery, blood and gore, I'd rather be here than back home, because I look upon most of the fellows I handle as heroes." She paused then added, "I mightn't if I had known them when they were whole and had to listen to their inane jabber. But when they are helpless and suffering, and when you hear a man crying below his breath for his mother . . . They all say it in different ways: or Mam, or Mammy, or just Ma. Some of them jabber their wife's name. And then they come round a bit and say, 'Oh, nurse, was I chattering?' Ashamed of their weakness. Sometimes I want to put my arms around them, or even"—she now pushed him to one side—"get into bed beside them," and her laughter rang out; and he joined her, saying gallantly now, "I'll have to get myself in a mess," to which she made no rejoinder until they had walked on further steps when she said, "I was going to give you an answer to that, but I won't." Then she added, "How would you like a cup of real coffee, and a boiled egg and toast?"

"Who but an idiot could refuse such an invitation?" he said.

"Well, come on, put a move on, because you know what might happen if the maiden"—she now pointed up to the moon—"keeps on doing her stuff."

Reaching the camp, they skirted the back of the hospital, then crossed a hard mud-ridged area that led them towards a line of low brick buildings which at some time must have housed an assortment of animals. Here, at the end door, she took a key from her pocket and still in keeping with the mood of such an evening, said, "Step in, sir."

Compared with the moonlight outside, inside it was dark. He heard her strike a match and when she had lit the hanging lantern, he looked around him in some surprise, saying, "Well, well; you're nicely ensconced, aren't you?"

"I'm privileged. I'm one of the old hands; in fact, next to matron who, by the way, and thankfully, is off on her forty-eight. So you don't need to fear someone knocking on the door and crying, 'Nurse! you know the rules.' "

"You've got a fireplace, too."

"Yes, it must have been some sort of boiler house, likely for pig food, because . . . look!" She pointed to the potboiler in the corner of the room.

He looked around the rest of the hut: a single bed stood against one wall; there was a dilapidated armchair to the side of it, and beyond that what looked like a folding card-table.

On the other side of the room, and looking grotesquely out of place, was a single mahogany wardrobe; also, and more in keeping, four large boxes, forming two open-fronted low cupboards. In one he could see odd pieces of crockery and a kettle; in the other what he imagined must be pieces of food wrapped in paper, a tin of jam and one of bully beef.

"Home from home."

"Sit yourself down," she said. "But don't flop in that chair else you'll go straight through the bottom."

"Can't I help you?"

"No. Do as you're told; sit down."

So he sat down gently and found himself sinking into the broken mesh of the chair seat; nevertheless, it was comfortable. He now leant his head against the back, stretched out his legs and sighed. But then he said, "How are you going to boil a kettle and your eggs on that fire? It's enclosed and it looks to be on its last legs."

"Be quiet."

She went to the far corner of the room to another cupboard and took out an oil burner. And after she had lit it and set the kettle on top of it, he remarked, "You're set for life here."

"You know nothing yet."

He sat looking at her. Without her overcoat and hat now, and in her blue print uniform with its big white apron, that wasn't very white any more, he thought, She's comely; only to ask himself why he had used such an old-fashioned word to describe her. Perhaps it was because of her shape. Everything about her looked round: her buttocks, her bust, her face; yet she wasn't fat. She was a comforting person, was Susie.

Sister Susie sewing shirts for soldiers
and soldiers sending missils they would rather
sleep on thistles.

Oh why did his mind prattle on so? And he didn't know the words of the song. Why was it taken up with such trivialities? And the answer came, Because you don't write any more. And the voice yelled back at him: What the hell will I write about in this madhouse! A thesis on the anatomy of spilled brains, rivers of blood and guts? For God's sake! shut up. Look at Susie; she's frying the eggs.

"I thought you were going to boil them," he said.

"I changed my mind. We can have them on fried bread with butter this way. Anyway, I thought you were asleep."

"I wasn't asleep."

"No? Likely, musing as usual. What do you think about, anyway? I've often wondered. Is it true your mother's a lady? David says she is."

When he started to laugh, half remonstrating him, she said, "Well, what's amusing about that? Is she?"

"Yes, I suppose so. But what do you mean by a lady?"

"Well, one with a title."

"There are lots of ladies without titles, and my mother would be a lady whether she had a title or not."

"Is she nice?"

"Lovely. Beautiful in all ways."

"Have you ever been married, Gerald?"

He chuckled now as he said, "Only to a smallholding."

"You had a smallholding?"

"Yes. Yes, I had a smallholding."

The bread sizzled as it went into the hot butter, and she turned it over on to the other side before she asked, "Been engaged?"

"No, I haven't been engaged, or anything like that."

"Never had a girl then?"

"Oh, yes, yes. I've got a girl back home."

"Oh."

He was amused now, and so he said, "She's rather lovely, too; different."

"Well! Well! a beautiful mother and a beautiful girl."

"Yes. Yes, I'm very lucky, and I'm sure my girl will grow more beautiful every day."

He saw her turn a sharp look towards him, her face now unsmiling. And his tone became lighter, a little teasing, as he went on, "She was always very bright and her letters show this. The only thing is she writes too often; I can't keep up with her. What she'll be when she grows up I don't know."

"What? When who grows up? Who?"

"My girl."

She lifted the eggs off a plate where they had been standing on the hob of the dying fire, slapped them on to the bread, then took them to the small table, pulled out some cutlery from a box to the side, then said, "Come and get it. No! Stay where you are. I'll lift the table round and I'll sit on the bed," and she continued to contain her feelings, at least until they had started to eat, when she said, "What did you mean, when she grows up?"

"Just what I said. She must be . . . well . . . oh, twelve, thirteen, going on fourteen now."

"Oh you! You're a funny fellow. You know that, Gerald?"

"Yes, I've been told that before. By the way, this tastes marvellous."

It was some time later. The meal had been finished with a cup of milky coffee. The greasy plates had been put into an iron pan half filled with water and placed at the front of the boiler fire, which prompted him to ask, "Won't it put it out completely?"

"No; it will still be on in the morning. I'll just have to give it a blow."

Again he remarked, "You are well organised, aren't you?"

"Just some parts of my life."

When later he was about to sit again in the chair, he hesitated, saying, "My next effort will find me through on the floor. You sit there."

"No; I prefer the edge of the bed."

And that's how they sat; and when she leant against his shoulder, he put his arm around her. And after a moment of holding her so, he said, "You're a very nice person, you know, Susie."

"How is it you've just found that out?" She didn't turn to look at him as she spoke, but nestled her head closer to him.

"I haven't just found that out; I've thought so all along."

"You've been rather backward in telling me then."

"Have I?" There was a surprised note in his voice. "I've always talked to you. I found you easy to talk to, comforting in a way."

"In a way? You're lost, aren't you, Gerry? I've always wanted to call you Gerry, but that would be classing you with them over there." Her head moved under his chin. Then she went on, "This is not your scene. It staggers you. I can see that every time you come back. You take things to heart too much. You put me in mind of a fellow that used to be on the trains just before you came. He was always spouting poetry. He'd be speaking ordinary to you, then he'd come out with a quotation or other. But when he started to go up and down the ward . . . oh well," she said with a small hunching of her shoulders, "they took him back home."

"And you think I'll go the same way?"

"Oh, no." Her tone was emphatic now. Yet she added, "It's the look of you at times, and you keep things bottled up. David says you do."

He brought her head up from his shoulder, saying, "Then I'm discussed between you and David? Why?"

"Oh, we have a natter at times. He's very fond of you. Well, he thinks you're great, your principles and all that. Quite candidly, I think all you fellows in that unit, in all your units, are great because of your principles. But you haven't got to let them get on top of you, not out here."

She now put her hand up and stroked his cheeks and her touch sent a quiver through him. She began to unloosen his tie and the last button of his coat that hadn't been undone, and he did not stay her hand. And when a few minutes later they were both standing up and her last piece of clothing fell to the floor, she stood looking at him for a moment before, stretching her hand behind her, she rolled back the blanket on the bed. And then they were both lying side by side, and when she whispered, "You hadn't to get wounded," he made no answer, but as his lips passed over her face he wasn't seeing it.

After rising from her side, he got into his clothes before, bending over her again, he kissed her on the brow and said, "Thank you, Susie. Thank you."

She was half asleep as she murmured, "You're welcome any time, sir."

There was no longer any moonlight as he stepped out into the night, but he stood looking at the stars in the sky. He was feeling greatly relaxed, changed somehow. Would anybody believe that had been his first night with a woman? No, he could hardly believe it himself. And now the question he asked was, why had he put it off for so long? Why? For it had been the most marvellous, most wonderful experience. He could face the morrow now and the days ahead on the train, for there'd always be Susie to come back to. And what about the seven days' leave? Yes what about it . . . ?

As it turned out, she wasn't able to get seven days off, but was given a forty-eight hour pass. And they spent it in a little village some long way behind the lines. And he experienced a feeling of comfort and ease that was like a soothing salve on his mind.

FIVE

$\mathcal{T}$hings were going from bad to worse. They all knew this and it was being voiced in many quarters: where were the bloody generals who were ordering them forward only for them to be thrown back on all sectors again and again? Exacerbating comments but, in truth, very telling when voiced by the wounded crammed now like sardines in the trains. Why didn't they come up to the front? No; they were sitting in their comfortable billets and drinking their bloody port after dinner, toasting the Royal Family . . . England . . . the Flag.

And the officers. Who did they think they were anyway? Young snots, hardly able to wipe their own noses. When it came to leading men . . . leading men, huh! Doing it in their pants, some of them, but they still looked down their noses at you.

Yet in the trains there was no distinction of rank, no officers and men, only a bloody mass of mutilated bodies. Even so, here and there, a voice would rise in defence of a particular officer, or even a sergeant who had perhaps risked his own life and in doing so had enabled a speaker to be on that particular train.

He had stopped writing so many letters home. Although he had the occasional comfort of Susie whenever she was free, the horror of the war seemed, at times, to be turning his brain: as David described it, the world had turned into a slaughterhouse and the abattoir was very messy. And to the comment of their latest addition, one Sydney Allington, "God made the back to bear the burden," David immediately retorted, "Yes, Mother Shipton," a reference which the young man did not understand, but nevertheless one which simply strengthened his growing opinion of Gerald, David and Jim as being strange company, and further made him question why any of them were there at all, at least in their capacities as non-combatants. And he continued to address them formally.

It was in March 1918 that three outstanding things happened, two of which were to propel Gerald's mind into the oblivion for which he would often crave in order to escape the horror of the everyday scenes he was forced not only to look upon, but to deal with.

The first took place when again the train was making slow progress back to base. They had taken on four sitting passengers, now propped up against the end partition of the carriage.

While entraining, he had noticed that two of these men had helped each other, one using his only usable arm to help his companion hop. And now bending down to the nearest man, he asked, "How's it going?"

"Not too bad. But Lawson, my friend here, I think his leg's giving him gip." And the tone of the man's voice made Gerald look more closely at the mud-covered uniform. Then he leant across to the man Lawson and said, "Feeling low?"

"Not too bad, sir. I'm all right, thanks to the captain here."

Gerald turned his attention back to the other man, saying now, "Rough show, sir?"

"Yes, you could say that." He was about to speak again when Allington, the odd man out of their particular team, tapped him on the shoulder, saying, "Mr. Ramsmore, you're needed further down; Mr. Mayhew requires your assistance."

After nodding at the soldiers, Gerald turned away, thinking to himself, Requires your assistance. That fellow got on his nerves more than did the war. He had almost said, bloody nerves and bloody war, and he must stop that: he was becoming as bad as the others in using such expletives with every other word.

He found David having trouble with a delirious and very ill man: "Get the needle," was David's greeting, and inclined his head further along the carriage to explain his call for assistance: "Jim's got his own hands full."

Gerald knew it was no use saying, "What about Allington?" because David couldn't stand the fellow. How odd that one individual could mar a team. Yet if they were to go into it, Allington's motive for being here at this moment was purer than theirs, for in his case God had come into it.

It was more than an hour later when he made his way back to the men propped up at the end of the carriage. The train had gathered some speed, and he could see that the private was dozing. The officer had his eyes wide open, and, on seeing him he put up his good hand to beckon Gerald down to him.

"Ramsmore?"

"Yes. Yes, that's my name."

"Strange coincidence, so is mine."

"Really? Well, well, it's a small world, as they say."

"May I ask if your Christian name is Gerald?"

"You may, and it is."

Gerald straightened up a little; then bending again, he peered into the young officer's face and said, "Don't tell me your father's name is Beverly?"

There was a small chuckle now as the young man answered, "No, but my grandfather's is."

"Good Lord!"

"I've heard a lot about you."

Somewhat stiffly now Gerald answered, "I bet you have."

"Oh, not in the way you're inferring." The words had been rapidly spoken. "Oh, no; I mean, along this route. Those over there know damn all about it. I'm . . . I'm very pleased to meet you." And when the hand came out Gerald shook it warmly.

"My name is Will. We must get together and have a crack after this. Are you on the same run all the time?"

"Most of it."

"My God! You chaps certainly have had your bellyful of war and no medals. How long are these runs?"

"Eight, ten hours; it all depends."

The young officer peered at his wrist-watch and remarked, "We've been going for five and a half hours. Good Lord!" And the next moment he asked, "Have you been home lately?"

"No; not since I came out here last year."

There was a pause; then peering up at Gerald, the younger man said somewhat thoughtfully, "You know, I have never seen my step-grandmother, or is she my step-great-grandmother? Yes, she would be, wouldn't she? They say she's a very nice lady."

"Yes, she is. And you must rectify your omission when you get back. She would be delighted to see you. Although, as I understand it, most of the house has been taken over by the military."

"My grandfather often talked of the Hall where he was brought up. But he seemed to think you had lost all the land."

"Not quite; there's still a few acres left. I ran a smallholding, you know."

"You didn't!"

"Yes."

"Good for you. You must be longing to get back out of this hell-hole."

Gerald did not answer but straightened up. Was he longing to get back? He'd had a strange thought in his mind of late that he would never get back, that he would never live in that house again. It had become an obsessive thought about which he could do nothing other than aim to ignore it.

There was a commotion further down the carriage: a man was crying out, not for his mother or father, but for someone called Little Jackie, perhaps a son.

He intimated that he must go, and the young man nodded and said, "We mustn't lose touch," in answer to which he himself nodded and muttered, "No. No . . ."

He saw his distant relative twice while he was in the base hospital prior to his being moved on down to the port when they had shaken hands and promised to meet up again. Will had also said he would go and see his step-great-grandmother.

The second thing that occurred shocked his system more than even war scenes and the ambulance trains had done.

The last stretcher had been passed over to the hospital orderlies, who had protested loudly as to where it was expected it should be put. "They're hanging from the ceiling," said one. "And if they don't soon clear some of them to the boats, you can put off your next run, for they might as well lie outside where they are, as lie outside here."

David and Jim had heard it all before, and they gave as much as they got, but Gerald had turned away. He was now making for the showers and his bed. But having to pass the nursing staff kitchen and day quarters, he stopped a nurse who was coming out of the door and asked, "Is Susie about?"

She glanced behind her into the room, then closed the door; and now, looking up at him, she said stiffly, "She's gone."

"What do you mean, she's gone?" He turned and looked about him. There was no evidence of a bomb having been dropped overnight.

The girl now said, "She left yesterday. She's been posted."

"Posted! Where to?"

She shrugged her shoulders; and when it seemed she was going to walk away, he said, "Well, do you know where she's been posted to?"

"Not quite. I hear it's back home . . . sort of training job or something." She now smiled and bit on her lip before walking away, leaving him standing perplexed.

It had been three days since he had seen her, and then only to have a quick word. Surely, she must even then have had an inkling it was about to happen. Why hadn't she mentioned it to him? Why? She had been a bit . . . well, offhand lately. He swung about to go hurriedly in search of David.

He met him emerging from the bunkhouse, and without any lead-up he said to him, "Do you know anything about this? Susie's gone, they say. Well, the nurse seemed to think that she might have been sent home."

"Yes." David glanced away before looking back at him, then said, "Yes, that's what I understand, she's been sent home. I think she's going into a training job there." He smiled now, rather sadly as he said, "She'll be a great miss, will our Susie. She was a great comforter. Oh yes."

Gerald's eyes narrowed and he moved his head slightly to the side without taking his eyes off David. There had been something in that tone he hadn't liked, that he wished he hadn't heard, that he didn't want to understand. Still he pursued with his questioning: "What do you mean by a great comforter?"

"Well, she was, wasn't she? Great girl, Susie. I knew it would come as a bit of a shock to you. It was to me, I can tell you. And not only to me. Oh, Susie's little grey nest in the West will be sadly missed."

He was seeing the room now: the boiler, the table, the oil lamp, the frying pan, the bed. Oh, yes, the bed, and the comfort of that bed. There wasn't much room in the bed . . .

David's voice seemed to come to him from a distance. Although it was in an undertone it was very loud in his head, for he was saying, "Don't look like that, man. You must have known. God! You must have known. And you know, you were favoured: it lasted a long time compared . . ."

When Gerald's fist shot out it was warded off painfully by David knocking it aside. But when he repeated the action, he felt the impact of David's fist on his mouth. And he not only tasted his own blood but smelt it, and it smelt as strong as a carriage full of mangled flesh. He knew he was now being pinned against the hut wall by David's thick stubby arms and chest and, with his face close to his he was spilling words over him: "All I can say, chum, is you're a bigger bloody idiot than I thought. Couldn't you see she was one of nature's bedwarmers? And I say, thank God for it. She knew what she was doing all right, and she enjoyed it. There are women made like that. And we knew what we were doing, too, the risks we ran with any of them . . . and what they ran an' all. Anyway, you're not an infant. You know what's going on. Why did you think she was any different when she came so easy, as she did? It should have told you."

David slowly eased himself off Gerald's shoulders, muttering as he did so, "Sorry. You'd better have your lip seen to. Funny, but you're the last person on God's earth I expected to battle with in this bloody war. The only thing I can say is, I didn't start it, and I'm not going to say now that I understand your reaction, because I just don't. I was always under the impression that you knew what you were doing and you knew who you were doing it with. Anyway, I know the matron's been on her track for some time. She was giving her girls a bad name. You know, some of them in there"—he jerked his head back towards the hospital—"are wearing chastity belts. Of course, I don't blame them, nor do I blame the Susies of this world, for God knows what we would do without them. The alternative, as I see it, has always left a nasty taste in my mouth." He now leant forward and looked into the white, stiff-drawn face of the man whom he liked and called a friend, and he said, "In spite of our high-falutin' moral stand against this wholesale slaughter, we remain men with the needs of men. There's no bloody saints among us. Some heroes mind, those who are back in the English prisons. Oh yes, those back there in the English prisons are the real heroes for you. Only yesterday I heard about the treatment meted out to a couple of them, and it's unbelievable that Englishmen are torturing Englishmen. Give me the Germans any day, rather than such individuals." He paused now before again leaning forward and saying, "Come on. Come on, old fellow. Say something. Let's forget about this. Come on."

But Gerald couldn't say anything. He pulled himself from the wall, wiped the back of his hand across his bloodied chin, then turned and walked away. And David stood looking after him for a moment, then he bowed his head and muttered, "Damn and blast!"

He was no fool. He was no simple-minded individual; he was an educated, highly intelligent man. Without being swollen-headed, that was how he saw himself. He saw the futility of war and the greed and the insensibility of those who created it and of those who kept it going. Like drovers driving their herds of cattle to the slaughterhouse. But then, not quite: they sent in their cattle, their battalions, but they did so from quarters well behind the lines, some even from as far away as London.

Yet being knowledgeable in this way, why hadn't he the insight to realise that first night that, unlike himself, she was well practised in the art of so-called loving. As she had admitted, she had wanted him for a long time, but then she hadn't said, as she could have, that he wasn't like the rest of her clientèle.

Clientèle.

My God! What had he just thought? He wasn't just a fool, he was an idiot; and more so, for marriage had crossed his mind. He had gone as far as to wonder if his mother would take to her. He did, however, recall the doubt there. But why should there have been a doubt? He had never gone into that, for he knew the words to describe her that his mother would have used:

cheap and slightly common. But would that have deterred him, the way he was then feeling about her?

How had he felt about her? Had it been love or just body hunger? Were you capable of distinguishing between the two when you were in that state?

During the following days different members of the unit remarked on the change in Ramsmore. He had never had a lot to say, unless you could get him into a conversation on books or poetry. But now he scarcely ever opened his mouth. That was, until around the 17th of March, when a long section of the front was pinned down for two days and nights by gas shells. And this was the third and final thing that sent him into oblivion, albeit not right away.

First, he had to experience the results of the gas attacks. The cases were horrifying: a choking, throttled mass of humanity. For two solid days and nights the Germans had bombarded the great stretch of the front with gas shells. And this was soon commonly recognised as being the prelude to their making a big push. The Red Cross and its orderlies, their own Friends' Unit and its orderlies, everyone available was mustered to cope with the influx, which soon developed into a mêlée. Even so, it became evident to many and was remarked upon that Ramsmore was not just talking, that he had taken to much swearing and blaspheming. And David made it clear he preferred the dour man, that to him the present pattern had all the signs of an approaching breakdown.

From this particular stretch, the trains ran every day to Rouen. If they left in the evening they didn't arrive there till about five the next morning. But what was worse, they had to pass several stations this side of Amiens and see hundreds of stretcher cases lying on the ground and hundreds on hundreds of walking wounded waiting patiently to be loaded into some vehicle or other.

When it was rumoured that the Fifth Army had been routed, spirits could not have been lower, and everyone waited for the end, telling themselves that whatever the outcome it couldn't be worse than this.

The end didn't come quickly. Nor, to David's surprise, did Gerald's final collapse; for not only through April and May did he continue to be very voluble, but at every available moment he could be seen scribbling in his notebooks.

It was on the 2nd of June that Gerald sent a batch of hand-written material to the War Office in London, and with its despatch his mind closed down on him. That night he lay in his bunk and a voice from a great distance told him not to get up again, and of a sudden, he was enveloped in a great peaceful silence.

So Gerald Bede Ramsmore, the conscientious objector, was called up before not a military court but a medical one, after which he found himself in hospital, where he lay quite content as long as no-one tried to get him back on to his feet, for then he became aggressive.

He arrived in England on a stretcher and heavily sedated. He was taken straight to hospital. And he knew nothing about the Allies preparing to advance again and doing so in August, and nothing whatever about the armistice on the 11th of November.

Part Two

ONE

"Where are the men?"

"I've let them go. Rob will be back later to give me a hand. There's a Victory Tea in the Hollow."

"It's three o'clock in the afternoon."

"I'm well aware of that."

"You're taking too much on yourself."

They were both standing in the doorway of what had been the old barn. And now Carl stepped into the open as if putting distance between himself and this man. And after taking in a deep breath, he said, "Yes, perhaps I am, but that wouldn't be necessary if you hadn't left the whole of this place on my shoulders for years now. When, may I ask, did you last turn a hand in this yard? You walk through it only when the fit takes you."

Carl watched Ward's colour deepen into an almost purple hue, and his voice was a growl as he said, "You forget who you are talking to."

"No, I don't forget who I am talking to. I only know that ten years ago I wouldn't have dared to address you in this way. But now, when you don't give a damn for man or beast, I consider it my right to speak my mind. And I've been wanting to do it for a long time, and there's no time like the present. I've been working for you for over thirty years and not only have I kept this farm going, I've turned it into a profitable business. Oh, yes,"—he made a wide gesture with his hand as if throwing something off, as he said, "There is the carrot of the half-share. Well, I don't give a damn for that, let me tell you, because I could leave here tomorrow and start up on my own, and the men would come with me."

"Huh! Start up on your own? Don't make me laugh. What would you pay your men with? Eh? . . . *My* men . . . with rabbit skins?"

A number of seconds passed before Carl, his voice low but his words steely, said, "The agreement was that I had a part of the profits over a certain amount. Yes; on top of this I had my wage and Patsy had hers, and we've saved."

"Huh! You've saved. I know what you've got over the profits and your wages. And what would that amount to? You couldn't run a house and allotment and one man on it, never mind livestock."

Carl's jaws were tight. He knew that this was true. However, it would be a start, and he knew he could rely on Mike and McNabb; they would go along with him, small wage or no. Then a thought struck him. He did not know from whence it came, unless it was perhaps from Janie's talk of the prospects that lay in the Hall acres when the young master was well enough to come home. And now he heard himself say, "I certainly wouldn't have to start at the bottom for land. There's an offer open to me from the Hall. There's land there and buildings that would house stock; all it needs is labour. And as I warned you, the men would be with me. So what d'you think of that?"

What Ward thought of it had silenced his tongue for a moment. He knew only too well what would happen to this farm if Carl left. But he couldn't bear to be downed in this manner. So he answered, "Talk. That woman hasn't enough money to hire a couple of servants, never mind stock a farm. And this is the gratitude I get. You forget what I took you from. You owe everything you are to me."

"I owe nothing that I am to you, sir, for from that boy that you took in, I worked for my keep, and more. But you owe me a lot, for you crippled my wife. Yes. Yes, you did."

"I did no such thing. It was the other one I was thrusting away. I did not cripple your wife, and don't you dare say that again."

"I'll say it, not only again, but with my dying breath." And now he leant forward and growled into Ward's face, "You crippled my wife. You could have murdered her, and the youngster, but in a different way from that you did your daughter. Oh, you can look like that, but I know what I know."

Ward now stepped back into the doorway as he muttered, "No! You're out of your mind. You're mad. You could be brought up for even suggesting such a thing. Do you know that?"

"I'd be quite happy if you did bring me up. I saw you taking the poison from the tins. You made one mistake, though: you left the milk glass on the wash-hand stand and there was sediment in it. And I'm not the only one who knows."

After saying this he realised he might be incriminating the doctor and so he added hastily, "I took it to a chemist and had it analysed." And then his imagination took him further when he added, "He put his findings in writing."

Carl now watched Ward put his hand out as if to support himself on the stanchion of the door, but felt no pity for the man, for now he was speaking his mind. "You became obsessed with your daughter, as you had been with your wife," he went on. "You could do nothing wrong. Your love for them became a mania. But for the child that your daughter gave birth to, and no matter who the father was she was the daughter of your child, and you are her grandfather, what have you done for her? I'll say what I've thought for years. It's a damn good job she didn't inherit any trait of either your wife or your daughter, else her mind would have been turned years ago under your treatment. But what she has inherited, God knows where from, has stood her in good stead and given her the strength and the power to stand up to you, because she doesn't fear you. As she herself said, she only hates you. And you're the one to know what hate can do. You had your first lesson from the village. But that first wave did nothing to what they felt for you after you ruined three families, one of them for the second time."

He stepped back quickly as he thought Ward was about to strike him. But when the hand left the stanchion of the door and was lifted forward like a blind man groping his way, he did feel a sudden pang of mixed guilt and sympathy.

He stood where he was and watched the older man walk across the yard and round to the front of the house. He never entered these days by the kitchen door, not since Patsy took to crutches.

He, too, now felt in need of the physical support of the barn wall, and he stood there for a full minute, his head back against the overlapping slats, his eyes tightly closed. And then he actually jumped as a voice to his side said quietly, "Carl."

"Oh! Miss Jessie. You startled me."

"Carl, is . . . is it true? I heard . . . I heard it all. I was just at the corner coming round." She could have added, "as clearly as I heard you and Patsy through the slats of what was the old barn years ago." But when he bowed his head and made no answer, she muttered, "Oh dear Lord! What next? This house is indeed doomed. But . . . but Carl"—she clutched his arm—"about you leaving and going to Lady Lydia's. Oh, please! Please, don't do that. Never leave . . . I mean, I just couldn't bear it." Her voice was breaking now and she didn't say why she really couldn't bear it, but she added, "To be left here with him alone. No! No! I would have no-one. Janie, I have lost her. I know I've lost her already. I lost her years ago, first to . . . to that man in the Hall, and now to his mother. And if you went . . ."

"There, there. There, there." He patted her hand where it still lay on his arm and as he looked into her tear-stained face he felt an ache in his heart for her, for he well knew of her feelings and her awareness of the hopelessness of them. And so by way of comfort he said, "I'll . . . I'll not go as . . . as long as I can stick it out. And anyway"—he forced himself to smile—"where would I find anyone to help Patsy as you have. You've been wonderful with her and she appreciates it. As for me, I'll never be able to thank you enough."

"Thank me enough?" She turned away now from him, her lips rubbing one over the other. "You to thank me when, as you said, Patsy's accident was due entirely to Father?" Turning slowly about and facing him again, she asked, "Has this ever been a happy house, Carl? Can you remember?"

He seemed to consider for a moment, then said, "It was a long time ago, shortly after your mother came, before things began to happen from the village. But when she died . . . well, I think all happiness went with her, at least for him. And yet there were times in your early childhood when you and Angela romped and played with him."

"I . . . I can never remember romping or playing with him. Angela used to, but not me. All I can remember of my childhood is feeling lost. Needing someone, wanting someone to love me." She brought her eyes fully on to his now, and in a very low voice, she ended, "But you know all about that, don't you?"

She turned away and walked briskly along by the barn and retraced her steps to the cottage, and there, to her surprise, she found Janie. And she expressed her surprise by saying, "Well! that was a short visit."

Janie was bending down warming her hands at the fire when she said, "Lady Lydia was away. She won't be back until tomorrow. She's gone to see Mr. Gerald."

"I thought she only went once a month, and she visited him last week, didn't she?"

"Yes. Yes, she did." She straightened up now and turned and looked directly at Jessie as she said, "Perhaps they've sent for her to bring him home. Perhaps he's well enough." She stopped herself from adding, "And you wouldn't like that, would you, Auntie Jessie?" Why, she was always asking herself, did her Auntie Jessie not like Mr. Gerald? She knew that she had been disturbed when she heard that he was being brought back from France. She also knew that she had been relieved when she found out he was to be kept in a hospital, not for wounded men, but for those that were sick in the head. She herself could never imagine Mr. Gerald going sick in the head. To her, he had always appeared so sensible and wise.

Jessie said now, "I'll have to go over shortly and help Patsy with the meal; Mrs. McNabb has gone to the Victory Tea in the Hollow." Then she added in a querulous tone, "They've all gone mad with their Victory Tea. I'll leave your meal out for you."

"I can see to it myself, Auntie Jessie. You know I can."

"Very well, very well, see to it yourself." She half turned away, then paused a moment before she said, "By the way, what's this talk about Lady Lydia turning the place into a farm?"

As this was absolute news to Janie, she just stared at Jessie, which only made her aunt snap, "All right! All right! If you've been told not to say anything. But don't tell me you don't know anything about it, when Carl says he's been approached. I think it's very bad of her ladyship, anyway, to try to take another person's men . . . staff. And I would tell her that if I met up with her." And on this she flounced round and went into the kitchen.

Lady Lydia starting a farm, and asking Carl to go and man it? Lady Lydia hasn't got any money. They had talked about it only yesterday. She herself had suggested how good it would be if they could engage two or three men to get the land back into shape for when Mr. Gerald came home, and what had Lady Lydia said? Her income was just enough to keep the house going, pay its rates and Nancy. What money she had received from the military for housing them she had put away for Mr. Gerald, because he had been given no actual pay, no money for the work he had done during the war years, which had struck her as being very odd, because even the wounded men in the Hollow got some kind of a pension. And in a way Mr. Gerald had been wounded. She must get to the bottom of this. She must see Carl.

She waited until she knew that Jessie would have reached the house, then she bundled herself into her coat and woolly hat and went out.

She found Carl in the cowshed; and now, leaning towards him where he was lifting a pail of milk away from a cow, she whispered, "Can I speak to you?"

Laughing at her, he whispered back, "Any time, any time. But it'll cost you." Then straightening up, he said, "Come on into the dairy. What is it?"

She didn't answer him until he had finished pouring the milk into the cooler, and then she said, "Auntie Jessie has just said something very odd to me. It is that you have been approached by Lady Lydia to start a farm."

She watched him now take his broad hat and pull it slowly down over his face; and then he said, "Oh dear me!"

"Is it true?"

"No, my dear, it isn't true"—he was bending down to her and whispering—"you see, I got so mad with your . . . grandfather"—he always hesitated when naming the man's relationship to her—"that I threatened him I would walk out. And when he pooh-poohed the idea that I could ever make a living outside this place, I thought of you and your chatter about the small-holding and what could be done there when Mr. Gerald came back . . . that was before he . . . well, went into hospital. And it just came out. I said I had been approached. And you know something?" He wagged his finger at her. "They've got enough land there and facilities to start a little farm of their own. I've thought that time and time again. A few men and a bit of money behind them and I wouldn't mind doing it."

"It's a pity Lady Lydia hasn't got that kind of money, for then you could start. But . . . but then what would become of this place? Everyone knows it's really your farm."

"Oh, no, no. I've kept it going. I give myself that much credit. But it isn't my farm. And as you know, I'm supposed to have a half-share in it when he goes. But I'd give that up tomorrow if . . . if I could work, if we could all work under happier conditions. You know what I mean?"

She stared at him for a moment before she nodded her head, saying, "Yes, Carl. Yes, I know what you mean."

He shook his head and then said softly, "Of course, of course. I know, lass. Yes, I know. Your years here have been tough going too. You know, when I look at you I can't believe you're still only fourteen. You've got a head on your shoulders that many a one hasn't at twenty. It isn't fair." He put his hand on her cheek now, then patted it as he added, "And it isn't fair either, no, it isn't, that you've had no childhood, no girlhood."

"I don't mind not having any childhood. As for girlhood, I don't feel like a girl, Carl." She turned her head away now as she said, "I passed some girls on the road a while back. They were chatting and talking and laughing before they came up to me. Apparently they had left school; they looked fourteen, but they sounded so silly. They were like . . . well, I really hadn't anyone to compare them with, but I knew they weren't like me, or me like them. And . . . and as I passed them they all stopped and stared at me as if I was something strange." She shrugged her shoulders. "I suppose I am. Yes, I suppose I am."

"Don't say that, dear, don't say that. *Now don't say that.* You're a normal, lovely-looking girl, and, with another few years on you you'll be a spanker."

She smiled at him now, saying, "You know what I did when they stood like stooks? I stepped past them and then turned quickly and went, 'Boo! boo!' And they scattered like frightened rabbits. And you know—" Both her expression and her tone now altered: "I should have laughed, but I couldn't. I just felt sad, like I did, you know, when I told you last year about that old man whom I'd seen standing by a stile a number of times. And . . . and when he came up to me he looked as if he was about to cry; then he said, 'Hello, dear.' You remember?"

"Yes. Yes, I remember."

"You still don't know who it was?"

His tongue moved in and out of his mouth before he said, "No. No. I never found out. And anyway, he wasn't there any more, was he?"

"No, I never saw him again."

No. No, you wouldn't, he thought. Poor old Mr. Mason, the man whose family had been torn asunder by this child's grandfather. His daughter was still in the asylum, his eldest son was God knows where, and his wife had died of a broken heart, and he was left with one son on a farm that had once been prosperous. The old man had likely wanted to see the child who could be his granddaughter: it was more likely that his son, not one of the others, would have been the first to take her mother, for his feelings for Ward Gibson had been those of real hate.

He said now, "Is there any news of Mr. Gerald coming home?"

Shaking her head, she said, "Not this year anyway. Perhaps next, Lady Lydia says."

"Do you know what is really wrong with him?"

"No; only that he is not wounded; he won't talk. And you know, that's very odd because he used to like to talk, as I do." She smiled at him now. "I always want to jabber, but I never really do until I get to the Hall."

"And you jabber a lot there?" He was smiling widely at her.

"Oh yes. Lady Lydia seems to like me to jabber. But—" Her tone altered, as did her expression, as she said soberly, "But I like to jabber sensibly. You know what I mean? When I once said that to Lady Lydia she laughed until the tears ran down her face, and she said, 'Never stop; never stop jabbering sensibly.' I . . . I like Lady Lydia," and she immediately added emphatically, "More than like her." And on this she turned and walked away.

And again Carl stood thinking, Yes, the girl had to more than like someone, and someone to more than like her in return. Jessie undoubtedly loved her but she couldn't like her because she didn't really know whom she was liking; in fact, whom she was loving: to her, the child must always have been a triplet of evil.

TWO

"How's the pain, love?"

"Oh, I hardly feel it when I'm lying down. My chest's worse than any other part of me."

"Well, that's your own fault. You're stuck in that draughty kitchen."

"Don't be silly." She slapped at his hand. "Draughty kitchen indeed! What about the draughty dairy. That's where I got it in the first place." Then, drawing in a painful breath, she said, "It's going to be some Christmas."

"Never mind about Christmas. Mrs. McNabb has everything in hand in that quarter, and Miss Jessie will see to the rest."

"There's another one that should be in bed. She looks utterly tired."

"Well," said Carl, "it isn't with work so much as with worry."

"Do you think there's any truth in what Rob says, that he's sure he saw Pete Mason?"

"I don't know, but I don't think so. Anyway, would he recognise him after nearly fifteen years? There'll always be rumours about him and his whereabouts. Remember, he was supposed to have been killed in the war—a good way of getting rid of him. Then, just a few months ago, that he had absconded from the Army. Anyway, from what Mike said, Rob was tight on the night he was supposed to have seen him."

"It's a terrifying thought. I can understand Miss Jessie worrying because of Janie."

"Oh, I couldn't see him doing anything to her . . . well, you know—" He lifted his hand expressively; then changing his tone, he said, "Never mind them; it's you that's worrying me. Now you've got to make up your mind to stay there, not for a few days but, as Doctor Patten said, for a couple of weeks or more." Then bending over her, he added, "Why don't you do what he says, love, and go to one of those hospitals. They do wonders. Well, the war has given them practice. They've got fellas walking who thought it would never be possible to put their feet on the ground again. And anyway, they could rig you up with one of these corsets," he said.

"Yes. Yes, dear, I've heard of them, and what I've heard I don't think I'll bother. Now listen to me. I'm all right. I'll . . . I'll do what I'm told." She gasped again, saying now, "I have no other choice. Anyway, I was managing fine on my wooden legs until this hit me." She stabbed her chest. "I've had bronchitis before but never as bad as this. Now get about your business, Mr. McQueen, and leave me to mine, which is reading the paper. By!" She flicked the newspaper that was lying on top of the counterpane, saying, "The way they're preparing for Christmas in some places, you'd think there had never been a war. They seem to have forgotten half the houses will have no man to play Santa Claus, or to see in the New Year. Oh yes; it'll be merry and bright, but just for some."

"Well, you cannot undo the past. There's a new generation coming up. They'll want their fling, and those who are lucky enough to come back alive, they'll have it. But talking of generations, I've got a few in the cowshed waiting to start another one, so I'll go and see if they've arrived yet." And with the back of his closed fist he punched her gently under the chin, then went to do the cows' bidding.

In the kitchen Mrs. McNabb greeted him with, "Look at that!" as she pointed to a tray. "He's hardly eaten a bite; well, just a mouthful of bacon and a bit of toast. He's not taking his food, Mr. Carl, at no time. And I set it out well enough."

"Yes. Yes, of course you do. But don't you worry, he'll eat when he's hungry."

"I don't know, Mr. Carl: he won't get very hungry sitting about in that room most of the day. He hardly moves until night-time. D'you know"—she leant towards him—"McNabb said he saw him leaving the cemetery again last night, and it was almost on dark."

"Well, he often goes to the cemetery."

"Oh aye; but not like he's been doin' lately. McNabb said he shouldn't wonder if he's found dead there one day," to which remark Carl only nodded before going out, but he could not restrain himself from thinking: that wouldn't be a bad thing either. He might even take with him the confounded curse that seemed to be on the place, because let him face it, that village would never forget or forgive Ward Gibson, at least while he was alive. It remained so strong that even he, when forced by the weather to drive the cart through rather than skirt it, would feel, even smell the fear his master must have engendered in it.

When he entered the yard it was to see Jessie and Janie crossing swords again. Jessie was saying, "There are plenty of things here to keep you occupied. We need all the help we can get, you know that."

"I've told you, Auntie Jessie, I shan't be long. I just want to catch Lady Lydia before she leaves; I have Mr. Gerald's Christmas present."

"Well, see that you aren't long. I'm . . . I'm becoming tired of this running backwards and forwards . . . Something will have to be done."

Janie had moved a couple of steps away from Jessie when she turned and said defiantly, "Yes. Yes. Something will have to be done. It could be my staying over there altogether. And I would like that. Yes, I would. *I would.*" And on that she turned and ran from the yard, leaving Jessie looking at Carl and saying helplessly, "What am I going to do with her?"

"Just leave her alone. She'll grow out of it."

"Oh, Carl!" Jessie tossed her head now as if throwing off the inane reply; then she muttered, "Grow more into it, you mean," and flouncing about, made for the kitchen, whilst Carl drew in a gulp of the icy air, shook his head, and went back to the byres . . .

When Janie actually burst into the Hall, which had now taken on a semblance of its old style, with some of the smaller pieces of furniture having been brought in and set in their familiar places, she came to an abrupt halt and looked up the stairs to where Lady Lydia was about to descend. And she cried, "Oh! I was afraid you'd be gone."

"No; the taxi isn't due for another fifteen minutes. You're out of breath, child."

"Well, I wanted you to have this to give to him." She now held out the brown paper parcel. It was tied up with narrow grey-silk ribbon, and she pointed to it, saying, "Men don't like fussy stuff, but it's better than string."

"Oh, I'm sure he won't notice what it's tied up with. But come into the drawing-room, it's a bit warmer in there. May I ask what the present is?"

"I've knitted him a scarf. I hope he likes it. But I'm not a very good knitter. I mean, the stitches are not even, you know. Sometimes they're slack and sometimes they're tight; it's according to how I feel." She laughed, a sound that, with her growing taller, was becoming more and more attractive, and which drew Lady Lydia into laughing with her and to put her arm around the girl's shoulder. And as she pulled her down on to the couch that was set at right angles to the fire, she wondered what she would have done these bleak years without this child. She dreaded to think how bare her life would have been.

"Are . . . are you going to ask if I may come with you next time?" The question was put very softly, and as softly Lady Lydia answered it, saying, "Yes. Yes, I am, dear. And I'll put the question straight to him." But even as she said this she could see the response: silence and that blank look in his eyes. Yet she would feel that he knew he was pleased that she was there, even though he might show no sign, not even the movement of a hand. Her heart was always heavy with love and pity for him, but it turned to lead in her breast whenever she sat beside him.

"Will you be back tomorrow? or are you staying longer this time?"

"Oh, I think I'll come back tomorrow. The weather is very uncertain and, as I've told you, the hospital is some way out in the country and I wouldn't want to be snowed up there."

Oh, no, no, she couldn't bear that. Although she loved him so dearly she could only tolerate the pain of seeing him in such a state for a few hours at a time.

And then there were the others, the poor others. Was there any God in the heavens that allowed men to go on living with only bits of their bodies and minds left?

They had said that if Gerald got even a little better they would move him, perhaps to Highgate; she would then be able to see him every week. But would he ever get better? Some of those men had been there since the first month of the war . . .

But the dear child was chattering again. "What was that you said, dear?"

"I said, I've been working on an idea. It's about the small-holding and putting it into shape again and getting it ready for when he comes home. He'd like that, wouldn't he?"

"Oh yes. Yes, I am sure he would. But . . . but you know, we talked about this before and . . ."

Now Janie patted the hand that was resting on her knee and said with some excitement, "But this is different. It wouldn't take a lot of money. Well, just a little, and you said you had a little that you were saving up for his return. Well, it won't do much good lying in a bank, will it?"

Lady Lydia threw her head back now and laughed; then, hugging Janie to her, she said, "You know, my dear, one day I can see you ruling a big company or some big house. Really ruling it, and all on your own."

"Huh! Huh! I don't see anything like that, Lady Lydia, not for me. Although"—she now pulled herself slightly away and affected a pose—"I wouldn't mind ruling over the gardens and telling men what to do, like Carl does. Carl's very good at telling men what to do. He doesn't demand: he doesn't say, do this and do that; he always says, We. "I think *we* should do this. What do you think?"

"Oh! Janie." She was laughing again.

"Do you find that very funny?"

Lady Lydia coughed, almost choked, then managed to say, "I'm more positive than ever, child, that one day you will be saying *we* would like this done, and *we* would like that done, and not only to gardeners, mind," and straightaway rose to her feet, pulling Janie up with her. But Janie did not immediately leave go of the holding hand; she slowly looked around the room as if contemplating, then said, "I'll never want to run a big business or do anything like that. You know what I would like to do?"

"No, my dear, I don't."

"Well . . . really and truly—"

"Well, tell me what you would like to do, really and truly."

"Live here for the rest of my life, with you."

"Oh, my dear. My dear." Lady Lydia bowed her white head, and as the tears ran down her lined cheeks Janie put her arms around her, saying, "Oh. Oh, I didn't mean to make you cry. And . . . and I wasn't being what you call—" She searched for the word before saying, "presuming. It is just that . . . well, I feel more at home here than I do—" Her voice breaking now, she muttered, "I'm very sorry."

"My dear child, you have nothing to be sorry for. My tears were really of gratitude. It's wonderful to hear you say that. But now look at me." She stepped back, dabbing her eyes with a fine lawn handkerchief. "Here I am about to go on a journey, and if I'm not mistaken there is the taxi man's hooter telling me he has arrived. Dear, dear! Where are my gloves? Oh, there they are. And my parcels. Come on, come on. Is my hat straight?"

Smiling now, Janie said, "Your hat's always on straight, m'lady, and you always look lovely. Will you tell Mr. Gerald that . . . that I love him and ask him, will he come back soon?"

"Yes, my dear, I'll tell him that."

It was four hours later when Lady Lydia was ushered into the matron's room with some ceremony. And the matron, rising from her chair, held out her hand, saying, "You must have had a very tiring and cold journey, m'lady.

Isn't the weather dreadful? Do sit down." Then turning to a nurse who was standing by the door, she said, "Bring Lady Lydia a coffee, please. No, bring two. I know I've just had one but I can always drink coffee." She smiled widely now; then she resumed her seat and from across the desk she said, "We're all getting ready for Christmas." But seeing the expression on Lady Lydia's face, her own changed and she said, "Yes, it does sound silly, doesn't it? It's ludicrous really, but, you know, a number of them do appreciate it."

"May I ask if there's any change?"

It was the same question on every visit and the matron said, "I'm afraid not; but it's early days. It's amazing how the change comes about in cases like that of your son. You know, I often think of the first two lines of psalm 130:

> Out of the depths have I cried unto Thee, O Lord.
> Lord, hear my voice,
> Let Thine ears be attentive to the voice of my supplication.

Sometimes it's as if the Lord's ears are open to the prayers and pleadings and supplications because quite suddenly something happens. Ah, here's the coffee."

Ten minutes later the matron passed Lady Lydia over to a nurse who, smiling, then led her along a corridor made up entirely, so it seemed, of a great number of doors. She had been down this way before and she knew to where it led, and she dreaded going into that room.

When the nurse opened the door a strange buzz of sounds assailed her ears. She sometimes likened it to an aviary of birds, cockatoos, mocking birds, parrots. It wasn't loud, just an overall hum, and as usual she concentrated her gaze on her son, who sat in the far corner of the room, because the faces looking at her created such a sadness it was unbearable; not the faces that were twisted up as if in pain, nor those of the disfigured or limbless, but those that smiled at her with that soft appealing look, like a child at its mother. The look always said: come and hold me. Please! come and hold me. Put your arms about me.

Sometimes hands would go out to her and it would take all her will-power not to jump aside. Sometimes she would take hold of one and pat it, and sometimes the nurse would have to loosen its grip on her.

Then she was with her son. He was sitting in a comfortable chair, a small table to the side of him. But this, she had noticed the first time she had come into this room, was fastened to the floor, as were all the other pieces of furniture.

"Hello, darling." She took the limp hand from the knee. "How are you feeling?" Oh, if she could only think of something else to say. But what?

"I've brought you some presents." She pointed to the table, but there was no response whatever from him.

She sat for some minutes stroking his limp hand while gazing into his thin blank countenance. His eyes seemed to have sunken deeper into his head each time she came. After a while she allowed her eyes to wander around the room. Nurses were to be seen here and there. They all seemed very cheery. One was sitting at a table showing a patient how to make paper chains, and the man was laughing as his fingers fumbled under her guidance.

And this is where her beloved son would have to spend the remainder of his life. It was unbearable, unbearable. She suddenly reached out to the table and, picking up Janie's present, she put it on his knee, saying, "Guess who this is from? She's knitted it for you." And as if she had received an answer to this she undid the ribbon, then unfolded the paper and took out the blue-and white-ribbed scarf with its tasselled edge. And now, putting it across his hands, she said, "It feels lovely and soft. You must wear it when you walk in the garden. She must have spent a long time over it because she's no knitter. But I must tell you she's full of ideas about getting the smallholding ready for your coming home. Anyway, she wants to come with me on my next visit . . ."

When his hand lifted suddenly and thrust her aside she could not help but cry out. But it did not drown the sound that came out of his wide-open mouth, like a wail from some injured animal, as it emitted one long drawn-out word: *"Noo . . . o! Noo . . . o!"*

Immediately two nurses appeared at his side, trying to restrain him. But when suddenly his head flopped and he coughed so much that she imagined he was going to choke, all the while clutching at his throat, she stood aside speechless. Then she watched the nurses lead him from the room, and as she went to follow she stepped on the scarf and the parcel she had brought, and, stooping, she grabbed them up and together with her handbag she clutched them to her before running from the room. When she reached his room the nurse said, "He'll be all right. He'll be all right. Would you like to go to the waiting-room?" and as if following some invisible signal another nurse appeared and, taking her arm, led her along the corridor and into a small, cosily furnished room. "Just rest there awhile," she said. "Matron is on her rounds with the doctor. Would you like a drink?"

Lady Lydia looked at her but did not speak, and the nurse said, "A cup of tea, eh? I'll get that for you. It always helps." And on this she went out.

She did not know how long she had sat there: she thought it was for hours, but it was only twenty minutes later when the matron and doctor entered the room and they were both smiling. And the doctor said immediately, "Well this is good news. A definite breakthrough. How did it happen?"

"How . . . how did what happen?"

"I mean, did you say something to him that caused him to react? or do something that all our gadgets have failed to do?"

She thought back for a moment, then said, "No; nothing startling. I just made small talk as usual, and I was talking about a present a young friend of his had sent him. She had knitted him a scarf and"—she paused—"it was just as I was saying she wanted to come and see him and would he like that, that he . . . well, a change came over him. He yelled something that was like, 'No! No!' "

"It was indeed, no, no."

"But then he seemed to choke. You . . . you said he wasn't gassed, but . . . but it looked as if . . ."

"He wasn't gassed, Lady Lydia. We've talked about it before: he went through a very bad time, being so long on duty on the ambulance trains and then with the sudden huge influx of gas victims, and he saw their suffering . . . well, that was the breaking point, I'm sure. And deep inside himself he is still suffering with them. Although he made a great effort to go into oblivion, and has succeeded for some time, nevertheless the suffering in his mind is still there. But—" And with a small toss of his partly bald head the doctor added, "It is the best news I've heard today. His has been a stubborn case, you know, and it really looked as if it were set in. You can go home with a lighter heart, today, Lady Lydia, for from now on we know that he is capable of thinking rationally. But"—he now lifted a warning finger—"everything must go slowly; don't expect miracles straightaway. And who knows, in time you will have him home."

Lady Lydia looked up at the matron. She was smiling at her and she could hear her saying:

> "Out of the depths have I cried unto Thee, O Lord.
> Lord, hear my voice,
> Let Thine ears be attentive to the voice of my supplication."

He had been attentive to her crying.

When she looked back into the smiling face and murmured something like, "Voice of my supplication" before bursting into tears, the doctor said, "That's it. There's no easing of tension like a good cry, especially over good news. You can go home happy now."

Quickly she dried her tears. His talk was just patter. He was talking as if she could walk out of here now with her son when he had previously said it would be a long job. But she should be grateful. Oh, she was. But what she wanted now was to be home and tell Janie. Yes, tell Janie, but not that he didn't want to see her, and that the very thought of the sight of her had brought him out of the depths. Oh no, not that.

THREE

$\mathcal{I}$t was about seven o'clock in the morning of the 2nd of January 1919, that a farm worker, taking a short cut across the cemetery, almost tripped over a prone figure lying across a grave. His flashlight showed that the man was lying with his blood-soaked head on the nine-inch ornate rim of marble that bordered the grave.

The farm-hand rushed to the vicarage and raised Parson George Dixon, successor to Parson Tracey, but of a different calibre, from his bed.

There was so much blood on the victim's face that neither the parson nor the farm worker could recognise him: so therefore, the parson had sent post-haste for the police. He had no doubt but that the man was dead and had lain outside in the bitter night for some long time, as the blackened and congealed blood showed.

It was broad daylight when the police arrived; just the one constable at first, but he immediately sent for his superior, who came accompanied by another policeman, by which time Doctor Patten had arrived on the scene. And there was no doubt from the first moment Philip Patten saw the figure and how it was dressed that he knew who the victim was, if the word victim could be put to it. This would become evident, he told himself, only when he examined the body, which he did some time later, in the church hall, when his assumption was confirmed. It was later still when the police doctor, accompanied by an inspector, arrived, although his findings were not as quickly given: Philip had to wait until the man had examined the stonework surrounding the grave, when he commented, "He is a heavily built man, and he must have slipped and come in contact with that." He pointed down to the marble surround. "It certainly could have done the damage, but he might have survived if someone had been with him. He must have lain all night for he's as stiff as a ramrod."

"You say he's a well-known farmer?"

"Yes; Ward Gibson. Farm's just a mile or so away," Philip said.

"Likely as drunk as a noodle," was another cursory conclusion.

"He must have been visiting his wife's grave."

"Oh? . . . Oh, yes. Gibson. Very odd situation. Yes. What do you think?" But Philip added nothing further, and the man seemed content to return to his surmising. "Well, his fall certainly did some damage to his skull. And there's no evidence of any other marks on his body that could indicate he might have been attacked. Apparently the search of the surrounding area shows no sign of a struggle. The footprints are all precise and still imprinted with a covering of frost." He nodded down to the grass around his feet. "If there had been any sign of a skirmish the ground would have been churned in some way. Well now, I suppose his people will have to be told."

"They've already been sent for."

As they walked back towards the church the police doctor said, conversationally, "You've been here some time then? You took over from old Wheatley?"

"Yes, that's so."

"By! he was a walking hogshead, that one." The man laughed. "I met him, you know, a couple of times. He really could carry some."

"Yes," Philip Patten agreed with the man, "he could carry some."

Just before they entered the church hall the man turned round and surveyed the cemetery to his right and the drive to the church on his left. He could see the lych-gate and part of the street beyond, and he remarked, "It's got a bit of a name, this village, hasn't it? if anything can be made of the old wives' tales, and they can't all be wrong." But receiving no comment he said caustically, "This business should have turned out to be a murder, for then it would have fitted into the picture, eh?"

And now Philip did speak, and there was bitterness in his voice that was not lost on the police doctor as he said, "Yes, yes, it would have fitted into the picture, indeed it would."

Carl and three of the men had come from the farm to take the body home. Jessie had come with them. It was her business to identify the dead man. And it was after they had gone and there was only the vicar and Philip left that the vicar said to him, "Can you spare a few minutes, Doctor?"

"Yes. Yes, of course," said Philip.

"It . . . it's something that no-one has commented on. But I wonder what you think, because truthfully I don't know what to make of it. If you'll come back to the cemetery I'll explain."

They were again standing by the grave, and, pointing to the headstone, the vicar said, "Do you see anything peculiar there?"

Philip looked at the writing on the stone, and then he said, "It says at the top quite plainly, 'Remember me.'"

"Yes. Yes," put in the vicar quickly now. "It is quite plain. But can you make out the rest of the inscription?"

Philip bent forward now and peered at the moss-covered stone, and what he read was

Remember me.
Agatha Hamilton,
aged 49 years,
left this cruel world
and took her pains to the Lord on
May 2nd, 1872.
R.I.P.

"Well?"

Philip repeated, "Well, all that strikes me is that 'Remember me' is very clear to read whereas the rest is not." He now leant forward again and looked at the two words heading the stone, and he said, "It looks as if these have been roughly scraped clean, or at least just the surface. A bit of emery paper or such could have done it. But then"—he turned to the vicar—"every now and again you have the headstones cleaned up."

"Not often in this old part; it must be two years ago since any cleaning was done here. Anyway, you know yourself, Doctor, he was a most hated man for many miles around. He had brought tragedy not only on his own house but . . . but on others. And this village, I have found to my dismay, is very prone to superstition, and somebody's just got to recognise that these two words have been made clear and the rumours will start again." He looked down at the old grave, at the frozen weeds, and pulling at one he managed to loosen some earth about it. Then taking a handkerchief out of his pocket, he put it around his fingers and scooped up some of the soil and rubbed it quickly over the two words. And the thought that crossed Philip's mind as he watched was, If this man had been vicar of this village the day Ward Gibson had come to him and asked to have the banns of marriage read, half the events that had happened since would not have come about. Oh, there would always have been Daisy Mason, but he was sure her actions would have been condemned in many more quarters and the knowledge that much of the village wasn't with her would surely have curtailed her venom. And now this kindly man shook out his handkerchief, rolled it into a ball and put it into his pocket, and, turning to him, said, "It may be just a coincidence, but when I earlier read the name Hamilton on this stone, I remembered it had been recalled to my mind some time earlier, and I wondered why; and I'm of such a nature, Doctor, that I always have to follow things to their source, if you know what I mean. So I have just looked up the name in the church register, and there I find that Mrs. Mason's maiden name was Hamilton."

"No! Never!"

"But we'll let it rest there, eh? Shall we, Doctor?"

Philip twice nodded his head slowly as his mind pictured two fiercely strong hands banging Ward Gibson's head against that stone. And whoever had done it, he couldn't have been alone, for as had already been noted, there was no sign of a struggle. He must have been knocked insensible before being carried to the grave. And whoever had done it had planned it.

Seth Mason was the only one left of the Masons, and he was a weakling, at least he would be on his own. And Pete was dead . . . Or was he? Every now and again there had been a rumour of his returning home and being hidden, and this was since the War Office had written him off as "missing, believed dead." And that was in France. If he had absconded, how on earth could he have got here? But hate, like faith, could perform miracles. And it wasn't unknown that men could feign loss of memory and be shipped over with a crowd of wounded, only to disappear.

It was all very strange and rather terrible. Anyway, Ward was dead, and all that was left of his family was Miss Jessie and the girl. He did not know really how Miss Jessie would feel about her father's going, but he knew that the child would be released from his tyranny and could not help but be glad.

As the two men walked back to the church, the vicar said, "I don't often see you at the services."

Philip turned to him, a wry smile on his face as he said, "I don't often have much time. As you know, it's a busy job. But I'll try to squeeze a visit in now and then . . . in the future."

"Do that. Do that. I'd be pleased to see you."

They parted at the church door, knowing that they understood each other.

FOUR

*J*t was said in the village that the day Ward Gibson was buried should be celebrated with another Victory Tea; for God, having seen fit to strike him down in the cemetery, was pointing out his final destination.

There was relief, too, among the families that had been for him, although perhaps with the exception of Fred Newberry. His comment was that Ward had been a fool to himself from the beginning in letting his fancy stray to Newcastle.

It had been said that on the farm, too, there was permeating a feeling of relief. It was as if the dark oppressive shadow that had been hanging over all their lives had been swept away. Never more so was this feeling evident as Carl and Jessie sat by Patsy's bed discussing the future.

The will had been read. It had not been altered from the time Ward had struck the bargain with Carl. That Carl was now the legal owner of half this house and its prosperous business seemed at the moment more unreal to him than when it had been just a promise that might never be kept. It certainly wouldn't have surprised him if Ward had changed the will after his outburst on that particular day at the barn.

What was being heatedly discussed now concerned Jessie and where she should reside in the future. She was saying, "We are quite comfortable where we are. Anyway, Patsy, I ask you, just think what it would mean if you went back there. You'd need someone with you all the time, you know you would. Here, there's Mrs. McNabb at hand and me, and you're within call of Carl from the yard, whereas . . ."

Patsy turned her face away on the pillow, at the same time raising her hand to stop Jessie's flow, and what she said was, "This is your rightful place. Even the two cottages put together make no more than a box. And then there's Janie, she . . ."

"Yes, there's Janie. And let me tell you, if I was dying to come back in here tomorrow, I couldn't do so, and because of her, for she absolutely refuses even to talk of the possibility of our living in this house. Do you know, she's been in it only once since the time I moved us to the cottage, and you know when that was. But—" and now she drew in a long breath and shook her head as she said, "believe it or not, she has given me an ultimatum: if you and Carl were to come back to the cottage, she would go and stay at the Hall, and nothing would stop her. I couldn't. It seems impossible to admit it, but she is past me, I cannot believe I'm just dealing with a fourteen-year-old girl. Anyway, she's just waiting for an excuse to be able to stay over there. She's obsessed with that place and those two. Thank God that madman isn't there."

For the first time Carl spoke, and now harshly, saying, "Oh . . . oh, no, he's not that. Well, what I mean is, it's something like shellshock he suffers from. God help him."

"Shellshock!" Jessie was indignant. "He was never in the war really; he was a conscientious objector."

Carl dared to say, "Don't be silly. From what we hear some of them had the rottenest jobs imaginable. They were in the thick of it out there, stretcher-bearing and such."

Patsy turned her head and was smiling at them as she said, "That's it, have a row. It'll make a good start." Then looking pointedly at Jessie, she said, "You know, you should be grateful that she found something to hold her interest. What life had she here as a child? It really broke my heart to see her locked up in that cottage every time you came out. And in this house it was the same; in fact, worse, for she only saw the bedroom."

Jessie looked down at her fingers where they were plucking imaginary threads from her skirt, and she muttered, "I know, I know, but what else could I do? Have her run in here and bump into Father? It was bad enough when they crossed paths outside." She did not add, "And you're lying where you are because of one such encounter."

But Patsy did not pursue this trend in their discussion, except to look at Carl and say, "You know that piece of fancy talk you often come out with, which means let things be, leave them as they are? Well, that's what you want to do now."

Carl laughed and looked at Jessie and said, "Status quo?" And when Jessie, with raised eyebrows, nodded and smiled at him, he knew that she had as little understanding of the term as Patsy. Her reading likely didn't touch on the daily papers, whereas his own got no further these days. And so he said briskly, "Well! to business. I'll leave you two to get on with your jabbering but I must get back to work. Somebody must do it." He pulled a face, turning from one to the other, and then went out.

It would appear that Janie had been waiting for him to come out of the house, for she was there by the door, requesting straightaway: "Come into the tack-room a minute, will you, Carl?"

In the room and with the door closed, she immediately excused her request: "I don't want Auntie Jessie to see me talking to you," she said. "She'll want to know what I'm saying, as always," and she wrinkled her nose, then astounded him: "How much do you pay the farm-hands?" she asked.

"How much do I pay the farm-hands? Oh well, it varies. They get good money now, you know, since the war." He pushed out his chest in explanation. "We're the feeders of the nation, you know. So we're being recognised at last. Well now, you want to know what they're paid. Mike and McNabb get thirty-five shillings a week each. Rob gets thirty-three. Then of course any extra male help in the summer in the fields is paid by the hour."

"Do women helpers in the summer get the same?"

"Oh no." The shake of his head was emphatic. "Women never get paid as much as men, because they don't do the heavy work."

She thought for a moment, then said, "In the summer they do, lifting the stooks and all that, and they rake with the men."

He tapped her cheek gently, saying, "Now we're not going into politics. Why d'you want to know all this?"

"Oh." She shrugged her shoulders, but she didn't answer his question: what she said was, "I didn't think they got all that. How about if they slept in; I mean, had a place to stay and got their food; how about it then?"

"Oh then, well, a pound a week or perhaps a little more, a little less, according to their experience."

"As low as ten shillings?"

"Oh no, you couldn't offer a man ten shillings a week, even with bed and board. Anyway, what's all this about?"

"Well, I can tell you. I was thinking about . . . well, I put it to Lady Lydia about employing someone, or perhaps two, to clear the ground and get some of it set for a crop or such. I'm going to pick all the fruit this year . . . I might need a little help. We'll bottle it, and it could be sold like they used to do when Mr. Gerald was at home. But during the war and the soldiers tramping over everything, and then those village children coming in and scrumping, there wasn't much left. But it will be different this year, because now they can't get in since the Army mended the fences and the walls. Well, they went through them, didn't they, with their trucks? So that part's all right; it's just clearing the ground and getting it into shape again."

He now placed his hands on her shoulders and looked into her face as he said, "You're taking something on, aren't you? And, you know, you should still be at school?"

"Oh, Carl, I'm at school every morning. History, geography, arithmetic, English. She . . . she keeps me on such childish things, Carl. If she knew of the books that I look at in the Hall library, she'd have a fit."

He laughed now as he asked, "What kind of books?"

"Oh, all kinds, about gods and goddesses. And then there's stories, marvellous stories. You could spend days reading the stories. But I hardly ever get one finished, because I can't stay long enough." She now turned from him and walking towards a saddle hanging on the wall, she stroked the leather for a moment as she said, "I'll never live in that house across the yard, Carl. Although he's gone I feel he's still there. You know what I'd do with it?" She swung round to him. "Set fire to it and make it into a sort of funeral pyre like they used to do in Egypt and put it on his grave."

"Oh. Oh, Janie, you shouldn't think things like that. Oh, my dear."

"I do think things like that, Carl. I hated him when he was alive and I can't stop hating him now because he's dead. And another thing, whichever one was my father he couldn't have been as bad as he was, not so cruel, so cold. He hated me because of what those men did to my mother and I was the result. But they only did that to my mother because he'd had a woman put in an asylum, the sister of one of them."

"Shh! Shh!" He had her by the shoulders again. "You shouldn't think about it. You shouldn't talk about it. And anyway, she was put in the asylum because she had done very wrong things to your grandfather. She had, in a way, killed your grandmother. Now there's two ways of looking at this matter. You should try to see the reason for your grandfather's actions."

"I . . . I experienced his reactions, Carl. I . . . I knew there was something wrong with me right back when I was a child and had to be locked in the cottage. And . . . and I wanted to be loved and"—she now bit on her lip—"Auntie Jessie's love was a different kind. I can't explain it. She was always saying she loved me then doing hard things."

"She had her reasons, too, dear; she was trying to protect you."

"Oh well"—she now flung her arms wide—"it doesn't matter any more, well not much. I'm me, and I've known I'm me for a long time. I'm . . . I'm different from others. I know I am. Yet—" Her expression now changed to one of slight pleasurable surprise as she said, "One of the girls from the village spoke to me the other day. Do you remember me telling you about the ones I went boo! to? Well, she was the tallest one. She was by herself on the road when she half stopped and spoke to me."

"What did she say?"

"She said, 'Hello,' and I was so surprised that I didn't answer. And then she said, 'Isn't it cold?' And I said, yes, it was. And then she said, 'Goodbye,' and I said, 'Goodbye.' "

"When was this?" His voice was low now.

"Oh, the day before yesterday."

Well, well! Could it be with the passing of the thorn in the villagers' flesh that their attitude would change towards the child and she would be finally accepted? But would she want to be accepted? Did they but know it, they were dealing with someone as strong-willed as ever her grandfather had been; only there would be no vindictiveness in her strength.

She was saying now, "If . . . if Lady Lydia decides to take on a man, would you . . . on the quiet, come and check him over for her? I mean, to tell us that he was capable of hard work and was of good character?"

He now put his two fingers to his forehead and flicked his hair back, saying, "At your service, ma'am. Any time, at your service, with no charge."

As she laughingly pushed at him so he put his arms around her and held her tightly for a moment; and he, laughing too, said, "Any time you want help, my dear, you come to me, and it won't cost you a penny." And now they were pushing at each other, their laughters mingled. And Mike, passing by in the yard outside heard the laughter and, as he remarked to the others, he had never heard such a gay sound in this yard since he first came into it.

FIVE

"We've made seventy-four pounds out of the fruit and jams this year, and there's still a month to go to Christmas."

"Yes, my dear." Lady Lydia nodded at Janie. "But that's only because Carl has been so kind as to loan us his transport and a driver. And we can't expect to take advantage of him again at Christmas and . . ."

"It isn't taking advantage, and he likes helping. It takes his mind off . . . well, Patsy's going. He's still mourning her, I think, and it's now over seven months. Anyway, he said we've just got to ask him. And so with the money that you've got, you could take this man on. It would be a start."

"It would mean buying extra food, my dear, and men eat a lot. And then he'd have to have a wage, and I read that some of them are demanding two pounds a week."

"I think this one would be glad to take anything. And anyway, as Carl once told me, it comes down by practically half if they have bed and board."

"But where's the bed, my dear? Those rooms above the stables have never been used for years. They are dank and . . ."

"If a man has been a soldier he's used to sleeping on anything, I should say. In any case, we could soon fix that up; in fact, he would fix it up himself, I think. And this one's young and strong-looking, not like some of the older ones that come begging. But his shoes are in holes. They must be because one sole is loose. I noticed that."

Lady Lydia sighed as she said, "What don't you notice, my dear? But there is another thing: I don't think I would be able to cope with labour; I mean, giving orders and seeing that they do their work. And, you know, I'm away a day or more in every week now that Gerald is closer to home."

"Well, I'm not afraid of giving orders."

Lady Lydia chuckled as she said, "No, you certainly are not. But you are still a very young girl for all your height and all your"—now she wagged her finger at the tall girl standing at her knee—"for all your height and for all your talk you are still a young girl. And that's how men would see you."

"Not for long they wouldn't."

Lady Lydia's chuckle became louder as she said, "You're an awful child, you know."

"I know I am. But, Lady Lydia, I don't feel a child. I can't remember ever feeling a child."

The smile went from the older woman's face and her voice was soft as she said, "That is a great pity."

"No, it isn't, because I'm able to see things that so-called girls don't. I mean . . . well, I'm not silly."

"No"—there was a chuckle again—"you're far from that. Well now, to get back to the business that I don't want to take on. I think we had better take advantage of Carl once more and ask him to come and vet this applicant of yours, because he's not mine."

"Well, you'll have to pay him."

"Yes, I'll have to pay him, but you will have to oversee his labour. You say you have stopped your lessons in the mornings?"

"Oh yes, some time back. Well, ever since Patsy went, because Auntie Jessie is taken up with re-doing the house inside."

"But she still lives in the cottage? I mean, you both live in the cottage?"

"I told you, didn't I? I would never live in that house. She might. Oh, yes"—she nodded now—"she might sometime."

"Well, away with you! and ask Mr. Carl if he can spare the time to come and see me; then, if he finds that the man is suitable, you will have to take him and show him where he's supposed to sleep, and that will likely turn him away."

"Not by the look of him, it won't." She bent slightly forward now and placed a light kiss on Lady Lydia's cheek, whispering as she did so, "I love you." Then, as any young girl might, so she acted and ran from the room, with Lady Lydia sitting shaking her head as she wondered, for the hundredth time, what she would have done without her. And yet, she thought, if it hadn't been for Janie, Gerald would have come back with her two months ago. During that visit, while she sat talking to him, she had happened to say that Janie now practically lived in the house, except that she didn't sleep there, and that her bright personality lit up the whole place.

For some weeks up to then he had been talking to her slowly and sensibly. But on that day, as they were sitting in the garden, he had one of his choking fits. It wasn't one that would need attention, but it was a signal that he was distressed. And when later he had calmed down he had said to her, "If . . . if I ever come back, it . . . it won't be to the house. I . . . I don't want to see anyone." He had then brought his face close to hers to say slowly but somewhat aggressively, "Do . . . you . . . understand, Mama? No one! When . . . when I come back it will be to the cottage . . . the woodman's cottage . . . alone, or else . . . I don't come . . . at all."

So vehement were his words that they were still imprinted on her mind.

When, later, she had spoken to the doctor about him, he had said she could take him home at any time. He might still be withdrawn and not want company, but it would be better if he had an occupation of some kind. And yes, there was no reason why he should stay any longer, unless he wanted to. He wouldn't press him either to go or to stay. And then he had smiled as he said, "You could say he is one of our successful cases. Would there were more like him."

But the very thought of putting Janie out of her life was unbearable to her, as was the thought of her son existing in the woodman's cottage that was again entangled in the undergrowth.

Dear, dear! She felt old and tired. She would be seventy next year, and what had she done with her life? Her marriage of convenience in order to have a child; and what a child! one who had been driven out of his mind because of his sense of moral right.

The house seemed dead. Yet since her father's death she had worked on it daily, returning it to something like its former state and even better: replacing curtains and covers, moving furniture around, even getting rid of some, such as the bed in her father's room and the one in the room which she had once shared with Angela. She hadn't replaced either bed. Carl slept in one of the two spare bedrooms. She herself still slept in the cottage; and that simply because of Janie's stubbornness.

At the moment the kitchen was empty, for Mrs. McNabb left with the men at five o'clock, at least in the winter. However, one or other of the men would return at half-past six to help with the last of the chores. But now it was six o'clock and there was nobody here in the house, or in the cottage, or on the farm. Carl had gone across to the Hall to look over a man her ladyship was about to engage, a man to do the clearing, so went Janie's garbled story.

Jessie walked into the hall, at the moment lit by the hanging gas lamp, then made her way along the corridor to the room that had once been her father's study, then later Patsy's and Carl's bedroom, but which was now a small and comfortable sitting-room. The fire was low in the grate but she did not immediately tend to it. She stood with her hands on the mantelpiece and gazed at her reflection in the mirror. It was long, white and drawn. She was thirty-three years old and she told herself that if she were to meet a woman who looked like her reflection, she would say she was forty at least. She had never been beautiful. Carl had once promised her beauty when she grew up, but that was only through kindness. All the beauty had gone to Angela, only to be marred, broken and wasted. Her life, too, had been wasted.

When there was no hope of her ever having Carl, she had grabbed at the child who had been born of cruelty as something on whom to shower her love and to receive love in return. But it hadn't happened like that. The measures she had had to take to confine the child had killed the return of love that she might have had from her. And now she had lost her. Oh, she had lost her a long time ago: to that man first, and then his mother, and now to the house itself . . . And what about Carl? It looked as if it was going to be the repeat of her father's story, for he had hugged his mourning to himself as if all the while embracing his lost love. And Carl seemed to be following the same route, for he never spoke of Patsy. He was civil and kind to her, but so were the paid hands.

She had a terrifying thought of him going into Newcastle and seeing a poster of a dancer on a billboard, as her father was said to have done, and falling madly in love with the girl it represented, maniacally in love with her, just as her father's loving had not been sane. Yes, the same thing could happen to Carl, for twice during the last three weeks he had been into New-castle and never mentioned the errand he had been on.

If he were to take another wife she would go mad. Yes, she would, she would go mad. She nodded into the mirror. She would go back into that cottage and lock herself in and she would go the same way as Angela had.

The gas mantle on the bracket to the right of her went plop, plop, plop, and the glass shade seemed to shiver, as did her reflection in the mirror, only this was shaking its head and its mouth was open, denying her last thoughts, saying, No! No! What was she thinking?

When the tears spurted from her eyes she looked upwards for a moment and whispered aloud, "O Lord, I am so lost, so lonely. Whatever happens, don't let me do anything silly, please." She could no longer see her reflection in the mirror and her throat was full; and she was about to turn away when she heard footsteps coming along the corridor, and almost in a panic now she dropped on to her knees, grabbed the tongs up from the hearth and began to take lumps of coal from the brass helmet bucket at the end of the fender. And when the door opened she did not turn around as Carl said, "Oh! There you are. I've just taken Janie to the cottage. She'll make a farmer one of these days. Anyway, the fella seems all right and he was more than willing to take on the job for a pound a week and his grub. He didn't turn a hair when he saw the condition of those rooms above the stables, even seeming to like what he saw and said that he would soon have one shipshape. And he kept thanking me, and I told him it wasn't me he should thank but the young lady."

He stopped now and watched Jessie plying the bellows until she had kindled a flame among the coals again. And when she still didn't speak or turn round, he bent over her, saying, "What's the matter? Are you all right?"

He could just make out the mumbling, "I'm all right." But when she pulled herself up from the hearth and did not turn towards him, he took her arm and pulled her gently round to face him. And he stood staring at her bent head, her face awash with tears and it was some seconds before he said gently, "What is it, Jessie?"

She now pulled herself away from his hold and, grabbing at the lawn waist-apron she was wearing over her woollen dress, she rubbed her face vigorously with it, but still she didn't speak.

Again he took hold of her, both shoulders this time, and made her face him; and when, looking up at him, she mumbled, "I'm sorry. I . . . I can't help it. I . . . I just felt so lost, the house, everything. Nobody here. Lonely. I . . . I seemed to have been born to be lonely. I . . . I have lost Janie and . . ." She couldn't bring herself to lie and say, "Patsy, too," because she had known for a long time that Patsy was nearing her end, and although she had grown fond of her over the years, she could not help but think and hope what her going would mean: she would have Carl once more. He . . . he would be bound to turn to her, if only for sympathy. But he hadn't, he didn't need her sympathy. And now she blurted out, "You . . . you hardly ever speak . . . you . . . you don't know I'm alive."

"Oh, Jessie, Jessie." He brought one hand now and cupped her wet cheek and his voice was thick and low in his throat as he said, "I know you're alive, dear. I know you're alive, only too well. But . . . but it's early days

. . . I mean . . . well, you know I cared deeply for Patsy and . . . and I have missed her. But I've known of late you can't live with the dead for ever. And she . . . she wouldn't want that, she told me she didn't. The last thing she said to me was"—his own voice was throaty now—" 'Be happy and don't be lonely. No . . . nobody should live alone,' she said." He did not add, "She knew how you felt for me and always had done," because he had immediately reacted by saying, "Never ever! I'll never put anyone in your place." And she had smiled at him and said that her mother had a saying: the heart has a number of rooms.

He went on now, saying, "It's seven months. I . . . I would have made it easier for myself if I had been able to talk about her to you, but somehow I . . . I couldn't make an opening. D'you know what? Twice lately I've been into Newcastle and got blind drunk, but it didn't help."

The tears were still running down her cheeks but more slowly now, and he took out a handkerchief, and as he wiped her face he said, "We'll take it from here, eh, Jessie?" to which she answered, "Yes, Carl." Then the meaning of his words and the tender look in his eyes as he had said them acted like the bursting of a dam.

And now her whole body was shaking and her sobbing was audible and he was holding her to him, and it was as if he was back in that bedroom all those years ago and asking if he could hold her. In some strange way she had belonged to him from then on. Even the beautiful Angela couldn't displace her in his affection, although she was never convinced of this. But then there came Patsy. Dear, dear Patsy. But now Patsy was no more, and he was holding that woman that had been the child, and he knew that he must go on holding her, for she had indeed been his from the day she was born.

SIX

Lady Lydia looked at the tall young girl standing before her. She was wearing a long, mole-coloured velour coat, with a fur collar. A green velour hat completed the outfit, the whole seeming to complement the face and the two deep brown eyes set in wide sockets and outlined by curved eyebrows. The nose was small in contrast to the wide mouth, and the hair framing the whole and covering the ears held a deeper tinge than the eyes, and it was drawn back and lay in a bun under the rim of the hat. The face had no claim to beauty nor could it be called pretty, but it was arresting. The eyes alone would hold the onlooker, as would the rest of her: the way she stood, the pose of her head, the chin tilted forward, created a picture that would draw the eye and hold it, for the whole expressed a vivid personality.

"Oh, my dear, you look lovely. How did it go?"

"Fine. Grand. They looked happy." She nodded now. "Yes, they both looked happy. And Auntie Jessie . . . well"—Janie gave a small laugh—"she looked so young. I've never seen her look like that before. And Carl looked . . . oh, so handsome. I went with them to the station. McNabb drove us. He and Mrs. McNabb are going to look after the place for the week."

"And they're going to Devon for their honeymoon?"

"Yes; and it will be the first time in their lives that either of them has been more than a few miles from the farm. And . . . and the place will be so different when they come back . . . I mean . . . well, happier. But," she added now with a straight face, "I'm still not going to live in the house with them. I've told them I can manage by myself in the cottage. Anyway"—her smile returned—"I'm not often there, am I? Auntie Jessie says that by being so stubborn I'm keeping the McNabbs and Rob and his family from good housing. Well, I said there was a solution, I could come and stay here, couldn't I?" Her smile was wide again.

"But what did your aunt say to that?"

"Well, up till now, you know, it's been because I'm all she's got. And that is a silly saying, isn't it? because nobody belongs to anyone, not really."

"Oh, my dear." The older woman slapped at her now, saying, "You're far too young to think things like that. But you do think she might change her mind now that she is married?"

"Yes. Yes, I think she might, because she will have someone else, someone she's always wanted. I think she has been in love with him all her life. Apparently he held her when she was born and so she claimed him, as I did. I used to follow him around. He became, in a way, my father, until I met up with . . . the nice man." The smile sliding slowly from her face now, she said, "How did you find him yesterday?"

"Oh, really very well. He's . . . he's talking much more now, in an ordinary way."

"Then why can't he come home?"

"I've . . . I've told you, my dear, it's . . . he can't stand being in the company of people."

"But he's with lots of people in the hospital."

"Yes. Yes, you're right, but they're different. They don't bother him. They . . . well, I suppose they don't want to talk to him or him to talk to them. The orderlies, I suppose, don't count. He's become used to them."

Janie now pulled off her hat and threw it on the chair, and with definite impatience said, "Well, is he going to spend the rest of his life there?"

"No. No, dear, I don't think so. But look—" Lady Lydia smiled now, saying, "I know what you're going to do next. You're going to throw your coat on top of that lovely hat, aren't you? Now take them both and put them in the hall closet, and then tell Nancy she may brew the tea."

With the coat over her arm and the hat on top of it, Janie turned once more to Lady Lydia, saying, "Have Arthur and Billy finished that patch?" to which the very quick reply was: "Oh no, dear. They've been in the loft lying on their beds; they can't work unless you're standing over them with a whip."

At this, Janie, tossing her head, walked quickly from the room, followed by her ladyship's laughter. Within a few minutes she was back and picked up the conversation as if it had never been interrupted by saying, "That could well be in Billy's case; Arthur would be willing to work all night if you let him. He said he knew Billy would, too, for Billy had been in the Army with him. But Billy is not the same as himself, and now that there are dozens of men on the roads begging for work, I'm going to tell him he'd better watch out."

"Oh! my dear; he does a good day's work."

"He doesn't, Lady Lydia. You know he doesn't. He gives us what he calls our pound's worth. He forgets about his bed and board, and there's many on the road, in fact, many have knocked on the door, who would gladly do what he's doing for good meals and a place to sleep. He thinks he's still scrounging in the Army. And I can tell you this, Arthur's disappointed in him, too. Anyway," her voice changed, "I shouldn't be a bit surprised if he ups and goes one of these days. I hope he does."

Lady Lydia looked at the slim figure of the girl who already had a woman inside her, and she said to herself, it shouldn't be. It shouldn't be. And looking back she thought that at her age, all she would have thought of was what dress she should wear for the coming ball; and would John Cook Mortimer be there? Or Jim Harding or . . . ? "What was that you said, dear?"

"What I said, Lady Lydia, was, if things improve the way they've done this year and we can send vegetables to the market as well as the fruit, then we'll need a horse and cart, just a small one."

Lady Lydia closed her eyes as she said, "My dear, I've dipped into the funds so much."

"You won't need to dip into the funds any more, Lady Lydia. What we make next year, even without the vegetables, now that we've got the orchard cleared and the vinery and the hothouses all going, there'll be more than enough profit to buy a horse and cart. Carl would pick an old one out that had still a lot of work left in it. You can get carts at any of the sales; and if you're in a position to buy at any time, there'll always be a cheap one. It would more than pay for itself, and quickly. I'm sure it would."

Lady Lydia stared at the girl sitting by her side. Was she only sixteen? In her day, a girl of sixteen . . . What was she thinking? The girls of her day were long, long past. They had passed before the war; nowadays they were a new generation. They were different beings. She had encountered them of late on trains and buses. They were flamboyant; their youth had age to it. And this girl here . . . well, she had never known youth, not with her upbringing. And then there was the questionable mixture inside her. Yes, yes, that mixture. Did she ever think about it? Oh, being who she was she would think about it. Perhaps that was why she was so different, even from the youth of today. She was beyond them. Her heritage, whatever it was, had forced her into adulthood.

"Nancy's a long time with that tea. You haven't been listening to what I've been saying."

"Oh yes, I have, dear. Oh yes. I always listen to what . . . you . . . say." She stressed the last words then added, "How could I do anything else?"

Now Janie leant her head against Lady Lydia's shoulder and, laughing, she said, "Do I always appear so forward?"

"Yes. Yes, you do, dear; you always appear so forward."

"But does it annoy you?" She was now sitting up straight.

"My dear"—Lady Lydia took her hand—"I couldn't imagine you ever annoying me. Surprising me, oh yes. Amazing me, oh yes. Yes, that, too, but never annoying me. What you are, dear," her voice dropped, "is a comfort. You always have been and I hope you always will." But as Janie went to embrace her, she exclaimed, "Oh! Ah! Ah! At last. Have you been to China for that tea, Nancy?"

"No, ma'am; I didn't get as far as that, only to Newcastle. And I hadn't me tram fare back so I had to walk." And Janie, jumping up to take the tray from her, laughed loudly, saying, "Well, you should have had enough money for the tram; what have you done with your bonus?"

"There you are, ma'am." Nancy was nodding to Lady Lydia, who sat smiling tolerantly on the sofa, "She'll not let me forget that bonus. And by! I had to work for it. I nearly lost me fingers pickin' an' bottlin'. I pity those fellas outside, I do that." Then looking Janie up and down, she said in a more appreciative tone, "I saw you coming in with your new hat an' coat on. You looked lovely, you did."

"Thank you, Nancy. Thank you."

But when, looking towards her mistress, Nancy bantered again, "She looked like a young lady for once, which is a change," Janie cried, "Oh, you! You would go and spoil it, wouldn't you?" and Nancy made for the door laughing, only to stop abruptly, saying, "Oh, I forgot, ma'am. That bloomin' telephone thing, bell, kept ringin' and when I got to it there was nobody there, and I shouted, twice I shouted, 'Hello! Hello!' "

"When was this?" Lady Lydia had risen to her feet.

"Oh, when you were upstairs restin', ma'am. If anybody had answered saying, 'It's me,' or some such, I would have come up for you, but there was nothin'."

The telephone was a new addition to the house and she'd had it installed because, earlier in the year, she'd had to miss two visits to Gerald because of his suffering from a severe cold, and she had said to him, "If another time you are not feeling well, would you phone me?" And he had nodded at her before saying, "Perhaps." So she'd had the instrument installed. But he had never used it; and the only other call she had received was from her stepson Beverly's daughter-in-law, the mother of the young officer whom Gerald had attended on the hospital train. The young man himself had written to her a few times and had commiserated with her on Gerald's breakdown, and always he had spoken highly of him. And a year later, after he died from his wounds, his mother had informed her and then taken up the correspondence. And it had been she who had phoned that once.

"Whoever it was, they'll ring again," said Janie, now handing her ladyship a cup of tea. "It could be someone from the market. I gave them your number."

Lady Lydia did not say, "I wish you hadn't," but she listened to Janie going on, saying, "Mr. Potter in the fruit shop said that's how business is done today." She smiled now as she added, "He was very funny. He said, all you had to do was to lift that thing, and he pointed to the phone, ring to the source, say what you wanted, and they put it on the carrier cart if it was for in the country, and Bob's your uncle."

The cup rattled in the saucer. It was impossible, Lady Lydia told herself, not to laugh or to be happy in this child's company. Yet why did she still think of her as a child when she kept telling herself that Janie Gibson had never been a child?

The sound of a bell ringing sent the teacup and saucer clattering on to the table. And when Janie cried, "I'll see who it is," Lady Lydia checked her quickly, saying, "No, no! I'll see to it."

In the hall she took up the receiver from the wall and said, "Yes? Hello." There was no answer for a moment; then the voice said, "Mama."

"Oh. Gerald, Gerald. Hello, my dear."

"Mama. Will you put a single mattress down in the cottage and . . . and a few cooking utensils?"

"Oh, Gerald . . . Ger . . ."

"Mama, I am not coming to the house. Either I go into the cottage or I stay here."

She had to draw in a long breath before she could say, "All right, dear, all right. When . . . when are you coming?"

"I . . . I don't know. Perhaps tomorrow or the next day. When . . . when I feel you've done as I asked."

"Yes. Yes, my dear, I'll do as you ask. Oh yes. Hello, hello, Gerald."

There was no answer. She replaced the receiver; then stood gripping the edge of the small table on which lay a telephone directory. Her eyes were tightly closed; but then she started when a voice behind her asked, "Are . . . are you all right?"

She turned and leant against the edge of the table. Her body was shaking slightly and she put out a quivering hand and gripped Janie's as, her voice seeming to come from high in her head, she said, "He's . . . he's coming home."

"Oh! Oh, wonderful. Wonderful!"

"But"—she pulled herself from the support of the table—"not here, not into the house."

"No? Why not?"

"He . . . he . . . Oh, my dear, let me sit down."

Janie supported her across the hall and to the drawing-room again and seated her on the couch, where she lay back, then said, "What you must understand, Janie, is that he doesn't want to see anyone. Those are his conditions. If he is not left alone he will"—she gulped in her throat—"well, go back to the hospital. He said as much. He wants a mattress and some cooking utensils put into the cottage. But"—she now shook her head—"it is in a dreadful state, so damp. But there it is, we must do something."

Janie remained silent for some time before she said quietly, "Not even me?"

And Lady Lydia could have answered, "You in particular, dear, because even the very mention of your name seems to make him retreat even further into himself." She couldn't understand this because he had been so fond of Janie. Hadn't he taken it upon himself to go to the aunt and threaten what he would do if she was locked in again? And he had been her confidant. She could have been his daughter, so close were they.

"Oh, dear, dear!" Lady Lydia put her hand to her head. "Now we'll have to get the men to help clear around that place, and take a bed down and put a fire on. The next thing is, it will be all over the village and they'll say he's . . ." She stopped.

"They'll say nothing of the kind," said Janie. "And I'll talk to those two and tell them what will happen to their jobs if they open their mouths down there. Anyway, Arthur won't jabber and he'll keep a watch on Billy's tongue. Now don't you worry." She leant towards Lady Lydia. "I'll go now and put my old coat on and change my shoes, and I'll see to things."

And this is what she did. In the hour that was left of daylight she had the two men clear a path to the cottage. She herself built a fire and swept down the cobwebs and the floor. Then the following morning, by daylight, she had the men at it again. They brought a single bed from the house and a small couch, an easy chair, and a straight-backed one, also a wooden table. She herself collected all the utensils needed for cooking and eating. And lastly, the men took down a double-doored cupboard in which food could be stored in one section and utensils in the other.

It was that afternoon when the things were in place that she thanked them both, while reminding them: "You know what I said about not talking about Mr. Gerald in the village?" And Arthur Fenwick replied, "There'll be no gossip from us, miss. But what about leaving a stack of wood outside the door?"

"Oh yes, yes. Thanks, Arthur. Yes, do that, please."

It was Billy Conway who now said, "What kind of a fella is he, miss?"

Janie thought for a moment, then said, "When I last saw him he was tall and thin, and very nice looking. And he wasn't a fella, he was a gentleman."

"No offence meant, miss, just a manner of speakin', like. But . . . but 'tis funny him wantin' to live down here when he's got that fine place up there."

"He . . . he stayed down here a lot before he went away. This is where he used to . . . write."

"Oh. Oh, he was one of them writers? Oh, I see. Well, that explains it," which brought another reminder, this time from Arthur Fenwick on a laugh: "Well, he won't be able to write if he's frozen, Billy. So let's get at it." And Janie, too, laughed, then left them to it, and walked back to the house, thinking to herself, Yes, he used to write, and he might again.

She met Lady Lydia descending the steps from the terrace; she was muffled up against the chill wind, and over one arm she was carrying a greatcoat and a woollen jumper, and in her other hand she was holding what looked like a large brief-case. Nodding first to the coat, she said, "He'll need this. And this is the writing case he used before."

Janie didn't say, "That's odd, I was thinking about writing materials;" instead, she suggested: "Let me take these and you go back indoors, it's so cold."

"Well, you can take the case." And Lady Lydia handed it to her. "It's rather heavy. But . . . but I'll carry the coat. And I want to see how it is down there."

"But it's very rough going. Although they've cleared a path, it's all ruts and stones."

"Well, if I fall, my dear, you'll only have to pick me up."

"I won't do any such thing," Janie said, taking her arm. "I'll let you lie there and I'll say, 'It serves you right. I told you so.'"

"Yes, I'm sure you'll do just that."

So, exchanging light chatter, Janie helped her along the pathway; and when they were standing inside the cottage, which to Janie looked quite habitable compared with what it had been when she had first pushed the door open, Lady Lydia looked aghast for a moment, saying, "Oh, dear me! Dear me!"

"I . . . . I think they've done very well. You should have seen it before."

"Yes. Yes, I know, my dear. I know you've done wonders, and the men too. But that he should choose this. Oh!" She gave a shuddering breath, then said, "I should be grateful that he wants to come back at all. But, my dear—" She turned to Janie now and, putting her hand on her shoulder, she said, "You won't—" She stopped as if searching for a word to substitute for "pester," then went on, "I mean, you won't come down here? He won't mind Arthur bringing what is necessary, but . . ."

"You were going to say that I mustn't pester him. Well, if you say I mustn't come down here, I won't. Although I still can't see why not. We got on splendidly before, like a house on fire. Why doesn't he want to see me?"

"My dear, it isn't only you, he doesn't want to see anyone."

"You mean females?"

"No, no; I don't mean only females, because there were nurses in the hospital as well as the orderlies. It's just people. He wants to be alone. He . . . he tolerates me, and that's about as far as he can go at present, but he may change."

Janie swung about and went towards the door, saying tartly, "Well, I hope he does, for your sake, if not for his own, because he's got you worried to death."

"Oh my dear, don't talk like that."

"I can't help it, Lady Lydia, because it's true. You can hardly eat for worry, you're all skin and bone."

"Ho! ho! Look who's talking. If I'm all skin and bone I would describe you as two lats."

"Yes, you might," said Janie now, her head bobbing; "but there's a chance that I'll develop in places, at least I hope so. But you'll just fade away if you're not careful. Then what will he do? Come on; you look frozen."

"Yes, yes. And he'll be frozen in here."

"No, he won't. That fire gives out a lot of heat. And if it's on night and day the place will soon be snug, and many a one would be glad of it, let me tell you."

"Yes, I suppose you're right, dear. Those poor men on the road. The war was going to make all the difference. But what has it done? Turned this country topsy-turvy, with young men who had commissions in the Army now having to do menial jobs, door-to-door salesmen, and glad to do it. It's unthinkable really. The world will never be the same again."

As they walked back to the house Lady Lydia exclaimed, "Something will have to be done to this path; you could break your neck on the ruts."

"Well, we'll have to see about that later," said Janie, again tersely. And then she added, "Because if Mohammed can't go to the mountain, the mountain should come to Mohammed. And let's hope it happens."

"Yes, my dear, yes." Lady Lydia could not help chuckling. "Indeed, let's hope it happens. But until it does, my dear, I must ask you to promise me not to go anywhere near the cottage. As I said before, Arthur will take down what is necessary."

For four days Arthur visited the cottage, only to report no-one was there, and that he had replenished the fire. But on the fifth morning he came hurrying into the kitchen and asked Nancy to inform her ladyship that he had found the cottage door locked and that there was smoke coming from the chimney.

On her way upstairs Nancy had met Janie coming down, and excitedly she had said, "He's back! He's back! Arthur found the door locked. He's back!" And as Janie made her way slowly down the remainder of the stairs and to the kitchen, she thought, for all the change it's going to make to me he might as well be still in the hospital. But what I'd like to know is why he doesn't want to see me. She could understand him not wanting to see people. But she wasn't people, she was Janie, his Janie, and he was her "nice man." At least that's how it had been before he went away. But now no more.

SEVEN

$\mathcal{I}$t was now May 1921, and Gerald had been ensconced in the cottage for seven months, and Janie hadn't seen a sight of him, even though she was now living permanently at the Hall.

This arrangement had been amicably made after Carl and Jessie's return from their honeymoon. It was Carl who had suggested tactfully to Lady

Lydia that Janie's Auntie Jessie was concerned for her future career and was urging that Janie take up a course of some sort or other, such as nursing, that would provide her with a livelihood later on, because she didn't want to stay on the farm. However, he wondered, would Lady Lydia consider taking her into a partnership, for the girl seemed to be adept at managing labour? He said he was aware that she, Lady Lydia, was giving Janie a generous portion of the profits, but again he pointed out that her aunt was concerned with her future security, and at the moment the part of the profits she was receiving did not suggest future security.

The thought that her protégé would leave her to start on some trifling course or other filled Lady Lydia with dismay, and so, "Yes, yes, of course," she said. But as for a partnership, she herself did nothing towards the business: the men did the work, but it was organised by Janie, who seemed to have great plans for extending the smallholding.

From this, Carl went on to say there was just one more point: perhaps she knew that Janie had refused to live in the farmhouse, and they didn't like her staying alone in the cottage, so would her ladyship consider Janie living at the Hall with her? Yes. Yes. Her ladyship was only too delighted to agree to this: and so it had come about.

As it had also come about, and you could believe it, that her ladyship had adopted "that one" and "that one" was running the place, ordering this done and that done. And the latest was a horse and cart, all out of veg and fruit . . . I ask you!

Then there was the son living in a broken-down cottage in the wood. He was still round the bend in his head. And this latter was the cause of another division between the patrons of the two inns. Some said he was still barmy, and some said he wasn't, that he was writing, and writers had to be on their own. He'd be doing a war story. He was at it every day . . . But what did he know about the war? it was questioned.

He was a conchie.

So the village gossiped as usual, and the recluse stayed in his fastness in the wood, seeing only his mother and a man called Arthur. Meanwhile, Janie went on building up the business of the smallholding and defiantly riding through the village by the side of Arthur on a Saturday morning, when they attended the market in Fellburn where, more and more, she was greeted with smiles and kind encouraging words.

She had never allowed herself to question Arthur about what happened when he took the stores down to the cottage, until this particular Saturday morning. It was when passing through the village and after the second unknown person had looked towards her and smiled and brought the remark from Arthur, "There now, people aren't as black as they're painted, are they? Things are changing, I understand, from what they used to be." It was then she asked, "Have you found any change in Mr. Gerald since he came?" And after a moment he said, "Yes and no. He's always civil and we have a word now and again."

"What kind of a word? What do you talk about?"

"Oh, the weather and the crops."

"Does he ask about crops?"

"Well, not exactly. I mention them with the weather, you know."

She now forced herself to say, "Does he ever speak about me and . . . what I do? I mean with the business?"

"Oh no, miss, no, nothing like that. He doesn't touch on the house, just the weather an' that."

Just the weather and that, she thought, and not without some bitterness. Why didn't he get himself out of that place and clear the shrub? He had started chopping his own wood, but that was about all. If he could do that he could cut the undergrowth and use a shovel. The more she thought about him the more mad she got at him. And Lady Lydia had to go along that path because it was impossible to cut back all the roots of the trees. That way was never meant for a path. The only reason why the men had made it was that it was a straight run from the front of the house, over the sunken lawn, through the shrubbery and into the wood. One of these days she would blow up, she knew she would.

And the day wasn't far ahead.

It had been a hard winter. There had been a heavy and unexpected fall of snow at the beginning of May. It was then that Lady Lydia caught her chill. And after a week of taking linctus which did nothing to alleviate her cough and the pain in her chest, she took it upon herself to ring for the doctor. When Philip Patten came, he ordered her to stay in bed for at least a week, threatening that otherwise her bronchitis might develop into something more severe. And when he finally said to her, "Now we understand each other, don't we, your ladyship?" she had said, as in an aside, "Yes, Doctor." And when he insisted, "You won't disobey my orders, will you?" and she had answered, "I can't promise you," he said nothing more. But when going downstairs with Janie, he remarked tersely, "If she goes out into the cold I won't be answerable for the consequences, so see she stays in bed. And by the way," he added, smiling at her, "I hear very good reports of you as an excellent businesswoman." Then he added further, "You don't miss the farm?"

"Oh! no." The two words were emphatic, and he said, "No, no, of course you wouldn't. But it's a happier place now, you know."

"It would have to be, wouldn't it, Doctor?"

"Yes, my dear, it would have to be. And . . . and how is the other patient?"

"I don't know. He keeps to himself. He does a lot of writing."

"So I understand. Anyway, he doesn't need a doctor, that's something."

"Yes. Yes, that's something."

"Now do what I say and keep an eye on her ladyship and don't let her get out of bed."

"I'll do that, Doctor."

She did that for a week; but when her ladyship said she felt better and able to get up a while, Janie was emphatic: "No, you can't! If you attempt to, I'll get on the telephone to Doctor Patten straightaway," a threat to which Lady Lydia seemed to accede, for she now asked Janie, "Has . . . has Arthur said anything?"

"No, he hasn't. But the person in question must know you are not well, and if he can't see fit to take his legs along that path just for once, then I feel he wants . . ." Oh dear me. She closed her eyes and turned away. She had nearly said, "Somebody's foot in his backside," a threat she had often heard

Mike use to Rob, a threat that worked. "If you don't get on with that you'll have me foot in your backside."

"What were you going to finish on, my dear?" said Lady Lydia with a smile.

"Something that would have shocked you, I can tell you that."

"No doubt, no doubt. Well, I promise you I'll stay put for the next two days. The weather has changed, and I'm so much better now, I've hardly coughed at all today. Just two days more and then I'm getting up."

As Janie went out of the room she remarked to herself, "That's what you think." Then downstairs, she pulled on her old field coat and a woollen hat and actually marched out of the door and thence along the rutted path. But when she came in sight of the cottage she stopped. Her heart was beating against her ribs. Why it should, she didn't know, only perhaps, she thought, it was with temper. Who did he think he was sitting in there all day? Even if he *was* scribbling.

When she reached the door she hesitated a moment; then determinedly lifting her hand, she knocked twice.

She heard a movement inside the room and she knew there was some-body now standing just behind the door. When there was no reply, she knocked a further three times; and when again she received no answer she put her face close to the door and yelled, "If you're afraid to open the door, I'll give you the message through it! Your mother is ill in bed, and you must know that, else she would have been along to see you. And why she should the Lord only knows, because you've still got two legs and you could walk. But no! you've got to hide yourself away. Well, there you have it. She's been ordered to stay in bed, but she's not going to because she has to come along here and see how you are. And to my mind you're not worth bothering about. You're cowardly . . ."

The door was pulled open with such force that she staggered back. And there he was, this tall, thin, spare-looking figure that gave her no semblance of the "nice man." He was glaring at her. His eyes looked black, whereas she remembered they had been grey. But now, like his face, they seemed ablaze. She didn't know this man. He was like no remembered image that she had retained of him and that she had conjured up during the years since she last saw him on the day she learned of her beginnings through the conversation in the cow byres. The "nice man" she remembered was all gentleness, whereas this man looked like a demon; and she stood gulping, her hand gripping the top of her coat, too terrified to turn and run now. Then she saw the man seeming to melt away and the figure lean against the stanchion of the door and close its eyes. And when his voice came low, saying, "Go away," she still stood. And when, in a croaking whisper, she said, "I'm . . . I'm sorry," he said again, "Go away, please."

She went to turn about but something stopped her. What, she didn't know. Whatever it was it made her take three steps towards him. And now in a trembling voice, she said, "I'm . . . so sorry. I shouldn't have said all that. I didn't know." She did not add, "you were still ill," or that, "I should not have called you a coward." Perhaps it was that word, because Carl had told her and explained to her about the conscientious objectors, and it would seem not one of them could be called a coward.

When she put her hand on his arm he jumped backwards as if he had been stung, and again she said, "I'm . . . I'm sorry." Then she watched him almost stagger to the easy chair and drop into it and lean his head back while his eyes stared straight in front of him.

She stood within the doorway now, saying softly, "I . . . I just came to ask you if you would come and see your mother. There's . . . there's no-one there after five o'clock. I mean, the men finish and . . . and go upstairs above the stables, and then out. You could come in the back way. There's only Nancy in the house, and you know Nancy. I'll . . . I'll leave the back door open for you . . . shall I?" She saw him now close his eyes and she could see a vein standing out on his left temple. It was throbbing. She said softly, "Shall . . . shall I make you a cup of tea?"

"No!" It was as if he were about to spring up from the chair again; but all he did this time was grip the arms. She had stepped further back, and now he said, but in a normal-sounding voice, "Please go away."

She stayed for a moment or two longer; then she backed out of the door and pulled it closed, and on the sound of it he opened his mouth wide; then gripping his chin, he muttered, "No, no," and slowly his mouth closed again. No more gas attacks. No, no. That part was finished with. But that she should appear at the very moment when he had just finished writing of that first night with Susie and how her face had turned into the child's, and in what followed he had felt the purity of the child in Susie. It had been the most wonderful experience. Nothing he had thought of before had ever come up to it. He had been glad he had waited for that ecstasy that hadn't ended in a moment but had gone on and on. And then to learn . . .

He now flung an arm wide as if throwing off the child who had become defiled, and he was the defiler, just as all men were defilers.

It had been following the shock of Susie and while on a forty-eight-hour pass that he saw them, a line of them, laughing, joking, going from one foot to the other while they stood in the queue waiting their turn. It had come to him in that moment the unfairness of the saying that man acted like a beast: beasts would never act like man; they were selective and there was a time arranged by nature to satisfy their needs. In that place there hadn't been much chance of selection. So they had lined up. To what? To a victim, or another Susie? The sight had created a stench in his nostrils that remained with him, a stench that was stronger than any of the blood-soaked, mutilated, gangrenous limbs that he had handled on the trains. And then he had asked himself if he was less of a man because he thought this way? He had wanted love, and to love, and to feel the essence of love, but it had ceased to be clean. It had become dirtier than the war had become, on a par with gas. *Yes, gas. Oh, gas.* That had been the end. *Gas.* The blind eyes, the choking throats, and agonised hands. The bursting lungs spewing forth.

But why had she to come at that moment? the moment he had dreaded to face up to and then to write about; and that word she used to him. He could have struck her. And she had looked so frightened. And yet where had the child gone? Where had the girl gone? She now looked a young woman. How old was she? Sixteen, seventeen? Oh yes, she must be that. She was so tall. Yet her face hadn't changed, nor had her voice. But why had she come? Oh, yes, yes; his mother was ill. Well, hadn't he known something was wrong with her, else she would have been here? Why hadn't he gone to see her? She did not represent civilisation, nor people, and chatter, and daily papers, lying daily papers covering up the faults of old men. But they couldn't cover up the graves, could they? Nor the numbers, hundreds, thousands, millions that would look upon the stars no more. Were they all looking down from heaven? The padre used to say that they were at rest now in heaven. Were they standing up, or laid out in rows, the hundreds, thousands, millions? Why weren't they falling through the clouds?

He sprang from the chair, put his hand on his head, drew in a long, long, slow breath and said aloud, "Stop it! No more! Get rid of it! Go on writing it out!"

He went into the other room and was about to sit down at the table on which, at one side, lay his writing case and a pile of papers, all sheets covered in a close spidery hand, and at the other books and loose-leaf folders. He didn't sit down, but he said, and again aloud, "Do it now! Don't put it off. You must do it now!" And with this he went to the door, took his greatcoat off a hook, pulled a cap on to his head, and left the cottage.

During the following week Gerald visited his mother three times, and each time Janie had been aware that he was in the house simply by going to the side entrance and finding the door closed; she always left it ajar until she was about to go upstairs to bed. But in no way did she show herself during his time in the house.

On his third visit he sat with his mother for almost an hour. In order to keep him by her side a little longer, she felt she could ask him about his work. Was he, for instance, going to compile his writings into a book?

Yes, he said, that was his plan.

And was it all about the war? she dared to ask him.

Yes, but the war of a conscientious objector. The title would be "My Conscience, My Cross."

"Oh. Oh." They looked at each other for a moment before she asked, "Has it helped you? Will you publish it?"

"Yes, definitely it has helped. But no, I won't have it published, because that would mean—" he moved uneasily on his seat before going on, "Well, you know what it would mean, and I couldn't bear . . . well, publicity . . . people."

"You could use another name."

He smiled wanly at her. "And this same address? Just imagine what would happen. The things that I've dared to say and . . . and expose would cause questions to be raised in Parliament and stir up the white-feather gang again."

"Oh, my dear, I don't think there are many white-feather individuals left, not now."

"O . . . h," the word was long drawn out, "you don't know, Mama. There was a young fellow in the hospital, he was one of us; in fact, we were the only two among soldiers and we were accepted by them. But this young fellow didn't break down until he returned home, when he was actually attacked by a herd of women from the street in which he lived, because they had lost husbands, or sons, or brothers in the war, and there he was, to them, whole and hearty. They smashed the windows and beat him up. The fact that his mother had to shield him finished him. It's unbelievable, yet women can be more fierce than men . . . or animals."

They sat in silence for a time, and then she dared to bring up another subject. She did it very diplomatically. "I . . . I am sorry that Janie disturbed you the other day. I told her that I should be all right in a day or two."

"It's . . . it's all right. She didn't disturb me. Well, at least . . . well, she surprised me. I . . . I thought I recognised her voice and then when I saw her, I didn't recognise her at all. She . . . she has grown . . . very tall."

"Yes, she is tall. I hope she doesn't keep on, she is five feet six already. But then, she'll soon be seventeen and one stops growing after that, I think. Yet," she smiled, "I don't remember what age I was when I stopped. I only know at the time I was glad I did, because very tall women were looked upon as oddities in my day. But Janie will never be looked upon as an oddity. She . . . she's such a charming girl. I don't know what I would have done without her during these last . . . Are you going, my dear?"

"Yes. Yes, I mustn't tire you."

"Oh, you could never tire me, but I must tire you with my chatter."

"It's good to hear you, Mama. Yes." He bent over and repeated, "Yes, it's good to hear you. Goodnight, my dear." As he kissed her softly on the cheek, she put her arms around his neck and held him to her for a moment, and it seemed to her he might be about to return the embrace, but then his body jerked away from her and he was standing straight, saying, "Goodnight, my dear."

"Goodnight. Wrap up well. It's . . . it's still chilly out."

He had backed a little way from the bed and now he nodded before turning abruptly and leaving the room. And she lay with her hands tight pressed against her chest, and she prayed, "Bring him back, dear Lord. Bring him back to what he was."

The raspberries had followed the strawberries and had given them a real bumper crop. And now it was the end of August and they had finished clearing the bushes. Arthur had gone into the town with fifty-pound punnets and there were still four large and two small baskets on the kitchen table. And Nancy, surveying them from her stool at the end of the table, said, "I thought I'd seen the last of them lot. D'you mean to bottle them all?"

"Well, I think we'll do three baskets, and"—Janie turned to Lady Lydia —"I would like to take one over to the farm and," pulling a face, she added, "get some cream in exchange."

"Yes, that's an idea," said Lady Lydia, nodding her head, her eyes sparkling their amusement, and Nancy put in, "A bit of butter when you're on."

"I brought a pound back the day before yesterday."

"Oh, what's a pound, miss, when those two hogs outside cut into a loaf?"

"You should give them some of your dripping."

"Now you know why I don't, miss, 'cos it makes better pastry than your farm butter. I've always said that, an' I always will."

"Well," Janie retorted, "as you say yourself, people say more than prayers and they whistle them."

"Oh! Janie."

And to this laughing reprimand Janie said, "I only repeat what she says, Lady Lydia. Anyway, I'll take this basket and we'll have one of the small ones for tea . . . with cream."

"Oh, get yourself away." Lady Lydia now pushed Janie gently in the shoulder, "And give your aunt and Carl my thanks for the eggs and their kindness."

As Janie made for the door Nancy called to her, "What do you want doing with the other basket then?"

"I want it kept to one side. That's for Mr. Gerald. I'll see to it when I come back."

"I'll take it down."

"You'll do no such thing." She had turned on Lady Lydia. "You nearly twisted your ankle yesterday." Then muttering, "Something will have to be done," she lifted the none-too-light basket and went out . . .

When she entered the farmyard she was sweating profusely and Rob, seeing her and taking the basket from her, said, "Coo! I could just do with a basin of those. By! they're big 'uns. The missis has just gone into the kitchen."

A moment later, Jessie, too, was exclaiming over the size and freshness of the raspberries, and she said, "I'll get a good few bottles out of that lot. But why didn't you tell Carl, and he would have come over and carried that basket? It's an awful weight. Sit down and I'll make you a cup of tea."

"I can't stay long."

Jessie sighed. "That's always your cry, you can't stay long."

"Well there's so much to do over there."

"You're still happy doing it?" Jessie turned from the table where she was spooning some tea into the teapot, and Janie said, "Yes, couldn't be happier. Well . . . I mean."

"What do you mean? Something else you want?"

She could have answered, Oh, yes, there's something else I want, and I mean to get it on my birthday . . . my seventeenth birthday, which is only a few weeks away. But were she to give Jessie an inkling of what she meant to do, she would see her aunt flying across to the Hall and confronting Lady Lydia; and then everything would be spoilt. And all under the heading of "I'm doing it for your own good." So she answered, "Yes. Yes, there's umpteen things I want. Anyway, you're happy, aren't you?"

"We're not talking about me, we're talking about you. Because . . . because I'm concerned for you, always have been and always will. I want to see you happy."

"Oh, I'm happy enough." Janie got to her feet now, adding, "Am I going to get that cup of tea or not? There's more raspberries waiting to be bottled."

It was noticeable that she never mentioned Gerald nor did Jessie refer to "that man down in the cottage." So fifteen minutes later she left the farm carrying the basket, now laden with butter, cheese, cream and eggs. And when, back in the Hall, she picked up the smaller basket, Nancy protested,

"He won't get through all of them on his own," and Janie answered, "With the help of half this cream he will." . . .

When Gerald saw the raspberries, he said, "You're still picking?"

"This is the last, thank goodness. My fingers are sore."

"Well—" he smiled wryly as he said, "that's your own fault. You should take on extra hands at this time."

She was standing near the table, and now she swung round and stared at him, and the look on her face caused him to say quickly, "Don't say it. Don't say it."

"Well!" She turned from him, her shoulders shrugging, and when she muttered, "Well!" he repeated, "Well!" Then she looked to the end of the table. It was clear. Usually it was littered with paper and books, but now it was clear, and she said in surprise, "You . . . you're not writing? You're finished?"

"For the present, yes."

"Are you going to send your book away?"

"No."

"Why?"

"Just because I've decided that the past is best left in the past."

"Then why did you go on writing it?"

His voice rose now and his words were rapid, "Just because I wanted to get things out of my system, and I prefer to write them down instead of jabbering."

She now faced him squarely, saying, "Well, don't you bark at me."

And his answer to this was, "I'll stop barking at you when you stop acting like a woman."

They were staring at each other, their bodies stiff. But then she said, "I . . . I am a woman, a young woman."

"You're nothing of the sort. You're a girl, a young girl."

"I'll be seventeen in October."

"Huh! Seventeen in October. You haven't started to live yet. You know nothing about life."

"Oh, don't I!" Now she was yelling, "I've known about life since I found there were locks on the doors, let me tell you. You think because you were in a war and it didn't suit you, that you're the only one who has experienced life, as you call it, and the things it can do to you inside. Well, let me tell you, you needn't go any further than this village to suffer all the pangs of life and none of the joys. That woman back there"—she thumbed towards the door—"she said years ago that I was the result of an unholy trinity. Carry that around with you in your mind. Do you remember the day when I asked you what an unholy trinity was? Well, almost every day since, I've asked myself, am I doing this because that one fathered me? or, because that one fathered me? or, because that one fathered me? You said stop being a woman. I was a woman before I was a girl. You and your conscientious objecting and your moral protesting. I've been protesting all my life and it's been a long one, and I don't have to wait until I'm seventeen to be a woman."

When he moved a step towards her and said, "I'm . . . I'm sorry," she moved swiftly back from him, her voice still loud as she cried, "You're not sorry. You're not sorry for me, you're only sorry for yourself. If you were sorry for anybody else you would stop your mother having to trail over here to see you, wet or fine. And she's an old lady, you seem not to have noticed that, and she's very fragile. And if you were really sorry you would do something about it." Now she flounced out of the room, across the other one and to the door. And when she had pulled it open, she finished her tirade by yelling, "And instead of sitting on your backside moping on your wrongs, you want to get a shovel in your hand and start digging outside here. So there, you have it! and I've been wanting to tell you that for a long time."

She left him standing outside the cottage watching her march away, and his whole body was yelling, "Janie! Janie! Come back! Please! I need you!" But he knew he must never say that. And now he turned back to the doorway and leant his brow against the stanchion. And his mind told him there were all kinds of crucifixions, and he was suffering another now as he faced the knowledge that had always been buried deep with him. But he saw no end to this form of torment: look at him, what was he? A middle-aged man, bewildered and still sick in his mind.

EIGHT

$\mathcal{A}$ week passed without Janie visiting him; nor would she tell Lady Lydia why, except that they'd had a few words. And anyway, she was too busy, and didn't Lady Lydia think it was time that he did the walking this way? "He's still not quite himself, my dear," Lady Lydia still maintained, only to be slightly amazed when her dear girl, who was so sympathetic in all ways, came back with, "Well, it's about time he was. And if people didn't run after him he might pull himself together."

It was half-way through the second week, after one of Lady Lydia's hazardous journeys across the rough, root-strewn path that she brought a letter from him. And it took Janie quite some seconds before she could open it, and there on a rough scrap of paper were written the words: "Please come back. I have something to show you." She now handed it to Lady Lydia, saying, "Why couldn't he come and say that instead of writing it?"

"Be patient, dear. You have got him this far; don't let him go back."

"Me? Me! got him this far?" There was definite surprise in her voice, to which Lady Lydia responded and said, "Yes. Yes, only you. With that sharp tongue of yours and that bossy manner, and you'll do it my way or else; of course, the latter softened by your own form of diplomacy."

"Oh, Lady Lydia."

"Oh, Miss Gibson."

Janie had to bite on her lip to prevent herself from laughing outright; then she asked quietly, "Am I like that?"

"Yes. Yes, dear, you are; together with being so honest, and true, and kind. Oh, my dear, don't cry."

"I'm not crying." She blinked her eyes rapidly. "And anyway, there's no time for that."

"No, of course not, dear. But . . . but will you go along today and see him?"

"Perhaps; after I've had a talk with Arthur. He broached a very good idea yesterday. It's about the bottom field: if a few huts could be put up there, he says, we could keep up to a hundred hens. And there's the pond at the bottom of the field. It's fed from the ditch and, as he pointed out, it only wants some of the silt clearing and there you have a place for ducks. Eggs are always a good market sale."

"Oh, my dear, my dear. I wonder what next?"

"I wonder, too, and among my wonderings I thought about your friend that you phone, the one who's asked you up to London. Now there's enough money in the coffers to give you a holiday anywhere you like, and you said you loved London and the theatres, and so . . ."

"Oh, my dear, I'm too old to explore London and do the rounds of the theatres."

"You're not at all. Anyway, I've settled in my mind that you're going to London. And I haven't time to waste talking," which left her ladyship gasping as usual and telling herself that the child was right: she wasn't too old to go to London and see a play. No, of course she wasn't. In fact, she was feeling better now than she had done for a long time. And that was because her dear boy was so much better . . . proof of which was to show itself that day.

It was four o'clock in the afternoon before Janie made her way to the cottage. And there he was, washing his hands and arms in a sawn-off tub of rain-water supplied by a spout at the end of the cottage. When he saw her he pulled a coarse towel from a hook in the wall and rubbed himself briskly before approaching her. "Hello," he said.

"Hello."

"Feeling better?"

"I've never felt bad."

"No. No, of course not. The . . . the kettle's on. Would you like some tea?"

"I don't mind," she said and he made to go into the cottage, but as he stood aside to allow her to enter, he said, "Wait a minute. The tea will taste better if there's some sugar in it. Come here." He did not put his hand out towards her, but motioned her to follow him, then led the way to the back of the cottage to the small stone-walled yard. The gate leading from this had been overgrown with weeds and here and there low shrubs had embedded their roots in the wall. But now, to her amazed gaze, the yard stood out clear amid a largish piece of ground which had not only been cleared but also tilled.

As she stood surveying it, he pointed silently to the spade leaning against the wall, and he was smiling as he said, "You provide good medicine."

"Oh." She bowed her head now and muttered something like, "I'm sorry. I shouldn't." But he came back at her quickly, saying, "Oh you should. You should. The time was ripe. The pen gets rid of some things but there's nothing like tired limbs to give you dreamless sleep . . . now and again. Thank you, Janie."

She flung round from him now, saying, "You're making me feel awful, you know. Lady Lydia said I was . . ." She hesitated.

"Was what?"

"It doesn't matter."

"I know what she would say, and that would be that you have been such a great help to her; she doesn't know how she would have got through without you, but," he added now, "at the same time you are inclined to be bossy and expect to get your own way."

"I'm not and I don't!" They were standing beside the cottage door now. "I am not bossy. I . . . I just know how things should be done, and I always ask and politely. I am not bossy."

"Well, that surprises me." He shook his head, at the same time directing his arm as if ushering her into a drawing-room. And like any annoyed young miss, she now flounced in before him only, immediately she was in the room, to point to the fire and declare, "It's nearly out! How do you expect the kettle to boil on that?"

"Oh, undoubtedly it will take a little longer. But in the meantime, madam, would you mind sitting down and stop acting . . ."

Her arm was already thrust out towards him and she was saying, "Don't you say that to me again. You know what happened the last time."

"You don't know what I was going to say."

"Oh, I do, I do. Acting like a woman."

"I wasn't."

"Well, what were you going to say?"

"Oh—" He gave a little shrug now, saying, "I've forgotten." Then he took a seat at the opposite side of the table and looked across at her, and as she looked directly at him for the first time since he had returned home, she saw the semblance of the "nice man": he had smiled more during the last few minutes than he had done during all the past months she had seen him.

He stared at her intently for some minutes until she said, "What . . . what's the matter?" She put her hand up to her hair. "I'm . . . I'm a mess? Well, I've been at it all day."

"You're not a mess. You're a beautiful young girl. Always remember that. Now I'm going to ask you something."

"Yes?" She waited.

"Can we, from this time on, become friends, as we were, I mean, before I went away?"

She swallowed deep in her throat, then said, "I'd like that."

For the first time his hand came out to her and she placed hers in it. She watched him bend his head for a moment; then he said, "Let us take it from here."

"Yes."

It was he who now let go of her hand and, rising from the chair, he said briskly, "If I don't put the bellows under that kettle it'll never boil tonight." And as she watched him she thought, I don't care if it never boils. Never, never, never.

It was her birthday, and she was seventeen. Lady Lydia had given her her own gold fob-watch and a ring that she had worn when she was a young girl. Nancy had given her half a dozen handkerchiefs with drawn-thread hems and her initials hand worked on them. And the men together had presented her with a bunch of roses and a pound box of chocolates.

Now she was in the sitting-room at the farm and there, facing her, were her Auntie Jessie and Carl. And she had just opened their present, at least one of two presents, and was exclaiming aloud as she held up in front of her the lovely pale blue taffeta dress, saying, "It's beautiful. It looks too good to wear."

"It could be a party frock." Carl was smiling widely at her. And she looked at him for a moment with a look that didn't exactly hold disdain, but something they both understood, for it said: what party?

"And the pearls will go with it." Jessie held up a double strap of necklet pearls.

"Yes. Yes. Oh, thank you both." And impulsively she kissed Jessie, then Carl.

And now Jessie said, "But these aren't all. You should see the lovely cake that Mrs. McNabb has made for you. She thought she would keep it till tea-time and we'd have a little party on our own."

"Oh, Auntie Jessie. Oh, I'm sorry. I . . . I won't be able to come, I don't think, not today."

"What! Why not?" It was Carl asking the question now. "Surely they can get on without you for one afternoon?"

"Yes. Yes, I know, but . . . well, I must tell you something and . . . well, it's this." Before she went on she turned and picked up the dress from where she had dropped it on a chair before she had embraced them, and she laid it carefully over the back. Then turning to them again, she said, "I'm . . . I'm becoming engaged to be married today."

They stared at her blankly, then glanced at each other. It was Jessie who said, "What! Engaged . . . who to? Who are you engaged to be married to? What are you talking about?"

"Just what I said, Auntie Jessie. I could have told you before, weeks ago, but I promised myself I would wait until my seventeenth birthday and then you couldn't say, Don't be silly, you're still a child or some such, as you always do. I'm seventeen today, Auntie Jessie, and I feel I've been seventeen, eighteen or nineteen for a long time. And as you know, I've been doing the work of someone older for a long time. And I know my own mind, I always have, always, for years and years."

"Who are you becoming engaged to, dear?" Carl's voice was quiet.

"Well, need you ask? To Mr. Gerald."

"No! No!" It was almost a scream from Jessie. *"No! I won't allow it.* You're mad, girl, as mad as he is."

"He's not mad. Never has been mad." Janie's voice was quiet but each word was emphatic. "He went through so much in the war that his mind closed up against it and all those people who perpetrated it. He is no more mad than you or I. But speaking of me, there's more chance of my going mad with my background than of his."

"He's old enough to be your father." Jessie closed her eyes tightly at this. What had she said? But Janie picked it up, saying, "But he didn't happen to be one of the three, did he, Auntie Jessie? He was, though, the one who found my mother, so I understand, and carried her back here. And he was the only one, let me tell you, who showed me any kindness, apart from you, Carl; because you didn't, Auntie Jessie, you were my gaoler, and I was just something to fill up the gap in your life. You see, the way I'm talking is not as a young girl would, Auntie Jessie; someone who doesn't know her own mind. Now, no matter what you say or what you do, you'll not stop me in my purpose."

"Has he asked you to marry him, dear?" The question coming from Carl was again quiet.

Janie looked away from him for a moment before answering, "No, he hasn't, and I know he never will. But what I do know is that he loves me. And I'm going to tell him today that I love him and we are going to marry. Not straightaway, but we are going to marry."

"Oh my God!" Neither Carl nor Janie went to Jessie's side as she slumped into a chair; but Janie looked at her, saying now, "You never liked him, did you, Auntie Jessie? For the simple reason that he told you your treatment of me was wrong. Well, there it is. I'm sorry I won't be over today, but if you still want me to, I will come tomorrow. And very soon"—she now turned to Carl—"if you'll allow it, Carl, we'll walk over together to see you . . . because, in a way, I've known he's always looked upon you as my guardian."

Carl said nothing.

But when she turned to look at her Auntie Jessie again she saw her actually shudder. Slowly she picked up the dress and the string of pearls, saying, "Thank you so much for the pearls." And then she added, "I suppose I may keep them?" which brought a grimace from Carl as he said, "Don't . . . don't say things like that." Then she walked out.

The minute the door was closed on her, Jessie sprang from the chair and, going to Carl, she said, "You . . . you've got to stop it! It's indecent. That man must be forty or near it."

"My dear"—he put his arm around her shoulders—"I can't stop it, and I wouldn't if I could. In fact, I've known it would come about some day. Yet, I must admit it was a bit of a shock, especially today and the way she put it over, when she implied he would never ask her. And what he says when . . . she proposes to him will never be known, I suppose."

"But he'll take her."

"If he's wise, yes he will, dear. She's loved him from the beginning, I know that; and that man had a most protective feeling for her as a child, which must have grown with the years, especially of late."

"Oh dear Lord!" She turned from him now. "More fodder for the village."

"Damn the village!" She almost jumped at the sound of his voice, and he repeated, "Yes, Jessie, damn the village. That village is not going to impinge on my life or on this farm any more. And she being who she is, it won't impinge on hers. I'll take a bet on that. So damn the village!" And on this he, too, walked out of the room, and she was left exclaiming to herself, "Oh, that girl! That girl! She's been the bane of my life. And now this. Is it ever going to end?"

The bane of her life was standing at the farm gate and Carl was saying to her, "I understand, dear. Yes, I understand."

"And . . . and he's not forty, Carl, he's thirty-seven or perhaps thirty-eight."

He smiled at her now, saying, "What does a few years matter? The main thing is that you love him. But how do you think he's going to take your proposal?"

"Not quietly." She smiled at him. "He'll argue a lot, put up more obstacles than Auntie Jessie would ever dream of, and . . . well, I'll take it from there. Whatever he says I'll point out to him that I consider myself engaged and . . . and that next year we could be married."

He suddenly pulled her to him and said, "You're one in a million. You always have been."

When she put her free arm around his neck and said, "Thanks for everything, Carl. Next to him I love you best of all. And oh my!"—she pressed herself from him—"my dress will be all crushed," she said, and she made motions of smoothing out the dress, then said, "Bye-bye, Carl."

"Bye-bye, love. Come over tomorrow. I . . . I want to hear the end of the story. No, no, not the end, the beginning."

"Yes, Carl, I'll do that . . . and the beginning. . . ."

It was an hour later when she reached the cottage. The weather had turned sultry, the sky was low and it promised rain. He was standing outside in his shirt-sleeves and he greeted her with, "Hello. I think we're going to have a storm."

"Yes, yes," she said; "we could have a storm."

"Happy birthday, Janie."

"Thank you."

"Do you feel any different?"

"Yes. Yes, I feel twenty-seven."

He laughed his gentle laugh. "You have a long way to go, my dear, before you come to that. But come in. Look, it's spotting rain."

"Have . . . have you been working?"

"Yes. Yes, ma'am, I've been working since early on. I should say that I have a quarter of an acre ready for planting. So watch out, I might beat you at your own business."

"It isn't my business, never was my business. It's your business. I've just been carrying it on for you."

"Now, now, now, don't start, it's your birthday. Look, I've got a little present for you. Stay there." He pointed to the couch, and she sat down.

When he returned to the room he dropped a parcel on to her lap, saying at the same time, "I'd better light the lamp. It will soon be dark in here."

As he lit the lamp she undid the paper and looked down on what, if it had been bound, would be the flyleaf of a book, and the heading was, "Conscience Crucified." And underneath was a pen and ink drawing of the Three Crucifixions. She looked up at him and said, "You're . . . you're giving this to me? You're not having it published?"

"No. No, I told you I wasn't having it published. And, although I am giving it to you, I would urge you not to read it for some time. Put it aside as one of those useless Christmas boxes that one gets, say, for about another year."

"Why?"

"Why?" He looked up towards the low smoke-dyed ceiling and repeated again, "Why? Well because I don't want your emotions to be torn to shreds by the wailings of a conscientious objector."

"They've already been torn to shreds by the wailings of a conscientious objector."

"Huh! Huh!" He was chuckling now. "I've never known anyone in my life to come back with answers to a statement that asks for further questioning. But in this case I am not going to ask you the question about your emotions."

"No, because you're afraid to."

"Now, now, Janie, don't start. We made a pact some time ago. Remember?"

"Yes, I remember, and that pact was we were to be friends. But friends can talk plainly to each other, otherwise they are not friends but just acquaintances who have to be polite and probably lie while doing so. Anyway, it's my birthday and you've given me a present. I . . . well, there's something else I want."

"Something else?"

"Yes, something else."

"Well, what is it?"

"I want to be engaged."

He screwed up his face. "Engaged? Engaged in what?"

She was on her feet now and actually yelling at him, "Don't be so damned stupid! I want to be engaged to you!"

"*What?* You must be . . . this is romantic nonsense, girl. You are seventeen years old and I'm nearing forty. *Stop it! Stop it! Stop it!*"

"I won't stop it, and you don't want me to stop it; you are just covering up again. You'll marry me some time, so it might as well be soon."

"I'll . . . I'll not marry you some time." He now held both hands up before his face, though not touching it. It was as if he were putting a shield between them. And when she grabbed them, saying, "You know that our ages have nothing to do with it. You love me, you always have. And I look back and I cannot remember the time when I started to love you, nor the time when I will ever stop."

It sounded like a whimper. "Out of the depths have I cried unto Thee, O Lord, Lord . . ."

"What are you saying?"

"Nothing! Nothing! Only remembering something that someone said, and I'm appealing to Him now to keep me sane, or, what is more important, to bring you to your senses."

When she stepped back from him his hands slowly dropped to his sides and, looking at her, he said, "You'll never know how much I . . . I am more than honoured, but I can't let you throw your young and clean life away."

"Will you stop talking like some character out of a book? We're standing facing the truth in this awful little cottage." She now flicked her hand to the side. "I am seventeen and you are thirty-seven and you love me. And what's more, you need me. And I love you and I want you, and it will come about some time. I know it will. And you in your heart want it to come about. And now, please, please, Gerald, hold me, just hold me."

He did not raise his arms towards her until she lay against his chest, her head under his chin; and then he was holding her, every fibre of his body shaking as he pressed her to him. And then he kept repeating her name, "Oh, Janie! Oh, Janie! My Janie! Oh, Janie!" And when her brow became wet she looked up at his face to see it aflood with tears, silent tears. And now she beseeched him, "Oh, don't cry. Don't cry, my love. Please, please don't cry."

But he went on crying and now taking her with him, he stumbled towards the couch, then dropped on to it. And when his crying became audible, she beseeched him, "Gerald! Gerald! Listen to me, it's all right. I'm sorry. Please!"

But between loud agonising sobs he gulped out, "Let me cry, my love, let me cry. I . . . I have never cr . . . cried, never. Hold me tight, Janie. Hold me tight. Don't ever leave me. And let me cry.

"Oh, let me cry. Let me cry, my love."

The Year
of the Virgins

Part One

ONE

"*I* just can't believe my ears. I just can't."

"It's a simple question for a man to ask of his son."

"*What!*"

Daniel Coulson bent over and looked at his wife's reflection in the mirror, and he saw a round flat face, the skin of which was still as perfect as when he had married her thirty-one years ago. But that was all that remained of the girl who had got him to the altar when he was nineteen, for the fair hair piled high above the head was bleached and her once plump, attractive shape had spread to fat, which now looked as if it were trying to force its way out at various points of her taffeta gown, an evening gown with a neckline just below the nape of her neck; it would be indecent to expose the flesh leading to her breasts. But any ardour those breasts would or should have aroused had died in him long ago. His attention was now focused on her eyes: pale grey eyes which at most times appeared colourless, except as now when rage was boiling in her. And as he stared into them he ground his teeth before saying, "You expect me to collar him and ask him that?"

"It's what any ordinary father could ask of his son. But then you've never been an ordinary father."

"No, by God! I haven't. I've fought you all the way, because you would have kept him in nappies until he left school. You had him at the breast until you were shamed out of it."

When her arm came out and her elbow caught him in the stomach, he stumbled away from her, the while thrusting out his hand, for she had gripped the lid of a heavy glass powder-bowl and was holding it poised for aiming. "You let that out of your hand, missis," he growled, "and I'll slap your face so hard you'll have to make an excuse for not attending his wedding."

As he watched her hand slowly open and the lid drop back on to the dressing-table he straightened his back as he said grimly, "You can't bear to think you're losing him, can you? Even to the daughter of your best friend. You tried to link her up with Joe, didn't you? But she had grown out of her schoolgirl pash and wanted Don. And, let me tell you, I saw that she got what she wanted, and what Don wanted. Although if there was anyone she could have had apart from Don I would have picked Joe."

"Oh, yes, you would have picked Joe. You saddled me with a retarded son, then you inveigled me into adopting a child . . ."

"My God!" He put his hand to his head and turned from her and walked down the long, softly carpeted room towards the canopied four-poster bed, a bed he had not slept in for more than fifteen years, and he bumped his head against the twisted column of one of the posts. Then in the silence that had fallen on the room he turned slowly; but he did not move towards her, he simply stared at her for a long moment before he said, "Me inveigled you into adopting a child? It's well seen it wasn't *my* father who ended up in an asylum."

When he saw the muscles of her face begin to twitch he told himself to stop it, he had gone too far, it was cruel. But the cruelty wasn't all on one side. No. By God! No. If she had been a wife, just an ordinary wife, instead of a religious maniac and an almost indecently possessive mother, then he wouldn't now be carrying the shame of some of the things he'd had to do because of his needs; and all on the sly, because one mustn't lose face in the community, the community of the church and the visiting priests and the nuns in the convent and the Children of Mary and the Catenians and all the paraphernalia that must be kept up . . .

He must get out. He must have a drink. He drew in a long gasping breath. He'd better not; he'd better wait until the company came, because if he started early his tongue would run away with him.

He was walking down the room towards the far door when her voice hit him almost at screaming pitch: "You're a low, ill-bred, common swab, like your father was, and all your lot."

He didn't pause but went out, pulling the door after him; only to stop on the wide landing and close his eyes. It was amazing, wasn't it? Simply amazing, calling him common and a low, ill-bred swab, she who had come from the Bog's End quarter of Fellburn! He could recall the day she came to the office looking for a job. She was fifteen, and Jane Broderick set her on. But after three months Jane had said, "She's no good, she'll never be able to type; the only thing she's good for is putting on side. She's got the makings of a good receptionist, but this is a scrap-iron yard." And it was his father who had said, "Give the lass a chance. You said she had a good writing hand so let her file the orders like that." And his father nearly killed himself laughing when it was discovered she was taking elocution lessons from a retired schoolteacher in town. It was from then that he himself began to think there was something in her, that she was different. And my God, he had to learn just how different she was. But there was one thing he could say for her; her elocution lessons had been put to good use, for she could pass herself off in any company. Even so, she chose her company: no common working-class acquaintances for her. Look how she had chummed up with Janet Allison because, although the Allisons didn't live in a blooming great mansion like this, they were middle-class down to their shoe laces. Catholic middle-class. Oh yes; Winnie could not have tolerated Protestants even if they *had* supported a title. She was faithful to one thing, at any rate, and that was her religion.

He went slowly down the stairs and as he walked across the hall the far door opened and there stood his adopted son, Joe.

Joe was as tall as himself, and they were very alike, only his hair was black, not just dark, and his eyes were a warm brown, not blue. Daniel had always felt proud that Joe resembled him, because he had thought of him as a son even more than he did of Stephen, or even of Don.

As he approached him he glanced at the two books Joe had in his hand, saying, "What's this? Starting to do a night shift?"

"No; not quite; just something I wanted to look up." They stared at each other for a moment, then Joe said simply, "Trouble?"

"What do you mean, trouble?"

"Well, unless it slipped your mind, the bedroom is placed over the library. It's a high ceiling in there," he jerked his head backwards, "but it's not soundproof."

Daniel now pushed past him to go towards the library, saying over his shoulder, "You got a minute?"

"Yes; as many as you want."

Joe closed the door after him, then followed Daniel up the room to where a deep-seated leather couch was placed at an angle facing a long window that looked on to the garden. But when the man whom he thought of as his father did not sit down but moved to the window and, raising one hand, supported himself against the frame, he walked to his side and said, "What is it now?"

"You won't believe this." Daniel turned to him. "You'll never believe what she's asked me to put to Don."

"Well, not 'til you tell me."

Daniel now turned from the window, walked to the couch and dropped down on to it. Then, bending forward, he rested his elbows on his knees and, staring at the polished parquet floor, he said, "She's demanding that I ask Don if he's *still a virgin.*"

There being no comment forthcoming from Joe, Daniel turned his head to look up at him, saying, "Well, what do you say to that?"

Joe shook his head as he said, "What can I say? Nothing, except to ask what you think she would do if you came back and gave her the answer that he wasn't."

"What would she do? I just don't know; me mind boggles. She'd go to some extreme, that's sure, even perhaps try to stop the wedding, saying he wasn't fit to marry a pure girl like Annie, or Annette, as her mother insists on calling her. These people! Or she'd try to yank him along to Father Cody. Oh no, not Father Ramshaw; no, he'd likely laugh in her face, but hellfire Cody would likely call up St. John The Baptist to come and wash her son clean."

"Oh, Dad." Joe now covered his mouth with one hand, saying, "That's funny, you know."

"Lad, I can see nothing funny in anything I say or do these days. To tell the truth, and I can only talk about it to you and one other, I'm at the end of me tether. I've left her twice, as you know, but she's hauled me back through pity and duty, but when I go this time, all her tears and suicide threats and for the sake of the children . . . Children!" He pointed at Joe. "Look at you. You were twenty years old when she last named you among the children. That was five years ago and she still had her child with her, because she still considered Don, at sixteen, to be a child. It's a wonder he's turned out the decent fellow he is, don't you think?"

"Yes; yes, I suppose so, Dad. And he *is* a decent fellow. But . . . have you thought, if you were to go, what would happen to Stephen, because *there's* someone who is a child for life. You faced up to this a long time ago. And you couldn't expect Maggie to take him on if there was no other support. And if you went, you know what Mam would do with him; what she's threatened many times."

Abruptly, Daniel thrust himself up from the couch, his shoulders hunched, saying, "Don't go on. Don't go on, Joe. Stephen will never go into a home; I'll see to that. But one thing I do know: I can't stand much more of this." And moving his feet apart and stretching his arms wide, he said, "Look at it! A bloody great room like this, full of books that nobody apart from you bothers to read. All show. Twenty-eight rooms, not counting your original prehistoric annexe. Stables for eight horses; not even a damned dog in them. She doesn't like dogs, just cats. Six acres of land and a lodge. And for what? To keep five people employed, one for each of us. I've lived in this house for fifteen years but it's seventeen years since I bought it, and I bought it only because it was going dead cheap. A time-bomb had gone off close by, and the soldiers had occupied it, and so the owners were glad to get rid of it. Funny, that. They could trace their ancestors back two hundred years, but they were quite willing to sell it to a taggerine man who had made money out of old scrap that was helping to kill men." He nodded. "That's how I always looked at it, because when my Dad and old Jane Broderick were blown up together in the works towards the end of the war, I thought it was a sort of retribution. And yet it's strange, you know, for even though it was going cheap, when I saw it I knew I had to have it. I can't blame your mother for that, for like me she jumped at it and then took a delight in spending a fortune furnishing it; and wherever she got it from, I don't know, but that's one thing that can be said for her; she had taste in furnishings. But it's funny, you know, lad, this place doesn't like me."

"Oh." Joe now pushed Daniel on the shoulder with his fist, saying, "Come on, come on, don't be fanciful."

"It doesn't. I have feelings about things like this. It doesn't. I'm an intruder. We are all intruders. The war was supposed to level us all out. Huh . . . ! But these old places, like some of the old die-hard county types, keep you in your place, and mine isn't here."

For the first time a smile came on to his face and he turned and looked towards the window again, saying, "Remember our first real house, the one at the bottom of Brampton Hill? It was a lovely place, that; cosy, a real home, with a lovely garden that you didn't get lost in. Do you remember it?" He turned to Joe who, nodding, said, "Oh yes, yes, very well."

"Yet you like this house?"

"Yes, I like it. I've always liked it, although when I was young, the 'cill' part of it, Wearcill House, always puzzled me. Yes, I've always liked it, but at the same time I know what you mean. There's one thing I must point out to you, Dad: you're lucky, you know, that it takes only five people to run the house, and that's inside and out. When the Blackburns were here, I'm told there were twelve servants inside alone. And *they* had only three sons and a daughter."

"Aye, three sons; and they were all killed in the war."

"Come on, Dad, cheer up. I'll tell you what." He again punched his father in the shoulder. "Go on; go and ask Don if he's a virgin."

Watching Joe shaking with laughter, Daniel began to chuckle, and characteristically he said, "Bugger me eyes to hell's flames! I'll never get over that. Anyway"—he now poked his head towards Joe—"do you think he's a virgin?"

"Haven't the slightest idea. But on the other hand . . . well, I should say, yes."

"I don't know so much. Anyway, where is he?"

"The last time I saw him he was in the billiard-room, playing his usual losing battle with Stephen. He's very good with him, you know."

"Aye, he is. And that's another thing she can't get over; that her wee lamb has always found time for her retarded and crippled first-born. Aw, come on."

They went out together, crossed the hall to where a corridor led off by the side of the broad shallow staircase, and at the end of it Joe opened the door and almost shouted at the two people at the billiard table, "I knew this was where you'd be. Wasting time again. Chalk up to the eyes and company coming"—he glanced at his watch—"in twenty minutes' time."

"Joe! Joe! I beat him. I did. I beat him again."

Joe walked round the full-sized billiard table towards a man who was almost as tall as himself, a man thirty years old, with a well-built body and a mass of brown unruly hair, but with a face beneath it that could have belonged to a young boy, and a good-looking young boy. Only the eyes gave any indication that there was something not quite normal about him. The eyes were blue like those of his father, but they were a pale, flickering blue. It was as if they were bent on taking in all their surroundings at once. Yet there were times when the flickering became still, when his mind groped at something it could catch but only momentarily hold.

"I . . . I made a seven . . . break. Didn't I, Don?"

"Yes. Yes, he did, and he made me pot my white."

"Never!" said Daniel. "He made you pot your white, Don? In that case you're getting worse."

"Well, he's too good for me; and it isn't fair; he always wins."

"I'll . . . I'll let you win next time, Don. I will. I will. That's a promise. I will. I will, honest."

"I'll keep you to it, mind."

"Yes, Don. Yes, Don."

Stephen now put his hand up to his throat and, pulling a bow tie to one side, he said to his father, "It hurts my neck, Dad."

"Nonsense. Nonsense." Daniel went up to him and straightened the tie.

"Dad?"

"Yes, Stephen?"

"Can I go in the kitchen with Maggie?"

"Now you know that Maggie's getting the dinner ready."

"Then I'll go with Lily."

"Not now, Stephen; we won't go through all this again. You know what the pattern is: you say How do you do? to Mr. and Mrs. Preston and Mr. and Mrs. Bowbent and, of course, to Auntie and Uncle Allison and Annie . . . Annette. Then after you've done that and had a word with Annette, as you always do, you can go upstairs and Lily will bring up your dinner."

"Dad." Don was signalling to his father as he turned away to walk down to the end of the room where a wood fire was burning in an open grate, and when Daniel joined him he stooped and, picking a log from a basket, he placed it on the fire, muttering as he did so, "Let him go up, Dad; he had an accident earlier on."

"Bad?"

"No, just wet. But he's all nerves." He stood up now and, looking at his father, said, "It's hard for him. I can't understand why you make him keep it up."

Daniel lifted his foot to press the log further into the flames, saying, "You know fine well, Don, why I keep it up. I'm not going to hide him away as if he were an idiot, because he's not an idiot. We know that."

"But it isn't fair to him, Dad. Let him go tonight. It would upset Mum if he were to have another accident, and in tonight's company. It's happened once before, you know it has."

"That was a long time ago. He's learned better since."

"Dad, please."

Father and son stood looking at each other; neither spoke, even though in the background there was Joe's voice still forming a barricade behind which they could talk, until Don said, "Look upon it as an extra wedding present to me."

"Aw! you; aren't you satisfied with what you've got?"

"Oh, Dad, don't say that, satisfied. I've told you, I can't believe it, a house of our own and such a grand one. And—" He paused as he now looked deep into his father's eyes before adding, "a good distance away."

"Aye, lad, a good distance away. But there's one thing I've got to say, although I don't want to. But it must be said: don't cut her off altogether; invite her often, and come back here whenever you can."

"I'll do that. Yes, yes, I'll do that. And one more thing from me, Dad: thank you for everything, particularly for bringing me through."

He did not have to explain through what, nor did Daniel have to enquire; they both knew. Turning quickly, Daniel walked towards Stephen, crying, "All right! You've got the better of me again. You're not only good at billiards, you're good at getting round people. Get yourself away up to your rooms; I'll get Lily to go up with you."

"No need. No need, Dad." Joe put his arm around Stephen's shoulders.

"We've got to get things straight here; he's backing Sunderland against New-castle. Did you ever hear anything like it? Come on, you! Let's get this worked out." And with that the two tall men left the room, Stephen's arm around Joe's waist now and a deep happy gurgle coming from his throat.

On their own now and with the opportunity for more talk, it would nevertheless seem that the father and son had exhausted all they had to say to each other, until Don asked, "Like a game, Dad? We've got fifteen minutes; they always arrive on the dot, never before."

"No thanks, Don. I'd better slip along to the kitchen and ask Maggie if she can send something upstairs before she gets the dinner going." And with this he turned and abruptly left the room.

A baize door led from the hall into the maze of kitchen quarters. He'd had the main kitchen modernised, putting in an Aga, but leaving the old open fire and ovens, which were still used and baked marvellous bread. It was an attractive kitchen, holding a long wooden table, a delf rack on one wall, a sideboard on the other, a double sink under a low wide window that gave a view of the stable yard. There was a long walk-in marble shelved larder, and next to it a door leading into a wood store and from this into a large covered glass porch, where outdoor coats and hats were hung and, flanking one side, a long boot-rack.

The kitchen was a-bustle. Maggie Doherty, a woman of thirty-seven, stood at the table decorating with half cherries and strawberries a trifle which had already been piped with cream, and she glanced up at Daniel for a moment and smiled as she said, "They'll soon be here."

"Aye. Yes, they'll soon be here . . . That looks nice. I hope it tastes as good."

"Should be; there's almost half a bottle of sherry soaking itself down-wards."

"Eeh! we mustn't let Madge Preston know, must we?"

"Tell her it's cooking sherry. It makes all the difference; you wouldn't believe."

"Aye, I would. Is it duck the night?"

"Yes; with the usual orange stuffing and the odds and bods."

"What soup?"

"Vichyssoise."

"Oh aye? That's something to swank about."

"Or shrimp cocktail."

"Oh, Betty Broadbent'll go for those."

He stood for a moment watching Maggie's hands putting the finishing touches to the trifle, then said, "I've sent Stephen straight up. He hasn't been too good the day, I understand. Would you see that he gets a bite?"

Maggie Doherty lifted her eyes to his, then looked down on the trifle again before saying, "Why you insist on putting him on show, God only knows; he suffers agony with strangers. How can you do it?"

"Maggie, we've been through this; it's for his own good."

The top of the trifle finished, she took up a damp cloth from the table and as she wiped her hands with it, he said under his breath, "For God's sake! don't you an' all take the pip with me, Maggie, 'cos it's been one of those days; a short while ago I just staggered out of another battle."

Again she looked at him, but her gaze now was soft as she said, "You know better than that," before turning away and calling out to a young woman who had just entered the kitchen, "Peggie! set the tray for Master Stephen and take it up. You know what he likes." Then she added, "Is everything right on the table?" And Peggie Danish replied, "Yes, Miss Doherty. Lily's just put on the centre piece; it looks lovely."

At this Maggie said, "Well, I'd better go and see if I'm of the same opinion." But she smiled at the young woman; then taking off a white apron and smoothing her hair back, she went from the room. And Daniel followed her. But once in the passage they both stopped and he, looking down into her face that was neither plain nor pretty yet emanated a soft kindness, said, "I'm sorry, Maggie, sorry to the heart of me."

"Don't be silly. I've waited a long time for that and I don't feel brazen in saying it."

"Aw, Maggie; but after twenty years, and me like a father to you."

"Huh! I've never looked on you as a father, Dan. Funny that"—she gave a soft laugh—"calling you Dan."

"You won't go then?"

"No." She turned her eyes from him and looked up the passageway. "I thought about it, then knew that I couldn't. But I'll have to watch my tongue and my manners, won't I? And that's going to be hard, because whenever she's treated me with a high hand I've felt like turning on her many a time and walking out. I never knew what kept me at first"—she was looking at him again—"and when I did I knew I was stuck here. But I never thought it would be for twenty years. Early on I used to imagine it was just because of Stephen because he was so helpless and in need of love, and still is"—she nodded at him—"more than any of us I think."

"I wouldn't say that, Maggie."

When she turned abruptly away he caught her arm and was about to say, "Don't worry; it won't happen again," when she forestalled him by looking at him fully in the face and saying, "As you've known for years, I go to me cousin Helen's on me day off. You'll remember it's at forty-two Bowick Road." She made a little motion with her head, then went from him, leaving him where she had left him, dragging his teeth tightly on his lower lip.

TWO

The dinner was over. The guests had spoken highly of the fare and congratulated Winifred on the achievement, and once again she had been told how lucky she was to have such a cook as Maggie Doherty.

As usual, the ladies had left the men to their cigars and port in the dining-room and had adjourned to the drawing-room. This was a custom that Winifred had inaugurated when they had first come into the big house, and this aping of a bygone custom had made Daniel laugh at first; but just at first.

Annette Allison sat on a straight-backed chair to the side of the grand piano and she looked from her mother to her future mother-in-law, then from Madge Preston to Betty Bowbent and, not consciously directing her thoughts as a prayer, she said to herself, "Dear God, don't let me turn out like any of them." And she did not chide herself for her thinking, nor tell herself that when next she examined her conscience she must repent for her uncharitableness to others, especially for not wishing to grow even like her mother; and she should have done for, educated in a convent, she had been trained under the nuns since she was five years old, and so such thoughts should be anathema to her.

Her mind wandered to Don, but she knew she wouldn't be allowed five minutes' privacy with him tonight; not only was her own mother like a gaoler, but Don's was too. Oh, yes. When she thought of Don's mother she became a little afraid of the future because, once married and with the added status of a wife, she might not be able to hide her feelings or curb her tongue.

When she heard Mrs. Bowbent mention the name Maria and her mother put in quickly, "Wouldn't it be nice if we could order the weather for next Saturday?" she saw an outlet for her means of escape and, standing up she said to Winifred, "Would you mind if I went up and had a chat with Stephen?"

After a slight hesitation Winifred smiled at her and answered, "No, no; not at all, Annette. He'll be delighted to see you."

The four women watched Annette's departure; then Madge Preston turned to Janet Allison and said, "Why put a taboo on the subject, Janet? She knows all about it; in fact everybody does."

"No, they don't." Janet Allison almost bridled in her chair. "And anyway, they moved, didn't they?"

"Yes; but not until Maria's bulge couldn't be hidden any longer."

"Oh, Madge, you are coarse."

"Don't be so pi, Janet. What if it had happened to Annette?"

Rising to her feet, Janet Allison said, "You have gone too far this time, Madge."

"Oh, sit down, Janet. I'm sorry. I'm sorry."

Winifred had not spoken throughout this discourse, but now, putting her hand on Janet's arm, she said quietly, "Do sit down, please, Janet, and we'll talk about something else. This is most distressing." And she cast a glance at Madge and made a small reprimanding motion with her head. Then, looking towards the door, she said, "Ah, here are the men," and sank back heavily into her chair, at the same time almost pulling Janet Allison back into her seat.

They filed into the room, led by Daniel: John Preston, round, grey-haired, and smiling; Harry Bowbent, thin and weedy, and looking like an old parochial Mormon father; then the tall, imposing, big pot-bellied figure of James Allison. Joe was the last to enter, closing the door behind him, and as he passed Winifred she screwed round in her chair and asked him under cover of the babble of voices, "Where's Don?"

"Oh, he just slipped upstairs to say goodnight to Stephen."

She had to force herself not to get to her feet, but when, turning her head, she caught Janet Allison's eye tight on her she knew they were of the same mind . . .

In Stephen's sitting-room on the second floor Don and Annette stood locked in each other's arms. When their lips parted he said, "I feel that I cannot live another minute without you," and she answered simply, "Oh, me too, Don, especially now."

"Yes, especially now." Then holding her face between his two hands, he said, "Can you imagine any couple having mothers like ours?"

"No, I can't; and I'm riddled with guilt at times. But you've been lucky; your father's on your side, whereas I've got two to deal with. And, you know, the only reason I was allowed up here on my own was because the ladies were about to discuss Maria Tollett once more. Honestly, Don, poor Maria. I remember her as a shy, quiet little thing. I could put a name to twenty that might have done the same thing, but not Maria. But then Maria did, and her people had to take her away and hide her some place because of the shame. I thought we were in a new world, a new era, and that kind of thing couldn't happen in nineteen-sixty. But, I suppose while there are people like your dear mama and mine, it could still be happening at the end of the century."

Suddenly she put her arms around him and gripped him tightly to her, and in a voice that seemed to be threaded with panic she muttered, "Oh God, bring Saturday soon."

"It's all right, darling, it's all right. And just think"—he stroked her hair—"three weeks in Italy. But of course we must go and see the Pope while we're there."

Her body began to shake, her head moving backwards and forwards on his shoulder, and, although laughing himself but silently, he said, "Shh! Shh! You let that laugh of yours rip and they'll be taking the stairs three at a time."

Her eyes were wet as she looked into his, and she had to swallow deeply, saying, "I promised faithfully we would go to Vatican City and to Mass every morning . . . both of us."

"You didn't!"

"I did."

"Oh, why didn't you tell her we'd be cuddling in bed until twelve?"

She giggled and hugged him as she said, "Oh, Don."

"Listen"—he pressed her gently from him—"there's someone coming. I'll go next door and see if Stephen's asleep and you make for the door." But as he went to move away from her he suddenly stopped and, putting his arm swiftly around her waist, he said, "No! by God, no! We'll do no such thing. Come on. There's a limit, and if I'd had any sense I'd have reached it a long time ago."

But when they reached the door, defiance expressed in their faces, it was Joe who confronted them, saying quietly, "I'm ahead of the search party. Come on you two, there's departures in the offing. They're all in the morning-room looking at the presents, but conversation has been forced." He now asked of Annette, "Was there a battle?" And she, shaking her head said, "No, I left to leave the way open for more condemnation of Maria Tollett, which I imagined would be opposed by Mrs. Preston because she's a close friend of theirs."

"O . . . oh! I see. But look"—he nodded at them—"take my advice and get that look off your faces, and don't go down entwined like that because there's been a fire smouldering all day and we don't want a conflagration, do we?"

As they laughed he pushed them both before him. And when Don said, "Come Saturday. Come Saturday," and Annette added, "Amen! Amen!" they would have been surprised to know that big Joe, their friend and ally, was longing for Saturday equally as much as they were, if not more.

It was just on eleven o'clock. The house was quiet. Winifred had retired to her room. Joe and Stephen were also upstairs. Lily had gone down to the lodge half an hour before, and Peggie had just said goodnight to him as she made her way to her attic room. There was only Maggie in the kitchen and he knew he'd be welcome there, and he needed that welcome. Oh, how he needed that welcome. But he couldn't take it, for his mind was in a turmoil: if he encouraged that, where would it end? The situation in the house would become unbearable, for he wasn't a great hand at hiding his feelings.

He wasn't feeling tired. He never felt tired at night; it was always in the morning when he had to get out of bed that he felt tired.

He went into the cloakroom and took a coat from a peg and, having put it on, he went quietly from the house and on to the drive. There was an autumn nip in the air; the long dark nights would soon be upon them. And this description, he thought, had been very like his life, one long dark night. But now a fire had been lit and he longed to warm himself at it. Yet in some odd way he was feeling ashamed of his need of it.

He walked slowly down the drive. He could see, in the distance, that the gate-lights were still on. That meant Bill and Lily hadn't yet retired.

He was near the lodge when the side gate opened and Bill White stepped out, paused, then said, "You gave me a bit of a gliff, sir."

"Just getting a breather before turning in, Bill."

"Your company went early."

"Yes; yes, they did the night. It's nippy, isn't it? We'll soon have winter on us."

"Aye, we will that, sir. I like winter meself, I'm partial to it: me feet on the fender, me pipe, and a book. I can never settle down like that in the summer somehow."

"No; no, I can see that. There's things to be said for all seasons, I suppose."

Bill was walking by his side now towards the open iron gates where, poised high on top of each of the two stone pillars, glowed an electric lamp, topped by a wrought-iron shade that sent the light spraying far into the middle of the road. They both stopped within the line of the gates, and there was silence between them until Bill, in a voice scarcely above a whisper, said, "I had to drive up Dale Street the day, sir."

Daniel remained motionless for a moment; then slowly he turned his head and looked at the face now confronting his, and asked quietly, "Do you often drive up Dale Street, Bill?"

"Twice before; but I never twigged then."

"When was this? I mean, when you drove up before?"

"Last week, twice."

"Is this just something new? You . . . you haven't been ordered anywhere else?"

"Something new, sir, although I've been questioned."

Daniel gazed across the road towards the open farmland that the gate-lights just touched on, and he thought, Will she ever let up? And what a situation for this man at his side having to obey the mistress's whims while bearing allegiance to the master. His voice was thick as he muttered, "Thanks, Bill."

"Any time, sir."

It was as he was about to turn and go back up the drive that a car made itself heard by its approaching rattle. He knew the sound of that car, and as it slowed opposite the gates he walked towards it, and when it stopped with a jerk he bent down and said, "Why are you out at this time of the night, Father?"

"Oh, business, as usual. Had company?" He pointed towards the lights.

"Yes, they've all gone. Care to come in for a drink?"

"Now since you've asked me, I think I would. A few minutes ago, all I wanted was me bed. So hop in!"

Daniel turned now and shouted to Bill, "Don't wait up, Bill. I'll see to the lights. Good-night."

As the man called, "Good-night, sir," Daniel got into the car and asked of the priest, "Where've you been to at this time of night?"

"Oh, at Tommy Kilbride's."

"Not again! He's a hypochondriac, that fellow."

"He was, but not this time. He doesn't know it, but he's for the hop, skip, and jump all right, and within the next couple of days or so. And you can believe me there'll not be a more surprised man when he finds himself dead. I bet he says, 'Look, it's all a mistake; it's all in me mind. It's a fact; they've been sayin' it to me for years. Let me go back.' And you know something? Life's funny in the tricks it plays on a man: he's imagined he's had every disease under the sun except the one that's crept on him unawares. I'm sorry for him, I am that, but he's brought it on himself; I mean the surprise he's going to get."

"Oh, Father." Daniel was laughing now. "I bet you are wishing you could be there to see his face when he arrives. And by the way, it'll be yourself that'll be arriving and very shortly if you don't get rid of this old boneshaker."

"I've no intention of gettin' rid of Rosie, so please don't insult her; she's a friend. Would you propose gettin' rid of all those elderly ladies with ageing bones who creak in every joint? Anyway, you've had a party or some such tonight; how did it go?"

"Oh, as usual."

"You'll be glad when Saturday comes and is gone."

"You've never said a truer word, Father. I certainly will that. And look, don't take . . . Rosie right to the door, else you'll have windows popping up and enquiries as to what's causing the rattle."

A few minutes later they were both ensconced in the library. Daniel had put the bellows to the fire and it was blazing brightly, and on a table between the chairs was a decanter of whisky and a bottle of brandy, two glasses and a jug of water.

Pointing to the bottle, Daniel said, "I thought you might like to try this. I know brandy isn't your drink but this is something special. I had it given to me by an old customer. It's all of forty or fifty years old; it's like elixir on the tongue. I've never tasted anything to equal it before." He now poured a good measure into the glass and handed it to the priest. And he, sipping at it, rolled it round his mouth, swallowed, then, arching his eyebrows, he said, "Yes. My! as you say, elixir on the tongue. But still, I think I'll stick to me whisky because I wouldn't like to get a taste for this kind of thing; you might have me robbin' the poor box . . ." He lay back into the deep chair, saying quietly, "Ah! This is nice. It's a beautiful house, you know, this. I remember coming into it first during the week that I arrived in Fellburn. The Blackburns were wooden Catholics, so to speak, and as such were never free with the bottle. A cup of tea, or a cup of coffee, and that watery, that's what you were offered. Of course they were living from hand to mouth at the time: it takes a lot of money to keep up appearances, you know, especially when you like horses."

"You're telling me, Father, even without the horses."

"Oh, aye." The priest put his hand out and pushed Daniel's shoulder. "I'm tellin' you. Anyway, how's life? Your life."

"As bad as it could be, Father."

"As bad as that? Well, open up."

"Oh, you don't want a confession here the night; at least, not after being with old Tommy. And you must have listened to many the day."

"I'm always open to confessions. But it needn't be a confession, just a quiet crack. What's bothering you, apart from all the other things I know of? Anyway, you haven't been to confession for some weeks, have you?"

Daniel took up his usual stance when troubled, his body bent, his elbows on his knees, his hands gripped together, and he stared into the fire as he quietly said, "I've taken up with a woman."

"Oh God in heaven! man, tell me something I don't know."

Daniel now turned towards the priest, saying, "Not that kind."

"What other kind is there that you can take up with?"

"There are some good women, Father."

"Are you aiming, Daniel, to teach a sixty-four-year-old priest the facts of life? What you seem to forget, and many more like you, is that we are men and that some of us weren't always priests. Meself, for instance, I never came into the racket until I was twenty-five."

"Then why did you—" and a small smile appeared on Daniel's face now as he added, "if you knew so much?"

"Because He wouldn't let me alone." Father Ramshaw's eyes almost disappeared under the upper lids as he looked towards the ceiling. "I nearly got married when I was twenty, but He put His spoke in there. The girl's father wanted to knock me brains out and her brother threatened to break me legs if I ran away. But run I did. And, candidly, I've been doing that inside me head ever since. Well, perhaps not so much these latter years. Yet at one time, and that's not so long ago, here was somebody frightened to go to confession to the Bishop because I was brought up to believe that you sin by thought as much as by deed. But of course you don't get as much satisfaction out of the former as you do out of the latter."

As Daniel now threw himself back into the chair, his body shaking with laughter, he said, "Father, I don't believe a word you say."

"That's the trouble, nobody does. They always think I'm joking; but you know the saying, There's many a true word spoken in jest. And all my jokes have a broad streak of truth in them. You can take it from me what I've just imparted to you is God's honest truth. Anyway, who's this decent woman that you're worrying about? Do I know her?"

A few seconds passed before Daniel said, " 'Tis Maggie."

"Oh no! not Maggie."

"Yes, Father. Now you see what I mean."

"Ah well, it had to come."

"What do you mean?" Daniel now shifted round on the couch and looked at the priest who was staring towards the fire.

"Just that. She's been for you all these years. Why do you think she's stuck here? and stuck Winifred? Because, let me tell you, it's bad enough for a man to have to put up with a woman, but for a woman to have to put up with a woman is, I should imagine, much worse, and with such a woman as Winifred. God Himself doesn't demand such devotion. And devotion of this kind is a sort of sickness, and there's a number around these quarters that's got the smit. Now, between you and me, and as if you didn't know it, Annette's mother is another one. As for her father, he's bordering on religious mania. There's moderation in all things. And you know Daniel, we've got a lot of faults, we Catholics. Oh dear God! we have that. And the main one, as

I've always seen it, is to imagine that we are the sole chosen of the Almighty. Now if we could only get that out of our heads we'd be the perfect religion. But there, I could be excommunicated for voicing such an opinion, because on the other hand there's not a more lenient or tolerant sect. Which other lot would give you leave to get drunk on your Friday night's pay, batter the wife, then arrive at confession on the Saturday night, then take Communion on the Sunday morning, before making for the club for a skinful? I tell you, we are the most tolerant of God's creatures and so we don't go in for extremes."

"It's a pity then, Father, you couldn't have put over that point of view to Winnie some years ago."

"Oh, me boy! I did. And I keep at it to this day, and with others of her kin. But do they take any notice? No. They would rather listen to Father Cody spouting his hellfire. Oh, believe me, Daniel, there's more thorns in the flesh than women. Why on earth did they send that young man to me? Now why am I asking the road I know? Things want tightening up around Fellburn. That's what was said in high quarters. People were forgetting there was a hell, at least that old fool Father Ramshaw had forgotten. Instead of folks being sat on hot gridirons minus their pants, that old fool was proposing a sort of nice waiting-room where the patients could just wait and think and ponder on their past life and be sorry for their misdeeds, sins, if you like; the worst, which I've always stated in plain language from the pulpit, as you know, being unkindness to one another . . . But to get back to Maggie: how did this come about after all this long time?"

Daniel again brought his body forward, and his voice low now, he said, "It was quite simple; it seemed to be all set up. It was her day off. I gave her a lift into town. Strange, but it was the first time she'd ever been in the car with me; I mean, alone. Years ago, when she used to take Stephen out on her day off, I would drop them at her cousin's. And there we were this day, and she invited me to go in with them. Outside this house she seemed different, and as she talked I looked at her and saw this smart woman that had lived in my house for twenty years, and the kindness emanating from her, and I knew then what I'd known for a long time deep within me that I not only wanted her, but I loved her too. And that was that. Apparently, as you said, she had the same feeling for me, even though it was well hidden. What am I going to do, Father?"

"Now what can you do? If I say to you, cut her out of your life, you'll say, how can you, living in the same house? If I say to you, if your wife gets wind of this there'll be hell to pay and no mistake, what'll you say?"

"I want to leave Winnie, Father. Once Don's married and out of her clutches"—he jerked his head towards the ceiling—"I mean to go. And I'll take Stephen with me, Maggie an' all. I've thought about it, and seriously."

"You can't do that, man, you can't do that; she'll never leave you alone. You know what happened the last time, and the time before that. And she would do it again, just to weigh on your conscience for the rest of your life, because once she's lost Don she won't have much to live for. I'll never know how she has allowed his wedding to come as close as it has."

"Well, I can tell you that, Father; I've seen to it."

"You have? I must have known all along you had a hand in it, for she would never let go of the reins on her own. I can recall her going to watch him play football on a Saturday and waiting to drive him home, hail, rain or snow."

"Yes, in case he spoke to some girl or other. And what do you think of the latest, Father? What do you think she asked me to do tonight?"

"I couldn't give a guess, Daniel. Tell me."

"She didn't only ask, she demanded that I go and find out whether or not he was a virgin!"

"No. Oh dear God! No." The priest chuckled.

"You can laugh, Father, but oh dear God! yes."

"What possessed her?"

"What's always possessed her? The mania that is in her to hold him tight to her for the rest of his life. Pure and unsullied, that's how she thinks of him. You know, since he was born and she saw that he was normal, you could say in all truth that she's hardly looked at Stephen or Joe; in fact, she dislikes them both, although for different reasons."

Father Ramshaw now shook his head before slowly saying, "But even if you were to leave her you couldn't be divorced. You know that."

"That wouldn't matter to me so long as there was space between us, more space, because as you know I haven't had her bed for years; she even shrinks from my hand."

The old priest sighed as he said, " 'Tis a sad state of affairs. But perhaps God has a strange way of working: after Saturday, when she knows she's lost Don, she might turn to you."

"Oh, never, Father." Daniel now reached firmly out and replenished the glasses with whisky and, again handing one to the priest, he said, "I couldn't stand that. I really couldn't. Not after all this long time. Oh, no, there'll be no reconciliation like that, I can tell you."

"What about Joe, should you carry out your plan?"

"Oh, Joe's a man in his own right; he'll order his life the way he wants it. He's in a good position now, being a full-blown accountant. And anyway, he's got his own little establishment in the cottage. There's days on end when he doesn't come into the main house here, not even for his meals. Oh, I don't worry about Joe; he'll get along on his own."

"Aye. Joe's a fine fellow, but nobody gets along on their own, Daniel. And that reminds me, I'll have to be after him; he's been neglecting his duties of late; I haven't seen him at Mass for a couple of Sundays. But then he could have been at Father Cody's. I could have enquired about that, but I didn't. The less that devil-chaser and me have to say to each other the better!" He gulped at the whisky now, then laughed and ended, "I'm a wicked man, you know. But there's only you and God know that, so keep it to yourself. That's a fine whisky an' all, Daniel, but it must be me last if I don't want to drive home singing, because then, believe it or not, Father Cody would have me on me knees, he would that, and thumping me on the back, saying, 'Repeat after me: Drink is the divil. Drink is the divil. Drink is the divil.' "

They both laughed, and the priest went on, "And I bet he would say that an' all, because he puts me in mind of Sister Catherine. They could be mother and son, you know, the way they deal with those who lapse, because that's what she used to do to the young lads. I caught her at it once, thumping a hapless little divil on the head for some misdemeanour and with each thump crying, 'Say: God is love. God is love. God is love.' "

"Oh! Father." Daniel wiped his eyes with a handkerchief. "I hope you'll attend my deathbed, because I'd like to die laughing."

"Ah, that's nice, that's a very nice thing to say. But seeing how the two of us are set in years it could be the other way round. Now, give me a hand up. Let me see if me legs are steady. How many whiskies have I had?"

"Three, and the brandy."

"It's the brandy, whisky never goes to me legs like this." He put out a leg and shook it, saying, "It's got the tremors. Come on, let me out quietly, and then get yourself away to your bed. I'll see you on Thursday at the rehearsal, then pray God Saturday will be here and it will all be over. We must talk again, Daniel. Do you hear? Promise me you won't do anything until we talk again."

"All right, Father, I promise."

And on that, Daniel led the way out of the house and saw this dear old fellow, as he thought of him, into his car, saying, "I'll see you to the gates; I promised Bill I'd put out the lights . . ."

Back in the house, he looked across the hall to the green-baize door. She was still in the kitchen—he had seen the light from the drive—but he didn't make towards it. Instead, he slowly went up the stairs.

THREE

It was a beautiful day; it could have been mid-July, for it was quite warm and there wasn't a breath of wind. Everyone said you would think it had been ordered.

The marquee had been erected on the lawn beyond the drive. A number of men were going quietly about their business unloading tables and chairs from a lorry; from a van outside the main door, a woman and a man were carrying baskets of flowers into the house, and another was taking armfuls of blooms towards the marquee; and on the drive, men were stringing rows of electric bulbs between the larches. There was no fuss, and everything appeared orderly, as it did within the house.

It was half-past nine. Winifred had breakfasted in bed; Daniel had been up for some time; Joe and Don had just left the dining-room, both dressed in light pullovers and grey flannels. They were crossing the hall towards the stairs when Maggie came down and, confronting them from the bottom step, she said, "He's in a tizzy, he won't get up. You'd better go and see what you can do."

"Well, if you haven't succeeded in rousing him, there's little chance for us."

Maggie looked at Joe as she said, "We don't want any ructions today, do we? Cajole, invite, or threaten, but get him out of that bed."

Don, passing her now to go up the stairs, said, "I would have thought it was the best place for him, seeing he's not allowed to come to the service. Anyway, he'd have been all right; he can hold himself if he likes."

Maggie said nothing but stepped down into the hall and walked away. And Joe, taking the stairs two at a time, was quickly abreast of Don and said in an undertone, "You know as well as I do, Don, what excitement does to him. And there's nobody would like him there more than I would."

"He never gets a treat of any kind."

"Oh, you know that isn't right. Look what Maggie does for him. And I take him out at least once a week."

"I didn't mean that kind of a treat. This, well . . . well, I would have thought today was special and she could have stretched a point, even taking the risk of anything happening."

As they mounted the next flight of stairs in a single file Joe, looking at the back of this younger man whom he couldn't have loved more had he been his own kin by birth, thought ruefully, he said, *she*, not Mam, or Mother as she more often demanded as her title. It was as well he was going, for although as yet there had been no open rift between them, he had long seen one opening. And although he had his own feelings concerning the woman whom he addressed as Mam, he had no wish to see her broken openly by the desertion of the one being she loved. And not only loved; there was another name for such a feeling; but there was not a word in his vocabulary that would fit the need she had for her offspring.

"What's all this? What's all this?" Don was the first to reach the bed where Stephen was curled up in a position such as a child might have taken, his knees almost up to his chin, his arms folded across his face. "Now look here, you, Steve. Are you out to spoil my day?"

The long arms and legs seemed to move simultaneously and the body lifted itself up against the wooden back of the bed, and the lips trembled as they muttered, "No, Don, no. But I want to come to the wedding. Don't I, Joe? Can I, Don? Oh, can I?"

Sitting down on the side of the bed, Don now said quietly, "I want you to come. We all want you to come, but you know what happened at the rehearsal, now don't you? And anyway, the wedding will be over like that." He snapped his fingers. "Then you'll see Annette in her pretty dress, and the first thing she'll do when she comes into the house will be to cry out, 'Where's Steve? Where's Steve?' She always does, doesn't she?"

"I . . . I wouldn't misbehave, honest, Don. Look, I haven't in the night. Look!" And with a quick movement he thrust the bedclothes back. "It's all dry."

Joe had turned away from the bed and now stood as though looking out of the window. It made his heart ache to see this big man reduced to a child. But no, not reduced, just acting his mental age. What would happen to the lad . . . man when Don was gone and he himself was gone from this house, for he couldn't stand the atmosphere much longer. Of course, there was always Maggie and his dad. But his dad was at the business all day, and out and about his own business most nights. As for Maggie, she was still a youngish woman. And he had just an inkling, too, of what might have kept her in this establishment all these years, and that it wasn't just Steve. But it was only an inkling. Altogether it was an unhappy house. He had been aware of this for a long time. Even so, in a way he was grateful that he had been brought up in it, otherwise he wouldn't be in the position he was today. Yet, should he be grateful for the ache that was racking his body at this minute? Two years ago he had imagined this day could have been his, but two factors had intervened in the shapes of his dad and Annette herself. But mostly his dad.

As he looked down on to the drive he became aware that the flower van was moving away and in its place was what he recognised as a Bentley. He was keen on cars, but the family tended towards Rovers and he couldn't recall one of their friends who had a Bentley. Then his mouth fell into a slight gape as he saw a man whom he imagined to be a chauffeur get out and then open the door to allow a woman to alight. Then his face spread into a smile as he exclaimed, "Aunt Flo!" But she was early. She wasn't expected to arrive until later. Then again his mouth fell into a gape, but a bigger one this time, and he called quickly, "Don! Don! Come here a minute."

When Don reached his side, Joe pointed down on to the drive where a very smartly dressed woman was talking to the man he had imagined to be a chauffeur, and he said, "Look at that! What do you make of that?" And when the man now slipped his arm into the woman's and began to walk her towards the door, they both looked at each other, their faces stretched into expressions portraying glee.

Pressing the side of his head with his hand, Don groaned. "Oh my God! We only needed this. Mam will go berserk."

As though of like mind, they were turning together as Joe said, "Get yourself down to her and warn her; I'll go and meet them." But at the door he turned again and stabbed his finger towards Stephen, saying, "Now you be a good lad: go and have a bath; make yourself smell nice; and put on your good suit. And then, yes . . . yes, you may come downstairs. Do you hear?"

"Yes, Joe. Yes."

"That's it. Be a good lad."

"Yes, Joe."

Joe now turned and hurried towards the stairway. On the first floor he paused for, standing at a bedroom door, Don was holding his mother by the shoulders and saying, "Now stop it! Stop it! There could be an explanation."

"Explanation!" Her voice was loud. *"He's black!"*

Don cast a worried glance at Joe as he almost ran past them towards the stairs; then pressing his mother back into the room and closing the door, he said, "Now listen, Mother. If you make a scene you're going to spoil everything. Come. Come on." And he pulled her towards the chaise-lounge at the foot of the bed, saying, "Sit down."

"No, no; leave me alone. Oh! what am I saying? what am I saying?"—she held out her hand in a supplicating gesture—"Saying to you, of all people, leave me alone, when this day you are leaving me. And . . . and she . . . she's done this on purpose. Yes, yes, she has." Her whole fat body was shaking in confirmation of her statement. "She has always tried to rile me one way or another. Now she's come here today with . . . with, of all things, a black man."

"But you invited her. And why? because she said she was engaged to a barrister. Now own up."

"He can't be a barrister; he's black."

"Mother! Mother! Don't be silly."

She turned from him now and began to pace the room. "This is your father's doing. Oh, yes, yes it is. They were supposed to bump into each other in London, and I hadn't heard a word from her for years, not since Harry died, and that's five or more years ago. And he came back with the tale that she was doing splendidly, doing something big in an office and was working for a barrister. He must have known the barrister was black. He's done this on purpose. Your father's a wicked, wicked man."

"Be quiet, Mother."

"I won't! I won't! And what's more, I'm going to tell you something. Yes, I am. It's he who's brought on this day."

"What do you mean, brought on this day?"

"Just what I say: he was determined to part us, and he's brought it about. You know he has. You know he has."

Yes, yes, he knew he had. He knew his father had brought about his wedding day, and he thanked God for it. But he had to lie, saying loudly, "That's utterly ridiculous." But having lied he now inadvertently spoke the truth, adding, "I love Annette. I have done for years. Why, I went through agonies when I thought she fancied Joe. And you thought she fancied Joe, didn't you?"

"Nothing of the sort. Girls are flighty; they don't know their own minds. And . . . and I ask you now, Don—" Her voice had sunk low, her lids were blinking, the tears were pressing out of the corners of her eyes as she stammered, "Do . . . do you know what you are doing to me? Do you? You're breaking my heart. You are leaving me alone. When you go I'll have no-one, no-one in the wide world."

"Oh, Mother, please."

"Don. Don." With a cry she had her arms about him, pressing him to her, her flesh seeming to swim around him, her lips covering his eyes, his brow, his cheeks.

It was with an effort he pushed her from him, then stood rigid, wide-eyed, looking at her body quivering from head to foot beneath her light dressing-gown. He watched her turn from him and fling herself on to the couch muttering brokenly, "You don't love me. You don't love me."

He made no response to this for a full minute, and then he had to force the words through his lips, saying, "I do love you, Mother. But this is my wedding day. And what is more significant at the moment is that Aunt Flo is downstairs with her fiancé. Now how are you going to greet him? That's what you've got to think about. How are you going to greet him? Because you know Aunt Flo: she'll stand no nonsense. If you make a fuss . . . well, she'll make a bigger one. So, please, put on a dress, anything, and come downstairs and see her."

"I won't. And I don't want that man in my house."

"He is in the house, and Father will welcome him. I say again about knowing people, and you know Father."

"Yes. Yes"—her voice was almost a scream now—"I know Father. God in heaven! yes, I know Father. I've known him for thirty tortured years."

After drawing in a long breath he turned away and walked towards the door. But there she checked him. Her voice was low now as she said placatingly, "I . . . I can't go down yet. You can see that, Don."

"Will I send her up?"

She didn't answer: instead she turned her head away, which he took as an assent, so he left the room.

Pausing at the top of the stairs, he put his hands across his eyes for a moment as if to shut out something, and then went quickly down the stairs and towards the drawing-room from where came the sound of voices.

His father was standing with his back to the flower-decked fireplace; and there, too, by the end of the couch on which Flo was sitting, stood the man. On this closer acquaintance, his colour seemed not to be as dark as when first seen, but more a deep chocolate-brown. He was perhaps a half-caste, a very handsome half-caste, over six feet tall and well-built with it: not heavy and not slim, but more like an athlete.

His father greeted him with an over-loud voice, saying, "Oh, there you are, the man of the day," and almost before the words were out his Aunt Flo rose from the couch and, coming swiftly towards him with outstretched hands, cried, "Hello there! My! My! I hardly recognise you."

Don took her hands, then bent towards her and kissed her on the cheek, saying, "Nor me you, Aunt Flo."

And this, he told himself, was true, because her voice had become a little a-lah, as he termed it, and her rig-out, which was a mauve velvet suit with a matching coat, he noted was lying over the back of the chair, and was indeed something. From what he remembered of his Aunt Flo, she had been a bit slovenly; cheery and nice, oh yes, but not at all the classy piece who was now saying, "Come and meet Harvey."

She turned and led him by the hand towards the dark man, saying, "This is my fiancé, Mr. Harvey Clement Lincoln Rochester." She emphasised each word as she smiled broadly up at her intended. And the man, now holding out his hand, said, "How do you do? And let me explain right away that the Rochester doesn't mean I'm any relation to Jack Benny's stooge; and the Lincoln has no connection with a past president either; nor Clement with an English prime minister, nor Harvey with an imaginary rabbit that you might have seen in the film."

They were all laughing, Joe loudest of all, and Don, looking at them, could not help but pick up the approval he saw in their eyes and allow it to register in his own. He liked this fellow. But by God! if he knew anything, he was going to throw a spanner into the works today because she would go mad. If the man had been a Protestant or an atheist even, he might have got by, but a black man who was likely to become her brother-in-law! Oh my, my, his being a barrister wouldn't make much difference in this case. But now, out of politeness, he asked of the visitor, "Being a barrister, sir, what kind of cases do you handle?"

"Rogues; mostly rich ones."

"Oh, Harvey, you don't! not all the time. You take on poor people too." She was smacking at the big hand which rested on the head of the couch, and he, looking down at her, said, "Woman, they are still rogues, all of them."

Joe stared at the man. He could imagine him in court: he would be powerful; even his presence would show strength. And that voice . . . that was the second time in the last few minutes he had called Flo "woman." But the way he split up the word, it came out like a caress, woo . . . man, as another man might say, dar . . . ling. When he heard Don saying, to Flo, "Mother would like you to go up and see her. She's in the middle of dressing, and you know how long that takes," he thought, Yes, it would be a long time before Mam came down those stairs to meet this visitor.

"Oh well," said Flo, rising from her seat, "here's the mountain going to Mahommed." Then she cast a sidelong glance at her fiancé, saying, "Do you think you'll be able to cope until I return?" And Harvey's reply: "You know how I am without you, so don't be long," must have perplexed the assembled company, thought Flo, as she made her way upstairs, not only because of his choice of words, but also by his tone.

The nearer Flo got to the door of Winifred's room, the straighter her back became. When her knock received no response, she gently pushed open the door, and there, across the room, and seated near the window, was her sister.

Flo closed the door behind her, and had walked halfway towards Winifred before she spoke. "Hello, there!" she said. And when Winifred's lips tightened, it occurred to her that the bombshell must have already dropped. Of course, Don would have told her; he would likely have seen them arrive.

"How are you?"

At this, Winifred swung round and through tight jaws said, "How dare you?"

"How dare I what?"

"You know what I mean; don't act the innocent: bringing a black man here!"

"Oh, that!" Flo shrugged her shoulders before going on, "He's no black man; he's a half-caste, as if it makes any difference; a good-looking, handsome, half-caste. He's a barrister, a gentleman, and well respected."

"Shut up! Well respected. They don't even let them into working men's clubs in this town. And you've done this on purpose, haven't you, you and him between you?"

"What do you mean, me and him? He knows nothing about you."

"I mean Daniel."

"Daniel? What are you talking about?"

"I was given to understand that you had bumped into each other in London and that you had told him you were a secretary to a barrister and engaged to him."

"Yes, yes, that's what I told Daniel. But he never met the barrister, though I see now that's why I got an invite to the wedding: you thought I'd gone up in the world and you thought it would be one up for you to claim that your sister was engaged to a barrister. My God! you haven't changed a bit, have you, Winnie?"

"Well, that makes two of us, for first time around you had to go and marry a cheap insurance agent, a drunk."

"Harry was no drunk, not in that sense; he was an alcoholic, and he was a decent enough fellow. But in your opinion he was somebody to be ashamed of. Just like Father. Remember Father?"

"Yes. Oh yes, I remember Father."

"Well, that surprises me, when you wouldn't go to see him even when he was dying. You hadn't even the decency to go and see Mam. No, you were out for prize money and you hooked on to it through Daniel. It really wasn't him you wanted but what he could provide you with. Which has been proved, hasn't it?"

Her nose wrinkling, Winifred said scornfully, "You . . . you know nothing about it. You'll always be cheap and common. When you came into this room a moment ago you had an accent that any ignoramus could detect was assumed, but now you are yourself again, aren't you? Well, as yourself, you can go down and take your coloured man out of my house. You can give the excuse that this is just a flying visit. You understand?"

Flo slowly drew herself up to her full height, so dwarfing the standing, fat figure before her, and remained silent for a moment; then she said, "I came up for Don's wedding and to Don's wedding I and my fiancé will go. And we'll attend the reception afterwards. And only then, perhaps, will we think of leaving. Mr. Rochester is a gentleman, an educated gentleman, far above your husband or your sons in education, and if you don't treat him at least with civility, then you can prepare for squalls, because you know me, Winnie: when I get going I've got a loud voice and I can put things over, especially home truths, in a very jocular way, and so make people laugh while they ponder. I have that knack, haven't I? Well, I can assure you I'll do my piece. If you are not downstairs within half an hour I'll promise you one of the best performances of my life, solely for your guests, one hundred and thirty of them I understand. Think on it, Winnie. Think on it." And on this she turned slowly about and left the room: and her step was steady as she went down the stairs.

As she entered the drawing-room her fiancé was saying, "My grandparents came over at the end of the last century. They were from California, and they went into service in a gentleman's family just outside of London. They had a son who grew up in the same establishment and became a sort of factotum; and just after the last war he married one of the housemaids. And they had a son, and about the same time the daughter of the house and her husband, who lived with her parents, had their third son. The young half-caste"—he now pointed his forefinger towards himself—"and the three boys grew up together. They were sent to boarding school, I was sent to the local school, from where I got to the grammar school. The only coloured boy there. I stood out, I can tell you." His smile was broad now. "And from there it was just a natural step to university. I didn't stand out so much there, for there were other dark faces to be seen. Well, I read law, and there you are."

Flo came quietly into the room at this point, saying, "And one of the sons of that house is a solicitor and he brings him cases. But there's not much left of the younger one, for he was blown up during the war. But we go and see him every month. And those three sons are his closest friends."

It was evident to Daniel, Joe and Don that, as they had expected, Flo had had a hard time upstairs, for her eyes were bright and her lips were trembling slightly.

It was also evident to Harvey, and when he addressed her, "Woo . . . man, come here," and she complied, he took her hand, and gazing into her eyes, he said, "Would you like to go home?"

Before she had time to reply, Daniel's voice broke in loud and harsh: "Home? She's just come." And he went quickly to her, took her by the shoulders and pressed her down on the couch, saying, "You've come for the wedding," then glanced up at the scowling face and added, "You've both come for the wedding and for the wedding you will stay. You're my guests, and"—he looked across at his two sons—"Don's and Joe's guests. Am I right?"

And together they said, "Yes, certainly."

Flo put out her hand towards Daniel, saying, "It's all right; I'm all right. Winnie's dressing; she'll be down shortly."

"Oh, well; in the meantime we'll have some coffee, it's too early for the hard stuff, at least for me. What about you?" He looked towards Harvey who, smiling, replied, "Me too. Coffee will be fine."

"Well, excuse me for a minute; I'll go and tell Maggie. You haven't seen her yet, have you?"

"No; nor Stephen."

"Oh well, we'll have to do a tour. There's plenty of time before the big show starts, although I think, Don, you'd better get outside and see how things are going in the marquee."

And so it was that Joe was left alone with them and, after a moment, looking at the man who was still standing at the head of the couch, he said, "Come and sit down; you look too big even for me."

With a slight nod Harvey took his seat on the couch beside Flo and immediately put his arm around her shoulders, drawing her tightly towards him, and as if he knew he had a friend in Joe, he said to her, "A bad time up there?"

And lying with a smile, she answered, "No, no, not really. But you know, as I told you, we've never agreed, not since I first lisped her name and called her Win instead of Winifred. I was three and she ten when she first boxed my ears. But I was six and she thirteen when I first hit her with the coal shovel. Since then our war has just been verbal."

"What a pity"—Joe, sitting opposite to them was laughing now—"because, believe it or not, Aunt Flo . . ." he now leant towards her and, his voice a whisper, he said, "you're not the only one who would like to use a coal shovel at times." Then straightening up and in a more sombre tone, he asked, "I can tell you seriously, at least, I should say, I can't tell you what life is going to be like once her favourite lad walks back down the aisle today because, as you only too well know, Aunt Flo, he's all she's lived for for years."

"Yes, I'm aware of that. But what puzzles me is how she came to approve of the marriage in the first place."

"Well, to be truthful"—Joe's voice sank—"Dad manoeuvred it."

"And she let him?"

"Well, it was a case of between the devil and the deep sea. You know Dad's got a cousin in America. Well, he's succeeded in much the same business as Dad's, only in a much bigger way, and two years or so ago Dad asked him to find a place for Don. At the same time . . ." He hesitated now and glanced towards the flowers in the hearth, then passed one lip over the other before turning back to them again and saying, "Well, in some way he found out that Annette was sweet on Don . . ."

"But she must have been still a schoolgirl, still at the convent."

"Yes, she was a schoolgirl of nearly eighteen, Aunt Flo. She could have gone on to college—I think she wanted to be a teacher—but apparently she wanted Don more, and so Mam had to decide whether she would have her son in America or ten miles away in Hazel Cottage in Northumberland. So, with bad grace she plumped for the latter."

"Ten miles away! And she still can't drive. I wonder she allowed that."

"Oh, she has Bill to take her all over the place. Still, it's not on the doorstep exactly. Again, it was Dad's doing."

As Joe pulled a face, Flo said, "No wonder she's on a high key . . ."

"And my appearance hasn't, I'm sure, helped matters," said Harvey.

"Oh, I don't know so much." Joe grinned at Harvey now, saying, "You've acted as a diversion."

"Like a red light depicting a road up, in this case black. Never mind." He squeezed Flo to him. "What I'll do is imagine I'm in court and she is the prosecuting counsel and I'm defending a lone woman"—he again pressed Flo to him—"who is not only beautiful, but kind and understanding. But her main attraction for me is she is the best secretary in the business."

They were laughing when Maggie brought the coffee in. She showed no reaction. They were again laughing when Stephen came into the room, and he, seeing the visitor, exclaimed, "Oh! you *are* a big black man." And Harvey, knowing all about Stephen's condition, replied, "And aren't *you* a big white man, and a fine looking one into the bargain."

They were still laughing when, in a group, they inspected the marquee with its pink cord carpet and its garlands of flowers looped from stanchion to stanchion . . . But their laughter and chatter dwindled away when Winifred appeared in the doorway, looking like a very overblown flower herself.

It should happen that Harvey was nearest to her, six steps from her, and when nobody moved or spoke he covered the distance and, standing in front of her, he held out his hand, and in a cultured tone, the like of which she had never heard in all her years in Fellburn, said, "I must apologise, Mrs. Coulson, for intruding on this your special day." Then, his deep voice dropping to a level that only she could hear, he added, "If you find my presence embarrassing I will take my leave, because I do not wish that you be upset, especially today."

Her lids were blinking rapidly. To the side, she took in Flo, her face straight, her eyes bearing a threat that she could not ignore. And yet, even if there had been no threat she would have found it difficult to order this unusual creature to leave. Such was her make-up that she was asking herself: how had their Flo come to be taken up by a man such as this, even if he was black, because there was something about him, not only the size of him and his looks, and that voice of his, there was just something. And she wasn't surprised when she heard herself say, "I . . . I am not in the least embarrassed. Why should I be?"

When her hand was taken and firmly but gently shaken, she could not put a name to this new feeling that she had for her sister, for she had never been jealous of her in her whole life . . .

Following the visit to the marquee a feeling of gaiety seemed to pervade the whole house.

It was just turned twelve o'clock when Don, fully dressed for the fray except for his grey topper, ran out of the side door and around the end of the house towards Joe's cottage. It was as he passed one of the small windows, which were original to the cottage, that he stepped back and his head drooped to the side, for there, kneeling by a chair, and obviously praying, was Joe.

Either Joe became aware of a shadow at the window or he sensed someone's presence, for he raised his head quickly, and they stared at each other for a moment.

On entering the room Don said quietly, "You worried about something, Joe?"

"No, no."

"But you were . . . well . . ."

"Yes, praying. Don't you ever pray?"

"Never in the middle of the day. You're sure there's nothing wrong? Anyway, you haven't been to church lately. You'll have the sleuths after you; or at least Father Cody."

"Well, if you want to know, young 'un, I was just asking that . . . well, that you'd both be happy."

"Oh, Joe." There was a break in Don's voice and impulsively he put his arms around his brother, for he thought of him as his brother in all ways, and Joe held him too before pushing him off and saying, "What do you want in this neck of the woods, anyway?"

"I . . . I just want to phone Annette, have a word with her, see how she feels, and I couldn't do it from the house, could I?"

"Go ahead." Joe thumbed towards the adjoining room, which he used as an office, and he waited until Don had entered it before he himself turned about and went into his bedroom. And there he stood with his back to the door, while his head drooped on to his chest.

In the office Don was saying, "Oh, Sarah? It's me. Could you get Miss Annette to the phone for a minute?"

"Oh, Mr. Don"—the voice came at him in a whisper—"she's getting dressed. Oh, and here's Mrs. Allison."

"Hello! Who is it? Oh, Don, what on earth do you want? You know it's unlucky to have contact in any way before your wedding."

"I thought it was only if we came face to face. Come on, Mother-in-law to be, just let me have a word."

"You're not thinking of jilting her, are you?"

He held the phone away from his face, grinning widely now. Fancy Ma Allison making a joke. His laugh was high as he said, "That's what I want to tell her. Come on, let me have a word with her."

"It isn't right; it's unlucky."

"Nothing's unlucky today."

There was a pause. He heard the murmur of distant voices, then there she was.

"Oh, Don, anything wrong?"

"Not a thing in the world, darling. I . . . I just wanted to know how you felt?"

"Oh, terrified, shaking, longing. Oh, Don, I can't believe we're nearly there." Her voice was low now.

"Another hour and I'll see you coming down the aisle."

"I love you. I love you very much."

"I don't only love you, I adore you."

"Eeh! You'll have to go to confession." There was a tinkle of laughter at the other end. "False idols."

"Oh, yes, false idols, but an adorable idol. All right, all right, I'll let you go. Goodbye, my love. No, not goodbye; *au revoir.*"

He put the phone down and stood for a moment staring ahead. The next hour was going to be the longest in his life. It would be the longest in both their lives.

FOUR

The Nuptial Mass was over. They were married. They were one. The hour that had seemed to have been an eternity was finally at an end. They had taken Communion. They had listened to Father Ramshaw's kindly words. The choir had burst its lungs in song; the young boy soprano had trilled so sweetly he had brought tears to many eyes. And they had just signed their names in the register: Annette Allison had become Annette Coulson.

They had looked at each other and the relief on their faces could have been painful to a keen observer. But everything was bustle.

The organ was soaring as they left the vestry and walked towards the two front rows of pews. Annette's mother was crying openly, but Winifred Coulson's eyes were dry and her plump face was pasty white, and it appeared that Daniel had to press her forward into and up the aisle and then to mingle with the crowding guests outside the church.

The photographer soon seemed to take control, endeavouring to line up the bride and bridegroom, with the close relations on either side; the best man Joe, and the two bridesmaids, Annette's school friends Jessica Bowbent and Irene Shilton, both hanging on to Joe's arms while they giggled and each hoping secretly that one day she would be standing there with Joe as today Annette was standing with Don.

The usual groupings had then been assembled and photographed when Daniel, who had been standing with Harvey, surprised everyone by crying out. "One more! Come on, let's have our men now. What do you say, Harvey?" And to the further surprise of everyone he arranged himself and Joe on either side of Harvey, so, in his mind, pre-empting the guests from making assumptions, or perhaps making them wonder all the more who or what this black man was.

And they *did* wonder about him, but they were not to know who he really was until almost an hour later when the toasts were being drunk and Daniel, with the devil in him, raised his glass to toast the happy couple and ended by saying, "I know they'll be the first ones to say they hope that the next wedding from this house will be that of my sister-in-law and her fiancé." And with this he indicated Harvey, who was sitting three chairs away from him on the top table. Then leaning forward, he looked along the row in the other direction to where sat Father Ramshaw, and he said, "Would you marry them, Father?" And the priest came back jovially, "Marry them? Of course, I'll marry them. I'd marry a Hallelujah to a Jew if it meant I could get them into the church."

A great roar of laughter arose. But Winifred did not join in; nor did Joe, because he was thinking: that wasn't very kind of you, Dad. She's suffering and you know it. But then, perhaps it was Daniel's way of being kind, a way of staunching the bleeding from the knife-thrust that was piercing her.

It was his turn to stand now, and what he said was to the point: he didn't aim to be funny. He said frankly that everyone in the room knew there was no blood-bond between Don and himself, but had they been born Siamese twins they could not have been closer. And while he was on the subject he would like to thank the man he called Father, and the woman he called Mother, for their care of him over the past twenty-five years. Lastly, he turned towards the bride and groom and, raising his glass, said, "To the two people I love most in the world."

It had been an unusual speech for a best man, with nothing amusing about it, not even one joke. There was applause but it was sober applause, accompanied by some shaking of heads here and there.

He was a strange fellow, really, was Joe Coulson, the sort of man you couldn't get to the bottom of. An excellent accountant; and always courteous and kindly, yet at the same time deep. Yes, that was the word for him: deep.

But of course this often happened with adopted children and it was understandable, for you never knew from where they sprang . . .

The bride and bridegroom were getting changed: in separate rooms, of course. They were leaving at five o'clock to catch a train from Newcastle, which would begin the journey for their honeymoon in Italy and three whole weeks together.

When Don emerged from his room he wasn't surprised to see his mother standing at her bedroom door, talking to one of the guests. Others were milling about on the landing and the stairs, and the house was filled with laughter and chatter. They must have overflowed from the marquee. On the sight of him, Winifred said to the guest, "Excuse me," and, holding her hand out towards her son, she said, "Just a moment, dear." Her voice was high, bright, like that of an ordinary mother wanting to say a last farewell to her son in private. But once she had drawn him into the room and closed the door she stood away from him, her hands, gripping each other, pressed into the moulds of flesh at her breast. "You would have gone without a word to me, a private word."

"No, no, I wouldn't, Mother. I meant to come."

"No, you didn't. No, you didn't. Do you know this is the end?"

"Oh, please. Please. Don't spoil this day," Don said, closing his eyes for a moment. But when he opened them she was standing close to him, her breath like a hot moist wind on his face as she said, "I mightn't be here when you come back. I don't think I'll be able to stand it. I could be dead."

"For God's sake! Mother." His tone was sharp; and when her head began to bob in agitation, he ground out, "Don't start. For God's sake! Mother, don't start that!"

"Oh! Oh! You've never used that tone to me before. It's happening already. Why do I have to go through all this? What have I done to deserve it . . . ? Oh! Don. Don."

Again he found himself in her embrace. But he couldn't bring himself to put his arms about her; he was repulsed by her nearness, and this was a new feeling. Putting his hands on her shoulders, he pressed her almost roughly from him, saying, "Look, you must try to be sensible about this: I am married now; I'm starting a new life of my own. Can't you understand?"

"Yes, yes, I understand. I've lost you already."

"You haven't lost me yet, but you're going the right way about it. I love you. You're my mother."

"You love me?" Her voice was soft. "You really do love me, Don?"

"Yes. Yes." He moved his hands on her shoulders as if to shake her, but her body didn't respond.

She stared into his face, whimpering now. "Promise you'll love me always? You'll keep some love for me? Promise?"

He had the desire to turn about and flee from her, from the house and everyone in it. Except for Annette. In his mind he had Annette by the hand running. But he heard himself say quietly, "I promise. Now I must go."

"Kiss me."

Slowly he leant towards her to put his lips on her cheek, only again to be enveloped in her embrace. But now her open mouth was covering his, his slim body pressed into her flesh.

A moment later he managed to stagger from the room; although he didn't go straight downstairs but into the bathroom, and there, locking the door, he bent over the basin and sluiced his face with cold water. His whole body was shaking. She was mad. She must be. He sluiced his mouth with a handful of water and rubbed his lips; then he dried his face, wiped the drops of water from the front of his suit, and in an effort to compose himself he drew in a number of deep breaths before leaving the bathroom.

At the head of the stairs there stood his father.

"I was coming for you. Where have you been? Annette's downstairs waiting. What's wrong?"

"Nothing. Nothing."

Daniel looked along the corridor, then said quietly, "Your last goodbye?"

Don drew in a long slow breath before he said, "Yes, Dad, my last goodbye."

"Well, lad, it's over; the cord's severed. And keep it like that. You understand?"

"Yes, yes, I understand." They looked at each other as might have two men of similar age and experience. "Come on then." Daniel took him by the elbow and led him down the stairs and into the crowded hall, where everyone was talking at once; and then they all spilled out on to the drive.

And now Annette was being hugged by her mother; then her father who, seeming to find difficulty in unbending his stiff body, kissed her first on one cheek then on the other, then characteristically said, "God go with you, child."

That there were two people missing from the crowd wasn't noticed in the excitement: the bridegroom's mother and Don's brother, Stephen. Stephen had had another accident, which would not have been generally known; in any case he was now waving from the upper window, and quite happily, because his father had promised him he could come down and watch the dancing on the lawn later on that night. Perhaps only Daniel, Joe, Flo and Don himself were aware of Winifred's absence.

Don and Annette were in the car now. Daniel and Joe were at one window, Flo at the other, all talking together: "Mind how you go."

"Make it a good life, lad." This was from Daniel.

"I'll have the house well warmed for you," from Joe.

"Thanks," they both said together, then turned their heads to the other window where Flo, her hand extended, gripped Annette's as she said softly, "Love each other."

They were both too full to make any remark on this; and now, as Don turned the ignition key and the car throbbed into life, Daniel's and Joe's heads disappeared from the window and their place was taken by Father Ramshaw's, crying now above the noise of the engine, "Being me, I'll have to have the last word. God bless you both." And with a mock serious expression on his face he now cried, "If you should drop in on the Pope, give him me kind regards. And look, will you tell him on the quiet that I have a curate that would suit him down to the ground as a first secretary. I'll send him off any time; he's just got to say the word."

They both laughed loudly and Annette said, "I'll do that, Father, with pleasure."

"Goodbye. Goodbye."

"Goodbye. Goodbye."

The voices sent the car spurting forward, and with the sound and feeling of a thump on the back of it Don said, "I bet they've hung something on there. Anyway, we'll stop along the road and see."

Annette now turned and looked through the back window, saying, "They're running down the drive."

"They can run, darling, they can all run, but they'll never catch us." He glanced at her, his eyes full of love. "We're free. Do you realise that, sweetheart? We're free."

"Oh, yes, yes, and in so many ways. Oh, darling, no more worry, no more fear of what might happen if and when . . ."

He lifted one hand from the wheel and, gripping hers, he pulled it swiftly to his lips.

They were nearing the gates that led into the narrow side road as Annette once more turned and looked through the back window, crying now, "There's Joe and your Dad. They're running side by side."

And these were the last words she remembered speaking. She saw the pantechnicon. It was like a tower falling on top of them, yet not falling but lifting them in the air, and their screams sounded to her ears like those of people on the high-flyer just before the car went over and into the dip, and she knew they were going into the dip, because the car had become a great horse, a flying horse. It mounted the railings bordering the fields, then hurtled into the sky, straight into it.

And all was quiet.

FIVE

It was half-past twelve, early on the Sunday morning. At the hospital, Daniel and Joe were seated at one side of a small table, Flo at the other. At another table sat Janet and James Allison, she leaning forward, her elbows on the table, but he sitting bolt upright, yet with his eyes closed. He could have been dozing, except that every now and again he would look with annoyance towards Winifred, who was pacing the room in the clear area in front of the doorway, sixteen steps each way.

No-one could have said when she had first started pacing, though all could have recounted how she had screamed at Daniel when he attempted to lead her by the arm to a chair, and then almost knocked Flo to the ground with that sharp flick of her forearm, with which she was adept; and again when Joe had said, "Please, Mother, you're not going to help yourself like this," that she actually bared her teeth at him.

The only one who hadn't approached her as yet was Harvey. It was he who now entered the room with a tray of tea, which he placed on a table, then handed a cup to each person. And when there were two cups left on the tray he picked one up, turned and, walking slowly towards Winifred, he blocked her pacing by standing in front of her and holding the cup towards her. For a moment he thought she was going to dash it from his hand. Then surprisingly she not only took the cup from him, but sat down in the nearest chair as if a crisis had been passed.

The tension seemed to seep from the room. But only for a moment, for they had barely started to drink their tea when the door opened and a night nurse appeared and, looking towards Mr. and Mrs. Allison and mentioning them by name, she said, "Would you like to come and see your daughter now? She has come round. But you may stay only a moment or so."

They both sprang from their chairs as if activated by the same wires, and as the nurse held open the door for them, Winifred caught at her arm, saying, "My son?" And to this the nurse replied, "He is still in the theatre, Mrs. Coulson. The doctor will see you as soon as the operation is over. Don't worry."

After the door had closed on the nurse, Winifred's pacing began again. But now she was muttering, "Don't worry. Don't worry. Stupid individuals! Don't worry. Don't worry." The words were emerging through closed teeth, and as her voice rose Daniel got swiftly up from the seat and, confronting her, gripped her by the shoulders and hissed at her, "That's enough, woman! Stop it! And try to forget for a moment that you're the only one concerned." And with a none too gentle push he thrust her down into a chair, stood over her, his face almost touching hers, and growled, "You start any of your tantrums here and by God! I'll slap your face until you can't see. Do you hear me?"

This was the second time within a week that he had threatened to slap her face, and as she glared back into his eyes, so deep was her hatred of him he could almost smell it and he straightened up and gasped as if he had just been throttled, then turned to where Joe and Harvey were standing side by side as if they had been ready to intervene and prevent him from doing her an injury.

After a moment they all sat down again and Flo, looking from one to the other, said quietly, "Here, drink your tea. It's getting cold." And like obedient children, the men took up their cups and drank from them.

Ten minutes or so later, the door opened and two men entered the room and introduced themselves as Mr. Richardson, the surgeon and Doctor Walters. Both men looked exhausted, particularly the surgeon, a man with a natural tan which, at that moment, looked as if it had faded.

Winifred sprang from her seat and ran towards them, and he patted her arm, saying, "It's all right. It's all right."

"How is he? My son, how is he?"

"Sit down. Sit down."

She shook her head impatiently and remained standing, and Mr. Richardson looked from her to the other woman and the three men and, his eyes resting on Daniel, he said quietly, "It's been rather a long job."

"Will . . . will he be all right?"

"I have to say that remains to be seen; he's badly injured."

"Will he live?" It was a demand from Winifred.

And now looking her straight in the face, he said, "That too remains to be seen, Mrs. Coulson." His voice was terse now. "One thing I must make clear"—he was again looking at Daniel—"he has lost the use of his legs. The spine is injured in the lumbar region. But that might not have been so serious except that one lung was crushed and his liver damaged. The latter, I'm afraid, could have serious consequences. However, it is very early days yet. Now, I would advise you all to go home and rest. There'll be time enough later on to . . ."

"I'm not going home. I must see him. I will sit with him."

"I'm afraid you won't, not tonight, Mrs. Coulson." The surgeon's tone was definite. "This is a very crucial time. Come back in the morning and we'll take it from there. But at the moment it's imperative that he is not disturbed in any way."

It appeared as if Winifred's body was about to expand to bursting point: her breasts heaved and her cheeks swelled as if she was holding her breath.

It was Flo's voice that seemed to prick the balloon, as she asked, "How is Annette . . . his wife?"

It was Doctor Walters who answered Flo. "Oh, she's been very, very lucky," he said; "a broken arm, bruised ribs and slight concussion. It's amazing how she escaped so lightly. She'll be all right. Of course she too needs rest and quiet. So, as Mr. Richardson has said, it would be wise if you all went home and got a little rest yourselves. As for us," he inclined his head towards his colleague, "we'll be glad to get to bed too. I'm sure you understand that."

"Yes, yes of course." It was Joe speaking. "We'll . . . we'll do as you suggest, Doctor. And . . . and thank you very much."

"Oh, yes, yes." It was as if Joe's words had reminded Daniel of the courtesy expected of him, and his voice was hesitant as he went on. "I . . . we're all a little dazed. It . . . it was so sudden. The wedding. They had just left the house. It seems impossible."

Mr. Richardson nodded before coming out with the platitude: "These things happen. We don't know why. But there's always hope. I'll say goodnight now." He inclined his head to Daniel, then went out, followed by Doctor Walters.

With the exception of Winifred, they all made ready to go; she remained standing, stiffly staring straight ahead. After glancing at her, Daniel walked past her and out of the room. Flo too glanced at her; she even paused in front of her before walking on.

It was Joe who stopped and said quietly, "Come on, Mother; I'll drive you back first thing in the morning." For a moment it looked as if she was determined to remain standing where she was, but when she glanced behind her at the black man standing a few feet from her and seemingly not intending to move until she did, she thrust her body forward, at the same time throwing off Joe's hand from her elbow.

Joe exchanged a glance with Harvey; then together, they followed her out of the room.

It was two o'clock in the morning when they reached home, and Winifred, still without speaking a word, made straight for her room. And a stunned feeling seemed to have descended upon the others too as they sipped at the hot drinks supplied by Maggie who, without complaint at the late hour, had set about preparing rooms for Flo and Harvey.

With the exception of Stephen, everyone was astir before eight o'clock that morning. Stephen had been heavily sedated the night before. Apparently he had witnessed the accident from his attic room and he had screamed and wailed and had become so obstreperous that the doctor had to be called to attend to him.

Maggie had been up since six o'clock. She had cooked a breakfast which no-one wanted. She was now in her sitting-room facing Daniel. Her eyes were red and swollen, her voice broken, as she said, "He didn't escape after all, did he?"

Daniel swallowed deeply before he replied, "No, he didn't escape."

"But if he's as bad as you say, she could lose him yet. We could all lose him, but I think I'd rather see him dead than helpless, because then he'd be back to square one, or even beyond that."

"Oh no! by God, he won't. They've got their own house, and, as I understand it, Annette hasn't been injured much, and she'll look after him. And there's always nurses. No, by God! Maggie, that's one thing I'll see to: in some way they've got to be on their own. She might never be off their doorstep but at least they'll be in their own home. And he'll have a wife."

She stared at him before turning away and going to the chest of drawers, from which she took out a clean apron. Putting it on, she said, "Will you all be back for lunch?"

"I doubt it," he answered.

"Will Flo and Mr. Rochester be staying on?"

"I don't know . . . What do you think of him? Were you surprised to see who she had become engaged to?"

"Perhaps at first, but later, no. I should imagine there's many a woman would be glad to link up with a fellow like that, an educated one an' all, and he so good looking. But then aren't they all? I've never seen an ugly man. Have you?"

"Come to think of it, no, not really. Anyway, we're both of the same mind: I think she's done well for herself, no matter what his colour is. Now, I must be off." He stood for a moment gazing at her; then, taking a step forward, he thrust his arms about her, and hers went around him, and they held each other close; and with his head buried in her shoulder, he muttered,

"Oh, Maggie, I'm heart-broken, not only for meself but for him. I dread to think what's in the future."

Pressing him from her, she rubbed the tears from her cheeks with the side of her finger before saying, "You can do nothing about that. Yesterday should prove that. Man proposes but God disposes. Go on now; and phone me from the hospital, will you?"

He nodded at her but said nothing more and went out.

In the hall Flo and Harvey were already standing waiting with Joe, and on seeing him, Flo walked quickly towards him, saying, "I've tried to speak to her but she won't open her mouth."

"Where is she?"

"In the breakfast-room drinking a cup of tea; she hasn't eaten a thing."

"Well, that won't hurt her." His voice was grim. "She's got plenty of fat to live on. Go and fetch her. Tell her we're ready and waiting."

"She's been ready and waiting for the past hour or more." Flo sounded somewhat upset at Daniel's attitude, but did his bidding.

Tension seemed to be rising, and so Joe turned to Harvey and asked, "Will you be going back today?"

"It isn't at all necessary. We're both on a week's holiday; we could stay on if we could be of any help." He now looked at Daniel, and Daniel replied simply, "You're welcome to stay, at any time. I'll leave it to you."

Flo now emerged from the corridor, followed by Winifred, who passed them all as if they were invisible and walked out of the house and took her seat in the car waiting in the drive; and as she settled herself she tucked the skirt of her coat under her calf as if preventing it from coming in contact with her husband's leg.

Daniel averted his eyes from the broken railings as they went through the gate into the road, and he did not utter a word until they were nearing the hospital. Then, as if he were whispering to someone, he said, "Don't you give us a show of hysterics in here this morning, because if you do I'll go one better: there's a simple cure for hysterics, you know."

She gave him no immediate answer; in fact, not until he had pulled into a line of cars in the hospital forecourt did she speak, and then, her hand on the door, she said grimly, "I'll see my day with you. *Oh yes, I will.*" To which, he replied, "We'll see our day with each other, and pray God it will be soon."

As she marched towards the hospital door, he turned to where the others were getting out of their car, and together they entered the reception area to hear Winifred proclaiming in no small voice: "I want to see Doctor Richardson," and the receptionist answering, "I'm sorry, but *Mr.* Richardson's operating at the moment, but if you take a seat in the waiting-room, I'll ask another doctor to attend to you."

Daniel was standing at the desk now, and he cut in on what his wife was about to say by asking, "Can you tell us which ward my son is in? You wouldn't have been here earlier; he was operated on. Coulson is the name."

"Yes, yes"—the receptionist nodded at him—"I know, but as I've said, if you would take a seat in the waiting-room, I'll get someone to attend to you."

"Thank you."

He turned away, followed by Joe, Flo and Harvey, although Winifred remained standing at the desk for a full minute before following them.

The waiting-room was busier than when they had left it earlier that morning; there were now at least a dozen people present, so that only three seats were vacant. What was more, two small children were scampering after each other around the tables.

After one glance, Winifred went back into the corridor and, after a quick exchange of glances between Daniel and Joe, the latter followed her.

Harvey now led Flo to a seat and sat down beside her, while Daniel stood near the door, and they each became aware of the silence that had fallen on the room. A white woman with a black man. And what a black man! And both dressed up to the nines, not like those mixed couples you might find in Bog's End who had to brave the community, these two were brazen. In some such way did the atmosphere emanate from the adults who, with the exception of a youth and a man, were all women.

But they had hardly been seated a few minutes when the door was pushed open and Joe said, "Dad," then beckoned towards Flo and Harvey. And there they were, all in the corridor again, standing before a young doctor who was saying, "Mr. Richardson would like to see you. He'll be free in about half an hour. In the meantime you may see the patient, but only for a moment or so. In any case, Mr. Coulson has not yet recovered consciousness. It will be some time before he does. If you will come this way. And . . . and just two at a time, please."

He led them along a corridor, then another, and into a passageway leading to a ward where there was a great deal of activity and the clatter of dishes on a food trolley being wheeled from the ward. The young doctor stopped outside a door. Then nodding first to Daniel, then to Winifred, he gently pushed the door open and they went inside.

Slowly Daniel walked up by one side of the bed and looked down on his son, who might have already been dead, so drained was he of colour. There was a tube inserted into one nostril, there were tubes in his arms, there was a cradle over his legs.

Daniel closed his eyes for a moment: his throat was constricted as his mind was yelling, "His legs! His legs!" He opened his eyes to a sound of a gasp and he looked across the bed at his wife. Her face was screwed up in anguish, the tears dripping from her chin. He heard her moan.

A nurse whom he hadn't noticed seemed to appear from nowhere and, touching Winifred gently on the arm, said, "Come. Come, please."

Winifred jerked the hand aside, muttering now, "I want to stay. I can sit by him."

"Doctor says . . ."

"I'm his mother!" She almost hissed the words into the nurse's face, and the nurse glanced across the bed towards Daniel as if in appeal. In answer to it he moved down by the side of the bed and Winifred stepped quickly away. She made for the door, muttering, "I want to see the specialist."

Not the doctor, not the surgeon, but the specialist.

Daniel made a small motion of his head, then asked quietly of the nurse, "When . . . when do you think he'll come round?"

To this she answered, "I don't know . . . there's no knowing."

He now asked, "Which ward is his wife in? Mrs. Coulson?"

"Oh, I think she's upstairs on the next floor."

"Thank you."

A few minutes later when he was ushered into a side ward, there, to his surprise, he saw Annette propped up in bed. Her eyes were open and as he neared her he could see that one of her arms was in plaster and that the right side of her face was discoloured, as if she had been punched.

Her voice was small as she said, "Dad."

"Oh, hinny. Oh my dear, my dear." He lifted her other hand from the counterpane and stroked it. And now she said, "Don?" then again, "Don? Is he very . . . very bad? They . . . they won't . . . tell me."

He swallowed some saliva before he lied, saying, "He'll . . . he'll be all right. I . . . I understand his legs were hurt. He's not quite round yet, but he'll be all right. You'll see."

The nurse who had followed him into the ward pushed a chair towards him, and he nodded his thanks to her and sat down. Still holding the limp hand, he said, "Oh, don't, my dear. Don't cry."

"We . . . we were . . ."

"Yes, dear?"

"Esca . . . ping."

"Oh, yes, yes, you were escaping. And you will again, dear. You will again. Never you worry."

"Why Dad? Oh, why?" The last word, dragged out on a higher note, acted as a signal to the nurse, for she motioned Daniel to his feet, saying to Annette: "There now. There now. You need to sleep again. I'll bring you a drink and then you'll rest. You'll feel better later."

Daniel walked backwards from the bed. Just a few hours ago she had been a bride, a beautiful bride, and now she looked like someone who had inadvertently stepped into a boxing ring and got the worst of it.

He waited in the corridor until the nurse came out of the ward, then he asked quietly, "How bad is she, nurse?"

"Surprisingly, she's got off very lightly. She's bruised all over, naturally, but the only bone broken is in her arm. She's had a miraculous escape, whereas her husband, I understand, is in a pretty bad way. You are . . . her father?"

"Her father-in-law."

"Oh, then he is your son?"

"Yes, yes, he is my . . ." But he found he couldn't complete the sentence, and when the nurse said, "It's a tragedy, isn't it? Just married for a matter of hours, and just starting their honeymoon. It's incredible the things that happen."

When later he emerged from the toilet his eyes were red but he looked more composed. And it was as he was making his way back to the waiting-room that he almost bumped into the surgeon.

"Oh, there you are, Mr. Coulson. I was wanting a word with you."

"Good morning, Mr. Richardson. I've just been to see my daughter-in-law."

"Oh yes, yes. Now, she's been lucky. It's amazing how lightly she got off. Would you like to come into my office for a moment?"

They were in the small room now and the surgeon, pointing to a chair, said, "Sit down a moment." Then, taking his seat behind a long desk, he joined his hands on top of a clean blotting pad and, leaning slightly over them, he said, "I'm afraid, Mr. Coulson, I'll have to ask you to speak firmly to your wife with regard to her visits to her son, at least for the next few days until we can ascertain fully the extent of the damage. You know, as I pointed out to you, that he is unlikely to walk again, and that his liver has been damaged too. Quite candidly he's lucky to be alive, if one can put it that way. Anyway, together with the liver problem he's likely to be incontinent. And added to this, we had to take away part of his lung."

Now he paused and, putting his hand out, he tapped the edge of the blotter, as if it were in sympathetic contact with Daniel, saying, "I know that sounds terrible enough, but there could be more. These are physical problems which, in one way or another, can be treated, but until he is fully conscious, to put it candidly, we won't know what has happened in here." He now tapped his forehead. "The point is, you have to ask yourself if you would rather see him dead and out of all the coming misery, or would you have him live, if only to be nursed for the rest of his life. And how long that will be . . . well, I am not God and I can't put a time to it. We don't know if there is damage to the brain, although we do know his skull was slightly cracked. And the same question will apply to him, you know, when he knows about his condition: will he want to go on living? The will is a mighty force both ways, but we must just wait for time to answer that question. And, as I pointed out, the next few days will be crucial: so I must insist that he be put under no undue strain, for I hold the theory that many a patient who is apparently unconscious can imbibe the emotions of those around him. And your wife . . . well, you'll know her better than anyone else, but she does seem to be a very highly strung lady. Am I right?"

Daniel stared at the surgeon for a moment before he said, "Yes, you're right, only too right. The fact is, he's all she's lived for for years. And to put it plainly, she was already in a state yesterday, feeling she had lost him through marriage. But now, if anything was to happen to him . . . Oh—" he waved his hand in front of his face as if he were flicking off a fly—"it's all too complicated. But I will see that her visits are kept short."

Mr. Richardson rose from his seat, saying, "Thank you. I shall leave word that only you and she are to be admitted to see him during the next day or so, and then for a matter of minutes only. But"—he shrugged his shoulders —"she seems determined that she's going to sit with him. You *will* impress upon her that this would not be for his good at the moment, won't you?"

"I'll do that." But even as he spoke he had a mental picture of the scene being enacted as he told her she was to carry out the surgeon's orders, or else. It was the "or else" part that made him visibly shudder, for he doubted that, were she to act up again, he'd be able to keep his hands off her.

In a kindly tone, Mr. Richardson now said, "And you, Mr. Coulson, I won't tell you not to worry, because that would be pointless, but you can rest assured we'll do everything in our power to bring him round; and when, or if, that is accomplished, to help him to accept the life ahead."

"Thank you. Thank you very much indeed."

They parted in the corridor; but there was no need for Daniel to go into the waiting-room to collect Winifred, for there she was standing at the reception desk. And what she had to say was drawing the attention not only of those behind the desk but also of other people in the hall.

"I will take this matter further. I shall write to the Medical Board. Other people can sit with patients, with their family. *Who is he*, anyway?"

Daniel's voice was scarcely above a whisper but the words came out of his mouth like iron filings as he said, "Only the man who saved your beloved son. Your son. Nobody else's. And nobody else is feeling pain or worry, only you. Have you been to see Annette? No. No. Now look! Get yourself outside."

After casting a ferocious glance at the staring faces, she stamped out of the building. And as she went towards the car she turned her head to look at him, hissing, "You! to show me up."

"Nobody can show you up, woman, because you're an expert at showing yourself up. Always have been. Now get into the car."

He had taken his seat and started the engine, and she still stood there, until the sound of his engaging the gears drove her to drag open the door and to drop like a heavy sack on to the seat.

Again no word was exchanged during the journey, but he had hardly drawn the car to a stop before she thrust open the door and swung herself out. And again he was surprised that with her weight she could still be so light on her feet, especially so now when she ran across the drive as a young woman might.

Joe had already arrived, and he walked quickly towards Daniel's car and, bending down he said, "Go easy on her, else . . . well."

"Or else what?"

As Daniel got out of the car Joe replied, "I would call the doctor if I were you. She can't go on like this or something will snap."

"It snapped a long time ago, Joe." Daniel's voice sounded weary.

"Yes, in one way, but this is different. She's never had to tackle anything like this before."

"None of us have had to tackle anything like this before."

"No; you're right, you're right there. But will I do it? Will I phone the doctor?"

"Yes, phone him. Not that it'll do any good."

Daniel knew it was too early in the morning to drink but he also knew he must have a stiff whisky before he went up and confronted her with the news that she could not baby-sit her son in the hospital.

He had just thrown off a double whisky when the door opened and a quiet voice said, "Dad."

He turned to see Stephen standing there hesitantly.

Daniel went towards him, saying, "You're down early," but stopped himself adding, "Why, and all by yourself?" Instead, he asked, "Where's everybody?"

"Maggie's in the kitchen, Dad. Lily's gone to church with Bill, and I think"—he paused as he put his head on one side—"Peggie is doing the bathroom. Not mine; I've been good. I have, Dad; I've been good."

"That's a clever fellow." Daniel put his hand on his son's shoulder, saying, "Well, what are you going to do now?"

"I . . . I want to see Joe. I . . . I want to ask him about Don and Annette."

It had been evident to Daniel for a long time that it was Joe whom the lad sought whenever he wanted help with anything, not him, his father. He said, "Well now, I think Joe will be busy, as we've all only just come back from the hospital, so you should . . ."

He was cut off by Stephen, who quickly said, "Don't . . . don't send me back upstairs yet, Dad. Don't; please don't send me back upstairs. I'm . . . I'm sad. I'm sad all over. I . . . I would like to go and see Don. I . . . I saw it happen yesterday. I . . ."

"Yes, I know you did," Daniel sharply interrupted, "and you are upset, but now I want you to keep quiet and be a good fellow. And I promise you this: as soon as Don and Annette are a little better, I'll take you myself to see them in hospital. What about that?"

"You will?"

"Yes, I will. I promise. Just as soon as they are a little better. But you will have to be good. You know what I mean?"

The man-cum-boy hung his head and in an almost childish whimper he said, "Yes, Dad. Yes, I know what you mean. And I will; I will be good."

"Well now, you go back into the kitchen and stay with Maggie while I pop upstairs, and then I'll come down again and we'll have a crack, eh? Or a game of billiards."

"You will, Dad? Billiards with me?"

"Yes; yes, I will. Go on now."

Stephen grinned with pleasure, then turned and at a shambling run made his way towards the kitchen. And Daniel, glancing back towards the decanter on the sideboard, hesitated for a moment before going out and up the stairs.

Rather than tap on his wife's door he called out, "Are you there?"

He waited, and when there was no answer, he opened the door and went in. She had taken off her outdoor things and was sitting at the dressing-table. He had often wondered why she sat so long at the dressing-table, but assumed she was admiring her unlined skin and the lack of grey in her hair. And this had made him wonder too why she didn't concentrate more on getting rid of her surplus fat, because without it she would have been a very presentable woman. Her eating problems, so the doctor had said, came from inward anxieties. And he could say that again—inward anxieties—anxieties with which she had affected the whole family over the years.

He moved no further towards her than the foot of the bed, and there, his hand on a post, he said, "I must have a word with you."

She made no reply, but simply stared at him through the mirror, as she was wont to do whenever she was seated at the dressing-table.

"It's about the hospital visiting," he said. "Mr. Richardson thinks it would be advisable if we make our visits very short for the next few days, just for a minute or two. It'll give Don a better chance . . ."

"A better chance?" As her body moved slowly around on the seat her flesh seemed to flow and ripple. He saw the muscles of her arms undulating under the tight sleeves of her dress. He watched her large breasts sway. On anyone else these motions could have suggested a certain seductiveness, but with Winifred, as he only too well recognised, they were but the signals of a rising rage.

Her words, like her movements, came slow at first. "A better chance?" she said. "A better chance? You're agreeable to giving him a chance? Is your conscience pricking you? You arranged his life: you arranged his marriage; you would have gone to any lengths to take him from me. But getting him married was a sort of legitimate cover-up for your own actions, wasn't it?" Her voice had risen but was not yet at screaming point. "You couldn't bear the thought that I kept him pure, that I saw to it that he didn't follow in your footsteps with your filthy woman."

"Shut up! Shut your mouth!"

The movement that she made now was a spring. She was on her feet and standing at the foot of the bed gripping the other post as if she would twist it and wrench it from its support.

"Don't you ever tell me to shut up! But you listen to me now. If my son dies I'll kill you. Do you hear that? I'll kill you." Her voice had risen to a scream. "You were longing for last night, weren't you, when he'd be defiled, made into a man, like yourself with your dirty whoring."

The blow caught her fully across the mouth; yet she didn't even stagger. Instead, her hands flashed out, and she was tearing at his face and screaming words that he realised were obscene, yet he could hardly believe his ears.

Gripping her throat now, he struggled with her; and as his rising hatred matched hers he would not have known what he might have done next, but for the hands pulling at him, and through a blur of blood he saw the black face close to his own and Joe with his arms tight around Winifred as she lay half-sprawled on the chaise lounge at the foot of the bed.

When Peggie's shocked face appeared in the doorway Joe cried out, "Fetch Maggie!" And it would seem that Maggie was already on the scene, for the next instant she was in the room, although she stopped and stared for a moment at the sight of Daniel, his face streaming with blood from the torn flesh of each cheek.

Turning swiftly to Peggie, she cried, "Get Mrs. Jackson; she's in the garden with Stephen. Then phone the doctor." And to Harvey she said quietly, "Take him out. Get him out," and Daniel allowed himself to be guided from the room. But on the landing they both stopped, surprised by the sight of the priest on the stairhead.

Father Cody was a man in his early thirties. He had the countenance of an ascetic, his tone was clipped, and his voice had no recognisable accent: "I heard the commotion," he said. "I just popped over between Masses to see how the young couple were faring. Dear God! I see you have been fighting. This is not a time for recrimination, I would have thought. Your wife has been suffering of late. Don't you know that? What she needs is comfort. And especially at a time like this. Those two poor innocents yesterday. But you know"—he raised a hand—"they do say the sins of the fathers will be visited on the children, even to the third and fourth generation. Everything in life has to be paid for. God sees to that. Yes, He . . ."

"Get out!" Daniel had pulled himself from Harvey's grasp.

"You wouldn't! You wouldn't dare!" The priest held up both hands.

"Don't take that attitude with me, Daniel Coulson. I am your wife's confessor and at this moment I'm sure she needs my help."

"Look! If you don't want me to help you on your way with my toe in your arse you'll turn about and get out. And I don't want to see you again, not in my house."

Father Cody now cast a glance at Harvey, expecting him to remonstrate with this perturbed individual; but all the black man said, and in a deep voice, was, "I would do what you are told, man, and quick, if I were you."

"You can't intimidate me." Father Cody looked from Harvey to Daniel. But when Daniel, with fists doubled, took a quick step towards him, the priest thought better of his stand and turned abruptly, saying, "God has strange ways of working: He protects His own, you'll see."

"You go to hell, and as far beyond."

The two men remained at the top of the stairs watching the black-coated figure cross the hall and out of the house. And Harvey, now taking Daniel by the arm, said, "Come on. We'll get you cleaned up." Then in an aside that at another time would have raised a laugh, he added, "There's no fear of him going to hell. Did you see him cross himself at the bottom of the stairs?"

The doctor gave Winifred a sedative almost without her realising it, for her rage was still blazing. And when he saw Daniel's face he said, "A tiger might have gone a bit deeper but not much; I'd better give you an injection." Then, later, as he was about to leave, he said, "One of these days she's going to need help, special help. You understand that?"

Daniel understood it only too well and prayed that it would be soon . . .

It was around two o'clock when Father Ramshaw came. The house was quiet, unusually so. He let himself into the hall, then made straight for the kitchen, asking Maggie, "Where's everybody?"

"I think you'll find himself in the study, Father," she said; "the others are in their rooms."

"Well, it's himself I want to see. Have you any tea going?"

"No; but I could have it going any time, Father."

"When you're ready I'll be glad."

He went out, crossed the hall to the far end where the door led into the study and, after tapping on it, he called, "It's me."

Daniel swung his feet from the leather couch and sat up, although he didn't rise to his feet; and the priest stopped in his stride, his mouth dropping into a gape before he said, "Oh, my goodness! no. What brought this about? But need I ask." He sat down on the edge of the couch and, shaking his head, muttered, "Something will have to be done. But what, God only knows. There's always a climax to these things, and your face, I should imagine, could be it. But will it? You're feeling rotten?"

"Not very good, Father. But have you come about your assistant?"

"Oh, yes. Yes." And adopting a severe expression, the priest said, "You've insulted my curate, do you know that? In fact, as far as I can gather you sent him to hell; you actually voiced it." He turned his head to the side, saying, "Oh, the times I've wished I was brave enough to say that." Then he went on quickly, "Don't try to smile; it'll hurt, I can see that." And they looked at each other for a moment in silence before the priest, his tone serious now, murmured, "She must have gone clean mad. What brought it on anyway?"

"She had made a scene in the hospital because she wasn't allowed to sit with Don, and the doctor took me aside and asked me if I would impress upon her that, for the next few days, her visits had to cover minutes not hours, or days and nights as they would if she had her way. And I went in and put it to her quietly. But then"—he sighed now—"she's holding me responsible for the accident. If I hadn't inveigled them into marriage and they hadn't been going away in that car at that special time, none of this would have happened. It's all at my door."

"Well, Daniel, look at it this way: she's right, you know, because on your own saying you brought them together; and you got them married yesterday. Strange, but in a way she's right. Your intentions were good. Oh aye, they were good. You wanted to save the boy from being swallowed whole by her. If ever there was an Oedipus complex in reverse this is it. It's probably the worst case I've known. And I've known a few. It isn't all that rare. Oh no; but a lot of it's hidden. How many women treat their daughters-in-law like dirt? Cause trouble? in fact, separate the couple? I know one who arranged a divorce. Yes, she did; and they were Catholics an' all. She had them separated, hating each other. Then the couple happened to meet by themselves on a street, and in his own words as he told me, he said to his wife, 'I must have been mad to listen to her and put her before you. If you'll only come back I'll tell her where she stands.' And you know, he did, and they had ten years of happy marriage. But it had a strange ending, for the young fellow up and dies and, would you believe it, the two women lived together quite amicably for years afterwards. Can you believe that now? There's nothing so odd as human nature. I see quite a bit of it you know, from the inside, you could say." He paused, rubbing a hand tightly over his clean-shaven cheeks, then said quietly, "One of these days, I fear, she'll have to be put away. You know that? At least for a time. She needs special attention. It'll be for her own good."

Daniel stared at the priest. He was surprised to hear put into words the very thought that had been in his mind for a long time. In his mind, yes, but then he had told himself that you couldn't class anyone to be in need of mental attention just because they had an unnatural passion for their son. Yet, couldn't you? Hadn't it in a way turned her mind?

"I hear Don's in a bad state. By the sound of it I think it would be better if the Lord took him . . ."

"How do you make that out, Father? The surgeon, Mr. Richardson, he didn't give up. What I mean is . . ."

"I know what you mean: where there's life there's hope. But I happen to know Freddie Richardson. I've known the family since I was a lad. I got on to him. I didn't know whether or not it was he who would be seeing to Don, but I sensed he would know about the case, and he said the lad's in a bad way. And I think, Daniel, you've got to face up to that. You'll be able to, I know, but I doubt if she will. You said to me a little while ago that you thought about walking out again and I was for putting you off, and I did put you off. But looking at you now, I wonder if I was giving you the best advice. Sometimes I wish I was nearer to God, then I would know what to do under such circumstances."

Daniel got slowly to his feet, and as he did so he said, "I think you're near enough, Father, as near as anybody can get."

"Oh, come off it. I wasn't implying sainthood or anything like that. I was pointing out my fallibility."

"I know what you were aiming to do, Father, and I'll tell you something now. Perhaps I'm saying this because I don't know if I'm walking or sleeping, but you are the best friend I've got: you know all about me, the bad and the good; and I don't think, whatever I told you, you would turn against me, even if I told you I wanted to finish her off this morning."

"Well, under the circumstances, that was a natural reaction, I'm sure, but you know we must curb such reactions. Yes, don't I know meself that one must curb such reactions." He smiled wryly, then said, "Thank you, Daniel, for calling me your friend. Thank you. Well, now I must be off, but"—and here he wagged his finger at Daniel—"but before I go I must admonish you for insulting my curate and sending him to hell. This has got to stop, you know; I'm the only one who can indulge in that privilege."

A sound that could have been a laugh issued from Daniel and he said, "Well, Father, you keep it up, and keep him out of my hair, for I've never been able to stand him. And today was the last straw."

The priest leant towards him now and, his voice low and a grin on his face, he said, "What annoyed him most was the black fellow daring to tell him to get out. I like that chap, you know. And what a voice! Lovely to hear. And he's too good-looking for his own good. You know that? He caused a stir yesterday, in a nice way you know, surprisingly; yes, in a nice way. People were enquiring about him. As one old faggot said, he talked like a gentleman. Huh! Women! But what would we do without them? One thing I do know, me confessional box would be empty or near so. Well, I'm away. I don't expect to see you at Benediction tonight. My advice to you is to take two double whiskies hot and go to bed and pray—and it'll have to be hard—that face of yours will look a little different in the morning, because what excuse you're going to give for it I don't know. I'll leave you to think that one up. Goodbye, Daniel."

"Goodbye, Father."

He sat down on the couch again. Yes, yes, he'd have to think one up, wouldn't he? But who would he hoodwink? Nobody, not those in the works, or out of it.

Part Two

ONE

$\mathcal{D}$on lay with his eyes fixed on the door, longing for it to open
to see one face, dreading for it to open to see another. How long had he been
here? Years and years; six years it must be, not just six weeks. But it was just
six weeks since the world had exploded.

He lifted one arm slowly from the counterpane and looked at it, then he
lifted the other one. He still had his arms, he still had his head, and he could
think. He still had his sight and his hearing, and he could talk. He had all
these faculties, but of what use were they to him? His body had gone. Well,
not quite; but he had to breathe heavily at times to know that he still had
lungs. And dear God, he knew that he had a bladder and bowels. Oh, that
was shame-making. If only, if only. But he had no legs. Yes, he had. Oh, yes,
he had; his legs were there, he could see his toes sticking up. But what use
were they? Why didn't they take them off? They had taken so much else from
him. Hurry up, Annette. Hurry up. Dear God, don't let Mother come today.
I'd like to see Dad and Joe. Yes, Joe was comforting. He had said yesterday
he was going to try and bring Stephen in just to have a peep.

Just to have a peep. That's what people did. They came in and peeped
and they were gone again. He wished some of them would stay longer. He
wished Annette would stay all day and all night. She did yesterday, at least
nearly all day, and the day before. No, not the day before. His mother had sat
there—he looked to the side of the bed—and she had stroked him and patted
him and whispered to him. That worried him. He was too weak to cope with
his mother. They should keep her out. He would talk to his dad about it.
Dad understood. So did Joe. And, of course, Annette understood. Oh, yes,
yes, Annette understood. He didn't like her people. He had just discovered
he didn't like her people. Her father was pompous and in a way her mother

was stricken with God as much as his was. That was a funny thought: stricken with God. Odd that he could think amusing things, like a short while ago when of a sudden his mind cleared of the fuzz that would constantly float across it and he thought, I'll get up and get dressed. Yes, he had thought that, I'll get up and get dressed. He would never get up and get dressed again, he knew that. *Never.*

He closed his eyes tightly; then appealed to God: don't let me cry. Please! Jesus, don't let me cry. Holy Mary Mother of God, don't let me cry.

"Don. Don."

"Oh! Annette. Oh! darling, I didn't know you were there."

He moved his hand in hers, his fingers clutching weakly at the softness of it. "Oh! my love, I've been longing to see you."

"I've only been gone an hour; I've been down to the surgery. Look they've taken the plaster off my arm. I have to have massage and therapy, but it will soon be all right."

"Only an hour?" He blinked at her.

"Yes, darling, only an hour."

"I'm very muddled, Annette; my mind goes round in circles. Sometimes I can think quite clearly then it is as if a mist blots things out."

"It will pass. You've improved marvellously in the last week. Why, every-body's amazed at the improvement in you."

"Are they?"

"Yes, yes, darling."

"Will I ever get home?"

"Of course you will, sweetheart."

"I mean, to our home?"

"Yes, to our home. It's all ready."

He turned his gaze from her and looked around the white ward, at the flowers banked up on one table, at the mass of cards arranged on another, and he said, quietly, "I'll never be able to walk again, Annette."

"Oh, yes you will. There's ways and means."

"There's not, Annette. I heard them, Mr. Richardson and the others. I heard them. I couldn't make out any words, but I could still hear. He was talking to the students about the operation, the lumbar section. I heard him say, 'And what happens when that is smashed?' "

"Darling, listen. Don't dwell on it. You're going to get well, really well. I'm going to see to it. And remember what we've got to look forward to. Remember?"

He turned his head and gazed at her. Then, his face stretching into a smile, he said, "Oh, yes, yes; I remember. Yes, Annette, I remember." And his voice changing, he said, "And you've only got a broken arm? I mean, that's what you said, just bruises and a broken arm?"

"Yes, that's all, darling, bruises and a broken arm."

"That's wonderful, wonderful." He turned his head on the pillow again and looked upwards and repeated, "Wonderful, wonderful. It had to be like that, hadn't it?" And she said tearfully, "Perhaps, darling, perhaps."

She bent over him and laid her lips on his, and he put his arms around her and held her. Then she twisted her body so that her head rested on the pillow facing his and softly she said, "I love you." And he said, "I adore you. Always have, and always will, as long as I live . . . as long as I live."

When the tears dropped from the corner of his eyes she said, "Oh, my dearest, you are going to live, you are going to get better. Listen . . ." But her words were cut off by the door's opening; and there stood his mother.

For a moment their heads remained stationary: then Annette, twisting herself back into a sitting position, stared back at the woman who was glaring at her now, and she said quietly, "Hello, Mother-in-law."

Winifred made no reply, but went round to the other side of the bed and looked down on her son for a moment; then, bending over, she kissed him slowly on the lips before drawing a chair forward and sitting down.

"How are you, my dear?"

"All right, Mother . . . much better."

"I've brought you an apple tart that Maggie made; your favourite kind." She motioned to a parcel she had placed on the side-table. "And I've told them out there"—she nodded towards the door—"which ice cream you prefer."

He closed his eyes for a moment, then said, "Mother, they know what I should eat. They are very kind."

"Yes, kind, but ignorant half of them. It is hospital food. Although you are now in a private room, it's still hospital food they dish out." She looked across the bed at Annette, saying, "Oh, you have the plaster off then?"

"Yes." Annette flexed her arm. "It wasn't such a bad break. I've been lucky."

"Yes, indeed you were lucky."

There was silence between them, but when presently beads of perspiration gathered on Don's brow and Annette went to wipe them away with her handkerchief, Winifred rose from the chair, saying, "That's no good," and going to the wash basin in the corner of the room, she wetted a face flannel, then returned to the bed and began to sponge her son's face, and all the while he kept his eyes closed. But when she started to wipe a hand, he jerked it away from her, saying, "Mother! Mother! I've been washed. Please, don't; I've been washed."

"Don't excite yourself. Lie still."

Now looking across the bed at Annette, she asked, "How long are you staying?" And when she was given the answer firmly and briefly, "All day," she said, "Oh." Then added, "There's no need for two of us to be here. And I thought you were seeing about the house being put in order."

"That's already been done. And this is my place."

They were both startled as Don cried, "Nurse! Nurse!" at the same time lifting his hand and ringing the bell.

When the door opened immediately and the nurse entered, he said, "Nurse, I am tired."

The nurse now looked from the elderly woman to the younger and said, "Would you, please?" And as they both made slowly for the door, Don's voice checked them, saying, "Annette. Annette."

And she, almost running back to the bed, bent over him. "Yes, dear? Don't worry. I'll be back in a minute or so. Don't worry."

In the corridor they faced each other. Before Annette had time to speak Winifred said, "Two are one too many in the room."

"Yes, I agree with you. And I have first place, I am his wife. Please remember that."

"How dare you!"

"I dare, and shall go on daring." With this Annette walked away towards a door marked "Sister Bell." And knocking and being bidden to enter, she went in and put her case to the sister in a few words, ending, "Who has first right to be with her husband, sister? The mother or the wife?"

"The wife, of course. And don't worry, Mrs. Coulson, I understand the position and I'll see Mr. Richardson with regard to the visits his mother can make in the future. You've had a very trying time." She came round the desk and, putting her hand on Annette's shoulder, she said, "There, there, now. You've been very brave. Don't cry. Leave it to me, I'll deal with her. Is she still in the corridor?"

"She was."

"Then you stay there until I come back."

A few seconds later Annette heard her mother-in-law's voice finishing on the words she had become accustomed to over the past weeks: "He is my son. I will see into this."

There followed a silence, but the sister did not return immediately. When she did, her smile seemed somewhat forced as she said, "The coast is clear now; you can go in to your husband."

"Thank you. Thank you very much, sister. By the way, sister"—she paused—"could you give me any idea when I shall be able to take him home?"

"Oh." The sister raised her eyebrows before she said, "I'm afraid that will be some time, some weeks. You see, he's due for another operation later this week; and also, once you get him home, there'll be continuous nursing for a time. You know that?"

"Yes. Yes, I understand that."

"But one day at a time. Take it one day at a time. He's progressing much more quickly than we had thought he would, and he always seems better when you're with him."

Annette could give no answer to this, but she went out and into Don's room again. He was lying with his eyes closed and didn't realise who it was until she took his hand. And then he said, "Oh, Annette. What . . . what am I going to do about her?"

"Don't worry, don't worry; sister's seeing to everything."

"She upsets me, dear. I can't help it, she upsets me. I dread her coming in now. What am I going to do?"

"You are going to lie quiet and have a little doze. And just think, in a few weeks I'll have you home. I mean to have you home." She squeezed his hand between both hers. "That's all I'm living for, to have you home as soon as possible."

"But how will you manage?"

"Oh"—she laughed down on him—"if that's all that's worrying you, put it out of your head this moment. How will I manage? I'll have plenty of help. And I could manage you on my own. I'll let you see what I can do."

"But . . . but for how long, dear?"

She stared at him. Yes, for how long. There were two meanings to that remark, but she didn't know to which one he was alluding. So she evaded it by saying, "As long as ever it takes. Close your eyes, darling, and go to sleep. You don't want them to throw me out too, do you?"

He made no answer but turned his head to the side and lay gazing at her. And with his hand held between her breasts she gazed back at him.

TWO

"Look, my dear." Daniel put his arm around Annette's shoulder as they walked from the hospital to the car. "There's nobody wants him to go straight to the cottage more than I do. Believe that, dear. But the only way the doctor's going to let him out is if we can promise him that Don will have adequate nursing. Oh, I know you can get a night and day nurse, but one nurse will not be enough. He's got to be lifted and turned. As you know he's incontinent and always will be. Then, with the damage to his liver and his chest, he hasn't got the strength to pull himself up and down. The only reason Mr. Richardson has agreed to letting him leave is because he is getting depressed, mainly because he can't see enough of you. And remember: it isn't that long since they took the plaster off your arm. You couldn't possibly help a nurse with lifting, whereas at home there will always be Joe and me. And we couldn't be on hand if you were in the cottage, you know. So this is what we have thought up. It was really Joe's idea. You know the games-room next to the billiard-room? It's large and airy, with those two long windows looking on to the garden. Then there is that other room that at one time used to store all the paraphernalia for the conservatory before it was turned into the sun-room. As Joe said, the games-room could be fixed up as a fine bedroom. He's even picked a bed from upstairs, and also pointed out that with a couple of mattresses it will bring it up almost to the hospital height for a bed; you know, to make it easy for lifting the patient. Then the other room can be turned into a sitting-room. And you know how handy he is with wires in rigging up things—he should have been an electrician—well, he said he can fix up an intercom from your room to his along the corridor and another to my room upstairs, so that we'll always be on hand if needed. But only if needed."

She stopped in her walk and with a touch of bitterness in her voice, she said, "And what of . . . Mother-in-law? She'll never be out of his room. There won't be any nurses or doctors or sisters to take my side. It's her house."

"It's my house."

"Don't split hairs, Dad. I . . . I won't be able to stand it. And there's enough warring as it is. And you know how Don feels about her."

"I know. I know, dear. But I promise you I'll lay down laws and that they will be obeyed. One threat will be that if she doesn't keep her place then you can move him to the cottage. Come on, love, try it for a while. It's for Don's benefit. Just think of it that way."

"No. I can't think of it that way, Dad, because most of his nervous trouble is through her. You've got to admit it."

"Oh, I admit it. Oh, yes, I do, lass. But at the present moment I can't see any other way out. He's either got to stay where he is or come back to his old home; as I said, at least for a time. Later on, we may be able to get him into a wheelchair. Now, think of that." He put his arm around her shoulder again and said, "Come on. Come on. You've been so brave all along and I want bucking up. I'm very low meself at the moment."

"Oh, I'm sorry, Dad."

"By the way, how are you finding things at home?"

"Oh, as usual, Mother's fussing, trying to find the answer to why it all happened. Father's just the same, although he just looks on."

He brought her round squarely to face him now, asking quietly, "Are they kind and understanding?"

And she answered as quietly, "Kind in a way, but not understanding. They never have been and they never will now." They stared at each other for a moment before he said brightly, "Oh, well, come on. I'll land you at your door."

"I thought you were going into Newcastle on business?"

"I am, but I can still land you at your door and turn round and come back."

"I can get a taxi."

"You'll do no such thing. Come on. . . ."

Five minutes later he dropped her at the gates leading to her home, saying, "I'll call in at the hospital about eight to pick you up. Will that be all right?"

"Yes, Dad. And thanks."

He waved to her, turned the car around and drove back into Newcastle and straight to 42 Bowick Road.

Maggie opened the front door for him as if she had been standing behind it waiting, which in a way, she had. Once it was closed they put their arms about each other and kissed long and hard. Then in a matter of fact way she said, "You look frozen. I've got some hot soup ready." And to this he answered, "We could have snow for Christmas, it's cold enough."

"Here, give me your coat." She took his outdoor things, went into the passage and hung them on an expanding hat rack. When she returned to the room it was to be enfolded in his arms again. But now they just held each other closely for a moment until she said, "Sit yourself down," and pointed to a two-seater sofa set at an angle to the open fireplace, in which a coal fire was blazing. And he sat down and stretched out his legs, then looked at the fire, and when his body slumped he leant his head on the back of the couch and his escaping breath took on the form of a long sigh. Presently, without moving, he called, "What time did you leave?"

And her voice came from the kitchen, saying, "Near twelve."

"What!" He brought his head up. "You were ready first thing before I went to the yard."

"Yes, I know, but there was a bit to do with Stephen. You know what he's like on my day off, or at any time when he knows I'm going out. Well, he came down in his dressing-gown. I was in my room when he entered the kitchen, but I heard him. You know how his voice cracks high when he's going to have a tantrum. When I went in it was the usual: he wanted to come with me or go and see Don. They should never have promised to take him to see Don; he remembers these things. It was decided long ago you know, not to promise him things he couldn't have or do. Well, who should give us a surprise visit at that time but herself, and at this he started one of his tantrums. He just wouldn't stop, throwing himself about, you know, in this three-year-old fashion. And so she slapped him."

"She what!"

"She slapped him. And she was right. Oh yes, on this occasion she was right. And it stopped him in his tracks. But he started to howl, so I took him upstairs, told him to have his bath then get dressed. And I went down again and saw her."

Her voice stopped, and he pulled himself up to the end of the couch, calling, "Well, what happened next?"

She came into the room now carrying a tray on which were two plates of soup and, laying them on a small cloth-covered table set against the wall opposite the fire, she said, "I went to her room. She was looking out of the window, with her hair hanging down. I'd never seen her with her hair hanging down, you know. She turned and looked at me. She had been crying, Daniel. She had been crying."

He rose to his feet and walked towards her, saying, "Well, she had been crying. She's got a good right to cry; it would be because she was sorry for herself, knowing she can't have all her own way and her son to herself."

Maggie looked away from him, then continued, "When I asked if she would mind if I took him out for a little run, she said, 'It's your day off.' And I said, 'I know that, but it doesn't matter, I've nothing special to do.' And you know what she said?" Maggie was looking at him now, and in a low voice she went on, "She said, 'This used to be a happy house at one time, didn't it, Maggie?' "

"Happy house be damned! It was never a happy house; never from the beginning. She wanted it to show off, and it was a large enough place to push Stephen out of sight."

"I know. I know. But I think she was making comparisons with then and now. And when next she said, 'Life isn't fair, is it?' I answered her truthfully, 'No, ma'am, it isn't fair.' And when she said to me, 'Are you happy?' what could I say? But I answered truthfully, 'Only at odd times, ma'am, at very odd times.' Daniel, for the first time in my life I felt sorry for her. In a way she has a side, she can't help feeling as she does about Don no more than I can help feeling as I do about you or you about me." She put her hands upon his shoulders now, saying, "Be civil to her, Daniel. You know, Lily tells me she hates to go in and serve the meals. You speak to Joe or she speaks to Joe; Joe speaks to you, or Joe speaks to her. She said that the other day the conversation was so stilted it was just like a puppet show. And it's better when you don't go in at all, because then Joe talks to her freely. It's not so bad when Annette's there, either, but better still when Mrs. Jackson and Mr. Rochester happen to pop down; he even makes her laugh at times."

He took her hands from his shoulders and pressed them together, saying, "It's odd that you should say you're sorry for her."

"Well, I am, and feeling guilty an' all."

"Oh my God! don't do that, Maggie. Don't be a hypocrite."

She withdrew her hands from his, saying, "I'm no hypocrite and you know that, but I'm in the house with her all day. I'm a looker-on, as it were, and I generally see most of the game. I don't like her, I never have, and not only because I've loved you; I don't like her as a woman. She's an upstart, she's selfish. She's all those things, but at the same time, because she's got this love; no, not love, but passion or mania for her son, I can understand in a way because, dear God, how many times have I wished I had a son that I could go mad over? Your son."

"Oh! Maggie. Maggie." His arms went about her again and he rested her head on his shoulder. But it was there for only a moment before she sniffed and said, "This soup'll be clay cold. Come on, sit down, you must be starved."

"Yes, I am Maggie, I am starved, but not for food."

"Well—" she smiled at him, then patted him on the shoulder gently as she said, "we'll have to see about that, won't we? But first things first. Sit yourself down."

At about six o'clock he was ready to leave and, standing at the unopened door, he said, "Maggie, not being the allocator of time, just like everybody else, I don't know how long I've got, but I can say this to you: I'd gamble away the rest of my life for just a few weeks in this house with you." Then on a smile he added, "Well, perhaps not exactly in this one, because I couldn't deal with Helen too. Give her my love, will you?"

"I'll do no such thing; I'll give her your kind regards. Good night, my dear. Mind how you go; it's freezing, the roads will be slippery. . . ."

He had hardly entered the house when Joe approached him from across the hall. It was as if he, like Maggie, had been waiting for him.

"May I have a word, Dad?"

"Yes, yes, what is it? Come into the study."

Once in the room Joe said, "Annette came here this afternoon. She went and had a talk with Mam. I don't know what transpired, not really, except that she made it plain that if she allowed Don to be brought here they would have to have a certain amount of privacy. There would be a day nurse but no night nurse, as she could call upon either you or me, and between us we'd see to him first thing in the morning and last thing at night. In the meantime what needed to be done the nurse herself could see to.

"She didn't say how Mam took that, only that it was settled. But since then, you wouldn't believe it, there's been so much bustle. Mam's had Lily and Peggie scrubbing away, and she even brought Stephen down to help me move furniture. I suggested that it would be better to wait until you came in, but no, Stephen would do, he was strong, she said. He is, you know, and he can do things when he likes. And of course he was delighted."

"Well! well! things are moving."

"Dad." Joe put his hand out towards Daniel, saying, "She seemed happy, changed, like her old self . . . well"—he shrugged his shoulders—"as happy as her old self could be. Dad, try to go along with her, at least until . . ."

Daniel looked into the face of this man who could give him inches and whose whole body was filled with kindness, and he thought it odd that these two people for whom he had love and who were of no blood connection could be pleading for his wife's cause, pointing out that she had a side. Quietly he answered him, saying, "I'll do my best; I was never a disturber of the peace. But what do you think is going to happen when the bubble bursts, as, knowing her, burst it will? I'm amazed it hasn't been pricked before now. It just needs a prick, you'll see. But all right . . . all right, I'll go along, and I promise I'll not be the one to use the pin."

THREE

$\mathcal{T}$he bubble burst just five days after Don had been brought home. And it was evident from the start that Winifred intended never to speak to her husband and to ignore Annette.

There had first been a little contretemps over the placing of another single bed in what was to be Don's bedroom, a bed that would have a double purpose: it would not only be a place for Annette to sleep near her husband, but be useful in being some place on which to lay him when his bed was being made. But on the evening before Don was due to arrive, the bed had been taken out and placed in the adjoining sitting-room. Apparently John and Bill had been called in from outside to remove it. But it wasn't Daniel who ordered it to be put back, because as yet he hadn't seen the move, but

Joe who, with the assistance of Stephen, himself in a high state of excitement about Don's return, had taken the bed to pieces and then reassembled it where it had been originally. And as soon as Winifred knew of this her temper became evident, for she naturally imagined it had been at her husband's behest.

But when she knew it had been Joe's doing, she had upbraided him with, "How dare you!" But what else she intended to say was cut off by his speaking to her in a fashion that stilled her tongue. "You can do nothing about it, Mam," he had said; "they are married; she's his wife and her place is by his side. You'll feel better if you admit that to yourself. In fact, things will be better all round."

She had certainly been, if not amazed, then greatly surprised because of all the members in the house it was he who always spoke civilly to her, and often in a placating tone.

She marched out and the bed remained where it was.

But each morning since, before the nurse came on duty, she had contrived to meet her in the hall and give her unnecessary instructions.

Nurse Pringle was a middle-aged woman. She had been in private nursing for years. She had met Winifred's type before, and so she would smile and say, "Yes, Mrs. Coulson," the while determined to do things in her own way.

Following the issuing of instructions to the nurse, Winifred would eat her breakfast. No calamity seemed to stop her eating: in fact, the more she was troubled the more she ate. And when the meal was over, and only then, she would visit her son's room. She had to suppress the temptation to go down in her dressing-gown as soon as she awoke, for she couldn't bear the thought of seeing that girl so near to him, even perhaps lying by his side.

During the past weeks she considered that Annette Allison had changed so much there was now no resemblance to the quiet, convent-bred girl who had been engaged to her son. It was as if, having married him, she had, at the same time, grown to maturity.

And there was something else she had to restrain herself from doing: to kiss her son and fondle him, for since his marriage he seemed to resent her nearness. She would not admit to herself that his stand against her proximity had begun a long time before his marriage.

She conceded to the arrangement whereby her husband and Joe saw to the changing of the bedding; but when she learned that the nurse would not be bathing Don, and she had told Annette that she would do it, the girl had answered, "He won't allow me to wash him down, so he won't allow you." There had been times during the past five days she had wanted to take her hand and slap that young, confident-looking face. She would not say "beautiful," because she didn't think she was beautiful; to her she wasn't even pretty.

And so now, as usual, she was bracing herself as she crossed the hall on her way to pay her morning visit, when her jaws stiffened at the sound of laughter coming from the direction of her son's bedroom. When she opened the door she saw the reason for it. Her eldest son—she couldn't bear to think of him as such, but nevertheless he was—was standing with his back towards the bed and laughing all over his face as he cried, "Go on. Go on, Don, pat me on the back. Go on. Maggie always does when I've been a good boy. Go on, 'cos I've been a good boy. Ever since you came home I've been a good boy. Go on.''

Neither the nurse nor Annette turned at her entry. They too were laughing as they watched Don reach out and pat his brother on his back, saying, "That's one extra for tonight.''

"Yes, Don. I'll be good tonight; you'll see, I'll be good. And you know, I'm goin' to help to lift you tomorrow. I asked Dad, 'cos he says, I'm strong as a bull. I helped Joe carry the other bed in. Yes, I did. I did . . .''

"Stephen!" The young fellow became quiet, and as he straightened up, his body became stiff and he said, "Yes, Mam?"

"Go up to your room."

"I've . . . I've just come down, Mam. And . . . and Don likes me to be here; I make him laugh.''

"Go on, go up to your room."

Stephen looked down on Don, who nodded at him, saying, "Go on now. Come down later. We'll have coffee together and chocolate biscuits, eh?''

"Oh yes, Don, chocolate biscuits, yes." He backed away from the bed, moving in an arc around his mother as he made for the door.

And now Winifred, addressing the nurse, said, "You must be firm with him: he cannot come and go as he likes; he'll tire him." She looked away from the nurse and back towards the bed, as though expecting no reply from the nurse; nor did the nurse answer, but Don said quietly, "He doesn't tire me, Mother. I like to see him.''

She ignored this and said, "How are you?" She had now moved to the head of the bed and was looking down on him.

"I've had a good night; not too bad at all, in fact, a hundred per cent better than I did in hospital. I'll soon be in that chair the nurse was talking about yesterday. What do you say, nurse?"

"Could be. It all depends. But like your brother, you'll have to be a good boy." Then looking from her patient to Annette, she added, "There now, you two, you can get on with your crossword. I'm going into the hall to do some phoning. There are some medicines I need and I want a word with Mr. Richardson.''

"What do you want to say to Mr. Richardson?"

Nurse Pringle looked at Winifred and she said quietly, "I want to report on my patient."

"You can tell me and I can do that."

"I'm sorry, Mrs. Coulson; this comes within the confines of my duty, and I'm obeying Mr. Richardson's orders in doing so."

"You're impudent."

"I'm sorry if you find me so. If you have any complaints . . .''

"Nurse." Annette was standing at the other side of the bed now; she had turned from arranging some flowers on a table near the window. "Do what you think is right. And I don't consider you impudent. My husband is very grateful for your attention, aren't you, Don?"

Don's lower lip was jerking in and out and he muttered, "Yes, yes, I'm very glad of nurse's attention. And . . . and you must forgive Mother; she doesn't understand the routine." He forced a watery smile to his face by saying, "She's never been stuck in a hospital for weeks."

The nurse went out leaving the three of them breathing the air that was thick with hostility.

"Something will have to be done; I'm no longer mistress in my own house," Winifred said, and emphasised what she had said by drawing in her stomach.

"Mother! For God's sake, stop it, will you? If you start again I'll ask to be taken back to hospital. No, no, I won't"—he shook his head in much the same manner as Stephen would have when in a tantrum—"we'll go to the cottage. Yes. Yes, that's what we'll do." He put his hand out and, gripping Annette's, he almost whimpered, "I can't stand this arguing. We'll have a night and day nurse and someone like John, a handyman. Oh"—his voice rose—"a male nurse. Yes. Yes, a male nurse."

"I'm sorry. Please, don't agitate yourself. I'm sorry. It . . . it won't happen again," said Winifred.

The words had cost his mother something, and both Don and Annette realised this. And it was Annette being placating now when she said, "Please, Mother-in-law, try to accept things the way they are. It could all run smoothly. He . . . he wants to see you. Don't you, dear?" She turned and looked at her husband, and when he nodded, she went on, "You see if you'd only try to . . ."

The look on the woman's face checked any further words, and Annette watched her turn about and go hastily from the room.

"It won't work, Annette. It won't work."

"Yes, it will, dear; she'll come round. I know she will. It will take time. In a way I know how she feels: I've stolen you from her. If someone tried to take you from me, I . . . I would feel the same as she does."

"Never!"

He was right, of course; she would never be able to feel the same way as that woman did. There was something about her that wasn't . . . She couldn't find a word with which to translate her thoughts, but what she said was, "You mustn't worry. That's the main thing, you mustn't worry. Because, as you've just said, we could go to the cottage. Any day, dear, we could go there. In fact, as you know, that's where I wanted to take you in the first place."

"I wish you had stuck out, dear. Oh, I wish you had."

So did she . . . But they were here now, yet not for long, she knew, for the scene that had just been enacted was but a pin-prick to the one that was bound to come.

It came that evening at half-past nine.

Winifred's mind was in a turmoil: there was another person in her household that had been set against her: the nurse. Now, only the servants spoke civilly to her, and she didn't think it was because they were paid to be civil. Even Joe was totally on the side of that girl. But of course, he would be, wouldn't he?

She felt hungry. It was more than three hours since she had eaten. She must have something.

She went downstairs. The house was very still: there was only the throbbing of the boiler from the cellar penetrating the quiet. She went into the kitchen. It was empty. Maggie would, of course, be in her room. Lily would have been down at the lodge this last hour; she finished at eight every night. Peggie Danish would not yet have gone to bed; she must be upstairs seeing to Stephen, hoping no doubt that Joe would be up there too. She'd have to watch that girl; she was too fresh by half.

She went to the fridge, but found only a shop-bought veal pie and some cheese that could be eaten immediately.

She hesitated on the cheese; it generally kept her awake. So she cut herself a slice of the pie, put it on a plate, then stood for a moment with the plate in her hand; she never liked eating in the kitchen. She went out and walked towards the dining-room, but then changed her mind. There was a moon out; it would be nice in the sun-room. She would eat there. And then she would look in on the sick-room; just a peep.

The sun-room was softly lit by the moonlight. She sat down in a chair and munched on the pie. When she had finished she licked her finger ends and wiped them delicately on her handkerchief. Then she sat musing for a moment as she looked out on to the garden, so thickly lined with frost that it looked like a layer of snow.

Although she rarely felt the cold, she shivered and pulled her dressing-gown tightly about her before getting up and making for the door, only to stop before reaching it and to look to the far end of the conservatory to the door that led into what was now Annette's sitting-room. Why shouldn't she go in that way? She did not add, and surprise them and see what they were up to; at least, what *she* was up to, for she wouldn't put it past her to be lying with him at night. That was why she had been against the night nurse. And in his condition. It was disgusting!

Swiftly, she walked to the other door. It opened quietly. She paused on the threshold. The only light in the room was that coming from under the door leading into the bedroom. But there was no obstacle in her way; the couch was to the side. She closed the door behind her; then, hand outstretched, she made her way towards the strip of light on the floor, sought the handle of the door and pushed it open. Then, at the sight of the tableau on the bed, she froze.

There was that girl, that hussy, that woman, stark naked! And there was her son, reaching out, his hand on her belly and her two hands covering it!

At the sound of the door opening, Annette swung round to grab at her dressing-gown, then Winifred heard her son cry, "Don't! Don't! Stay as you are." And the girl, the dressing-gown trailing from her hand, stayed as she was for a moment.

Winifred found it impossible to accept what she was seeing: it couldn't be! It couldn't be! her mind was screaming at her. The car accident had happened at the bottom of the drive; it would be impossible for them to have been . . . The words were cut off in her mind by a dreadful thought that seemed to spiral up from some dark depth in her. And when it reached the top of her head it pierced her brain and sent thoughts splintering in all directions. She could read them but she could scarcely believe them. And so she screamed, "You dirty slut, you! You filthy creature! You're pregnant and you're putting it on to my son. You low down . . ."

"Stop it!" Don's elbows were pressed into the bed, supporting his raised shoulders now as he cried at her, "Shut up, woman!"

She took five steps into the room, and these brought her almost to the foot of the bed. And there she screamed back at him, "Never! Never! I know you. I'm your Mother, remember? You were *good, clean, pure* . . ."

"Pure? Hell!"

"Don. Don. Lie down; I'll . . . I'll deal with it."

Annette had by now pulled the dressing-gown around her; but Don ignored her and dragging himself a little further up the bed, he yelled at his mother in a voice as loud as hers had been, "Listen! woman. Listen! for once. The child is ours . . . *mine*. We've been together for a year, a whole year. And what do I mean by being together? I mean, having it off under your nose. Having it off. You couldn't expect anything else, could you? her mother treating her like a vestal virgin and you trying to tie nappies on me. A full year we've been together. When this happened"—he jerked his head—"it was no mistake. I wanted it. I wanted an explosion. Yes, do you hear? an explosion *to blow you out of my life.*"

"Don! Don! Enough! Stop it! Lie down."

"I've lain down long enough. It's got to be said, and I'll say it: it's been a wonderful year, a time I think of as a year of the virgins."

Winifred's mind was refusing to recognise the man in the bed as her son. This man was talking common, dirty, just like her husband, and her son wasn't like her husband. But there was one thing certain: he was so much enamoured of that creature that he would like just to save her face and name.

Now she screamed at him: "I don't believe a word of it! You can't hoodwink me. You're just shielding her."

There was the sound of a door banging in the distance. It must be the door at the far end of the corridor, the one that led into the cottage, she thought. Yes, that was it. Joe. And so she cried, "It was him, wasn't it? Joe. It was Joe. He always wanted you. And he would drive you here and there, wouldn't he? Even when you two were supposed to be engaged he would drive you. It was Joe. Tell me, girl. Speak the truth. But there's no truth in you. You're a dirty, filthy slut. You're a . . ."

The opening of the door and Joe's appearance did not stem the flow of vituperation, but simply redirected it, and now she screamed at him. "Getting my son to hide your filthy deeds, were you?"

Joe's face screwed up. He looked perplexed for a moment before asking of Don, "What's this?"

But it was Winifred who interrupted her son as he was about to answer, yelling, "Don't you ask 'what's this?'. Look at her stomach! But of course, you know all about that, don't you? Being a bastard yourself, you've given her one too!"

"Oh my God!" Don gasped and fell back on to his pillows the words, garbled, tumbling from his mouth. "She's m . . . mad, clean mad. She . . . she always has been. Get . . . get her out of here, Joe. Get her out . . ."

Joe didn't move towards his adoptive mother, but stood gazing at her, wishing to God that what she was saying were true. And then, through gritted teeth, he said to her, "You were glad to take in a bastard baby at one time. But there's more ways of being a bastard than being born on the wrong side of the blanket. Think on that. Now I'd get yourself away to bed."

For answer she swung round, grabbed the carafe of water from the table at the side of her and threw it at his head. It struck him on the ear and sent him reeling to the side, and as she came at him, her arms outstretched, her fingers clawed, the door opened and Daniel rushed in shouting, "In the name of God! what's up now?"

It took both Joe and Daniel all their time to hold her and drag her from the room as she screamed abuse at them, using the same words she had previously yelled at Don.

In the hall, she brought Peggie Danish's eyes popping and her mouth agape, but the language made no impression on Maggie as she tried to avoid the kicking legs and helped the men get her up the stairs.

At one time Maggie thought the four of them would come tumbling down backwards, and as she clung to the banister with one hand, she shouted down at Peggie, "Phone the doctor. Go on, girl, phone the doctor."

Once on the landing, they propelled the wriggling, screaming woman to the bedroom; and there Daniel, kicking open the door, shouted at Joe, "Let go!" Then he thrust her forward on to the floor and, turning quickly, he pulled the key out from the inside lock of the door, pushed Joe and Maggie into the corridor again, then locked the door from the outside. And as the three of them stood panting, a high scream came from the room, followed a few seconds later by the sound of articles being thrown about. When something heavy hit the door they all stepped back, and Daniel, looking at Joe, said, "What brought this on?"

Joe was still gasping but his voice snapped, "She opened her eyes at last and actually looked at Annette. I came in at the tail-end. I don't know what had happened before."

When something again hit the door, Maggie said, "She'll wreck the room."

"Let her."

Daniel turned and went down the stairs, and they followed him into Don's room, to find his son white and shivering.

"What actually happened?" he asked Annette. "How did the news break?"

She bent her head a moment before she said, "I was undressed and she could see Don had a hand on my stomach. She must have been in the sun-room; she came in that way unexpectedly."

"Well, she had to find out sometime, hadn't she?"

Annette looked up now and said, "I'm moving him tomorrow, Dad."

"There mightn't be any need, lass; when the doctor comes, he'll need to take a second opinion, but she's got to be put away. It's been coming for a long time."

When, half an hour later the doctor, together with Maggie, cautiously entered Winifred's room, he stopped on the threshold and gazed around him in amazement. The only item seemingly to be in one piece was the four-poster bed, and sprawled across it was the woman whom he had attended for years and to whom he had doled out pills that he knew would do her no good whatever.

He moved towards the bed, and avoiding the side over which her legs were hanging, he went round to where her head lay. And cautiously he touched it, saying quietly, "It's all right, Mrs. Coulson, it's all right. Sit up, there's a good woman."

She raised her head and stared at him. Her face was empty of expression, quiet; yet her voice belied this when, as if he knew all that had transpired, she said, "I tell you he was a virgin. I watched over him. Except—" She turned her head to the side and screwed up her eyes as if trying to recall something and then, springing from the bed, she cried, *"He* did it! He was going to make him like father like son; he couldn't bear to see anything pure. No, no." She shook her head wildly now and, putting her hand out and gripping his arm, she appealed to him: "No; it was Joe. *You* see that he owns up. Joe gave it to her. Joe always wanted her."

"There, there. Sit down. Come on, sit down." He drew her gently down on to the side of the bed again; then glancing towards where Maggie stood, he motioned his head towards his bag, which he had dropped on to the floor, and she brought it to him and placed it on the bed. And when he opened it and began to pick out one thing after another, Winifred jumped to her feet, saying, "You're not putting me to sleep; I haven't finished yet. Oh, no, I haven't finished yet, not by a long chalk. I'll destroy them and everything in this house. It won't be fit to live in when I'm finished with it."

"Well, we'll talk about that tomorrow. Come, sit down."

As she backed away from him, he stood for a moment, looking at her helplessly; then, without turning his gaze towards Maggie, he said quietly, "Fetch the men."

As they were both outside the door it was only a matter of seconds before they were in the room, and when Winifred saw them she looked wildly about her, searching for something to throw. And when she made towards the dressing-table and the glass bottles and powder jars scattered around it on the floor, both Daniel and Joe rushed towards her and held her as best they could, trying to ignore the volume of obscenities once more pouring from her mouth, while the doctor inserted a needle, none too gently, into the thick flesh of her arm.

Winifred struggled for another few seconds before finally subsiding on to the floor.

As he stood looking down on the huddled form, Doctor Peters let out a long slow breath before saying to Daniel, "She'll have to be admitted, of course. And before she comes round. I'll phone the hospital and arrange for an ambulance."

"The County?" Joe's voice was small as he continued to stare at the crumpled heap of flesh, more animal than human.

"If not the County, then Hetherington. In her case I think the Hetherington would be preferable. It will depend on which one has a vacancy, though, so I'd better find out," Doctor Peters answered.

While this was going on, Daniel hadn't spoken a word, and he didn't break the silence that followed when left with Joe and Maggie.

They both watched him as he stared down at his wife, and he was unaware of Maggie's touching Joe on the arm and of their leaving the room, for he was searching deep into his mind, asking questions, giving himself answers. Was he to blame?

No, no. He couldn't say he was to blame because he would never have taken up with anyone else if she had behaved as a wife.

But had she ever been a wife, a willing wife? Wasn't it that she hadn't wanted a husband so much as security and position?

But when had the big rows started? the recriminations?

From the time she knew that Stephen was retarded.

Had she been a wife to him during the time she had played mother to the adopted boy, Joe?

Only under protest.

How many women had she caused him to use? Because he *had* just used them; there certainly had been no feeling of tenderness or love in his dealings.

Perhaps Father Ramshaw could answer that question better than he himself, for he had a good memory for confessions. Following each time he had gone off the rails, he had gone to confession.

Had it been just fear of the retribution of God that had driven him to confession? Or the fact that he had liked the priest and thought he would understand? And he did understand, even about Maggie.

How was it that he loved Maggie? He must have loved her all the time, but had only become aware of it during recent years. Now, if she had given him some hint, he wouldn't have had to sully his soul as much as he had done, for he had never kept up a connection with any one person for long.

Looking at his life, it had been hellish. He had money, a thriving business, a fine house and, except by a few men, one being Annette's father, he was highly respected. Yet what did it all amount to? He could only repeat: hell. The only thing that mattered in life was love. It wasn't even essential to be able to write your own name; you could be deaf or blind, or just dim; but if you really loved that's what got you through.

He stretched his body now and looked away from his wife. Hadn't she loved? No; that wasn't love, that was a mania, a possessive mania; more than that, it was almost incest. Love was something else. What else?

He looked around the room as if searching for an answer and then said aloud, "Kindliness. Aye, that's it." To be kind, that was love. To give comfort, that was love. To like someone for themselves, forgetting their faults, yes, that was the best kind of love. And he would have never known anything about it except that Maggie had come into his life. Odd that. She had always been there, but she had just come into it.

He turned and, stooping, righted an upturned chair; then as he was about to pick up a broken picture from the floor, he straightened, saying to himself, there'll be plenty of time for that tomorrow, for the house will be at peace tomorrow, and for the next day, the next week, the next month, please God.

He turned again and looked at his wife. And now the knowledge that she would soon be gone, as well as the sight of her lying in that undignified heap, brought from him the urge to go and lift her on to the bed, to straighten her limbs, to bring back to her a little dignity, because this heap that now represented her had stripped her of all dignity. And he recalled that when she walked she had done so with dignity. Fat she may have been, fat she was, but she carried it well.

He could not, however, make the move towards her; for now an overwhelming feeling of revulsion was preventing him from touching her. When the ambulance men came they would see to her, or perhaps Joe, or the doctor, or anybody.

He scampered from the room, tripping over broken furniture as he went. Joe was waiting outside. It was as if he was always waiting, waiting to be of help, and it was natural for him to put his hand out towards him, saying, "I'm going to be sick, lad." And Joe, taking his arm, hurriedly led him across the landing, pushed open the bathroom door and guided him inside. And he continued to support his head while the retching continued, and even after the stomach had given up all it held. Then he sat him down on the bathroom chair and sponged his face with cold water. This done, he said, "I would go to bed if I were you, Dad; I'll see to things."

"No, no; I'll see it through." Then he added, "The doctor's been a long time on the phone."

"He had to go and see Don; he was in a state. He gave him a sleeping draught. He's with Annette now; and she's not much better."

Daniel got to his feet and adjusted his clothes. Pulling his tie straight, he said, "It's odd that Stephen should sleep through all this."

"He hasn't slept through all this; he's downstairs in the kitchen with Maggie. He must have run down when we were all in the bedroom. He was stiff with fear."

The sound of a commotion in the hall now brought them both out of the bathroom and down the stairs, there to see two ambulance men and the doctor in discussion. And the doctor, turning towards Daniel and taking in his blanched face, tentatively said, "Do you think you'll be able to accompany us to the hospital? Someone must come along. Perhaps you would rather your son . . ."

"No, no; I'll come."

"Very well." The doctor and the two ambulance men, preceded by Joe, went up the stairs, while Daniel, standing in the middle of the hall, grappled with the fact that it wasn't all over yet; he'd still to see her into the place.

There was a weird stillness on the house, a kind of stillness that exaggerated the ticking of the tall grandfather clock, which now boomed three times, announcing that it was a quarter to twelve. Don was in a deep sleep which would take him through until the morning. Stephen too was asleep, as also was Peggie. Maggie was in her room, but she wasn't asleep. She wouldn't go to sleep until she heard Daniel's car draw up in the drive. And Joe and Annette weren't asleep. They were in the drawing-room, sitting on the sofa opposite the log fire. They had been sitting there for some time, both wanting to speak but not knowing how to begin. It was Annette who first made the effort. Looking at Joe, who was sitting bent forward, his elbows on his knees, his hands hanging between them in his characteristic fashion, she said softly, "I'm sorry that you are implicated, Joe. She . . . she didn't know what she was saying. You understand that?"

Joe now slowly turned his head towards her and he gazed at her for a long moment, in which his thoughts were racing and shouting at him: if only there had been even a vestige of truth in the statement. But what he actually said was, "I know that, dear. It was an utterly ridiculous suggestion to make. But as you say, she didn't know what she was saying. And . . . and you've always been like a little sister to me."

She smiled wanly now, saying, "Oh, I didn't think of you at one time as a brother! Remember when I used to follow you about? I had a kind of pash on you when I was fourteen."

He made himself smile, saying, "And it would be a *kind* of pash."

"Don't be silly, Joe; you always underestimate yourself. You always have done, and there's no need. There's Irene, Irene Shilton. You would only have to lift your little finger. And Jessica Bowbent's another." Then, her voice dropping, she said slowly, "You should marry, Joe, and get away from here. Yes—" She shook her head now and turned and looked into the fire, repeating, "Get away from here, from all of them . . . from all of us, from Stephen, he's Dad's responsibility, and from Don; he's . . . well he's my responsibility now, and from Dad himself, because if you don't, you'll find us all on your shoulders."

When she turned her gaze on him again he wanted to put his arms out and pull her into them and say, "I'd carry you on my shoulders at any time. I'd wait a lifetime if I thought there would be any chance of bearing you as a burden."

She went on, "They take advantage of you, Joe; you're too kind. You've always been kind. You think you owe them a debt because they took you in when you were a baby. To my mind you owe nobody a debt; you've paid it by filling a gap in their lives."

"Maybe, but only for a short time." He shook his head ruefully. "From the moment Don arrived, the gap was closed. I faced up to that as a child, but it didn't make me think the less of Don. I loved him. I still do."

"Joe. Oh, Joe." She put her hand out to him, and he hesitated a moment before taking it; then he gripped it and said, "Don't cry. Oh, please, please, Annette, don't cry. It'll all work out, you'll see. We'll get him better in the end."

The tears now were raining down her cheeks; her lips were trembling and her words came through her chattering teeth as she said, "Don't hoodwink yourself, Joe, or try to hoodwink me. He'll never be better. If it was just his legs there'd be some hope, but he's all smashed up inside. You know he is. He knows he is. We both know he'll never get better."

"Annette. Annette. Oh, my dear." Her head came on to his shoulders and his arms went about her, and as he felt the nearness of her he made a great effort to disbelieve her words, because it was true what he had said: he loved the man he thought of as his brother, the brother who had usurped his place in her life.

He let his mouth drop into her hair as he said, "He'll live a long time yet. Between us we'll see to it that he holds his child, and see it romp an' all." And he was about to mutter more platitudes when she drew herself away from him; and after she had dried her eyes she put her hand out and gently touched his cheek, saying, "You're the kindest man in the world, Joe. I could tell you anything and not feel ashamed. I didn't feel ashamed when I told you about the baby coming. And now I can tell you of my fears too. I'm afraid of going home tomorrow—I still think of my parents place as home—and giving them my news. Because you know what will happen, Joe? They'll disown me."

"Never! Never!"

"Oh, yes, they will, Joe. In a way, my mother is akin to Mam; she's got religion bad. I never pray now, you know, Joe, I never pray to God for Don or for anything that I want because all my young life it was prayers morning, noon, and night, at the table and away from it; and religious books, The Lives of the Saints, the martyrdom of this one and that one; then life at the convent school: Mass and Communion every morning during Lent. I would feel faint with hunger but she would make sure I went to Communion. Even the nuns didn't expect me to have Communion every day; but they could see me as a potential saint, such a good little girl. And all the while I was getting to hate God. Dreadful, terrible feelings inside. As for the Virgin Mary, I suffered agonies in what I thought about her. And I longed, longed for escape. And on our wedding day we both thought we had made it. But as Mother always says, God is not mocked, and after the accident I began to believe it was true, and that what had happened to us was retribution. But not any more. It's people who bring retribution, not God. And you know, Joe, it's people who turn us away from God; it's the talk and actions of others that turn us against Him. Anyway, you can see why I'm dreading tomorrow . . . And . . . and you know, Joe, I fear this house. There is something evil about it." She raised her eyes and gazed round the room, saying, "It looks lovely, but I'm afraid of it. I want to get away from it, or from her. She's just gone, Joe, but already I feel she'll soon be back. And then we couldn't possibly stay here; I'd have to take him away. You understand that?"

"Yes, my dear, yes, I understand. And don't worry. But in the meantime, you must take care of yourself and the baby . . . and Don."

"Yes; yes, of course. You know, we were going to ask you something before this last business happened. We had made up our minds to leave and we were going to ask you if you'd come to the cottage with us. Would you . . . would you have?"

How much pain could one put up with without wincing? or even crying out? Here he could retreat to his rooms after doing what was expected of him morning and night and saying, "Hello, how are you, old fellow?" and smiling, and talking small talk. But to live with both of them!

He stalled by saying, "Now that won't come about. The way things are, you'll have no need to take him to the cottage."

"You wouldn't have come then?"

He took her hand again and, looking into her face, he said, "I'd do anything you ask, Annette; anything to make you happy." He qualified this by adding, "And Don."

FOUR

*T*he Mass was nearing its end. The Missal was moved from one side of the altar to the other. The priest covered the chalice and genuflected before the tabernacle before being preceded from the altar by two small altar boys. It was eight o'clock Mass and there were no more than twelve people present and they were regulars, all except one.

After Father Ramshaw had taken off his surplice he didn't as usual go through the side door into the yard and across the lawn that led to the presbytery and his breakfast—he was always ready for his breakfast—but instead went back into the church, knowing there would be one of the congregation still seated.

At a pew near the back of the church he sat down beside Daniel, muttering, "If you'd got any further, you'd have been out of the door. How are you? You look awful."

"I feel awful, Father."

"What's happened now?"

"Winifred went off her head last night, clean off her head. She found out . . ." He paused.

"Well, what did she find out?"

"That Annette is pregnant." He paused again, then said, "She's going to have a baby."

"Yes, I understand; there's no need to spell it out for me. Only one thing surprises me and that is she took so long to twig Annette's condition. What happened to her?"

Daniel looked towards the altar. "She wouldn't accept it, that it was Don's. She pushed the blame on Joe and went for him. And when we got her upstairs screaming, we had to lock her in her room where she smashed up everything movable. She was taken to The County."

"Oh dear God! The County. I'm heart sorry to hear that it's come to this. Although it's no surprise. But God help her when she comes to herself in that hell-hole. I'm telling you, I hate to visit there. It isn't the real mad ones I'm sorry for. Oh no. They're happy in a way being Churchill or Chiang Kai-Shek or merely one of today's television so-called stars. No; it's the ones that have snapped temporarily through breakdowns and the like, because they are conscious of what's happening to them. And she'll be in that category."

Father Ramshaw now put his hand on to the back of the seat in front of him as if for support; then, narrowing his eyes, he asked of Daniel, "Is it guilt that's brought you here this morning?"

"Why . . . why should I feel guilty? You know what my life's been like. You . . ."

"Yes, yes, I know all right. But you're not free from blame. And ask yourself what's brought you to Mass this morning when, to my knowledge, you've never been to week-day Mass in your whole existence. Yes, Daniel, you've got to share the blame, it's not all hers. In a way we're all accountable for another's sins. More so are we accountable for our thoughts, for they prompt our speech. And do we ever say anything, I ask you, that doesn't have a reaction on something or someone? All right, all right, we don't do it in all cases with the intention of bringing disaster in its train. But look at you, look at yourself, Daniel. You wanted to free your son from his mother's apron strings, and what happens? Yes, I know I'm laying it on thick, and at this time too when you feel you need sympathy. But I want you to realise that you are not free from blame."

Daniel stared at the priest. He had come here to find comfort. He'd not returned home from the hospital until almost two this morning and he hadn't been able to sleep. He had glimpsed only one ward in that place but the sight and sounds were haunting him. He had said to the doctor, "Isn't there any private place she could go?" And he had replied, "Not in her present condition. And there's none such around here." And now for his dear friend here to take this attitude! His voice was stiff as he said, "You seem of a sudden to be siding with her, Father."

"I'm on nobody's side, Daniel. As always, I'm on the touchline, running meself skinny, asking the referee to see fair play done. But I've got to catch His eye, as it were, for most of the time He's under the impression, like many another, that it's up to me, so He doesn't look the side I'm on. I'm an ordinary man, Daniel. I'm not one of God's chosen and I've no aspiration to be, and I don't see the world divided into saints and sinners; there's always a lot of grey in the middle."

Daniel remained silent. He had never known the priest's parables to irritate him before. But now he was finding that this outlook of a middle man was anything but helpful, particularly this morning when he was feeling desperate.

"I won't keep you, Father," he said; "you'll be wanting your breakfast."

As he made to rise the priest's hand pushed him none too gently back on to the seat while he said, "Me breakfast can wait for once, and I wouldn't be able to stomach it if I knew you were going off in a huff. Look—" He leaned towards him and, his hand now on Daniel's shoulder, he said, "I know what you've been through all these years. I've even condoned in me own mind your antidote against her, when I should have been condemning you for your rampaging with women. I've thought many a time, as I've listened to her ranting on about her son and God and goodness, that in your place I would have done the same. God forgive me. But Daniel, I'm sorry for any human being who has to shoulder the burden of an unnatural love like she has. She couldn't help it no more than those two youngsters could help giving in to nature. If you want to know, I'm on your side, but at the same time, as I said before, we're all accountable for another's sins. And you can't come into church here and make your confession, talking to God through me or anyone else and think, that's that, the slate's clean. It isn't. You know"—his tone lightened—"that's what Protestants think we do. They think you just have to go to confession, tell the priest you've committed murder and he says, 'Oh, you've committed a murder? Well, it's all right. I'll have a crack with God about it, and he'll wipe your slate clean. Carry on.' That's extreme, I know, but it applies to drunkenness, whoring, and coming in here to Mass on a Sunday while refusing to speak to your neighbour or relative or some such. Anyway—" He now patted Daniel on the shoulder, saying, "Everything in this life must be paid for in one way or another. But I'm with you, Daniel, all along the road. Just remember that. Now get yourself home and I would suggest that you have a bath, for you don't look your usual spruce self this morning. Eat a good breakfast, then get off to work. Yes, that's it; work, there's nothing like it."

They were back on their old footing. And the priest took Daniel's outstretched hand, then he walked with him to the door; and there he shivered, saying, "By! it's cold enough to freeze the bacon in the frying pan. We'll surely have snow for Christmas. I'll tell you something, I hate snow. Mind how you go; the roads are like glass."

Odd, people were always saying that: mind how you go, the roads are like glass. It was like a warning against life.

"Goodbye, Father, and thank you."

"Goodbye, Daniel."

Lily and Peggie were clearing up the debris of the bedroom, and Peggie, holding the cut-glass powder bowl in her hands, said, "My God! She did go at it." And to this Lily said, "Her brain must have completely turned. It was the shock of finding out."

"Oh, to my mind her brain was turned a long time afore that. Anyway, she must have been blind not to notice. And Miss Annette being sick an' all and lookin' like a sheet most of the time. But wait till it gets around; it'll set the church on fire. . . ."

Standing in the greenhouse, John Dixon and Bill White were discussing the events.

"We hadn't gone to bed," Bill said, "when we heard her. I didn't like to go up because I thought it was an ordinary shindy they were havin'. But when the ambulance came, well, I ran up then, and I couldn't believe it. There she was on a stretcher. I thought they were taking her to hospital, but no, it was The County. My God! To end up there. But in a way I'm not surprised, for she's been a tartar both inside and outside the house for years. Oh, the airs she used to put on when she was in the car. D'you know what she suggested just a while ago? That I should wear a uniform. I put it to the boss and he said, 'You don't want to wear a uniform, do you, Bill?' And I said, 'No fear, boss.' 'Well, you're not going to then,' he said. And that was that. By! he's had a life of it. I would have done her in afore now if I'd been him."

"Oh, he's seen to it that he's had his compensations."

"Who's to blame him? Not me. Anyway, things will be quiet now for a bit, I hope."

"Quiet for a bit, you say. Wait till it gets round about the youngsters. My God! If it had happened only one day after the wedding they would have been in the clear. I wonder how her people will take it? Now, there's a pair for you. Have you ever seen a fellow like her father? He stands there, doesn't say a word, but just looks. Ah well, let's get on; there's wood to chop. We'd better get a stock in afore the snow comes, because I can smell it; it's in the air."

Nurse Pringle had just left the room after saying, No, no; she wasn't surprised at what had happened last night. It took a lot to surprise her. And almost before the door had closed, Don said to Annette, "She's a cool customer."

"She has to be."

"Are you all right? You look white."

"Of course I'm all right. Don't you worry about me, please."

"Who else have I to worry about?" He stroked the hand he was holding and, looking at it, he said, "Strange, but that scene last night, it's just as if I'd had a nightmare, that it wasn't real. But then, it's not even like a nightmare, because I've had a good night's sleep. I should be feeling terribly sorry for her, but I can't; I'm just glad that I won't see her face coming in that door. It's dreadful, isn't it?" He looked up into Annette's face. "It's unnatural in a way. Yet nothing about our association has been natural." He let his head fall back on to the pillow, saying, "Strange but it's the first morning I can remember that I haven't had any pain. I feel as if—" he smiled wryly, before adding, "I could get up and walk."

"That's good. That's a good sign."

"How long do you think they'll keep her there?"

"Oh, I don't know. Dad will be going today. He'll find out more. I should think it will be some long time; she needs treatment."

Oh yes, Annette thought, she hoped it would be some long time. Enough time to let her baby be born and for her to be strong enough to insist that she take Don to their own home, because she knew that the case put forward both by Daniel and Joe that it was necessary for Don to stay here so that they would be on hand to help, was only part of their strategy; she knew it was also because they didn't want to lose touch with him. As long as he was here the family, as it were, was still together.

She felt knowledgeable about things and people now. Four months ago such thoughts would never have entered her head. Yet from the moment she woke up after the accident she had felt so much older, as if it had made her into a mature woman. But then, hadn't she been made into a woman months before that, as Don had yelled at his mother; a whole year before that? She recalled the time they had first come together. It was the day on which they had escaped her mother's vigilance, and had supposedly gone to the pictures. If only her mother had known that day what had happened, she too would have gone insane.

Oh dear me! She still had that journey before her and that inevitable scene.

She said now to Don, "Look, dear, you know what I've got to do this morning."

He screwed up his face for a moment, then said dolefully, "Oh, yes, yes. It isn't fair that you've got to stand this on your own. I should be there. I should. I should . . ."

"Now don't get yourself agitated. If I know anything it'll be over before it's hardly begun. That'll be that. And it's not going to worry me."

"You're sure? Because, after all, they're . . ."

"Don't say it: my parents. We've discussed this, haven't we?" She bent over him and kissed him; then smiling down into his face, she said, "Do you remember the day that I told you what I thought of my parents and you nearly choked yourself laughing? And I felt dreadful at saying the things I did. But the tears were running down your face, remember? And then you told me about your mother. I'd always known that she smothered you, more than mothered you, but at the time you made it sound so funny, and we clung to each other laughing. Remember?"

"Yes, yes." He traced his fingers now around her face, and there was a break in his voice as he asked, "Why had this to happen to us?"

She did not immediately answer him; but then she said, "I've asked that every day for weeks."

The muscles of his face tightening now, he asked the dreaded question: "And you have told yourself, 'He'll never be able to love me again.' "

"No, no"—her voice was firm as she pulled herself upright—"because you do love me and I you . . . even without that."

"Oh, Annette"—again he put his hand out to her—"don't delude yourself. It's all part of the process."

"Well, we've had a good share of the process, haven't we?" There was a break in her voice now. "Just think of that. I'm carrying the results of the process, aren't I?" She patted her stomach and, forcing back the tears, she brought laughter into her voice as she said, "And tonight I'm getting into that bed with you, so move over, Don Coulson." Then giving his face a light slap, she turned swiftly away, saying, "I'm going to get ready. . . ."

Half an hour later she got into the car. It would be less than a five-minute run to her old home, and she knew exactly where she'd find her parents when she reached there at about ten o'clock. Her father would be in his study, going over the previous day's reports from their shops: four grocery and three greengrocery establishments, as well as an antique shop in the upper quarter of the town, and a junk shop near the market. At half-past ten he would leave the house and do spot checks on the establishments, varying his time of arrival so as to catch out someone, as he saw it, not doing his duty. It was said that he had the quickest turnover of staff in the town: misdemeanours, however small, were not tolerated under his management.

Her mother would have already been in the kitchen and given Polly orders for the meals of the day. She would have examined the larder and the refrigerator. She would have checked the stores in the cupboard. And it being Thursday, and with the Catholic Ladies' Guild meeting being held in the afternoon in the drawing-room, she would likely have given Janie and Sarah their weekly admonishment as to their duties—she still insisted on their wearing frilly caps and aprons after lunch. She had often wondered how Janie had reigned so long in the house, because she hated wearing them. She had watched her snap one from her head and throw it on the kitchen floor, then pick it up and, laughing, say, "You won't split, will you, miss, will you?" And she could hear Polly saying, "She won't split, else she won't get a jam tart at eleven." There had been no eating between meals in her home.

It was Sarah who opened the door to her. "Oh, hello, miss," she said. "But isn't it cold? Freeze the drops in your nose, this would. How are you?"

"I'm fine, Sarah. How are you?"

"Oh, you know, miss; you know me, waiting for that rich man to come along and sweep me off my feet."

It was her usual remark, and Annette said, "Well, if I meet him on the road back, I'll tell him to hurry up." This was their usual banter. Sarah, Polly and Janie and their predecessors were the only light relief she had found in this house.

"Where's Mother?"

"Oh, in her rest-room, miss; you know."

"Polly all right . . . and Janie?"

"Yes, miss." Sarah's voice was subdued now. "Nice if you could pop in afore you go."

"I'll try, but I doubt it will be this morning."

"Oh." Sarah's mouth was pursed . . . which said a lot for her understanding of the situation in the house.

For such an imposing house it lacked a hall; in its place was a very broad and long corridor, at the end of which was a similar but shorter one. She turned into it and knocked on the first door. It was several seconds before a voice called, "Come in."

She entered the room that had always appeared to her to be partly a chapel, for in one corner stood a small altar, in the centre of which was a crucifix flanked on one side by the figure of Mary and on the other by the figure of Joseph, and to the right of it, attached to the wall, a glass holy water font. In front of the altar was a padded knee-stool from which she knew her mother had just risen.

"Hello, dear."

"Hello, Mother."

"You're visiting early."

"Yes, yes, I suppose I am."

"How is Don?"

"Much the same . . . Mother?"

"Yes, my dear?"

"I have something to tell you. Sit down."

Mrs. Allison stared at her daughter. She wasn't used to being told to sit down, at least not by this child of hers. She sat down, but noted that her daughter didn't. And now she said, "Well, I'm sitting down, so what have you to tell me?"

"Mother-in-law was taken to The County asylum last night."

"*What!*" Mrs. Allison half rose from the chair, then subsided again, to sit breathing heavily for a while before saying, "Well, it's really not surprising, Winifred has always been very highly strung. But what brought this about? Some kind of fracas?"

"Yes, you could say that."

Her mother stared at her and her mouth opened and closed twice before she said, "Concerning you?"

"Definitely concerning me . . . You see, Mother, I'm pregnant. I'm going to have a baby. I'm surprised you haven't noticed. But then, of course, I've been wearing loose dresses and coats. And you've very rarely looked at me, have you, not properly?"

She watched her mother's hand move slowly across the lower part of her face; she saw the thumb press into one cheek and the fingers into the other, forcing colour into the pale skin around them.

"Oh, my God!" she cried, the words muffled by the palm of her hand. "I . . . I knew there was something . . . something that I should have seen, but not this. Oh! . . . Oh! your father." She now took her hand from her face and placed it on the top of her head as if pressing herself down into the seat and muttered, "Dear God."

For her mother to mention God's name twice, apart from in a prayer, was an indication of how the news was affecting her. Yet she had not raised her voice. And that was the difference between the two mothers: her mother-in-law had screamed her anger, whereas her own mother was able to contain herself. Appearances must be kept up.

Annette watched her mother press a bell on the wall, while she continued to stare at her daughter. She said nothing until the door opened and Sarah appeared; and she listened with amazement at her mother's composure, as in a perfectly calm voice she said, "Ask Mr. Allison if he can spare a moment; I would like to speak to him."

"Yes, ma'am."

When the door had closed the shock returned to Mrs. Allison's voice as she said, "This will have a terrible effect on your father and his standing in the church. Oh!" She closed her eyes for a moment. "Do you realise what you have done, girl? You have ruined us. We won't be able to lift our heads up again. And that wedding! All those people at that wedding, and you in white . . . purity. Oh!" She jerked herself up out of the chair and began to pace the room.

It was just as Annette was about to defend herself that the door opened and her father appeared. As usual, his presence seemed to fill the room and make it appear smaller: his height and breadth, and his sheer bulk . . . the stiff, quiet bulk of him which she could never recall being disturbed in any way. "Good morning, Annette," he said. His tone was level.

"Good morning, Father."

"You're early. Is everything . . . ?"

That his wife dared to cut him off in the middle of a sentence by saying, "James, this is no time for niceties; she has something to tell you," caused him to breathe deeply before he turned his enquiring gaze from his wife to his daughter, at whom he now stared for a full minute without speaking, and then he said simply, "Yes?"

Her stomach had trembled all the way here; she had felt sick with it. But the fear was not new; she had always been afraid of this man. He was her father; yet, unlike other fathers, he had never put his arms about her. He had never held her head against that broad chest. When he had kissed her, it was on the brow, and that was rarely. More than once since she had conceived the child within her she had wondered how her own conception had come about: what had stirred his bulk to create, and how had her prim, composed mother responded? Had they both later been ashamed of the act? Yes, yes, she could imagine that. And ever since they must have prayed to expunge it, for she had never seen them kiss. She had never even seen them hold hands. They slept in separate beds. As far back as she could remember they had always had separate beds. Her mother, she knew, undressed in the dressing-room and under her nightie, and had taught her to do the same. Her mind now gave a jump back to the previous night, when she had stood naked with Don's hand on her stomach. Would that sight have broken down her father's façade?

"I'm going to have a baby, Father."

No muscle of his face moved, except that his eyelids seemed to droop slightly.

"You've heard what she said, James? You've heard what she said?" Her mother was clutching the front of her woollen dress with both hands as if she was suddenly very cold. "You see, it must have happened . . ."

"Quiet!" The word itself was said quietly, but it was a command. "You say you are going to have a child?"

"Yes, Father."

"Conceived out of wedlock?"

"You could say so, Father."

"I could say so? But what have *you* to say? You who were brought up in strict piety—have defiled yourself."

"We'll have to move. I couldn't bear it," her mother put in.

He cast a glance at his wife, but his attention was brought back swiftly to Annette for she was exclaiming, "Oh yes, follow the Tolletts. They too couldn't stand the shame of Maria having a baby. She was another one who had been brought up in strict piety. You're hypocrites, both of you." Now she did see a change in her father's face: she watched the purple hue take over and she saw that for a moment he was unable to speak, staggered apparently by the accusation and audacity of this child, as he thought her—at least, he had until a moment ago—for she went on, "I've thought it for a long time and I'll say it now: it's all show; stained-glass window in the church; offering to pay for the new organ, but begrudging your shop staff a shilling or so rise. It's all show. And look at you." She flung her hand from one to the other. "Have you ever been happy together? I was glad to be at school, just to get away from this house."

Her father was now speaking through tight lips: "Do you know what you have done, girl?" His voice was thin and sounded deadly, with a deep finality about it. "You have severed yourself from me."

Annette stood staring, her eyelids blinking, her throat full. She had thought she could get through this meeting without breaking down, but now the tears rained down her cheeks and she cried, "My mother-in-law was taken to the asylum last night, not only because she came upon me standing naked before my husband, but also because, like you both, she has religious mania, and is an unnatural parent. And you needn't worry about severing me from the family. That certainly works both ways."

If she had turned into the devil incarnate they could not have looked on her with more horror and distaste, and it appeared to Annette at this moment that her father was actually swelling, his whole appearance so frightening she felt she must get out of the house at once.

She turned and pushed her way from the room and along the corridor to where Sarah was waiting near the front door. And on the sight of her, Sarah exclaimed, "Oh, miss. Oh! Oh, miss. Don't take on. It'll be all right. You just stick to your guns. We're all for you."

Annette could say nothing in reply. She ran blindly across the drive to the car, but once she had seated herself, she would not allow herself to set off until her spasm of crying had stopped when, having dried her eyes and face, she turned the car about and drove away from the home of her childhood, knowing that whether they stayed or went, her parents would never recognise her again.

FIVE

*I*t was nearing the end of March. The sun was bright and the month had ceased to keep to pattern, for there was no high wind today. It was Saturday and visiting day at the County Mental Hospital. Daniel, Flo, and Harvey were standing in the hallway amid a gentle toing and froing of patients and visitors. The grounds outside were already dotted with people walking between the flower beds, and as Daniel glanced out through the open door, he said, in an undertone, "If the inside was half as attractive as the outside of this place it would do."

"Why do you think we have to wait?" asked Flo.

"Your guess is as good as mine and you know it, Flo: somebody's just mentioned my name to her and she's had a screaming fit."

"She seemed much improved when we were last here."

Daniel looked at Harvey. "Yes," he said; "no offence meant, but she could even tolerate you, whereas I'm still the thorn in her flesh and always will be apparently. So it would seem there's not much chance of her improving unless I could be got rid of in some way."

"Don't talk like that, Daniel," Flo said sharply. "Anyway, the impression I got is that they are very good to the patients."

"You've only been here twice, Flo, so we have different opinions on that.

From what I've seen, if you're not quite round the bend when you come in you'll certainly have travelled the distance before you're ready to go out; I'm sure they must imbibe one another's disorders. I hate the place." Daniel turned quickly towards an approaching nurse who, smiling broadly, said to him, "Matron would like to have a word with you, Mr. Coulson." She passed her smile over Harvey and Flo, then turned away; and Daniel followed her down a bare stone corridor and into an office where, behind a desk, sat a comparatively young woman and, to her side, a middle-aged man.

The man stood up and held out his hand to Daniel, saying, "How are you, Mr. Coulson?" to which Daniel replied, "Quite well, doctor, thank you," then inclined his head towards the matron.

When seated, he waited for one or the other of them to speak. And it was the doctor who said, "Naturally you'll be wanting to know how your wife is faring. Over the last two or three weeks . . . it is three weeks since you were here?" He now turned his head to the matron. "That so, matron?" And, looking down on a ledger, matron said, "Yes; yes, it is three weeks since Mr. Coulson's last visit."

Thinking they must be blaming him for his neglect, Daniel now put in, "I've been under the weather myself; sort of 'flu.' "

"Oh. Oh—" the doctor wagged his finger at him now—"we are not criticising you for your absence, don't believe that for a moment, but matron felt that you should be put in the picture as to your wife's progress and what might impede it . . ."

As he paused Daniel put in, "And what is that?"

"Well"—it was the matron who now took up the conversation—"I'm afraid Mr. Coulson, it is yourself; you know what happened the last time she saw you. Well now, it's any mention of your name or that of your son that puts her . . . well, puts her back, we'll say. The only persons she seems to appreciate a visit from are her sister and her friend." And the doctor, nodding in agreement, said, "It's strange, isn't it? We had thought that in her condition she would be against all men, but it seems no, for the twice he has been here she has greeted him quite normally, and there has been no reaction. Otherwise she has progressed in that she no longer goes into tantrums; in fact, she has responded to treatment amazingly well. So, what we think Mr. Coulson, is that it would be better if she doesn't see you for a while but that her sister could, if possible, visit her more frequently. Up till your last visit we had hopes that she would soon be well enough to go home, at least for a day or even a week-end. That won't be possible, I'm afraid. We are sorry about this."

"Oh, you needn't be sorry; I quite understand. But tell me: if her attitude towards me and the mention of her family upsets her like this, how long do you imagine that it will go on?"

"Oh, that is hard to say in these cases," the doctor answered. "It's a time-taking business. We are hoping that she will respond to the electric treatment in that it will eventually tone down, if not obliterate, her animosity towards you."

Daniel made no comment, but his thoughts were: only death would obliterate her hate of him. He rose to his feet now, saying, "It will be better if I don't come at all then?"

"For the time being." The doctor moved towards him. "But as I said, if her sister could come more frequently it might be helpful."

"She lives in London. It would be impossible for her to come up every week."

"Well, as often as she possibly can would be appreciated."

"I'll ask her. Thank you." And he nodded to one then the other and went out.

In the hall, Flo was standing at the window watching Harvey talking to a patient. She turned at Daniel's approach, saying, "Isn't it sad? She's been talking to him, that woman out there, quite normally, as normal as you or I, more so I should say; then she asked him if he would like to go out and see the garden."

Daniel's mind was not at the moment sensitive to such feelings, and he said abruptly, "They don't want me to visit her again, but they're asking you to come more often. How about it?"

Flo paused for a moment; then shrugging her shoulders, she said, "Yes, it's all right. We may not be able to manage it every week, but we'll try. Anything to help her. May I go to see her now?"

"Yes. Yes, I suppose so."

She was turning away when she stopped and said, "You shouldn't be surprised at her not wanting to see you, Daniel."

"No, I shouldn't. I don't know why I come."

"Because you feel it's your duty, I suppose."

"Yes, I suppose so. But now, apparently, I'm relieved of it and the burden's been passed to you."

"Oh, don't look at it that way. Anyway, we'll talk about it later."

When she was gone he stared through the window, to see Harvey was now strolling with the woman; then presently he went out and joined them.

"Oh, there you are." Harvey did not go on to ask why he wasn't visiting Winifred, but said, "This is Mrs. Deebar."

The lady in question, who was in her early sixties, leaned forward towards Harvey and, smiling broadly, she said, "You haven't got it right. It's De . . . bar. It's not like the De in Debrett."

"Oh, I'm sorry." Harvey now turned to Daniel, saying, "Mrs. Debar is a novelist. She's had a book published called—" He paused and looked at the woman, and she, still smiling a very sweet smile, said, "Manners and Decorum in The Victorian Era."

Daniel made the required motion with his head now, saying, "That sounds very interesting," to which the lady replied, "Well, one tries one's best. I've had a lot of help from Mr. Disraeli."

Daniel and Harvey exchanged glances. They said nothing, but continued to look at the lady. And she, turning to and giving all her attention to Harvey, said, "Thank you for your company. It isn't often one has the opportunity to meet and converse with the uncivilised, but it is nevertheless very enlightening, even instructive. Now, if you'll excuse me, I'm expecting Mr. Macmillan to tea. Good day, gentlemen."

They each muttered something that was inaudible, then watched her walking, in fact, tripping between the flower beds and across the drive towards the main door. Not until she had disappeared did they look at one another; and then it was Harvey whose voice held a chuckle as he muttered, "I . . . I should have guessed, I suppose. But she was talking as sanely as you or I."

"God help her!"

"Oh, I don't think you need to be sorry for her. If it could be analysed I think she's happier in her world than we are in ours. You only had to look at her face; it was quite serene. And—" his voice taking on a sad note now he said, "She must have been quite beautiful in her day. But that last bit"—he chuckled—" 'uncivilised'. Well, it's only what a great many still think, I suppose."

As they both turned to go back inside, Harvey asked, "What has happened?"

"Something that mightn't please you. Apparently the onus is going to be on Flo. They've worked it out that the sight of me only makes matters worse, and that the only one they think it advisable for her to see is Flo."

"Well, I can see no obstacle to that. It's all right with me. I certainly don't mind coming; in fact, I'm glad to get away from London."

"But you don't know how long it's going to last."

"Well, we'll just have to wait and see, won't we? But if that's all you've got to worry about, Daniel, you can stop now. As you know, Flo and Winifred never got on, but since this happened, Flo has . . . well, become sorry for her."

"Most people have."

"Yes, yes, I suppose so. It's like an assault case: the victim is often forgotten; the main objective is to get the perpetrator off. Anyway, don't worry about us; you have plenty of that to do back in the house. It's just on Annette's time, isn't it?"

"Well, no; she's a bit longer to go yet. And that's another thing: how will she take the news of a grandson or daughter? I've little hope that it will revive some sort of interest in her. I can't see anything stirring that apathy of hers now, except the sight of me."

But there Daniel was wrong. Winifred was sitting in the large room, Flo by her side. There were other people, seemingly family groups all about; some were talking together, others were just sitting still staring at the patient while the patient looked into space. In one group two small girls were laughing. It was a strange sound because it was ordinary laughter.

Flo, looking at her sister, felt pity rising from the depths of her. She had never liked Winnie: they had nothing in common, but she wouldn't have wished the devil in hell to find himself in a situation like this . . . in a place like this. Winnie, she knew, had always been good to herself, had her fill, food-wise and comfort-wise, but had remained empty. She had needed love, oh yes, she had needed love, and to love. But she had centred this on the wrong one.

She now put her hand on Winifred's and said, "Don sends his love."

"Who?"

There was no insanity in the eyes that looked into hers; at least, the look in them was not that which she would have expected in the eyes of anyone insane. Whatever this new attitude was she felt it didn't stem from madness.

And her voice was slightly sharp as she said, "Now Winnie, don't act like that! Don is your son and you love . . ."

"I have no son."

"You have three sons."

"Huh! Three sons you say? Would I be mother to an idiot, a bastard, and a cripple?"

Inwardly Flo felt herself shrinking away from the hate showing on her sister's face as she hissed out the truth, for indeed, she was mother to an idiot, a bastard and a cripple. But put like that it sounded horrifying. She stared at Winifred now realising that her sister wasn't mad in that sense, she was just burned up with hate. Hate was a terrible emotion, a consuming fire that in Winifred's case could never be douched. That would mean she would remain here for . . . Oh! She actually shook her head at the thought of her sister having to spend the rest of her life in this place, a place which gave her the creeps even to visit.

Thinking as she did, she was afterwards to ask herself what made her make such a remark, as "Don't talk like that, Winnie; you could have so much to look forward to. There's a child coming; you will be a grand-mother," for her hand was thrust away so quickly that it hit the edge of the chair and she had to hold her wrist tightly to stop herself from crying out. And now she was gaping at Winifred, whose body was shaking as if with an ague, and through her trembling lips she was hissing: "It's you who should be in here, daring to suggest I will be a grandmother to a child with a whore for its mother and fathered by the other bastard. My son was pure, do you hear? My son was pure . . ."

Flo was aware of the approach of a nurse who said nothing, but with a slight motion of her hand conveyed to Flo to take her leave; which she did hurriedly. Yet she was not quick enough to escape Winifred's voice yelling obscenities after her, and causing an uproar in the room.

Both Harvey and Daniel came towards her as she entered the hallway.

"What is it? You're as white as a sheet." She looked at Daniel for a moment then, lowering her head she said, "I was a fool. I brought up things I shouldn't. I thought to create . . . to . . . Oh dear!"

Harvey said nothing but, putting an arm around her shoulder, led her outside.

In the car, Daniel said bitterly, "It will be better if nobody comes; let her stew in her own juice."

"Oh, Daniel, don't be like that. One could go insane just being in that place and among those people."

"Come; don't upset yourself; don't you cry."

Harvey pulled her tightly to him. "And don't be sorry for those people. Listen, I'll tell you what happened to me and Daniel." And he went on to tell her about Mrs. Debar.

But he failed to make her laugh, or even smile. Instead, she said, "God help her. God help them all."

They had just finished their evening meal. Throughout, the conversation at the table had been stilted; and now Daniel, looking at Annette, said, "You all right, hinny? You look a bit peaky."

"Yes, yes, I'm fine, Dad."

"She's tired." This came from Joe. "She's been on her feet all day. Why do nurses insist on the week-end for their days off? Of course, yes, don't say it." He closed his eyes and flapped his hand at them. "That was a silly thing to say because we are all on hand at the week-end." And poking his head forward across the table towards Annette he said, "We can manage you know, and when I say we I'm including Stephen, if you'll leave us alone."

She smiled now as she said, "I think you need supervision, both of you."

Flo now said, "It's amazing how that boy has changed, isn't it, seemingly in all ways." She was looking at Daniel and she emphasised, "Well, it is. We are not with him all the time so we notice it, don't we, Harvey?"

"Well, yes; we can see it: he's no longer the child, or shall I say childish."

"You're right there." Joe was nodding at him. "The amazing thing to me is he's had a dry bed for weeks now. You could say it was from shortly after"—he paused, not quite sure of his choice of words which would have been, "since Mam left," so he substituted, "since Don had to be seen to."

"He loves being with Don," Annette put in, "and the nurse is wonderful with him. She calls him the superintendent. He glows at that. And Don likes him to be there. Imagine, a few weeks ago we couldn't have left them for this length of time. What is it?" She turned and looked at the clock. "Over half an hour, which tells me I must return to duty." But in a low voice, she added, "But it's no duty."

"Duty or no duty, you sit where you are and have a natter. I'm going along now, so do as you're told." Joe stabbed his finger at her and repeated, "Do as you're told for once, stay put." Then turning to Flo, he said, "And you see she does, woman." Then his laughter joined Harvey's as Harvey cried, "Be careful, you big fellow, I'm the only one who has the right to call her woman, me being uncivilised."

Joe left the room amid laughter that had its basis in an attempt to bring normality into the atmosphere, and as he entered the sick-room he was greeted with more laughter, the hiccupping kind, from Stephen, who cried at him, "I've been tellin' Don about that time, you remember, Joe? when Mrs. Osborne came. You remember? And I told her she could drink out of the saucer and blow on her tea if she liked."

He was laughing again, and Don too was laughing, and Joe said, "Oh, yes, I remember that day. You got your backside twanked, didn't you?"

As he spoke he was seeing Stephen not as he normally thought of him, as the lad or the boy, but as Harvey saw him now. He did indeed seem to have aged a little. And it was true, he hadn't wet his bed. And, now he thought of it, he hadn't had a crying fit for months, either. And then he could help lift Don as well as he himself or his dad did, and help to change him too, and with gentleness.

Looking at the tray on the side table, Joe remarked, "You didn't get him to eat his dinner though, did you, clever clogs?"

"I wasn't hungry." Don now put his hand out towards Stephen, saying, "You know that game we used to play?"

"Tiddleywinks, Don?"

"No, no; the one you call bumps, you know with the checkers. It's up in your room. Do you think you could get it, because I would like a game?"

"Oh, yes, yes, Don. I'll go now. I'll go now." And he was about to rush from the room when he turned and looked at Joe and said, "All right?"

"Yes; yes, all right. Go ahead and get it."

Once they were alone together Don, with the aid of his elbows, edged himself on to the pillows, saying, "I . . . I want to have a word with you before Annette comes in. We never seem to be alone, do we? I've been wanting to . . . well say something to you for some time now, Joe. Sit down and listen, will you?"

Joe drew the chair up close to the bedhead and, looking tenderly down on the white face, he said, "Fire ahead."

"It's . . . it's about Annette."

"What about her? She's all right, she's doing fine. You won't have all that long to go before you see your . . ."

Don's hand came on to his now and pressed it as he said, "You've put your finger on it, I won't have that long to go."

"Oh, now, now!" Joe pulled his hand roughly away. "Stop that nonsense. Don't take me up wrong. You've been doing fine since you came home."

Don now turned his head away and said slowly, "Joe, please. If . . . if I can't speak the truth to you, who can I speak it to? You know as well as I do time's running out." He now tapped the counterpane in the direction of his stomach, before saying, "They were thinking of taking me in again with that. But if they do, it'll be a quick end, so they suspect. That's why they're putting it off. But I don't suspect; I know. And my breathing's getting . . . worse. Now, now!" He was looking at Joe again. "Please, Joe. She'll likely be back at . . . any minute, and it's about her I want to speak. And listen to me, don't say a word until I'm finished. No matter what you think, don't . . . don't say a word. And it's just this. By rights you should have married Annette . . . Please!" His fingers went into a fist and when Joe was about to emphatically check his words, Don put in, "If Dad hadn't manoeuvred and pushed me forward just because . . . because he thought it was best, I know that, to get me out of . . . Mam's clutches, she would have continued to admire you. She always did, you know . . . from when she was a schoolgirl. But even when . . . when she turned to me, I was afraid at first that it was only a flash in the pan and then there would be you again. I loved you, Joe, but I loved her too. So I—" He paused for breath, gasped for a moment, then almost in a rush he said, "I deliberately made sure she would be mine. I was the one who made the first . . . move, not her. And . . . and once done, it went on. Then that didn't seem enough. I could have continued like that with no results, but . . . but I made up my mind there *would* be a result; at least, I hoped there would and that would clinch it. And it did. But then I was scared, we were both scared, very scared. That's why I insisted on the wedding being brought forward . . . 'The best laid schemes o' mice an' men gang aft a-gley.' God, there's never been a truer saying . . ."

"No more. No more. I know all about it."

"You do?"

"Yes, yes, I do: Dad being supposedly with you all the time when you went out, but him going off too, leaving you two alone, and you went straight to the cottage."

"How did you know that?"

"Intuition, partly, but I happened to go to the cottage one day with the plans. You remember Annette wanted the kitchen extended, and before I turned up the farm track I happened to see the car outside. And that night both you and Dad talked as if you had been together all the time. So, what are you worrying about? Tell me something I don't know."

"Yes, yes, I will. When . . . when I'm gone I . . . I want you to look after Annette and the child, to do what you've always wanted to do: marry her."

Joe got slowly to his feet, saying now, his voice firm, "You're alive, Don. You're going to be alive for a long time yet. What you haven't taken into account is that Annette looks upon me as a brother, a big brother. She loves you and always will."

"Sit down, Joe, *please*. This business of . . . of love and death, I've given them a lot of thought of late. Yes, Annette loved me during that year we were together. Funny, but when I went for Mam that time I called it 'The Year of The Virgins'; and yes, we were both virgins. But love can still be love even if it changes. Annette still . . . still loves me but in a . . . a different way. She is my nurse, my companion, and yes, she even plays the mother, strangely while waiting to be a mother herself. And because she . . . she is waiting for that I think she is somehow apart. I think if the accident hadn't happened I would have learned to understand that . . . because she was carrying the child she had in a way grown apart, somehow self-reliant, taken up with what she is nourishing. All . . . all women must feel that. And you know, lying here thinking, I don't believe that love can ever be the same once a woman has a child . . . because . . . because she's housed it in her body and in some way the man has lost a piece of her. Strange thing." He smiled wanly now. "But along those lines I can even understand Mam, although, oh God! I don't want to see her again, ever, Joe." He turned and groped for Joe's hand. "That might s . . . sound awful of me, but I dread the thought that she'll ever come back here."

"I don't think you need worry very much about that. By what Dad's said and by what Flo confirmed, the very thought of facing your Dad again would indeed send her mad."

"Well, with treatment, she will likely get over it some time. But I hope I die before that time comes."

"You're not going to die. Will you stop it?"

"No, I won't stop it, Joe, because, let me tell you, I'm . . . I'm not afraid of dying. I was some months ago, but not any more. It's those who are so healthy and strong and . . . and all people like you who are afraid of dying. But when you lose your body and you've only got your mind left it puts things in perspective. The only thing . . . I want to live for is to see my child born. And then I'll be quite glad to go, because"—his voice ended on a break—"I'm in pain, Joe, deep pain. The pills don't erase it entirely. The injections do, but I don't want too many of those."

Joe was unable to speak and it was with relief that he greeted Stephen when the door burst open to admit the young fellow who was carrying a narrow wooden box and saying, "I had a job to find it. It was on top of the cupboard. You remember, Maggie put it up there because it made so much rattle when we played it."

"That wasn't why she put it up there," said Joe, "it was because you cheated."

"I didn't, Joe. Did I, Don?"

"No, you didn't Stephen, you never cheated."

"You were just jokin', Joe, weren't you?"

"Yes, big boy, I was just joking."

Joe ruffled the head that was on a level with his own and, in a quieter voice, he said, "I don't think I would play the game with Don tonight; he's a bit tired."

"You tired, Don?"

"Yes, I am a little, Stephen. We'll have a game tomorrow. Ah"—he looked towards the door—"here's the boss, and she wouldn't let us play on the clean counterpane, would she?"

"What's this about playing on the clean counterpane?"

"I . . . I brought the checkers game."

"Oh, that rattly thing."

"There you are." Joe nodded at Stephen now. "I bet you don't reign long with that one."

"Ah! you." Stephen now punched Joe in the chest, saying, "You would get me into trouble, wouldn't you?"

"Yes, if I could, but it's so difficult to catch you out in anything these days."

He watched the big form wriggle as a younger boy might, then say, "Oh! Joe; you're teasin' me, aren't you? Pulling my leg, you are, aren't you?"

"I've never touched your leg. I wouldn't touch your leg with a barge-pole."

As Stephen laughed it came to Joe that legs were a tactless topic. But Don was smiling and saying, "Go on, you two, get out. I never seem to get a minute alone with my wife; there's always one or the other of you here. All right. All right." He wagged his finger towards Stephen. "I'll play you a game tomorrow."

"Come on, big boy." Joe marshalled Stephen from the room, and Annette, taking the chair that Joe had vacated, said to Don, "Don't you think there's a change in Stephen; I mean, for the better?"

"Yes. Yes, I do. I thought I was imagining it, but since you mention it, yes." He looked up at her now and paused a moment before asking her: "How are you feeling, really? Tell me; don't just say, all right."

"To tell the truth, darling, I don't know exactly how I'm feeling, never ever having had the privilege of being in this condition before." She tweaked his nose now. "I suppose it's natural to feel . . . well . . ." She screwed up her face now. "Sometimes I think that he or she could come tomorrow; but I've got several weeks to go yet."

"Do you feel ill? I mean, just a . . ."

"No, I don't feel ill. And stop worrying. Here, let me put your pillows straight."

As she rose from the chair she asked herself, "Do I feel ill?" And the answer she was given was, "Yes, in a way more like feeling odd; so odd I should go and see the doctor on Monday."

SIX

*I*t was the last week in March 1961 and very cold. Some were saying they could smell the snow, while others countered with, Don't be ridiculous; all that's happening is we've had two nights of keen frosts.

It was after seven o'clock and the house had dropped into its evening quiet when the front door bell rang. Maggie happened to be passing through the hall and, on opening the door, said, "Oh, good evening, Father."

"Good evening, Maggie. And what a snifter! I shouldn't be surprised if we have snow; I shouldn't at all."

"Oh, the times I've heard that today. We're touching April, the daffodils are out. Anyway, are you better, Father? I hear you've had a nasty time of it."

Maggie was helping him off with his coat now as he said, "I'm the fellow who created the saying, 'Swinging the lead.' They say it was originally a timing device; don't you believe it. I've had them all run off their feet for the past two weeks or more and I've enjoyed every minute of it." He coughed now, a deep rumbling cough, and Maggie nodded at him, saying, "Yes, yes, I can believe that, Father. At the sound of that chest I can believe it." She laughed now as she took his coat and placed it over the back of a chair. "What I can believe, too, is that you're a very queer individual, Father."

"I am that, Maggie, I am that. And anybody who says different I'll call him a liar. There's nobody queerer than me. That's another saying that sprang with me birth: 'The Queer Fella.' Where's everybody?"

"Oh, scattered around, Father."

"Well, I'll find them, I suppose." And he was on his way when he swung round, saying, "Got a minute, Maggie?" And when she turned enquiringly and walked towards him, he said, "Lent's nearly over and we're supposed either to give up something that's dear to our hearts or do something that could be dear to our hearts. And you know, Maggie, there's one thing I've always craved to do and that's make a convert. I've never knowingly made a convert, not in my whole career. Now wouldn't you like to please an old man and step over the wall?"

She pushed him as she gurgled with laughter, saying, "Go on with you, Father. If anybody could have got me into your tribe it would have been you; but even you and all the tea in China wouldn't make me take that step."

"You're a hard woman, Maggie. I've always known that you're a hard woman." His smile denied his words. Then leaning towards her and lowering his voice, he said, "When you produce the bottle, bring some hot water and sugar with it, eh?"

She was chuckling too as she said, "Hot water and sugar it is, you queer fella. Hot water and sugar it is."

As he turned, laughing, from Maggie, he saw Annette coming along the corridor and she greeted him with, "Hello, Father. You're up?"

"Well, if I'm not, I must be walking in me sleep with all me clothes on. How are you, my dear?" He put his hand on her shoulder. "The last I heard, you were ordered to bed for a time."

"Yes, but I'm fine now."

"Sure?"

"Nearly sure."

"Like that is it?"

"Like that, Father."

"Strain telling?"

"No, not really; it's just that . . . well"—she smiled now—"I'm not used to this business, you know." She put her hand on her high abdomen, and he, serious now, said, "No, no, you're not, child; but I'd go careful, it's a critical time. Obey the doctor's orders. I had a word with him the other day when he was trying to find out what was wrong with me, and he couldn't, so he said, 'Get up on your pins because I'm not coming in any more.' He then told me you were tired. And it's no wonder, so—" his voice serious again, his hand on her head, he said, "Go careful; he would like to see his child. You know that, don't you?" He did not add, "That's what he's hanging on for." But she answered, "Yes, yes, I know that, Father."

"And you know there's a possibility he will have to go into hospital again?"

"Yes, yes, I know that also, Father."

"Ah, well, we all know where we stand, don't we?" And his voice rising, he ended, "Where's the head of the house?"

"The last time I saw him he was making for his study."

"Well, I'll slip along and see him, then have a word with Don."

"He'll be pleased to see you, Father. He's missed you these last few weeks."

"Ah, that's nice to know. It's nice to be missed. I'll tell you something, though: there's one who didn't miss me. He's had the time of his life, I understand, in that pulpit. You know who."

"Yes, I know, Father. The church has been very warm these last few Sundays."

His laughter rang out as he said, "Ha! ha! That's a good one. Opened up a few more furnaces, has he? Well, let me get back on to that stand and I'll cool 'em down. You take me word for it."

"I've no doubt of that, Father."

They went their separate ways laughing, and the priest, knocking on the study door, called, "It's me! May I come in?"

"Oh yes, yes, come in, Father," Daniel called, and on the priest's entering the room, he said, "I never expected to see you; I didn't know you were up."

"Nobody seems to expect to see me except at me funeral. I've disappointed a lot of people, I can tell you. Anyway, I'm here and I've just given Maggie orders about the hot water and the sugar. Is that all right?"

Daniel made no answer to this but said, "Sit down. Come up to the fire."

The priest sat down and gazed at the flickering electric logs, saying, "They give off a good heat; a little imagination and you feel you could stick a poker into them. I'm going to treat meself to one of those some day and put it in me bedroom, because, believe me, Iceland's nothing compared with that room. That's what's given me this." He tapped his chest. "Now the damage is done, they're going to put in central heating. The belief that freezing cold is good for the soul and dampens the emotions is poppycock; there's more people jump into bed together in cold rooms than there's ever been counted. Anyway, how are you?"

"Oh, I'm all right, Father. But how are you? How long have you been up and about?"

"Oh, for the last three or four days. By the way, if you don't mind me saying so, I don't like the look of Annette. She looks peaky, very tired. It's natural of course to be tired at this stage of her condition, but she doesn't look right to me."

"She's been worrying about Don, as we all are."

The door opened and Maggie came in with a tray on which stood a decanter, a jug of hot water, two glasses and a bowl of brown sugar. And the priest greeted her with, "Ah, here's the soul's solace. Thanks, Maggie, you're one in a thousand. You're still determined not to come in?"

When Daniel looked from one to the other in enquiry, the priest, with a solemn expression, said, "I made her an offer to be my first convert, but she refused; threw it back in my face. She doesn't know what she's missing. You know, when I was a lad I believed, at least so me mother used to tell me, if you could make one convert in your life it was as good as the key to heaven, no matter what you did after, for it could never be taken from you. I worked hard at it as a lad, because I understood that once I had the key I could rampage about as much as I liked and me heavenly future was fixed: a house with a billiard table, the lot . . ."

"He's a dreadful man, isn't he?" Maggie was looking at Daniel now and he said, "The worst I've come across. Thanks." He nodded down at the tray.

Maggie now said, "When you get through that lot, ring for refills." And at this both men burst out laughing.

With the room to themselves again, the priest said, "She's a good woman, that Maggie, and you're not a good man towards her. You know that, Daniel?"

"It all depends, Father, on what you term good. Good for what? Good for whom? Good for each other? Or not good for each other? I've had a lifetime, as you know, of not being good for each other."

As Daniel poured out the whisky the priest watched him, then took the glass from his hand and sniffed it appreciatively, before taking a long drink. Then he lay back in his chair, staring ahead for a moment as he said, "I saw her this afternoon."

"You did?"

"Yes; I was over there, and I looked in on her."

"And how did you find her?"

The priest sighed. Then, placing his glass on the table, he said, "I think it would take a miracle, a large one, to bring her back to normality. And yet she talks sensibly enough, at least until"—he flapped his hand—"this house is mentioned, or any person in it. Perhaps I shouldn't have brought it up, but I did. I pointed out that her beloved son was soon to be a father and she a grandmother, and wasn't that marvellous?"

"And she went wild."

"No, no, she didn't. She just sat there and stared at me. But I couldn't bear to see the look on her face nor watch her body go rigid, so I called a nurse and left. On my way back I was set to thinking of the things we do in the name of morality, such as persuading people to stick to a recognised code, to follow a line of duty, and I thought if I hadn't persuaded you to stay, but let you do what you wanted and leave her that first time, things mightn't have reached this state today."

"Oh, don't trouble your head with that, Father. They would have reached this state in any case, because don't forget, she had a son who—and I'm not blaspheming when I say this, Father—I'm sure she had convinced herself she had come by the Immaculate Conception, or the Virgin Birth, or whatever. It wasn't only the fact of losing her son to another woman, but the fact that he had bespoiled himself—that is a favourite word of hers—with a woman before marriage, and that this filth, as she used to term it so often, had been going on for a year, practically under her nose. That's what finished her. Of course, I've known for a long time that she couldn't stand the sight of me, but at the same time she didn't want me to leave because she wouldn't then have been able to bear the thought of being the deserted wife, nor the covert satisfaction of all her friends in the church seeing her brought low. We both know, Father, that she wasn't liked even among her own kind, because right from the beginning she played the lady, and the veneer was so thin it could be seen through. Moreover, she was one of those women who wanted to rule, whether it was a Mother's Meeting, or the Children of Mary, or the Holiday Committee for Poor Children. Oh yes, she liked to be thought the good doer of good doers."

"Don't sound so bitter, Daniel, because, God help her, she's paying for her vanities. And in a way, she knows it, and that is the worst of her troubles: she is not mad, only deranged with hate and bitterness and failure. It takes a strong man or woman to face up to failure and come out of that battle unscathed. Well, what I want to say is this: that as things stand, and from what I gathered from the matron in our chat later, she's going to be there for a long time, because were she to be sent home as she is now, she would be a danger to herself and to everybody else."

"I can't say I'm sorry Father, I'd be a hypocrite otherwise, but once she entered this house again, I'd have to leave. And definitely Annette and Don would too." He looked to the side, saying, "But, as you know only too well, Father, Don could go at any time soon. So it would be better for us all if she was never let out."

The priest made no comment on Don, but hypothesised further: "Say she did come out and you left and Annette left, what about Joe and Stephen?"

"Stephen would come with me; he's my responsibility. And Maggie would come with me, Father."

The priest did not take his eyes off Daniel's face and said, "And Joe?"

"Oh, Joe wouldn't stay here on his own, nor would he come with us. Joe would start a life of his own, because, somehow, he's always lived a separate existence. He looks upon me as his father and I think of him as my son, but it's a game, really. He's one alone. You know something? We found out only recently that he had been looking for his parents; at least, trying to find out who his mother was. I just happened by chance to come across an old nurse who, for years, had been at the Catholic Home we took him from. She retired last year and she was well into her seventies, and she was very forthcoming and said what a fine fellow my adopted son had turned into. I didn't realise she knew him, and I said as much. Oh, she said, he had been to see the matron some time before, but had got no joy out of her. She said she could have told him what he wanted to know, but said he hadn't asked her. In any case, she said, they were supposed to keep closed mouths. But she didn't agree with this; she thought they should know."

"And did you ask her who his mother was?"

"Yes, I did."

"And what answer did you get?"

"The correct one. She gave me the married name and last address she knew of."

"And have you taken it further?"

"Yes, in a way. I went to the house, but the occupants were an Asian family and they had lived there for eleven years. The previous owner, they thought, had emigrated to Australia."

"And you haven't told him?"

"No."

"Do you think you should?"

"I'm in two minds. He could easily go off to Australia on a wild-goose chase. What would you do, Father?"

"I'd keep me mouth shut and mind me own business, because, let me tell you, it isn't anything unusual you're talking about. And I can also tell you its only one in ten who turn out to be glad they've made the search; most come away ashamed of their findings. It's a strange thing about illegitimates, you know, they've got to have something to cling on to bigger than themselves, because society has made them have a low opinion of themselves. So, who do they pick for a father? or a mother? but mostly, who do they pick for a father? It's never a docker or a bus driver or a window cleaner or a lavatory attendant. Oh, no, no, no. They usually start with doctors, climb the ladder to surgeons; or if it's in the teaching line, then they are likely to go for one that's been to Oxford or Cambridge. It's not unknown for them to imagine they are in line with a family connected with the Crown. Oh, you can raise your eyebrows, but a priest is a receptacle for lost ideals and idols. When a nice girl with a nice job in an office and with nice adoptive parents, has the urge to find out from where she sprang, it's usually a mother she's after, and then she finds out that her mother is from a large family, and a family who don't want her. Why? Because she's been on the streets for years. I'm not giving away confession confidences here by relating that, because it happened to my sister and brother-in-law, who adopted a child and doted on her. The girl was never the same afterwards. Did she stay with her adoptive parents? No; she broke their hearts as *her* heart had been broken. But then you might say a man like Joe would look at matters differently; he could take a blow like that and survive. Don't you believe it. Men are more critical of their mothers than any woman could be, because every man, at the bottom of it, wants to feel that his mother is a good woman. A wife could be a whore but never a mother, and knowing that he was conceived on the wrong side of the blanket, he carries a feeling of shame in him for the rest of his life. I've got proof of this; I'm not just talking through me hat. So my advice to you is to let sleeping dogs lie, in Australia or in Timbuktu, or wherever. Well, now—" His tone changed and he held one hand out towards the warmth of the artificial logs, saying, "I'm so comfortable, I don't want to move. But I must go and have a word with Don. Would you like to lead the way?"

They both got to their feet. Then the priest, after a moment's pause, during which he looked up towards the ceiling then down at his highly polished black boots, said, "About the last rites for the boy. You'll let me know, won't you, if there's a sudden change? I don't want to administer them too soon, because although in ninety-nine cases out of a hundred it brings peace, I know it does, there is a chance in his case he might just let go. And we want him to hang on, don't we? So when you think his time has come, any time of night or day, just let me know."

"I will, Father. But I don't think you need be worried about it precipitating his going, because he knows he's due to go, and soon. As I said, he's only hanging on to see his child."

Later that night Daniel stood in the kitchen facing Maggie, saying, "What difference does it make, here or at your place."

"All the difference in the world to me, Dan. This is still her house. To tell you the truth her presence is thick in it. And you're askin' me to go upstairs to your bed. That's insensitive of you."

"I don't see it that way. I've just told you what the priest said: she's not likely to come back for a long time, if ever, so are we only to be together once a week? Oh! Maggie"—he put his arms about her—"I need you. I need you, in all ways. There are even times in the day, in the thick of business in the yard, I want to break off and go to the phone just to hear your voice. When I come in at night I want to come straight to the kitchen and hold you. I just don't want you for one thing alone: you represent everything to me, companion, friend, lover. And yes, and lover, very much that. At night up there"—he jerked his head—"I toss and turn knowing that you're just a staircase and a corridor away from me. Look, my dear, if you won't come upstairs, will you let me come to your room?"

Standing within the circle of his arms, she bowed her head until her brow rested on his shoulder and her voice was a mutter as she exclaimed, "You don't want me any more than I want you, Dan, and in all ways, for I, too, lie down here thinking of you up there and I long to gallop up those stairs. Yes, I do, I do. But there's something in me that won't allow it. I have scruples about it."

He released his hold on her and stood back, and there was a suspicion of a sad smile on his face as he said, "There was Winifred who wouldn't let me in to her room for fear my body touched hers, and there is you who won't come into *my* room for the same reason."

"Oh, that's unfair, Dan, and you know it. You're twisting things. I'll come into your room anywhere but here."

"Well, don't come in up here, but let me come into yours down there. Look, Maggie, this state of affairs could go on for years; I mean, her being where she is and likely to stay there. What are we going to do? Live our separate lives, as you said? Being with each other once a week? Making ourselves love then as if to order, mustn't miss an opportunity? As much as I need you, I don't need you to order. As I said, I need you in so many different ways: to sit quiet with you, to lie peacefully with you, just to know you are there."

As they stood looking at each other in silence for a moment they heard the phone ring from the hall, and Daniel said, "Who can it be at this time of night?"

"I'll go and see."

He pressed her aside, saying, "No, no; I'll see to it," then hurried into the hall, picked up the receiver and said, "Hello."

"Daniel, this is Flo."

"Flo! What's wrong?"

"Nothing's wrong at this end; everything's very right. At least, I've got some news for you: Harvey and I are to be married."

He paused a moment before saying on a laugh, "Well, I'm not surprised at that."

"Well, you may not be, but it's going to be quick. It's to be next Saturday and I'd like you to come down."

"Next Saturday! Why the rush? You're not . . . ?"

"No, I'm not pregnant; but he's had a wonderful offer. And it's come at the right time, a time when things aren't busy here, at least for him. It's in Canada and naturally he wants to take it."

"Oh, yes, of course. I'm pleased to hear that, Flo. But on the other hand we'll be losing you. Oh, I'll miss you and Harvey. I've taken to that fellow, you know."

"So have I. Apparently he's known about it for some weeks; at least, about the impending offer, but he didn't tell me in case it fell through. And Daniel . . ."

"Yes, Flo?"

"You understand there won't be any more weekly visits to Winnie? You'll have to do something about that."

"I can do nothing about it. Father Ramshaw was in earlier this evening. He had seen her today and from what I gather, even my name sends her round the bend. But don't worry on that score; I've got to thank you for what you've done over the past weeks. Anyway, I'll be down on Saturday. If not me, it'll be Joe."

"Couldn't both of you try to come? Oh, no; I suppose that's too much to ask. I understand. I'll be glad to see one of you. How's Annette?"

"Not very bright at the moment, I'm afraid. Doctor has ordered her to bed for a week. Well, she stayed there about twenty-four hours. Between you and me I'll be surprised if she goes her time, although I hope she does. By the way, how long do you mean to remain away? Are you going to make that your permanent home?"

"Yes, as far as I know. But of course we've got to go there first and see how we are received. You understand?"

"Yes. Yes, I understand. But once they get to know Harvey they'll accept him wholeheartedly, I'm sure."

"I wish I could be as sure. He won't go to any of the main hotels. You know that, don't you? Or any clubs. And I've always thought him wise that way, because Gerry Morley—you know, the friend we've spoken of—he was turned away from a working men's club. You wouldn't believe that, would you? And he's not a bit like Harvey, who is contained and can take it. He caused a bit of a rumpus and it just missed getting into police hands. So with regard to Canada, we'll have to wait and see, won't we?"

"Well, I wish you both all the luck in the world, you know that. And I shall miss you both. We'll all miss you both, because quite candidly, Flo, you and Harvey have brought a little lightness into this house over the past months. And that was badly needed."

"Thanks, Daniel. Well, until Saturday. You'd better come down on the Friday night, because it'll be an early do on the Saturday morning."

"I'll do that, Flo. I'll do that. Good night. God bless."

Back in the kitchen Maggie, on being told the news, said, "How wonderful for them. Yet I doubt if they'll have an easier time there than they have here. It's awful to think of, for they are two of the nicest people in the world. And I've never met a man like him before, with the manners that he has. He's a gentleman of gentlemen, but he has to be persecuted because of his colour. By! when you think of some of the swabs round about it makes you want to spit, and them in high places. And you don't have to look far, do you? Look at Annette's father. He's the only one who never spoke to Harvey. But then he's not speaking to his own daughter. Is it true that he's trying to get rid of his businesses?"

"No, no; that was just a rumour. They are too profitable for him to let go."

"But it's true that they're moving, isn't it?"

"Yes, as far as I can gather, that's true enough."

"Somewhere around Carlisle, somebody said."

"Well, they can move to hell for all I care. But to get back to us, Maggie; what about it?"

She turned from him and went towards the fire and, bending, she pushed in the damper to the side of the boiler, then said quietly, "I'll . . . I'll have to think about it, Daniel. Leave it for the present, will you?"

She turned and looked at him, and he, walking over to her, put his arms about her again, saying, "Then make it a short 'present' will you? Please, Maggie, make it a short present."

SEVEN

𝓘t was half-past six on the Thursday morning that Annette took ill. She felt a sharp pain at the base of her abdomen, and for a moment she felt she was going to faint. Slowly she brought herself up to the edge of the bed and looked at the clock. Daniel and Joe didn't normally come into the room until seven o'clock and the nurse didn't arrive until eight. She got out of bed, looking towards where Don was still sleeping under the influence of the night pill and walked carefully past the foot of his bed and towards the door leading to the sitting-room. She just managed to reach the couch there before the pain gripped her again and she was brought double, her hands hugging her abdomen.

She looked at the bell pushes on the wall; then, making an effort, she took stumbling steps towards them and pressed one, and it seemed only a minute before she heard footsteps running along the corridor, and there was Joe, saying, "What is it?"

"Joe."

"Yes, dear? Take it easy. Take it easy." He had guided her back to the couch, and now sat down beside her, his arm about her. "You've got a pain?"

"I . . . I think it's coming, Joe. You . . . you had better get the doctor."

"Are you sure?"

She gasped now before she said, "Dreadful pain."

He rose immediately and went to the phone that was placed on a side table.

Presently he came back to her. "He's coming," he said. "He won't be long. Lie down."

"I . . . I can't, Joe. Oh dear!" She groaned out the words. And he was now holding her tightly to him, saying, "There, there. It'll be all right. Look; just rest easy, I'll ring for Dad. He'll get you a hot drink. That might help."

He stretched out his free arm and pressed the other button, and within a minute or so Daniel came hurrying into the room, only to hesitate for a moment before he approached her, saying, "This is it then?"

"Dad . . . Dad, it's too early."

"I know. I know, love. But it's all right; these things often happen. You'll be all right, you'll see. The doctor?"

"I rang him; he's on his way."

"Oh my! Oh dear!" Her face was screwed up in agony now, and they both held her twisted body while Daniel muttered, "Why the hell doesn't he hurry up!"

"He was asleep. I woke him. He has to get dressed."

"He's only a five-minute car-ride away."

"Look; go and wake Maggie. But go carefully, we don't want Don to know about this; not yet, anyway."

Maggie and the doctor arrived in the room almost simultaneously. Annette was lying back on the couch now, her body heaving, and she put her hand out to the doctor and, gripping his, she said, "Please! Please, do something."

"We'll do something, dear, don't worry. How often have the pains been coming?"

"It . . . it seems to be all the time . . . all the time."

He turned from her, looked around the room, then pushed past Daniel and went to the phone. Then after a moment, he said, "The ambulance will be here in a few minutes."

"The ambulance?" Annette went to pull herself up into a sitting position, and he said, "Yes; the ambulance. And lie quiet, you're going into hospital."

"I . . . I thought . . ."

"Whatever you thought, you can think in hospital, my dear. That's the place for you, and you'll be all right in no time. There's nothing to worry about." He turned to the men now, saying, "I would get your clothes on; one of you had better go in with her."

As they both made to go from the room Joe said to Daniel, "You stay here, Dad, and see to Don. I'll take her in." Strangely, Daniel made no objection, but just said, "All right, lad. All right." And each hurried to his room to dress, as both missions were equally urgent.

Before the ambulance arrived Annette, hanging on now to Maggie, had three more painful spasms. But when the men brought in the stretcher, she waved it to one side, saying, "I . . . I can walk. And . . . and I want to look in on my husband."

The doctor and Daniel between them helped her to her feet, then led her through to the bedroom. Thankfully the hustle and bustle had not awakened Don, and she bent over him and kissed him on the cheek. But when he stirred and muttered something, the doctor turned her quickly from the bed. Once in the corridor, however, he said, "Now you've walked far enough. Lie down on the stretcher and we'll tuck you up, then you can forget about everything but that you will have a fine baby. I'll be along to see you later. I've been in touch with Doctor Walters, so he'll be waiting for you."

When, overcome by another spasm, she began to groan, the ambulance

men stopped and she, gasping, looked up at Joe, saying, "You'll stay with me
. . . Joe?"

"I'll stay with you. Never fear, I'll stay with you."

Two hours later, Joe had had four cups of tea and had explained at least six
times to three expectant fathers in the waiting-room that no, he wasn't the
father, he was the brother-in-law. And when a young fellow asked, "Where's
the bloke, then? Scarpered?" he had answered good-humouredly, "No; he's
still in bed," to which the reply, after a moment's hesitation, was, "You don't
say!"

"I do."

"Drunk?"

And to this Joe had said, sadly, "No, not drunk—I wish he were—he had
an accident."

"Oh." The enquirer was obviously very sorry. "Hard lines, that," he
said. "It's every man's right to know what's going on, don't you think?" And
when Joe had said, "Yes. Yes, I suppose you're right," the young fellow had
pointed to the far end of the room to a pacing expectant parent and, in a low
voice, had said, "That bloke demanded to be in on the show. Can you believe
it? He can't have gone through what I have else he'd bloody well want to
steer clear of that. Eeh! some folks."

Part of Joe was laughing; but only part of him; the other part was bitterly
engaged in alternately begging God and demanding of Him that Annette
would be all right; and if it should be either her or the child, to let the child
go. This business of the child at any price was all hooey to him. The church
was wrong there, and he would tell them so the very next time he saw Father
Ramshaw; or, yes, Father Cody. He would be the one to throw it at. If they
let anything happen to her to save the child, what light was left in his life
would be extinguished.

He had had to wage a constant struggle to carry on, even behind the
façade he had put up: for as he had watched her abdomen swell, so his own
envy of Don had grown. Although he knew that never again would Don give
her another life to carry, he was still, in a way, jealous because, he would keep
reminding himself, it needn't have happened. He should have been strong,
forceful, shown his hand before his Dad set to work developing his own ideas
for his son's escape. If he had come into the open and declared his love, Don
wouldn't be on his back now, nor would his own adoptive mother be in an
asylum.

"Mr. Coulson?" The nurse was tapping him on the arm. "It's all right.
It's all right, Mr. Coulson. Don't look so worried; everything's fine."

"She's . . ."

"Yes, she's all right, I tell you. She's asleep now. We had to give her a
caesarian. You have a little girl . . . I mean"—she laughed—"you have a
little niece."

"A girl?"

"Well"—the nurse laughed again—"if she's a niece I suppose she's a girl;
there're only two types."

His relief and thankfulness showed as a deep exhalation of breath,
enough to bring a number of heads turning in his direction, and as he fol-

lowed the nurse out of the door, one of those heads turned to another, saying, "Funny bloke, that. He's supposed to be the brother-in-law. Huh! He's been more stewed up than me."

The brother-in-law was now gazing through a window to where a nurse was pointing to a cot in which he could just make out a small wrinkled face like that of an old woman.

When the nurse at his side said, "She's beautiful; small, just over six pounds, but beautiful," Joe smiled down on her, saying, "Can I see her? I mean, Mrs. Coulson," and she said, "It wouldn't be any use, she'll sleep for some time yet. If I were you I'd go home and give the father the news, then have a bath and a big breakfast, by which time she should have come round."

"Thanks, nurse. I'll do that. But do you think I could have a word with the doctor before . . ."

"Oh—" she cut him short by saying on a laugh, "you'll have a better chance when you come back, because he's still in the theatre bringing another one . . . out of the depths."

He laughed with her, nodded, then said, "Thank you very much, nurse," and walked away.

Out of the depths, she had said. Was she a Catholic?

Out of the depths I have cried unto Thee,
O Lord: Lord, hear my voice.
Let Thine ear be attentive to the voice of my supplication.

How many times of late had he said that, and at the same time wondered why he was saying it, because he had his doubts, his grave doubts, about anyone or anything being there to listen to the voice. What was more to the point, he knew that if anything had happened to her this morning, it would undoubtedly have made him realise that for years, like millions of others down the ages, he had been talking to himself, and that would have been the finish of "I believe, help Thou my unbelief," for never again would he have prayed for faith.

But she had survived.

He stepped out into the cold morning and took in long breaths of icy air. He looked upwards. The sky was high and blue but it was still cold enough to be deep winter.

Having arrived in the ambulance, he took the bus home, one that would leave him nearest the house. The bus was full of people, all remarking on the sudden cold, apart from one passenger, the woman that was sitting next to him, for she turned to him and in a low voice said, " 'Tisn't sudden at all; it's been like this for two or three mornin's now. I said last week we'll have snow, and we will: end of March or no end of March, you'll see. I'm gettin' off here." He moved his knees to let her pass and she said, "Ta-ra."

He answered likewise, "Ta-ra." And he remarked to himself that you missed a lot when you had a car: not only did you fly through the countryside without seeing anything, but also you missed people. "Ta-ra," she had said. Nobody had said "Ta-ra" to him for a long time. The three fellows and the two girls in the office would say, "Bye! Be seeing you." The nearest they got to "ta-ra" was, "so long." He sat now looking out of the window. That woman, she could have been his mother. He cast his glance backwards. Anyone of these women could have been his mother. But then, no; they all looked very working-class, and his mother had been . . . What had she been? Oh! not again. He should stop deluding himself, because it wouldn't end there; once he found her he would want to find his father, wouldn't he? Anyway, to stop the nagging there was only one way to tackle it: he'd go back to the home and ask.

During his teens he had thought that, as he grew older the questioning would lessen, but it hadn't. It had grown in intensity. But what if he *did* find her and she turned out to be a disappointment? He'd have to risk that. But could he? He'd been rejected by his mother, he'd been rejected by his foster-mother. He had, in a way, been rejected by Annette. Could he risk another rejection or disappointment? But he had this great emptiness inside. He needed something . . . someone to fill it, and no matter how soon dead men's shoes became vacant, he couldn't see himself jumping into them, no matter what Don wanted . . . it wouldn't be decent. Anyway, there was Annette, to whom he was just a brother.

Oh, he wished he hadn't got on the bus. No, he didn't really, because he liked to be among people. Yet that was a contradiction, wasn't it? Why had he asked to have his rooms in the cottage, separate from the family? Oh, he knew why, because he had to get away as much as he could from the rejection by her; and also from his dad breaking his neck to make up for the rejection which, in a way, was just as bad.

What about Jessica? Jessica Bowbent; or Irene Shilton . . . yes, what about them? No, not Irene. So that left Jessica or, better still, Mary Carter. Yes, better still, Mary . . .

Maggie was waiting on the doorstep, with Daniel behind her, and Peggie and Lily behind them.

"Well?"

"She's fine. It's a little girl."

Daniel closed his eyes and he, too, exhaled loudly; then his voice almost attacked Joe as he cried, "Why the hell didn't you phone, then? We've been on tenterhooks." But then he showed his surprise when Joe barked back at him in the same tone: "There's a phone at this end; you could have phoned the hospital yourself, couldn't you?"

"All right, lad. All right. Calm down." Daniel patted him on the shoulder. "You've been there and I can understand you must have been worried. But quite candidly, I was afraid to phone. Come on. Come on. Have something to eat."

"I will in a minute; I want to go along to Don."

"Of course. Of course. He's been on hot bricks. He couldn't believe that she had gone and that he hadn't woken up."

Joe went swiftly along to the sick room, but before entering he braced himself, then thrusting the door open, he cried, "Who's a papa then?"

The nurse turned from the bed, crying, "She got it over?"

"Yes, she got it over." He was standing now looking down on Don; but Don didn't speak, and so he cried at him, "Well! say something, man!"

"How . . . how is she? Is she all right?" Don's voice was thin, weak.

"She's fine." Joe didn't know if this were true or not; but for the moment she had to be. "You have a daughter," he said.

"A girl?" The words were short, but Joe's voice was extra loud as he said, "That's what a daughter means: yes, a girl. Anyway, that's what the nurse said to me."

Don now pressed his head back on the pillow, looked up while his teeth drew on his upper lip, and the nurse asked, "What did she weigh? Is she all right? I mean, not sick or anything?"

Joe, and still in a loud voice, said, "Of course she's all right. I don't know what the baby weighs. Oh yes, I do. I think the nurse said just over six pounds. I was in a daze. I tell you, the room was packed with men all striding about waiting to be dadas." His voice low now, almost at a whisper, he said, "Oh, don't, man. Don't." He looked down on Don's closed eyes and the tears running down his cheeks. "It's wonderful news. Come on. Come on."

"Well, why can't a man cry with joy? That's what he's doin'. Aren't you?" The nurse now wiped Don's face as if he were a child, saying, "What you need now is a celebration. In fact, we all need one. What about it?" And she cast a cheeky glance up at Joe, and he, catching her mood, said, "Yes. Yes, that's a good idea." And he hurried from the room.

He had been surprised that Daniel hadn't followed him along to Don's room and so, as he made his way to the dining-room and seeing his father coming down the stairs, he stopped and said, "What's the matter? Why didn't you come in with me?"

Daniel now ran his hand through his hair as he said, "I . . . I somehow couldn't face him . . . I felt I'd break down. I'll go along there now."

"I'm going to get us a drink."

"That's an idea." Daniel smiled now, saying, "And we'll have them all in. I'll shout Stephen down an' all. Peggie's up there with him."

As Joe was about to turn away Daniel said, "Just a minute. Look, could I ask you to do something?"

"Well, you don't have to ask, you know that. What is it?"

"Would you go up in my place on Saturday to Flo's wedding? It means leaving on Friday night. Would you do it?"

"Yes. Yes, like a shot; but I thought you wanted to be there."

Daniel turned away for a moment and looked across the hall before he said, "Yes . . . I would like to be there, but I've got a weird feeling on me: I don't want to leave Don; I think he's failing fast, Joe. What do you think?"

It was some seconds before Joe said, "He's fading, we know that, but not, I would say, fast. He could go on for some time yet and the birth of the baby will give him an incentive."

"I don't think it's up to incentives. But there, perhaps you're right. I feel, though, I'd rather be on the spot. You understand?"

"Yes, yes. But I'll not stay up there; I'll come straight back after the wedding. I'll be back here on Saturday night. By the way, I think we should ring Flo and tell her about the baby."

"Yes, I suppose so. But what about letting him do that; Don himself? We'll bring the extension in from the other room."

"Yes, that's an idea. Go and tell him; I'll get the drink and I'll call the others in."

Ten minutes later they were all standing around the bed: Maggie, Lily, Peggie, the nurse, Daniel, Joe, and Stephen. And they had glasses in their hands, except for Joe, who had just dialled Flo's number, saying as he waited for a reply, "She's bound to be somewhere in the office." Then his chin went up and he said, "May I speak to Mrs. Jackson, please?"

"Mrs. Jackson speaking. Who's that?"

"Well, don't you know by now? It's your secret admirer, Joseph Coulson."

"Oh, Joe. Joe. What is it? Something wrong?"

"No, no. There's a gentleman wants to speak to you. Hang on."

He now passed the phone to Don and he, pulling his shoulders up from the bed, said, "Hello there, Flo."

"That's Don!"

"Yes, it's Don. Who did you think it was? And . . . and put a little respect in your tone, for you're speaking to the father of a daughter."

"Oh my goodness! She's had her baby. Is she all right? And the baby?"

"One thing at a time, woo-man." He said the word as he had heard Harvey say it, which caused laughter from those around the bed; then he went on, "Yes, she's all right, and we have a baby daughter."

"Oh, that's wonderful, wonderful. Oh, I'd love to come up now, Don, but I'll make it sometime next week."

"Flo?"

"Yes, love?"

"We're going to call her Flo."

As he spoke he looked at the surprised faces around him and he nodded as he spoke again into the phone, saying, "Annette and I said if it was a boy we would call it Harvey, and if it was a girl she would be Flo; not Florence, just Flo."

There was a pause on the line before Flo's voice came again, saying, "Oh, that's wonderful. Oh, I'm so proud. And to think you would have called the boy Harvey. Oh, if only he had been here when you phoned. He's just gone into court, but he'll be over the moon. You know we're going to be married on Saturday?"

"Yes, yes, I know, and I hope you will always be happy. I know you will; he's a fine man, your Harvey."

His breath began to get heavy and he said, "I'll pass you back to the big fellow." And of a sudden he dropped back on to his pillows.

Joe, speaking now, said, "Isn't it wonderful news?"

"Oh, yes. And how is she really?"

He paused before he could say, "Oh, she's fine. I've only just come back from the hospital and I'm going to have something to eat and then I'll call in again on my way to work."

"Give her my love, won't you? And thank her and Don so much. I'll hear all the further news tomorrow night when Daniel comes."

He did not say, "I'm coming in Dad's place," but said, "They are all straining at the bit here, Flo, all with glasses in their hands to toast young Flo. Bye-bye, dear."

"Bye-bye, Joe. Bless you."

He put the phone down, then picked up his glass and, holding it out towards the gasping figure of Don, together with the others, he said, "To young Flo," and he added, "And her mother and father."

They had hardly finished their drinks when Nurse Pringle took over, saying briskly, "Well now, we've all got work to do, so I'd be obliged if you would let me get on with mine, with a little help from you, Mr. Coulson, so you two big fellows can go and have your breakfast."

Joe understood her urgency, for Don was now finding it difficult to breathe and so, guiding Stephen, he made his way quickly from the room. And Stephen did not protest. He was very quiet these days. He would remain for hours in the sick-room, making himself unobtrusive when the nurse was there, sitting in the corner just looking towards Don and smiling when their eyes met, but once the nurse left the room he would slip quickly to the side of the bed and hold Don's hand as long as he would let him. And, strangely, he didn't chatter.

The nurse now said to Daniel, "Help me lift him, will you?" And when he did, she said, "Hold him there while I get some more pillows." And Daniel, holding his son and watching his heaving chest, suffered with him, but more with remorse than with physical pain, for more and more he was blaming himself for having brought his son to this pitch, this hard way of dying. The question now seemed to be: had he really wanted to free him from his mother or merely to get the better of her in the parental war?

Some minutes later, after swallowing two pills washed down with a thick brown liquid, Don's breathing eased, and he opened his eyes and looked at his father, saying on a weak smile, "I would have to break the party up, wouldn't I?"

"Never mind about that. Pain gone?"

"Yes, nearly. Ain't science wonderful!" He drew in a long slow breath now, saying, "I . . . I shouldn't be making game of that because I often lie here thinking what it must have been like before there were such pills and potions; because, you know, Dad"—he looked up into Daniel's face— "there's only so much one can take, of everything; happiness too. Oh, yes, that's sure. Isn't it wonderful about the baby? When do you think they will be home?"

"I don't know, son. I'm going to slip along with Joe on his way to the office, but I won't stay long. I'll hurry back and give you the news of them both."

Don pulled his chin into his chest and looked down the length of the bed to where his useless legs formed a valley in the counterpane, and for a moment he saw his toes as the tops of two mountains and the dip in the counterpane a gorge. It wasn't the first time his mind had played tricks with him like that. The other day he had watched a fly crawling on the ceiling. It was the first fly he had seen this year and he wondered where it had come from; and he realised that its view was limited, but then he realised also that it had more power than he had. He had a mind that could think about it, but he couldn't move. It was at the time the pills weren't having the desired effect; they had been slow to act that day because the nurse hadn't given him the brown liquid at the same time. He was only supposed to have so much of the brown liquid, whatever it was. He had never enquired, but it was on that day he realised the wonder of the fly, but more so of an ant or of a mosquito because, as he had pointed out to himself, in those minute frames there were digestive tracts. They could suck and evacuate. And strangely, he realised he had never thought like that before; not along those lines anyway. And the wonder of the construction of a workable system in a pinpoint of a body had in a strange way brought him near to God for a moment. And he had asked Him to take the pain away, and strangely it had gone; or perhaps he had just fallen asleep. He didn't seem to be responsible for his thinking these days and sometimes could not even restrain himself from expressing his thoughts, as now when he said, "They must have taken Joe for the father, Dad."

"*Oh no, no*. He told them who he was."

"No. He said they were all walking up and down together, all those fathers waiting. He wouldn't have told them; they would have thought he was the father." He turned his head fully now to the side, then looked up into Daniel's face as he said, "And he should have been, shouldn't he, Dad?"

"Nonsense. Nonsense. What's put that into your head? There's only been you in Annette's life; Joe and she were like brother and sister. That was the relationship there. Now, now, don't you be silly. Anyway, I think you want to rest now. I'm going to leave you in nurse's hands; she'll make you toe the line."

Why did one say such silly things. He flapped his hand now at his son, saying, "I'll pop in again before I go to the hospital. Perhaps you would like to write her a note."

"Yes. Yes, I'll do that, I'll do that . . ."

Twenty minutes later, as Daniel was about to leave the house, Maggie hurried towards him across the hall, saying, "I've been thinking: if Flo won't be here on Saturday to go and see her, I think you'd better phone the hospital, for she'll likely be waiting for her coming, seeing that she happens to be the only one she ever wants to see."

"Yes. Yes, I suppose they must be told." He nodded at her. "Do you think you could do it? I've got to be off now, but I'll pop back after I've been to the hospital, and then I've got a full day ahead of me."

"Yes, I'll do it." Then, after opening the door for him, she said, "My goodness! It's starting to snow, and at this late date too! Take care." And he smiled at her and said, "For you I will." They exchanged a long look, and he went out. And after she had closed the door she picked up the phone and got through to the hospital and asked if she could speak with the matron: she wished to enquire about a patient, a Mrs. Coulson. When she was told the matron was in conference but that Nurse Pratt from Mrs. Coulson's ward happened to be at the reception desk and would she like to speak to her, Maggie said, "Yes, yes, of course."

When she heard the nurse's voice she said, "I just wanted to tell you that Mrs. Jackson won't be calling on Saturday to see Mrs. Coulson. The fact is, she's getting married."

"Oh, that is nice. I'll tell Mrs. Coulson. It'll be something of interest for her."

"Would you also put it to her gently, please, the fact that she is now a grandmother? Her daughter-in-law had a little baby girl this morning."

"Isn't that exciting!" said the voice on the other end of the phone. "Oh yes, I'll tell her. And as you say I'll put it to her *gently*. Goodbye."

"Goodbye." Maggie stood looking down at the phone for a moment. Was that nurse being sarcastic when she repeated her own word "gently"? No; she didn't think so; she sounded very nice.

She turned towards the kitchen again. It was one of those weeks; everything seemed to be happening at once. She was sorry that Flo and Harvey would soon be leaving the country. She'd miss their visits; they brought lightness to the house. That was an odd thought when he was a black man. She wished something would happen to bring lightness into *her* life. And yet it would be so easy to go up those stairs at night. But wouldn't it be just as easy to let him come down at night and into her room?

Yes, she supposed so, and she knew she wouldn't be able to hold out much longer. But it was their coming together in this house that was the trouble. Why she should feel like that she didn't know, for she had never had any liking for Winifred Coulson, not from the first day she had entered the house to look after Stephen. And she could say there were times when she had been a bitch of a mistress. And look how often she'd had to bite her tongue to prevent herself from telling the woman just what she thought of her. An upstart would barely be the beginning of it. So why was she standing out against Daniel? Was it conscience?

She had become a little tired of that word over the years. This was a Catholic house—she was the only non-Catholic in it—and it seemed to be the privilege of Catholics to have a conscience. But she knew that her conscience was more alive than that of any member of this household. Yet no; Daniel had a lot on his conscience, but with reason. Yet she could never blame Daniel for anything he had done or would do. She had loved him for so long and so hopelessly that now their association should be filling her with delight, yet it wasn't. It was too furtive and she couldn't bear the thought of the others finding out about it. But that must come some day. Oh, yes, it must . . . some day.

Daniel was sitting by the side of his son's bed. He was in his dressing-gown, as was Stephen, who was lying on the single bed reading a comic from which he would look up every now and again and smile across at his father or Don.

Daniel, having answered the smile, found himself again saying in an undertone, "It's amazing the change in that fellow these last few months. Have you noticed it?"

"Yes. Yes, I have. He seems to have grown up in his mind."

"Well, it's all because of his feelings for you and . . ." He didn't go on to add, the release from his mother, because in a way Stephen had needed that release as much as Don had done, although whereas it had helped the one, it had . . . He shut off his thoughts, saying now, "You look grand the day, you know."

"I feel grand. You know something, Dad? I've even been able to pull in a long breath." And he smiled as he demonstrated. But then, the smile disappearing, he said quietly, "You know, there are days when I wake up and wish I hadn't, but since hearing yesterday about the baby and that Annette is all right, and then the news today that she is sitting up and as chirpy, as Joe said, as a linnet, it's quite amazing the effect on me: I've hardly had a twinge of pain all day. And I've only had one lot of pills, and I'm not taking those—"

he pointed to the side table on which were two small white pills on a plate and next to it a medicine glass with brown liquid in it, and he said, "If I continue to feel like I do now I'm going to go to sleep naturally for once, because that lot makes me so thick-headed in the morning. You know, Dad, feeling like I have today I've had to ask myself if pain can be controlled, because since I heard about the baby and Annette, as I said, I've felt different altogether. In fact, if the pain were to start again I don't think I would resort to the pills. If I can do it one day I can do it another."

"Oh, I'd take your pills, lad. The thing is, as you get stronger you'll have less pain."

Don now looked at his father and repeated, "As I get stronger . . . we are kidding each other, aren't we, Dad? Today is only a flash in the pan; tomorrow I'll be in the pan again and all the high thoughts about pain being controlled will, like most of me in the morning, have gone down the drain."

"Now don't talk like that; miracles do happen."

"Oh, Dad." Don made an impatient movement with his shoulders. "Don't come pious on me, for God's sake. The only miracle that can happen to me is that I live long enough to see my child crawling towards me on the bed here. Oh, now, now, don't you get upset; it's only you and Joe I can open up to. By the way, what made you send him off in your place? I thought you would have loved to see Flo married."

"Oh, I don't know. A number of things: I wanted to be near you and my grandchild"—he pulled a face now—"and I didn't fancy that journey, and I knew once I got to yon end I'd be kicking my heels to get back again. Anyway, Joe likes travelling."

"It isn't so much what Joe likes, Dad, it's what he does for others. We're lucky to have Joe. You know that."

"Yes, I know that."

"And Maggie."

Daniel knew that his son was holding his gaze, and he thought, Oh, no, no. Then he almost muttered aloud, Oh, my God! when Don said, "She's a good woman, Maggie. I don't know why she's stayed here all these years, Dad, do you?"

For a moment he felt stumped, then said, "Well, she hadn't a family of her own; she looks upon us as her family," as he again held his son's penetrating gaze. But then the head turned slowly away as Don said, "You know what I'm going to do? I'm going to read myself to sleep just like that big gowk over there." He thumbed towards Stephen, and Stephen cried, "You want one of my comics, Don?"

"No, I don't want one of your comics. Get off your lazy backside and hand me that third book down on the table over there."

"This one with the blue cover, Don?"

"That's the one. Fetch it here."

After Stephen had placed the book on the bed Daniel leant over and looked at the title, then at Don, saying, "Plato's Socrates? You're going deep, aren't you? What do you want to read that for? But there, that stuff should put you to sleep."

"You should read it, Dad. I read it in my last year at school. I didn't understand it then, only that there was a lot of truth in it, but now I do. It's the story of a man about to die."

"*Oh, lad,* for God's sake!" Daniel sprang to his feet, but Don's hand stayed him from moving from the bed as he said, " 'Tisn't like that at all; 'tisn't mournful."

"No? But why are you reading that kind of book?"

"It was among my books upstairs and I used to look at it every now and again because of the man's knowledge of human nature. But then a while ago I got Annette to bring it down because I knew there was something more in it for me. And there was: it's how to die with dignity."

"Oh, God Almighty! boy."

"Don't act like that, Dad. Would you rather I was lying here squirming because of my coming end? You must read this book. You'll learn a lot; if nothing else, you'll stop being afraid of the other fellow. I was always afraid of the other fellow, you know, right from when I was small. Everyone of them was cleverer than me, better than me, taller than me, broader than me . . . especially Stephen. I loved Stephen, yet at times I hated him. But this book is about a man who is ugly, in no way prepossessing, yet he attracted the greatest respect, even from his enemies. Fear is not the antithesis of liking or of love or of respect; it's really envy of those qualities. Oh, Dad, don't look like that. Look, I'm happier tonight than I've been for a long time, believe me."

As Daniel looked at him he thought, yes, he is. Strange, but he is. But how altered his son was, still so young and talking like an old man. "I'm going along to have a hot drink now," he said. "And you, Stephen"—he looked across to the smiling figure on the other bed—"don't you go to sleep until I come back. Do you hear?"

"I'll not go to sleep, Dad. I never do when I'm with Don. Do I, Don?"

"No, you don't. You're a good watchdog."

"There you are, Dad, I'm a good watchdog. And do you think, Dad, that the snow will lie and there'll be enough to play snowballs in the morning?"

"I doubt it. But then you never know, it's cold enough. Well, if you want me you know what to do: ring the bell. I'll be in the kitchen for a little while. . . ."

He had expected to find Maggie still up, but apparently she had already retired, for the kitchen table was set for the breakfast and the fire was damped down. He took an enamel pan from the rack and held it in his hand for a moment, staring down at it. Then thrusting it on to a side table, he went out of the far door and along the short corridor. And after first tapping on Maggie's sitting-room door he pushed it quietly open.

The room was in darkness, although there was a light coming from the bedroom door, which was ajar.

"Maggie." He was holding on to the handle of the door as he gently pushed it further open and quietly stepped into the room.

She was sitting up in bed and her voice was a whisper as she said, "Something wrong? You need me?"

He was standing over her now looking down into her face as he said, "Yes, Maggie; I need you. Let's not have any more talk."

Swiftly he threw off his dressing-gown and pyjamas and, pulling the clothes aside, he lay down beside her and took her into his arms.

EIGHT

*I*t was barely ten minutes later when the large, white-coated figure emerged from the kitchen garden, groped its way along by the low wall that ended at the beginning of the courtyard. It slunk past the two stables that were now used as spare garages, then turned and crossed the yard towards the door of the glass-fronted store-room. Knowingly, a hand went up on to the low guttering and pushed the snow away until the fingers came in contact with a key. The door was unlocked and pushed gently inwards, and the figure groped forward.

When it tripped over some wellington boots it kicked them to the side and went on until it came to a further door. When it entered the wood-room, the figure put its hand out towards the stacks to the right of it and guided itself towards where a light was showing beneath the bottom of a further door. Here it stood listening for a moment; then quickly swung round and groped at the top of the wood-pile until it found a longish piece of wood, and then, gripping it tightly, moved towards the streak of light.

With its free hand it flung the door wide, and almost sprang into the room, only to stop dead.

Winifred Coulson surveyed her kitchen. It was as she had seen it day after day, year after year: everything neat and tidy as she had demanded it should be.

She moved swiftly across the room to the green-baize door, opened it, then stood with her back to it for a moment looking through the muted light coming from the standard lamp at the far end of the hall.

For one so big and heavy, for her bulk had not diminished over the past months, she ran up the stairs, past the room that had been hers, to stop outside her husband's room. Slowly she put her hand on the knob of the door, then with a jerk she flung it open and burst into the room, only to come again to a standstill.

The light was on but the room was empty. She took in the fact that his shirt and pants were lying on a chair, his trousers laid over the back of it, and on the floor to the side of the chair were his socks. She took a step forward as if to pick them up, then stopped. She had never been able to stand untidiness; it was a fetish with her: everything had to be straight, even handkerchiefs had to be laid in straight edged piles in the drawers. She stood now, the piece of wood across both hands as if she were weighing it; then, swinging round, she went out on to the landing and made for the stairs. But before she reached them a thought seemed to strike her and she ran quickly back and thrust open her bedroom door. She snapped on the light, thinking perhaps to find him in her bed, but this room was empty too, and tidy. Everything was just as she had left it, except that the cheval-mirror was gone . . . She had smashed that.

In the corridor again she made for the stairs; but instead of running down them, she crept slowly and softly, and when she reached the hall she turned in the direction of her son's room.

At the door she stood listening, but when no sound came to her her hand went to the knob and, turning it, she thrust the door open. Then yet once more she was standing still.

Seemingly taken aback that she was not being confronted by Daniel, she stood, her mouth agape, one hand gripping the piece of wood held at shoulder height and for a moment deaf to the silence coming from the two beds in the room; just for the moment, for Don had raised himself on his elbows and exclaimed in a voice no louder than a whisper, "Oh my God!"

But the cry that Stephen gave was loud. He had jumped from the bed and was standing near Don now, crying, "Go away, Mam! Go away, Mam!"

She didn't appear to see him as she walked towards the bed, because her eyes were on her son. "Where is he?" she demanded.

His breath coming in gasps, Don said, "Mam! Mam! Sit down."

"Your father; where is he?"

Don was unable to answer, for his breath was choking him, and it was Stephen who said, "D . . . ad, is in . . . in the kitchen."

"He's not in the kitchen."

She was still staring at her son, all the while brandishing the stave.

"He is. He is, Mam. Go on, go away. Get out! Leave Don alone."

Like a child now he put both hands out to push her away, and the next moment he was screaming as she brought the piece of wood down on his shoulder. She had aimed for his head, and she tried again, but his arms were up. Thwarted and like a wild beast now, she sprang at him, flailing him with the stave. And when he fell to the ground, still covering his head with his arms, she took her foot and kicked him, and he stopped crying out.

She now turned to Don, who was lying back, deep in the pillows, his arms hugging his chest as he fought for breath. His face was contorted with pain, and she stood over him, her eyes boring into his, and after what seemed an age she said, "You never loved me, did you? You never loved me."

He made an effort to speak; but finding it impossible, he groped for the pills on the table at the other side of the bed.

Like a flash, her hand went out with the piece of wood held in it and with a swipe she overturned the table, and the pills and the medicine fell almost soundlessly on to the carpet.

"You're dying, aren't you, and in pain? Well, now you can suffer as you made me suffer. *Yes you did. Yes you did.*"

It was as if he had contradicted her. "And you've got a daughter, they tell me. Well, she's a bastard. You know that? She's a bastard. And she's not yours, she's big Joe's and the daughter of a bastard." She smiled now, a terrifying smile, as she said, "You are going to die, you know, and slowly, because there'll be nobody to come to your aid this night, not when I'm finished with them. You've all hated me, all of you, you even made the servants hate me. That Maggie running my house!"

She lifted her head back now as if listening: then she said, "That Maggie. Yes, that Maggie. John wouldn't take me, would he? He said he didn't know the address. He could have asked her, couldn't he?" She looked down on her son again. Don's eyes were closed, his hands lying limp at each side of him. She pulled herself back from the bed, looked down at the twisted form of Stephen, then turned and left the room.

When she reached the hall the phone was ringing. As if none of the events of the past months had happened, she lifted the receiver and in a quiet tone said, "Yes?"

A voice at the other end said, "May I speak to Mr. Coulson?"

"He's . . . he's not available at present."

"This is important. Could you please get him or someone in the household. Who's speaking?"

She paused before saying, "This is the maid."

"Well, try to find somebody in authority and tell them that Mrs. Coulson has got away. We don't know how. She is not in the grounds, so he must be on his guard. Will you tell him that?"

"Yes; yes, I will tell him that at once."

She put the phone down and kept her hand on it for a moment, and as she looked at it she squared her teeth, and her lips went back from them as if in a snarl, and she said, "Yes, I'll tell him that at once."

Quietly now, she crossed the hall and went through the door into the corridor leading to the kitchen, stopping outside Maggie's room. Very quietly she turned the handle of this door. There was no light on in the small sitting-room, but there was a light coming from the bedroom, and also a murmur of voices. She went to the partly open door through which, by standing to the side, she could see her husband and her housekeeper in bed.

She had always been light on her feet, but the spring she made from the doorway to the bed could have been likened to that of a panther onto its prey.

They both screamed at the terrible apparition above them, but it was too late for Daniel to escape the blow to the side of his head. It was as if his ear had been wrenched off. In attempting to pull himself out of the bed, his hands went towards his wife and she brought the stave across his arms, all the while her mouth spewing out obscenities. Maggie had jumped from the other side of the bed and, screaming, she made for the door, only to be stopped by a blow on the back of the neck that silenced her screams and brought her to the floor.

Returning now to her main target, Winifred Coulson almost threw herself on to Daniel, who had struggled from the bed, his naked body bent forward, one arm supporting his blood-covered face, the other hanging limply at his side.

When she came at him he brought his hand from his face and flung it around her neck. But when she used her knees and her feet on him he crumpled up by the side of the bed. And now she flailed him with the blood-soaked stave until he lay quiet. Then her body heaving, she stood over him and turned him on to his back, and her lips curling at the sight of his nakedness, she lifted the stave again and was about to bring it down on to his loins when she heard a distant voice, crying, "Dad! Dad!"

Wildly, she gazed around the room as if looking for a way of escape. The next minute she was running through Maggie's sitting-room, pulling the door to as if hiding what she had done, hurrying through the kitchen and out the way she had come . . .

Stephen was half lying on the bottom step of the stairs. He had stopped calling "Dad! Dad!" and was now crying, "Peggie! Peggie!" then changed to "Maggie!" And his whirling mind hanging on to the name seemed to give him the urge to pull himself up from the stair and to stumble, zig-zagging towards the kitchen door, and when in the room he leant against the table, crying again, "Maggie! Maggie!" his face awash with tears.

He was about to sit down on a chair when he stopped. Where was his Dad? Maggie would know.

He went from the kitchen into the dark corridor. But there was a dim light streaming out from Maggie's sitting-room.

"Maggie, where's Dad? Maggie?"

He stopped at the bedroom door and stared at the naked, bleeding form of his father and the huddled body of Maggie. He did not move towards either of them, but there escaped from his lips a thin sound that could have come from a weary, pain-filled animal. And now, at a shambling run, he made for the hall again.

In his present state of mind he deduced that, having to climb the attic stairs to Peggie's room and then to waken her, for she slept so soundly, it might be too late to help them all. But there was the phone: yet he didn't know numbers, for he had never tried to ring anyone on the phone; although somewhere in his mind he recalled an adventure story in Children's Hour where the clever boys had caught the thief because they had used the telephone and rung the number nine.

He had the receiver in his hand. He pressed his shaking finger in the dial and turned it to nine. But nothing happened: nobody answered.

It was nine, he told himself; or was it two nines? or three nines? Again he stuck his finger in the dial and turned it to nine twice. Still no voice came to him. Almost angrily now he swung the dial for a third time. There was a silence and then a man's voice said, "Yes, can I help you?"

Holding the receiver from his face he now cried, "Will somebody come; my Mam's been here."

The voice said, "Speak up, please. Can I help you?"

He brought the receiver close to his mouth and yelled, "Mam's been here! She's killed them all!"

"Tell me your address."

He paused a moment before he said, "Wearcill House."

And a voice said, "Wearcill House? Now where is that? Which road?"

"Fellburn."

"Yes, but which road?"

"Oh, Telford Road runs at the bottom."

The voice said, "Wearcill House, Telford Road. Don't worry; somebody will be there very soon."

He went and sat on the bottom stair again and stared towards the front door. He knew he should open the front door to let them in, but if he did his Mam might come in again.

It seemed a long time that he sat there, but it was only ten minutes before he heard the car draw up outside; yet not until the knock came on the door did he move to open it.

There were two policemen standing on the step, and as they came in he backed from them. They were looking at his blood-stained face and hands. The taller policeman said in a quiet voice, "Are you the young man who phoned?"

Stephen didn't speak but just nodded his head.

"Well, tell us what happened? You said your mother was here."

Stephen now shook his head, saying, "She's gone. She's gone. She hit me with the wood." He put his hand to his head. "But she's killed Don and my Dad and Maggie."

The policemen now exchanged glances; then one said, "Show us."

Stephen looked one way, then the other, as if wondering who was most in need, then when he said, "They've got no clothes on," the policemen again exchanged glances. Who had they here, a big fellow talking like a child?

It was the shorter policeman who said now, "Come and show us where your Dad is, lad." And Stephen moved shakily to obey him.

When the two men entered the room, just as Stephen had done before, they stopped dead for a moment, and one of them muttered, "God Almighty! Somebody's been busy."

The shorter policeman knelt down by Daniel's side, put his hand on his blood-stained ribs, waited a moment, then said, "He's still alive. What about her?"

"I don't know if a pulse is there, it's very faint. Go and ring for an ambulance."

Then rising from his knee, he said to Stephen, "Is there anyone else in the house?"

"Don. I tried to save him but she hit me."

"Where is he . . . Don?"

"At the other end, in his room. He's bad, he can't move. His legs won't work."

"What's your name?"

"Stephen."

"Stephen who?"

"Stephen . . . Coulson."

"Coulson."

The policeman now raised his eyebrows as if he was recognising some thought, and he said, "Oh, yes, yes; Coulson. Come and show me where the young man is."

As they passed through the hall the other policeman had just put the phone down, and he said, "This is the Coulson place?" And his companion nodded, adding, "Yes, it's just come to me."

When they reached Don's room one of them said, "God! It looks as if she's finished this one off an' all."

"This is her son; the one that had the accident, remember? on his wedding day."

"Oh, aye. Aye, yes."

They turned now and looked at Stephen. "Is there anyone else in the house?"

"Peggie. But she's asleep."

"Asleep through all this? Show us where she is."

Stephen had to be helped up the second flight of stairs; and when Peggie, shaken out of a deep sleep, saw the two policemen staring down at her, she let out a high scream. And one of them said, "It's all right, miss, it's all right."

"Wh . . . at . . . wh . . . at do you want?"

"We want you to get up. Come downstairs and see what's happened in the time you've been asleep."

"Oh, my God!" She was now staring at Stephen and his blood-stained condition and she cried, "What have you done?"

"It was Mam. It was Mam, not me."

"All right, old fellow, all right." The policeman was patting Stephen on the shoulder now.

Looking at the policeman, Peggie said, "Couldn't be her, she's . . . she's in the asylum."

"Apparently she got out of the asylum, miss. Now will you put something on and come downstairs and prepare yourself; there's one or two nasty sights."

"Oh, my God!"

They were turning from her when one said, "Is there any one else about we could get in touch with?"

"There's Lily and Bill in the lodge. But oh"—her head bounced back—"they're in Newcastle. They've gone to a show and that, it being Friday night, their night out. And John . . . Dixon, he's a gardener and handyman, he lives out."

"No other friend of the family?"

"Well"—she blinked her eyes—"Mr. Joe is in London at Mrs. Jackson's wedding and young Mrs. Coulson, she's just had a baby; she's in hospital. That's the lot."

"Well, get something on and come down."

They were making for the door when Stephen turned round and in a high voice cried, "You thought it was me, Peggie. That was nasty. I'll tell Maggie about it."

"It's all right, son. It's all right." They both put their hands on his arms and led him out.

A few minutes later, when Peggie entered Maggie's room, she let out a squeal, putting her hand over her mouth and closing her eyes and almost collapsing.

"Come on. Come on." The tall policeman led her from the room and, seating her on a kitchen chair, he said, "Now, tell me where we can get in touch with this other member of the family, the one who's gone to London."

She sat gasping for a moment before she was able to say, "Mrs. Jackson's; it's in the phone book. He'll be there with her. But she's to be married tomorrow."

"Well, I'm afraid that she'll be one man short. It wasn't him she was marrying, was it?"

"Oh, no, no. She's his aunt. She's marrying a black man. He's nice, though."

Whatever comment the policeman might have made at this was cut off by his companion saying, "There's the ambulance. By the way, who's their doctor? I mean, the young man's at the end; who's his doctor?"

"Doctor Peters."

"Well, come on; be a good lass and go and ring him. No; on second thoughts, just give me the number. I'd better speak to him."

And now the other policeman said, "Yes, I think he'd better come and see the damage afore they are lifted. . . ."

When Doctor Peters pulled down the quilt that was now covering Daniel his teeth gritted for a moment before he lifted up the bloodstained hand and felt for the pulse. He then went to Maggie where she too lay covered up, and after feeling her pulse he looked at the ambulance man, saying, "Get them there quick."

"What about the young man; the invalid?"

"I'll tell you when I've seen him. But first of all, get these two off."

"And the young fellow?"

"Oh, Stephen? I'll have a look at him and I'll ring you if you're needed again."

When the doctor looked down on Don he thought for a moment, as the policeman had done, that he was already dead. But when the pale eyelids flickered, he leant close to the face, saying, "Don. Come on. Come on. You're all right."

In raising his head and looking beyond the bed he noticed the pills on the floor and so, turning to the policeman, he said, "Would you get those pills, please; then help me to raise him up just a bit. Come on, Don. Have this drink."

The eyes flickered, then opened and now the head moved slightly. After taking in the presence of the policeman, his eyes came to rest on the doctor, and his lips moved a few times before he said, "Mother. Mother . . ."

"Yes, yes, we know. Don't worry."

"Stephen?"

"Stephen's all right. He's all right. Come on, take this drink of water, then swallow your pills."

Don sipped at the water, then painfully swallowed the pills. And as he lay back again, he said, "Mother," then added, "mad."

"Yes, Don. Yes, we know. Now, just rest. Go to sleep; you'll feel better in the morning."

Don kept his eyes on the doctor for a moment, then he sighed and closed them.

Out in the hall again, the doctor spoke to the policeman. "She's done a thorough job. Now she's got to be found before she does any more harm, although I don't think she'll be back here again. But then, there are two other members of the family . . ."

"We've contacted the son in London. He's catching the midnight train back. He seemed in a bit of a state, naturally. But that's one who escaped unharmed, anyway."

"Oh my God!" The doctor put his hand to his head. "If she knows about the child she'll make for the hospital, and she's mad enough to act sanely to get what she's after."

He grabbed up the phone and got through to the hospital and within a minute or so was explaining the situation to the doctor on duty, who assured him that they would be on the look-out and would put a nurse in charge of Mrs. Coulson and the baby.

Next, he phoned the superintendent at the asylum, telling him in direct words that he had better get his men out and start looking for her, for she had played havoc in her home and he didn't know if two of her victims would survive the night, only to be told they were already searching.

Following this, he now turned to Stephen, who had been hovering in the background all the while, and said, "Go upstairs, Stephen, and Peggie will run you a bath. Now get into it, and then I'll have a look at you, because at the moment I can't see where the damage has really been done. That's a good fellow."

Peggie had him by the arm when he turned and, looking at the doctor and the policeman, he said, "Will she come back?"

"No, no, she'll not come back. Never."

"You mean that, Doctor?"

"Yes, I mean that."

Yet, even as he said this, Doctor Peters wasn't quite sure in his own mind, because it was as if he had been waiting for this call for a long time. What he was sure of was that until she was safely under lock and key, there would be no accounting for the events of this night as having ended here and now . . .

His examination of Stephen revealed that the main source of blood had come from a three-inch cut in his skull behind his ear. Fortunately it was only surface deep; his thick hair had cushioned the blow; but his arms, back and legs were covered with bruises, which tomorrow would be giving him more pain than they were at present.

When the doctor was making for the door, Stephen said, "Don't like her. Nobody likes her."

And the doctor paused, then looked down for a moment, thinking, that's the trouble, nobody likes her. Nobody has ever really liked her. And she knew it.

Joe arrived at half-past seven the next morning and was dazed by the turn of events that had taken place during his short absence, as related by the garbled descriptions coming from both Stephen and Peggie.

Peggie and Lily had taken charge of the house now. A new day nurse had just put in an appearance, because the last thing the doctor had done before leaving early in the morning was to get in touch with Nurse Pringle and ask her to come and take over again in the sick-room . . .

It had snowed heavily in the night: there was all of three inches lying. Everyone said it had been expected; it was cold enough for it. But here it was, the end of March. Really! it shouldn't happen.

Bill White came up to the house and half apologised to Joe, saying it wouldn't have happened if he had been on duty. But as Joe assured him, there was and could be no blame attached to him for, apart from it being his night off, she hadn't come in by the drive-way but had got in through the wood-room. Naturally she had known where the key was kept.

There had already been men from the asylum asking for exact details of when this and that had happened. But Peggie didn't know anything, and Stephen couldn't tell them how long he had been lying on the floor before he himself came to.

There was now a police guard on the gate, but that hadn't stopped two reporters getting through to the house at half-past six this morning. Bill White, however, had given them short shrift.

Everyone was glad to see Joe back, because now there was someone who could take the responsibility.

And this is what Bill White said to John Dixon as they stood in the warm greenhouse discussing the events of the past night. "Joe'll see to things. Anyway, at bottom, he always has."

"This'll put her away for life," John said.

"Well, it's not afore time, if you ask me, because from what our Lily tells me she was a bitch to him; no wife at all for years. And, you know, our Lily was right about more than one thing. She's been saying for some time now she suspected there was something going on atween Maggie and the boss. Then, of course, there they were found like that, him stark naked, and her an' all. You surprised?"

"No, not at all." John Dixon shook his head. "I've known which way the wind was blowing in that direction for a long time. She had him followed, you know, when he used to go to Bewick Road. I tipped him off once or twice."

"You did? You never said anything to me."

"Well . . . well, you've got a wife an' all, you know"—he grinned now —"and you would have likely told her and it would have been passed on to Peggie, because she's your niece and you know Peggie's got a mouth like a pontoon; and I thought, well, the boss had enough to put up with; it's best to keep a still tongue sometimes. Anyway, I wonder where she got to after she went through the house with her mallet or whatever she had in her hand." He paused before saying, "What's the matter with Larry?" and he pointed through the glass door to where a small Scotch terrier was barking furiously. "What's up with him?"

"Smelt a rat or something. He's always like that when those devils are about." Bill White opened the door and the dog ran to him and jumped up, then darted back, turned and waited, and Bill said, "All right, all right. Come and show me."

"I haven't seen any rats for weeks," John Dixon said. "Likely it's rabbits coming in from the fields."

They both went out, pulling the collars of their duffle-coats up around their necks, and as they crunched over the snow in the wake of the dog, Bill said, "Who'd believe this, snow at this time of the year? You know it's my opinion it's those atom bombs they're dropping all over the world. It's altering the seasons."

"Where's he going?" John Dixon now asked.

"He's going for the hen-crees. I bet you what you like a fox is around."

They passed through an opening in a low hedge and so into a small field, at the end of which were a row of hen-crees; although only one or two hens had come through the hatches.

"They don't like the snow, but I bet if we put the food outside they'd come out fast enough. What's he after?"

They now followed the dog along by the side of the crees to an open shed used for storing boxes and crates. The front ones were partly covered with snow that had fallen during the night. Then they both stopped within yards of the place and looked at the two feet sticking out from among the tumbled boxes.

"*Eeh no!*"

"*God above!*"

At a run now they reached the shed and, pulling the boxes to one side, they exposed the stiff body of their mistress.

"Is she dead?" Bill White was bending over John Dixon as he was tentatively putting his hand inside the crumpled coat; and after a moment he said, "Can't feel anything. Look; dash back to the house and tell Joe to ring for an ambulance. And you'd better bring a door or something. We could never carry her like this."

Bill raced up the garden, straight over the frozen herbaceous beds, and made for the front door. He didn't ring but banged on it, and when Peggie opened it, he gasped at her, "Joe . . . Mr. Joe, where is he?"

"Along with Mr. Don. What's happened now?"

"The missis. She's in the garden."

"Oh my God!" She put her hand over her mouth. "Close the door."

"Stop it!" He pushed her. "As far as I can tell she's dead. Get Mr. Joe. Go on!"

Within seconds Joe was standing before him, saying, "What! In the garden? Where?"

"In the box house. We must get a door or something; couldn't carry her, the weight she is. And . . . and you'd better call the doctor an' all."

Joe stood for a moment as if dazed; then, looking at Peggie, he said, quietly, "Ring for the doctor. Tell him it's urgent."

Peggie ran to the phone, crying, "He'll know it's urgent if it's anything to do with this house."

But Joe was already following Bill at a run to the out-houses; and there, Joe said, "There's no doors here except that big glass one, and that's too heavy as it stands."

"Aye, you're right, Mr. Joe. But there's a sling . . . well, it was a hammock, like. It's up in the loft. . . ."

It was a full twenty minutes later when they brought Winifred back into her home in a sling and laid her on the hall floor. The doctor was waiting; then as he knelt down by her side he shook his head slowly. But after a moment he looked up at Joe, saying, "She's still alive. Phone for an ambulance. . . ."

Sitting by her side in the ambulance, Joe pondered on the events of the last few days. There was Annette and the baby in one part of the hospital, and his Dad and Maggie would be in another part. And he still didn't know whether they were dead or alive. And now here was his adoptive mother being taken to the same hospital. It now only needed Don and Stephen to go and they'd all be there; and by the look of him Don could soon be joining them. And poor Stephen, black and blue from head to foot and yet still carrying on. He had experienced an awful night; and, as Doctor Peters had just said to him, if it hadn't been for him they could have all lain in their battered condition and would very likely not have survived the night.

What had come upon them? It was like a curse. But it was no curse, it was simply mother-love, twisted mother-love. As he looked down on the dead-white face, the ambulance man who was sitting near him said, "She's in a bad way. Lying out all night in that; it would kill a horse. It's amazing she's still breathing."

Yes, it *was* amazing she was still breathing, and some part of him wished fervently that she wasn't, because, after this, what would her life be? They certainly wouldn't send her back to the County but to some other place of high security, especially if either his Dad or Maggie died. And then there was Annette. How to tell her? because she was still weak. The birth had taken it out of her more than somewhat. His talk of her sitting up and being perky had been diplomatic bluff.

There was more bustle at the hospital, and as his mother was being wheeled away he was surprised to see in the hallway a nurse whom he recognised as being from the County Asylum, accompanied by a man. And she, seeing him, approached him immediately, saying, "Tragic, Mr. Coulson, isn't it?"

He nodded. "Yes, nurse, tragic," he said.

And as if somewhat apologetically, the man said, "We searched the garden last night. Although it was dark we went over it thoroughly after we knew she had been to the house."

"Oh, you wouldn't have thought of looking among those crates and boxes," excused Joe; "but how did she get out?"

He turned to the nurse and she replied, "Apparently with the help of two of her room-mates. They're wily . . . they're all wily. They had done the old trick of packing pillows in her bed, and they did it thoroughly because, as you know, she's a size."

"But she'd have to get through the gates?"

"Oh, she didn't go that way. She must have had this in mind for some time and had looked around the garden and the strip of woodland. She climbed over the wall. There's a tree grows near the wall and one of the lower branches touches the top of it. How she managed to get up there with her weight, I don't know, I just don't know, but they think that's the only way she could have escaped. She was very agile on her feet, you know, very light.

Still, to climb that tree! But in that state they'll do anything, and can achieve anything once they set their mind to it. Do you think she'll live?"

It was on the tip of his tongue to say, "I hope not," but he answered, "I can't tell." Then, saying, "Excuse me," he turned away and went to the desk and said, "May I see Mr. Coulson and Miss Doherty?"

"If you'll just take a seat, I'll enquire," said the receptionist and lifted the phone. Presently she beckoned to him, saying, "If you go to number four ward, Sister Bell will see you."

"Thank you."

Sister Bell took him into her office and, after offering him a seat, she said, "What a tragedy. I've just heard that your mother, too, has been brought in."

He made no answer to this but said, "How's my father, and Miss Doherty?"

"Well," she sighed, "it appears there's little change from last night. Yet they're both alive and we can only hope for the best. But I would say your father is in a much worse state than Miss Doherty."

"May I see them?"

"Yes; if you stay just a moment and don't start a conversation." She shrugged her shoulders now, adding, "Not that it would be of any use."

When he stood by his father's side he looked down on a face that was swollen and so black and blue as to be unrecognisable. There was a tube up his nostril, one in his arm, as well as what appeared to be wires attached to his arm. He looked much like Don had looked after the accident. He wanted to put his hand out to him and say, "Oh, Dad. Poor Dad," for the words were like whimpering inside of him. Stephen had said she had been carrying a lump of wood. Well, it must have been a hefty stave, but then she was a hefty woman, and in her madness she could have wreaked havoc with a hair-brush.

When, next, he stood by Maggie's bed, her eyes were open and peering out from the bandages around her head and face. He said aloud, "Oh, Maggie." And she went to raise her hand from the bed cover, but the effort seemed too much.

Looking down on her he felt his throat was full: Maggie of all people, why did she have to suffer like this? But why not? She had, in a way, made his mother suffer, for she couldn't have been unaware of her cook's feelings for her husband. Yet she must have, or else she would have sent her packing years ago. If she hadn't been mad to begin with, that bedroom scene would surely have tipped the scales.

He brought back to mind the sight of Stephen standing there in the corridor that morning, almost before he had got into the house, and gripping the lapels of his coat as he stammered, "Dad was on the floor, Joe, with no clothes on. And Maggie, she was an' all, with no clothes on. That was bad, wasn't it? Maggie shouldn't have been there, not without her clothes. I haven't told Don, as he's still asleep. Anyway, that new day-nurse wouldn't let me in."

Joe had shaken him gently, saying, "Now, be quiet, Stephen. Be a good lad. And from what Peggie tells me you've been a very brave fellow getting the doctor and the ambulance." He didn't mention the police.

"My head aches, Joe, an' all over. I'm paining, Joe."

"Well, go upstairs and get into the bath and I'll be with you in a minute or two."

"But I've had a bath, Joe."

"Well, go and have another." He had only just stopped himself from yelling at him, but keeping his voice level, he went on, "Lie in it: it'll help to take the pain away. Then I'll come up shortly. Go on now."

"You won't go away, Joe, will you?"

"Go away? What are you talking about? Don't be silly. Go on now. . . ."

He had to cross the hospital yard to get to the Maternity Ward. At one point he stood on the frozen grass verge and pondered what he should say to Annette. It wasn't likely that she'd heard the news already, so he decided he would say nothing until later in the day, and not even then unless either of them died. He didn't include Maggie in his thinking, nor yet Don. He remained standing as he thought: four of the household in this hospital; five, if one counted the baby; and back in the house Don lay as near death as made no odds. There seemed to be only himself and Stephen left whole. What had happened to the family?

When love, all kinds of love, came as the answer, he jerked himself from the verge and hurried towards the Maternity Ward, and strangely, Stephen's words came to the front of his mind: "You won't go away, Joe, will you?"

Annette was propped up in bed. She showed her surprise immediately by saying, "You're supposed to be at the wedding."

"Oh, Dad changed his mind and thought he should be there. So we swapped around again."

"But you would have liked to go, Joe."

"Not all that much. Anyway, they'll be coming up this week. How are you feeling?"

He drew up a chair to the side of the bed and took hold of her hand, and after a moment she answered, "Up and down. I've had an uneasy night, they tell me. Temperature popped sky high around midnight. I felt awful. I couldn't explain it, so they made me take a sleeping tablet. You know how I hate sleeping tablets. And then I had sort of nightmares. Oh, I'm glad to see you, Joe."

But he did not pursue this line; instead, he asked, "How's her ladyship?"

"Well, I saw her half an hour ago and she said she'd like to stay here with me, but they wouldn't let her. And I told her to put on some weight and then she could defy them, and walk in all on her own." She smiled wanly, and he said, "You'll be surprised how soon that'll come about."

Her eyes tight on his now, her face unsmiling, she asked, "How is Don?"

He paused a moment before answering: "Well, he was still asleep when I came out."

"He's worse? Tell me, tell me the truth, Joe, he's worse?"

"Now, now; don't be silly, he's not worse."

"You know what, Joe? With that weird feeling I had last night I was sure he had died. I must get home soon. They said it might be ten days or a fortnight but I can't possibly stay that long. And . . . and he must see the child. Joe, you understand?"

"Yes, my dear"—he was stroking her hand now—"I understand how you feel, and I'll have a talk with the doctor and find out just how soon they'll let you go. But you must remember this was no ordinary birth, as I think you know. It wasn't plain sailing." He smiled at her, but her face was straight as she answered, "Nothing I seem to do is plain sailing, being clever and getting pregnant for a start." She turned from him now and looked down towards the foot of the bed. "Getting married and having such a wedding day. And I blame myself for that because if . . . if I hadn't been pregnant there would have been no hurry. And what did it do to Don? Killed him slowly."

"Be quiet. And don't talk like that. What you did, what both of you did, was out of love for each other." There was that word again. What a lot it had to answer for. He went on, "Stephen sends his love. I'm going to have to bring him in one day to see you. It's a job to get away from him when he knows I'm coming in and he keeps yammering on about the baby." How easy it was to create a story; and once started he went on, "The girls send their love, and . . . and Maggie. They keep asking when they'll be allowed to visit. They've all been knitting like mad." That was true; he had seen them at it in the kitchen.

The nurse entered the room now with a tray and, looking at him, she said briskly and in an exaggerated Northern accent, "This is chucking out time. Will you go peacefully or shall I have to use force?"

He smiled at her, saying, "Well, I don't know; I might make a stand for it." Then bending over Annette, he kissed her on the cheek, saying, "I'll be in this afternoon."

As he backed a few steps from the bed she said, "When will Dad be back? I want to hear all about the wedding."

"Oh . . . oh." He scratched his brow now, saying, "Well, I think he might stay on until they come up. I . . . I really don't know. But anyway, you'll have to put up with me for a day or so."

"Give my love to Don, won't you?" Her voice was small and he said, "Oh, yes, yes, I'll give him your love, dear."

Once again out in the grounds, he stood breathing deeply of the icy air. He knew he must now go back into the hospital and find out what was happening to his mother, when all he really wanted to do was get into the car and drive, drive away from it all . . . from everyone. Yes, even from Annette, because every time he looked at her he was torn between love for Don and desire for her.

Back in the reception area of the hospital he was making his way towards the desk when a sister hailed him; then standing in front of him she looked at him and said quietly, "I'm afraid, Mr. Coulson, we weren't able to save your mother. She . . . she didn't regain consciousness. She died from the effects of exposure."

Was he sorry? Was he glad? He didn't know. But after a moment he asked, "What is the procedure now?" And she answered, "Well, she'll go to the mortuary and you'll have to make your own arrangements. They generally lie in the undertaker's chapel, you know."

"Yes, yes. There's nothing more required of me now?"

"No; unless you would like to see her."

"*No.*" The word was emphatic. Then he added, "Thank you. I'll . . . I'll be back." And on that he turned abruptly from her.

The sister went to stop him with a movement of her hand as if she had something more to say. Then, turning towards the desk, she leant on it for a moment as she said to the receptionist, "He's upset naturally, but if you ask me it's just as well she went. She could have been certified as insane and then she would have spent her life inside. And if she wasn't . . . well! by what I understand she did to those other two last night, she would have gone along the line for that. Oh well, it's all in a day's work." And on a small laugh she said, "One day I'll write a book and I'll call it, 'She Died At Her Post,' because I don't know how I'm going to get through this session. My head's lifting off."

NINE

*I*t was Sunday evening. Flo and Harvey had arrived earlier in the day, and it was Flo who was now standing in the hall talking to Father Ramshaw.

Helping him off with his coat, she said, "I'm sorry, Father, to get you out at this time of night, and such a night, but I don't think this is a case for the doctor. As I said to you on the phone, he swears she's in the room with him."

"Well, she might be at that, Flo, because she was a very forceful woman. She's shown that in more ways than one. Dear God! she has that. But who would have thought she would have gone to the lengths she did. But there, human nature is as unpredictable as the weather, for who would have thought we would have snow at this late time of the year. But then again we should have remembered we've had it before as we should also remember that human nature is a very strange mixture of the good, the bad, and the 'I can't help it.' "

"Will you come in to the dining-room and have a drink first, Father?"

"No, no; later perhaps. What's the latest from the hospital?"

"Daniel has regained consciousness. They think he'll pull through."

"Thanks be to God for that at least. And Stephen?"

"He's asleep, Father. I gave him a tablet. He's been through it, poor boy."

"He acted very sensibly by all accounts."

"Yes, yes, he did. You know, Father, I must confess, if I'm sorry for anyone in this world I'm sorry for Stephen. Just that little something . . . just that tiny little something up here"—she tapped her forehead—"and he'd be a splendid fellow."

"God picks his children, Flo; they come in all sizes. By the way, I'm forgetting you were married yesterday."

"Yes, Father, I'm pleased to say."

"In a registry office?"

They had been walking towards the corridor and Flo stopped, saying, "No, Father, not in a registry office; we were married in a church by special licence."

"Oh! Oh! But"—he poked his head towards her—"the other side?"

"Yes, Father, the other side."

"Oh, well, I've heard He pops in there now and again when He has time."

"Oh, Father." She pushed him in the shoulder, and he grinned at her, saying now, "I'm happy for you anyway. And he's a fine man, what I've seen of him. But you know . . . well, I think you know, that life won't be easy."

"I'm well aware of that, Father, and he more so; but we'll get through."

"That's the way to look at it."

When they entered the sick-room the nurse seemed to be relieved at the sight of them, and she said immediately to Flo, "He won't take his tablets."

"Go and have a bite."

"I've had my supper."

"Well, go and have another one." The priest pushed her gently towards Flo, then went towards the bed and, pulling a chair up close, he sat down.

Don was propped up against the pillows, although his eyes were closed and he kept them closed as he said, "Hello, Father."

"Hello, son. Misbehaving yourself again?"

"So they tell me, Father."

It wasn't until the door had been closed for some seconds that Don opened his eyes and, looking at the priest, he said, "She's here, Father."

"Now, now, now."

"Don't say that, Father. My body's in a mess, I'm only too well aware, but my mind isn't affected. She's here. I . . . I said it isn't affected, but how long it will stay that way I don't know."

"What makes you think she's here?"

"I saw her, Father. She was standing there at the foot of the bed."

"When was this?"

"Last night. No, no, yesterday, sometime. Can't rightly put the hour to it. I thought I was imagining it at first because she looked just like an outline. And then, towards night-time it got stronger. She stood there looking at me, with no smile on her face, just staring. And I was glad to take the sleeping tablets; but then, in my dreams, she became more lifelike. Oh yes." He moved his head on the pillow. "She sat on the edge of the bed where you're sitting now and she talked to me, the same kind of stuff that I'd listened to for years, how she loved me . . ."

"Well, she did love you, and that's what you must remember."

"There's love and love, Father. She must have been insane half the time."

"No, I don't think so."

"You didn't have to live with her, Father."

"No; that's true. But she's gone now, only God knows where; she's not here any more."

"She's here, Father."

"All right, all right, don't get agitated. All right. To you she's here. But I can promise you this, she'll go."

"When? Tell me that, when?"

The priest paused for a moment, then said quietly, "Tomorrow morning I'll give you Holy Communion. But in the meantime, should she return, talk to her. Tell her that you understand how she felt. Yes, yes, do that. Don't turn your head away like that, boy."

"Father, you don't understand, she's waiting for me to die, then she'll have me again wherever I go."

"She won't. I promise you. Listen to me." He gripped both of Don's hands now tightly and shook them as he said, "After tomorrow morning she'll go. You'll never see her again. But your main job now is to give her peace. Send her away in peace. Tell her you forgive her."

"Forgive her, Father! She doesn't think that she's done anything to me that needs forgiveness."

"You know nothing about it, Don. Only she knows how she felt for you, and likely the main reason she's coming back is to ask for your forgiveness. Give it to her."

It was some time before Don answered; then, his chin on his chest, he murmured, "I'm frightened, Father."

"Of her? Is that all?"

"No, no. Of everything. Where I'm going shortly . . . Everything. I thought I wasn't, but I am."

"Well, you needn't worry about the latter; God's got that in hand."

"And Father, there's something else."

"Yes?"

"I've . . . I've already spoken my mind to Joe about it. I . . . I want him to marry Annette. I want him to have the care of her. You could manoeuvre that for me."

"I'll do no manoeuvring. No such thing. If it's so willed that they should come together, they'll come together without any more manoeuvring being done in this house." He got to his feet. "I suppose you know you are where you are at this minute because of manoeuvring. You're aware that your Dad manoeuvred you towards Annette. Oh God forgive me." He put his hand to his brow. "I don't want to lose me temper at this stage; I'm too old to get worked up about life's foibles." He stopped here for with some surprise he saw that Don was actually smiling, and so, his voice now taking on a purposely rough note, he said, "And what are you grinning at? I have a pretty rough time of it. You're not the only one you know."

"You always do me good, Father. You know, I've always thought you've been wasted as a priest; you would have done much more good on the stage."

"For your information, boy, I *am* on the stage. What do you think the priesthood is but a stage and all of us enacting a play . . . ?"

The last word trailed away and his head drooped and he said softly, "I didn't mean that." Then his chin jerking upwards, he said, "Yes, I did. God isn't fooled. He's looking down on this stage all the time and watching His lead players. Like a good producer, He's picked us. But He doesn't take on the directing; He's left that to each individual, and some of us find the act harder to play out than others. I'll tell you something." He leant both hands on the bed now and, bending, brought his face close to Don's, and almost in a whisper he repeated, "I'll tell you something. You know what I would like to have been if not a priest?"

"A psychiatrist?"

"Psychiatrist, no! A clown, a simple clown. Not a magician; you know, one of the clever clots; just a simple clown. And I would like to have acted solely before children under the age of seven, because it is then we are told they come to the use of reason and reason wipes out wonder. Have you ever thought about wonder? It's a gift that's given only to children, but they lose it so quickly, so quickly." He sighed now, pulled himself up straight and, his voice changing, he said, "You know something: you're bad for me. You're like Joe. He's the kind of fellow that makes you go to confession every time you talk to him." He chuckled now, then said in a deep but soft tone, "Good night, my son, and God be with you every minute of it." And on this he left the room. And Don, pressing his head back into the pillow, said, "Yes, God be with me every minute of it."

Joe met the priest in the hall, saying, "Come in here, Father; I've got a hot drink for you."

"Don't have a shock, Joe, but I'm going to refuse it. I've got two visits to make and it's getting near me bedtime. See that he takes his tablets early, will you? Do you know, he . . . he thinks she's come back and is waiting for him."

"Yes, Father. I got an inkling of it a while back, and I believe he's right."

"Oh, now, don't you start, Joe. You with a head on you like a spirit-level."

"Does that mean, Father, that you're insensitive if you're level-headed?"

"Not a bit of it, not a bit of it. You know what I mean."

"Harvey sensed something, Father. He didn't know what. But he wasn't in the house very long before he said, 'I can't believe she's gone. I've got the feeling she's still upstairs, and not in the ordinary way. I just don't know.' "

"Well, coming from his culture, they're nearer the earth than we are."

"Or the gods."

"Oh, Joe, don't egg me on to theology at this time of night and in my present state. Still, I know what you mean and although I'm throwing doubt on everybody's opinion, let me tell you I too know she's here. There are more things in heaven and earth than this world dreams of. One more thing and I must be off. How soon can Annette come back? because he wants to see that child and it's only fair that he should."

"It'll be some days yet, Father, I'm afraid."

"Oh, well, there's no doubt about it, he'll hang on if at all possible. I'll be round in the morning at eight o'clock for Holy Communion. And it wouldn't do you any harm to take it either. Two for the price of one."

"I'll buy it, Father. Good-night."

"Good-night, Joe."

TEN

On took Holy Communion the following morning, but his mother remained with him.

They buried her on the Wednesday and it was noticeable how few of her friends attended the funeral, for had she not been insane and tried to murder her husband and other members of the household? Besides Joe, Flo and Harvey, you could have counted another twenty people, half of them Daniel's workmen. Nor did any of these, other than Joe, Harvey and Flo make their way back to the house.

From the talk around him, Stephen had known that his mother was to be buried that day, but he had shown no desire to attend the funeral; in fact, he had remained in his room until Joe had gone up to him. "It's all right," Joe had said to him, "for I want you to stay and look after Don till we get back." And Stephen had jabbered with relief, "Yes, yes, Joe, I will, I will. I'll see to Don. Don likes me seeing to him. Yes, I will."

On arriving back, Joe went immediately to Don's room. Inside, however, he did not approach the bed, but looking towards the nurse, he said, "Mr. and Mrs. Rochester are going to have a bite of food; would you like to join them?"

Taking the broad hint, the nurse smiled and left the room; and Joe, now standing close to the bed, looked down on Don but found it most difficult to speak for the moment. It was Don who seemed the more composed, and he said quietly, "Well, you got it over?"

"Yes, yes, it's over."

"So now we'll see. But . . . but somehow it doesn't matter; I'm not afraid of her any more. I haven't been for the last few days. I think it was after I took Holy Communion I seemed to get quiet inside. It was like Extreme Unction. He hasn't brought that up yet." He smiled wanly. "Father Ramshaw, I mean. He's sort of putting it off until the last minute. I've always thought Extreme Unction must be like signing your name to a death warrant. Oh, Joe." He slowly lifted his hand and caught Joe's wrist. "Don't look like that, man. Don't you think it's as well I can talk about it? You know, it's like people who are afraid to mention the name of anyone who's just died. I always think that's silly; it's like shutting them out. I don't want to be shut out, Joe. I don't want you to talk about me when I'm gone, behind my back." He gave a small laugh.

"Oh, for God's sake, Don!" Joe pulled his hand away from the weak grasp. "You know what? You break my heart at times."

"Oh, Joe, I'm sorry. Look at me. Come on now. I'll tell you something. You know what the doctor said this morning? He said my heart's steadier than it's been in weeks. Now why is that? And I said to him, I'm going to get better; I'm sick of paying your bills. Come on, Joe. Joe, please."

Joe did not turn round, but muttered, "I'll . . . I'll be back in a minute." And with that he went into the sitting-room, and he was about to ring the bell that could be heard in the dining-room and the kitchen and which would summon someone back here, when he heard Don's door open and Stephen's voice say, "Oh, I thought Joe was here. He said we could play billiards."

"Come and sit beside me for a while." Don's voice came as if from a far distance. "Joe'll be back in a minute; he's gone on an errand for me."

Joe slipped out through the conservatory, along the corridor, and so to his own apartment. And there he sat down and drooped his head into his hands. He couldn't stand much more of this; the turmoil inside him was tearing him apart. Again he wished he was miles away. At one time he had loved this house for itself, now he hated it. He, too, was certain that although her body might be in the grave her spirit was still here.

After a moment or so he rose to his feet and stood looking out of the window on to the garden. The sun was shining brightly. The week-end winter had gone; it was even warm. That unfailing announcer of spring, the bed of crocus just below the window, was pushing through, and a border of daffodils, their buds now showing but still pointing straight up, on the other side of the path. The garden was beginning to smile. He drew in a long breath.

But down to earth again: in an hour's time he would be going from one to the other in the hospital. And yet, did he need to? They all knew she had been buried today.

Annette had had to be told of her father-in-law's and Maggie's sojourn quite near her. When he told her what had happened to them she had become fearful, saying, "She'll come here and try to get the baby." And so, to calm her he had been obliged to tell her that her mother-in-law was already dead.

It had also lain with him to break this news to Daniel, and that had come about only yesterday. The doctor had advised against it, and when he had received this advice he had wanted to say, "He won't be shocked. He'll be glad to hear it."

His father had spoken to him for the first time two days ago: "She did it at last, Joe," he had said.

What Maggie had said was, "I think I would have done the same in her place."

Well, Joe told himself as he gazed down on the spring flowers, it would be over once Don was gone.

But what then?

Well, he'd just wait and see. But did he want to wait and see? There was a change taking place inside him: it was as if he too had been battered, and into insensibility, for it came to him that once Don died he would be free, and being free he knew what he would do.

*E*LEVEN

*I*nside the hospital they separated, Flo and Harvey visiting Annette while Joe made straight for Daniel's room.

Daniel was sitting up in bed. It was as if he was waiting for him.

"Well, Joe?" he said.

"How are you feeling?"

"Relieved, in a way. I'm all right inside apparently, so the X-rays say. And they've stitched me up here and there . . . she was always methodical. What happened this morning?"

"What could happen, Dad? We buried her."

"Well, don't look at me like that, expecting me to say I'm sorry or I feel any guilt, or poor soul, or what have you. What I've been feeling over the past few days is deep bitterness and regret for the wasted years in having to put up with her. Forgive and forget, they say. Let them try it after living with someone like her for half your lifetime."

"She's dead, Dad. And the past is dead with her. You've got to look at it like that."

Daniel made no reply to this, only cast a sidelong glance at Joe before he did say, "How's Don?"

"About the same. But I think Annette should try to come home as soon as possible. I'll see the doctor before I leave."

"Maggie will be home tomorrow. She was in just a little while ago . . . I'm going to marry her, Joe."

"Yes, yes. Of course, I understand that you'll marry her."

"But we won't go on living there. That's one thing sure. She doesn't want it and I certainly don't."

"I can understand that an' all. What about Stephen? Where does he go?"

"He'll come with us. He's my responsibility, after all."

Joe felt the urge to speak his thoughts by saying, I'm glad you see it that way; you've practically made him mine over the years.

What was the matter with him? He was tired. He must be careful of his tongue. Yet the next moment he was saying, "Have you worked out what's going to happen to Annette and the baby?"

"Why are you using that tone on me, Joe? That doesn't need any working out. Once she's . . . left alone"—he paused—"she'll go to the home that was intended for them. That only leaves you. What do you intend to do? Would you like to stay there? I mean, I can pass the place over."

"Thank you very much. Stay in that house! Me? Alone?"

"Well, you've always said you liked the place, loved it even. Apart from . . . her who wanted it in the first place, you considered it the best house in the town, not only from your architectural point of view, but because of the house itself."

"Things change. People change. I don't want the house. As soon as you're on your feet I'm off."

"Off? Where?"

"It doesn't matter much where." He moved a step from the bed; then turned and said, "Perhaps I'll try to find my own people . . . me ain folk, you know."

He was going out of the door when Daniel called to him, "Joe! Joe!" But he took no notice. He found he was sweating. He took out a handkerchief and wiped his face, the while chastising himself: Daniel was still in a bad way and he had gone for him like that. Well, Daniel's body might have been knocked about but his mind was just the same. And at this moment he was seeing him as a man who had gone his own way all his life. Perhaps he had bowed to duty once or twice by staying with his wife, but for the rest he had lived on the side, whereas he himself had never tasted that kind of life. He had wanted one girl, one woman, from when he had first held her hand and taken her across a road. And he would have had her, he felt sure of that, if the man behind that door who had acted as father to him, and whom he had thought of lovingly for years, had not had the urge to get back on his wife in some way. And so he had made plans. And his son unsuspectingly had carried them out.

Well, here he was, twenty-six years old, and he could have been the virgin that his adoptive mother had desired in her own son, for, as yet, he hadn't known a woman. Not that he hadn't wanted to. My God! Yes, he had wanted to. Then why hadn't he? Hadn't he told himself that once Don and Annette were married that would be that? And then if he never married he would certainly taste the fruits of it. But what had happened? Well, the result of what had happened was all about him. And now he was waiting for his brother's dying.

No, he wasn't.

Once again his thoughts were spurting him forward and along the corridor and into the new ward to which Maggie had been moved.

She was sitting in the chair by the side of the window when he entered, and she turned to him, her face and voice eager as she said, "Oh, hello, Joe. I am pleased to see you. I'm coming home tomorrow."

"So I understand."

He sat down opposite her and, after a moment while she looked at him, she said, "I called it home, but, you know, I'm afraid to enter that door. I want to be away from there as soon as ever I can. Do you understand that, Joe?"

"Yes, Maggie, I understand that."

She pressed her head back, looking hard at him for a moment; then she said, "You understand most things, Joe. Somehow you've been forced to understand. I've sometimes thought that it was a good thing for the family when you came into it but a bad thing for yourself."

"That's life, Maggie. And isn't that the most trite remark in the English language? Yet, like many another, it's true. I had no say in it, had I, whatever power that ordained my life, and I often think there's more than one on that committee up there and that some are blind and others cynical."

"Don't be bitter, Joe. That's not like you. What's the matter?"

"Aw, Maggie." He waved his hand at her and then laughed. "Fancy you saying that; what's the matter?"

"Well, I mean"—she bridled a little—"I know what's happened only too well. Dear God! I know what's happened. But as long as I've known you you haven't had an acid tongue."

"That's because I swallowed my thoughts before they slipped out of my mouth."

Sadly now she shook her head; then she asked, "Has . . . has something happened that I don't yet know about?"

"No, Maggie, I think you know about everything, except that Dad has suggested that I take on the house when he leaves. I think that stopped me swallowing my thoughts."

"Oh. Oh." She nodded now before saying, "That was a damn silly thing to say."

"Well, I suppose, as he says, I'd always appeared to like the house when everybody else was trying to get away from it. But under the circumstances, me there . . . and who else? Eh? Who else? Oh, I'm sorry." He took her hand, saying, "Don't look so troubled."

"Did you have words with him?"

"No, no; no words. Well, not really. Anyway, I'm glad you're coming back tomorrow, for however long or short."

"I'll have to stay until Don goes."

"Yes, yes." He rose to his feet and sighed now. "We'll all have to stay until Don goes. Poor Don. We're praying that he won't die, yet all of us are waiting for him to go."

"You *are* upset, aren't you, Joe?"

"Perhaps. Anyway, I'll see you tomorrow, Maggie. Goodbye."

"Goodbye, Joe. Joe." He turned as he was opening the door for she was saying, "If I hadn't been in love with your father I would certainly have fallen for you and said so, no matter what the age gap."

He jerked his chin up and laughed as he said, "Thanks, Maggie. That's nice to know. And I'd have been honoured to have you."

When he reached the Maternity Ward and Annette's room, Flo greeted him with, "It's about time you came and talked some sense into this one here; she's for discharging herself against the doctor's wishes."

"Oh?" He stood by Harvey now and looked at Annette, and he said, "Well, by the look of her she seems fit enough to me. Do you feel fit, Mrs. Coulson?"

"Yes, Mr. Coulson, I feel fit. And the baby's fit. We want to come home."

"Well, I think we'd better see the doctor, hadn't we, and leave the decision to him?"

"May a man of the law speak?" They looked at Harvey now, who was smiling widely, and it was Flo who answered, "It wouldn't be any use trying to stop you, would it, sir?"

"Well, as I see it, I think the person in question should be regarded as her own doctor. Put the said person in a wheelchair, transfer her to an automobile, carry her and the said child into the house and put them straight into bed. What could be simpler?"

Annette smiled at Harvey and said, "That sounds sensible. Well, what do you say, Joe?"

"I still say we should leave it in the doctor's hands. Anyway, I'll go and have a word with someone in charge and I'll be back."

After he had left the room Harvey and Flo exchanged glances and looked at Annette, and she said, "I've never known Joe to be in a temper. But . . . but what do you think? He's in a temper, isn't he?"

"He's in something." Flo pursed her lips and turned to Harvey, saying, "Don't you think so too?"

"Well, if you want to know what I think, ladies, I think that everybody, I mean everybody, puts on Joe. As far as I can gather, he's been a dustbin for everybody's woes, the sorter out of troubles. Oh, Joe'll do this and Joe'll do that. And something must have happened that's made Joe think that he's tired of being a dustbin. Perhaps I'm wrong; it might be something else. I don't know. But in my short acquaintance with him, this present Joe is not the Joe that I had come to know."

Getting up from where she was sitting on the side of the bed, Flo said, "I wish I wasn't going, that we weren't going." She looked across at her husband, and he said, "Well, we made a decision."

"Oh . . . oh, yes, yes, I know, and I'm looking forward to it, and although I said I wish I wasn't going, it's because I just want to see Annette settled." She put her hand out and stroked Annette's hair back from her forehead, adding, "But once you're in your own home you can start a new life." Her voice trailed off; then jerking herself away from the bed, she said, "Oh my God! the things I say."

"Flo, I'm not upset. Things like that don't upset me. I faced up to it a long time ago. Don will soon go. That's why I want to get back. And you must go too and be happy in your new life. And who couldn't help but be happy with this big handsome fellow here." She put out her hand and Harvey gripped it. "Write to me every week, won't you? And perhaps in a little while I . . . I could come out for a holiday with young Flo."

They were both standing over her, silent now, until her arms came up and went round their necks and Flo's tears mingled with hers and, brokenly, they said their goodbyes. And the last words Harvey spoke before leaving her were, "I'll always be grateful to you, Annette, for being prepared to give your son—had he been a son—my name. You'll never know how much that means to me."

Left alone, Annette gulped over the lump in her throat, telling herself she mustn't give way, for if she got upset it would stop her going home. And yet, in another way, she was dreading going back to that house, even though it still held Don. But she wouldn't be able to leave until he left it too. And Joe. What was the matter with Joe? She had never seen him as he had appeared a short while ago; distant. He wasn't the Joe she could rely on, the Joe that was always there. What if he too wanted to leave? Everything was changing. It was natural, she supposed, yet she had thought that Joe was the kind of person who would never change: he was there, stable, someone you could rely on. But he had his own life to lead. She recalled that only a few weeks ago she had seen him in the town talking to Mary Carter. She was a very smart girl, about his own age. She was a Protestant, though. But then she couldn't see religion standing in Joe's way if he really wanted her. Then there was Irene Shilton. She had trailed him for years, and she was a Catholic. She was very pretty, younger than him. Strangely, she had never liked her.

The door opened and the nurse entered carrying the baby, and when the child was laid in her arms and the nurse said, "She's putting on weight every day. Isn't she lovely?" she looked up at her and said, "I'd like to see Sister as soon as possible, please. I . . . ."

"Is something wrong?"

"No, no, nurse; nothing's wrong. And you've been so kind, but I want to go home. My husband, you know, is very ill. I want him to see the baby."

"Yes, yes, of course. I'll tell Sister."

TWELVE

*I*t was eight o'clock the following morning. Flo and Harvey were ready for leaving: they had said their goodbyes to Don and the staff, and now they were standing outside by the car, with Joe and Harvey shaking hands.

"You'll come and see us, Joe? You promised. And you will?"

"I will. I will. Don't worry about that." Then he laughed as he added, "For two pins I'd pack my bags and come along with you now except that, at this time, two's company."

Flo didn't laugh; but now, putting her arms around Joe's neck, she kissed him and, looking into his face, she said softly, "Everything comes to him who waits, Joe." And she jerked her head back to where Harvey was standing, the car door in his hand. "Look what happened to me." Again she kissed him, and he returned her kiss.

He watched the car moving down the drive, Flo's arm out of the window and, for a moment, Harvey's hand out of the other. And then they were gone and he doubted if he'd ever see them again.

Slowly he went back into the house. Everything comes to him who waits. Waits for what?

When he entered Don's room the nurse had just finished washing her patient and was stroking a thick quiff of hair back from his brow as she piped, "Who's a pretty boy then?"

The sound grated on Joe's ears. What effect it was having on Don's didn't show. But he, looking up at Joe, said, "They've gone then?"

"Yes, they've gone."

"She doesn't know it"—he drew in a gasping breath—"but things aren't going to be easy out there." Another gasp at the air. "I . . . I shouldn't wonder to see them back in . . . in no time."

"Oh, I think they know what they're up against. They've got through it here so they'll manage."

"You're . . . you're all dressed for out."

"Yes, I have to go to work sometimes, you know"—Joe smiled—"if it's only to put in an appearance."

"Nurse said your . . . your light was . . . on at half-past two . . . this morning."

"She's a Nosey Parker, like all nurses." He glanced towards Nurse Porter and she turned, smiling, towards him, saying, "I'll tell her tonight what you said. She's a hefty piece; you'd find your match."

"That would be nice." He returned her smile; then looking at Don again, he said, "Well, I'm off. I'll be back at lunch-time. Behave yourself, mind. Do you hear?"

"Joe." Don's voice was a thin whisper now. "When . . . when is she . . . coming? I mean . . ."

"Any time now. I'm going in this afternoon; I'll likely bring her back with me then."

"Do. Please do, Joe."

"I will." He patted the thin shoulder. "Don't you worry, just behave yourself." And with this, he turned and went out and along the corridor to his own cottage.

Having thrown some papers into his case, he stood looking down at it for a moment and repeated to himself and grimly, "Everything comes to him who waits." My God! Flo must have thought he was hanging on for that . . . Well, wasn't he?

No, No! He wasn't going to have that said of him.

He entered the hall at dinner time to see Maggie coming slowly the stairs. She stopped, and he stood at the foot smiling up at her, saying, "You've made it then?"

"Yes, I've made it. But I hadn't realised just how much it had taken out of me until I stepped outside the hospital. I would prepare yourself before you go along there"—she thumbed towards the sick room—"there's visitors."

He glanced in the direction she had indicated, then said, "Who do you mean? Annette?"

"Yes, Annette."

"But how?"

"Oh, quite easily. She phoned Lily. Lily brought her clothes and mine in a taxi, and Bob's your uncle, here we are. Now, now; don't look like that; it's all right."

"And the child too?"

"Yes, and she's doing fine. She's put on a pound or more in a week."

Maggie descended the rest of the stairs and stood in front of him, saying, quietly now, "Oh, you should have seen his face when he took the child from her. You know, it's sort of given him a new lease of life. I shouldn't be surprised if"—she shook her head now as if denying her thoughts. "Anyway, it's given him a reprieve, I know that."

He made no comment on this but turned from her and walked towards Don's room. His step was not hurried nor yet slow and he prepared himself for the tableau before opening the door. And there it was: father, mother, and child, close together.

It was Annette who spoke first. Getting to her feet, she said, "Now don't be annoyed with me, Joe; I just couldn't stand that room a minute longer.

And I'm fine. We're both fine. Look at her!" She pointed to where the child was held in the hollow of Don's arm, a finger of his other hand stroking the wisps of hair. And Don looked at him, saying, "This is . . . the happiest day of my . . . my life, Joe. Isn't . . . isn't she beautiful?"

"She is that, she's beautiful." He was bending over them now, and when he put his hand out towards the tiny one groping at the air and it hung on to his thumb the restriction in his throat seemed to expand and cover his chest, making his own breathing difficult for a moment.

It was the nurse who broke the tension by saying, "Not that all babies don't do that, but, there you are, she's claimed you straight away. So look out! If she howls in the night you know what to expect."

"She doesn't cry at night," Annette said. "They told me she sleeps soundly."

"And that's what she's going to do now," said the nurse. "So here! Give her to me. And you"—she nodded towards Annette—"go and have something to eat and then it's bed for you this afternoon. Now do what you're told. I've had my orders and I'm giving them to you."

When the nurse had taken the baby from Don's arms Annette leant over him and, after looking into his face for a moment, she kissed him. And his arms came around her and held her close. Then he was lying back with the tears oozing slowly from beneath his lids.

Joe, taking hold of Annette's arm, drew her from the bed and out of the room. They didn't speak until they reached the dining-room; and there she sat down before, looking up at him, she said, "You're vexed with me?"

"No. What makes you think that?"

"Because . . . because I came home on my own and didn't wait another day or so as I promised. But I'm all right and I felt I must be here near him. You understand?"

"Of course I understand." He sat down beside her. "I was going by what the doctor said was best for you; but if there had been any noticeable change in Don you know I would have brought you home immediately."

"He looks dreadful, Joe."

"Do you think so? I thought . . . well, I thought he was even looking better?" he lied firmly.

"No, no. And it's not just because I haven't seen him for a week or so. But now, seeing the baby, perhaps he'll rally. What do you think?"

"I think just that, he will rally, he'll go on."

She shook her head as she looked away from him. "You don't believe that. Neither do I. I looked in on father-in-law . . . or Dan, as he insists I call him. He says he's coming home too, but he still looks awful. He . . . he told me he's selling the house: he's already told his secretary to put it on the market. I'm glad of that. I hate this place; I wish I could take Don and the baby straight to the cottage. Oh, it's all right, it's all right." She closed her eyes and put out her hand towards him. "I know I can't but . . . but I did think Dad might have waited until . . . well—" She shook her head. Then looking at him again, she said, "What will you do?"

"Oh, don't worry about me; I have it all worked out."

"You won't leave the town?" There was a note of anxiety in her voice, and he answered, "No. No, of course not; my work's here."

"You could set up your work anywhere. Newcastle for instance. Durham, anywhere . . . or even Canada."

Her head drooping on to her chest now, she murmured, "I felt so lost in there, Joe. I . . . I thought perhaps Mother might come and see me. Father I knew would never come, but . . . but somehow . . . But there, she didn't. When the papers were full of it last week one of the new nurses said to me, 'It's a good job your parents weren't in the same house when your mother-in-law got going. I bet they were relieved that you were in here at the time.' And when I burst out crying she patted me, saying, 'They'll likely be in soon. Don't worry. Don't worry.' "

Her face flooded with tears and he steeled himself not to draw her near to him, but just took her hand and patted it, saying, "There now. There now. Don't cry like that, please. If he sees you upset it'll only make him worse. And . . . and you've got the baby to think about."

"By the way"—she was drying her face now—"where's Stephen? I haven't seen him."

"Oh, he's been in bed these last few days. He's been having accidents again, you know. I think he heard Lily and Peggie talking about the likelihood of this place being sold and the old fear about being put in a home has erupted again. He's been threatened with that so many times. I've tried to tell him that wherever Dad and Maggie go, he'll go with them. You understand about them, don't you, Annette?"

"Well, I do now, Joe, if I didn't before. I must admit I was a bit surprised, but I don't blame him, either of them. Oh, no, I don't blame them, Joe." She squeezed his hand tightly and paused before she said, "Do . . . do you think Don's mind is becoming affected too?"

"His mind? What makes you think that?"

"Well, it happened as soon as I put the baby into his arms that . . . that he held it up as if showing it to somebody, and he looked towards the foot of the bed and said, 'And this is the result.' It . . . it was as if he was seeing someone. You don't think . . . ?"

He took her other hand now and pressed them between his two large ones, and he shook them gently as he said, "He's not going off his head, dear; it's just that he imagines his mother has come back. And it isn't just imagination, you know, for at times I too feel she is here. Now don't . . . don't. Please . . . please don't shake like that. You have nothing to fear. She's gone. She's dead. But you know how she felt about him, and these things happen whether we like to believe them or not. I wouldn't have believed it a few months ago. In fact, I wouldn't have believed any of this." His voice was harsh now. "But I know as well as he does that she's there in that room. And that's what's troubling poor Stephen as well. We try to put it down to the fact that he doesn't know what's going to happen to him, but whereas once he wouldn't leave Don's side, he now seems afraid to go into the room. The last time he was there he actually wet his pants on the spot. Now, that's never happened before. Did you feel anything strange when you went in?"

"No. No, I didn't. Perhaps I hadn't been in the room long enough. I was only so pleased to see him."

"Well, if he does mention it to you don't let him see that you're afraid.

Just tell him that she can do him no harm. And you know, it's odd, but I'm sure she doesn't want to do him any harm; she just wants him. There's one thing, though, I know, and I've got to say this, that once death comes to him she'll be gone too, because it's mostly in his mind."

"But if it's mostly in his mind how do you too feel that she's there?"

"Because it's in my mind as well, I suppose. Love and hate can create a sort of ethereal body. At least, that's how I've explained it to myself: there's the three of us, three men. Don's love, or any feeling he had for her, turned to hate because of her abnormal obsession with him. As for me, her attitude towards me over the years created dislike. And yes, that could have bordered on hate too. But in Stephen's case it's fear: fear has created her for him. Well" —he sighed—"that's the only explanation I can give. But what the three of us know is that her presence is still in that room. But the strongest emotion is between her and Don, and through this he almost sees her, if he doesn't *actually* see her. But as I said, once he goes . . . and he'll go in peace, she'll no longer be there. Nor, I imagine, will she be able to hold him, for there'll be no coming together."

"That's an odd thing to say, Joe." Her voice was quiet. "It's against all the tenets of our religion, isn't it? The coming together, the meeting up with the loved ones, the forgiveness of sins, life everlasting, the mansions of God. What do you say to all that?"

"That it's mostly myth. Don't look surprised. Yes, I know I attend Mass, I go to Confession, I say the Rosary. But I'm protesting all the time. I've talked it out with Father Ramshaw and in his kindly, God-like way he tells me the doubts will pass. Every true Christian goes through this stage, he says. Well, I've been through it for some time now and all that has happened is the doubts have become almost certainties. Still, it takes strength to throw over God, to do away with him altogether, and I doubt if I'm all that strong. But, don't look so worried."

"I'm not worried, Joe, I'm only surprised, because you've put into words the feelings I had in the convent. Some of those nuns were like angels, some like devils. And if it hadn't been for Father Ramshaw I would have rebelled openly some time ago; especially after a rating from Father Cody. And do you know, that man tackled me about my sin, Don's and my sin together, and he told me I should do a long penance and berate my flesh."

"He didn't! You should have told Father Ramshaw about him."

"Oh, I don't think Father Ramshaw needs to be told about him. Odd, isn't it?" She smiled now. "I know that those two hate each other like poison. Disciples of God and living in the same house and can't stand the sight of each other. Oh, but what does it matter? That's all beside the point really."

"Yes, dear. Yes, it is. Now come on, have something to eat, then as the nurse said, you go back and you feed Flo. . . . They went off this morning, you know."

"Yes, I know. They called in at the hospital again."

"They didn't!"

"Yes. Yes, they did."

"That was nice of them. I thought they were going straight on. Anyway, you're going to have a rest, but not in that room. You're going upstairs.

Peggie had already fitted up a guest-room with a dressing-room attached, and now she's fixed that up as a kind of nursery. So it's all ready for you."

"Oh, that *is* nice." She rose now and went towards the dining table; then quietly she asked, "Have you been along to the cottage lately, Joe?"

"Yes, I've looked in at least every other day. I had business with a client up that way, so it was easy. And I don't know why it's called a cottage, with nine rooms set in an acre and a half of land. It's like a little manor house. You'll be happy there, dear."

She looked at him for a long, long moment, but said nothing; nor did he, for he felt it had been a tactless remark to make: happy in a nine-roomed house on your own with a baby.

THIRTEEN

$\mathcal{F}$rom the moment of Annette's and the baby's return Don seemed to blossom, inasmuch as his breathing became easier. He complained less of pain; the doctor seemed pleased with him; and he exchanged quips with Father Ramshaw. And a fortnight after Annette's arrival home his father stepped into the room and he held out both arms to him and returned the hug that Daniel gave him.

One side of Daniel's face was still discoloured, he walked with a slight limp and it was evident that he had lost some weight.

They talked about everything that didn't matter until the day wore on and it was time to say good-night; then, appertaining to nothing that had gone before, Daniel, from where he was sitting at the side of the bed, leant his elbows on the coverlet, took hold of his son's hand and said, "She's not here. Get it into your head, lad, she's not here. She's gone forever."

"You don't feel her, Dad?"

"No . . . no, I don't feel her; except where she's left the bruises all over me body. That's where I feel her. But not anywhere else."

"She's here, Dad. She's been here from the minute she died."

"Now, Don."

"It's no good talking, Dad. And I'm not the only one. Why do you think Stephen isn't down here chatting away? He hasn't been near the room for days. He's in bed, supposedly with a cold. He knew she was here; and so does Joe."

"Oh, not Joe. Joe's too level . . ."

"Joe's not too level-headed, Dad. He feels her almost as much as I do. And I know one thing for sure: she won't go till I go. But I'm not afraid, I mean, of her. I've become so that I pity her. But she knows she can't hold me. I've told her that and she knows it. It is as if knowing it she's determined to see the last of me here."

"Don't talk like that, lad."

"Dad . . . you grew to hate her. You hated her for a long time, and the more you hated her the more she loved me. And in the end, you know, I've come to think that love is stronger than hate because it's her love, or whatever name you could put to it, that's keeping her here. I don't mind her now. I was petrified at first, sick at the thought of her being here, but not any more. And even her appearance is altered. She's sort of pathetic. I'm sorry for her. And don't look like that, Dad, as if you were scared; my mind's not affected, it's the only place that's been left whole. I know it's whole."

"Have you talked to Father Ramshaw about it?"

"Yes; yes, we've discussed it openly and often. He understands. As he says, there's more things in heaven and earth than this world dreams of, and he's right. Have you had any takers for the house yet?"

"Yes . . . yes, I understand there's been takers."

"Well, they'll have to wait a while, won't they?"

"I hope they have to wait for years, lad."

"Oh, no, not as long as that, Dad, not as long as that. It'll be funny, this house breaking up; it seemed so solid at one time. Dad . . . ?"

"Yes, son?"

"You and Maggie will get together, I know that, and Stephen will go with you. Well, let it rest there; don't interfere in any other way, will you? Will you not?"

"What do you mean, interfere?"

"Just that. Let . . . let the rest of them run their own lives."

"The rest of them? Who do you mean? There's only Joe and Annette."

"Yes . . . well, I know, there's only Joe and Annette. But whatever happens, Dad, let things take their course."

Daniel got to his feet and, looking down on his son, he said sadly, "I don't like that, Don, not the way you're saying that. Whatever I did in the past was for your good."

"Yes, yes, I know, Dad, but that is what most people say, you know: I did it for . . . for somebody's good."

Daniel narrowed his eyes as he looked down on the thin pale face with the sunken eyes, the face that a year ago had appeared like that of a young boy . . . well, at most, a young man about to enter his twenties. But the eyes, as they gazed back at him from the deep-set sockets, could have been those of an old man and one who had lived a life and had experienced many things. He said quietly, "Good-night, son. Sleep well."

"Good-night, Dad. You too."

* * *

It was a fortnight later and around seven o'clock in the evening. Father Ramshaw was sitting in the library with Joe. Each was drinking a cup of coffee and the priest was saying, "I'm sorry I missed Daniel, I wanted a word with him. You say he's gone to look at his old place at the foot of Brampton Hill?"

"Yes. It's odd, isn't it, that it should become vacant at this time? He never wanted to leave that house really. It was one of the smallest on the hill and one of the oldest. I think it was the first one built before the élite of the town got started with their mansions."

"Yes, so I understand. And he's going to set up house there with Maggie and Stephen? Well, that's one part of the family that'll be settled. What about you?"

"Oh, I'm settled too."

"What do you mean? Have you got a flat?"

"Yes, sort of. It'll all be settled soon."

"Well, I don't think you have very long to wait. He's near his end; I feel that he should have the last rites tomorrow."

"But . . . but he seems bright, Father. I thought he could go on for some time yet."

"It's a forced brightness, Joe. I thought you would have seen that. But he knows that his time is running out and fast. The doctor said to me when we had a crack the other day, he's amazed that he's lasted so long. It's Annette and the child that's kept him going, and he's happy. It's strange but he's happy and quite ready to go. If I were you I'd sit up with him for some part of the next few nights. By the way, what's going to happen to the staff, Bill, John, Peggie, and Lily?"

"Well, Peggie is going to stay with Annette, and John is going with Dad. Bill and Lily will stay in the lodge, and if the new people, whoever takes the house, want to keep them on, well and good, if not, Dad's going to see to them in some way. So they are all going to be accounted for."

"Well, that's good to know. And you, are you going to live in this flat of yours alone?"

"Well, what do you suggest, Father?" Joe pursed his lips now as he waited for an answer. And the priest, raising his eyebrows, said, "Well, from what I gather you wouldn't have far to look for a partner. There's two in the church I know of and one outside."

"How do you know about Miss Carter?"

"Oh, I know lots of things, lad. It's amazing the news I get and where it comes from. Well, are you going to pick one of them?"

"I may."

"So you've been thinking about it?"

"Yes, Father, I've thought about it a lot; in fact, I've already made a choice. I made it some time ago."

Father Ramshaw's eyes widened. "Well, well! That's news. No inkling to who it is?"

"Not as yet, Father. I'll tell you when the time comes."

"Inside or out?"

"I'll tell you that too when the time comes."

"Well, that's something to look forward to. Now I must be on my way. I enjoyed that meal. It was always a good meat house this. And it's sad, you know." He stood up and looked about him. "It's a beautiful house, especially this room and all those books. What'll you do with them? Send them to auction?"

"Some of them, but I'll keep most of them."

"For your flat?"

"For my flat that could be a house."

"Oh, oh, we're getting somewhere now. The flat that could be a house. Well, well! You know me, Joe: once I get my teeth into anything I hang on until I know whom I'm biting. But it's going to be a surprise to me. I know that, because I thought I knew all about you both inside and out."

"There's always a depth, Father, in all of us that only the owner can plumb."

"Yes, yes, you're right there, Joe, you're right there. Nevertheless—" He chuckled now and shook his head, turned away and went down the room and out into the hall and to the front door. And there he stopped and, looking back towards the stairs, he said, "If your Dad doesn't sell this place to one of the tribe then my visits here will be cut short pretty soon. Good night, Joe."

"Good night, Father. And Father, you're a great believer in the efficacy of prayer, so you should see what it'll do about the new occupants."

The priest threw his head back now and laughed, saying, "That's good advice, Joe. Yes, I'll do that. Yes, I'll do that."

At ten o'clock Annette said good night to Don and when he took her face between his hands and said, "I love you," she answered brokenly, "And I you, Don. Oh yes, and I you." And when he added, "Be happy," she drew herself from him, and going to the nurse who was at the other end of the room, she said, "I . . . I think I'll sleep down here tonight."

"There's no need, Mrs. Coulson. If there was any change at all I'd call you immediately."

"I'd rather."

"Annette."

From the bed, Don said, "Go to bed upstairs, please. I'm going to sleep. I feel fine, really fine."

She went back to the bed again. "I'd rather, Don, if you . . ."

He took her hand, "Do as you're told, Mrs. Coulson. Go to bed. If you are lying on that hard mattress I'll be aware of you all night and I won't rest. Moreover, I want my daughter seen to." He continued to look at her long and hard, then said, "Please."

To hide her emotions she turned and hurried from the room. But instead of going to her own room she went along to Joe's apartment.

When there was no answer she went in and called softly, "Joe." And when there was still no reply, she turned about and went hastily along the corridor, through the hall and towards the kitchen. He'd likely be there talking to Maggie. Strange, she thought, that Maggie should still be carrying on what duties she could in the kitchen and sleeping in her own room while her father-in-law slept upstairs: the proprieties must not only be kept, but be seen to be kept. And after all they had gone through it seemed silly to her.

However, Maggie was not in the kitchen. Peggie said she was in her room and she had last seen Mr. Joe in the library.

She found Joe in the library. He was at the table thumbing through some books, and at the sight of her he raised his head and rose to his feet, saying, "What is it?"

"I don't know." She gave her head a little shake. "He seems all right, but . . . but it was the way he acted. I wanted to sleep there but he won't let me."

"Well, I'll be staying up, and if there's any change whatever you know I'll come for you."

"Yes, yes, I suppose so. But he seemed different, sort of very calm and, in a strange way, happy. It . . . it was puzzling, even weird."

"Now, now. He's in a weak state and he's bound to react like that at times. Go on, get yourself to bed. I promise you, at the slightest change I'll come and fetch you post haste."

"Promise?"

"I've said so, haven't I?"

Turning abruptly, she made for the door; but there she stopped and, looking back towards him, she said, "Odd, isn't it, that Dad's going back to the house that he first lived in? It seems that everything is falling into place for everybody, even you; I heard Dad say that you had told him you had got a place, a house of some sort. Is that right?"

"Yes. Yes, it's right, Annette."

"Are you going to furnish it from here?"

"No, no. The only things I'll take from here are my books and papers, because there's nothing here that really belongs to me."

"It's all settled then?"

"Yes, it's all settled. For once in my life I'm going to please myself and do something that I know I should have done a long time ago."

"Yes. Yes, I understand, Joe. You've never been able to please yourself. As I said the other night you've been at the beck and call of everybody, even of me of late. Well, I'm happy for you. Good-night. And . . . and you'll call me?"

"Yes, I'll call you. Good-night."

He returned to the desk, gathered up his papers, put the books into their respective places on the shelves, then left the room and made his way to his own quarters. There, he took a quick shower, got into his dressing-gown and slippers, then went along to the sick-room.

He had hardly closed the door before the nurse greeted him with, "We've got a naughty boy here; he refuses to take his pills. What are we going to do about it, Mr. Coulson?"

"Hold his nose. I think that's the only way."

"He's not going to like that." She was looking towards the bed and smiling. And Joe said, "We've got to do lots of things in life we don't like."

Joe took his seat beside the bed and Don looked at him and said, "All right, then; let's have them. You look very fresh and handsome tonight, Joe."

"I don't know about handsome; fresh, yes, because I've just had a shower."

"Yes, your hair's still wet. Funny, I could never stand my hair being wet; I always had to dry it with the electric drier. Remember?"

"Yes, I remember."

"What's the weather like?"

"Oh, it's a very nice night: calm, not even a breeze, and quite warm."

"That's nice. I feel very calm, Joe, very calm. Nurse!" He now looked towards the nurse. "Do you think I could have a cup of hot cocoa?"

"A cup of hot cocoa? Why, of course. But you've never asked for cocoa before at this time of night."

"That's what I would like, nurse."

"Well, that's what you'll have."

She went out smiling.

"Hot cocoa?" Joe gave a small chuckle. "What's this, hot cocoa?"

"I just wanted to say something to you, Joe. Time's up. She's gone. I told you she would stay until I was ready to go. Oh . . . oh, dear fellow, dear dear friend, and yes, dear brother, don't look like that but be pleased that I'm going this way. Do you know, I haven't got an ache or pain in my body: in fact, you would think I hadn't got a body. I haven't said anything about this, but I haven't had a pain, nor an ache, for two or three days now. I seem to have got lighter and lighter. And I have no fear, not of Mother, or death, or the hereafter. It all seems so settled. Oh, please, Joe, be happy for me. Be happy that I'm going like this. I want you to stay with me tonight. Sit just where you are."

Joe's voice was breaking as he said, "I should bring Annette down."

"No, no. I said my goodbyes to Annette. She knows it too. I couldn't bear to see her weep. I wouldn't go easy then. But with you, Joe, it's different. You're the only one I've ever been able to talk to, properly that is, to say what I think. I'm going to close my eyes now, Joe, and when the nurse comes back you can tell her that I've fallen asleep. In a short while she'll sit in her chair over there and she'll drop off. She does it every night."

"But . . . but I thought you've just taken your pills?"

"I've become very clever at that, Joe. You know, you can hold things under your tongue for a long time."

"Oh, Don, Don."

"You know I want to laugh when I hear you say my name like that. You sound just like Father Ramshaw. There's a man for you. He knew, too, that I don't often take my pills at night, the sleeping ones. The other one and . . . and the brown stuff . . . oh yes, yes; I've had to take them sometimes. But, as I said, for the last three or four days I haven't needed them. You know, Joe, when I was first put into this bed I was bitter. Oh dear God, I was bitter, and when they let me up out of the drugged sleep, I wanted to scream. And I can't look back and tell you when that time changed. You know, Joe, I've lived a longer life these past few months than I ever did in all the years before. And I know that if I had lived to be ninety or a hundred I wouldn't have understood half as much as I've come to understand in these past days. I've learned so much lying here, so I'm not sorry all this happened. Strange that, isn't it? for me to say that I'm not sorry that all this happened. And here I am leaving a beautiful young wife and a child. But I'm not worrying about them either. It's all right, Joe, it's all right, I won't go on. What will be will be. I hold you to nothing; you have your own life to live. And Father Ramshaw let it slip the other night that you had your eye on somebody. He was quizzing me to find out which one it was, but I couldn't tell him and I'm not asking you now, Joe, either. Every man has a right to change his mind, and Annette and the child are in God's hands. He'll take care of them. Don't look so worried, Joe, and don't say anything. Please, don't say anything. I understand everything."

"You don't, you don't. Who do you think you are anyway? God, already?"

"Oh, Joe, Joe, don't make me laugh. That's funny, you know. I ache when I try to laugh. Oh, she's coming. She's heavy-footed, that one; she thumps the carpet. Hold my hand, Joe, and keep holding it, will you?"

Joe took the hand extended to him and when the door opened it was all he could do to turn and look at the nurse as she entered with the steaming cup of cocoa on a tray. He couldn't speak to her but he signalled to her that the patient was asleep, and she shrugged her shoulders, smiled, laid the cocoa down on a side table, then settled herself in an armchair.

At what time Don died, Joe didn't know. He had sat wide-eyed for a long period, the pale hand held in his. Once, he glanced at the clock, which showed a quarter past one. And it was at about this time that the nurse roused herself and apologetically said, "I must have dropped off. He's sleeping quietly?"

He nodded at her. She didn't come towards the bed but busied herself at a table for a little while; then sat down again, wrote something in a notebook, and within a short while, if not quite snoring, was emitting quite heavy nasal sounds.

His arm and wrist were in a cramp but still he didn't move. What he did do was try to edge his chair a little nearer to the side of the bed to relieve the tension on his shoulder. It was some time after this that he closed his eyes and some time again before a voice said, "Oh! Mr. Coulson. Mr. Coulson!"

His eyes sprang wide open and he stared at the nurse on the other side of the bed as she had Don's other wrist between her fingers.

"I'm afraid . . . I'm afraid, Mr. Coulson . . ."

He looked at the face on the pillow. It appeared to be warm and alive, yet stiff, as if it had been set into a mould. It could have been a sleeping face, but it wasn't.

"He's . . . he's gone, Mr. Coulson."

"Yes, yes, I know." Slowly, he lifted the thin white hand and unwound his fingers until they were straight, then just as slowly eased his cramped arm from the bed.

"I'd . . . I'd better phone the doctor."

"Yes. Yes, nurse."

"And . . . and call his father and his wife."

"Leave that to me."

Why was he so calm? It was as if he had imbibed the feelings that Don had expressed a short while ago: he was feeling no sorrow, no remorse, just a quietness that was expressed in the face on the pillow and that seemed to fill the whole room, for, it was true, she had gone too. Definitely she had gone.

He flexed his arms and went towards the door; but he found he couldn't grip the handle with his right hand, so opened it with his left.

Instead of making for the hall and up the stairs to alert both Annette and his father, he turned the other way and towards his quarters. And from his sitting-room he opened his door into the conservatory; then he opened the conservatory door and stepped out into the night, which was bright with moonlight: the full moon was hanging like an enormous yellow cheese in a pale blue sky. The air was cool and there was just the slightest breeze. He felt it through the sweat on his brow. He put his head back and took in the great expanse of nothingness in which just the moon floated and the stars twinkled and into which Don and his mother had gone, but in their separate ways.

FOURTEEN

$\mathcal{W}$ithin seven weeks the house had been sold and almost completely denuded of furniture. Daniel had furnished his new home with the better pieces, and Maggie and Stephen were already installed there.

The new owners of the house agreed to keep on Bill and Lily in the lodge. All that remained was for Annette, the baby, and Peggie to be moved into the cottage. And it was strange that, although it was weeks since Don had been buried from the house, Annette still seemed hesitant to move permanently away from it. She had driven backwards and forwards to the cottage almost every day, returning to the house at night to sleep. Today, however, was her final day here; as it was Joe's. And where was Joe going?

Only this morning he had filled his car with cases holding his clothes and boxes holding his books, and had driven them to his new home. Where was this? As yet no-one knew, and the question was now being put to him by Daniel. They were standing in the empty drawing-room, and when Joe told him where he was to live Daniel didn't speak for a moment; then he said, "You can't do that, man."

"Why can't I?"

"Well, there'll be talk."

"My God! Dad, for you to say that to me: there'll be talk."

"Oh, I know, I know, but my life's mine and I'll have to stand the racket for it, I always have. But you're different. Here you are twenty-six years of age and no-one could raise a finger to you."

"Dear God! I just can't believe it."

"I'm only speaking for your own good. There'll be talk."

"Yes, there'll be talk. And what the hell does it matter to me who talks? What is amazing to me at this moment is the way *you're* talking."

"All right, all right. I don't want to argue with you, Joe. I'm past arguing in all ways."

"I wouldn't have thought so."

"I'm only thinking of you."

"Only thinking of me? and Father Cody? and Father Ramshaw? Well, let me tell you, you can cut Father Ramshaw out."

"I would doubt it in this case."

"We can wait and see then, can't we?"

As Joe turned away Daniel said, "Joe. Joe, we are breaking up. It's as if a bomb had hit us, a time bomb left over from the war, and it's knocking us to blazes one way or another. You and me, we don't want to part like this. You're all I've got in the way of a son, and it's because of that I've said what I've said."

"Well, you've still got a son, Dad, if you want one, but he's got to live his own life, as you've lived yours. And don't forget it, you have lived it, and right to the full. I haven't sipped at mine yet, but I'm going to. But don't worry, I'll be along to see you later, perhaps tonight or tomorrow. So good-bye Dad, for the present."

In the hall Annette was standing with the baby in her arms and he said, "Are you ready, then?"

"Yes, Joe. But . . . but there's no need for you to drop me off; Peggie will be back with the car at any time. She's just slipped into the town to see her mother. I can wait."

"Well, I've got nothing else to do at the moment."

"Is your place all fixed up?" Her voice was stiff as she asked the question, and he said, "Yes. Yes, all fixed up and very nicely."

"You've been very secretive about it; why?"

"Oh, you'll soon know the reason. It'll be all out shortly."

She cast him a sidelong glance, then went towards the front door. But there she turned and looked around the hall and towards the stairs and, her voice grim now, she said, "If ever there was an unlucky house, this is it. Pray God I'll never know such again."

"Pray God you never will."

He opened the rear door for her and settled the baby on her knee; then took his seat behind the wheel. And they had gone some distance before she said, "Wherever this place of yours is, will you be near enough to drop in now and again?"

"Oh, yes, yes, definitely."

"Joe."

"Yes, Annette?"

"Can't you tell me? Why have you kept this place secret?"

"Well, Annette"—he paused, for they were approaching a corner—"I thought it the best policy. And, you see, there is this young woman concerned, and I felt I've dallied with her long enough; I wanted to bring things to a head sort of abruptly."

"I don't understand you, Joe, not lately I don't."

"Well, Annette, for a long time I didn't understand myself, but now I do and I know what I'm about."

"Well, that's all that matters, isn't it?"

"Yes, that's all that matters, Annette."

There was nothing more said between them as the car sped the rest of the journey through pleasant countryside. And then there they were bowling up the short drive and stopping in front of the long, grey-stoned two-storey house.

He opened the front door into the small hallway and she went in before him, then stopped abruptly and looked down at the four suitcases standing side by side near the telephone table. Swinging round, she looked up at him, and he said, "Yes, yes, they're mine. There are a number of boxes, too, books you know, but I've put them in the loft."

She took three steps back from him, and he said, "Look out! you'll fall over the chair. Come and sit down."

He pushed open the door of the sitting-room, then took the baby from her and, entering the room he laid it on a deep-cushioned armchair.

She hadn't followed but was still standing at the door, and so he walked back to her, took her hand and brought her to the couch. And here, pressing her down into it, he sat beside her and said, "This is my new flat; I'm staying here. I've already picked my rooms at the end of the corridor upstairs. They'll do for a time. What do you think about it?" His hand spread out, taking in the room with the gesture. "Quite a nice place?"

"Stop it! Joe. Stop it!"

"No, I'm not going to stop it." His own voice had changed now, all the banter gone. "I'm doing what I should have done many years ago. I shouldn't have been pressed aside. You know it, and I know it. And Don knew it. Oh, yes, Don knew it. You were mine long before you were his. We both knew that. I don't know where you come in in that part, but I knew that if I had spoken before Dad started his manoeuvres, I would have had a wife by now, and a family. You grew to love Don. I'll not deny that. And he loved you. Oh, yes, he loved you. You loved each other. But it was an interlude. As I see it now, that's all it was, an interlude. In looking back, you belonged to me right from the beginning. Can you imagine what I felt like when I was forced to take on the big brother role? Can you? Oh, don't cry, my dear. Don't cry. I want to talk to you. I've got a lot more to say and it's this: I've waited so long now I can go on waiting until you're ready, but I've got to be near you, and I've got to know that you are mine, and that one day we will marry. And I can't help but add I hope it will be soon. But you know something? Dad warned me just before I left the house that there'd be talk. He was upset when I told him what I was going to do. He of all people to tell me that there would be talk. Can you imagine it? Now, the point is this, Annette. The talk could have substance, or it couldn't. I leave that to you and in your own time. Just know this. I love you . . . I've always loved you, and I can't see myself, after all this long time, ever stopping. And because I love you so much I feel that it would be impossible for you not to love me in some way, some time."

"Joe. Joe." Her eyes were tightly closed. Her head fell against him and rested on his shoulder as she muttered, "I do love you. I love you now. I've

been full of guilt with the feeling. I loved Don. Yes, I did. But I loved you too. All through I've known I loved you, and not just as a brother. Oh, Joe. Joe."

His chin lay on top of her head, his eyes were screwed up tight, his teeth biting into his lower lip. Then pressing her face upwards from his shoulder, he brought his lips gently down on hers. And when she clung to him Flo's words sprang into his mind: "Everything comes to him who waits." Then his eyes twinkling, he said quietly, "You know there'll be a field-day. Are you prepared for that?"

"Yes, Joe." Her face still wet, the tears still running, she repeated again, "Yes, Joe. And the stalls and the coconut shies."

"With Father Cody pelting us?"

Once more they were enfolded in each other's arms and Joe added, "And by God! he will that. Even if we get no further than this"—he kissed her on the tip of her nose—"he'll flay us as only he can flay with his tongue . . ."

She looked at him steadily now as she said, "Well, we'll have to see that we are flayed for something, won't we, Joe?"

"Oh, my dear. My dear."

Gently now they enfolded each other and lay back against the couch. But when a small cry came from the chair, their mouths opened wide and they laughed aloud. Then, springing up, Joe picked up the baby and, rocking it widely from side to side, he cried, "Listen to me, Flo Coulson, your mother loves me. Do you hear that? Your mother loves me. Everything comes to him who waits. Your mother loves me."

THE END

ABOUT THE AUTHOR

Catherine Cookson was born in Tyne Dock, the illegitimate daughter of a poverty-stricken woman, Kate, whom she believed to be her older sister. She began work in service but eventually moved south to Hastings where she met and married a local grammar-school master. At the age of forty she began writing about the lives of the working-class people with whom she had grown up, using the place of her birth as the background to many of her novels.

Although originally acclaimed as a regional writer—her novel *The Round Tower* won the Winifred Holtby award for the best regional novel of 1968— her readership soon began to spread throughout the world. Her novels have been translated into more than a dozen languages and more than 40,000,000 copies of her books have been sold alone in Corgi. Four of her novels—*The Fifteen Streets, The Black Velvet Gown, The Black Candle* and *The Man Who Cried*—have been made into successful television dramas, and more are planned.

Catherine Cookson's many bestselling novels have established her as one of the most popular of contemporary women novelists. After receiving an OBE in 1985, Catherine Cookson was created a Dame of the British Empire in 1993. She and her husband Tom now live near Newcastle-upon-Tyne.